THE
DARKENING
STORM

L. J. HUTTON

ISBN-13: 9781719994408

First published 2012
This edition 2021

Copyright

Acknowledgements

As every writer knows, books don't appear without the help of others. So first and foremost I must thank Karen Murray for being the chief reader and guardian of the Islands world. She enthusiastically reads everything I send her, and her perceptive comments have made this a better book than it would have been otherwise – not least because she keeps the historian in me in check!

I must also say a big thank you to all of you readers who took the plunge with *Chasing Sorcery* and have come back for more. Rest assured that there is an end!

My husband John has yet again tolerated my substantial absences while writing, sometimes to the detriment of domestic matters. He hasn't starved yet!

And finally to my lovely lurchers, Minnie, Blue and Raffles, who have kept me company while I've fought the computer – albeit with them asleep most of the time!

Thank you all!

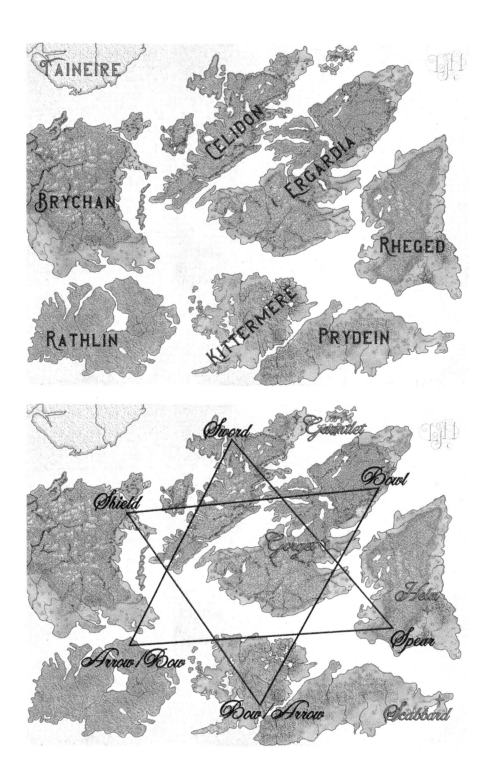

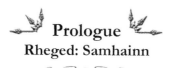

Prologue
Rheged: Samhainn

The burnt out shell of the castle sat gloomily guarding the promontory, which rose above the junction of the two rivers. At first glance it looked desolate and forgotten in the chill, grey early winter day. To anyone approaching Montrose along the main track from the north, there would appear to be little change since its razing by King Oswine's men. Yet a closer observer would realise that all was not lost. From behind the smoke-blackened great curtain wall there came sounds of hammering on wood, and chipping at stone. The lone rider by the ford knew that if he completed the part circuit to bring him in view of the great gate, then he would see a difference. The torn and twisted hinges bereft of their companion gates had been taken down with care, and in their place new ones were being fitted. By the end of this day, if the Spirits willed it, the repaired gates would once again stand guard at the vanguard of the defences.

Osbern of Braose, however, was more worried by the ford. Having taken over the defence of Montrose Castle and its village from his friend and former fellow soldier, Edmund Praen, he had been given strict instructions about this stretch of water. When Edmund and their other friend Ruari MacBeth had arrived here to find the wreckage, Ruari had been most insistent that the ford be as deep as possible. Of latter years the Montrose family had drained the waters and rearranged the stone causeway into a straight track, but Ruari had told Edmund it must be returned to its original state.

Back then the stones had veered off on a zigzag route as soon as they had disappeared under the murky water, instead of running straight across. Anyone attempting to ride fast and hard into Montrose would have become mired in the boggy ground, but that was not the only reason Ruari wanted the water back. In his journey across Rheged he had been pursued by a deadly spectre. The creature hunted in a dense fog which had nothing to do with any natural weather, but, having deduced that it was a farliath, Ruari had assured Edmund that it could not cross water. Despite being controlled by a war-mage of the DeÁine it could not be distanced from its master by water, or the war-mage's grip would be broken.

More worrying even than that had been the discovery that the village had been infiltrated by one of the DeÁine Tancostyl's acolytes, posing as a replacement priest. Ruari had summarily dispatched the impostor to the Underworld, but before his own departure, had warned all to be on their guard against further strangers under the influence of the distant malevolent sorcerer. The water was supposed to ensure protection from that threat too, and Osbern could only wonder at the extremes Tancostyl was going to to find the former owners of the castle.

Personally, he cordially disliked the uncouth Will Montrose, even though he had to admit that Will was an excellent general for the army of Rheged. On the odd occasions when they had met, he had tolerated Will for the sake of their mutual friend Ruari, while inwardly disdaining the immorality of the man and his coarse manners. Yet if anything, he disliked Will's wife even more. Lady Matilda Montrose behaved, in his eyes, in a manner most unbecoming to a chatelaine of her standing. The woman rode and bore arms like a man! She even read old books on military tactics! And worst of all, she was trying to interfere in his marriage, along with that sharp-tongued redhead whom his friend Gerard, for some unfathomable reason, doted upon.

It had therefore been something of a shock to find that the Montroses had put their lives at risk in order to protect the small boy who was next in line to Rheged's throne. Try as he might Osbern could find no ulterior motive in their actions; which was why he was here while Ruari, Edmund and Gerard searched for the missing pair and their precious companion.

He looked at the water again and shuddered. His horse – well-trained though she was – refused to set a hoof in the still expanse, shying away with eyes rolling and coat shivering, no matter what the urging. The first sign of trouble had been when two villagers had left to go to the next town's market two days previously. No-one had seen them off since nobody had thought there would be any problem. It had been the terrifying shrieks of agony, overlaid by eldritch keening, which had sent villagers and Osbern running out of the castle. All they found was empty clothing drifting on the surface, and the two packs lying forgotten in the shallows undisturbed. No footprints or hoof marks disturbed the ground on the other side, and even the sharpest-eyed amongst them could see no intruders in the distant woodlands.

It was only when one of them stepped forward to reach for the packs that the fate of their fellows became clear. Barely had his foot broken the water's surface than it began to roil and rise in a column to encase the leg. The young man had leapt back, but found himself held fast by the water. Others had sprung to his aid, but it was only the combined strength of half a dozen burly men which finally hauled him free. As they had pulled him backwards to dry land, the water had remained entwined around him like transparent weeds, stringing out unnaturally without ever dripping a drop on the bank of the ford. The turning point seemed to come when the man landed on his back on the ground in a pile of fallen leaves, and others piled on top of him to hold him there, while two more hacked at the gelatinous liquid with axes, more in desperation than any hope of cutting it. Suddenly, as it came into contact with the leaves, the thing loosed the leg with an audible snap and shot back into the ford.

Shaken and distraught the villagers had retreated, demanding answers of Osbern which he could not supply. That night he had prayed for guidance with all his might in the castle chapel. A deeply devout man, Osbern was shaken to the core by the knowledge that Tancostyl had infiltrated the Church, and felt cast adrift by the lack of priestly guidance at this time of crisis. His personal inadequacies seemed all the worse for wondering why he had changed into the man he was now. Once upon a time he had been as daring as any of his friends, but that had all changed the day he had been almost fatally wounded by an arrow in the chest. In dark times like this he desperately longed for his old decisiveness, but it seemed to have evaporated like morning mist as his wound had healed.

Both Edmund and Gerard had been badly wounded at least once during their soldiering careers, and he had lost count of the times Ruari had appeared bandaged or on a stretcher. Yet they seemed to shrug it off and carry on as normal. Indeed it had been a standing joke that Osbern must have a guardian spirit, for until that fateful day, he was the only one who had remained unhurt through the most dreadful frays. He had verbally savaged Ismay, his wife, when she had suggested that maybe it was exactly that lack of experience of feeling vulnerable until he was middle-aged that made it so overwhelming – but now he was less sure. Maybe it would have been better if he had taken a few wounds earlier and accepted that he was mortal. Whatever the rationale, though, as he prostrated himself before the altar he would have given anything for Ruari to ride in and take over, allowing him to retreat into the sanctuary of his home and the world of the sacred texts. Why was his faith no comfort or support in this hour of need, despite his deep devotion?

Instead, as the night wore on, he was disturbed by the sound of torrential rain. Winter showers turned to a long, raging storm, battering the castle with sheets of driven rain which ran in rivers through the holes in the roofs, soaking everyone to the skin. At one point Osbern could have sworn he heard the hideous cries again, only for them to be drowned out by the rain. As daylight sullenly appeared, the storm exhausted itself and the villagers crept out of their hiding places to see the paved courts full of puddles and the surrounding farmlands awash.

Fear of what might lurk in the water paralysed everyone for the first few hours, but as the surface water drained away without incident, their courage returned and they ventured out. Finally, a few brave souls and Osbern made the walk to the ford, which was twice its normal depth and unsafe for use. With the run-off from both banks, and the tributary streams swollen with rain from off the hills behind the castle, the whole of the long stretch of water was far from still. It swirled in eddies, fallen leaves, twigs and branches engaged in twirling dances as they span east, or west, to the respective draining points over the high cliffs.

Looking around, one of the men spotted the two packs now caught on a fallen branch near their bank. With great caution he used the staff he was carrying to hook under one of the straps and managed to pull one pack up onto the bank. Everyone held their breath, but nothing moved. The same man exchanged glances with his friends then, with two others hanging onto his one arm, he stepped into the edge of the floodwater. Nothing happened. Loosing their grip he waded swiftly to the branch, grabbed the second pack and ran back across the flooded grass to the edge, water splashing mightily but normally at his passage. Retreating back several yards they all watched the ford intently, but nothing abnormal appeared.

That had been the previous day, however, and now Osbern feared the monster in the ford had returned. All he could think of was that the torrential downpour had swollen the waters so much that the infestation had been swept to the rim of the headland, and over the edge in one of the waterfalls to the rivers below. However it had been dislodged, though, its master had obviously detected its absence and had restored its lurking presence to terrorise them all. Moreover, if it was inhabiting the water, then this was no farliath, and Osbern wracked his brains trying to remember the catalogue of monsters that he had heard Ruari talk of the DeÁine being able to summon.

In his piety he had consciously held himself aloof from such studies, believing that the Blessed Martyrs would protect him from such beasts of the Underworld – if Ruari wished to imperil his immortal soul by digging in the dirt then that was his affair. But here he was, starring down the maw of one such beast (metaphorically even if it was not in evidence today), not a scrap of divine intervention in sight, and all Ruari's warnings about being prepared for the worst coming back to haunt him.

In the dim recesses of his memory he thought he recalled a monster that lived in water, but what was it? There was something called a bansith, but he fairly sure that this one was not one of those, despite the fact that he could not remember exactly what a bansith was either. And there were bleizgarves and grollicans, but he did not think it was them, either. Was it a baneasge? The name sounded right, yet he could not recall if it could leave its watery retreat to hunt on land. If it was confined to the waters of the ford it was bad enough for them all, but if the monster could leave it for forays, however short, then he would be expected to come up with some plan for defence against it.

Morosely Osbern turned the mare back towards the castle wondering how he was going to explain to the villagers that he could no longer go for more supplies; and that unless they could summon another violent rainstorm, they were marooned for the winter. He would have to wait and see whether the baneasge ventured out of its watery domain, and in the meantime he was heading back to the castle to pray – not in the chapel to the Martyrs this time, since they seemed to have deserted him, but for the reappearance of his courage or Ruari.

NEW LOCHLAINN (DeÁine controlled West Brychan)

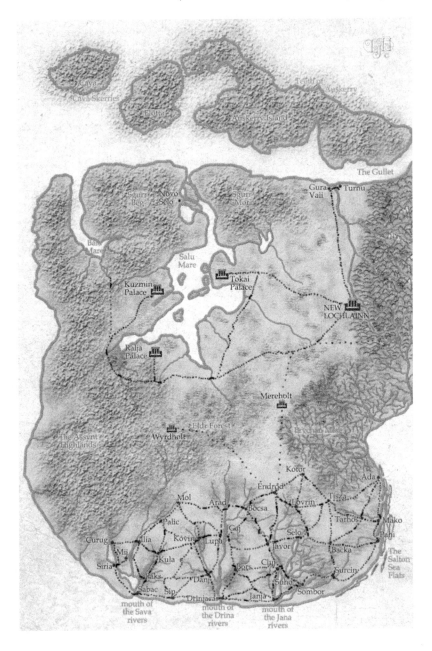

Chapter 1

Schemes within Schemes

Four women sat in conference within a great palace in New Lochlainn. The room alone would have held several small dwellings of the Island folk, even though it was by no means the largest or most splendid within the vast assembly of joined buildings. The seat of DeÁine power in the western half of Brychan was the massive fortress-city of Bruighean within New Lochlainn. However, the female cadre of the Abend declined to spend the winter months there. It was too drearily functional, too close to the mountains, and far too cold. The four had little in common, and for the most part disliked one another with an intensity that could only come from being thrust into each others' company for centuries. Yet it was still preferable to migrate to this smaller pleasure palace further south, than endure months of being cooped up with the rest of the DeÁine elite.

Mereholt Palace had once been the winter hunting lodge of the king of the Islands, although no former king would now recognise his residence had he seen it, so greatly had it been enlarged. Lying with the vast marshes of Brychan Mere to the east, the huge forest of Eldr to the west, and the waterways and strange channels to the south, Mereholt was in a valley with a micro-climate all of its own. Temperate throughout the year, it rarely saw frost let alone snow, and only in the summer – when the humidity rose all around with no breeze to relieve it – was it unpleasant here. A series of courtyard gardens now encircled the main building, each with their own suites of rooms surrounding them, and the four Abend witches tended to keep to their individual spaces rather than socialise with one another. However, at present they were assembled in Geitla's rooms for two reasons. This was the one room not only faced with marble slabs, but also backed with other rooms whose walls were solid stone, and the Abend were nothing if not suspicious. Wood could too easily contain peep holes and cavities in which eavesdroppers could lurk, and they wanted no listeners at this meeting. The other reason was that they were waiting on Geitla herself to finish satiating her voracious sexual appetite. At present the other three were within the chosen room, while Geitla was riding a young male slave to a climax on a silken chaise beneath exotic fruit trees in the orangery beyond. Indifferent to the presence of her fellow witches, Geitla's diaphanous gown had slipped from her shoulder on one side, and her naked full breasts were bouncing unrestrained in rhythm with her exertions.

Masanae watched with distaste from her position by the ceiling-high tiled stove at the rear of the room. The tall black-haired woman was as different from Geitla as it was possible to get. With red lips and fingernails contrasting against alabaster skin, a wig of black hair which shone like raven's wings, and dressed in a black sheath dress which followed the lithe contours of her perfect body, Masanae should have been an arousing sight to the young men whom Geitla kept about her. Instead, she was guaranteed to freeze their ardour on sight. For Masanae was cold. As cold as the deepest ice-flow and then some. The beautiful face had a hardness about it that made the high cheekbones seem like stone, and the black-ice eyes as mutable as jet. Not a shred of compassion or passion entered her soul as far as most observers could discern.

Masanae was the oldest of the witches, and she alone of all of them could remember the DeÁine's first coming to the Islands six hundred years past. Rumour had it that back then she had been Quintillean's soul-mate and bedfellow, and although whatever bond they had had was now weakened, he was the only one known to occasionally share her bed. What they did to one another Geitla would have loved to find out, for their coupling often brought about wild blasts of Power, which had been known to tear through stone and bury unsuspecting servants beneath piles of rubble. Masanae's orgasms were rough on the buildings, and everyone was glad that she only seemed to feel the need once a decade at most.

Geitla, on the other hand, needed constant pleasuring. To Masanae's impatience this was the sixth man in a row that she had required brought to her, but finally the voluptuous redhead was coming to an orgasm.

"At last!" Helga's icy drawl came from the left-hand couch, as Geitla's moans rose in pitch. "Maybe we can get down to business now."

Helga was cut from the same cloth as Masanae – another tall, lean and cold woman, icy-blonde and equally as disinclined to sexual excesses. Where they differed was in application. Masanae approached the Power with academic rigour, endlessly building her skill, and looking for new subtleties which would allow her to draw another strand from here, and another from there. All the time refining her talent to razor-edged sharpness. Yet if Masanae was the quill, Helga was the sword. While Masanae strove to elevate herself, Helga perfected the skill of cutting others down. She was the unquestionable expert at torturing, and her rare smiles were usually confined to the torture chamber which was her own domain.

The fourth member of the coven lounged on the right-hand couch, legs neatly curled up, and looking for all the world like a cat waiting to pounce on some unsuspecting mouse. As dark as Masanae, she was more delicately built, with a froth of soft, curly black hair (a wig, of course, as with all the Abend, but a choice reflecting what she had once had) framing a winsome, heart-shaped face. Except that Magda's pretty face was marred by a permanent pout, unless she was snarling with rage or on those terrifying occasions when she truly smiled. And Magda's smiles were terrifying, for she was the most unpredictable of the four and the most randomly vicious.

The fiery one of the four, in many ways she was the most unstable, but not so much so that she was incapable of having flashes of brilliance. Some of the witches' greatest successes had started with one of Magda's inspired moments, and for that they were prepared to tolerate her nastier quirks and odder peccadilloes. Almost as old as Masanae, she was becoming more querulous with age, which showed in her mind if not in the ageless body. Nobody had said anything to the male members of the Abend, but Masanae and Helga had privately agreed that there might come a time when Magda became too unstable and would need to meet with an accident. Her channellings of Power were strong but often indiscriminate, and too often in the last century had wildly missed their aim, leaving havoc in their wake where none was needed or wanted.

In response to this, Helga had found a most promising recruit amongst the acolytes whom the Abend kept under close supervision. As the ones who shouldered by far the greatest part of the burden of teaching the underlings, Masanae had needed little convincing by Helga that they alone should be the ones to choose who the next member of the inner circle should be. Geitla was also proving to be burdensome to them, and they rued the day that their former comrade and leading witch, Gamaleda, had raised Geitla so high that upon her death Geitla's inclusion had been a foregone conclusion. Her main qualification being that of all of them, Geitla could hold, both in capacity and length of time, more Power than any of them, and almost more than Helga and Magda combined.

Yet that was not enough to make a good member of the Abend in the eyes of Helga and Masanae. Helga had been raise a mere fifty years after Geitla, and yet she was infinitely more trusted and of use despite her notably lesser strength in using the Power. In the two hundred years she had been one of the Abend, Geitla had done little to further their cause, preferring instead to indulge herself in every way possible. She had never been known to plan anything alone, and was willing to spend her days in promiscuous gluttony as a way of relieving the tedium of longevity, awaiting the moment when the others would tell her when and how they wished her powerful drawings to be directed. The best part of a century ago the icy pair had therefore begun searching for another person more suitable.

It pained Masanae that they had lost Taise. That young woman had had so much potential, if only they could have broken that infernal conscience of hers! Taise's intelligence would have made her an ideal replacement for the weak-minded Geitla. Another fifty years of fine tuning and she might well have been ripe for elevation to their ranks. And the Power she was capable of holding! She would have surpassed Geitla easily in strength and with more control over it too – perhaps because she had never had the opportunity to over extend herself while she was young, who was to know? They had not had a novice of her strength even in Masanae's long life, and had been reduced to referring to the surviving training manuals of the time before the sundering, rather than calling upon experience.

Masanae sighed quietly. Ah well, no use crying over the waste of such talent now. Helga was doing great work bringing on a sadistic young acolyte named Dagmar, while she herself had taken great delight in reclaiming one of Taise's friends and turning her back to the right path. Fenja had pleaded for mercy like all the others of her group, when the Abend had first suspected them of the betrayal which they finally laid at Bres' door. Unlike Taise, she had shown a wily streak of character in asking how she could benefit from telling them what they wanted. She had known nothing, of course, but Masanae admired the way her mind had twisted even under torture. Now Fenja felt not a shred of loyalty to her former friends, and Masanae had great hopes for what she might achieve if they were ever able to bring one of them back for questioning.

Geitla had risen from the chaise, splashed cooling water from the tinkling indoor fountain to freshen her sweat-dampened body, and sauntered in to join them. Masanae felt her customary surge of revulsion at the sight. Curse the woman, could she not even have the decorum to swiftly bathe afterwards before joining them? Now they would have to endure the stench of her once the doors were closed, and it was all Masanae could do to prevent herself retching at the thought. Oblivious or indifferent to the disdainful looks she created, Geitla flopped down on the couch beside Magda and asked in her irritating little-girl voice,

"What are we doing, then?"

In response, Magda gave a little wrinkle of her pert nose and flashed her a smile, before drawing a manicured, razor-sharp nail down the slope of Geitla's nearest bare breast. As the blonde squealed, Magda purred nastily,

"Well put them away then, sweetling, before I start sucking on them!" As Magda's current taste was definitely to other women, and Geitla had seen the mess she left after one of her all-girl sessions, it was no idle threat. Wriggling her ample breasts back into the flimsy dress and retreating to the farthest end of the couch, Geitla glared back and began to pull in Power.

"Enough!" snapped Masanae, sensing what she was doing. "Let go of that *now* Geitla! You deserved that for keeping us waiting so long!"

Geitla's mouth was now drawn down at the corners in a sullen sneer, but her sense of self-preservation was acute enough to know that the three others combined could still overwhelm her. And at times like this they *would* combine, as she knew from bitter past experience.

"Well sorreee…," she sulked. "It's not my fault I got me more hot blood than all a' you together. I got me a bad itch and it needed scratchin'!" At times like this her upbringing in a rustic corner of the DeÁine's first land of exile showed, however impeccable her bloodline was.

"Well next time you get one, come to me and I'll cut it out for you!" Helga shot back frostily, and not remotely in jest, while Magda tittered crazily and whipped out a claw again to pat catlike at the protruding nipple she could see through the sheer cloth. She giggled even more at Geitla's second squeal, and edged closer to the redhead, who was now as far down the couch as she could get and trapped unless she moved.

"Let's get on with it, shall we?" Masanae said firmly, drawing their eyes to her and away from the closed, transparent silk-screen panelled door to the orangery opposite, beyond which she could see Dagmar creep in to slip a poisonous marsh worm into the ear of Geitla's still recumbent lover. Masanae's eyes briefly met with Helga's in affirmation, and both felt more relaxed knowing that the six young men, whom Geitla had so recently entertained in front of them, would soon be screaming in madness and agony as the worms devoured their brains. Geitla must learn that when they called a meeting she should come, and come alone. Abend business must never be compromised by the risk of idle chatter by underlings. Geitla, meanwhile scurried across the plush carpet to sit by Helga, leaving a sticky damp patch on the other seat which Magda recoiled from.

"Nasty man-smell!" she declared, screwing up her nose and resuming her catlike position at the other end.

"Abend, attention! We have much to discuss," Masanae began, bringing a small leather stool in front of the ceramic heating stove and finally sitting down herself, her back straight and her bearing regal. "We have received word from Eliavres that he believes he has traced the Gorget, and it's at Caersus."

"Why didn't I know of this?" interrupted Geitla petulantly.

"If you'd get up off your cunt and do some work with the rest of us for a change, you *would've* known!" Helga spat savagely, cutting off any further comments from her neighbour on the couch, who belatedly realised how much she had antagonised her fellow witches and turned pale.

Masanae permitted herself a tight little smile at Geitla's discomfort as she continued. "As Helga has rightly pointed out, Geitla, had you been taking *any* interest in the messages arriving, you would know that he also sent a message by speaking-bird to the Donns. They've been in touch with us and seem quite willing to act on Eliavres' recommendations."

"The Donns are, indeed, unusually co-operative," mused Helga, all icy focus again, "which is amazing considering the way they've cut us off since that fiasco in the Pass. I think we can assume that they're only considering the proposal because Quintillean is known to be far afield."

"Where did he go?" Magda asked, her eyes suddenly going distant.

Helga and Masanae exchanged glances as Helga calmly repeated that he had gone in search of the Treasures. Neither was going to reveal that they knew more than that with Geitla in the room, and with Magda getting lapses of memory now as well as becoming eccentric.

"We can't let the war-mages get all the pieces!" Magda suddenly snapped back into focus. "Not after that scheme of Anarawd's. A super-DeÁine fathered on the little bitch Taise! That's what he wanted and still does! I'll not be pushed aside for anything with a prick!"

"Maybe she'd have had a daughter, then you could have fumbled her witless! Turned her to *your* ways!" Geitla riposted, going for Magda's weak spot.

Before Magda could rise to the bait, Masanae drove over the top of them. "No! None of us want a super-DeÁine! Of whatever persuasion!"

"Not under any circumstances," agreed Helga. "We now know that with all the Power someone like that could summon, we'd all be reduced to the state of *its* servants in no time. Our lives are long, but one like that could be, to all intents and purposes, immortal! A lifetime of servitude appeals to none of us, and that includes Eliavres. That was implicit in his message too."

"So, we're going to take advantage of this willingness on the part of our dear unloved warlords," Masanae continued. "It's too good an opportunity to pass up. The intelligence from our spies confirms much of what Eliavres has said – except for the Gorget. The new king of Brychan fancies himself above the guidance of his experienced advisers, is arrogant and can be easily lured. Eliavres assures us he knows how to neutralise the Knights for several weeks at least, and by the time they can rally we should be in an unassailable position."

"I bet he uses poison," purred Magda. "He does like his poisons, does dear little Eliavres." It had been Magda who had brought Eliavres on to the point where he could ascend to the Abend, and he had acquired many of her tastes along the way. "But do we trust my poppet?" she asked coyly. "No we don't! He's a hungry boy and more subtle than the others." She looked up at the others from under her long, dark lashes coquettishly and tittered maniacally again. "He'll have plans, oh yes he will!"

Going mad or not, Magda had hit upon the key point which Masanae reinforced.

"We have to have plans of our own. No it's not poison, Magda. He's asked us to control the winds. To keep the way clear for the army moving around the southern end of the mountains. To ensure that *all* the snow gets deposited on the mountains of Brychan and snows in the Knights for the winter. Then to blast a route for this puppet king when he marches – a narrow channel through the drifts which our own army can then use to enter through. This is all possible."

"Oh yes, and with me doing all the work, no doubt!" pouted Geitla.

"Considering how little you normally do, you have little room to argue," Masanae reproved her with such icy calm that Geitla's mouth snapped shut and stayed that way. "Indeed, with a little of your fine tuning, Helga, I think we can ensure that Brychan will get every drop of snow destined for the whole of this island and more, since we've been already creating extra snow to aid Tancostyl and Calatin in subduing their chosen Islands. But we need something up our sleeves, I feel. Something only we have control over. It's obvious that we shall have to travel with the army, since we shall need to have the utmost control over conditions. It simply will not do to be still back here when the army reaches Brychan. Quite apart from the fact that we cannot afford another fiasco (which would alienate the remaining pure DeÁine from us forever), do you want to find out that Eliavres has taken everything east of the mountains from under our noses?"

"With the army?" Geitla was aghast. "Marching?"

"Yes poppet, with the army. That way they won't need to take the whores with them! A few thousand men should keep even you happy for a week or two!" Magda scrunched up her shoulders and nose with a big smile in an almost childlike expression of excitement, totally belied by the malevolent glee in her eyes at the thought of Geitla being passed round the troops. Then her mood switched again and her head went on one side, birdlike. "The clouds are ours, we could use them. Jolnir! We could ask my darling Jolnir to help. Oh I'd love to see him again," she sighed wistfully.

Masanae and Helga looked to one another conspiratorially and saw they both agreed. These two considered themselves the decision makers and would make a united front in the presence of the others, even if they disagreed in private later.

"What would we have to offer him as enticement?" Helga asked Magda.

What was not commonly known was that one of the most promising male acolytes they had ever had had gone suddenly, and irrevocably, insane and disappeared. Four hundred years ago, give or take a decade as the DeÁine thought of time, a gloriously talented student named Othinn had been guaranteed a place within the Abend, even ahead of Eliavres. He and Magda had been inseparable, and he had delighted in exploring the darker recesses of the Power with her. He was also fascinated by Island folklore, and had been enthralled with the legend of Jolnir and the Wild Hunt when he had found it. Deeper and deeper he had dug into the Islands' legends, and there he had found references to the elder race, from which time he had become obsessed. It drove him frantic that he could not decipher whether those he found named had been simply extraordinary people, or gods with all the attendant powers – and, if gods, he wanted that power.

While Magda had been deeply in love with her student, he had become more and more infatuated with the idea of a legendary elder female named Vanadis. Eventually he was seeing her form in women all over the place – bizarrely, even in their then current place of exile – bedding them wherever he could and driving Magda wild with jealousy. Magda had finally entrapped him and had used all her resources in the Power to try to break into his mind. Instead, he had siphoned the Power off her to add to his, and, at the instant she was left with nothing more to give and was drawn within his mind, she saw that he was attempting to enter the world of Vanadis in the persona of Jolnir. The balance had tipped, Magda had been cast aside, and Othinn's worldly body had gasped its last breath. But when she had been revived, Magda had confessed to Masanae that she had felt Othinn's soul become irreversibly entwined in the Power.

Masanae had subsequently told Helga she was sure Magda's current decline was due to this experience, and that a part of Magda had also been torn apart in the moment of Othinn's conversion to ephemeral matter. The broken-hearted Magda had never taken another male lover – although, as Helga had pointed out, since they had been coupled at the time of his ascension, having your lover suck your soul dry, and then die on top of you, was enough to turn anyone off men. Careful experimentation had resulted in their ability to make brief contact with the ethereal Othinn, who by now had totally transformed himself into the persona of Jolnir, capable of brief manifestations but nothing more substantial. He was also completely mad. Yet he still craved power in his alternative form, since from his psychic ramblings the witches had gathered he still believed that if he could prove himself powerful enough, his goddess Vanadis would call him to her side.

"As Jolnir he must want more souls," Magda speculated, having taken over his research work on Island legends in a frantic attempt to find a way to undo what had been done. "We could give him some of those! There are lots going spare in the Islands."

"Mmmm…" Helga was thinking furiously. "A glamour attached to the front of a sending. One with a compulsion to kill. Then have Jolnir ride behind it harvesting what he can."

"New Year's Eve!" Magda exclaimed excitedly. "That's his night! His special night! And the Islanders expect him then. *Ooooh*, they'll be *soooo* scared!" And she rubbed her hands together like a naughty little girl, and bounced up and down on the cushioned seat. "Then I can see my poppet again! Watch my boy do his worst. *Ooooh* I do love him when he's being wicked!"

"And what does that achieve, except your sticky knickers?" Geitla grumbled sulkily.

"No, she has a point," Masanae said thoughtfully. "Helga's also right. If we summon Jolnir and offer him souls by means of Helga's glamour, I don't think he'll refuse to manifest. New Year's Eve would suit our timing nicely, too. It gives the Donns time to get our army up to the border, and us time to get the Knights snowed-in. If we have the Islanders falling on one another and killing themselves, there'll be less opposition for our army. And best of all, having done it once, we can threaten to summon him again if any of the war-mages get too full of their own importance. They can use the Treasures, but we shall have control of their armies. If they try to cut us out, we'll threaten to decimate their troops. They might take the Islands with the Treasures, but they can't hold them without flesh and blood soldiers."

"And not a word to Anarawd!" Helga cautioned them, but looking most pointedly at Geitla. "They all should know nothing of Othinn-Jolnir's involvement, and that's the way it must stay. We need to keep them full of doubt. Keep them wondering whether we've summoned the real gatherer-of-souls or not! It's the one way we can keep control no matter what, even if they find the Treasures."

They all agreed and then rapidly left the room and its scent of Geitla's excesses.

Magda retreated to her own suite and the fireside couch draped in thick furs. Wriggling her slender frame deep into the warm pile, she sipped hot mulled wine as one of her female slaves massaged her feet with warm, scented oils. Watching the flames dance, she took delight in how easily she had led the others the way she wanted them to go. They had no idea that she had found a way to communicate with Jolnir away from their joined channellings of Power.

Tonight, my sweetling, she thought with delight, tonight I shall come to you again! I've been so lonely since you've been gone, my wicked boy. They don't know about us, oh no they don't! But we'll be together again soon! The Treasures are out again. I can feel them on the tides of the Power, sucking it into them! And when I get close enough to one of them, all that Power is going to send me to you, my poppet. Forget your snow-white queen! You shall have a dark queen to match you and then some more! And what fun we shall have then! Oh they'll be sorry they laughed at me. Especially that dirty little whore, Geitla! She'll wish she'd never been born, oh yes she will poppet, because you'll show her what a really naughty boy can do!

Geitla herself had retired to the luxury of a hot tub to ease the soreness between her legs. It was taking longer and longer for her to climax these days, yet the craving for the intensity of the moment was no less than when it first began. It had all been Anarawd's fault. Until he had turned his attentions on her she had had normal desires, but then he had begun to show her what it could be like when the Power became the third party in their couplings. He had soon moved on to some new dalliance, but she had been left with an intense craving for the highs she had reached with him as desperate as any drug addict's.

Was it that fusion of Power which had turned Masanae and Magda's eyes that intense black instead of clear like other DeÁine's? Quintillean's eyes were also black on black, so that the pupil was indistinguishable from the iris, but she had never seen Othinn close enough to see before he had left them. As far as she had been able to tell, none of the other male DeÁine had entered into long term sexual partnerships with any woman with real Power, and none had the black irises. But then those three were also far older than any of the rest of them. Was it age alone did that? She regularly pulled every ounce of Power she could summon into herself during her matings, constantly driving herself to absorb more and more, but it was never enough. Once she had asked Masanae if the Power was gendered, and had received a look of such derision that she had never asked again. Yet if the Power did not distinguish between the sex of its drawers, it still seemed to be only in that moment of physical unity that the blending between two separate strands took place.

As she climbed out of the water the old cravings began again and, unable to face the prospect of riding another man, called her masseuse to her. The woman had a way with her hands that unknotted the tension in Geitla's limbs, and she needed to be restrained over the next couple of days to conserve her energy until they met with the Donns. Two of those generals had turned out to enjoy threesomes with her, and she was going to make sure that in return for giving them what they wanted, they told her everything that was going on ahead of the other witches. Because when they found those pieces the cursed Islanders had hidden, she was going to show them just how much Power she really could control.

So Anarawd wanted a super-DeÁine? Fool of a man! He was all focused on breeding one and yet here she was. Thanks to his depriving her of her drug, she was now far more powerful than when he had last taken her. Now she was sure she was strong enough to control the pieces without his help, and she would have her revenge on Anarawd! Yet even as she daydreamed on this, the screams from down the hall disturbed her, and, when she stormed down there to berate her servants and found the wreckage of her six lovers instead, she too forgot her plans and screamed.

Helga heard the screams even in her suite and made a mental note to congratulate Dagmar. For now, though, she was planning. Helga was not so naïve that she had not guessed that Masanae would still back Quintillean when the time came. Alone Masanae could not rule the Abend, nor did she have the strength in any form to overthrow Quintillean as leader. Helga knew she would therefore back him as a means to retain her position as second-in-command, and that left little room for Helga in the greater scheme of ruling the Islands. And Helga wanted to rule – but not the Abend or even the DeÁine, for she knew she would never be able to have the absolute power she craved with others watching over her shoulder for the slightest slip. No, she wanted an Island of her own, one where she could be queen and she alone.

To this end she had sized up the war-mages and decided that Tancostyl was the best potential ally. With him there was no need to pretend sexual attraction as she would have had to do with Anarawd – and anyway, Anarawd had his own scheme so firmly in his mind he would share opportunities with no-one. Calatin was even colder than Masanae, and such an aesthete that he wanted one of the Treasures so that he could delve even further into the Power itself, not for what it could bring him in worldly status or pleasures. Helga wanted her power in forms she could hold in the here and now.

Eliavres was even more junior than herself and Geitla, and so slippery she trusted him less than any of the others and then some. Helga had her suspicions that Eliavres coveted King Ruardan's role and had been courting the young DeÁine king's mother, Eriu, whom everyone knew was the real power behind the throne. It would not have surprised Helga if Eliavres had not made some secret proposal of marriage to the old king's concubine, to be consummated once he had something worth bargaining with – and Helga suspected that would be control of the other half of Brychan. As the stepfather of Ruardan and controller of the Islanders' Brychan, he would be in a very strong position.

Well let him have Brychan. By the time another war had rolled over the top of that Island there would be little of value left. She, on the other hand, had set her sights on the wealthiest of the Islands, Rheged. It was the only Island to produce an excess of grain and export it – and everyone needed bread – and while the other Islands all produced wool in great quantities, it was in Rheged that the valuable dyes were produced. It was also through Rheged that the merchants from the vast continent to the east came to buy the high quality woollens and trade them for exotic spices, oils and silks.

It had been inevitable that Tancostyl would be the one sent to Rheged. He was next in seniority and experience to Quintillean, and the most capable of operating under the difficult conditions in Rheged, which was also the farthest away from any aid by the rest of the Abend. Indeed, in many ways Tancostyl was as qualified to lead the Abend as Quintillean. Except, that was, for one small flaw – Tancostyl made mistakes. He was oddly impatient for someone with so much time at his disposal, and often failed to think things through to their ultimate possible conclusions. Quintillean, on the other hand, could make a snail look hasty if he thought it was necessary to exercise caution.

And Helga was counting on Tancostyl to make a mistake somewhere along the line. Separated from Quintillean's restraining influence, she was certain that sooner or later Tancostyl's own nature would get the better of him, and he would leave something undone or move too fast. Now he had sent word back that the Helm was in Rheged and in his possession, and Helga could have jumped for joy. Of all the pieces the Helm was the one she coveted the most. The thinker's Treasure! The Helm gave direction to the wielders of the other pieces. That much she had discovered from the acolytes' research programs before the debacle which had led to the defeat at Gavra Pass, and the breaking of the coven of acolytes.

It rankled that time and again she had warned that the acolytes might know more than they were passing on to their tutors. Taise had been the one Helga had especially mistrusted because of her high-minded principles. Once Anarawd's previous indiscretion with Taise had subsequently come to light, Helga had tried to insist that she be segregated from the others and put out of his reach, but to no avail. There had been little joy in being proven right when the woman had then disappeared, and Masanae was hardly the kind of woman to say 'I told you so' to – at least not if you wanted to see the next dawn. Nor was she overly happy that her prediction had come true that they would have to expend valuable Hunters tracking the woman down. Two of those triads sent she had personally spent much time with tuning to her own ways, and she resented that they had been dispatched on a wild goose chase which need never have occurred, had they listened to her in the first place.

So now she was counting on Tancostyl getting the Helm to within her grasp, and then she was going it alone. Let the others take over the rest of the Islands if they wanted. She had overheard Quintillean and Masanae talking about moving the court into the east of Brychan so that they would have easy access to the other Islands, and had laughed to herself. Had Masanae taken more notice of the Island histories, she would have known that Ergardia was useless to them. The only way they would ever gain any sort of hold on that cursed Island was through brute force exercised by Hunters and half-bloods. None of the pure DeÁine could ever set foot on its soil without getting very sick indeed. And whoever would want Celidon? All bare rocks, snow and sheep!

That only left Prydein and its poor little cousins, Kittermere and Rathlin, with the forsaken Attacotti always nipping at the heels of any ruler. How would the mighty Quintillean and Masanae deal with itinerant tribes of freedom fighters? Fighters who would indulge in guerilla warfare, slipping out of their marshes to strike, and disappearing again. Never in big enough numbers to warrant pouring all the DeÁine military resources in to cleanse the islands completely – and at the risk of one of the main Islands seizing the opportunity (as they had done centuries ago) to strike the first blow for freedom – but enough to be an eternal headache. But then the DeÁine, and the Abend in particular, had proven that they were hopeless at learning from history. Those lessons Helga had studied in private, long and hard, so that she would not do likewise.

So now she wanted her glamour to be truly lethal. She did not intend to spend her long and prosperous reign fighting running battles with rebels. The Islands would be softened up in readiness for her to take the Helm and walk into Rheged as the unopposed queen. Until then, all she was waiting on was word from Tancostyl, upon which she would summon the wind which would give him the quickest sea crossing back to Brychan in the history of the cursed Islands.

Tancostyl wanted that fast crossing so badly he would have sold his soul to the real Jolnir and back again if he had thought it would help. Instead he had almost bitten Helga's hand off when she had offered him the bait. He was particularly prone to the sea's poison, but the crossing could not be avoided unless he wanted to stay in Rheged, and Tancostyl always wanted to be keeping an eye on Quintillean. So cross the sea he must, and Helga was counting on him being as weak as a kitten by the time his ship docked. Weak and disorientated, she would take the Helm from under his nose and find a likely scapegoat for when he woke, while she retraced his steps to Rheged.

A suite of rooms away, relaxing in the monastic austerity of her garden room, Masanae inspected her collection of dwarf trees with satisfaction. Artfully pruned and wired until they resembled perfect miniatures of their larger cousins in the forest beyond, she found them a living example of how patience and application could tame even nature. Just as she and Quintillean would soon tame these Islands and reclaim their Treasures. She allowed a small smile to play at the corners of her mouth. She was well aware that Helga schemed behind her back, but at least it showed the younger witch had spirit and intelligence. More than that liability, Geitla. And thinking of Geitla, she made a mental note to check on the reports her spies within Geitla's household had sent her of late. It would be all too easy to dismiss the nymphomaniac altogether, but Geitla was not entirely stupid and she was greedy – a powerful incentive in Masanae's experience.

Not that Masanae was worried about what they wanted. She was quite certain that none of the other Abend had a clue as to what she and Quintillean really intended. Let them plan and scheme to take their bites of the Islands – they were welcome to them. Once the old folio of a manuscript, bound out of context in another ancient book, had been found, their paths had taken quite a different direction. The acolytes had reported back and then carried on with the work they had been set, but the two most senior of the Abend had been intrigued.

In secret they had worked on it and finally they were sure they had the meaning. Four DeÁine Treasures – the Gauntlet, the Gorget, the Helm, and the Scabbard – were all capable of being worn together, and yet to do that was to invite death, even for one as powerful in the Power as Quintillean. Yet here was a ritual which, if done right, would enable the performer to control and channel the Power contained within the pieces without ever coming into contact with them.

Frustratingly, all they had was a reference to another manuscript in which was written the full ritual, and this was what Quintillean had gone to find. Anarawd had got wind of the fragment and had gone off on totally the wrong tack, as far as Quintillean and Masanae were concerned. It had been at this point that he had become fixated on the idea of fathering the super-DeÁine on Taise. A DeÁine who would be capable of wearing all four pieces at once, both in order to control the combined DeÁine Treasures, and to annihilate the last vestiges of Island power.

But that was not how Masanae and Quintillean had interpreted it. Each of the four required the blood of a person of pure lineage. Pure in every sense. The quest was on, therefore, for four virgins who represented the pure bloodline of the ruling house of the Islands. Ideally the pieces would be immersed in the blood while having Power channelled into them, and in doing so the blood would absorb the essence of the pieces and their individual qualities. Who so ever then drank deeply of that blood would then control all. All the DeÁine Treasures! And with them the power to destroy whatever vestiges there were of that bastard wild thing the Islanders called Power. No ruler would ever have ruled so absolutely as they would after then. Resistance would be futile.

Their spies in Brychan had been most useful in trying to track down potential targets. The royal lines of Brychan were tangled and complicated to unravel, that was true, but essentially they all could trace their roots back to the ones who had taken control when the DeÁine had first been repulsed. At first Masanae and Quintillean had feared that the bloodline might have become so diluted that it would no longer serve their purpose.

However, they had breathed a sigh of relief when an easily corrupted prior had revealed the extent of the intermarriage between the various branches. Masanae had had her house slaves checking and double checking the interbreeding of the collective houses of Brychan nobility – indeed it transpired it was amazing that they were not all swivel-eyed simpletons given the closeness of some of the marriages which had been repeated over the generations. And none closer than the current ruling family. In fact it had been the self-obsessed king who had led them to the perfect candidates.

Edward himself was useless for their purposes, being some sort of mongrel from his dam's time on the border and not a true Mar, but the Earl of Mar's bloodline was the truest of all and there were half-siblings. Edward was determined to wipe the men out, of course, because of the threat they presented to him. Well let him have his fun with the males, gender was not important for their own purposes and the female line would do as well. Finding two from the same family had been an unexpected bonus and left only two more victims to track down. However, they now had no doubts that the rest of the Islands were ruled by the descendants of the same high ranking Islanders who had had the temerity to repel the DeÁine over five hundred years ago. Islanders who had wielded the perverted Island charms, or whatever they were.

Quintillean had therefore set out to scour the northern isles. The southern royal families they had dismissed because of the interbreeding with the Attacotti, for they had no idea from the ancient texts whether Attacotti blood was any use, but the in the north who else had they had to breed with but themselves? It was unthinkable that ruling families would deign to interbreed with the lesser folk – however would they retain their natural superiority if their blood became debased with that of commoners?

Even as Quintillean searched, Masanae was preparing things here. She had had four slaves bled to death to determine how much blood they were going to need to contain – which was less than she had anticipated, and something of a relief, given that they then had to drink it! (They were certainly not going to leave any lying around for others to partake of!) Always better to check, she believed, than to make a critical mistake. She had had a deep basin crafted of black obsidian, with special sacrificial tables containing channels to drain every last drop of the precious blood into the basin. And finely wrought glass goblets and a ladle to fill them with as well. Not here though! Not where the other Abend might find out. The sacrificial room was in her own palace on the western coast of the great sea loch which penetrated New Lochlainn in the west.

She smiled again. Eliavres could have the Gorget for now, until Quintillean got back. He was too naïve to understand fully how to use it anyway. Then they would send the messages which would trigger the collection of the other pieces by their very own triads of Hunters, and return to perform the ritual. At that point they would have the Treasures and full control of them. That would be the time when they could afford to be magnanimous. Let the others have the Islands.

She and Quintillean, however, would return home. Time to go home to the real Lochlainn, and at last to the society once more of others of refined tastes like themselves. Home to beautiful Lochlainn! With its beaches of white sand and great, slow moving fertile rivers; its shining pyramids, pagodas and temples; its fabled, immaculate gardens; and its endless supply of passive, responsive slaves, who never even knew what rebellion was, let alone to be possible, after millennia of institutionalised servitude. The humiliation of being the last surviving members of those who had lost the Treasures would be wiped out at last, and their exile revoked. Time to go *home*.

ERGARDIA

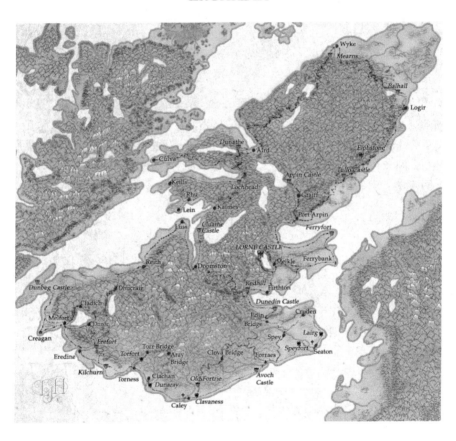

Chapter 2

 ## *Waiting to Depart*

Ergardia: Samhainn

Lorne Castle sat wreathed in winter mists, white tendrils wrapping themselves around the towers, then drifting off across the loch obscuring the icy water. Muffled in a heavy cloak, a small figure stood at the battlements of the great keep and stared into the swirling white. The door to the roof space opened and closed behind him without him noticing until a hand grasped his shoulder.

"Have a care, Andra! If you lean out any further you'll be over the edge!"

The speaker stood head and shoulders above the slightly built monk. He had disdained to don a cloak, and the immaculate black uniform of a Knight of the Order of the Cross stood out starkly against the surrounding pale background. The triple lightning flashes of the rank of ealdorman showed clearly on his collar, and his whole bearing was of someone used to taking control of situations.

"How do you stand it, Ruari?" Andra asked his friend. "The waiting, I mean. Don't you want to be *doing* something? This is driving me mad!"

Ruari needed no further explanation of what Andra meant, knowing that what consumed the younger man was fear for the pupil he had had snatched from his care. To know that the small boy, Wistan, was abroad in the depths of winter with only his naïve older cousin, Kenelm, for company was bad enough. Worse was the news they had received that the two were last seen in the company of the DeÁine sorcerer Quintillean. Everyone in this great fortress, which was the headquarters of the Knights in Ergardia, was worried about what Quintillean might have planned for the two innocents – especially given that they were the two nearest heirs to the kingship of Rheged – but for Andra it was much more personal.

"Well you don't need to wait much longer," Ruari said with an encouraging grin. "Grand Master Brego's had a message. Oh don't get too excited!" he warned quickly, seeing the eager light appear in Andra's eyes. "It's only a probable sighting, it's not confirmed, but Brego thinks it's enough to make more serious plans now. We're all meeting in his office when the next hour bell gets rung. Come on, let's get you thawed out before we have to go in."

When the single toll of the bell rang across the castle complex, there was a fair press of people squeezed into Brego's spacious office. In part this was because the Master had had a table placed in the centre of the room, which had a map of the whole Islands on it. Weighted down at each corner, it was a masterpiece of the cartographer's art – detailed and clearly drawn. Its presence signalled to everyone that events had moved on a step.

When he was sure everyone who ought to be there was present, Brego rapped sharply on the desktop and the buzz of conversation died away.

"Good afternoon everyone," he began. "I know we've all been waiting for far too long, so I won't keep you in suspense. A message has arrived from the castle at Dunbeg. It appears that Quintillean has outfoxed us in part." A collective groan rose from his audience, but died swiftly away again. "Indeed," Brego intoned grimly, then more positively, "however, it's not all bad news. We thought that Quintillean would make for a southern port where he could find passage on a ship directly to Brychan. Those who know the high-powered DeÁine only too well agreed that he would dread a sea journey, but we failed to recognise how badly. Apparently he was in no fit state to attempt such a crossing at all. The time he spent here in Ergardia was more injurious to his health than anyone could have guessed, it seems."

People began to look to their companions hopefully as Brego pressed on.

"Our commander at Dunbeg, on the west coast," everyone peered at the map to find it, "finally found out where he'd disappeared to when a fisherman's wife came to him, fearful for the safety of her husband. Apparently four nights before, a stranger with two young companions had come to their isolated cottage, and asked for passage just across the channel to Celidon. Even in a small fishing boat it should've only taken a day each way, so he was long overdue. The woman said there'd been something unpleasant about the man, and she'd pleaded with her husband to refuse, but he was won over with the promise of a generous payment. Now she feared that the stranger had done away with him once they reached the other side.

"The captain sent men across to Celidon and unfortunately found her fears had materialised, and the fisherman with his throat cut. The Knights then went on to Carndu and Bellhaven to warn the locals of the dangerous man abroad in their country, but also to seek further word of him. Our captain already had his suspicions of who it might be, and primed his men before they left. Consequently, we now know that Quintillean and the two youngsters left on a boat from Bellhaven only the morning before our men got there.

"The company made all speed back and sent birds on ahead, although those got delayed by the weather. We think that Quintillean must have attempted to reach the far west coast of Celidon, but was forced back by the heavy snow. Yet Bellhaven still leaves him with an unpleasantly long winter crossing. But notably, it also means that if he takes the first available landfall, he'll arrive somewhere in the middle of Brychan, and that's a long way from either of the two passable routes to New Lochlainn."

Brego now moved closer to the map. Pointing out the potential landings of the Brychan ports of Sandbay and Medrim, his finger then moved to the south.

"This is the route which will be most passable at this time of year. The whole of the range of mountains down the centre of Brychan will be a mass of drifting snow and ice by now. Utterly impassable, even for a well-equipped company of men. And even Quintillean should realise that while his powers might enable him to survive, his captives won't." Andra stifled a sob, yet Brego gave him an encouraging smile as he went on. "But given that he's gone to such lengths to keep both boys with him, we don't think he'll be so reckless as to endanger their lives. Whatever ritual he has planned for them, our guess is that he needs them alive.

"So, which way will he go? The southern route around the end of the mountains will be the most passable, because they can travel down near the coast where the salt air will keep the ice at bay. The danger for Quintillean in taking this route is that the Knights in Brychan have a whole chain of castles guarding the border, and nowhere more densely packed than at the weak point of the southern lowlands. He has to get through territory heavily trafficked by trained men, who all know only too well what a DeÁine looks like. On a different Island he might excuse his unnatural pallor by pleading illness, but down there he'll be spotted in an instant if he encounters any troops."

Ruari MacBeth, as acting Grand Master of the fragmented Rheged sept, took over as the next most senior Knight in the room.

"For that reason we think it's important that we cover the northern route too. In terms of the prevailing weather, it's a much tougher route. The snow will be deeper, and there'll be less traffic to break trail for them if it gets any worse. This road you can see running along the coast serves the Knights' castles of Peruga, Clodoch, and Borth and is well paved most of the way. The bad thing for Quintillean is that it's the *only* road, and it often runs through country where there are no side turnings or places to hide if a company of Knights appears. The good thing – for him – is that the Knights will be as hampered by the weather as he is, *and* they're on their guard for people coming *out* of New Lochlainn. He might decide that they won't be bothered about anyone going *in* and risk it. Once he gets near Borth he'll have a rough couple of days off road, but then he's in home territory where no Knights' patrol will go. It may be desolate, but it doesn't contain the mass of displaced folk who might betray him that the southern borderlands do."

"So," Brego took over again, "we're going to send *two* parties after our fugitives."

An excited buzz ran around the room, which the two senior Knights allowed to run its course before continuing. The group who took the southern route would be the larger party because of the size of territory to be covered. Brego anticipated sending as many as thirty men to allow for the need to split up if the trail seemed to fork with no clear indication of which way Quintillean might have gone. The depth of the prior preparations was revealed in the careful anticipation of all eventualities. Surprising to all but the inner circle of planners was the announcement of Labhran as one of the leaders of the southern force. For the first time, many heard of his experience as one of the Covert Brethren, deep undercover in the heart of DeÁine territory at the court of the former king Nuadu.

"Do you think Quintillean will get that far, then?" Andra asked anxiously.

"The honest answer is, I don't know," Brego told him. "Ideally we should intercept him long before then, but it would be foolishly arrogant to assume that as a certainty."

"More to the point," Labhran himself joined in, "once the party sets out from here and crosses the sea, it's too late to find they need a guide if they haven't got one. Our best chance of catching Quintillean is to make the best speed possible, and that means taking everything we think we might need, because then we won't waste time waiting for others to catch *us* up. I know it's distressing to think of those two innocents in the hands of that evil bastard, Andra, but I promise you I'll use all of my skills to help bring them back safely. If it comes to it, and we have to cross the border, no-one else here apart from Sioncaet has been as deep into enemy territory as me. And Sioncaet would be too easily recognised – anyway he's more useful here."

The second surprise announcement was that the Knights from Prydein would be amongst his party. Oliver Aleyne would be the joint commander with Labhran, and Friedl, Bertrand, Theo and Hamelin would go with him. Alaiz looked stunned at this announcement, not realising that she lay behind the Prydein Knights' selection. Oliver had long confessed to his seniors his worry that his friend Hamelin was rushing in where Spirits feared to tread with his growing affair with Alaiz. The young queen of Prydein was married to King Ivain – as long as he still lived – however much of a miserable match that was proving for her. Oliver feared for his friend's life if any of the senior nobles in Prydein found out about Hamelin's involvement, and Master Brego had agreed that the two should be separated for their own sakes. Nobody was happy about the pain they were going to cause, but it seemed the least of all evils.

Consequently, Oliver stood before the assembled witnesses and repeated his orders from the former Grand Master of Prydein, Hugh de Burh, to find and protect Wistan. He felt that it was cheating somewhat to lay the blame at Hugh's door for their departure, but it was another way of ensuring Hamelin would obey the order. It also gave Alaiz less room to protest in front of the assembly, although Oliver had no doubt that substantial pleading would be made to him to exempt Hamelin from joining the others once the meeting broke up. Five lances – each consisting of a Knight, a senior man-at-arms, another man-at-arms and two archers – would go with them. Brego added another surprise by announcing their departure first thing the next morning. The older man had guessed how much pressure Alaiz might bring to bear on Oliver, and hoped to avoid putting the young captain in the position of having to refuse a direct order from his queen. By sending them off straight away, the rest of the day would be too busy with preparation for Alaiz to get them aside alone. What none of the Prydein group knew was that Brego had plans to keep Alaiz busy too, but first things first.

It was Andra who once again drew the meeting back to the fugitives.

"But what if they take the northern route?" he asked anxiously.

"I'm going after them that way," Will Montrose spoke up. "I promised you I'd go after Wistan, Andra, and I keep my promises."

"I didn't doubt that," Andra said, feeling mildly chastised. "But you are a general, albeit in exile. I did wonder if there was something different that Master Brego needed you for."

Brego shook his head. "No, Brother. Where Will's concerned there's a limit as to what he can do anyway. In terms of experience you're right, he'd be best used going back to Rheged and rallying whatever troops he can find. But with his previous nasty brush with the DeÁine Helm, there's no way that we can send him back across the water while that thing is still active. Especially with that Abend, Tancostyl, at large and drawing on its power. Ironically the safest way for him is west, because that's the greatest distance from any of the DeÁine Treasures if any of the other Abend get hold of one and start trying to use it."

Everyone coyly avoided mentioning who would go with Will, except to say that he would not be going alone. It was Kayna who finally asked,

"Well what about the rest of us. Are we supposed to sit around here waiting for them to come back?"

Ruari shook his head.

"Far from it. We've been considering the information that Taise and Sithfrey have been continuing to work on. They'll get a week or so more to see what they can come up with, but do you want to tell them where you've got to, Taise?"

The tall DeÁine woman glided elegantly to the table where she could see most of the people.

"As you know," she began in her mellow contralto, "we got as far as realising that the piece of gibberish that was in the scroll we found, probably related to the Island Treasures. For days we couldn't think what it was supposed to be telling us, but then Sioncaet had a bright idea. He suggested that, although the location of each of the Island Treasures was supposed to be known to the Grand Master of each of the Knights' septs in each Island, they must have guessed the current crisis could happen. They prepared so well for everything else, it seemed unlikely that they would ignore the possibility that a Grand Master might die without passing on the information to his successor. So Sioncaet wondered whether the garbled message might be some form of coded way of informing people where the Treasures were.

"The bad news is that Andra then realised that we're looking at anagrams. This would be fine if all we had to do was unravel them. Even with Sithfrey and myself being so unfamiliar with Island geography, it would only be a matter of sitting with a map of each Island until we found a name that matched. Unfortunately this code is exceedingly ancient. What we have is probably a copy of an original."

"Why do you think that?" Matti Montrose asked curiously.

Taise sighed. "Because anagrams are hardly the hardest thing in the world to work out. As a form of protection it may be defeating us now, but at the time it was written it wouldn't have been that hard to decipher."

Sithfrey stepped reticently up to Taise's side. Speaking in front of these formidable Knights always gave the DeÁine scholar the jitters, just in case they forgot he was supposed to be on their side and filleted him in a fit of pique.

"Because of that it seems likely that this was written very early on in the days of the very first DeÁine invasion. Probably before the gravity of the situation was really realised, and it struck home to them that the DeÁine were planning to overrun *all* of the Islands – when nothing would be safe. The manuscript we saw over in Celidon wasn't *that* old, even though it was ancient. The problem then, you see, is whether it was copied correctly from the original.

"Kayna and Labhran were most meticulous in their copy of the Celidon manuscript, but there's no guaranteeing that the person who copied it from the first was as careful. If they had no idea what it was they were copying, there's always the possibility that a letter was missed out. With this sort of problem, letters switched about isn't so bad, because we're going to jumble them up ourselves, but if we don't have all the pieces of the puzzle, we could be in real trouble. Add to that the problem that the names of places change when you're looking at over five hundred years, and you begin to see the complications."

Everyone looked grave at this. One thing they had already agreed upon was that the Island Treasures must be found.

"I'm guessing, then, that you've not got anywhere with deciphering them?" Bertrand asked from his place at the corner of the table.

Taise allowed herself a smug moment as she was able to say,

"Actually we have made a *little* progress. Going on the rest of the poem, which implies that the Sword is in Celidon, we got Maelbrigt involved on that one. The words after 'sword' are 'its high iron where the'. Well, at first we tried all the words together and got nowhere. There were just too many letters for any name in Celidon. It's taken days of whittling them down, but we finally decided that the key words were 'high iron', which if juggled around comes to Rhionigh. Maelbrigt assures us that this is very probably the ancient form for Rionich up on the north coast of Celidon."

"That it is," Maelbrigt agreed. "It's a desolate spot where only the seals and the gulls go. The surviving castle is inland a bit, but there are the ruins of an ancient fort out on a rock that's now separate from the mainland. Five hundred years ago it was probably still connected by a narrow causeway of rock. It would've been a formidable place to have to attack. As a place to repel the DeÁine it would be ideal. Not only was it supremely defendable as long as there were some form of cisterns to catch rainwater for drinking, but the surrounding sea would make any high ranking DeÁine queasy at the sight of it. Certainly distressed enough to have trouble drawing the Power to attack it that way. I'd guess that once the old fort became dangerous as the sea carved away the rocks, that the Sword got moved to the replacement castle. That's now been deserted for decades as far as I know, but the walls still stand and there's a small preceptory up there. The Sword is probably still safely hidden there. All I have to do is find it."

"You?" asked Taise in surprise. "You mean you're going away?" She felt her heart leap in alarm at the thought of her beloved Knight going off alone into who knew what danger.

Maelbrigt smiled weakly at her.

"You and Sithfrey are safe here," he told her, "but you have to remain here for your own protection where the DeÁine can't reach your minds. The others have tasks that they need to do. I'm the obvious choice because I know the territory like the back of my hand. If I have to go to ground and hide, I can do that far more effectively than anyone else – anyway Sioncaet is coming with me, and it shouldn't take us long."

Taise's expression let him know that he had not heard the last of this, even if she was too tactful to take him to task in front of the others. Meanwhile Matti was looking pensive.

"Are there any others that you can make a good guess at?" she asked the three researchers. "Because the Sword is only one of six Treasures. Granted we have the Bowl because that's part of the landscape, and Master Brego knows where it is, but that still leaves the four others missing. I don't mean to demean what you've done, Taise, but we're going to need more than two if we're going to turn the DeÁine back – especially if Quintillean and the other Abend succeed in finding their own Treasures."

Sioncaet spoke up.

"Alaiz has been of real help with the Prydein clues. It's lucky that she grew up in a castle where the maps were all ancient and decrepit, because she knows some of the old names. Like with the Sword, the three words between 'arrow' and 'bow' are 'met air the', but it's only the first two that matter. Unfortunately, although Alaiz easily identified them as meaning Temair, the bad news is that Temair is a near-deserted settlement on a northerly point of Rathlin, across the water from Brychan."

"Oh bugger!" Bertrand swore, getting him a disapproving look from some of the others, to which he remained oblivious. "Right in Mad Magnus' patch. That really puts the cat amongst the pigeons doesn't it!"

"Too true," his companion Knight, Theo, agreed. "That means the Arrows are going to take some finding. We can hardly go in and start rummaging around on Magnus' doorstep without him getting suspicious. And I can't see him being wild about helping us – even against the DeÁine."

"I'm afraid it doesn't get much better, either," Alaiz piped up reluctantly. All eyes switched to her and she felt herself starting to blush. "Once we had Temair, we started to do a bit of geometry to try to place the six-pointed star Taise saw back when she was studying in New Lochlainn. By putting one point on Rhionigh, and one on Temair," she pointed to them on the map, "...once Master Brego had told us a third – the location of the Bowl at Emain Macha – we could get a rough idea of where the other three points must be, and so the Treasures too."

"Indeed," Taise carried on to spare Alaiz the scrutiny. "Alaiz was so right when she told us to remember that Rathlin and Kittermere were once considered to be part of a triple Isle of Prydein. I'm afraid even though we don't have the exact location, it's fairly certain that the Bow is either on the east coast of Kittermere, or just on the west coast of Prydein. We think Kittermere is more likely, but that means it must be within an approximate twenty mile radius of Alaiz' old home of Osraig."

The Prydein Knights groaned almost in unison. Osraig meant that the object they most needed to find was deep in the territory of Alaiz' brother Turstin. He was presently joined with another member of the DeÁine Abend in attempting to overthrow Ivain (the rightful ruler of Prydein and Alaiz' husband) for Ivain's cousin Brion. Once more the problems of even accessing the land, let alone searching it, looked insurmountable.

To add to the spreading sense of gloom, Taise confessed that none of them had the faintest idea where the Shield was, except that it was somewhere in the far north of Brychan across the water from the island of

Ynys. Similarly the Spear was lost somewhere in the heart of Rheged, deep in the mountains over which Matti and Iago had made their escape earlier in the year. Sithfrey even admitted that the settlement or castle which had once contained the Spear may have been abandoned for centuries, for they could find no sign of anything at all marked in the rocky wastes, even on the oldest maps.

They therefore had to face the grim possibility that a previous Grand Master of Rheged had moved it, and to who knew where. Ruari confessed he thought that his own predecessor may not have know it, even had he had the chance to pass such information on before he died. Rheged could turn out to be the worst to search yet.

"You see," Brego summarised for them, "there are no shortage of tasks to keep us busy. I'm sure that in the coming days each of you will find that there's more than enough to keep you occupied! Although Labhran and Oliver's men will set out tomorrow, I anticipate Will will be only a day later, because, although he can go overland far more, the weather is still against us. If he's to keep up with Quintillean, he'll need to make a landfall somewhere near Ynys as soon as possible. Maelbrigt and Sioncaet will go on their journey then, too, along with a message for the granges on Celidon to warn them that I intend to start sending Knights back there soon."

An excited buzz ran around the room, especially from Brego's own commanders. The Celidon sept had been forced to close after severe losses at the battle at Gavra Pass, over eight years ago, had reduced their numbers to a mere fraction of their former strength. Many of the surviving Knights, who had been forced to relocate to Ergardia, had wondered whether the day would ever come when their return would really happen. Brego was forced to explain that the arrival of the Knights from Rheged, whom Ruari had led out of the east, had swelled their own numbers sufficiently to make it a realistic proposition.

The Knights in temporary exile from Rheged would stay in the eastern part of Ergardia, ready to return to their home if the chance for action presented itself, but in the meantime guarding the coast against possible actions by Ruari's avaricious half-nephew Oswine, and the Abend war-mage Tancostyl. Yet given that more than one triad of DeÁine Hunters had got through to Ergardia from Celidon, that was now seen as a weakness which must also be addressed. It also meant that those searchers travelling west would have to do so covertly if their search was to remain secret from the Abend.

"As for the rest of you," Brego wrapped up the meeting, "Taise, Sithfrey and Andra have another week to come up with something we can use. After that I intend to start putting people into the field, and we'll just have to use the old method of trial and error to find the Treasures. Someone following a hunch based on what they've seen is just as likely to get lucky, and we don't have enough time on our side to be able to wait indefinitely."

He took in Taise's downcast expression and felt sorry for her. "It's not your fault Taise. You three have worked wonders with very little. If anything it's our own faults, or at least those of our forebears, for not taking more care of our records. We're all very grateful to you. Without your help we'd be in even more of a mess than we are now. It's no discredit to you or your work that we're just running out of time."

For now, though, he dismissed the assembly, and the different groups drifted out, animatedly discussing forthcoming departures or possibilities. As the great dragon-carved door swung shut behind the last man, another much smaller door opened at the back of the room and Brego's servant padded softly in bearing a tray. From the pot a subtle aroma of tea wafted out, and, as Brego groaned and lowered himself into his chair, a cup was poured and placed before him.

"Oh thank you, Angus," Brego breathed with relief. "That's just what I needed!"

As the Grand Master, Brego was the one man in the Order who was entitled to a personal servant. Past Grand Masters of Island septs, he knew, had chosen servants skilled in providing the kind of luxuries and services found at royal courts. Angus, however, was a burly highlander whom many thought taciturn, which was not the case at all. It was simply that he had never found the need for idle chatter – something which Brego found profoundly relaxing. Angus had perfected the knack of knowing what his master required and when, and was as likely to simply appear with a drink, put it on the table and go, rather than engage in conversation. Yet he also knew when his master needed to say out loud those things he nonetheless could not say to his aides and commanders. In their long years together, Brego had never known Angus be indiscreet and repeat anything he had heard in confidence, and welcomed a familiarity that was elsewhere denied him.

"It went well?" Angus asked, lifting a napkin off the top of a slab of rich fruit cake, which it had been covering to stop it drying out while it had stood waiting for the meeting to finish.

"Aye, as well as could be expected." Brego sighed wearily. "By the Trees, Angus, this conspiring is wearing work. They're all good people, but that's the trouble! None of them got to be here by being stupid or easily led, and they've formed bonds that are deeply binding."

"Do you think your plan will work?"

"Well so far it's been alright," Brego answered hopefully. "At least we've got young Hamelin separated from his queen without a scene – or until tonight, anyway! Giving them so little time to prepare means that this evening is going to be very busy for them. There isn't time for him to come up with ways of circumventing my orders when his friends are all pushing him to get packed so as not to delay them. Then the day after, we'll get Montrose and MacBeth packed off on their travels. It's not just Quintillean that's making me rush them off. That Shield is far too vulnerable in Brychan. Sacred Trees preserve us if the DeÁine come through the north, because it'll be cut off. MacBeth got the DeÁine Treasure away to safety through hostile territory, let's hope he can do the trick a second time!

"Thank the Rowan Maelbrigt is the steady sort too, and Taise. They at least won't throw any rocks in our path. So we can justify him and Sioncaet leaving with the other two, so as to chivvy them along, because they'll be travelling the same route at first."

"Do you think Maelbrigt suspects you're sending Kayna off on a mission?"

"Probably. ...He's not daft. But he has great confidence in Kayna being able to look after herself, and the one he would worry about is staying here anyway. I wouldn't be surprised if he's already talked with MacBeth about us sending Kayna across to Rheged with Iago. Just as long as neither he nor Will suspect she'll have Lady Montrose as company, we should be in the clear."

"So once those four go the day after tomorrow, who's going next?" Angus asked, as Brego held his drained mug out for more tea while devouring the cake.

"Depends on the weather," was Brego's cake-muffled reply. Swallowing the last bite, he took another grateful swig of tea. "I want to get Alaiz out of here and off to Kittermere as soon as possible, because I'm sure it's our best chance to strike while the worst of the winter lingers. Come the spring we may be faced with all-out hostilities in Prydein. Let's face it, we've no idea how bad things got after she and the others left – the messages we have had have been cryptic at best. The Island may've already descended into full scale civil war, we just don't know. But I daren't let her out of the castle until I've had word back that Labhran and Oliver's party have embarked and set sail. Nothing would be worse than to have them delayed, and meet up with Talorcan and Alaiz on the quay and find that we're sending their beloved queen into the jaws of a monster, so to speak. Can you imagine the ruckus that would cause?"

"Aye, I can!" Angus said sagely. "So you'll send the others to Rheged first?"

"Probably. I've thought it over, and having seen how Kayna and Lady Montrose have taken young Queen Alaiz under their wing while she's been here, I can't help wondering whether they too might baulk at her being sent into something they'd perceive as being so dangerous."

"Isn't it, though?" queried Angus. "She escaped Mad Magnus once, but he didn't know who she was then. Can you be sure he won't find out if they get caught this time?"

"No. I can't guarantee it," admitted Brego, "but that's why I want them to go so soon, while everyone's attention is distracted with this power struggle on Prydein. I wish there was another way, …but she's the one person we've got who knows Kittermere well. All her Knights are natives to Prydein, but they've never served on Kittermere or Rathlin. She's been to both. If anyone can trace the Bow, it's her. And with Talorcan's sergeant and the other man coming from Rathlin, she's going to get the best help I can give her. Unless, of course, a miracle happens, and Taise and Sithfrey come up with another clue in the intervening days.

"If I honestly thought it would help, I'd send a small army in with her, but I can't see any way that would change things other than draw far too much attention to them. Seven people can go unnoticed in a way that a company of soldiers never could. In fact seven is making a fairly big party by civilian standards if they're always seen together. I'll just have to trust to Talorcan's experience at covert operations to break them up in different combinations if they go into villages or towns, so they won't stick in people's minds. This sort of thing is what he excels at, and I know he'll protect her with his life without being obvious about it."

"Well that's a good thing," Angus murmured, as he cleared away the tray, "because he just might have to!"

Chapter 3

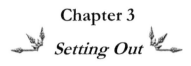

Setting Out

Ergardia: Aer-Yule

The next morning, on a cold and frosty first of Aer-Yule, a great assembly slowly took place on the northern shore of the loch. Where the river ran from its highland spring down the steep valley, the Order's stables lay, shielded at their back and sides by the towering walls of the mountains. A small force of expert mountaineers might launch an assault from across the treacherous crags, but even then the crumbling mountain faces threatened to betray marauders with rock slides and loose boulders. The Knights kept a substantial reserve of mounts here to cater for all eventualities, although this was but a small part of their herds. Many more were located at farms on the lusher valleys of the far north of Ergardia, where the mountains became softer and the new grass richer, and the horses were often rotated amongst locations but always keeping Lorne fully stocked.

Now preparations were under way for a full half-battalion to depart for Celidon. One hundred Knights, each leading a lance of enlisted soldiers required a huge number of beasts, and Brego was anxious that those travelling farther afield be provided for before all the horses disappeared. The last thing he wanted was to find that eager captains had emptied the stables, leaving Oliver and Hamelin to face Alaiz' pleadings for a week until more mounts arrived.

The chain ferry from the northernmost isle in the loch had transported those about to depart, and those who wished to see them off, to the shore. Alaiz stood red-eyed and pale in the watery early light, flanked by Kayna and Matti. Both were obviously being supportive of their new friend in her hour of need, which Brego was grateful for. He had little experience of tearful girls and was in no hurry to expand it, however much he liked and respected Alaiz. Hamelin was evidently faring better for, although he was quieter than his fellow travellers, he was going about the task of loading his saddlebags onto the horse and checking his gear with a workmanlike steadiness.

Privately, Brego wondered whether the same would have happened if he had known that Alaiz was not staying safe in the confines of Lorne. The odd comment that Oliver and the others had let slip, led him to think that the young Knight was slow to anger but formidable once roused, and Brego had no desire to get into a battle of wills with him. Especially as it was clear from Hugh de Burh's letter, which had come with them, that Hugh considered Hamelin had the potential to rise high within the ranks of the Order if given the right opportunities. The last thing he needed on his record was a face to face confrontation with a Grand Master.

Labhran finally swung into the saddle of the spirited roan he had chosen, triggering the others into mounting up. Alaiz gave a barely audible sob and Matti and Kayna moved closer to her, but she remained outwardly calm, giving Hamelin a simple little wave from where she stood. Behind Labhran and Oliver, the Prydein Knights drew up in pairs, then the additional five Knights and their lances who were going with them, plus the grooms who were to bring the horses and pack-mules back once they had embarked on the ship. On such a long voyage there was little to be gained by putting the horses through the stress of a rough winter crossing. Then the two leaders heeled their mounts up to level with where Brego stood on a low mound at the beginning of the road out.

"Goodbye, sire, and thank you," Oliver said, his words carrying a multitude of meanings known only to him and a few others.

"Safe passage to you all," Brego replied solemnly, then addressed Labhran directly. "The commander at our docks at Firthton is expecting you within the week. I fear you may have a miserable voyage in this weather, but with the strong winds you'll have a quick passage to Brychan. You have the papers?"

Labhran nodded and patted the left breast pocket of his heavy boat-cloak. "I'll convey this to the first ealdorman we meet once we land. If the chance presents itself, I'll send a bird when we make our last landfall on our south coast before setting out across the open sea."

"That would be helpful," Brego replied, neither needing to say why, but Labhran's eye strayed to Alaiz, returned, and gave an imperceptible nod as he declared to the assembly at large,

"This may take some time but we'll be back, never fear."

The surrounding troops cheered them off then swiftly turned to their own preparations, but Alaiz lingered looking longingly down the road as if she hoped to see Hamelin's horse return at any moment. When they judged she had stood there long enough, Kayna and Matti finally took her away, kindly but firmly propelling her to the ferry back to the castle. As soon as it pulled up to the castle quay she leapt off and ran, her sobs ringing out before she got out of earshot. Kayna and Matti looked at one another sadly. Neither liked to see their friend so distressed but let her go, instead heading for the refectory and hot mugs of caff.

"May the Sacred Trees protect him and bring him back in one piece!" was Kayna's heartfelt prayer.

"Make it so!" Matti agreed. "She's been through enough already, and she's so unprepared for the blows fate can hand out, I don't know how she'd cope if she lost him forever."

Kayna handed her friend a brim-full mug and picked up her own as they wandered over to a spare table, where watery sunlight was creeping in through the high lancet windows which looked onto an inner courtyard.

"What about you?" she asked Matti nonchalantly. "How do you feel about Ruari and Will going off together? Will I can imagine you'd be glad to get some space from, but what about Ruari? You don't say much about how you feel about him, but I've seen the way you look at one another."

Matti shrugged. "In a way I've got used to it – well, as much as you ever can. Right from when I was married off to Will, he's been disappearing off on some mission or other. Some more dangerous than others, I'll grant you, but he's been declared missing, even dead, before now. The same with Ruari. It's not that I don't worry, the Spirits know how many sleepless nights I had when the war in the east was on and the news came back that Jarl Michael was dead. I ought to be grey-haired by now! But you can't live like that, Kayna. Normal people just don't have that much energy to spare! At some point you have to start carrying on doing all the normal stuff, even as mistress of the house.

"And I always thought it was selfish for me to indulge myself weeping and wailing, when the ordinary women who worked in the castle had to get up and get on with life, even when they really were widowed. I've never had to face that certainty. So I sort of resolved to take stuff one day at a time. I'd worry about things when they actually happened, instead of wasting all my energy on something that might never come to pass.

"It sounds grand in theory, mind you, but it's a lot tougher to do in reality," she admitted ruefully a second later. "When I was Alaiz's age I found it a lot harder to maintain some semblance of composure."

"I can't imagine you ever being quite that naïve, though," Kayna contemplated. "I'm only five years or so older than her, but I can't ever remember being like that."

"No, but you were brought up in a garrison," Matti reminded her. "Poor Alaiz was closeted and cosseted, not out of any concern for her as Alaiz, but to protect that political bond between Prydein and Kittermere. Her relationship with Queen Gillies was hardly normal either, was it? Most people aren't brought up by their mother-in-law! And not only as a surrogate mother, but with Gillies and Ivain as her only real friends as well. The boy she played with as a child was the man she was supposed to have a fully functional marriage with! Can you imagine how that must have messed with her mind? Courts are a little self-contained world of their own as it is, but most people only go there as adults. I can't imagine what it would be like for that to be the only world you know until you're in your twenties. All your ideas of love and romance coming from minstrels' songs and arranged marriages, *uugh*!" She shuddered.

"I suppose so," Kayna admitted. "No wonder she thought she was in love with Ivain. It'd be hard to know otherwise, wouldn't it? Finding out that he didn't care two hoots for her really must have been a harsh blow. No wonder she's fallen so hard for Hamelin."

"Which is something else I suspect Ruari and Master Brego have taken into account," Matti said knowingly. "Both of them must be able to be ruthless when the occasion demands, but they're not unkind men. I'd bet that they've discussed the possibility that Hamelin was the straw of hope offered to a drowning woman. I have no doubt that *his* feelings are real and constant, but then Hamelin's almost ten years older than her, and he's been out in the big wide world for most of his life and taken a few more knocks. Can you imagine how hurt *he'd* be if she then decided, after a bit longer out in the world, that her feelings towards him had changed?"

"Sacred Trees!" Kayna swore. "I must admit I hadn't thought of that possibility, but it's the sort of thing Maelbrigt would think of, and he and Ruari seem very alike in that respect. Yes, I see now that however much it seems harsh, someone had to give her time to stop and think."

They sat in silence for a few minutes drinking the last of the caff. It was only as they got up to go that Kayna pressed Matti,

"What about you, though? When this is all over will you be willing to go back to just being Lady Montrose again?"

Matti laughed. "I don't know." Then looked at her friend's wry expression. "No really, Kayna! …I don't know. So much depends on what happens. If Will died then, yes, I think Ruari and I could be very happy together. But whatever he is, I've never yet truly wished Will dead, and I don't now. And to complicate things, all that's happened to Will recently has made him behave very differently to me here and now. After all these years I'm *finally* seeing the man who could draw Ruari into being best friends with him. There was always a huge wall there before. A part of him that he kept out of my sight, as if he was desperately trying to act out the role of husband without having a clue as to what to do. He was so uncomfortable in my presence I think we both stopped trying to find a bridge.

"It's taken me stepping into his world – away from any husband and wife situation – for him to find a way to talk to me. Sacred Trees, we've talked more in the weeks we've been here than in all the last ten years put together! So I'm not sure I could be so heartless as to cast him aside now – and for no better reason than he's been a lousy husband in the past – and I'm sure Ruari wouldn't be comfortable with that, either. ...Anyway, I thought you were chasing after Talorcan? You can't imagine that that one will sit at home waiting for the world to end!"

Kayna blushed despite her nonchalant tone. "Well, I guess I'm not so different from Alaiz after all," she admitted ruefully. "Talorcan always seemed so romantic. I totally misread him! I thought that if I waited long enough he'd wake up and see me. See that I was far more of a match for him than the frail little doll who had up and died on him. I'd always thought they must've been on the verge of marrying, or at least announcing an engagement. You could have knocked me down with a feather when Sioncaet told me, on one of those nights down in the great hall here, he'd never even kissed her! Yet she's the only woman I've ever heard him being associated with, even if it was back when he was barely out of his teens. And I now realise that he doesn't even see 'me', except as Maelbrigt's little hanger-on. The brat his friend should have let go years ago."

"Ouch!" Matti breathed. "Oh Kayna, I'm so sorry. No-one should find themselves cast aside for such a reason."

"Oh don't worry, I'm not badly burned, just a bit singed around the edges," Kayna said with a flash of her sardonic humour. "I'll live! The difference between me and Alaiz is that I could see that there wasn't much hope to start with. I only hoped I could make him *start* to love me – I never fooled myself into thinking he was pining for me. Now it's my pride that's dented more than my heart. I feel like going out and proving I'm just as good a Knight as him – even if I haven't taken the vows – not going and jumping off a bridge in desperation!"

There was a second's pause and then both women independently said, "No man's worth that!" Which resulted in them folding up in laughter as they left the refectory, to the puzzlement of the men behind them.

It was harder to remain quite so cheerful the next morning, though, when they assembled once more at the stables to see the next party off. Matti had forgotten quite how handsome Ruari looked in full uniform, for, as he was now to travel through Islands where the Knights were still a force to be recognised, there was no need for him to travel in disguise. Will, too, looked different from the last few times she had seen him leave Montrose Castle. The hardships of his journey to Ergardia had shed pounds in weight, yet he looked healthier than he had for many years, not least because Ruari had had him training hard every day. He had been loaned a spare uniform, and if he was shorter and squarer than Ruari, he nonetheless looked every inch the experienced and formidable soldier.

Beside them, Maelbrigt sat on his horse like a bridge between them. Taller and slimmer than Will, he was still broader in the shoulder than Ruari if a couple of inches shorter. Dark where the other two were fair, he appeared the thunder to Ruari's lightning. Sioncaet sat in total contrast to them all. In the depths of Lorne's armoury he had found breeches of a densely woven sage-green fabric and a tunic to match. His battered leather over-tunic was still there, but had benefited from some expert repairs from the master armourer, so that the steel rings now lay as neat rows of scales once more. The little man was dwarfed by his friends, even sat on one of the Knight's great destriers, but somehow looked both otherworldly and every bit as dangerous.

As on the previous day, a large number of soldiers prepared themselves to accompany the main party. However, this time each man led a packhorse laden with supplies. Oliver and Labhran's group would be accommodated at granges on the direct road to the sea, but their friends would have few such comforts. They planned to take the road north, making the bleak climb over the mountains to the fort of Appin, during which time they would for the most part have access to granges. But beyond that, they had a cross-country trek around the great inland loch of Appin down to the fort at Dunathe, and only then join more roads on to Culva.

They and Brego had spent hours contemplating the advantages of different routes, yet they had always come back to this one as the quickest means to get them across to Celidon while avoiding Abend spies. For Ruari and Will landing at Gigha made sense, as they could cross Celidon to

Ardfern with Maelbrigt and Sioncaet guiding them, although no-one pretended that in the heavy snow this would be easy. Yet avoiding this difficulty meant either an even worse journey over the higher mountains and a longer sea journey, or a truly lengthy trek around the coast of Ergardia. Both alternatives were slower and ultimately no easier or safer.

After witnessing Alaiz' forlorn roadside vigil the day before, Kayna and Matti were glad that Taise had said her goodbyes in private beforehand and had declined to come across to the stables. This time both felt that had she collapsed in tears, they would have joined her – partly because they knew how deeply Taise and Maelbrigt were attached to one another, for this was no new passion, but also because this time they too had people they cared about leaving.

Kayna found a reason to go and check Maelbrigt's horse's bridle and whisper to him,

"You be careful, big brother! I know you've gone up against the DeÁine before when I was too young to protest, but if you do something stupid this time to be heroic, I might have come after you to kill you myself!"

Maelbrigt laughed and squeezed her hand.

"You're a fine one to talk! You just remember that when you're off on Brego's mission – I don't want to come back and then have to come and bail you out!"

Kayna stepped back torn between sadness and curiosity. So Brego had a mission for her, did he? Typical Maelbrigt to drop a big hint like that and then ride off leaving her to stew on it!

Matti meanwhile had walked with studied calm over to Ruari and Will.

"You two take care of one another," she told them. "No competing to see who can out do who!"

"Yes mother," Ruari said with mocking servility, which earned him a slap on the leg.

"Ouch!" Matti exclaimed shaking her stinging hand. "What in the Islands have you done to those breeches? They're like iron! Surely that can't be comfortable to ride in?"

"They've just been treated on the upper leg," Will explained. "To stop a sword cut while you're riding. And it's your own fault if your hand hurts if you will go around whacking people! ...Ouch!" as Matti smacked his hand hard. "You see, Ruari? I'm a battered husband!"

"*Pffff!*" Matti snorted. "Battered, indeed! Get on with the pair of you!"

Then felt tears come in her eyes as she realised that this was the first time in years, if not ever, that she and Will had exchanged easy banter like this. Curses! Why did this have to happen now when they were both going away and might not return. All that wasted time and now no time to make up for it. She hurried back to Kayna and slipped her arm through Kayna's and held onto her friend for dear life.

Kayna was sharp-witted enough not to need to look at Matti to know what was wrong, and instead covered her hand with her own and gripped her back. As soon as Maelbrigt, Sioncaet, Will and Ruari had disappeared around the bend in the track, they turned back to the ferry, not waiting for the rest of the troop to file past. By the time Brego had joined them on the ferry, both had gained a modicum of composure, although it was a silent trip back to the castle.

The riders proceeded at a brisk walk, but as they reached a gap in the trees on the northern bank of the loch they could see the towers of the castle, and on the roof of one something red fluttered. Maelbrigt slowed, drew his dagger and let the sun flash off the polished blade. The red waved frantically again before they were deep in the trees again. His three friends looked meaningfully at one another but said nothing. All knew that there must have been some arrangement for Taise to be on the battlements around the right time, but nobody felt like teasing him about it. The whole day felt far too solemn for that. However much they might have made light work of the farewells, they all knew that both journeys were fraught with danger.

Back at the castle the day dragged on into another and then another. Alaiz slowly crept out of her room for longer periods, but looked endlessly red-eyed, white and shaky. Taise was subdued even by her calm standards, Matti quiet, and even Kayna had lost some of her bounce, but all three worried about Alaiz. All attempts to cajole her into coming down to the great hall had failed, and even Brego privately confessed to Angus that he might have misjudged the depths of her feelings. In the end it was Taise who won her over by getting her to come down to the library, and carry on trying to decipher the anagram for the Bow hidden on Kittermere.

In such a way a week passed. The next day a messenger arrived in the evening to say that the first group had safely embarked on board the boat and had left Firthton quay. Apparently they had made good time over the first four days, arriving in the grange for the fourth night's stay only to find a messenger there. The captain had sent word that the roads to Firthton were almost clear of snow, and that if they would ride on with all speed there was an advantageous tide on the next two mornings.

So Labhran had decided that they would ride through the night. Men and horses could rest the next day, he declared. Had the horses been going with them he would not have pushed them so hard, but they could take a couple of days to recover before going back to Lorne. The men, he announced could sleep once they were on the ship. Indeed there would be little else for them to do, and a tide in their favour was not to be missed. Consequently the grange found torches for every fifth man and they had carried on, arriving saddle sore and freezing at Firthton at dawn, just in time to grab saddlebags and proceed on board. Others from the grange attended to the horses, and no sooner was the last man aboard, than the gangplank was hauled up and the sails shaken out.

The three women expected Alaiz to decline even more at the news that Hamelin was truly departed, but instead she seemed to rally now that no chance of him returning early remained. She still seemed to be sleeping an inordinate amount but she was crying less. Brego had considered delaying Kayna and Matti's departure because of Alaiz' frail state of mind, but her slow adjustment gave him hope that it need not be so. By the end of the second week he felt confident enough to call the two women into his study, where the Forester, Elidyr, stood studying the great map shoulder to shoulder with Matti's old friend, Sergeant Iago. Angus drifted silently in and offered them all mugs of caff and hot, fresh, fruit buns before retreating tactfully to the back room.

Here it comes! thought Kayna, and gave Matti a conspiratorial grin.

"Well, I'm sure you all have a rough guess at why I've called you in here," Brego began, then looked at the grinning faces. "Alright! You needn't look quite so smug!" but could not refrain from smiling back. Thank the Trees that this foursome was as eager as hounds too long in the kennel. There would be no protests from them, he could see.

Elidyr gestured towards Iago and Matti and said,

"If they're involved would I be right in guessing we're going to Rheged to look for the Spear?"

"Absolutely!" Brego confirmed. "You'll depart in a couple of days for Ferrybank and go back across to Bridgeport. We've had word from Ruari's friend, Ron, that they have the next batch of rescued soldiers from across the sea in the east, safely ashore in Rheged. They're making their way to Bridgeport by the back way so the Jarl's men don't see, but should be there by the end of the week. You'll be going to stay with your old friends, Gerard and Rosin of Urse."

Matti's grin got broader at that, while Brego continued,

"We know that Edmund Praen went back with Ron to help him, but he should turn up with the new refugees. When he does we're recruiting him, with Gerard, to help you. I understand from Ruari that there's a third man you may call on for help, but only in dire need?"

Matti nodded firmly. "Oh yes. Osbern of Braose was a valiant knight and served the Jarl faithfully for many years."

"What went wrong?" Elidyr asked. "I assume by that frown that something did go wrong."

"He got wounded, almost fatally." Matti recalled. "It was touch and go for months as to whether he'd make it. But that's not the problem, physically he's fine. When he regained his strength some Spirit-forsaken priest got his hands on him, and convinced him that he'd been especially chosen by the Spirits to live. But that he should also consider himself forever beholden to them and their earthly representatives afterwards."

"You don't like priests?" Elidyr asked, curious at Matti's bitter tone.

"Not when they warp a man's mind like that I don't! These days Osbern doesn't fart without confessing it the family priest, and don't even *think* about getting me started on how he now treats his poor wife! Gerard's Rosin and I could go on all day with a catalogue of misguidedly cruel acts he perpetrated on her!"

"Sacred Trees!" an astonished Elidyr muttered.

"Yes, well it would be no bad thing if he turned to them once in a while for inspiration instead of the Blessed Martyrs! Bloody fool's probably itching to die some gruesome death to join their ranks! But we have to be careful, because what Osbern knows, sooner or later his priest will know, and if Tancostyl has a strangle hold on the archbishop and the Church, I'd be amazed if he hasn't got someone checking up on Osbern's priest."

"By the Wild Hunt!" Elidyr could only swear again.

"It's a mess and no mistake," Iago agreed. "I met Sir Osbern years ago. Back then he was as good a leader as you could hope to find. Not in MacBeth's class, of course, but then few are. Always was a bit on the serious side, mind, but I don't think anyone anticipated he'd go this way. He's not the man he was."

"So you see," Matti concluded, "we can depend on Edmund and

Gerard without any reservations, but I know they'd be the first to say let's keep Osbern at arm's length."

"Is there anyone else we can call on for help if we need it?" Elidyr asked Brego.

"Abbot Jaenberht, of course. He's beyond corruption and our best hope for holding things together in Rheged if it looks like civil war. Your problem is that you're going to be at the other end of the Island to him. His current stronghold is the abbey at Mailros up in the north-east, but you'll be heading for the south-west. If it becomes imperative that you consult old maps, for instance, then I'd advise you to make for him – unless Iago or Matti know of another safe source to approach. Your problem will be that it'll take you weeks to get there, losing you valuable time from your search."

"We may lose time anyway," Iago said thoughtfully. He pointed to the map and drew a triangle with his finger between Airey, Crauwel, and Underdale Castle. "Taise's best guess is that the Spear is hidden somewhere in this area. But look at it! It's all high mountains! We can only go there and hope for an early thaw. There's no way that we can hope to start searching while there's heavy snow on the ground. I know, because I've been up there in winter! On top of that, we must be extremely careful if we venture into Crauwel, especially you, Matti. It's crawling with Oswine's men, the last we heard, who were searching for General Montrose. We daren't take a chance on you being recognised, although you're easier to disguise than Sir Gerard or Sir Edmund – they'll definitely have to stay away if we go into the town."

"No new developments on the location, then?" Elidyr asked.

Brego shook his head. "They think it must be an anagram of 'tend wander', but look at the map! Do you see *anything* written there, let alone something that could be made up of those letters? That's why I fear you may have to go to Jaenberht, and see if there's some old map lurking in the dusty depths of his library that can shed some light. But I think you should at least go and scout round first, because there's no guarantee that such a map exists anyway."

"We'll just have to hope that by the time we've trudged back down there the worst of the winter will be over," Iago tried to be optimistic.

Brego gave them a list of supplies at their disposal and encouraged them to take as much as they thought they might need, for he could let them take packhorses to help with the load. What he dared not do was send more men with them.

"I wish I could send half a dozen lances with you," he sighed. "But Rheged is a taut bow string at the moment. One slip and the arrow will be away, and who knows where it might end up. With Gerard and Edmund, there'll be six of you – enough to discourage idle vagabonds, but not a big enough party to excite the curiosity of those wanting to flex their muscles. Of all the folk I'm sending out, you four are the closest to home, and if you're in any danger I want you to come straight back. Commandeer a fishing boat if you need to. That's not being an old worry-guts! We daren't provoke Jarl Oswine – or King Oswine as he now wants to be known – into launching an open attack on us. All our reserves must be ready for whatever the DeÁine have planned. I'd rather you came back if you felt your disguises had been compromised, and then make a second attempt later, rather than end up before Oswine and Tancostyl."

All four agreed to the need for caution, but once outside the office it was hard to be subdued. However, saying goodbye to Alaiz and Taise was hard. Taise had been expecting such an announcement, but was sad to be losing more people she knew. It was hard for her and Sithfrey to be the lone DeÁine in a fortress dedicated to training DeÁine killers, though they were now accepted by all the men openly, even if some had reservations in private. Alaiz was harder to console, and both women hoped that Brego would soon find her something to do to take her mind off her ever-departing friends. For someone who had spent so long with no-one at all, to find herself with a whole bunch of new friends had been almost overwhelming, but it was harder still to let them go. At least there was some consolation in knowing that it would be easier for these particular friends to come back.

Yet when it came to the day of Matti and Kayna's departure, Alaiz found herself unable to face going to see them off. Instead they all breakfasted together, and then Taise, Andra and Sithfrey led her off to the library while the others went to get their packs. This morning was very different to the previous departures. The snow was falling in large powdery flakes rendering visibility down to a few yards, and the four travellers with the same number of pack horses, slipped silently out of the stables to Brego's lone farewell. Before they had even turned the corner to the road they had become mere grey silhouettes in the white, with not even the sound of their horses' hooves to trace them by.

For the remaining occupants of Lorne there was little to do but train and wait, and Brego had great difficulty restraining Talorcan. It irked the younger man to be trapped in the castle when others were out pursuing his favourite quarry, DeÁine. In the end Brego summoned him to his office and revealed the mission he would lead, but conditional on him telling nobody else of it. However, by the third week of the month a much-delayed bird had arrived in the calm after several more days of heavy snow, with a message from Labhran saying they had reached Caley in good time. If the weather and tides stayed favourable, Brego believed that within the week they should hear that they had made the final landfall at Creagan, on Ergardia's south-west point. From then on they would be on the open sea and communication impossible. Nonetheless, it seemed to him that there was little chance of the Knights now returning to Lorne to find Alaiz gone, and he consented to Talorcan's plea to allow them to depart.

Whereas Labhran and Oliver's group had found transport on a merchant ship whose owner was bound to the Order, Talorcan's party would be taken by a very different vessel. Those heading for Brychan needed to slide into port unobserved in case Quintillean was using creatures to watch for them, and a regular merchant ship would excite no comment. The journey to Kittermere was far shorter but subject to a different kind of danger. The Attacotti might be normal mortals but they were formidable seamen, and even the foul weather of winter was no guarantee that their ships would not be out raiding. The only surety was that the galleys would not be able to put to sea. Those sleek craft, propelled by banks of huge oars as well as the sail, could produce a turn of speed and manoeuvrability which outclassed most vessels in calm seas. But the great disadvantage of them was that in high seas the oar ports shipped water badly, causing the galleys to capsize. However the Attacotti had a few single-sailed vessels, and by island-hopping they covered surprisingly long distances in search of places ripe for plunder.

Brego feared that the Attacotti leader, Mad Magnus, might be enjoying more than usual freedom of movement because of the conflict in Prydein. Kittermere had long been sparsely populated on its western side and Brego wonder whether Magnus might have men camped there. Even worse, he dared not send Alaiz by ship to either of Kittermere's ports, Osraig or Draynes, as they were her brother's holdings. Instead, one of Ergardia's mere handful of warships was to take them in their friends' wake to Caley, but then cross covertly to Kittermere. The vessel had been chosen as the shallowest draughted available, and it was Brego's hope that the captain and his master would be able to find a passage through the interminable saltwater marshes of northern Kittermere. Even so they would have to take horses with them, for there was no guarantee that there would be any to hire.

Although Taise, Sithfrey and Andra pleaded with Brego to allow Alaiz to spend Yule with them, he gently but firmly declined. Instead, he called Alaiz to join Talorcan and the men of his lance in the office. The rough and ready soldiers seemed more overwhelmed by Alaiz than their Grand Master, young Ad squirming uncomfortably and never looking up from the ground except to give her darting curious glances. Brego could not refrain from smiling as he heard him whisper to the older, fatherly Tamàs,

"If she's a queen, where's her crown?"

And Tamàs' soft reply, "Back at the castle lad, so as she don't lose it!"

Decke, the other archer besides Tamàs, was always dour, so there was little surprise that he said nothing, but Talorcan's sergeant, Barcwith was already studying the map with his fellow man-at-arms and brother-in-law, Galey.

As Brego explained what they were seeking, he could see questions already being formulated by the men. This was what he had wanted for Alaiz's companions. Men who would not blindly follow orders, but pursue the mission with intelligence and forethought. When he had finished the briefing, he summoned Angus with refreshments and gave them a few minutes to confer. Before he needed to call them back to the map, Barcwith and Galey were already there with a question.

"Are you sure, begging your pardon sire, that it's Temair that's the place you want?" Galey asked, peering over a battered pair of spectacles he had produced to look at the map with at Brego.

"Yes, we're sure," Brego replied. "In fact it's the only location we *are* sure of."

Alaiz spoke up nervously.

"It's the one place where the name hasn't changed in all the time since the scroll was written. We might have a possibility for Kittermere…"

"Oh yes?" Brego was suddenly alert curiosity. "Taise hasn't mentioned that before!"

"Because we're not sure, sire," Alaiz apologised in a fluster. She pointed to an area to the north-east of Osraig where another river ran into the sea. "Over here there's a sunken valley called Glen Rossen. The nearest we've got the words from Taise's manuscript to is Llin Rossing." She wrote both out on a work slate from Brego's desk. "You can see they don't look that much alike."

"No they don't." Talorcan said sharply, making Alaiz blush.

"Maybe," Barcwith said thoughtfully, "But when you say them with the local accent," he ran them both off in a lilting accent, "they sound like the one could have come from the other."

And indeed, said like that they did sound closer related, for which support Alaiz gave Barcwith a grateful smile. It gave her the confidence to continue.

"The problem is that it's a *flooded* sunken valley. Back when I was very small I have a vague memory of being taken there by my father with my brothers. He'd taken us there in the summer to see the tower of a church, which still stood beneath the water, and that's what I remember – peering down into the water at this great stone tower. If that *is* our place, we may have to wait until the water is warm enough to swim in to search it."

"Oh wonderful!" Talorcan commented sarcastically as he looked daggers at Brego. "We're going on a fishing expedition! How challenging! What else would you send a Knight for?"

Yet before Brego could chastise him it was Galey, with a familiarity born of years of fighting together, who cut across his commander's sarcasm with some of his own.

"Oh I think you'll find enough to keep even *your* sword happy, sire, when we get to northern Rathlin."

Talorcan turned to him and quirked and eyebrow.

"Oh indeed, so you will," Barcwith seconded Galey with a twitch of amusement on his lips. "You see, this is where the DeÁine ships run aground when they miss Brychan. No-one's left of the folk who lived at Temair – we buried them before we left, didn't we Galey? The most recent DeÁine slavers and their desperate charges massacred them while we and most of the other men were far away at the market in Brychan. There wasn't much to choose between the slaves who were desperate to find some place to call their own, and those herding them, who weren't much better."

He paused and both he and Galey had a faraway look in their eyes. "After the body count when we got back, it was clear that they must have taken some villagers to replace those they'd lost. Not my wife, nor Galey's, thank the Trees – they at least are at rest and beyond more torture. But among the slaves were murderers and other hardened criminals, and they escaped recapture as far as we could tell. Last we heard, most of the DeÁine slavers had made it back across the water in hijacked boats, but others were chasing the miserable souls they'd lost and were hiding in the hills from Magnus and his men. Not that he's bothered with that side of Rathlin much. The Brychan ports are all too well-defended to be easy pickings for the likes of him, so he leaves the poor souls who live there to fend for themselves. Some bloody leader! …Pardon the language, ma'am! …So if you want to search Temair, sire, you'll have to kill the DeÁine hiding there first!"

Chapter 4

Dark Horizons

Ergardia: Aer-Yule to Yule.

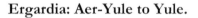

Talorcan's men set about preparing for their departure with practised thoroughness. Ventures into enemy territory were the norm for them, and they were used to having to be self-sufficient for weeks on end, but what did worry them was having Alaiz along. So much so, that they sent a request to Talorcan to meet them in a small private room, normally used for small-scale briefings, where they could talk openly. The tall dark-haired Knight entered the room to find them already seated around the fire, and a pot of caff warming on it. Without a word Barcwith poured another mug out and handed it to Talorcan, who hooked a spare stool out with a booted foot into the gap which completed the fireside circle, and sat down.

"Alright, what's this about?" he asked in a neutral tone. He knew and trusted his men, and however much he might be the commander – whose word was final – he valued their insights.

The men all looked to Barcwith, as inevitably happened on these occasions, although Talorcan knew that once they started talking everyone would find a way to have their say. The bulky sergeant bent his head to stare into his caff which he gave a swirl, as if to stir up his thoughts, before speaking.

"Well it's like this, sire …it's the wee lassie. Now me and the lads, well, we're up for this mission – even if it does turn out to be nothing more than a grand fishing trip. We've been on dafter missions than this – like that time we went chasing all over Celidon, that turned out to be some poor old chap selling a few harmless charms, instead of a DeÁine wizard on the prowl!"

"But it's the weather!" Galey picked up eagerly. "We can rough it. It won't be easy – this is severe weather even for here, let alone in the south which she's used to – but we know how to survive. It's going to be rough, but doable. But she's just a slip of a thing! How in the Islands is she going to cope with living rough?"

"Aye!" Tamàs' slow, thoughtful voice agreed. "We've all heard how she snuck out of Magnus' court, but she got rides in carts after that. Will she be able to take a full day in the saddle?"

"The talk in the messes is that she's been like a little ghost since that young Knight left," Galey added. "What are we going to do if she starts pining away again?"

"Slap her arse!" Decke muttered sourly.

"You can't do that! She's a queen!" Ad exclaimed, shocked at his fellow soldier's lack of respect.

"Bloody can!" Decke grunted.

"Bloody can't!" Talorcan declared firmly. "Absolutely no arse slapping! Under any circumstances!"

"What, not even if she takes a fancy to your handsome mug and decides she might like a bit of slap and tickle?" Barcwith teased his commander.

"Oh Spirits help me! Not that!" Talorcan moaned forlornly, his mood instantly switching from assertive commander to unwilling object of adoration. One smitten female was quite enough to contend with, he beseeched the Trees, although he hoped he had managed to put Kayna off without causing too much grief. The last thing he needed was for the young queen to attach herself to him emotionally when he had to be stuck with her for weeks on end.

"Don't worry, sire," Tamàs said comfortingly. "She's lonesome, there's not much doubt about that, but she strikes me as the faithful type. I don't see her shiftin' her feelin's about like some wenches we've knowed. No, it's more the practical stuff that worries me and Barcwith. What happens when …well …when women's things start happening? We could be on the road for months, if you sees what I mean."

"My wife, Trees bless her, used to be flattened for days each month," Galey reminisced sadly. "She wasn't putting it on, either! At any other time she was as hard a working woman as any in the village, but for those first few days it was all she could do to put some food on to cook, and then she couldn't face eating it! They say this Alaiz was in bed all day last week."

"Aye," his brother-in-law Barcwith agreed, "and although my Maura wasn't taken so bad as her sister, she still couldn't have ridden hard at that time. Someone's going to have to talk to her about it." He looked significantly at Talorcan who blanched.

"Oh, fuck off!" Talorcan exploded. "I've had to do some things in my time but there's nothing in the rules that says a Knight has to do *that*!"

"Well *someone's* going to have to," Barcwith said firmly. "We've been talking it over and there's no getting around it. If we have to make camp somewhere for three of four days it's got to be somewhere secure, and that means we have to have some kind of plan. We can't just wake up one morning and have her declare she can't ride that day – or the next – when we're somewhere exposed and two days from fresh water. We need at least some idea of which *week* she might have trouble travelling. That way we can pace our journey. I'm sorry, but you're the one who can go up to the guest rooms. You know we aren't allowed up there."

Talorcan had gone paler than any of them had ever seen him. The Knight who would face a pack of DeÁine Hunters single-handed was looking positively sick at the thought of discussing such a subject with a strange woman.

"No," he said. "No! I absolutely can't! ...There's no way! ...No way! I am *not* doing that!"

Barcwith shook his head in amazement at his commander. Even after all these years there were still the odd moments when Talorcan could surprise him, and this was one of them. Perhaps, Barcwith wondered, it was because of his upbringing that Talorcan could be so utterly defeated by the thought of having to deal with an intimate conversation with a woman.

"Couldn't you ask another woman to ask her?" young Ad asked innocently.

"No, I bloody couldn't!" Talorcan exclaimed, going red now. "Great Maker, that would be just as bad! 'Oh excuse me madam, but could you ask your friend when she's due 'on'?' Hounds of the Wild Hunt, Ad, are you trying to get me killed before we even leave the castle?"

Poor Ad cringed and buried his nose in his mug of caff at his admired captain's rebuke, but Tamàs nodded thoughtfully.

"Nay lad, that's not such a daft idea. What we need is an older woman. Someone who'll understand *why* we need to know, and can ask in a ...well, sort of motherly way."

"Mmmm..." Galey thoughtfully picked up a small scroll that had been put on the table behind him. "You know, Taise is a sensible sort of lady. I've been talking to her about wanting to get the chance to read more and she got me this out of the library. I've finished it and I was going to take it back to her anyway. I could try asking her to help, if you like?"

"Trees yes!" Talorcan said with alacrity, thankful to pass that problem on to someone else and swiftly changed the subject. "Was that all?"

"No, but it was the big problem, although it would be best if Galey says he's asking with your approval," Barcwith admitted.

"Approval given!" Talorcan hastily assented.

"But what are we going to call her?" Ad asked anxiously. "I don't want to be strung up for not being proper around the queen! But if we call her "your highness", or some such, then aren't we going to give the game away if someone overhears us?"

Talorcan growled, fit to spit nails. This mission was turning into something more befitting some creeping diplomat than a soldier.

"We'll just have to call her by her own name, Alaiz," he said firmly.

"But what if she objects?" Ad fretted.

"Tough!" Talorcan retorted, privately wondering whether Decke had not had the right of it after all, and what dire punishment there would be for turning the queen of Prydein over his knee and slapping her arse. Then shuddered at the thought of the chaos that would cause in his faithful band.

Tough men every one, they still had some very fixed ideas about how to treat women, and he doubted he would even get chance to raise his hand. After losing their wives in violent raids, the only thing that turned Barcwith and Galey into death-on-legs quicker than an attack on a woman, was one on a child. And Talorcan knew that it was the one time his seniority would count for nothing. Decke might say the words, but Talorcan had no doubt that doing the deed would be seen in a very different light. And gentle Tamàs might be slow to anger, but Talorcan had seen him roused, and never more so than in the defence of those whom he thought incapable of standing up for themselves. No, he would have to tread very carefully on this mission, or else he would end up with all his men jumping on him, verbally if not physically.

His mood was not much better two days later when they took the ferry across the loch to the stables. The horses that had taken Labhran and Oliver's party to the coast were once again waiting to do the trip, carefully held on one side from the seething mass of riders milling around in every available space. Alaiz was awe-struck by the sight, as were Taise, Sithfrey and Andra. The three researchers had decided that they should make the effort to see Alaiz off, however painful it was for themselves, for it seemed unfair that she should go feeling that there was nobody left would care whether she came back or not.

As they stood there, almost on the jetty, they saw the ferry coming back across with Brego on board, and as it left the castle a great bell somewhere in one of the towers tolled three times. The sound resonated across the water and suddenly order appeared out of chaos. Ten pennants were raised on lances, distributed in a rough line heading towards the start of the road. Riders now moved into formation behind them until a column of two riders abreast snaked back behind the imposing figure at the front, with ten knights behind each pennant.

Between each pennant and the lances formed on it, there was an equal-sized line of pack-mules. The little cluster of onlookers could see carefully strapped on many of them wrapped bundles of swords, shields, and quiver upon quiver of arrows. And scattered amongst the Knights were their trained battle-birds of prey – some apparently dozing on their perches on the saddle pommels, others watching alertly – which was a sure sign of something major happening. In this weather the hawks were normally only regularly exercised close to the castle, for a fully trained hawk had taken years of work to produce.

Taise grasped Alaiz' arm in excitement.

"It's the Knights going to Celidon!" she exclaimed softly. "Oh how I wish Maelbrigt could see this! He'd be so pleased!"

"Don't worry, my dear," Brego's voice sounded beside her, as he stepped up from the ferry. "He knew! I could hardly have persuaded him to leave otherwise! You of all people know how strongly he felt about defending his homeland. If I'd sent him off after the Sword without first promising him that I'd see to putting the Celidon granges on alert, well, he'd probably get there by next summer! Because he'd have felt obliged to take the warning to as many places as he could on the way. He's a stubborn man, your Maelbrigt!"

Taise felt a warm glow of pride at hearing him called 'her' Maelbrigt. At times like this it was almost hard to believe that he was the same person she had known for years as the unassuming man who farmed the land of the old castle, and whiled away the long winter hours telling her funny stories. And yet it all fitted. Looking back now she could see that he had never lied to her. She had been the one who had assumed that he was just some obscure soldier, living the quiet life and building a few incidents into a larger than life tale.

Instead he had turned out to be a force to be reckoned with, not only in his home but over here in Ergardia too. Brego was not a man to be easily swayed in his decisions, yet Maelbrigt had driven a hard bargain with him for the price of his co-operation and got away with doing it – which spoke volumes of Brego's respect for Maelbrigt. It would not have surprised Taise if Maelbrigt had been chosen to be the one to lead the return of the Order to Celidon, but in his absence another sat at the head of the column of men.

"Who's the leader?" she asked Brego, inclining her head towards the stranger who sat in the distance with his back to them.

"Baderon of Castle Sligo," Brego answered. Then realised that the name would mean nothing to any of those he was speaking to. "He's a good man, proven in battle, as Maelbrigt would tell you if he was here. Before the Knights of Celidon were cut down at Gavra Pass there were half a dozen Knights in line to become the next second-in-command to the Grand Master, when the current Master retired and his second, Grimbald, took over. Baderon and Maelbrigt were two of them."

He sighed sadly. "Now they're the only ones left. The others died at Gavra with their Master, and Grimbald took over as Master for a few short years before he had to take over the running of all of Celidon. Back then Maelbrigt, having already been inducted into the Foresters, took them over, while Baderon tried to help Grimbald re-form the rest of the Order." He smiled and patted Taise reassuringly on the hand. "You needn't worry, Taise, Maelbrigt was solidly behind Baderon taking the first wave of Knights back – in fact he said there was no better man for the job. We haven't forcibly deprived Maelbrigt of anything he wanted for himself!

"Now, I must go and set these men on their way so that you folk have room to move." He turned his attention to Alaiz. "I think you'll find that the men have been most solicitous for your well being and have tried to pack everything you might need. But if you feel there are things you lack, then I've given my authority to Talorcan to purchase extras – within reason of what you can carry, of course – before you embark on your ship."

Alaiz smiled wanly at him and nodded. At which point it occurred, somewhat belatedly, to Brego that she might be so intimidated by Talorcan that she would never ask, even if she was desperate.

"You mustn't be put off by him, you know," he added kindly. "Talorcan's bark is much worse than his bite." Then offered up a silent prayer to the Trees to forgive him for telling such a whopping lie, and to watch over Alaiz. That Talorcan was the right man to go undercover into Attacotti territory, and seize two Island Treasures from under Magnus' nose, was never in doubt. Yet without the modifying influence of his particular band of men, Brego feared that Talorcan would put expediency and the mission above any consideration of Alaiz' comfort or stamina. Not that Talorcan was a cruel man. Rather, he just saw the big picture more clearly than most. If one person had to suffer for the good of many – even if it was himself – then Talorcan would make the sacrifice, and worry whether he was thought callous afterwards.

Sometimes, in the depths of night in the privacy of his own room, Brego wondered what would happen to Talorcan if the ghosts of his past ever caught up with him all together. Somewhere deep inside the walls that Talorcan built around himself there was, Brego was sure, a vital spark of humanity which still burned bright. Ever hidden behind the sardonic mask he presented to the world, the genuine warmth of his personality remained reclusive. And to all but a few, Talorcan was an iceberg in human form – someone who brought wreckage and despair to those who stood in his way, and burned like ice those who tried to touch him. Yet there were times still when even he could be moved, and Brego prayed that there would be someone who would melt that ice enough to allow the inner flame to breathe again, before it was extinguished forever in the frozen depths where Talorcan kept it locked away.

The problem was that Master Grimbald had found Talorcan too useful as a DeÁine killer during those dark days after Gavra Pass, to worry about what it was doing to the man himself. So that by the time Talorcan had arrived in Ergardia with the rest of the Celidon Knights who had elected to come across, the damage had already been done. And it had taken Brego years to whittle away at the ice-face before glimpsing the real man beneath, let alone try to vary the missions he was sent on.

As Brego strode to the head of the column and spoke to Baderon, Talorcan appeared leading two horses, with his men behind him.

"Mornin' miss!" Barcwith called out cheerfully, as though they were going on nothing more than a pleasant ride in the woods.

Tamàs handed his horse's reins to Galey and cupped his hands to give Alaiz a leg up onto the horse.

"Up you go, miss!" he said gently. "She's a good-tempered beast, is this one. We picked her special for you."

Galey was already mounted alongside her by the time she got settled into the saddle, and as Tamàs adjusted her stirrups to a comfortable length, he reached over and draped an oiled cloak over the top of her existing one. Alaiz looked at him in surprise until he reassured her that, while the soft fur-lined cloak she had chosen was wonderful for warmth, it would be soaked through in no time.

"Wear the oiled one over the top," he instructed her, tucking it around her. "It'll help keep the wind as well as the rain out. There's nothing more dangerous in this biting cold than getting wet. You'll get to the point where you never get warm again if your wet clothes start to freeze on you."

Taise was having trouble not smiling at the way these soldiers were fussing over Alaiz, and her fears for her little friend's safety were evaporating like the morning mist. Talorcan, however, sat glowering to one side, wondering what in the Islands had turned his usually formidable lance into a bunch of lady's maids.

"Are you *quite* finished fussing?" he demanded as the last packhorses of the column of Knights passed them by.

"Oh I think that just about does it," Barcwith declared, letting his commander's foul mood run off him like water off a duck's back, and maintaining a resolute cheerfulness. Nudging Decke to take up position behind Talorcan with Galey alongside him, Barcwith put Alaiz in the middle of their group next to Tamàs, bringing up the rear himself with young Ad. As they passed Taise and the others he leaned down from his saddle and said softly to her,

"Don't you fret, now! We'll take good care of your wee friend."

"Bless you!" Taise responded from the heart, and on impulse Andra ran forward and pressed a small book into Galey's hand.

"It's some poetry," he said hurriedly. "You take it to read! Alaiz likes it too."

"Thank you," Galey responded, instinctively realising that it was no small thing for Andra to let such a prized possession go, and that he was trying to help in his own small way. He tucked the tiny volume into an inside pocket where it would remain dry and then waved in salute to those on the jetty as he rode on.

The little book had been the only thing Andra had carried with him from the monastery where he had grown up, given to him by the old monk who was the nearest thing to a father he had known. For years he had never realised the worldly value of what he had carried around, or wondered what a monk was doing with a book of somewhat lusty love poems. It had only been sharing them with Matti and then Alaiz that had opened up their full meaning to him. Only then had he remembered distant conversations with the monk, and pieced together the realisation that his mentor must have been the younger son of a very wealthy noble, given to the church despite his love of a woman. A woman he had never been allowed to see again, let alone marry as he must have wanted. Suddenly it had seemed appropriate to Andra that Alaiz should have the book which had been such a comfort to his 'father' in all those long years of separation from someone he'd loved.

Talorcan, meanwhile, had said his last farewell to Brego and was glad to be on the road once more. Yet no matter how much he tried to set a blistering pace on that first day, he kept finding himself way ahead of the rest of his party. No number of commands to Barcwith and the rest to get a move on improved their pace, but it was not until they coincidentally reached one of the more comfortable granges just as night fell, that he tumbled to what his men were doing. No matter what he said, they were making sure that Alaiz had a warm bed to sleep in while there was still a comfortable rest to be had. The result was that while the rest of the lance enjoyed a cheerful night in the refectory, allowing Alaiz to be the centre of attention of all there, Talorcan retired to his room with a flask of wine and fumed alone.

His health and temper were not improved the next morning by a stinking hangover. With a whole smithy of anvils pounding behind his eyes, he rode out in disgruntled silence, and maintained a frosty disinclination to talk all day. But it did no good. Once again nightfall found them at the large grange some ten miles back from the simple wayside resting place that he had hoped to reach. As he took out his temper on the roast chicken before him at the table, he spied Barcwith's humorously quirked eyebrow at his wrenching off a leg, and growled in frustration.

"Spirits take you to the lowest levels of the Underworld!" he snarled at Barcwith.

"Aaghhh …goin' there already," Barcwith lightly brushed the curse off with a chuckle, and despite his best intentions to the contrary Talorcan could not avoid grinning back.

"I'm not going to win this one, am I?" he asked resignedly.

"Nope!" Barcwith rejoined.

Talorcan crooked a summoning finger at his sergeant, as they stepped away from the long table and over to the corner bar, where a steward was dispensing ale.

"Are we going to carry on at this snail's pace all the way to Rathlin and back?" he demanded, now that they were out of earshot of the others.

"No," Barcwith replied calmly, "But we *are* going to give the wee lassie time to get used to being in the saddle all day. Look at her! She's falling asleep where she sits!"

Talorcan sighed in frustration. "That's commendable sergeant, but we have a boat to catch and the tide's not going to wait on a queen's sore arse!"

"Well we'd figured *that*," replied Barcwith with studied patience. "Me and the lads found some of the Order's sailors in the mess on night before we left, and asked them about the tides."

"Oh you did, did you?" growled Talorcan, irritated at being outwitted again.

"Oh yes. We've plenty of time. The first good tide's not for another three days, and it'll only get better over the next two after."

Barcwith was not to be swayed, Talorcan could see, and he grunted his assent before grabbing his plate and retiring to the back room. Half his foul mood was because he was not particularly proud of the way he was behaving, and yet he could not help it, because the other half of his temper came from this mission. Leaning wearily back against the settle he recalled the countless times he had pleaded with Master Brego to be allowed to be one of those going to Brychan. He wanted to hunt DeÁine. It was what he was good at. Even the memory of fighting the Hunters who had attacked Maelbrigt on the way to Lorne made his pulse race. He was good at it, maybe the best, although he was not so arrogant as to believe that in his heart of hearts. Yet what was he doing? Shepherding some lovelorn girl on a futile quest to find weapons they might not be able to even find, let alone use.

In his mind's eye he still recalled the face of the woman he had thought of as his mother. The only one who had shown him real affection as a child. And he also remembered her face and her screams as his natural mother had had her taken away to some prison cell as punishment for caring about him. He would never forgive or forget that act. Long ago he had worked his way past the feelings of guilt that it was somehow his fault that his foster mother had died, but the anger never left him. DeÁine blood might run through his veins, but he felt no kinship with that race. His whole life, from the time the Knights had found and rescued him, had been dedicated to clearing the Islands of every DeÁine he could find. As a Knight now himself, he was as skilled as he could be, and he seized every opportunity to put that skill to good use. Sometimes it was in a planned ambush, sometimes fortune played them into his hands. On those occasions the rage he felt at finding decent, ordinary folk dead and wounded, for no other reason than they had had the misfortune to cross the path of a DeÁine, lent him even greater strength.

What irritated him even more, though, was the fact that he knew that every one of his men was with him because they too had very personal reasons to hate the DeÁine. Yet somehow they had found it in themselves to accept this mission with good grace. So why could he not? None of them were given to false optimism any more than he was, so it was unlikely that they believed that this hunt would drastically change the course of the fight against imminent invasion. He grunted as he shifted position on the settle and felt the tension-knotted muscles in his neck and shoulders protest. Well, if they were going to carry on at this creeping pace, he would make sure that when the boat put in to Caley that he got chance to use the steam cabins. Maybe that would sweat some of the ill humour out of him. But for the coming nights he would just have to rely on the soporific quality of the hops to get him some sleep.

When they finally rode into Firthton, it was to a day as foul as Talorcan's mood. The sea was grey as slate, lopping in oily waves against the quay, but farther out he could see great dark rollers churning, promising a miserable crossing. The sky was an unremitting bank of towering charcoal-grey clouds which could not quite decide whether to rain or snow, and even just across the bay was indistinct with the low cloud. The ship, the *Craken*, lay tucked away in an unassuming berth at the far end of the harbour, and as they wandered down the quay towards it, they were all relieved to note that she pitched less than some of the other craft.

The captain turned out to be a middle-aged man made to look older by his wreath of grey whiskers, but who obviously knew his business well. In short order he had arranged for all but the things they would need for one last night ashore to be stowed away. He intended to depart on the morning tide and suggested that they rise early enough to give the horses a short exercise before they were swung on board. Hopefully the main crossing would be swift, and after that they hoped to be able to find places where they could moor up at nights to allow the animals off the ship for a while. While Talorcan and the captain discussed their route, the others took Alaiz back to the grange and made the best of the plentiful supply of hot food, and a warm fire to sit by.

In the dark, bleak, early hours, long before the late winter dawn, they were all gathered on the ship's deck, watching by torch-light the horses being swung aboard in rope cradles. None of the animals looked happy about it, but at least being the Order's own beasts this was not the first time it had happened to any of them and they went quietly. As soon as the loading was complete, Captain McCormack shooed his passengers down to their cabins out of the way of the crew as the ship was got underway.

For Alaiz it was something of a shock to find what the Order thought of as cabins. The last time she had set sail, on the ill-fated trip with Gillies, her accommodation had been the size of a small room, complete with normal furniture. Here she had something which was only as long as the bunk bed, and as wide as the bed plus a wooden trunk. The trunk was bolted to the deck, and had to both contain all her possessions and serve as a table. For all that Alaiz knew that she was lucky to have this to herself, she found it profoundly claustrophobic when the door was closed. There was not even a porthole to look out of. Perhaps because of this she found her stomach beginning to churn even before they left the relatively calm waters of the bay. She managed to hang on to her breakfast until they approached the wider channel between Ergardia and Rheged, but then had to run up the ladder to the deck and the side. It was little comfort that both wind and tide were with them, racing them down Ergardia's eastern seaboard. For Alaiz it was beyond misery. She had never thought she could feel so ill. Even water barely made it down to her stomach before going back over the side into the waves, for nothing seemed to ease it.

The men of the lance also found the journey uncomfortable, and for the first day Ad kept Alaiz company at the leeward rail. However, he slowly grew accustomed to the rolling motion, and by the second evening was able to eat the stew the sailors prepared, even if he did not enjoy it much. In the days it took to reach Caley, though, Alaiz' seasickness never abated, and by the time the ship eased its way into the harbour the men were deeply relieved that she would have some respite. Barcwith and Galey took their turns at looking after her, Galey reading from Andra's book of poetry to her to try to distract her, but it was Tamàs who eased her suffering most. There was no way that she could remain at the rail in such bitter cold, and Barcwith had carried her sobbing back to her cabin accompanied by a bucket.

Tamàs' gift with calming animals turned out to be as effective with people, for he swiftly realised how suffocating Alaiz found the small cabin space. Some careful negotiation with the sailors resulted in Alaiz being moved to a hammock slung right up in the bows of the main deck. Here she still had to bear the up and down motion as the fast ship crested wave after wave, but the screwing motion was less noticeable than further back in the ship. A simple curtain of old sail gave her some privacy without leaving her in panic-stricken claustrophobia.

Tamàs had a soulful tenor voice and an extensive repertoire, which he softly crooned as he placed cool cloths on her aching brow. It was not much but it relaxed his patient a little, and there was nothing else to be done. For most of the time she was so exhausted she slept, only waking to vomit. What concerned him more was that Alaiz was frightened by her incapacity, having told him that previously she had always been an excellent sailor.

"I don't understand this," she wept in despair. "I grew up by the sea. I remember going on long sea journeys around Kittermere when Father was still alive. Even when I went to Prydein, on the odd times we had to sail somewhere I was one of the only ones who *didn't* get seasick. What's wrong with me, Tamàs?"

As they docked at Caley, even Talorcan was forced to admit that Alaiz needed at least a day on shore. He had not seen her since they had come on board, and it had been a shock to see how white she was, and how much weight she had lost in such a short time when Barcwith dragged him down to see the state she was in. The captain had convinced him that, having made such good time around the foot of Ergardia, they now needed the wind to drop a little to facilitate their crossing to Kittermere. There was therefore nothing to be gained by making Alaiz suffer by putting out to sea straight away, and it gave him time to complete business of his own.

Leaving Alaiz in the care of his men at the grange, he went ashore and headed into the town to one of the bathhouses. Stripping off his uniform and placing it in one of the lockers, he took up a clean white towel off the pile by the entrance arch and headed into the first tiled chamber. Dousing himself, he used the plentiful hot water and soap to thoroughly scrub the grime of the journey off, then headed further back and found one of the pine built cabins. In the confined space there were two benches facing one another, and a brazier in the middle burning a mixture of coals and pine needles. Resting in the glowing embers was a bowl of stones which radiated heat too, and Talorcan took up a ladle of water from the pitcher standing by the door and splashed it on the stones. The air became filled with steam and he stretched, luxuriating in the warmth. Unbraiding his hair, he shook it free and looked forward to being really clean for the first time in a week. He was determined to savour this all the more because he knew it was likely to be the last time in much longer before he would have the chance to do this again.

It was not the only reason he was here, though. The cabins were heavily insulated with packed wool shavings (detritus from shearing and the looms) between the two wooden walls to keep the heat in, but what kept the steam in also kept sound in too. Nobody walking past would be able to hear what was being said inside. Before long the door to the cabin opened and another man walked in.

"Ah, Talorcan! Here at last, has Brego been keeping you on a short leash?"

"Oh, if only you knew!" Talorcan joked in only part mock desperation.

"How have you been?"

"Frustrated!"

"Well, I'm sure we can do something about that!"

Talorcan smiled for the first time in weeks. Most of the times he came to the steam rooms it was purely for the pleasure of getting truly clean, although he knew that other services were available if you knew who to ask. However, Talorcan had never been able to stomach the idea of paying for such personal entertainment, largely because he was convinced that those who sold themselves did so out of desperation not for the joy of it. He preferred his partners to be willing and to keep business where it belonged. Just occasionally, though, business could be combined with pleasure, and this particular informant was one of those times.

Had he known it, the seller of clandestine information was thinking the same thing. Some days he despaired of the lengths he had to go to to acquire even the most meagre of snippets, and more frequently of the kind of folk he ended up spending much of his days with. But the Knight in front of him was one of the ones who made it worthwhile. He had no interest in salacious tittle-tattle. Talorcan paid hard cash for one thing and one thing only – news of the DeÁine. Information hard come by and rarely of guaranteed reliability, and the Knight was not a wealthy man, but what went on while they did business sweetened the deal immensely.

Later, Talorcan left the cabin before his associate and went through to where a hulking albino kept the massage table. For the next half hour, Talorcan allowed his muscles to be pummelled and his joints manipulated, but by the end of it he had finally lost the last dregs of the blinding headache which had been steadily increasing on every day of the journey so far. As he dressed he even found that he could reach up to braid his hair at the temples, and then tie it all back in a neat queue once more, without his shoulders feeling like they were made of oak boards about to split. Pulling his uniform back on, he finally felt able to face the world again.

Reaching the inn where they were staying he found the others sitting in the common room. The men had obviously enjoyed a hearty meal, judging by the leftovers, and, although she still looked dreadful, Alaiz was nibbling on crusty bread and sipping a light beef broth, having slept the day away. While they had been at sea the Yule festival had begun and the old year seen out, yet there was no way that Alaiz could enjoy the cold cuts of the leftover rich meats that the men had gorged themselves on. The plentiful mulled wine, however, was at least putting a little colour into her cheeks, and she was eyeing the rich fruit cake with interest.

"Well here he is, the man himself," Barcwith greeted him cheerily. "Either you've slaughtered a few DeÁine around the corner there, or you've got some interesting information to be looking so cheerful." With feigned innocence he asked, "Did someone give you a Yule present?"

Talorcan took a playful swipe at Barcwith which missed by a mile, but making him duck so that Talorcan could steal his tankard of ale and take a long drink.

"Hey! Get your own ale, you!" Barcwith protested, grabbing his tankard back, then winked at Alaiz as he said, "Bloody captains, you can't trust them not to take advantage of their rank!"

Talorcan rolled his eyes and called across to the barman to bring another flagon over, before sitting down at the table.

"Well you're right, I did get some interesting information! The DeÁine haven't been seen hide nor hair of in Brychan all summer!"

"What? Not at all?" Barcwith was amazed.

"No, not even a whisper."

"That's weird!" Galey agreed. "There's usually some hothead on their side trying to start the next war even if the main army isn't on the move. Your man's sure?"

"Absolutely. Which means …"

"…there's something going on that's keeping even the wild ones happy." Tamàs finished thoughtfully.

"An invasion?" wondered Galey.

"That's what I think," Talorcan concurred. "There has to have been some promise of action to have kept the young bloods off Brychan's back all the time the mountains have been passable. That hasn't happened in decades! I wonder if it's all tied into the sudden appearance of the Abend in the Islands? Maybe they've decided that if the Donns won't support them with the regular army, they'll recruit their own men? There must be the best part of a generation of DeÁine lads for whom Gavra Pass is just old men telling tall tales. Lads who want a chance of glory of their own. Maybe if they think the traditional guard legions are too cautious …too hamstrung by the Donns and politics, …then they've been easy pickings for the Abend to recruit?"

"Then we have to find the Island Treasures even more!" Alaiz croaked, her throat hoarse from retching.

The others expected some protest from Talorcan when she said this, knowing his antipathy to this mission, but he simply nodded. It was not until Alaiz had retreated for an early night, and Ad had also crept off to enjoy a bed which did not move, that Talorcan spoke of it again.

"I've been thinking," he confided to the others in a quiet corner of the refectory. "If Alaiz is right and that sunken valley looks like being the place where the Bow was hidden, then there'll be nothing we can do at this time of year. DeÁine or no DeÁine, we won't be able to get to it while the winter rains raise the water levels and it's freezing cold. If that's the case, we should get across to Rathlin as soon as possible. I'm wondering whether our captain would consider sailing around Kittermere while we do our searching. That way we could meet him on the far side of the Island and take us by sea to the north of Rathlin.

"I know that Master Brego thought it would be less conspicuous if we persuaded a fisherman to take us across, but do any of you see an upstanding local wanting to sail into Magnus' home territory? It's always worried me that if we follow that course that the only folk we'd find willing to take us across might just deliver us straight to Magnus. And where will we be then? We certainly can't go hunting for the Arrows if we're locked up in one of Magnus' cages."

"The righteous have no dealings with evil men," intoned Decke, his pious inclinations to the fore. "Magnus is under interdict from the Church on every Island."

"I doubt the folk are as worried about the Church as Magnus' men's swords," was Tamàs' dry comment.

"It makes sense," Barcwith agreed reluctantly, but could not refrain from saying, "but unless you want to be seen to be openly defying Master Brego, we have to make a genuine effort to find the Treasures."

"I know," conceded Talorcan, "and we will give it our best shot."

"He'll not forgive you if he thinks you've disobeyed orders and gone chasing off after DeÁine on some information of your own." Barcwith warned again, worried that Talorcan had heard of some potentially juicier mission from his contact. Normally he knew his captain would think things through, but the enforced wait at Lorne, and watching others go on missions he wanted desperately to join, made him wonder whether impulse had got the better of the Knight.

"It's the information that bothers me," Talorcan admitted, making Barcwith groan in anticipation of what might be coming, but then explained himself. "My informant was talking about strange goings on in Brychan, and it struck me that if the Abend have found all their own Treasures, they may be trying to get them back to New Lochlainn. If they feel they need to use force, then they'll have to bring some kind of army into Brychan, and that'll mean the southern route round the mountains. But what if those friends of Taise's have been forced to carry on working on whatever manuscripts the Abend have? By Taise and Sithfrey's own admissions they've heard nothing of the others who were with them.

"They also said that they all used to work as a team. So what if these others have also worked out what Taise and Sithfrey have? That the Island Treasures are important? They don't need to know every last detail to see they're significant. And Temair was the easiest anagram to work out. But it's also the closest to the DeÁine territories."

"Oh shit!" Galey gasped. "Of course! Temair is only a step across the water. Spirits save us! Barcwith and I used to go to the Brychan markets from there every month! The DeÁine soldiers we fought …some of them went home! Not all, but probably enough for the Abend to be able to find out that most of the locals were dead, or fled like Barcwith and me."

Talorcan nodded. "Until now your home being savaged was important to you, but few others. Even the Abend being on the loose wasn't enough to cause concern over what was happening on Rathlin, because there are only four of them on our side of the mountains and we were sure they were going after their own Treasures first. But this unnatural stillness worries me. And if the Abend have soldiers, albeit novices, at their disposal, then would they think that sending some to Temair and relieving us of one of our

Treasures would be an easy victory to blood the new ones with? If they outnumber our troops three or four to one, they don't have to be good to win! And how many men are there to guard Rathlin anyway?"

"Few," sighed Galey, "far too few and most are the very young and the very old up in the hills, and Magnus won't notice until it's too late."

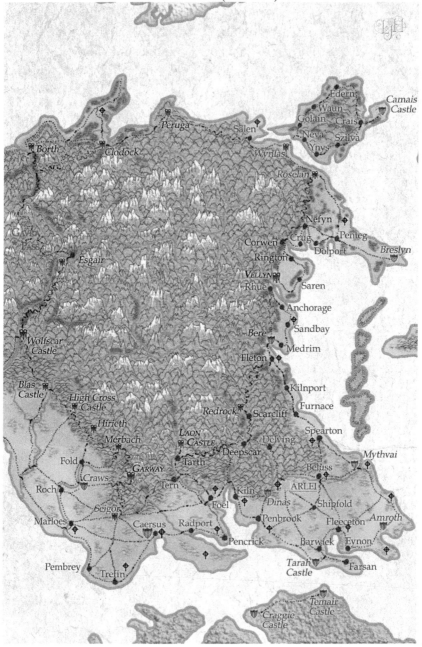

Chapter 5

 *Cloistered Secrets*

Brychan: Aer-Yule

The riders' horses ploughed gamely on through the deep snow up to Seigor Castle's gate. Normally the heaviest falls of snow came after the festival of Yule, but this year it had begun snowing early and kept on going. Not in great storms, admittedly, but every day there would come a point when what little daylight existed at this end of the year would disappear under thick, dark clouds. As the heavily-laden clouds rolled in from the west like icy, aerial lava flows, the snow would start. Big thick flakes, soft as goose-down, rained down in swirling curtains, at times obscuring all identifiable features in the landscape.

At such times Cwen was grateful that on the mountain roads they were travelling on, someone had planted tall wooden poles at regular intervals along both edges. It was not so much the times when they had a high cliff on one side and a near vertical drop on the other which bothered her – then it was simply common sense to stay as close to the wall as possible. It was crossing the floors of the valleys, when they were more exposed and the snow had drifted to form deceptive lumps and bumps. Then it would be so easy to step off the road into a hidden stream bed thinking that the ground was solid, only for a horse to break a leg and its rider to get doused in icy water.

Berengar and Esclados rode on either side of her, sheltering Twigglet with the bulk of their much larger horses all of the way from Redrock Castle down to Seigor. Having thought that travelling south would save them from the worst weather, this was a more arduous journey than any of them could have anticipated. However, the one compensation was that the further south they got the more they were in well-populated territory. This resulted in every castle being interspersed with granges and wayside hostelries, run by and for the Knights, at a distance which it was possible to accomplish in one day, even in the worst of weather.

There was therefore no necessity to even think about camping out in such bitter conditions. Had that been the case, Cwen knew that there would have been no way that they could have carried on, for to sleep outside would have been certain death. Even during the day the temperatures rarely rose to above freezing, yet Cwen grew to dread the warmer days even more than the others. While it remained so cold the snow fell and remained powdery, but once it started to melt, it meant that as soon as the temperature dropped again the melt re-froze as lethal sheets of ice.

There had been days when they had had no choice but to stay an extra day at some of their overnight stops, resulting in the journey taking several weeks. Now, though, they had made it to the huge castle of Seigor – in good weather one day's ride from their destination of Caersus. Also, if nothing, else the dreadful conditions had convinced Berengar and Esclados that the pursuing DeÁine war-mage, Eliavres, would find it near impossible to create any form of disturbance; instead probably using all his strength to survive in the circumstances of his final sighting high in the mountains. They could therefore focus all of their minds on how they were going to get sight of the all-important documents in the care of Caersus's great cathedral.

That night, as they stood before the roaring fire in the castle's refectory, Esclados sniffed appreciatively.

"Mmmmm… That smells like roast venison for dinner!" he rumbled in delight.

Swein took a sniff and wrinkled his nose at the pungent aroma wafting up from the kitchens. Once upon a time he would have been as enthusiastic as the old Knight, but all that had changed when he had walked in on the carnage wreaked by his former lord and lover, King Edward. What Edward had done to the young man whom Swein had thought was an actor – and who in reality was most likely to have been Edward's younger half-brother – haunted Swein's nights. Since then the sight of red meat made his stomach churn even when it was well cooked, whilst a bloody steak was enough to send him running from the room. He made a note to sit well away from Esclados, pulling his new friend, Jacinto, towards the head of the next table along.

Jacinto had come to realise the effect of meat on Swein and said nothing. If the slender, white-haired man was somewhat strange at times, Jacinto was not prepared to make a fuss over it. After all, Swein had turned his world upside down since the day they had met. The nights had been even more of a revelation though, and Jacinto – used to unsatisfactory encounters with women – had found in Swein's knowing company an unexpected, exquisite pleasure.

Berengar noted their move to the next table and said nothing too. As leader of this expedition he had more to worry about than the strange reversal of Jacinto's opinion of the man he was supposed to be guarding, and whom he had once despised. For much of the way Berengar had had to focus all of his mind on the getting here. Now the worst was behind them and he needed to start thinking about how he, a senior ealdorman with the Order of the Knights of the Cross, was going to persuade an equally senior man of the Church to divulge secrets which had been kept well hidden for over thirty years. When the meal appeared he sat down with Cwen next to him and Esclados opposite, but before he could say anything Cwen voiced his concerns for him.

"Who do you think we should approach tomorrow?" she asked.

"Well, I doubt it will be tomorrow," Esclados replied for him around a mouthful of hot meat. "By the time we've ridden across to Caersus we'll have used most of the daylight. I think we'll probably have to stop on the outskirts of the city, because there aren't any of our places inside the walls, and there's certainly no way we can bring all these men into the city without causing a massive stir. And do we want to do that? It would almost certainly mean that Edward would hear of it in no time."

"Agreed," Berengar said thoughtfully. "You know, I've been thinking that it would probably be best if we left most of the men here. If we take half a company to the grange outside of Caersus, with several set up as messengers to come back in case we need them, we'd probably be safer in a strange sort of way than if we took the lot. In this weather, nobody's going to be moving fast enough to come up on us unexpectedly. Our reinforcements will be only a short ride away if we need them, and here they're out of sight of prying eyes. Edward's spies will have no word of them from anyone here, which is more than we could ever hope for inside Caersus' walls." He looked kindly at Cwen. "I know you wanted to act before Edward had a chance to do something dire again," he told her, "but I think a little caution will bring greater rewards than rushing in."

Cwen sighed, "I know, and the weather has already delayed us more than I'd ever have dreamed possible. At this stage I can't see that one day more or less is going to be so critical."

Berengar nodded and went on to outline his plan for the next few days. With a third of his original company from Vellyn, they would ride towards

Caersus and overnight at the grange near there. At first light some of those men would go in groups of three and four into the city and make a reconnaissance, checking for signs of unusual activity which might indicate that Edward had anticipated someone coming for the proof of his illegitimacy, and set a trap.

If all was well, then the men would return by midday, at which point Cwen, Berengar and Esclados would ride into the city with a small, but formidable, armed escort, and go straight to the cathedral. There they would use the excuse of trying to find someone baptised in the same few months as Edward, to see the list in the great book. Esclados had come up with the idea that they might use part of his own family history, and say that they were looking for a boy, born of a DeÁine mother and an Islander father, who had been adopted as a small infant by a noble family. By bringing the DeÁine into the equation, it gave the Knights every reason to be involved in the search.

Consequently, midday two days on found them mounting up in the yard of the well-proportioned grange outside of Caersus, ready to ride in through the great gates of the city, having had the all-clear from the scouts. Berengar wore his cleanest uniform, as did the rest of their escort, in an endeavour to disguise how hard they had travelled to get this far. As they passed under the massive, deep gate arch, Cwen felt a shiver of fear at the thought of how easily they could become trapped in here. Swein had declined to come with them, and Cwen and the others knew it was because of how much of a close escape he had had from the capital, Arlei, when Edward's men had been hunting him.

Nothing would have got him back inside the unscalable walls and the triple-guarded gates of any city loyal to the king, and looking about her, Cwen could see why. They passed through the arch of the iron portcullis first, with its spouts for boiling oil, then the pair of thick oak gates, and finally a second portcullis defended by murder holes for archers to fire down through from the guardroom above. Cwen shuddered and wondered how many men over the years had lost their lives at this fearful spot.

Inside, however, it was all peacefulness. The busy sounds of the city were overlaid with a wet swishing everywhere, as the snow was worn to slush. Carters and tradesmen were going about their daily business, with no sign of agitation, other than wanting to get into the warm and dry. The party's horses splashed along through the icy wet, their destination easy to spot even in the press of buildings all around them. Only four things rose high above the cluttered roof-line. One was the castle keep, home to the king's garrison in this area, and the others were the cathedral towers. Over its western door two towers rose, each capped with a spire tiled in slate, but the dominating tower was the one which rose over the crossing. Massive and impressive, it loomed over the houses kept at bay by the wall of its enclosure, and its gate, which was almost as forbidding as the one they had passed through into the city. The difference here was that the arch was low, preventing anyone from riding into the sacred space.

Leaving their horses in the care of their escort, Berengar and Esclados led Cwen and five men-at-arms to the gate and rang the bell. A portly monk came almost immediately. He was full of his own importance at being the guardian of the gate and able to grant or deny access as he sought fit. However, even he would have had to have very good reason to deny an ealdorman of the Knights access – a reason he most definitely did not have. Within moments, the small party was walking across an open court on paths swept clear of the snow. Off to one side, they could see some lay brothers toiling with brooms on another section of path, clearing as much watery slush as was possible before it re-froze. Behind the sweepers, two other laymen scattered straw to provide some purchase on the flagstones, as had been done on the path they were treading.

At the cathedral, their guide turned right and led them along the cathedral's north wall, around and across in front of the west doors, and around a corner again to the south-facing cloisters. Here they were taken in through an unassuming door and along the enclosed walkway, until they came to the south range of buildings running off the cloister walk. The young monk guide gestured them to stone benches running along the wall and disappeared through the second door. Esclados looked disapprovingly down at the chilled stone, rubbed his aching lower back, and said feelingly,

"I think I'll stand! My bones are too old to be sitting on something that cold!"

Berengar smiled and remained standing also, his fingers playing with the pommel of his sword that hung in its scabbard at his side. No matter that this was a holy place, Berengar was obviously anticipating trouble, which made Cwen wonder whether there might be the danger of blood being spilt, and not just by the armed men who had come with her. However, they did not have long to contemplate the possibilities, for the monk reappeared and gestured them to enter the room beyond.

Passing into the room, it was revealed as an office with a huge desk in the centre and several smaller ones lined up beneath the series of lancet windows along the opposite walls. At them scribes were copying with great concentration, never even glancing up as they came in. Behind the great desk a whale of a monk sat, podgy hands clasped over an enormous belly, and beady, greedy eyes watched their every step over the rolls of pasty-white cheeks. There was nowhere to sit on their side of his desk, making the visitors feel that their host intended this would be a very short audience. They were not wrong.

"What do you want?" The imperiousness of the demand was only diluted by the squeaky voice that delivered it.

However Esclados was not deterred a jot. Striding straight up to the desk, he scowled down at the bloated being from under his bushy black eyebrows and growled back,

"And who wants to know?"

That brought a few heads up from beside the window. They had evidently not heard anyone give the fat monk his own back before, and going by the expression on his face neither had he.

"I beg your pardon!" he spluttered irately, his colour rising to a florid cerise.

"I said, who wants to know?" Esclados repeated, as though talking to a particularly dense child, then leaned forward towards the monk by putting his massive, scarred knuckles on the table. Cwen had to smother a smile, for Esclados seemed to have correctly read the fat monk as a bully who would ride roughshod over weaker folk, but who was now starting to quake under Esclados' ferocious scrutiny. Unable to resist his glee at the spectacle, one of the monks piped up with,

"He's Prior Poer. The abbot's away at Arlei."

It earned him a furious glare from the prior, but the young monk seemed to think was worth it for the treat he was seeing. Esclados snorted like a bull about to charge, and a tremulous ripple ran through the prior's rolls of fat.

"Well …Prior Poer," Esclados' voice dripped disdain over the name, "…*this* is Ealdorman Berengar of Vellyn, who answers to no-one below the Grand Master. So, if your master's away, I suggest you start thinking about the ways that you can be helpful to our mission."

Poer coughed and spluttered for a second as he levered himself into a more upright position, then cocked his head up in a gesture he no doubt thought of as defiant, and said,

"Mission? Well what might *that* be that brings *Knights* here?" In return he had managed to put every ounce of venom he could muster into the word 'Knights', so that it sounded downright derogatory. This was an insult which Berengar could not ignore. The prior could call him what he liked and be ignored, but the Order was sacrosanct. Three strides took him to the desk and three more had him round on the prior's side.

"On your feet!" Esclados bellowed in his best parade ground voice as Poer's attention was deflected to Berengar, the shock almost levitating the prior, who toppled and tottered out of the chair.

"I want to see your baptismal records for thirty to forty years ago," Berengar said in a silky-smooth voice which dripped danger.

"Records?" Poer squeaked. "No, no, that's quite impossible!"

"Who says?" Berengar was like a hawk waiting to strike at a particularly plump rabbit frozen in its gaze.

"Laws," whimpered Poer. "Church laws. Only those who've said the vows may read the records."

"Well that's just fine then, isn't it," hissed Berengar, "because Esclados has said his vows, haven't you, old bear?"

The old Knight grinned malevolently at the prior who had turned to look at him when Berengar had.

"Sometimes the Spirits need a little muscular help here on this earth," Esclados intoned, cracking his knuckles as he spoke. "They like to be prepared for all eventualities – like pompous priors!"

The knuckles flexed and cracked again, while Poer contemplated that being eaten by a bear might be one of the more original methods for a man of his standing to end up dying of. Berengar lifted a massive ring of keys from off Poer's desk and stepped back to wave the prior towards the door. As they exited into the cloister and closed the door, Cwen, who was last, heard an eruption of laughter from within the room, and thought with mischievous glee that it must have been a long time since the monks had had quite so much to tell their brethren at the next meal.

Sandwiched between Berengar and Esclados, Poer waddled as fast as he could down the cloister, even then struggling to match the pace of the taller, fitter men. At the corner, where the east cloister walk joined them, there was an extension of it leading away to the domestic areas of the monastery.

A few paces down this passage they came to a heavy wooden door, and Poer nervously rummaged through the key ring until he came to the right key. With a solemn clunk the lock opened and the door swung open. Small lancet windows, high in the wall opposite, let in a measure of light. Enough to see the piles of manuscripts on shelves around the walls, but not enough to read them by.

"I'll go and find someone to get us a light," one of the soldiers said, and headed back towards the office.

Esclados gave Poer a none too gentle shove to get him into the room, as Berengar said,

"Right! Where are the baptismal records?"

Poer gave him a look filled with resentment and hate, then wobbled his way across the room to wave his hand at a stack on the left.

"The ones for thirty to forty years ago?" Berengar made the imperative query.

Poer scowled again, but reached up and pulled several sheaves of documents down.

"Leave us!" Berengar commanded. "And don't go too far from your office. If we have to come searching for you, it won't go as well as this time!"

The oblique threat was enough to make the fat man go paler than ever, even though he was scowling furiously at his treatment. Without a word he turned on his heels and could be heard shuffling back down the flagstones. Berengar heaved a sigh of relief, then waved Esclados forward.

"We might as well respect the Church's edicts," he said. "You're the one who was once contemplating the priesthood, so it's up to you."

"It'd be quicker with you lot helping," Esclados grumbled in protest, looking at the number of scrolls before him.

"Yes, but if we need to use this evidence to bring Edward down," Berengar spoke softly in case of eavesdroppers, "then we may need the Church to act with us, and that will be much easier if we've not trampled on *all* of their toes!"

Cwen had stepped up to the small desk, meanwhile, and was looking at the scrolls.

"Wait a minute, though," she said. "These look like they're dated on the outside. We can sift through them until we come to the right one without opening them. That won't hurt, will it? Then Esclados only has to read the one!"

"Smart lass," Esclados breathed with relief. "Here you go then!" He shovelled a third of the heap towards Berengar and another to Cwen.

The three of them started inspecting the scrolls as the remaining escorts kept watch at the door. The last thing they wanted was some curious monk walking in on them just as they found the damning entry. It did not take long to find the scroll for the first half of the right year, and Esclados began to read it by the available light until the soldier returned with the scribe who had spoken up in the office, this time bearing an oil lamp with a glass lantern around it. The light was not bright, but it improved the visibility noticeably nonetheless. Placing it up on a stone ledge which was obviously there for just such a purpose, he turned back with a beaming smile to Esclados.

"By the Spirits! That was a treat!" the scribe chortled. "I never thought I'd see anyone get away with talking to that pious bastard Poer like that!"

Esclados' eyebrows shot up. "That's hardly language I'd expect someone of your calling to use!"

The monk snorted sardonically. "No it isn't, but it is honest! He's made every abuse of his office that it's possible to make in the time he's been prior. Many of the brothers think even the abbot is frightened of him, he gets away with so much. Once upon a time this was a happy community, but not anymore, and it's all that malicious leviathan's fault. The Spirits only know how he came to be in the Church, because it certainly isn't through any deep abiding faith. Even worse is that his bullying and tormenting have made many of the brothers begin to lose theirs, and even the most ardent are wondering what in the Islands we could've done to deserve having him afflicted on us. Personally, I think he's only here because this is a wealthy and comfortable monastery to put someone of the king's family in."

"One of the king's!" Cwen exclaimed. "You're joking!"

The young monk shook his head. "No. He's one the younger sons of one of the lesser branches of the Mar family, although don't ask me which one. Those of us who have to copy the documents think that he's here to keep an eye on the family interests down here, if you know what I mean."

The rest of them exchanged worried glances. Did this mean that more people knew of the records and of the danger if they became public knowledge? Suddenly Berengar's head whipped around.

"Where did Fattie go?" he demanded. "Did he go back into his office?"

"No, sire," the monk replied. "We never saw him after he left with you

– and we were certainly expecting him to come back after we'd heard him being humiliated, so that he could threaten us not to tell."

"Shit!" one of the men-at-arms swore, and with a look to Berengar which was replied to with a nod, he and the others ran off to search for the prior.

Berengar looked furious, and Esclados' black looks could have done justice to a thunder cloud.

"Can I help?" the scribe asked tentatively.

Cwen exhaled despairingly, then thought again and said cautiously,

"We're looking for records of anyone from the Mar family who was baptised here."

The scribe raised an eyebrow, but said nothing, prompting Cwen to go on,

"We have good reason to think that back before the Battle of Moytirra one of the Mars had a …liaison …with a DeÁine woman and it's possible the child was brought back to Brychan and baptised in secret." She leaned in conspiratorially towards the scribe. "The Knights have heard rumours that the DeÁine might be getting restive again. But the trouble is we don't know who this child's grown up to be. Well, you can see how difficult that might turn out to be! Of course the child might never have come here, or it might've been baptised just before it died to ensure its spirit a safe journey onwards, but they need to know for certain!"

The scribe's eyes were wide with awe at being let in on secrets of such great importance, and his mouth had dropped open. Then after a moment he seemed to pull himself together, and gave his head a little shake as if to clear his mind. Then he looked again at what the three were doing.

"Oh no!" he gasped. "You shouldn't be looking there!"

Berengar groaned in exasperation, thinking he was going to have to explain again the legitimacy of Esclados' right to read the scrolls, but before he could speak the scribe had carried on.

"It's no use you looking in those! They're only the ones for the common folk – or at least the ones who merit recording, the really poor just get shovelled into the graves down by the river with a novice priest to say a few words and that's it. That's so terrible, isn't it? We're all equal in the sight of the Spirits according to the Book, but you'd never know it from that!" He stopped and coughed nervously, having found himself being scrutinised by the two Knights.

"What do you mean? We're looking in the wrong place?" Esclados asked with measured patience.

"Oh the grand folk, and especially the Mars are recorded in Books of their own. There are about half a dozen copies of The Book kept in the chantry chapel of the cathedral, one for each of the major families. They were made especially with lots of blank pages in the back so that the witnesses would have room to have their names included."

Berengar leapt forward and seized the scribe, almost taking him off his feet as he spun him around.

"Show us!" he commanded, hustling the scribe out of the room and towards the door into the cathedral at the north end of the cloister.

With Esclados and Cwen at their heels, Berengar and the scribe dashed into the vast empty space of the nave. Their boots rang on the flagstones as they ran across the aisles towards the far north-east corner, the noise attracting the attention of one of their own men-at-arms who poked his head around a door on the opposite side at the far west end. Berengar gestured for him to find the others and to join him, and the man disappeared as they in turn exited the cathedral and came into the southern side-chapel. The scribe rushed to the east end and pointed to one side of the ornate altar, beneath a marble figure of a praying young woman pierced with arrows, to a shelf containing seven luxuriously bound books.

"Under a Holy Martyr! The cheek of it!" Esclados muttered in disapproval, even as he pounced on one of the books.

In moments he held up the second one he had looked at. "Got it!" he exclaimed triumphantly.

Wasting no more time, Cwen and Berengar shoved the books they had been investigating back onto the shelf and turned with him, Berengar grabbing the arm of the scribe.

"You're coming with us, brother!" he said in a voice that brooked no questioning. "Once Poer realises you've told us where to look for what we wanted, despite his attempts to deflect us, your life will be in danger. I'll not have another preventable death on my conscience – I've failed to protect someone else, and the knowledge of others who may now be in danger, by being too complacent and that won't happen again."

The statement intrigued Esclados, for although he knew Berengar was probably referring to the actor and the records at Breslyn, he could not figure out why Berengar would think he could have prevented any of it.

However, he was forestalled from asking for as they rushed out of the chapel they nearly collided with their escort.

"Quick, sire!" the one called. "The Prior went to the castle to fetch the King's men! Scully's waiting at the opposite gate we came in by with the horses."

All of them now ran through the cathedral and out of a small door at the south-west end. Offering up prayers of thanks for the brothers' hard work at clearing the paths, they were able to run at full tilt to the gateway, where the young Knight called Scully had his knife drawn and pointing at the throat of the gatekeeper, who had evidently protested at their anticipated departure. Berengar picked Cwen up bodily and threw her onto the horse she had ridden down on, blessing the fact that they had decided to give the valiant Twigglet a rest for the day and bring a bigger horse; for now Esclados shoved the scribe up behind her, commanding him to hold on tight. With two men-at-arms riding stirrup to stirrup with her, they all wheeled their mounts and charged off down the main street, scattering people and carts left and right. The rest of their escort joined them in short order, which was when Berengar learned that his second-in-command had taken the initiative and gone on with ten men to secure the town gate for them.

As they tore up to the stone bastions they could see that he must have come not a moment too soon. Their own men were keeping the sentries at bay with drawn bows and arrows aimed at them, although it was only a matter of time before one of the guards decided to be a hero and chance moving. And with that, the shout came from behind them to hold the gate. No doubt it was the difference between having a messenger from the Prior telling them to detain the strangers, and having their own officer command them to which made the sentries break the stalemate. They sprang forward only to die on the Knight's men's swords, or to fall after a step, impaled with arrows fired at such short range they could hardly miss.

Berengar and those with him pelted out under the gate without pausing, and the men holding the gate only waited until their companions were all through before reversing their horses through too – those who were dismounted speedily vaulting back on. Sergeant Scully leapt from his horse as he drew level with the last gate, throwing the reins to his companion. With a mighty kick he knocked the break off the chain which held the portcullis up, then dived and rolled under just in time as the great iron grill descended with an almighty crash to the ground, sealing in their pursuers.

He shrugged himself out of his mail coat which was pinned to the ground by a spike of the grill, revealing the narrowness of his own escape, before springing back onto his horse and rejoining the ranks.

"Well done," Berengar praised him, making a mental note to keep an eye on such a promising soldier who could show that kind of initiative. Now was not the time for idle chatter, though, and everyone concentrated on putting as much distance as possible between them and the town. However, the light was already failing, and the going became more treacherous as it grew ever colder with the coming night. Soon they were forced to slow their horses to a walk, at which time Berengar got to ask Esclados,

"Do you still have it?"

Esclados patted the front of his jacket. "Safe and sound," he confirmed. "By the Spirits, Berengar," he added softly out of Cwen's hearing, "but I never expected the evidence to be so obvious. So blatant!"

"You saw that much even in that one glance?" Berengar asked in amazement.

Esclados nodded, as if he too was having trouble believing what he had seen. "It's all there, just like she said! Edward's immersion into the Faith, and the only people there were his father and a priest! It wasn't even the archbishop or the abbot. Even Mar's wife wasn't there! And they were hoping to pass him off as her son? The whole of the entry is a couple of lines, and there are no more after that."

"I'm not surprised," Berengar wondered aloud. "If it's that obvious, would you risk having another member of your family baptised here? So that the next set of witnesses could see there was nobody present at the ceremony of the man who'd been named heir to the king, when they came to make their mark in the book? Not likely!"

At the grange, they made the decision to ride on with the full complement of men back to Seigor. The grange was a useful overnight stop, but its defensive capabilities were limited. Fearing reprisals against the small number of men manning the grange, Berengar went so far as to order the captain in charge to make his men ready to evacuate. They would wait to see what the morning brought, but for the first time in a long while they were to set pickets out on the road, despite the cold, alternating them every hour. At the first sight or sound of a major force arriving from Caersus, the captain was to mount everyone up and make all speed back to Seigor with the news that Edward's men had been ordered to attack. Even so, Berengar still hoped that there was enough respect left for the Knights that the incident at the gate would be seen as a minor aberration, and that full scale hostilities would not break out.

However, he was not prepared to leave anything to chance. They would have to keep the horses at a walk, but, with so well a maintained road as the one from Caersus up to the start of what was known as the Castles Road, a night ride was feasible even in such foul weather. Bracing themselves for a very cold night, the troop rode on. The sky cleared and they were treated to a spectacular star-scape, creating a magical scene as they rode through a white landscape under a moon-less black night, frosted with a myriad twinkling lights. Time seemed to stand still, as the only sound came from the rhythmic plodding of the horses' hooves. Under such a vast display of the wonders of nature, Cwen almost had the feeling that they were not moving at all, except for the swaying walk of her mount giving her the sensation of motion.

In the early hours of the morning they arrived back at Seigor, the ealdorman in charge rising from his bed to find out what had caused Berengar to make such a journey. Once informed, the castellan left to set preparations in hand for Seigor's defence, at which point most of the party went to bed. Berengar, however, could not rest until he had had chance to see what Esclados was carrying. By the light of flickering candles, they and Cwen laid the Book on a table and careful opened it up. There at the back were entries for the Mar family, starting over a century ago.

"Look at this," Cwen whispered in awe. "They must've started this when the first Mar acquired lands here in the south. See there! That one's heir just to Radport. He must've been the younger son of a younger son to inherit so little."

"And you can see how some of those lines died out and the lands reverted to the main branch until they had almost all of it," Esclados observed. "But look at the witness lists! Even the most minor ones are finding as many people of note as they can to be fosterers for their sons. They were networking – building alliances and associations – and by the time you get to the last generation look how many witnesses they have! Old King Lothar wasn't even a contender for the throne when he got brought into the Faith, yet he's got how many? Twenty! And the old Earl of Mar – your Richert's father, Cwen – he's got nearly as many, and he was the next branch away from the main earldom and not a whiff of the crown when he was born."

"Cross of Swords!" Berengar breathed, "Earl Richert was right. There's no way that anyone with any legitimate claim to the family lands would've been baptised in such a hurried and covert way. Not a single witness. Not one! Only a bastard would have been treated so. Someone whom they thought would be set aside once a real heir came along. What a tragedy that it was so many years before Richert was born, and they'd decided to acknowledge Edward in case there was no heir."

"The question now, I suppose, is who do we show this to?" mused Esclados.

"Well, given that our own Grand Master is only a couple of days' ride away at Garway," Berengar replied, "I'd say he was the obvious starting point. He'll believe us if no-one else does. Once we have his backing it's a much more straightforward step to go and speak to the archbishop. I can't think that we have any choice but to get the Church's backing, do you?"

"We could go to the monks first," Cwen proposed. "Don't forget that those monks at the cathedral were part of the main Church. The Order of Learned Brothers might not be much in the way of a political force any more, but don't you think it would be useful to have a religious group on our side, in case those Churchmen decide to dig their heels in and refuse to act?"

"It's a thought, isn't it," Berengar agreed. "All right, let's get some sleep. I think we need to have a good rest while we're behind these stout walls, because once we set out we'll be vulnerable again. I want to make the ride from here to Garway in two brisk rides, not resting exhausted men and horses at the grange halfway in case we meet up with some of the king's men."

In her room, Cwen wrapped herself in the blissful warmth of her blankets and gratefully snuggled into her bed. Although her fight was nowhere near over, it was good to feel that she had achieved her first goal. The evidence that Edward was a usurper was safe in the hands of honourable friends, who had seen it with their own eyes. Now they had to convince others that the man they called king was the cold-blooded murderer of his brother, his wife, and of the two small children whom the outside world had thought were his sons and heirs. Justice for that brother's death – the man who had been the light of Cwen's life – had just moved one step closer.

Chapter 6

 Faith in Friends

Brychan: Aer-Yule

A full day later, the company and a half of Knights set out once more, in the cold, dark, early morning, for the Knight's headquarters at Garway preceptory and castle. They were all feeling somewhat relieved that they had not yet found the Knights from the grange outside Caersus knocking on the door, proclaiming that the king's men had arrived, armed and dangerous. Of course, as Esclados pointed out, that might mean that they had simply delayed coming in order to rally reinforcements. Whatever the reason, though, it ensured the Knights a trouble-free journey.

Arriving at Garway, Cwen was awe-struck by the size and position of the place. She had always expected that this of all castles would be big. What she had never anticipated was that it would be partly built into the mountain which towered over it. A deep gulch had been ripped through the mountainside by the ferocious torrent which tore down the slope, and the road to the castle clawed its way up the southern side of the ragged scar on the landscape. Garway Castle was built on the northern cliff of the gulch, and the only way in was over two drawbridges. The first was over a tributary torrent, leading to a square platform carved out of the rock of sufficient size to enable a full company of over five hundred men to ride onto it in one go. From there it was a right-angle turn to a partial bridge and second drawbridge over the main chasm, which could be raised to make an additional reinforcement to the great gate of Garway Castle.

Towering above it, a battlemented wall ran in a circuit to encompass a long half-loop along the ravine's side. But that was the least of Garway's strengths. The keep was a massive edifice rising four storeys above the walls, and keyed into the rock-face behind it. The mountainside which rose above the fortifications was nearly sheer, and only a bird could have assailed it. Yet up there it was possible to see windows cut into the very rock face, proclaiming a network of rooms that went back into the mountain itself. Rumour had it, Esclados told her, that there were even tunnels that only the Foresters knew the full extent of, which would be used in dire emergency to bring foodstuffs into the castle. In such a spot there was no chance of the defenders ever running out of water, and the possibility of bringing siege engines in to bombard the walls was nil, so potential besiegers could only close the lone road out and sit and wait. If there was a safe place to be in Brychan if the DeÁine came, Cwen thought, this would be it. For now, though, it was good to know that her evidence would be kept safe here.

No sooner had they crossed the first drawbridge, having been challenged by a sentry high above them, than trumpets rang out announcing their arrival to the garrison. An alert sentry had no doubt gone to alert the Grand Master, for as soon as they came into view a commanding figure promptly appeared on the battlement above the gate. Cwen saw that he was a bulky man, not particularly tall, but imposing, with a bushy beard wreathing his face.

"Berengar!" his hearty voice boomed in welcome. "What brings you here in such company?"

Berengar leaned back in his saddle so that he could look up to the top of the gate.

"Ill tidings, sire, I fear," he replied. "The Abend are on the loose, and we bring evidence of a dangerous nature as well. We must speak immediately."

"The Abend out?"

"The Abend are out!"

"Did he say the *Abend*?"

The Grand Master's response was echoed by all those within earshot, and passed along to others farther away in a ripple of anticipation. He himself gave no further response, but turned on his heels and disappeared. By the time the leading rider had crossed the second drawbridge, he was standing waiting at the doorway of the gatehouse in the small courtyard before the gate. Straight ahead, the wall of an inner line of defence rose before them, blocking their path and forcing them to the left or right. Even if attackers got through the gate there was no clear run into the heart of this fortress.

Berengar gestured their escort to the left, where Cwen could see the path sloped down to where there looked as though there might be stables. Their own band of companions, however, only rode far enough from the gate to avoid congestion and then dismounted. Men came forward to take their horses, although Cwen was reluctant to let Twigglet go. He looked too small to be amongst all the great war-horses mingling in the confined space. However, the groom who came forward took an instant liking to the chunky little pony and fished in his pocket for a piece of carrot, which Twigglet snaffled with great gusto. Reassured, Cwen let his reins go and allowed herself to be ushered inside by Berengar.

No-one said a word as they climbed broad, spiral stairs onto landings which at each level seemed to be leading them ever further back into the mountain. Finally they stopped climbing just as Cwen was about to ask for a rest, as she became alarmed by Esclados' increasingly strained breathing at the exertion. The old Knight leaned against the wall and gasped for several minutes before he could speak, leaving the Grand Master an opening to say,

"You're out of practice, my friend! Too much ale, that's your trouble!"

Esclados snorted and turned to Cwen.

"We trained together," he told her by way of explanation for the teasing. "Even back when he was just another novice squire like me, Rainer, here, couldn't resist climbing everything in sight!" He looked back to his old comrade. "I suppose you still go out climbing these Spirit-forsaken rocks at every chance you get?"

Grand Master Rainer gave a hearty chuckle. "But of course! Not that I get much chance these days. By the Trees, Esclados, you wouldn't believe the paperwork that goes with this job! Requisitions for this, orders for that – I'll be as fat as you in a year or two!"

"Fat!" Esclados exclaimed in indignation. "That's muscle! Every inch! …Well nearly. Our trouble is we're getting old, Rainer, and the weight of the world we carry is forcing what used to be on our shoulders down to our waists! …Well that's my excuse and I'm sticking to it!"

Rainer burst into booming, good-humoured laughter as he opened the door into a room, and gestured them in before him.

Berengar and Esclados had, of course, been here before, but Cwen was joined by Swein and Jacinto in her surprise at the place. This was obviously one of the high rooms carved into the rock, although now that they were up here, the windows were much bigger than they had seemed from below. Their two beautifully carved, pointed arches were decorated with tracery and leaded lights which illuminated the whole room. The room behind, however, was downright stark. Then it dawned on Cwen that the cost of bringing wood this far into the mountains, when they were already above the sparse tree-line and with no forests nearby, would be enormous. Thick, plain wool rugs warmed the stone floor, and the walls were covered with heavy, plain-dyed woollen hangings in ochres and russets. Simple iron brackets held candles in waiting for the light to fade, and the only wood was the campaign chairs and the tables.

One was evidently serving as Rainer's desk, located by one of the windows so that he only had to turn to see out onto his domain. Dropping into his chair, he gestured the others to take a seat.

"Well now," he rumbled pensively, when they had all sat down, "what's this about the DeÁine getting frisky?"

With great economy of words, Berengar told him of their reasons for coming here, interspersed occasionally by Esclados. Hearing all the details for the first time, it was almost as much of a shock for Swein as it was to Rainer to find out that Cwen – his rescuer and travelling companion – had been the mistress of the king's brother. He had never even considered *that* possibility, although it made him realise how much he had been willing to accept without question as long as it took him ever farther away from Edward. Yet it made much more sense now as to why Cwen was so driven to bring Edward down.

What did confuse Swein was what kind of relationship she must have had with Richert. When Edward had spoken of his brother it had always been with disparagement, and Swein had gained the impression of a stuffy, haughty man, full of pious homilies and criticism. Yet the man these Knights and Cwen had known seemed very different. They spoke of his honour and valour, and his kindness and consideration to the late queen and her small sons. Which, given Swein's bitter guilt at having said nothing to prevent their murders, gave him some comfort to think that at least someone had tried to save them. It was also a strange sort of consolation to think that if someone as powerful as the king's own brother was unable to stop Edward, there was probably little Swein could have done which would have changed the outcome.

It was in the midst of this reverie that Swein became aware that they were now talking about him too, as part of the debate which by now had been raging for over an hour, and looked about him worriedly. But there was nothing to fear, and yet again these men surprised him with their lack of censure for his previous lifestyle. A surprise that was felt, but not shown, by Jacinto as well. Given that his own world had been thrown into turmoil by his feelings at being seduced by Swein, he was even more confused by the fact that these high ranking and demanding officers could reprimand himself so severely for some of his flaws, yet not bat an eyelid at Swein's. Deep down that rankled and offended his sense of the rights and wrongs of the world, and there was even more than a small touch of jealousy for the sympathy they gave to Swein, however justifiable that was.

As Berengar summed up their exploits so far, Rainer sat back in his chair and stroked his beard in contemplation. At the end his first comment was one of deep concern.

"Cross of Swords, Berengar, this is nothing but bad news all the way, and I don't know whether you'll like what I'm going to advise you to do. I certainly don't think you should act without much more thought! Although I will agree with you that we have to think very hard about what we do now."

Cwen began to have a nasty feeling about this. This argument had already gone round and round already without getting anywhere. They had gone to all the trouble to retrieve evidence of Edward's bastardy, and now it was beginning to sound as though the Grand Master might not back them.

"What do you mean, much thought?" she challenged him, head up and eyes flashing.

Rainer sighed deeply. "Just what I said. ...Oh my dear, I quite understand why you feel that Edward is unfit to rule, and you've made a very persuasive case. I don't doubt for one second that Edward is the dangerous, perverted, and possibly unstable, sadist you say he is. But ..." he sighed deeply, "what of Brychan? You see you've also brought news that the DeÁine are planning something again. That's a much bigger threat than ever Edward can be. There's only so much Edward can do without the backing of the Church and ourselves, and the men at the top of the Church are no fools. I'm sure they're not oblivious to Edward's growing instability, being closer to the goings on at court than we are. So they're unlikely to give him a totally free rein, and may even use their powers of persuasion on many of the nobility. But what happens if we get rid of him? Do you see the dilemma?"

"Actually, no I don't!" Cwen snapped fiercely.

"Who do we put in his place? The DeÁine could be coming, and that means we have to have someone as a figurehead. Someone, and *only* one, who at least *appears* to making the final decisions, so there's no debate. The one who has the casting vote. At a time like this we need stability at the top, not turmoil. And can you prove, beyond a shadow of doubt, even to Edward's supporters that what you say is the truth? All you have is an entry in an old book, and the word of a distraught and grieving girl, and a disenchanted catamite."

Even Berengar gasped at this. But before he could protest Rainer went on,

"Because that's how his supporters will portray you! Make no mistake about that! If you think you'll shift support away from him with this alone, you're deluding yourselves. Edward has far too many self-serving and greedy men at his heels who'll weigh up who can offer them the most rewards, and then, and only then, if they think there's more in it for them to back you, will they move against him."

"Does that include you?" Cwen demanded, stunning the other Knights with her bitter challenge. "Are you going to think about what I have to offer *you*? Well, let me save you some of the struggle. I've got nothing I *can* give you, and nothing I *would* give you when all I have is me! If you think I'll warm your bed for you in return for doing what I want, you can go to the Underworld! I was *never* Richert's whore, and I won't be anyone else's!"

Rainer was so taken aback he was unable to respond as she stormed on. "We came here *because* we're not so utterly brainless as to think we could just wander into Arlei, waving that book, and expect to have Edward's head at our feet within the day! Nobody said it would be easy, but with the right men behind us it would be *possible*. Men who would see the sense in removing Edward before anything else can happen to make things worse.

"Can't you see the folly of depending on Edward to do the right thing? All I keep hearing is of the danger of the coming DeÁine, but that blinds you so much you can't see that Edward is part of that problem. He won't be guided by you! He won't be guided by anyone! You could stand in front of him and tell him the DeÁine were knocking on the gates of Arlei, but if he was peeved at you at that moment *that* would be what swayed his decision to act – and it wouldn't be against the DeÁine! He wants to be the focal point, alright, but you'll never get him to act the way you want because he thinks of no-one but himself. You've been persistently stupid in thinking he's the right man to lead Brychan in a war against the DeÁine. The only way *I've* been stupid is in thinking that you lot are the right men to stop him!"

She was so angry she could feel the tears coming. After all the trust she had put in these men, to be so dismissed! Nobody was saying a word in her support – not even Esclados, and that hurt. She must not cry, though, because they would never understand that it was in sheer fury. She would just be even more of a weepy, hysterical girl in their eyes. Then to her amazement she heard an equally emotional voice to her right.

Spurred on by Cwen's speech, Swein was on his feet and quivering with a mixture of fear and anger.

"She's right! You have no idea what you're saying!" he spat at Rainer, jabbing the finger of blame at him. "Edward is already far beyond some old fart of a bishop stopping him. You didn't see what he did with his own hands! I did! To his own brother no less, too! If you think he'd even pause for breath before murdering anyone who stands in his way – priest, bishop, or otherwise – you're even more demented than he is. And as for leading the army against the DeÁine, you've got to be joking! Edward thinks that you lot overplayed that hand long ago. He thinks – and I *know* because he told me so *himself* – that you and the Church have used the threat of the DeÁine to frighten everyone so that they'll do what you say. He thinks the DeÁine are *cultured* and *sophisticated*, and people who really know how to use *power*. And you think he'll lead the fight against them? Dream on!"

With that Swein turned on his heels and followed an already retreating Cwen to the door. As she flung it open and stormed out, he turned for his parting shot.

"*She's* the only one who can see it! All the rest of you think you're still dealing with some good little boy who'll do what you tell him." Hand on hip and the other finger wagging furiously at them, he snapped, "Well, you'll still be waiting for him to move at the same time he's throwing an open party in his play-dungeon for those nice DeÁine, who think the same way he does! And then it'll be one of *you* who's strapped face to the wall while they get a hard-on!"

He stormed off down the corridor in Cwen's wake, having to trot to try to catch up with her, but the further they got from the room the faster she was going. In the end the only way he caught her was when she missed her footing and stumbled down the last few steps of the third flight of stairs, falling headlong. At that point he then realised it was because she was crying so hard she could not see properly. As he helped her to her feet she hugged him tight, then clasped his arm to help her keep moving.

"Bless you, Swein," she hiccupped, "you're the only one who can see it apart from me, aren't you."

He simply nodded because words seemed superfluous.

"Come on," she said, cuffing the tears away. "We have to get out of here *now*! Before that miserable old man can issue orders to stop us. I'm not having him lock us up here so that we can't rock the boat somewhere else.

Let's get away fast. We can worry about what we'll do next when we're sure we've got the freedom to do it."

With that the two of them picked up speed and ran as fast as they could down to the lower court. As they reached the open yard they turned right and found the stables where they could see Twigglet and Bracken tied up at a net of hay, luckily still outside of the actual stables and still saddled. As Cwen undid Twigglet's halter the groom came up looking quizzical.

"We're leaving!" Cwen said bitterly, then in a moment of inspiration Swein added,

"Apparently *we* aren't fit to be in the company of the high and mighty," and sniffed sarcastically. "The Grand Master's sensibilities are offended by the likes of us! *We're* not welcome guests!"

"Well I'm not staying to be called a whore and sent all the way back to sleep down in the nearest village!" Cwen added, quickly picking up on the opening Swein had given her, as they led the ponies out to the gate and mounted up.

It was only once they were well down the road that they dared to speak again, when Cwen praised him for his quick thinking.

"That was inspired improvisation Swein – making them think the Grand Master was actually turfing us out! With any luck they won't think about following us until the Master actually sends someone."

"Which way *are* we going, though?" Swein wondered.

Cwen thought for a moment. "I don't think there's much choice. There's only this road except for a few tracks up into the mountains, and we aren't equipped for those. I've still got some of my money. In fact there's a lot more than there might've been, because we haven't had to pay for our lodgings with the Knights. Although I think we should avoid the inns for a night or two if we don't want to be easily traced. Better if we offer to pay isolated farmers for a night in the barn, with the tale that we're brother and sister on the way to see a sick relative …a grandmother, do you think?" For a second she hesitated and looked back. "It doesn't look as though any of the others are coming after us," she said sadly.

Swein looked back and shrugged. Inside he was wishing that just for once he had found someone in Jacinto who would care enough to come after him. This time, for a change, he was actually in the right and not asking someone to do anything dubious. It would have been nice if he could have had some reward for that.

Then he sighed. Oh well, in the last day or two he had begun to wonder how deeply Jacinto cared for him. Whenever they were together it was always him pleasing Jacinto. The other man might have the body of a god, but he was singularly unwilling to change roles and be the one pleasuring Swein. And having heard about Cwen's total partnership with Richert, it had brought it home to him just how one-sided his relationship was. Well let Jacinto stay there if all he could do was follow orders. Swein needed someone who would help him, not stand there waiting to be told what to do, so he looked at Cwen and shrugged again. Then realised that he also had been passively depending on her to tell him what to do, and silently vowed to try to do better for the one person who had helped him without any expectation of getting something back.

"Never mind," was all he could think of to say at the moment, though, and she gave a bitter smile in response. In agreement they rode on down the hill, unaware of the chaos they had left behind.

Back at Garway, Berengar was stamping mad. It was rare he ever lost his temper, but just at the moment he was fit to kill Rainer. Esclados, too, was ready to explode. In the midst of the uproar between Rainer's senior men and their own, Esclados rounded on the friend from his youth.

"By the Spirits, Rainer, what's got into you!" he raged. "We weren't asking you to launch a full scale civil war! But those two youngsters have more of a grasp on reality than you seem to have."

"Oh come now!" Rainer blustered. "This is foolishness. A girl who took the royal prince's eye – and now thinks she's got the right to influence Island affairs – and a boy who got himself on the wrong side of the king come to you, and all of a sudden you swallow every word they say! Listen to yourselves! So the king killed some random actor. Well, we've known all along that Edward had strange tastes, but there are bigger things to consider than him snuffing out an actor's flame, even if it is immoral."

"Snuffing out a flame?" Berengar hissed, turning on him as he heard the comment. "Have you taken in *nothing*? That would be a blindingly bright sign to any right-minded person that Edward is out of control all by itself. But he wasn't *just* an actor, was he!" Berengar was leaning closer, a face like thunder, almost reaching for Rainer's throat across the desk. "This was his *brother*! Do the ties of kinship mean *nothing* to you, Rainer? Because they do to me! This so called king is a monster, and the death of a *brother* cries out for vengeance."

"Oh, and I suppose you think you're the one to do it?" Rainer scoffed, but before he could give his disparaging speech on how Berengar was likely to achieve this, the ealdorman had picked up the heavy rock which served as a paperweight and hurled it through the paned glass.

"Get a breath of that cold air," Berengar snarled, "and wake up! If you leave Edward in place you're almost *handing* Brychan to the DeÁine, not defending it!"

Turning and near colliding with Jacinto, Berengar shoved the young squire so hard that, big as he was, he fell back into a chair and tripped to fall headlong on the rug.

"I can't imagine what possessed me to think you'd understand the dangers," he snarled as he reached the door. Addressing the senior men of Garway collectively his parting shot was, "You've been too long up here in your eyrie! The world's moved on and so have Brychan and Edward! You ignore those changes at everyone's peril!"

Esclados glared at his former friend, as he scooped up the book from Caersus.

"How *dare* you dismiss that brave girl like that!" he stormed at Rainer. "She's risked life and limb to come and warn us, and all you can think of to do is to dismiss her as though she was some camp follower. *Shame* on you, Rainer! This will come back to haunt you, wait and see!" Then his gaze went to the hole in the glass and the view it gave of the distant road across the valley, and two small figures riding down it. "Oh Holy Spirits!" he exclaimed in horror and turned away. "May *they* forgive you for what you've just done Rainer," he cried over his shoulder as he hurried out of the door, "because I can't."

On the landing he dashed to the top of the stairs and heard Berengar's boots below him.

"Wait, Berengar!" he cried out, ricocheting down the flights stairs as fast as his bulk would allow. "They've gone! …*Oooff*!" He collided with Berengar at the bottom turn of the stair.

"What do you mean, they've gone?" Berengar asked, grabbing his shoulders and fixing Esclados with a gaze of frightening intensity.

Esclados explained what he had seen from the window as he spun Berengar towards the stables. Once outside he put a whistle to his mouth and blew, and, from far above where she had been freed to hunt with the other Knight's hawks, Sybil plummeted down to settle on his wrist, a freshly killed stoat in her beak. Reluctantly she let Esclados take it from her and stow it in the saddlebag when they got to the horses, while one or two of the other trained war-birds swooped and called to her, sensing a hunt in the air. Swinging into the saddle, the two Knights headed straight out of the gate and set their horses to a brisk trot, which was as fast as they dared go in the icy conditions. Clattering over the bridges they hurried to reduce the distance between themselves and Cwen and Swein, Esclados frantically thinking as he rode.

He knew why he was doing this. He had never fooled himself into thinking that his past was not his weak point. The missing child he had unknowingly left behind years ago haunted him, and meant that he would never wittingly abandon someone else's to a grim fate. In his moments of contemplation before the Sacred Trees in the chapels, he had always hoped that the Spirits would take that into consideration, and would direct someone to protect his child if he showed he was willing to do the service back for another. Cwen was just the sort of girl he would have wished for as a daughter. It was easy to care for her when she was so full of caring for others.

Yet Swein pulled at him in a different way. Abused and exploited, he represented a nightmare of abdicated parental responsibility. How anyone could see their child on such a path, and not move heaven and earth to stop the pain was beyond Esclados.

What now urgently perplexed him, though, was Berengar's motives. Until recently Esclados would have said he knew his commander better than almost anyone. It was true that if there was ever a man who would do the right thing it was Berengar. In that sense it was no surprise that he was here, riding alongside Esclados in pursuit of their fleeing younger friends.

But Esclados was sure there was something more. Back in the north, when it had become apparent that the man Edward had murdered was not just some random actor but the king's own half-brother, Berengar had been distraught. Far more than a battle-seasoned veteran would be expected to be. It seemed to be personal to Berengar, and upstairs in Rainer's office Esclados had had the same feeling again. What was all that about family? And a brother's death crying out for vengeance? As far as Esclados knew Berengar had never said he had a family, but then if his family had been killed maybe that was why. Now was surely not the time to ask, but Esclados was getting the feeling that the time was rapidly approaching when he would have to find out – for all their sakes.

Meanwhile, up in Rainer's study Jacinto was nursing his hurt pride. It was too much that he should have been tipped up by his commander right in the Grand Master's view. And what was Swein thinking? Why had he not come back for him, or at least called for him? It was always the same. *They* were always the same! (And 'they' was the term he used to encompass everyone who had chastised or upbraided him in his life.) Jacinto do this, Jacinto do that. Never giving him the respect he was due, only abandoning him at the first sign of trouble. Then he realised he was the only one of the original party still in the room, and the Grand Master was all his. Straightening his uniform he sauntered up to the desk.

"Excuse me sire, but shouldn't we send a warning to someone?" he asked as innocently as he could manage.

"Like whom?" Rainer asked, still in a daze.

"Well, the archbishop for one," Jacinto replied, thinking quickly, "you know, in case they turn up there acting like they have your backing."

Rainer looked him up and down, managing to hide his dislike of this squire who would so swiftly desert his ealdorman, however misguided that man might be.

"Yes …yes, indeed. Go and wait in the dining hall and I'll write a message for you." Jacinto looked as though he was about to query the wait, making Rainer add waspishly, "I doubt they'll go directly there, so you should take the time to go and eat."

He dismissed Jacinto with a wave of his hand, gesturing his puzzled second-in-command to come back in as they passed in the doorway. Sinking into his chair Rainer groaned. What a mess! He was shocked by the strength of Berengar and Esclados' feelings on the matter, and it had him worried. Neither of them were fanciful men, or given to rushing around blindly – Berengar in particular would never have got the rank of ealdorman if he had been. So maybe there was something in all of the story? If Edward really had contemplated an alliance with the DeÁine, then that was a whole new danger he and his senior advisers had never dreamed of. Arranging for someone to come and mend the hole in the window, he also issued the order for a message to be sent to the heads of the nearest castles at Seigor and Craws to join him in council the following day. This was too big for one man to decide alone, and in the meantime he asked for birds to be sent to the snowed-in castles along the border running north along the Castles Road, warning of the DeÁine.

Three bitterly cold evenings later the senior Knights from the nearest castles arrived in much haste with their attendant escorts. Ushering them into the small dining hall he kept for entertaining guests, Rainer had supper served while he told them of his fears. When the mead appeared at the end of the meal, the collected men were engrossed in debating the problem and took little note of how it tasted as it was passed around. It was only when Rainer felt his eyes blurring that he noticed an unusual flavour in the normally smooth drink. Before he could decide what it was, however, he pitched forward onto the table. Yet his collapse came too late to warn the others, who had all also partaken of the mead. In swift, silent succession the eight senior Knights slumped helplessly where they sat. When the servant came to clear the meal away his horrified calls for help proved in vain. Every one of the eight was already dead before the castle physician could be fetched.

Frantic inquires by the remaining most senior captain could find nothing amiss – except that somehow someone had managed to put poison into the barrel of mead which sat in the anteroom of the Master's chamber. Suspicion immediately fell on the most recent visitors, yet nobody could see how they would have had access to it without drawing attention to themselves. It was complicated by the fact that Rainer was known to only use that barrel of the finest quality when he had important guests. No-one was even sure if it had been previously offered to Ealdorman Berengar and the others who had come with him, but most thought not. So the poison could have been there for days or even weeks. All other barrels in the castle were carefully checked, but the only lethal one was Rainer's. There could be no doubt, the Grand Master had been the target, and with winter set in and most of the other ealdormen cut off, choosing a new Master was going to be incredibly difficult.

The most senior captain remaining sat at the Master's big desk, hoping against hope that he would find out what that meeting was about – because now there was nobody left alive who could tell him, yet it must have been desperately important for Rainer to send so many messages out. When the master of the birds came up to see him and told of the warnings sent out, the captain's blood ran cold. The DeÁine on the move and the Brychan sept leaderless! What a disaster! All he could do was send word out to the other castles letting them know that they needed to think of who would succeed Rainer.

It should have been done by elections, with all those eligible to vote at Garway in person, but in this weather that was impossible. Could he even call a vote? He was certainly not senior enough in normal circumstances, but then this was hardly normal. Then he thought of Berengar, and called for messengers. He was the one ealdorman who could come back here. Surely in the light of the murders and the danger to the Island he would come?

Far away in a warm room of an inn in Arlei, Eliavres put his feet up before the fire and wondered if his minion's work had taken effect by now. It had not been hard to see that the arrival of the party at Garway would soon have the pestilent Grand Master flexing his authority again. Except this time he had the means to silence him permanently. So easy to have the one he controlled slip over to the barrel sitting innocently on the side while all the confusion was going on. So easy to slip the poison, previously acquired in a town on the sly, into it. His only regret was that the group had split up so soon before he had eliminated any more of them, and with their departure he could not watch all of them at once any more. But that hardly mattered now.

He took an appreciative sip of mulled wine. These Islanders were so easy to stir up, one just needed to know how – something he had never fully got across to Quintillean, he mused. He had been here for such a short time, and yet already he had turned the place into a hornet's nest of activity. Eliavres worshipped at the altars of the goddesses Rumour and Gossip. Such useful tools, yet so under-used. A drink in an inn where merchants gathered was all it took to drop the words that the DeÁine were coming. When the men left the rumour went with them, spreading like a common cold to everyone who came into contact with them. Add to the contagion the question of what was the King going to do? And, would the Knights save the day? And, hey presto, an epidemic of fear ensued.

Now he was summoning his minion to him. That one would be sent into the court, although at the rate things were moving it might not even be necessary. Watching the royal palace, and the barracks around it, it was already possible to see the increased activity. Perhaps this King Edward had taken the bait without any enticement?

He stretched luxuriously and gave a cadaverous laugh. His birds should have reached New Lochlainn long ago with the news that he had found out that one of their Treasures was at Caersus. With only the witches and

Anarawd there, he could not imagine there being much resistance to mobilising an army. Quintillean's problem was that he always took the sledgehammer approach to the rest of the DeÁine hierarchy. So much so that the Donns who commanded the army would never move for him without a struggle first. But Eliavres was smarter than that.

Tell them that the Knights were snowed in. Tell them that a Treasure was in a cathedral in the south which was still accessible and almost undefended. Tell them that there would be minimal resistance and that it would be an easy victory – something they could work out for themselves without labouring the point – and again, hey presto, the army would move. Did Eliavres ever want to command the army, he had been probed suspiciously before he had even set out on this mission. Oh no, he had replied, and quite truthfully too! Command the army? No thank you! And the Donns, ever jittery regarding usurpation of their authority over the army they had nearly lost in the last Abend fiasco, had breathed a sigh of relief and dismissed him as no threat.

What they had not asked, and he had not said, was that he saw no reason why he should do any of the butcher's work. When they had the Treasure, when the Gorget was in DeÁine hands, then it would be different. Because then they would find that it took someone not just with power, but someone who could channel the Power, to wield a Treasure. And at that time he would be there, on hand and ready to help them out. Nice, compliant Eliavres, not like that power-seeking Quintillean. That would be until he put the Gorget on. Then they would see a different Eliavres, but by then it would be too late.

He did some mental calculations again. Yes, by now the DeÁine army should be well on the way to the southern sea coast route around the end of the mountains. If they had set off when he sent the messages, they should've been long on the move before the snow arrived on their side of the mountains. He rubbed his bony hands before the fire. He would sit here in the warm, and let that fool of a king in his castle up on the hill deliver Brychan into the arms of the DeÁine army; he would then take that army, and then the Islands would be his to rule! King Eliavres the First, and – with all that Power running through his veins – forever!

Chapter 7

Family Reunion

Brychan: Aer Yule

By the late afternoon Cwen and Swein became aware that there were riders behind them. In a small hamlet, where the snow had already been muddied and churned by passing cattle, and where the change in direction of their tracks would not be noticed, they slipped off the road. Hiding behind a rickety barn they watched to see who would appear.

Listening to the approaching crunching of horses' hooves on the icy ground Swein whispered in Cwen's ear, "It doesn't sound as though there are many of them."

"Good!" Cwen whispered back. "At least that means that the Master isn't sending a couple of lances after us." Then she thought about what she had said and added worriedly, "But maybe that's even more evidence that he doesn't take us seriously at all?"

She sighed at that. What was it going to take to get people to believe them? If it was only herself and Swein who would be affected, then it would not have mattered that much. But when the safety of the whole of Brychan hung in the balance, it worried her immensely. Then she had no more time to fret for the lead horse's nose came into view. When she saw Berengar with Esclados hard on his heels she almost started crying all over again – this time with relief that she had not been so mistaken in her trust. Hurrying out onto the meagre street, she waved to them and they reined in only a couple of paces away.

Berengar vaulted to the ground with more grace than she had credited him with up to now, and in a swift movement had swung her into his embrace.

"Thank the Trees we've found you!" he exclaimed, the relief in his voice audible.

Esclados' descent was more sedate, but his greeting no less heartfelt. To Swein's astonishment he found himself being clasped in a bear hug by the big old Knight as he said,

"By the Wild Hunt, laddie, you showed some spirit back there! Well done!"

Such unaccustomed praise totally threw Swein, but he also felt a warm glow inside at receiving such impromptu genuine praise for the first time in more years than he cared to think on. When it came to Cwen's turn with Esclados, she managed a choked,

"You came after us!"

"Good Spirits above!" exclaimed Esclados. "Did you think we'd desert you now? After all we've been through?" He shook his head in bewilderment.

"Yes …well, no. …But we weren't sure whether you'd disregard orders when they came from the Grand Master himself," she told him, feeling rather feeble for doubting now.

However Esclados gave an ursine growl, and held her back at arms' length to regard her with mock severity.

"The Grand Master? *Phfaah*! He may be the supreme commander, but he's not infallible. He's as human as the rest of us – he doesn't shit gold! And he can make mistakes. Rainer needs to remember that we elected him, and we can un-elect him if we feel he's going against the best interests of the Island. There aren't many reasons which allow for demoting a Grand Master, but that's one of them!"

"Well hopefully it won't come to that," Berengar said optimistically. "Rainer's no fool – however it looked back there. I'm betting that once he thinks about it, he'll see sense. What worries me more is this feeling I have that we're running out of time."

With that, he urged them back on their horses to ride on to the grange for the night. As he reasoned, they were the first to leave, and there was little chance of anyone from Garway catching them up there that night, so they could safely take advantage of the facilities without the danger of being restrained. Indeed, it was only another hour's ride before they were tucked up in the warmth of the stoutly protected grange, enjoying a much needed hot meal. Luckily, the fact that they arrived without their massed escort helped give a reasonable explanation for their hurried return to the commander there. The troops were staying to supplement those at Garway for a major action, Berengar hinted conspiratorially. But they were hurrying on to Arlei with messages of the utmost importance for the ealdorman there, he added. As he outranked the commander of a mere grange, the man was in no position to question Berengar, and so offered all the help he could.

What Berengar did not feel he could do was to ask the commander for access to his office in order to study the maps there. So it was with great relief that he saw Cwen produce Richert's folded travelling maps from her cloak, when they all adjourned to his bedroom to confer. Spreading the maps out on the bed, the four of them poured over them by the flickering candlelight.

"What are we going to do?" Swein asked tentatively, not wanting to appear stupid if he had missed something obvious.

Instead, though, Berengar and Esclados seemed as undecided as he and Cwen had been. In fact it was Cwen who came up with the first suggestion. With her brow furrowed in concentration as she stared at the map, she spoke pensively.

"Would it help if we decided where we *can't* go?"

The two Knights looked up at her, and seeing their questioning eyes she carried on.

"Well let's put it this way. Every day at the moment we're losing a bit more daylight to travel in. On top of that the weather is worse than I've known it down here in ages for this time of year." She tapped the map. "My folks are down here at Radport and I grew up in this area, but I can't remember the snow coming so early and so heavy since once when I was a little girl. On top of that, what are we going to do if the Grand Master *doesn't* wake up to the threat? Do you think he'll try to stop us? Because, if that's the case, then I think *he'll* think we'll take the most direct and fastest route. He seemed to think we'd dashed into this whole course of action in a mad rush and without considering the consequences, so personally I think he'll act on the assumption that we're more worried about speed than anything else. In which case, do we really want to take the straight, moors road towards to Arlei?"

The others nodded in agreement at all she had said, Berengar leaning in to the map again.

"That's a fair summary," he agreed. "Which leaves us with two choices of route. We could take the northern road we came on, that runs through the foothills of the mountains to Tern and then Tarth. Thinking about what you said before, Cwen, I think the next people to try are the monks. The Learned Brothers of the Holy Martyrs are a bit distant from the real world, but then maybe that will mean they have a better perspective. Their main abbey is right down in the south-east beyond Eynon," he explained, suddenly remembering how little of the outside world Swein sometimes knew. "They probably have the most credibility with the archbishop, so they'll be important allies, but it wouldn't hurt to have the two other minor orders on our side too. The problem there, as far as I can see, is that the Preaching Friars are too dispersed to do much except carry the word about Edward – although that could be a real bonus if they can convince the ordinary people he's untrustworthy."

"Indeed," Esclados rumbled pensively, "but it's unfortunate that we're now all the way down here in the south, because," a large finger prodded the map in front of Swein, "their main friary is back up here on the road to Vellyn at Sandbay. Given how long it took us to get down here with the bad weather, I think we need to plan things very carefully, or we'll be spending all our time travelling and getting nowhere fast."

"I agree," Berengar said worriedly. "The same thing applies for the Brothers of the Sacred Cross, because their love of isolation," he added for Swein again, "has meant that their head abbot is even farther north from us in Salen. So I think we need to think about getting to Eynon and out to the monastery first, and then worry about whether we can get to the others when we've crossed that first bridge.

"The road through Tarth will be tough in this snow, but at each of the crossings we have the option of coming back down to the main road if the weather really closes in. The bad thing about that route is that the snow was already drifting dangerously when we came that way from Redrock. We could end up getting snowed-in at one of the granges, and although speed isn't the overriding factor we certainly don't want to be stuck somewhere for a month!"

"So that leaves the southern route. Do we really want to ride back to Caersus when the men of the king's castle are after us?" Esclados wondered.

"Maybe that's the safest way, though," Swein said hesitantly.

All eyes turned to him and he could feel his colour rising. Oh why did he have to make a fool of himself, he thought as he cringed, but instead Berengar said, 'go on,' in an encouraging voice.

"Well they won't think we'll be so daft as to go back there, will they?" Swein said, gaining confidence. "I mean both lots. The soldiers in that castle are probably looking for a small army, because that was what we were when they last saw us. But more importantly, will that Grand Master Rainer expect us to go back to the place we were running from? Especially carrying that!" He pointed to the great book lying in state on the tiny bedside table.

Esclados started to grin, and gave Swein a congratulatory pat on the back that was so enthusiastic it nearly shot Swein over the bed and into Berengar's lap.

"There's another thing too," Cwen chipped in. "We've only got a week or two to Yule. I know you Knights are probably used to spending that festival in one of your own places, so you won't know this, but it's going to cost an arm and a leg to stay in an inn at that time. People travel to visit relatives, and if there isn't enough room in the family houses then they go to the nearest inn. Usually the villagers have a word with the landlord long in advance, and locals get first refusal on rooms at decent rates. But to outsiders the price will shoot up, because they know it's one of the few times of the year when rooms are hard to come by. Ma and Pa were always run ragged and we all had to muck in and help, even my little brothers had to sweep floors and carry towels up to rooms.

"So I've been thinking. If we can get to Radport by Yule, maybe we can go to my folks? We wouldn't have rooms. It would be a case of sleeping on the floor of our little parlour upstairs, or sharing with my brothers, but I could help Ma in the kitchen, and if you'd help out with the horses, I bet Pa would be grateful."

She looked hopefully at the others. Swein was already looking more cheerful having heard Cwen talk fondly of her mother's cooking. The two Knights exchanged glances then gave their agreement.

"You're right, lass," Esclados rumbled. "I'd forgotten what time of year it was with this weather being more like what we'd expect to get after Yule, but we surely don't want to get stuck on the road with nowhere to stay in this freezing cold."

"Are you sure of your reception, though?" Berengar asked gently.

Cwen drew a deep breath and thought carefully before answering positively, "I think so. Some of the villagers – like my stuck up aunt – disapproved of me going off with a nobleman, and I can't pretend that Pa wouldn't have been happier if I'd married some local lad. But both my parents liked Richert once they'd got over their awe of him. To be honest, I've been feeling terrible for not letting them know I left Amroth. When they heard about Richert's death they'll have been upset, and worried sick about me – and it's not the kind of news that will have taken long to get there. I feel I owe it to them to set their minds at rest that I'm still in the land of the living, and I think that will be their overriding concern. It won't hurt that two of you are Knights, either. We've had a lot of custom over the years from both the ancillary workers who pass through with horses and supplies, and some of the soldiers – and I know Pa likes them as guests, because they're less rowdy than some of the drunken merchants he gets."

The upshot was therefore that they set out for the grange before Seigor, where they spun the same story for their overnight stop, and then headed for Caersus. On this stretch of the road they were all jumping at shadows, and there was much debate as to where they should stay at Caersus. On the one hand they feared the grange might be being watched, but equally it could raise suspicions if two Knights turned up at a local inn when there was a perfectly good grange nearby. In the end the grange won, simply because they reasoned that once within its walls they would be safe, whereas they thought they might be informed on by someone at an inn, and find themselves being roused in the middle of the night by the castle guard. From there it was a slow trudge across to Radport, the one consolation being that this near to the sea, the salt wind kept the worst of the ice at bay.

The week before Yule they found themselves riding down the broad paved streets of Radport, and heading through the wide market square and on to an inn standing in an adjoining small square. Cwen's parent's inn was built out of the local grey granite, and stood solidly along one side of the square, with a central archway through to the stables beyond. Two floors of stone were topped with one of timber and wattle in-fill, and from a projecting beam the sign swung asthmatically in the gusting wind. Two rather inebriated hounds gazed down from it, one looking even more comical where a patch of snow had stuck and given him a big white nose, while the curly script above proclaimed it to be *The Brace of Brachets*.

As they rode in under the arch, Swein stared in a mixture of envy and delight at so homely a place – so very different from the cold, austere house he had grown up in. Cwen dismounted and tied Twigglet up to a rail obviously intended for such use, and the others followed her lead, while Sybil winged her way silently up to the stable roof. A pair of lanterns illuminated the main doorway, from which there issued the sounds of carousing, but Cwen walked past it and headed for a smaller door on the opposite side of the yard. Easing the door open gently, she looked inside and then stepped forward into the light.

A plump woman with a cheerful face was directing two younger women with platters of food out to the room beyond, and Cwen waited until they had gone, and the woman had put down the pot she was moving off the range.

"Hello Ma," she said tentatively, suddenly not so sure of her reception despite what she had told the others. The woman turned and, seeing Cwen, clasped her hands to her mouth for a moment, then with a gasp of delight rushed forward and pulled Cwen into her arms.

"Oh my girl, you're safe!" she exclaimed in a voice that was half laughing and half crying. Her hug was nearly cutting Cwen's breath off, and it was several minutes before Cwen could get a word in between her mother's alternating scolding and delight. By this time the others had stepped into the kitchen and closed the door, and finally Cwen's mother realised that there were others there.

"Ma, this is Ealdorman Berengar, and Esclados of Rhue, who's a Knight, too. They've been looking after me," Cwen got in quickly, thinking that this was the explanation that would endear them quickest to her mother.

"And who's this young man?" her mother inquired of Swein.

"His name's Swein and he's travelling with us because they're protecting him as well. It's a long story, Ma, and I'll tell you and Pa more later on. The thing is, can we stay here over Yule? We'll have to leave afterwards, but I wanted to come and see you to explain, and I've told them that there won't be any fancy rooms and that they'll have to help out."

"Oh, of course you can, my sweet," her mother said joyfully, cuffing a tear, yet acting as though it was the most normal thing in the world for her daughter to turn up with three strange men and ask to stay for over a week. "Go on upstairs, and I'll bring your father up as soon as we can leave the others to cope."

Swein was flabbergasted. He could not imagine what would happen if he turned up at *his* parents and asked for even one night. To turn up with a bunch of strangers and ask for a whole week – even if they were going to work for their keep – simply did not bear thinking about. He was still mentally wincing at his mother's imagined tirade when he realised that the others were moving again. Leading them out of the kitchen by another door, Cwen took them along a corridor which ran behind the main rooms which fronted onto the square, to a stair that lead upwards. Climbing up, shouldering their packs, they passed the first floor which held the guest rooms and on up to the family's rooms. Opening the door at the top of the stairs, Cwen showed them into a comfortable parlour which looked onto the yard.

"People always used to ask why we didn't have the bigger rooms below this one on the middle floor for ours," Cwen said. "But these rooms in the timber part are much warmer in the winter – when the inn's for the most part quieter – and Ma and Pa's room also looks onto the yard so that Pa can see what's going on down there. In an hour or so he'll bolt the gate into the yard, but every so often there's some thief who thinks he can climb in, and either get into the inn or steal the horses. The shutters at the front are very strong and the square is well used, so they don't usually try that way. The stable is lower so they try to come over that, but Pa keeps some of the slates loose so they make a racket when they're disturbed.

"My old room's over to the right, but my second oldest brother got married last year, so he and his wife have got what was his and our oldest brother Giles' room as theirs, and mine as a separate parlour. My two youngest brothers always used to share a room next to Ma and Pa's. If we're lucky there might be a couple of beds in the attic. When the boys were younger there used to be a barman who lived in, and a couple of barmaids at busy times, but, now that my brother Gus and his wife Yvette are working here, the rooms might not be being used."

It was not long before they heard Cwen's parents coming upstairs.

"Promise me you won't shout, dear," they heard her mother saying anxiously as they got closer. "At least not until they've had chance to explain."

"It's my house and I'll shout if I want to," the deep voice which obviously belonged to Cwen's father grumbled back, although without much malice.

The door opened and they walked in. To her friends it was immediately obvious that Cwen took after her father. The same corn-coloured hair, although in his case going grey, and the same eyes and mouth, which was trying hard to look stern but which broke into a mirror of Cwen's smile.

"Oh Pa!" she gulped and threw her arms around his neck.

After the first emotional reunion, the family sat down to hear what had happened. As Cwen had suspected, they had heard quite quickly that her beloved Richert had been murdered, and had been worried stiff that she had died with him. Her explanation was much helped by additions by Esclados and Berengar, so that her parents soon realised why she had not dared to send them word. They were shocked to the core to realise that

Richert had been murdered by his own brother in cold blood, and the lengths he had gone to to disguise the fact. When Cwen explained that Swein had seen the dismembered corpse that Edward had used as a distraction to make the rest of the court think he was dead, in order to give him time to carry out his plan, her mother was all sympathy.

"Oh you poor lamb!" she cried. "Oh how awful for you!" And for the first time in his life Swein found himself getting a taste of what it would have been like to have a real mother to fuss over him. It felt very strange, and a mite overwhelming, but very comforting all the same. No wonder Cwen was so calm and self-possessed, he thought. She had had all the nurturing she could possibly have needed in this happy home, and for the first time it occurred to him to wonder if he would have been very different if his own childhood had been like hers. No beatings, no constant degradation and abuse, no endless bullying from older brothers and his father. This kind of world had been something he thought only existed in dreams until now. Listening to Cwen's father half-heartedly scolding her for still having left it so long to get in touch with them, and so obviously not meaning anything other than his relief at having her back safe and sound and in one piece, was a revelation.

It took them several hours to finally get to bed, as Cwen's brother and sister-in-law came up after locking-up downstairs along with the two youngest brothers, and so the tale had to be told all over again. By that time Swein was beginning to wonder how anyone survived so many emotional encounters all the time — he was totally worn out! The two youngsters volunteered to go up to one of the upstairs bedrooms, and Swein was found a cot bed with them. Meanwhile Cwen had the tiny attic room, and Esclados and Berengar shared the lads' normal bedroom. Both parents were mortified that they had nothing better to offer so senior a member of the Order as Berengar. But he managed to convince them that he should remain incognito, and that it would be better if he remained up here as a family guest, rather than taking over a paying guest's room. That would cause too much comment, he told them, although Cwen's father, Roger, still took quite a bit of convincing that this would not bring the wrath of the Order down on him.

The next morning, Roger took Berengar and Esclados down to the stables. At first he was still much in awe of the two Knights, and it was not until Berengar picked up a shovel and rake and began mucking out the stalls in a way which spoke of plenty of previous practice that he relaxed. The inn's stables had been fully used the previous night, with travellers heading back to their homes before the festive season. This would be the pattern for the next few nights, Roger explained. The guests who were staying longer did not usually appear until a day or so before the festival. It made their lives easier for their first day, since the stalls had emptied by mid morning and they were able to muck out without having to shift horses out.

Come Yule, though, both Knights could see why Roger would need a hand, as the horses would need to be taken out in relays into the yard, while the bedding and feed was brought in to each group of stalls. Adjoining the wings of the inn were two short stretches of stalls, with the main run of stables connecting them to enclose the square. The hayloft ran the length of this long stable and was serviced by a flight of stone steps at each end, for which Esclados was very grateful. He did not fancy the idea of struggling up and down a ladder with bales of hay anymore. The nimble lad who could swarm up and down ladders all day without running out of breath, and minus aching muscles, had long gone.

Indeed by midday Roger had spotted the older knight rubbing his sore back, and tactfully sent his son out to swop roles. Cwen's youngest but one brother, Jes, was a strapping lad of nineteen who hefted bales of hay like feather mattresses, but hated making small talk with the customers and was glad to escape back outside. In contrast, Esclados proved to have a natural talent for chatting to the guests as he carried trays, laden far heavier than the kitchen girls could handle, out to the tables.

Berengar, however, was enjoying working with the horses. Over the years he had forgotten what it was like to be able to just get on with a job, without being interrupted every five minutes by someone wanting instructions or an opinion. As the horses began to arrive late in the afternoon, he found himself humming softly to himself as he stripped off saddles and brushed mud out of coats. He was surprised how quickly the time had flown when Cwen came to fetch him for the evening meal, and, even though it was late, there were still horses coming in afterwards which he went back outside to willingly.

Swein had been adopted by Cwen's mother, Jane, as a kitchen helper, and he found himself confronted by buckets of hot soapy water and piles of used plates and cutlery. Until this point, he had never really thought about what had gone on behind the scenes when he had eaten at the King's table. Now he was appalled at the work that went on to just serve a simple meal. Most of the travellers were hungry, and Jane's cooking lived up to his expectations, so there was little left over, but even what there was soon accumulated in a couple of large buckets. Cwen's youngest brother, Eli, came in every so often and carted them out to behind the stables to where the family had pigs grazing in their cider orchard. Going by the delicious bacon which Jane had sizzling on the skillet, the pigs lived well on the scraps, and she told Swein that the animals also got the draff from Roger's brew-house. If you had to be slaughtered, Swein thought, there were worse ways to go than to be happily sozzled on Roger's malty beer as you went.

The first few days passed in a blur, with the friends falling into bed at night too tired to talk much. The day before Yule Eve, the inn was exceptionally busy, and they came to understand why Roger closed for a few hours in the afternoon. Until then Esclados had wondered why they did not just keep going when trade was so good. Now, though, he could see that it was essential to have some time to clear up and replenish the stock. Walking into the second parlour he viewed the chaos with dismay. A family of merchants had dined in here, alongside a couple of senior moneylenders on their way west and a trio of celebrating journeymen weavers, yet the room looked like a whirlwind had passed through. Scraps of food lay on the floor, drink was spilt across the tables, mugs stood abandoned on any available surface, and some fool had thrown some of the decorative pine sprigs onto the fire which was now smoking and spluttering.

"By the Hounds of the Wild Hunt!" Esclados growled. "If any of our men left the mess in this kind of state, I'd have them back in here and scrubbing it until it shone,"

Roger chuckled. "Why do you think I like having folks from your Order as guests? They don't leave the place like a pigsty! The training obviously sticks even when they're out of the granges. Not like the King's army. Dear Spirits, you should see it when they've been through! We think we've been lucky if they make it outside to puke and piss."

"Bloody animals!" Esclados sniffed. "Where in the Islands do you start with this?"

"Find all the things that need washing-up for a start," Roger directed him. "I'll try to sort the fire out. Then when you've done that, get a big bucket and just shovel the rest of the rubbish into that and dump it on the manure heap outside. Then we'll get a bucket of hot soapy water and wash the tables over, and then the floor. Cwen will show you where to find the stuff."

For the next two hours Esclados ploughed through the detritus of other peoples' lives, amazed at what people could do in public. He had occasionally thought that when he retired from active service with the Order, he might find a nice little inn to settle down and run beside one of the castles. Seeing this was making him think twice about that for sure. This was a well-established inn with a good reputation, but it took the whole family to keep it that way. One man on his own would stand no chance, and Esclados could see how, once the standard dropped, so would the kind of clientele frequenting the place. His retirement plans did not include throwing out a constant flow of washed-out drunks! No, the innkeeper's life was not for him.

It was with great relief all round that they closed the doors on Yule Eve at the end of trade. On Yule itself, Jane would cook the traditional dinner for the family and the few guests who were not going out to visit family in the neighbourhood. A plump goose was plucked, dressed and stuffed with a rich assortment of fruits and berries, whose juices would cut the fat of the water bird and enhance its flavour. A great joint of pork was also just waiting to go into the oven in the morning, its flesh scored for the crackling, and apples in readiness to be baked with it, along with honey-glazed parsnips and carrots. Red cabbage was marinating in ruby wine and spices, while breadcrumbs and herbs had been blended ready to make a side-stuffing.

For Swein it was amazing. The meagre portions his parents had thrust at him had coloured his view of how ordinary people ate – poor food boiled to the point where whatever flavour it had once had had long disappeared. Only the rich had such an assortment of flavours so expertly prepared in his world. In contrast, Jane's sure touch with anything eatable meant that he had found himself tucking in ravenously at every meal so far, but those had been relatively straightforward dishes. For the first time since he had fled Arlei he found himself able to contemplate the thought of meat without heaving.

To see such fare as Jane had spent the day preparing was a whole new experience, especially as her philosophy was to use her seasonings, stuffings and glazes with a delicate touch that enhanced rather than overwhelmed the food. The heavy pungent sauces slathered over everything from the court kitchens meant that this was the first time he would actually be able to taste what goose was like, and he was sure he would be able to tackle the paler breast meat, even if he found the sight of the fleshier-looking pork daunting. And he could not wait to try the great cake which had appeared from a cool pantry once the inn's doors closed. That was worthy of the castle's master-baker back at Arlei, except that Swein was sure that this would be far more wholesome fare. But that was part of the lure. Anything that came from this hospitable and secure refuge had none of the overtones of fear and danger which dragged the bad memories back up to the front of his mind. For the first time in his life, Swein was excited about having a proper family Yule.

Beyond the staying guests they would not open their doors on Yule Day, and even then, there were strict laws down here in the south-west on the hours that Roger could serve ale to paying customers on this day. Cwen's oldest brother arrived last thing on the Eve from the farm he helped his wife's family to run, bringing with him his wife and two small children. For once the family took over one of the large parlours downstairs, and Roger thrust pokers into the fire to be plunged into mugs of rich, dark porter to heat it for the traditional toast. When the nearby church bell tolled for midnight, the family raised their mugs and solemnly toasted the end of the old year on this solstice. After seven days of feasting they would welcome in the new year, but for now it was the time to reflect on all that had passed in the last twelve months.

For Cwen it was a terribly sad moment, as she remembered how happily she had spent the last year's festival with Richert, especially seeing the happiness of her two married brothers. His memory was toasted with real feeling by all the family, with each of them hugging Cwen in turn, as was traditional for those who had suffered bereavement in the past year. It was therefore the most natural thing that Berengar should also take his turn after Swein's shy embrace and Esclados' bear hug. Taking Cwen in his arms seemed like the most normal thing in the world to do, and he found himself having to make a conscious effort to let her go. Now was not the time, he reminded himself. On this night she had too many memories, she did not need him making it worse.

Jane, however, noticed the lingering embrace with approval. She had taken a liking to the battle-scarred Knight, even if he was a bit older than she would have hoped for a new partner for Cwen. It was not that she had not liked Richert – far from it – but she had always thought that he had not thought of the consequences to Cwen of their relationship. The king's brother who was already married, albeit unhappily, was always going to have many other calls on his time, and Jane had worried about what would happen if they had had children. It was one thing for Richert to have his mistress, but would his wife have stood by quite so indifferently if Cwen was producing heirs whom Richert might want to acknowledge and provide for out of the estates?

And now look at what had happened. All this political intriguing, Richert gone, and Cwen caught in the middle of it with no home to go to when it all ended. From what she knew of the Knights, Jane guessed that married quarters would be made available to Berengar, and there was no reason why he should not marry – she had carefully probed Esclados for information on that score over the last days. To have her suspicions of Berengar's interest confirmed therefore filled her with a warm glow. With any luck the coming year might actually see her free-spirited and much-loved daughter settled with someone who would really take care of her this time.

Roger did not know quite what was making Jane look like the cat that had found the cream, but he was sure she would tell him soon enough. For himself he was also glad to find his adored daughter alive and well – although he was doing his best to leave the gushing expressions of delight to Jane. Now he was torn between being worried sick about what Cwen was going to get mixed up in, and being fit to burst with pride at her. His healthy conscience was appalled at what they now knew King Edward had done. That Cwen was the one who had found the way to ensure justice was done was something that he wholeheartedly approved of, and was the source of his pride in her. Many a girl he had known, in a life of dealing with people from all walks of life, would have been too absorbed in their own grief to think of others and the greater consequences of their bereavement. But not his girl! Yet the knowledge of the immensity of the task before her was enough to turn the remainder of his blonde hairs grey to match the rest, and he urgently wanted to make sure that she was not going to end up facing things alone.

With this in mind, he bided his time until the following afternoon when the family were relaxing after second portions of Jane's glorious roast goose and pork. Esclados was telling tales of soldiering that had Cwen's brothers in gales of laughter down one end of the table, with Swein to one side listening shyly but still smiling. The women had rearranged themselves, after the food, at the other end near the hearth where they could keep an eye on the toddlers playing on the rug before the fire. That left himself and Berengar somewhere in the middle. Under the pretext of replenishing everyone's drinks Roger ambled around the table with a fresh batch of mulled wine and then sat himself down next to the Knight.

"Tell me something, then," Roger began genially, sloshing a generous measure into Berengar's goblet. "No offence meant, but why are you doing this?" Hastily softening the question with, "Of course, if you don't want to tell me, I can't argue. You've protected our Cwen, and for that I'm eternally grateful. But in a week or so you're taking her off again, and while I'm sure you can protect her better against the king than ever we could, I'd like to know whether this is just duty, or if it's something more. …As Cwen's father, you understand…"

Berengar gave his wry smile and took a swallow of the excellent wine before answering.

"No, I don't mind you asking. In your place, if I had a daughter and someone was going to drag her off into danger, no matter who he was I'd be asking the same question."

At the end of the table Esclados heard the exchange and refrained from starting another tale, leaning forward to hear the reply. Berengar saw him and gave a small chuckle.

"You've been very patient, old bear, haven't you!" He turned to the family. "Esclados probably knows me better than anyone else, and I him. I know exactly why he's doing this. Do you mind if I tell them?"

Esclados shook his head, and Berengar told his old friend's story simply and without adornment.

"And you have no idea what happened to your child?" Jane asked in horror at the end.

"No," Esclados answered. "I don't even know whether it was a son or a daughter. I'd been posted away from the area, and by the time I got back the villagers could only tell me that the pregnancy was well advanced when the girl I'd loved was taken back over the mountains by her family."

"Over the mountains? Then your child is living under the DeÁine!" Jane exclaimed. "Good Spirits protect him or her then!"

"Which is why Esclados has said the first of the religious vows," Berengar carried on. "He's not a man to leave things to chance, are you?" he affectionately teased his old friend. "But I know he's been wondering why I'm here. I could've sent him with a full armed escort, and that would've been what duty dictated. In fact it's pretty much breaking with protocol, if not actually our rules, for me to have left Vellyn to others and come here myself."

"Why did you come, then?" Cwen asked softly, suddenly feeling that she was about to find out something of great importance.

Berengar looked at her and smiled. "For very similar reasons as yourself." Then turned back to Esclados. "Forgive me for not telling you this long ago, but I grew up knowing it was something never to be mentioned, and then later I thought we'd been forgotten about, and it didn't matter anymore." He took a deep breath.

"I was born in a small town that's now in New Lochlainn, just about. Being on the border, the war rolled backwards and forwards over us. I don't know who my father was because neither did my mother. It's never a good thing to be an attractive young woman when there's an army in town and nobody's sure who's on which side. I can still remember, as a child of about their age," he gestured to the toddlers, "seeing both the DeÁine army and then the king's army coming through. One day a group of DeÁine Hunters came into town and began questioning folks, then my mother caught their eye. They're used to being treated as the elite – able to do what they want with whoever they want – and they wanted her! Lucky for us there was a company of soldiers from Brychan on their tails, and they got to us just in time."

Suddenly Cwen knew where she had heard this story before and gasped, clasping her hand to her mouth but not daring to interrupt as he went on.

"One of the young noblemen took a liking to my mother when they'd killed the DeÁine, and before we knew it we were on the way back to Brychan. All of a sudden we were in a big castle, with servants and people running around all the time ...Funny, but as a child that was more frightening than the DeÁine! ...I kept getting lost and having to have strangers come and take me back to the rooms we shared. Then mother announced that I'd be having a new brother or sister. I was too disorientated to feel anything much about that, but as far as I was concerned, the good thing was that we got moved again to a smaller manor that wasn't so frightening for someone who was small enough to get trodden on in the crush.

"Then the baby was born and I remember my mother being in tears all the time. Then there were the rows between her and the nobleman. I didn't understand at the time why, although she told me later on. Back then, however, all of a sudden we were on the move again. This time, though, the journey was a really long one. For the first time I met Knights, and they were the ones who took care of me, because my mother was in no fit state to. The baby had disappeared and I thought it had died, as sometimes used to happen to other families back when we lived in the town. In the end we found ourselves up in the far north at Breslyn.

"We had a house that became our home and after a few years my mother married one of the enlisted men from the Knights." Berengar laughed at the next memory. "When my mother said she was having another baby, I remember I asked her not to have it because it would only upset her when we had to send it back again. It took the arrival of my brother and then two sisters before it sunk in that they were all here to stay!"

Suddenly Berengar choked up, and it was Esclados who said what Cwen had guessed, to the astonishment of the others.

"Dear Spirits, *you're* Edward's older brother! Sacred Trees, Berengar, no wonder you were so upset over the murder. That was *your* little brother too! Now I understand why you've kept making all those references to a brother's murder. This is personal for you too!"

Berengar pulled himself together and nodded.

"You see now why I've always said I had no family, and that I was found and raised by the Knight? But do you know something strange? I never knew that Edward – the king – was my half-brother until Cwen arrived."

"Sacred Trees!" Esclados exclaimed. "Really?"

"Really! You see, I knew that we were being hidden because my mother had crossed the royal family somehow, but because it never really came back to haunt us in any tangible form, it was just something we lived with in an abstract way. I knew I wouldn't be able to pursue a career at court or anything that got my family tree looked into in any depth, but as I wanted to join the Knights as soon as I was old enough to think about a career, it didn't really matter much to me. My little brother was happy being apprenticed to a minstrel who worked the north of Brychan, and for him and my sisters it was different anyway, because they had a living father whose name they bore. There was no reason to look beyond him, any more than with any other family – and our stepfather had a real and visible family in the north whom we were associated with. My family's just been a bit more careful than most, until now."

"But what about Edward? I mean did your mother never want to see him?" Swein asked timidly, afraid of the answer and yet desperate to know about his former lover and persecutor.

"Ah…" Berengar breathed dolefully. "Well one day, when some soldiers were coming back from a cross-border fight, the wounded were being brought to Breslyn as soon as they could manage the journey, but many of them had to rest for a while there. Until I heard my mother talking to them as she helped dress their wounds, I'd no idea how passionately she hated the DeÁine. One evening I got her alone and asked her why. It was then that she told me that she'd been raped by DeÁine soldiers. She asked me if I remembered the baby she'd had before we came north. Of course, I said. Then she said that she'd begun to suspect that it was the DeÁine Hunters who'd got her pregnant, not the nobleman who took her away. He'd been obsessed with her, but I got the impression that at first she'd been too distraught to care much. As long as I was being looked after and we were away from the war, she was rather past caring about herself. But after a few months – when she began to show and they moved her to the manor – she'd begun to take a bit more notice of things.

"She said what shook her out of her daze was the fact that she began to realise there was something strange about the pregnancy. Having had me already she knew what to expect, but the second time was different …too different. Apparently she tried to tell her lover that the child wasn't his, but he was so fixated he thought it was just a ploy to get him to marry her or something, and just showered her with more gifts.

"When the baby was born she took one look and knew it was DeÁine. She'd seen enough back home to know! Too pale. Eyes that were clear as water instead of blue. And thinner than a normal baby. She rejected it. Told the servants to take it away. Her lover was furious. He failed to see that to her it represented all the rapes and the beatings. It was the final abuse to force her to bear this alien creature. However strong her maternal instincts were, the circumstances of his conception overwrote all that.

"It was nothing but a relief to her to be sent away by her lover's father, and leave the child behind. What became of it she never asked or wanted to know. Of course, she heard that her lover had succeeded to the family title, but she'd never say his name to us. And she died before him, so she never got to hear of Edward's succession that came within the year of her passing."

Berengar sighed. "At the time he then became king, we were busy mourning her still. First my stepfather and then her within twelve months made it a double tragedy in our family. Much more important than some person we knew nothing of. My stepfather was a good and kind man who never distinguished between me and his own children. And she'd been a loving mother to us, and we all missed her terribly – my sisters especially, because the younger was still in her teens and the older was only just twenty." He took a restorative gulp of the wine, which Roger immediately replenished.

"I haven't seen much of my sisters in the last few years. A career in the Knights doesn't allow for much in the way of family visits, but if my sisters are anything to go by, I can see why Mar was attracted to Mother. They're only averagely pretty, but they both have a real vital spark – a zest for life – that makes them great fun to be around, if a bit exhausting if you're their older brother and trying to keep them out of mischief! I was always getting frantic letters from B…" His voice failed him for a second, "from Ben. He used to joke that he'd be grey by the time he was thirty from those two. Now I haven't dared to write to them to ask if they know he's gone. One letter traced and it could kill them too. I just keep hoping that they're so invisible by now that Edward won't find them. Ben was the only one living where he'd expect to be found."

Silence settled on the room for several seconds, then Swein let out a horrified yelp.

"So Edward's *half*-DeÁine! No wonder he thinks they're more civilised than us! …He must have realised!" Then another thought occurred. "Oh Spirits, no wonder he was so proud of the fact that he had no hair anywhere except on his head and that was so fine." Then blushed as he realised what he had revealed of his relationship with this man, but was too caught up in the moment not to carry on. "He said he'd be recognised as one of the highborn – that they'd know him for what he was and he'd have nothing to fear from them! I just thought he meant that he thought they'd think he was important as a figurehead for Brychan, but it wasn't that at all, was it? He knew they'd recognise his bloodline and he'd be allowed to live, even if everyone else was killed."

Berengar nodded his head but said nothing, and Esclados, looking at the expression in his old friend's eyes got the impression that there was more he knew but was not prepared to tell yet. He let it lie as Cwen's affectionate family was already positively smothering Berengar in expressions of sympathy for his brother's death. Only when they were alone in the shared bedroom, and the house had gone quiet did Esclados speak up.

"Are you awake?"

"Yes," Berengar sighed in the dark. "Too many memories tonight."

"Then can I ask you one last question?"

"Only one?" Berengar chuckled, "that'd be a first!"

"Was there something more you didn't tell everyone downstairs? Something you didn't feel you could say out loud in front of them …but you can tell me?"

The silence was long. So long Esclados wondered if Berengar had nodded off despite his protest of being unable to sleep. Then he spoke softly.

"Edward isn't half-DeÁine. My mother was a half-blood. Her mother had the same thing happen to her. My grandmother wasn't out of her teens when she had my mother after the DeÁine army went through New Lochlainn. Their family were refugees making the trek east. The only thing Mother was sure of was that my father wasn't a pure-bred DeÁine soldier. But you see, don't you Esclados, that it makes Edward nearly full DeÁine between both his father and his grandfather."

"Yes I do," Esclados sympathetically, "and I know what it makes you, too. In fact, if your father was of mixed blood as well, it's something you don't want to advertise either, is it? Rest easy, Berengar, I won't repeat a word. You'd still be my friend even if you'd turned out to be one of the pure bloods! But if someone wants to cause mischief, it would be too good an opportunity to miss to make something of, an ealdorman of the Knights being as good as half-DeÁine!"

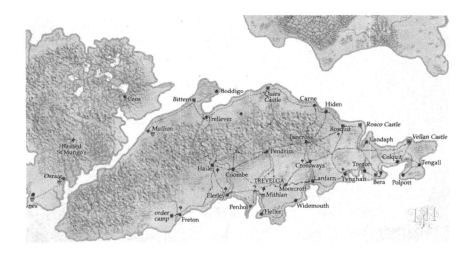

Chapter 8

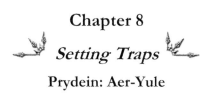

Setting Traps

Prydein: Aer-Yule

Hugh de Burh stared at the two messengers in undisguised horror. In all the years he had been Grand Master of the Knights of the Cross in Prydein he could not remember receiving worse news. Each piece of news alone was bad enough, but together they left him feeling paralysed in a way he had only ever felt once before in his life, and that had been when his beloved wife had died. The two men, both frozen and exhausted from their headlong gallop across the Island to him, had been waved to comfortable seats, and were now being plied with hot mulled wine and toasted cinnamon buns by one of the serving men. But Hugh barely registered the comings and goings. It took all of his will power to pull his mind back to the present in order to thank the men profusely, and have them led away for much needed rest. No sooner had the door closed behind everyone than he sank his head into his hands, elbows resting on his desk.

There was no doubt about the news – he had cross-examined the messengers and their stories fitted all too horribly together to leave much room for doubt. The first rider had had an exhausting ride from Bittern all the way along the northern coast to catch up with Hugh at Vellan. Sent by Commander Dabhi, the second-in-command at the Knight's great fortress and preceptory, the rider had worn out horse after horse, changing them in relays at granges along the way, but never sparing himself.

The news he brought was that Amalric de Loges, the Order's current Grand Master in name if not reality, had lost what little sense he had ever had, and ignored Hugh's carefully laid plans to draw out the men who were attempting a military coup. All he had had to do, according to Hugh's plan, was to ride in force to Mullion – home of Duke Brion, the leader of the rebellion against the rightful king, Ivain. From all the intelligence which Hugh had acquired, Mullion was relatively undefended and should have provided an easy victory for the force of Knights and men sent against it.

Why then, in the name of all that was holy, had Amalric decided to lead the small army towards the capital and the huge number of enemy troops stationed there? The written message that had come from Dabhi was tactfully worded, but left Hugh in little doubt that Amalric had some deep abiding resentment over the fact that while he was the named Grand Master, the real power still lay with his predecessor, Hugh. Yet why now, Hugh wondered? Why, when at last there would be ample chance to prove his ability as a leader once and for all, had Amalric chosen such an ill-considered course of action? Hugh had explained his reasoning to Amalric in great detail, so surely the logic of what they had planned had not escaped the man?

The one great consolation so far, for Hugh, was that he had not confided in Amalric about the DeÁine Treasure which was hidden away here at Vellan. Something had always stopped him just as he was about to tell his successor. Something that he had never been able to rationalise, but for which he was now incredibly thankful. Brion was supported by the DeÁine war-mage Calatin, and Hugh knew beyond any shadow of a doubt that Calatin had no real interest in who ruled Prydein.

Calatin's one and only objective was to get the DeÁine Scabbard, and at the moment he had no idea where it had been hidden. So for now he was using his unearthly powers to support Brion as a means of searching the great fortresses of Prydein. Calatin had been desperate to gain access to the main palace in the capital. Being one of a powerful elite who had dominated the DeÁine people for millennia, he had assumed that the Islands would function the same way, for no high ranking DeÁine would have let such a powerful weapon out of their close grasp. By his reasoning, the Treasure would be in the hands of the leading family and in one of their castles.

Hugh would have loved to have seen the expression on his face when he realised that not only the Scabbard was not there, but that (because of the way its Power tainted wherever it rested, leaving traces the Abend could sense) it had *never* been there. Hugh was sure that would have been an unsettling blow to the mage when he reached Trevelga, and Hugh wanted to strike before he regained his equilibrium. By sending a small force against the great fortress of Mullion, Hugh had hoped he was sending a heavy hint that the Knights going on the attack had the Scabbard with them, and were attacking with such confidence because of it.

All he had intended to do in this first gamble was to provoke Calatin and Brion and see if they took the bait. Mullion should have been an easy nut to crack, and as it was Brion's home, he was sure that Brion would not want to lose it. He had also hoped that if Calatin refused to support a retaking – a strong possibility since Calatin already knew that the Scabbard was not there – that it would drive a wedge between Brion and the mage, becoming a bone of contention.

Now all that lay in ruins thanks to Amalric's folly. And worse news had followed on its heels. The second rider had come up from the capital with equal speed, arriving at the same time because of the shorter distance he had had to cover despite having set off many days later. As one of a small group of scouts, he had been dispatched by the head of the Order within the capital, Trevelga, when they had seen vast numbers of troops riding out, fully armed. To the men's horror they had witnessed the slaughter of half of their Order's entire troops on the river plain at Haile. From their vantage point on a rise behind Brion's army, they'd watched the massacre of the vastly outnumbered Knights, and seen the few lucky ones escape south onto the inhospitable, freezing cold, winter moors. Separated by Brion's victorious army they could do nothing to help, and had little hope that those who had survived the mayhem would last long afterwards with no shelter and no supplies.

As Brion's victorious army turned for home, bearing the Knights' colour-flags as trophies at their head, the scouts had ridden with all speed back to Trevelga, but not to safety. Calatin had not needed to be present at the battle. The superiority of numbers had been sufficient to guarantee success except under any but the most incompetent commanders – and Brion was certainly not one of those. Instead, Calatin had waited in Trevelga. In rapid conference afterwards the Knights deduced he must have used his powers to watch the battle from afar, for as soon as the day was won, Calatin made to move against the Knights in the capital. With a body of men left behind for the purpose, he struck unannounced at the preceptories within the city, and the granges just outside, obviously intending to complete the wholesale slaughter of his most feared opponents.

The saviour of the unprepared Knights had been the leader of a gang of street urchins, called Tiny Arthur. His ragtag bunch of followers had no memory of home or parents and ran in a feral pack, occupying the alleys and drainage gullies of the dark underside of the teaming city. At various times, citizens intent on good works had attempted to catch, clean and re-home these small savages, but inevitably the kindly folk who took them in were no match for these experts in survival who escaped at the first opportunity. Yet even Tiny Arthur's gang could not control the weather, and two years previously a vicious winter had nearly been the end of them.

It had been a stroke of good luck that in desperation, some of them had crawled out of the icy streets into the Order's stables, and encountered the shrewd sergeant-farrier in charge. He had instantly realised that they had more in common with the wild horses he sometimes had to train, than the vast majority of the populace around them. Instead of overwhelming them, he had set them up in the hayloft, and sent them hot soup and fresh bread. Meagre fare to most men's eyes, this was a feast for the starving urchins. Soup that was not mostly water, but made from proper beef stock with fresh, not rotten, vegetables was a revelation, as was bread fresh from the oven and not several days old and heading for the pigs. At the end of the great freeze the waifs and strays had slunk back out of the loft as silently as they had come, but an understanding of sorts had been reached. Each morning the Knights left a fresh loaf by the stable gates at each of their places, and shortly afterwards a wisp of a waif would dash in and seize it, running off to the rest of the gang with the huge, warm loaf clasped in grubby arms. And the next winter the waifs and strays had returned to the warmth of the hayloft with more of their friends.

In payment (for then it was not charity and put them on more of an equal footing), every so often, Tiny Arthur or one of his minions would appear out of nowhere with information that might be useful to the Knights. Often very useful, since little that went on in Trevelga was missed by Tiny Arthur's gang. And they hated the new men in town with a vengeance. With King Ivain's men there had been a kind of truce, with each ignoring the other, but Brion's henchmen had viciously hacked down five of Arthur's pack on their first patrol through the streets, as though they were mad dogs.

It had been Arthur and his gang on the roofs pelting Calatin and Brion with rotten eggs, for, as far as Tiny Arthur was concerned, this was now open war. So he took it personally when he heard the Knights were to be slaughtered like his friends. A skinny little girl had raced into the dank hideaway, breathlessly panting that she had heard Calatin addressing troops outside the palace from her lookout point. The Knights were to be rounded up immediately and without warning, and brought to the palace for execution.

Calatin had moved fast, but not as fast as Tiny Arthur. His companions had dispersed with all haste, across roofs and through rat-sized gaps between buildings to the Knights bearing warnings. It said much for Tiny Arthur's standing that the warnings had been heeded. From the preceptories, riders were sent flying to the granges with orders to abandon them with all speed and retreat to the east and safety. Meanwhile, the men within the three small preceptories armed themselves and prepared to fight their way out through the guarded city gates.

The scout had left before the rest of his companions from the preceptory by the west gates, and had no idea whether they and others made it out alive, although he had made it through the gates by the skin of his teeth just before the order came to close them. On his headlong flight, he had seen two other riders tearing across the countryside, and guessed the warnings had reached most of the granges. The last he had heard from within the city, Tiny Arthur and his gang had been up on the roofs signalling the position of Brion's men to the Knights, and keeping them at least a street apart. The Knights feared for the brave lad and his friends if Brion ever found out what they had done, and the scout told Hugh that they had hoped to bring the gang out with them to safety, but that knowing Tiny Arthur's resistance to authority, there was no guarantee they would come.

Hugh found his hands moving to clasp in prayer as he offered up a heartfelt plea to the Spirits, the Sacred Trees, and anyone else who might be up there listening, to spare these brave children and bring them out to safety along with his men. If this little lad of something like ten years old was this much of a force to be reckoned with now, Hugh wanted him trained and in the Order when he was a man. If ever there was an ideal candidate for the Foresters or the Covert Brethren then it was Tiny Arthur.

Yet his prayers were very much for his men as well, for he saw only too clearly that it would take little short of a miracle for them to get clear of the city without heavy losses. Once the gates were closed there were only so many hiding places within the walls, even in a city the size of Trevelga.

Yet of everyone his thoughts were most often of Ivain. The young child left to rule after his father and grandfather's deaths had had great difficulty with what life had thrown him into, and the young man he had grown into was still struggling to find his place in the world. On the one hand, Ivain could be hopelessly naïve, as could only be expected with his protected upbringing. On the other, though, there were times when he could surprise everyone. When dealing with the ordinary people he had a natural talent for drawing them to him, and Hugh was hoping against hope that when it came to a full scale battle there would be some of his father's survival instinct lurking undiscovered in a corner of his mind.

Did Brion know that Ivain had ridden out with the Knights? Hugh had no way of knowing, but all his experience screamed out that if Brion knew, then the battlefield would be scoured until Ivain was found. And once found, Ivain's life expectancy would be numbered in minutes not hours. With Brion having already publicly executed a look-alike of the young king, most people thought Ivain was dead anyway, so who would suspect one more corpse on a field of slaughter? There was the faint hope that Brion had not found out before the battle, but how long would that last? The scout said the man next to him had seen Amalric being led away as prisoner of Brion once more, and given that Calatin had broken the Grand Master the last time he had had him in his grasp two months ago, Hugh had no illusions as to how long it would be before Amalric was babbling like a fool and telling all he knew. Then, and it may have been only an hour or so after the battle, Ivain would have been on the most-wanted list again.

Though it broke his heart to think of the young man whom he had loved like a son as dead, Hugh knew that it would be little short of another miracle if he had escaped. For his own part he could now no longer make his plans on the basis of the royal house of Prydein having survived in any but the perverse line which Brion represented, and there was no way that Hugh would ever sanction Brion as king. No, he must think and act on the premise that Prydein had descended into anarchy, and with that the master tactician buried his grief deep within his heart, and began to plot the downfall of the treacherous duke and the perverted war-mage.

In the small hours of the dawn, he put the final touches to his plans. Every possible Knight, man-at-arms and archer in the Order would be pulled back to eastern Prydein, focused on the Order's two great preceptory fortresses at Rosco and Bera. The River Tan, which was a major waterway from the town of Tancross down to its outlet at the sea at Lanfarn, would become the dividing line. It rose further north in the high tumbling rocks of Carne Moor, which until the spring would provide a barrier no army could cross in force at speed or without casualties, even undefended. The men from Quies castle could retreat to the town of Carne and fortify the coastal route. Quies was too accessible via the well-farmed river valleys which ran north from Trevelga between the east and west northern moors. There was no way that Hugh wanted to find the large number of men in Quies besieged, not now that they were so badly needed if he was to retake control of the Island.

If there were men still at Freton they were already beyond his reach, severed from the rest of the Order by Brion's army. Would Brion attack Freton? Hugh had no way of knowing for sure, but he feared that it would seem like another easy victory having already slaughtered most of those from Bittern. They caused him much worry. Should he order them on what would be a fearful march in the depths of winter north-west to Mullion, and hope that they could take the more substantial fortifications there? Freton was essentially a huge barracks supplied by substantial peripheral granges, with just one keep standing guard over them as a remnant of battles long ago. Nobody had ever expected to have to defend the place, especially from their own countrymen. Apart from an ancient inner curtain-wall it had no defences, since it was largely used as a training camp. And that was another of Hugh's worries. Of all the Order's holdings, Freton had the highest concentration of inexperienced men led by just a few veterans.

He paced the room beset by doubts, weighing different courses of action, and still worrying that none seemed the clear answer. *Flaming Trees, I'm getting old!* he thought. *I'm dithering around here like an old woman. I never used to be like this, surely? If I'd been this indecisive at Moytirra the DeÁine would have made mincemeat of us! Come on, de Burh, pull yourself together and think! This is no time to go all woolly-headed!* And as he warmed his bones before the re-stoked office fire he came to a decision. Harsh winter or not, the men must march.

Freton would not survive any sort of serious attack, and the men they would lose in that eventuality would far outnumber the casualties from a forced winter march. They must march north-west, going around the worst of the moors to Mullion, for there was always the possibility that the supporting men he had already dispatched there (to meet Amalric's troop who had never arrived) might still be there. If it still proved possible to take Mullion, then that was what they would do, and withdraw behind its mighty walls in safety. However, if Mullion was held against them, then they must march on to Bittern. The castle there was not such a mighty fortress as Mullion, but it did sit astride the neck of the heavily-wooded peninsula. With enough men, the narrow stretch of land could be fortified well enough, and there was plenty of fuel and shelter to help them outlast the worst of the weather.

So that took care of one problem, but how to win back the rest of Prydein from Brion and Calatin? First thing in the morning he called a council of war in his office. The commander of Vellan, a deceptively amiable looking man of middle years called Thorold, had been in Hugh's confidence for more years than either of them cared to remember, and stood shoulder to shoulder with him behind the desk. Ivain's two former rescuers, Captains Grimston and Haply, were also there, as were the commanders of Rosco and Bera, respectively Ealdormen Piran and Wulfric – originally summoned for very different reasons to meet Hugh here, but fortunately on hand now the crisis had come. The final man there was the senior Forester in the west of Prydein, a solemn, dark-haired, weatherbeaten commander known as Aeschere. Together the seven of them poured over the large-scale map of Prydein which lay spread over the desk.

All agreed that the Tan was the place to make a stand, the question was how to bring Brion to battle and counter the power of Calatin.

"We've already seen one example of those fireballs he can summon up and throw at us," Haply reminded everyone. "I for one wouldn't want to send men in to face that. There's nothing we have that even begins to qualify as a defence against them."

"I think we have to concentrate on a way to separate Calatin from Brion and the army," Thorold said thoughtfully. "That's the key, isn't it? Without Calatin we face an army of ordinary men, and I have no doubt that then our superior training will give us an edge over Brion's troops."

"Don't dismiss them too readily, though," Grimston warned. "Remember that out on the west coast there, they've had plenty of experience of real fighting against the Attacotti. I know the Attacotti aren't in the same league as us, but the majority of our army will be made up of young men who've trained and trained but never seen blood drawn in battle. Experience may make a big difference and even the odds."

"Agreed," Hugh spoke up, "but Thorold's right in the sense that they're only flesh and blood, and they can be killed. Who knows what evil surprises Calatin might be capable of? Even after all the years I've spent fighting the DeÁine, I still have no idea what the stamina of a member of the Abend might be. Collectively the Abend and their Power-wielding acolytes seemed to be capable of hurling bolts of energy, and mobilising their ghastly summonings against us, for hours on end at Moytirra. But we still don't know whether or not that was achieved by sucking the life out of the bodies of the hundreds of slaves we found afterwards, who seemed to have died without a blow being struck against them."

"Mmmm, …so you're saying it might be the case that against a big enemy Calatin might either expend his energy quite quickly, or be forced, in effect, to consume large numbers of his own army to fed himself if he wants to continue throwing this stuff at us?" wondered Wulfric of Bera.

"It's possible, …" Hugh pondered.

"… But do we really want to find out?" Thorold asked.

"I for one say no!" Piran of Rosco said emphatically. "It's no use to us that Calatin sucks half his own army dry, if half of ours have been wiped out by magic before they even get chance to come to blows with the remnants of Brion's lot!"

"Exactly," Grimston agreed. "I don't think there's any way around the fact that we cannot afford a set battle until we're very sure Calatin's had his claws cut – hopefully permanently!"

"But just how, *exactly*, do you plan to do that?" Piran demanded.

"What of the King and Queen?" asked Wulfric simultaneously.

"You're not thinking of using them as bait?" a horrified Haply gasped.

"No, no," reassured Wulfric, "I'm just thinking of whom we have to protect *before* we start dangling baits."

Hugh found his voice wavering as he forced himself to answer. "Thank the Rowan, Queen Alaiz is safe in Ergardia – although that's more due to her own actions than to anything we need to be proud of – but I fear King Ivain is dead."

"Dead? No!" Haply and Grimston cried in distressed unison.

"How?" demanded Haply alone.

"I sent him with de Loges," Hugh told them bitterly. "I thought it would restore his confidence if he had a real victory under his belt after what Calatin did to him. If they'd gone to Mullion, as planned, he'd have been as safe as anywhere in Prydein."

"De Loges is asking for a knife in the dark to take him out!" Aeschere growled, and all eyes swung to him. "Well don't all look so horrified! I'm only saying what we're all thinking! No blame on you for raising him up, Grand Master – and that's what you are again now, Master Hugh! Because if de Loges lives through what Calatin has in store for him, I doubt he'll be in any fit state to lead a Beltain feast dance, let alone the Order. But if it were possible, I'd dispatch him to his Maker before he can spill everything he knows into Calatin's lap. And he deserves eternity in the Underworld for the lives he's cost by his folly. And all for his own ego!"

Haply snorted, "I can't disagree with you on that! Who'd have thought the man would've had his head turned by power like that! I suppose it just goes to show that you never really know what someone will be like with that much power until it happens."

"Well thankfully he's the first we've had go dark on us for generations!" Thorold replied. "For the most part the men who get elected live up to their promise and beyond." His eyes swivelled to Hugh who was deep in thought and missed the collective sigh of relief. If Amalric had turned into a disaster in the making, it was a blessing that he did it while Hugh was alive and still spry enough to take up the reins of command again. But Aeschere cleared his throat to draw them back to him and said,

"I wasn't just wishing aloud over de Loges, you know. I'm volunteering here and now to find a way to get into the palace and do the deed." Six sets of startled eyes turned on him as he continued, "I'm saying this so that if you agree to me going, I can leave before you decide what to do next. That way I can't reveal anything if I'm caught and tortured. Think about it! Because you have to decide whether de Loges can compromise any future plans. If he's a real danger he has to go, Grand Master or not."

"Sacred Trees! I can't believe we're having to do this!" Wulfric gulped. "This is mutiny!"

"No it isn't!" Aeschere snapped. "Mutiny is when men rebel against a leader who still has full authority. It has nothing to do with an egomaniac who's lost the plot entirely, and has caused the Trees alone know how many deaths, and may cause even more!"

Hugh sighed. "You're right, Aeschere," everyone else gasped, "but don't you think it's too late for that now?" The others sighed, but with relief. "However much it would weigh heavy on my conscience, I'd send you on your way if I truly thought it would save that many lives. And I commend your courage, because I know *you* know what's in store for you if you go. But think about it …Calatin's had de Loges for over a week already, and more than two by the time you could hope to infiltrate the palace. Do you really think it would take that long for Calatin to get what he wants? I'll not have your death on my conscience for no good reason, for I fear it's too late to think of this now. No, my friend, stay and join in the debate, you'll not be going."

Aeschere bowed his head in acknowledgement. "Very well. I just wanted you to be sure you knew there was an alternative."

A servant knocked at the door and brought in a large pot of steaming caff and fresh mugs, and confirmed that men had been sent to take up position near the Tan in case the fleeing men from Trevelga needed assistance against pursuers. When he had gone the seven got back to the main problem.

"I hate to say this," Thorold said mournfully, "but the one thing I can think of that would draw that fiend out would be the lure of the Scabbard."

"Trees! We can't let the bastard get hold of that!" Haply swore.

"No we can't, but do we need to?" Aeschere mused. Once more all eyes were on him as he continued. "Master Hugh, am I right in thinking that he would sense the Scabbard once it came up out of the depths it's buried in now?"

Hugh suddenly brightened up. "I see where you're going with this! Yes, it might well work if we just got the Scabbard out and moved it around."

"Well, I was thinking more of moving it by sea to Bittern," Aeschere offered. "That way it would stay well out of reach of his sticky fingers, but the sense of it being somewhere in the north in general might well draw him out."

"By the Oak that protects, that might well work!" Thorold enthused. "By sea, yes, that *would* work. It might just drive him mad enough to act rashly – being able to sense it and yet being separated by salt water. It'd be like hanging a juicy ox bone high out of reach of a hungry hound. There'd be no way he could miss sensing it was there, and he'd not be able to resist going after it because he craves it so badly."

"And I doubt Brion would want to waste men by moving them randomly northwards," Hugh mused. "If Calatin could give him a definite destination he might agree, but out on the sea there'll be no markers to tell him where we're planning on sending it. Indeed, I think it would be good if we moved it in short hops around the coast. That would have two advantages. Each time the ship puts into harbour Calatin will have no way of knowing if the Scabbard is about to disembark, and it also means that the ship won't be so far from shore that if the winter storms get truly dire, they can't take refuge. We don't want the cursed thing ending up at the bottom of the sea where some fisherman can dredge it up in years to come, or turning up as wreckage on an unidentified beach, for the Spirits know who to pick up."

"Then it's agreed," Thorold asked, "we move the Scabbard by sea to …Bittern?"

Everyone nodded.

"Very well," he continued, "then the next question is: where, how, and with what do we neutralise the wizard?"

All eyes turned to Hugh and he in turn appealed to Aeschere.

"Do the Foresters have any information that might help us with this one?" he asked hopefully. But Aeschere had to admit that they had had little experience of actually capturing a member of the Abend down here in Prydein.

"The man you want to talk to is Warwick, our head over in Brychan, or maybe Grand Master Brego or Master Arsaidh in Ergardia. I'm ashamed to admit it, but we're a pale shadow of our compatriots up in Ergardia, Celidon and Brychan when it comes to knowledge of the arcane arts."

"But you must know something?" Haply remonstrated with him.

Aeschere looked profoundly uncomfortable, but after much thought said he was fairly sure that the wood of the Sacred Trees was pretty toxic for those wielding the Power.

"What about iron?" Grimston asked. "I thought I heard something about an iron stake through the heart being guaranteed to kill them?"

"Isn't that something else?" Piran wondered, "You know, like the un-dead or something?"

"I thought that was a *wooden* stake through the heart?"

"Anyway, how do we pin him down so we can stake him through the heart with …whatever?"

"Wooden cage?"

"Iron cage?"

"Throw sea water over him?"

"Lost Souls! How many buckets of that would we need? And does it have to be fresh?"

"Throw him *in* the sea?"

"Oh, bugger this!" Wulfric exclaimed in frustration. "We're totally in the dark, let's admit it!"

They all sat in glum silence for some time. Finally Hugh broke it, speaking with great care as if measuring his idea out word by word.

"I think we can assume that just moving the Scabbard will lure Calatin to wherever we want him to end up. That being the case, we can't be too obvious or he won't fall for it. So I think we can't expect him to come right up to the shore unless it looks really convincing. Amalric knows I've been based at Quies for some years, so why don't we attempt to catch Calatin there? We know we'll move the Scabbard to Bittern if necessary, but he's not to know that, and if he has Amalric he'll know that Bittern is drastically undermanned at the moment. So it won't make sense to him if he thinks we're taking it there. On the other hand he doesn't know – because Amalric doesn't know – that we're emptying Quies and bringing the men east. And it's a good location because it's not right on the coast, so it doesn't look like a trap. What Calatin doesn't know either, though, is that where the land falls away from the castle, the marshy land is actually salt marsh and in winter the high tides often wash over it, albeit not in huge waves.

"If we can get him there then we can think of something like a poacher's trap – or better still several, strategically placed on all possible routes to the castle. If we put the Scabbard in the east dungeons, there are barred windows venting them that give onto the marsh side. Hopefully he'll think he can blast the wall with his Power and just walk away with the thing, so we can lay traps in that area. When we've got him we can try everything we can think of as long as it is all to hand and can be got at quickly."

"Too right!" Piran agreed. "He's going to be one angry war-mage when he finds himself cornered. We won't have much time to act before he tries to fry us!"

"Right, so we need wizard traps – like a bear trap only …well …different?" Haply asked.

"Bear traps is a good analogy," Aeschere began with a wisp of a smile beginning to appear. "Yes! It'll be cold, wet work, but if we get the castle carpenters to make some cages out of rowan in particular, maybe reinforced with oak, then anchor them just below the water level in the marsh. …No …even better, let's make them look like a causeway! Most of it will be just ordinary wooden walkway. It doesn't have to be that substantial, because it only has to take one man's weight once going one way, so it needn't take long to construct. Then we can have two or three points where there's a trick floor. He steps on it, the planks give way, and he's down in a cage up to his knees …hips …waist …neck – no that would be too lucky! – in brine."

"Yes, and I've been thinking," Grimston added. "Why don't we get the armourer to make us some spears? Good solid wooden shafts. *Long* wooden shafts! With barbs on! Put a sharp steel head on them, so they'll penetrate well, and find men with a good throwing arm. Spears would be better than arrows because once they're in – if you get my drift – then there's enough shaft for whoever uses it to put their weight behind it and make sure it goes right through him. That way we can make sure he gets wood and steel, and long shafts will keep him wedged in the cage because he won't have space to move."

"And when we've got him?" Haply asked.

"Take him wholesale – cage and all – out to sea and drown the bastard," his friend said.

To their surprise Hugh was quite emphatic in agreement with the last. "Yes, we can't pierce his flesh if he has any Power drawn into him– so thrown spears are fine, but no stabbing until we're sure he's not full of it. The reaction could kill those of us close to him, too! And, no Aeschere, I won't countenance you sacrificing yourself, even to rid us of a war-mage. In the sea is the best place for him. He mustn't be buried! Burned or drowned are the only ways. Those of us old enough to remember Moytirra, know that some of the Abend have been known to have the power to raise the shades of the dead. We don't want to dispose of his earthly body only to have the monster come back as a malevolent ghost with an army of Spirits at his back just at the worst possible time!"

With the decision made, Aeschere offered to go with as many carpenters as Vellan could spare to prepare the trap at Quies. Since he had the best idea of how it would work, Hugh reluctantly let him go. In the meantime the armourers at Vellan and Rosco would set to work on the spears, and those heading for Quies would take the results with them when they went. Hugh and Aeschere estimated that if old wood was used – partly for speed by using what was available, and also to make the causeway look more convincing – then the traps should only take a week to make. The plan was therefore to aim to have Calatin and the Scabbard at Quies for the start of the New Year.

A week before the start of Yule, Hugh would therefore go with a small, but very visible escort, and start riding openly westwards. All the others agreed that while he was another excellent bait to dangle before the war-mage, Hugh was now too valuable to the Order to be endangered by being present when Calatin was trapped. Reluctantly he agreed, but only because he was outnumbered, and so as soon as he arrived at Quies, Aeschere was charged with spiriting him away again and, if necessary, bringing him back in secret to Vellan. Haply, Grimston and Thorold being the ones who were charged with the task of wizard baiting, while the others set the Order in readiness to retake control of Prydein.

They were consequently all kept busy for the following days making their preparations, taking little notice of the news of men from Trevelga making it to safety except to offer up prayers of thanks whenever they had chance. So Hugh was in the armoury with Haply and Grimston, when a rider hammered into the frost-decked bailey demanding to see him at once. The messenger refused any refreshment until he had seen the Grand Master and was brought straight to Hugh. Even stranger was the tiny figure trotting at his heels as they entered the stone vaults, warmed by the fires of the anvils. Leaning wearily against one of the great work benches the messenger spoke.

"Sire! You'll not believe this. De Loges walked into the camp a week ago!"

"What?" his audience exclaimed in unison.

A stunned Hugh dropped the spear he had been holding onto the bench and stared in amazement at the messenger. "You're telling me he just appeared? What of his capture? Is he well? Is he wounded?"

"He just appeared, sire. A bit tattered, but acting like nothing happened at all."

"Did he say what happened to King Ivain? Where's Ivain?"

"I don't know, sire. He's said nothing of him and he just doesn't answer some questions. He's started giving orders though!"

"What?"

"Oh don't worry, sire, the camp physicians are saying that he's not fit enough to be in command and so, while everyone is saying yes to his face, his orders are being ignored. I've written copies of all the ones he'd given before I left, though. The commander thought you should see them – especially when this person appeared with his story." The messenger gestured to the rather grubby little boy who stood quivering with impatience at his heels. "This is Tiny Arthur, sire."

Hugh's face broke into a smile. "Is it, indeed! Well, young man, you're most welcome! I understand we have you to thank for any of our men getting out of Trevelga at all."

"Aye, well never mind that!" Arthur brusquely brushed aside the thanks. "I didn't come bouncing all this way at the back of this chap like a sack of spuds for chit-chat! Your man's been turned!"

Hugh was taken aback as the little figure stepped forwards to stand right in front of him, small fists on hips, and a ferocious scowl on his face as he went on.

"We talked to the lads who clean the shit out of the privy shafts. They 'eard the wizard talking to that bastard duke. 'E was bragging how easy it'd been to turn your man again. Squealed like a stuck pig when 'e saw the wizard, 'e said. Didn't even have to break him. That's what you get for doing the job properly the first time, the duke says, and laughs. Now we'll gets rid of them Knights for good, they say. That's when the lads thought I should 'ear about it. They don't like it when that wizard does things. They've been seein' strange things of late. The ghosts of folks that're supposed to be dead 'ave been seen at night in the quiet places. And there's strange noises coming from the dungeons – not people noises, we knows about them.

"Turns out that wizard can crawl into men's minds if 'e breaks 'em right! That's what 'e's done to that stuck up prat of yours. 'E's inside 'is head! What your man sees, 'e sees! 'E's sent him 'ere to spy on you, and 'e don't even need to send messages by birds or nothin', 'cos 'e's right there with him. They thinks 'cos 'e's valuable you won't leave him out at the camps, but'll bring him right in 'ere and then they can listen in to what you's doin'. You gotta kill him, mister! Or else we're all dead!"

"We should have listened to Aeschere," Haply said bitterly.

"Mmmm …" Hugh murmured distractedly. "Amalric a spy, well, well." Then the others saw the twinkle in his eye as he said with relish. "I think our adversary has just made his first mistake. This could be turned to our use! Yes indeed it could! Come, young Arthur, you and I have plans to hatch. A young man of your talents shouldn't be wasted."

Chapter 9

The Bait is Taken

Prydein: Aer-Yule – Yule

The first thing to happen the day after Tiny Arthur's arrival, was the sending of a message summoning de Loges immediately to Vellan, couched in the most welcoming terms. The best carpenter and armourer in the castle were also summoned to Hugh's office. From there they were taken under escort to a small room beneath the west tower and shown a beautifully made wooden scabbard, inlaid and rimmed with rich metal tracery, which contained a second steel scabbard within it (also beautifully decorated), and told to make an absolutely accurate copy of them that had to be finished within the week. They could have all the help and tools they required until the job was done, and the sooner the better.

Aeschere had already been planning on leaving within days, but now he was to be sent on his way the next day with as many craftsmen as the castle could spare. If they were making wizard traps none of them wanted Amalric to catch even the slightest glimpse of them. The manufacture of the spears was also transferred to be undertaken at Quies out of sight.

In a late-night session with Thorold and Aeschere, Hugh reworked their time-scale. With Calatin evidently full of overweening confidence, and believing he had taken the initiative away from the Knights, they wanted to move fast so that he had no time to get suspicious at how easily things seemed to be falling into his lap. The bird-sent message summoning Amalric expressed delight at his fortunate escape, even going so far as to hint that he would be needed to take charge of one of the castles or something more important – a bait really for Calatin. If he set out without delay, as they were sure he would, then he would arrive at Vellan in mid Aer-Yule. By that time the real Scabbard had to be ready to sail away. A sleek warship was already anchored in the bay below Vellan, and her handpicked crew were being briefed as to their mission.

At first Hugh had thought to wait to welcome Amalric personally, but Thorold and Aeschere dissuaded him of the advisability of that. Nobody knew how far Calatin could reach through one of his familiars, and now was not the time to find out. His own departure was therefore brought forward to the eleventh of the month, by which time Amalric should be only a couple of days away. At that point the real Scabbard would also be brought up out of the subterranean room and taken on board the *Grendel*. Even far away in Trevelga, Calatin should sense its presence, and therefore when Amalric de Loges arrived shortly afterwards and saw an armed escort waiting to take the fake Scabbard out of the castle, through him Calatin would see what they wanted him to believe he was seeing – the Scabbard on the move. Amalric would be told by Thorold that Hugh had ridden out with an advance guard to prepare Quies to receive the Scabbard. They believed that there was little chance that Calatin would worry about attacking Hugh when the thing he had desired for so long was finally coming within his grasp, unless they made it ridiculously easy for him.

In reality the *Grendel* would be shadowing Hugh along the coastline, exchanging signals regularly – a precaution so that it kept pace with what the riders could reasonably achieve in the current weather at any given time. The last thing they wanted was for the roads to slow the riders down while the *Grendel* flew on ahead, so that Calatin became suspicious as to why he was sensing the Scabbard in one place and seeing it way off somewhere else. No-one was taking the chance of underestimating the war-mage's intelligence. A handful of Foresters were going to ride between the parties as well, complete with signals for the ship, in case they needed to warn Hugh to adjust the pace. By their calculations, if Calatin left Trevelga as soon as he sensed the real Scabbard appear on the eleventh, he would reach Quies at Yule. Aeschere was therefore working towards having the traps made and baited well before then, and to be out of the way before Calatin set foot in the place.

The only point they still fretted over was bringing the real Scabbard ashore, but all agreed that this was something they could not hope to plan in advance. If the Forester scouts Aeschere was going to send out to watch for Calatin's approach warned that he was within a day of Quies when the real Scabbard arrived, then it seemed prudent to leave it on board the *Grendel*, and have it anchor close to shore with the security of the brine around it. They could only pray that by then, Calatin would be so intoxicated by the aura of the Treasure that he wouldn't be aware of the switch unless he, in person, actually got within a few yards of the replica – and nobody had any intention of letting that happen if at all possible.

In the end the waiting was the worst torture that the Knights endured, for everyone wanted to be up and at the business now that it was begun. It was therefore with great relief that Hugh donned his heavy winter cloak and boots, and went down to the waiting escort at daybreak on the appointed day. Once mounted on his favourite war-horse, Scythian, the muffled figure of Tiny Arthur was lifted up in front of him. Hugh was taking no chances that Calatin might work out that the Knights had been warned and by whom. It was also some salve to his grief that if he had not been able to save Ivain, he could at least save this boy. Arthur had at first been reluctant to go along, fearing he was being bundled off out of the way just when things were getting interesting, but had cheered up immensely when he was told he was going to help set wizard traps.

Their party set off in yet more falling snow, and were soon lost to sight, leaving Thorold, Haply and Grimston waiting for the arrival of Amalric. Wulfric had returned to Bera already, and, once he was sure de Loges had passed them going east, he would be heading west to take command of the men who had fled from Trevelga and fortify the crossings of the Tan, along with every man he could get along the way. Even though he was following the same route as Hugh, Piran too had gone ahead to Rosco. He wanted to create the impression of scouts scurrying around the countryside, as they might do if they were actually moving the Scabbard across hostile territory. This would also give him the ideal opportunity to move many of his men out of the great Order stronghold, and disguise the number of men who had been held in reserve there.

Many of the outlying buildings at Rosco could be mistaken for ordinary farms built close to the castle for protection, especially in such awful weather when everything was disguised under layers of snow which blurred outlines. The full strength of the Knights in the east was something to be kept from Amalric's, and therefore Calatin's, eyes at all costs. Once the second party, led by Haply and Grimston with Amalric in tow had passed, Piran and his great force of men would be joining Wulfric by moving down from the north with all speed. Strength of arms would make little difference against a war-mage, but the line would be held against his all too human army at the Tan, and Brion would rue the day he ever aspired to rule Prydein, that they vowed.

For the first few days Hugh suffered agonies of frustration at not knowing whether the bait had been taken. Progress was slow, for they had to ride over the windswept headlands in order to miss Amalric, instead of taking the road, and to maintain the appearance of covertly moving the Scabbard but also to stay in sight of the *Grendel*.

"Don't you worry," Arthur kept reassuring him. "'E's too full of 'imself is that wizard. 'E don't think nobody's got no brains 'cept him, and you dangled a big bone for 'im to bite at. 'E'll want to bite, don't you fear!'"

Nonetheless, it was a huge relief when on the sixth day, one of the Foresters rode into the camp just as they were leaving with the news that Amalric was exactly where he ought to have been. Haply had risked slipping a message out to the Foresters to say that Amalric was definitely behaving strangely. For those who knew the now demoted Master, the hardest part was acting as if there was nothing wrong. The ordinary Knights simply kept their distance in a play of deference, but poor Haply and Grimston were with him most of the day, and were walking on eggshells in case they looked askance at something he said when they should not have. Luckily the weather had stayed grim, with the snow giving way to sporadic sleety rain which kept everyone huddled within their hoods, and scarves over their mouths, halting much in the way of conversation. It was going to be a long ride, though.

On that same day, Hugh's party reached Rosco and found that Piran had had a message by bird from Thorold. Apparently Amalric had practically fallen over himself in his haste to join the party escorting the fake Scabbard. He appeared to be taken in by the pantomime the men had put on of not handling the 'Scabbard', but using blacksmith's tongs to place it carefully in a lead-lined box which was welded shut once it was inside. Thorold confirmed that Amalric had had a good chance to look at the fake as it was ceremonially brought to its casket, and that one of the men had splendidly faked feeling ill in its presence by acting 'vomiting' something which looked disgusting with diced carrot in it. Amalric, ever delicate stomached, had been quite distracted by that – war-mage in his mind or not – and before he could get close enough to handle the fake, the farrier had been welding down the lid.

After that even Thorold had been hard put not to show surprise at Amalric's willingness to suffer cold and discomfort to travel with the casket, when in the past the ex-Master had been notorious for enjoying his creature comforts. Yet when the time came, de Loges had mounted up with the others, and ridden away from the comforts of the castle without so much as a backward glance.

Thank the Maker, he's swallowed the bait! Hugh thought. *Sacred Trees but I feared he wouldn't. Not de Loges. Him I would guarantee to hoodwink on all but the unluckiest of days. But Calatin! Hounds of the Wild Hunt, it's been a long time since I had to think to deceive an Abend, and I feared I wasn't up to it any more. Oh for the certainty of youth like young Arthur! To not know how badly you can fail, and at what cost. Age definitely has its drawbacks! I feel like some mummer in a play, putting on a mask to reassure the men while all the time I'm quaking inside. Trees, are you listening? If I live through this — if we all live through this! — I'm through with juggling all these lies and deceits, I promise. I'll find a nice quiet abbey and spend the rest of my days worrying about my immortal soul, and planning nothing more than whether I can still get up off my knees after prayers, and what's for dinner.*

For Haply and Grimston the ride towards Quies was equally as wearing. During the day they could avoid conversations for most of the time, but once they stopped for the night it was much harder to put off. They had hoped that once they were back on the main road across the north of the Island and were stopping at granges along the way — as befitted Knights with a precious package — that things would be easier. However, they inevitably found that Amalric was unwilling to associate himself with men whom he thought of as beneath him, and this included mere captains in charge of humble granges. There was some respite at Rosco in the form of Piran, and the two friends thankfully disappeared to bed early that night, leaving Piran to crack his jaw with false smiles instead of them.

Yet once they left the last major grange at Carne behind, they were truly forced into his company on the barren stretch of coast leading to Quies. By now the two were scared to death that they might make a slip when all was so near completion. They covered the source of their anxiety easily enough by hinting at fears that Brion would learn of their mission, which Amalric seemed to accept as reasonable. That did not help them during the long evening meals, though, and finally on one night Haply brought up the subject of Ivain in a valiant attempt to find some topic which was less fraught with danger, believing that Amalric too would mourn the young king's passing.

"We were impressed with how the young king handled himself, all things considered," Haply began. "It's a tragic waste he's been taken from us so soon."

"Tragic waste? *Phfaah!*" snorted Amalric.

"I thought you were close to him?" Grimston asked in genuine surprise at Amalric's reaction.

"Hardly," was Amalric's disdainful riposte. "He really was hopeless you know. If you'd ever seen him trying to lead men you'd have near fallen off your horses laughing. Sacred Martyrs! If his grandfather was watching from the next world, he'd have been tearing his hair out at what a useless pup his son spawned."

It took all of Haply and Grimston's self-control to not bite back and say that actually they *had* seen Ivain in action, and against Calatin himself, but if Calatin/Amalric did not know that then they were not about to reveal it.

"Someone will have to break the news to Queen Gillies," Grimston forced himself to go on pleasantly through gritted teeth.

"Well that won't be me!" snarled Amalric. "By the Wild Hunt, the woman is clingy! Do you know, I don't know how I kept the pretence up all those years? Really I don't! Paddling palms and giving meaningful glances to pander to her besotted attentions …*uuurgh*!"

"Yet she's a good-looking woman," Grimston remonstrated. "Many men would be flattered to have the attention of someone who's still comely and attractive for her age, *and* the dowager queen as well."

"Flattered? Well 'many men' can have her, is all I can say! And she isn't the dowager queen, because she was never *crowned*, you dolt! Geraint never became king and so, thank the Spirits, we never went through the farce of having a woman who was little short of notorious held up for our praise and adulation as queen. Not that that dim-witted girl they married Ivain off to is much better. All she's fit for is painting pretty pictures and sewing things. Do you know she actually thought she could decide what to do with her life? Witless creature!"

The two captains thought this was a bit rich considering that they had heard how it had been Alaiz who had galvanise Amalric into action on the moors. As Grimston went to replenish their wine and kick the side trestle to relieve his anger at Amalric's derisory comments, Haply valiantly tried to keep a light tone in his voice.

"You don't like women much then, do you?"

"What's that supposed to mean?" Amalric snapped, whipping round to glare at him.

"Well you're the only one who doesn't seem to have a good word to say for two women who're otherwise well liked for their feminine charms, if nothing else." Haply desperately countered – belatedly realising that Alaiz had affronted Amalric's substantial ego, even as he wondered if there was any topic the man would not take offence over.

"And what use are 'feminine charms', eh?" sneered the ex-Master. "If you've got the urge you can satisfy your needs with a whore, whom you can pay to keep quiet while you're about it, and then leave where you found her as soon as it's all over."

"Lost Souls! That's a cold way of looking at things!" Haply could not stop himself saying. "If you hate women that much why go with them? There must be men who you'd find more welcome company?"

"What are you suggesting?" an outraged Amalric demanded. "You're not saying I'm one of those shit-stabbers, are you?"

By now Grimston had been pushed beyond endurance and could not resist baiting the pompous bigot before him.

"Well people did say you were very fond of young Ivain, even made a pass at him." He did not say that it was Hugh who had told them of his odd conversation with Ivain. However, it was amply rewarding watching Amalric turn so red they wondered if he might explode.

"A pass? A pass! What in the Underworld are you talking about? That I fancied that …that …that arrogant, self-important, prick?"

Grimston gave a nasty smile and found he was enjoying himself for the first time since they had set out.

"Oh not fancied," he said with false innocence, "loved. You know, *lurrrved!*" and grinned lasciviously.

"This is intolerable!" Amalric was on his feet shouting by now, and the men around them were having trouble containing their mirth at his apoplectic rage. "This is the thanks I get for trying to show him the error of his ways? I should've known better! Just like that fool of a brother of mine, always trying to get people to like him, and saying whatever he thought they wanted to hear. Never mind what harm it does to others, oh no! Just because you're the legitimate heir it doesn't mean you can walk over everyone else. But where are they now, eh? Feeding the worms like all the others, that's where!"

Grimston set his wine cup down, having lost all desire for any more.

"I'm off to bed," he said in disgust, unable to stomach any more of the same.

"Hold on, I'm coming too," Haply quickly added, unwilling to remain in the sole company of de Loges when he was like this.

"Oh I see," sneered Amalric nastily, "it's like that is it? Just *friends*, are we? No wonder you were so quick to see me as another perve…" but was cut off as Haply spun and with a right hook caught Amalric right on the nose, which began to bleed profusely.

"You'd better get cold water from the pump on that," Grimston said icily and they left him to it.

As they crawled into their beds in the cramped room they were sharing with a sergeant and two archers, so that nobody had to share with Amalric, a thought came to Haply.

"You don't think that de Loges was thrown out of his family and sent to the Order for murdering his brother, do you? If they suspected but couldn't prove anything?"

Grimston was just about to blow out the solitary candle but paused and gave his friend a horrified look. "Rowan save us! I hadn't thought of that, but it did sound like it, didn't it? ...Ivain obviously misunderstood what he meant. Perhaps de Loges wasn't so much upset when Ivain said he loved Alaiz more than him as much as disgusted? Disgusted that he was actually trying to do things the right way? He seems to have little time for love and relationships. Maybe he thought he could be the one controlling Ivain and get everything he missed out on the first time?"

"It makes more sense that way, doesn't it?" Haply thought aloud. "I think Master Hugh needs to know what we suspect as soon as possible." He swung his feet back out of bed and pulled his outer clothes and boots back on. "I think I'll slip out and see if I can find one of our guardian Foresters to relay the message."

When the Forester caught up with Hugh, he had just ridden into Quies on Yule Eve with Aeschere escorting him for the last mile. Aeschere's reaction was one of, 'Well we need have even less conscience about disposing of him, now!' Hugh, however, found it a little harder to be quite so detached, but he nonetheless made a mental note to check more deeply into Amalric's background when he got chance. He thought he'd been sufficiently thorough before he elevated Amalric as his replacement, but after all the years de Loges had been in the Order, his old life had seemed to be of little importance, especially as he'd had nothing more to do with his family. Maybe that was more a case of them never wanting to see him again rather than him renouncing his ties, though, Hugh belatedly thought?

However, of more immediate concern was the inspection of the traps Aeschere had created with the carpenters. From the castle they walked down to the marsh with young Arthur in tow, who inspected the fake walkway with great earnestness and even more care than Hugh. Considering the time and conditions they had had to work in, the duck-board walkway across the marshes looked as though it had been there for years and had been well used. Some of it even had moss growing on it!

"We got that from an old sheepfold which was gradually collapsing," Aeschere explained. "Master Kilburn just lifted it wholesale and cut it to shape out here so that the planks never got separated and the moss disturbed. We used another side from the same pen a bit further along in the same way."

"I must say, I'm impressed!" Hugh announced. "This is way beyond what I expected to be achievable."

"Woah, no further!" Aeschere caught his arm and stopped him in mid step. "The next plank is the first one of the nearest trap."

Kneeling down on the boards he pointed out to Hugh and Arthur the box-like construction beneath, which was altogether newer looking and made from a mixture of woods.

"We made this and four others from the sacred woods. They're sunk down into the marsh and we had to dig out the mud to get them in. There are men in the castle who had a very grim time of it doing that job, but they set to it with a real willingness. Being up to your waist in mud and freezing water in midwinter is numbing work, and they could only stand it for an hour at a time, even with oilcloths on. The good news is that these traps have already filled up with sea water. Depending on the state of the tide when it happens, Calatin will find himself at least up to his waist – and probably deeper – in the stuff, which should keep even a war-mage of his calibre unable to use his Power on us."

Inside the castle, Hugh found that there was also a goodly stock sacred-wood made weapons hidden away where Amalric was unlikely to find them. To his delight the trap was as prepared as it was possible to be. Only Arthur was unhappy, and that was because he now realised that Hugh had no intention of letting him be part of the company which would skewer Calatin.

"I'm sorry lad," Aeschere agreed, "but it's off to the *Grendel* for you two as soon as she docks."

The *Grendel* was sitting out in the bay already, but her captain was waiting for the tide to turn before he risked bringing her closer in to shore. The weather was foul and a high wind was gusting around the headland, making it dangerous to try to sail her in at the moment, but the taint of the Scabbard was surely enough for Calatin to pick up by now? The spies out on the roads had had no sightings of him as yet, but there were a full two days to go before they could realistically expect him to appear.

They could hardly believe their luck exactly two days later, when, only hours after a very harassed Haply and Grimston had arrived with Amalric and the fake Scabbard, a signal from the hidden watchers indicated that Calatin was in sight. The Foresters out on the open moors now made themselves scarce with all possible speed and secrecy. The danger of Calatin being able to sense their presence outweighed their limited ability to make any effective strike against him, if he showed signs of going on the offensive.

Aeschere himself stayed well away from Amalric, leaving him to the hospitality of the reluctant Commander Breward, acting on Hugh's behalf. Breward had reverently led them down to the basement level and the dungeon they had designated should be the 'Scabbard's' resting place. With great solemnity they had placed it in the centre of the room, and then made great play of locking and barring both the door to the room, and that of the corridor leading to it, and placing a guard beyond.

Breward played his part with great aplomb, hinting darkly that Hugh had rushed off on a secret mission and would be back for the Treasure in a day or so when the 'plans' had been put into play. Amalric had stroked the lead-lined casket almost lovingly before being prised out of the dungeon room, saying,

"I can promise you, gentlemen, that within the next couple of days this thing of great value will be in the hands of those who will do most good with it."

"Oh indeed, sire, Master Hugh has some great design for this, he assures me," Breward had replied with feigned innocence, perfectly played.

"Oh I'm sure he has," Amalric had agreed with the smile of a snake about to swallow its prey whole.

Up on the roof with two of his most trusted Foresters, Aeschere watched Calatin's approach. The DeÁine war-mage was showing every sign of caution, but that was to be expected. Aeschere would have been more worried if he had strolled in without a care in the world, for that could have signalled that their hand had been tipped. If he could have done, Aeschere would have arranged a signal which would have got all of their men out of the way once Calatin entered the castle. However, the sight of men scattering hither and thither would also have aroused suspicion, being totally out of character for men of the Order known to carry on fighting even against impossible odds.

Instead, every man in the hall with Amalric and those on the route to the dungeon was a volunteer. Men who knew that they might end up giving their lives to protect something which was utterly worthless, but were willing to risk that in order for the charade to be convincing. Hopefully they would be able to put up a good show and then retreat, but Aeschere knew that they would be fortunate indeed if they got away with no fatalities at all.

With his diaphanous black robes swirling in the wind, Calatin strode up to the castle's great gate and with a blast of Power simply took them off their hinges. Aeschere winced as the gate guards were flattened against the walls by the impact of the timbers, and offered up a prayer to the Sacred Trees to heal their wounds or care for their souls, even as he took to the stairs. Foresters Saeric and Nazar were twin brothers with an ability to sense one another's thoughts which could be unnerving to those who had never seen them in action before. Tall, lithe and dark, they bounded down at Aeschere's heels like sleek deerhounds with the scent of the hunt before them. Ahead they heard the deep throated *crump* of another explosion, and guessed that Calatin was now inside the keep.

By the sound of it the men were making a good job of it seeming like a surprise, although some of the screams worried Aeschere. They sounded too real for comfort, and he hoped nobody was trying to be too heroic and attack the war-mage. Racing along the upper corridors, Aeschere, Saeric and Nazar got to the far stair and descended another flight, before leaving the castle by the small picket gate at ground floor level. Now they were on the opposite side of the castle to the gate and facing the marshes.

Aeschere lifted his bow and waved twice and saw some white feathers wave back. The archers out on the marshes now knew to expect Calatin at any time. They had been Aeschere's own touch. Spears were good, but an archer could fire with equally lethal effect from a much safer range. They were there to make sure Calatin stuck to the seaward route and was not tempted to turn back inland, rather than to kill him. There were also men on the land-ward side blowing trumpets and shouting orders, as if rallying troops – also to distract him from turning away from the coast. Until Calatin was in the water, Aeschere knew he could turn aside arrows or spears with a mere flick of the Power, but hoped the war-mage would be focusing that on bigger targets, and would regard the arrows as an irritant to be avoided.

A stunned man staggered out into the corridor behind them, blood dripping from his ears, his eardrums burst.

"He just blasted us!" he yelled, unaware that he was shouting. "He didn't wait for us to attack. He just started throwing men against the walls with the Power!" Then turned and staggered off towards the infirmary.

"Bastard!" Saeric swore softly, but before anyone else spoke there was another crash from within and below them.

"He's going straight for it!" Nazar exclaimed with glee.

Another crash within heralded the demise of the dungeon door. Aeschere risked a glance out away from the wall, and was relieved to see that the men with the spears were well away from the dungeon wall. Which was just as well, as seconds later a whole section of massive stone blocks flew outwards in a deafening blast, as if as light as dandelion clocks on a breeze. There was a heart-stopping moment when one block flew farther than the others and crushed the steps up onto the causeway, but it was still accessible. Out stepped Calatin, with de Loges at his heels puffing with the strain of carrying the casket. Instantly there was a tingling sensation in the air, and Aeschere knew that Hugh had unveiled the real Scabbard on the deck of the *Grendel*, which lay easily seen but inaccessible across a quarter of a mile of salt-marsh. They had expected Calatin to be able to be able to feel it, but no-one had thought ordinary men would, and that was worrying. If they could feel it here, what was it doing to those on board?

Yet there was no time to worry now. From within the castle someone was firing out of the gaping hole, and although the arrows fell uselessly to the ground a yard away from Amalric's back, they nonetheless prompted the pair to move on. Calatin was acting like a man drunk on too much good wine, reeling forwards as the tingling on the air increased. *Oh Flaming Underworld! He's drawing Power from it!* thought Aeschere, *this could all go bottom up in a hurry!* But to his amazement, Calatin was so preoccupied sucking in as much Power as he could that he was being guided forward by Amalric.

From behind the castle, the trumpets sounded again and Calatin frowned, turning away from it. For an awful moment Amalric took the lead, and Saeric and Nazar groaned in unison in the expectation of it being Amalric who took a ducking in the brine first, so warning the war-mage. Calatin, however, was used to his serfs knowing their place, and roughly shoved Amalric back with a snarl.

Out onto the walkway they went while the watchers collectively held their breaths. To his left Aeschere could hear Nazar whispering "keep going

…keep going," like a mantra that voiced all their prayers. At the first trap the floor gave way right on cue, plunging Calatin knee-deep in the water.

"Get me out you fool!" they heard him screaming to Amalric, who carefully set the casket down before reaching down to the DeÁine. Amalric was not a big man, and the weight of the tall war-mage was too much for him. Even as he got Calatin upright he was pulled in, but the DeÁine simply used him as a stepping stone to climb upon and get out. Without even a glance at Amalric, he picked up the casket and began to retrace his steps. This was the signal for the archers who immediately put down a volley, and appeared screaming out of the marshes at an angle to him. At the same time the spear-throwers broke cover and began charging towards him.

The war-mage lifted his hand and made as if to release one of the fireballs at the men. The ball appeared in his hand, and Aeschere held his breath again in horrified anticipation of the slaughter to come. But the ball only flew a few yards before dissipating on the wind. And it was then when Aeschere and the twins realised that they could no longer feel the tingling of the Power on the air anymore.

"He's caged the real Scabbard," guessed Saeric. "Master Hugh's locked it up again. The crafty old fox! Now Calatin thinks his Power is draining away with his water-filled robes!"

"By the Trees, you're right!" Aeschere exclaimed with delight, and sure enough, Calatin took to his heels and began running back along the duck-boards. Amalric had hauled himself out and was ahead of him, then tripped on the trigger of the next trap and went flying, but because he fell headlong onto it it failed to drop. Calatin sprinted up and cleared him with a nimble leap, and with a false sense of security that he was outpacing his pursuers did not realise what was happening until it was too late. Master Kilburn's artistry played out in balletic grace. Calatin's lead foot hit the slippery moss and he performed a series of frantic skating movements even as he hung onto the casket. In half a dozen steps he reached the next trap just as his feet finally shot out from under him so that he sat down hard, but continued to sink arse first into the icy brine.

For a moment there was stunned silence all around and then a massive cheer went up. In the blink of an eye they saw a boat being swung out from the *Grendel*'s side, which was no doubt Hugh returning to see their prize for himself. The spear-men raced forward to the caged Calatin and stood poised to skewer him, but there was no need. The feared war-mage was screaming piteously as the fresh brine covered him up to his neck. Once Hugh and Aeschere had joined them, the men removed more planks at either side revealing the trap to be a completely self-contained cage. Someone brought up the top piece, which was lashed over the top, before twenty strong men hauled the whole thing, Calatin and all, up onto dry land. At this stage his wrists were lashed to opposite sides of the cage and the same with his feet, while poles of rowan were slid into craftily designed holes so that Calatin became surrounded by the shafts to completely restrict his movements.

"Well good afternoon to you Calatin," Hugh said politely as the member of the Abend writhed in agony, his skin coming up in great festering blisters. All he got in answer was a gob of spittle which did not even reach his feet. "Charming!" Hugh breathed. "Right lads, let's get him into the boat!"

With the aid of some wooden rollers they trundled the cage out to where the ship's boat waited. It settled rather deeply in the water once the cage was on board, but the pull out to the *Grendel* was across wave-less water and was managed with minimal shipping of water into the boat. The experienced crew soon had the cage swung up onto davits on the side, where Calatin remained swinging in the salt breeze.

"I don't quite believe this," Aeschere said, grinning like a schoolboy at Hugh, "but we've caught ourselves a DeÁine! Happy Yule!"

"Yes and we'll celebrate the New Year by drowning the bastard in the depths of the seas!" Hugh grinned back. "He deserves nothing less for all the suffering he's caused."

Walking back to the castle with the war-mage's ululating cries echoing across the marsh they were treated to Arthur's excited dialogue.

"That was the *best!*" the lad enthused. "Can y' hear his caterwaulin'? 'E's had that comin', by the Maker 'e has! Are y' goin' to drown that thing with him? You should have seen it, Aeschere! There was that big bang at the castle, then Master Hugh threw back the lid and tipped that thing out onto the deck. 'E picked it up with a boat-hook and it started to glow all weird like! There was this nasty green light – like somethin' festerin' – and it ran in waves up that thing and into the air! Like big oily ripples running upwards! The sailors were all afeared and got as far away as they could get, but I stood by Master Hugh! Y' could even see that puss-green light on the air fer yards! An' it was headin' for that bald bastard!"

Both men grinned at one another over Arthur's head with wry amusement. Life on the streets had given Arthur a colourful vocabulary in advance of his years and an uncompromising attitude. Hugh was nearly as bald as Calatin, but Arthur was blissfully unaware of the comparison in his focused venom towards the war-mage.

"Indeed he did stay with me," Hugh confirmed, "even though he'd been told to remain below decks!"

"Well I wasn't goin' to miss all the fun after being bounced all that way from Vellan behind you like a sack of turnips, was I?" was Arthur's retort. "Anyhow, where are you goin' to drown him? You gotta give the captain a place to go, ain't ye?"

The two men stopped and exchanged startled glances, realising that they had not give that any thought, being too focused on actually capturing their quarry first. Back in the castle, as the clearing up process began, Hugh called Grimston, Haply and Aeschere to one of the out of the way tower rooms to make the decision. It was somewhat complicated by Amalric's presence, for they had assumed that Calatin would discard the ex-Master at the first opportunity. However, the bond between servant and master had become stronger if anything. Amalric had clung like a drowning man to Calatin's cage, and had begun to writhe in agony when several burly men had begun to drag him in the opposite direction back to the castle. There had been little choice for the moment but to send him on board the *Grendel* – although in his case it was to confinement in the strong room of the lower deck recently vacated by the real Scabbard, which was now under guard in the other half of Quies' dungeons.

"I'm hoping that when Calatin meets his watery end the distance of several hundred feet of brine will break the connection," Hugh explained.

"I don't know why you're bothering," Grimston muttered darkly, "as far as I'm concerned the fishes can have him right now!"

"*Tsssk..*! 'Cos we gotta find out what he knowed," Tiny Arthur's exasperated voice came from under Hugh's arm. The small head appeared at the map table, glaring up at the Knights with the kind of frustration of someone explaining the blindingly obvious to somebody very dense. "You *fink* that wizard knowed about the king ridin' inta battle, but you don't know for sure. We gotta grill him so as we know just how far the wiz' was in the know, and how far back. Once the wiz' is in the water, yer man will be in too much of a state to start argufyin'. 'E won't know if 'e's on 'is head or 'is arse! Master Hugh'll get the truth outta him then, don't you fear!"

"Thank you for the vote of confidence," Hugh smiled wryly at the vehement small face. Then to the others, "but Arthur's right." The small head bobbed emphatically in an, I-told-you-so, sort of way. "We have to know exactly how far we've been compromised by Amalric. We're all assuming that the first point was when Calatin hauled Amalric into the palace dungeons at Trevelga and had some fun torturing him. But we have no real idea when Calatin may have first had contact with him. The war-mage was certainly with Brion much earlier than that, and if you remember, Brion made a visit to the capital back in the summer for Ivain's birthday celebrations."

"Surely we would've heard of someone as noticeable as Calatin there then?" Haply wondered.

Tiny Arthur was practically dancing on the spot with eagerness to join in as Hugh said, "Yes, but that's assuming he came in his normal form. Tell them Arthur."

"My gang was watchin' the Duke when he come – 'cos he's always been a nasty bastard to us! This time 'e had a bunch of priests wiv 'im. Now we fought that was odd, 'cos the Duke don't spend no time in churches on account of the roof would fall round 'is ears 'cos of bein' so wicked!" The men all smothered laughs at Arthur's earnest belief in divine intervention in this form.

"So we watched them priests. Some of 'em went into the cafedral and was on their knees most of the day. But this one big fella and a couple of others, they never went near a church! They was ferretin' around in all sorts of odd places. We didn't fink nufin' of it then. Some of them holy bruvvers ain't so holy, as some of my little mates know, if yer get my drift."

He wiped his nose on his sleeve, Hugh swiftly retrieving a handkerchief from the boy's pocket and pushing it into his hand. "Not the sleeve, Arthur!"

"But it's quicker!" Arthur protested, then at Hugh's stern frown, sighed melodramatically and used the handkerchief. "Anyhow…" he checked with a glance at Hugh that he could carry on, "we just fought they was a bunch of perv's like we sometimes met before. But now I see'd 'im again, I'm sure that the big fella was that wiz'. 'Specially as sometimes my gang said they felt all funny if they got too close on his trail. Didn't know what to make of that then, but I do now!"

"So you see gentlemen, we have to rethink how long Calatin has been watching us." Hugh was quite firm on this. "We now have to consider the possibility that Calatin had begun to befuddle Amalric long before we first thought. Not control him, I think, since that kind of behaviour *would* have been noticed. But chipping away at his subconscious, so that when he got him in his clutches properly it didn't take him long to drain him of everything he knew."

"Oh crap!" Grimston murmured.

"Moreover," Hugh was continuing, "we need to get the *truth* from Amalric, because we need to know what he honestly thought of things."

"Whatever for?" Haply asked in astonishment, but Aeschere was starting to nod in understanding.

"I see where you're going with this, Master Hugh. Calatin could get into de Loges' mind, but what he found there would be *de Loges'* viewpoint of things. *His* perceptions! If de Loges' thinks – and thought – that someone was a useless fool, then that would be the impression Calatin would've been given too. De Loges couldn't deliberately lie to him, but if de Loges really truly, deep in his heart of hearts, believed that that was the truth, then Calatin's understanding would've been skewed that way. If de Loges thought that …oh I don't know …let's say a training exercise, for argument's sake, had gone badly because of the incompetence of two of his junior officers, then Calatin would think them incompetent too. The reality might be that de Loges mucked it up for everyone by giving the wrong orders in the first place, and that the officers actually did a good job of rescuing the whole thing from becoming a total fiasco. But Calatin would never see that, because de Loges would never believe deep down inside that he was to blame."

Haply and Grimston suddenly saw the huge implications of this. It might just mean that any other plans Brion had made with Calatin's aid were flawed at a fundamental level in a way that they could exploit.

"So we need him alive, and not just a breathing vegetable from having his mind shattered by wrenching it free from Calatin's," Hugh emphasised. "I therefore think that wherever we decide to drop Calatin has to be somewhere not more than a couple of days' sail away from these shores, so that we can get Amalric quickly back and to a physician if he needs one."

Together they all now peered at the map. The deepest water was in the basin which lay off the southern tip of Celidon. There they could guarantee Calatin would sink into more fathoms than any man had been able to measure, and under other circumstances that would have been their first choice.

However it was way too far for Amalric to be brought back with any speed, and they all wanted that information now. Weeks delaying its arrival could give Brion valuable opportunities to strike at them without intelligence to help counter him. The sea-basin between southern Rheged and Ergardia, and Prydein's northern coast, was not as deep but it would suffice. Their only concern was that there were rip tides running through there which frequently dredged things up from the sea floor and deposited them on the coasts of Prydein and Rheged. They could only hope that after several weeks at minimum at the bottom of the sea, Calatin would be beyond even the Abend's ability to resurrect him.

However, they decided that the cautious thing to do would be to sail to Boddigo first. That way Hugh could accompany Amalric part of the way, and it also meant that they would be sailing north well clear of the southwest of Rheged. The last thing they wanted was to have a storm come up and blow the *Grendel* onto Rheged's shore and wish their problem onto the already hard-pressed folk of Rheged.

Come the following morning, Hugh led quite a party on board the *Grendel*. Aeschere, with Saeric and Nazar, would remain on board to see the drowning of Calatin was thoroughly carried out. Haply and Grimston, with eight men-at-arms would watch over the Scabbard, which was once again brought on board. Everyone was jumpy about having it so close to Calatin, but Quies was no longer secure enough for the Treasure to be left there. With Brion possibly on the move it was deemed imprudent to send it east again, for Calatin might have primed Brion as to its movement in case he required an escort after he retrieved it. No-one wanted to win against Calatin only to lose such a dread weapon to their adversary. Using it would kill Brion for certain, but how many of their own he might take with them in the process was something they had no desire to find out.

Hugh had decided that once they reached Boddigo, he would leave Haply and Grimston with the Scabbard, and take Tiny Arthur with him to see the state of affairs at Bittern for himself. By now he had given up hoping the lad would stay put if he tried to send him somewhere safe. Arthur had a quick mind and a thirst for adventure tempered by years of successfully fending for himself, but it worried Hugh that the lad had little idea of just how much trouble he could find himself in if he went up against Brion on his own. It was much better to keep his small shadow with him, for at least there Arthur was content that he was with someone who was at the heart of all the big decisions.

For two choppy days the *Grendel* fought the tides westwards, having to go almost down to Treliever in order to ride the current safely into Boddigo's narrow harbour. During those days Hugh went repeatedly to visit the manacled Amalric without success. His former protégé was incoherent, sitting rocking himself on the hard wooden bench and mumbling words randomly. In a brief moment of optimism Hugh had wondered whether the occasional word was in DeÁine, revealing Calatin's mind if not Amalric's. Once his ear became attuned to the babbling, though, it was clear that it was nothing of the sort, and Hugh became concerned that too much damage might have been done for Amalric to ever return to normal.

Between Amalric's gibbering and Calatin's nerve-grating yowling, everyone was glad to spend the night ashore – Hugh even arranging for a guard from the castle to go on board to allow the sailors time ashore for a respite. As the *Grendel* pulled out on the following morning's tide, Aeschere hoped that leaving the Scabbard behind would improve their lot, and indeed Calatin was quieter even if Amalric continued his lonely dialogue. Saeric and Nazar took over his care and declared that if he was not truly mad, then he was the best actor they had ever come across.

Through rising seas, the *Grendel* fought its way north into huge waves which threatened to capsize them if they had not tacked back and forth – either beating into the grey slopes which towered above their mast, or flying down their sides as they turned back on the opposite tack. In such weather they could not leave Calatin swung up on the side, for the cage made the ship lopsided and threatened to drag them all down to watery graves. Instead, it was lashed to the grating in the centre of the upper deck, Aeschere checking the bonds that held Calatin as often as he could with waves washing across the decking.

By New Year's Eve the *Grendel* was not much further north than a day's sailing in normal weather, despite having been at sea for nearly twice that time. They were way further east, though, and there was the grandfather of all storms brewing up out of the west.

"I'm sorry, Commander Aeschere," the ship's captain told him, "but we're going to have to do it soon. I'm going to have to get the sail furled and ride this one out, and who knows where we'll end up then. We're already much too far east. If we're not careful we're going to end up on Rheged for the New Year!"

"Very well," Aeschere conceded, for there was no way to avoid it. "We'll stand by for your signal when you're sure we're over deep water. I'll get Saeric and Nazar up here with me, and if your bosun will stand ready with an axe on the fourth side, we'll hack the ropes off at your command and shove him overboard. I'd hoped for something more ceremonious for dispatching one of the greatest enemies of the Islands, but this will have to do."

The valiant captain sailed on, desperately trying to make sightings, the sail furled and three men at the wheel. Shortly after midnight there came a break in the clouds at which he and the master began frantic calculations based on the stars they could see. Aeschere saw their look of horror, and gestured the two Foresters and the bosun forward with the axes.

"We're even farther off course!" the captain cried. "We're far too close to Rheged for safety with that thing coming!"

Looking westwards the men now saw a huge thunderhead leading a storm-front their way, and despaired at their prospects of surviving an even worse battering.

"I saw a light!" a man in the stern suddenly called out. "Over there!"

"Sacred Trees and Holy Martyrs protect us!" the captain prayed. "That's east. That can only be Rheged on the horizon!"

"Now!" Aeschere yelled, swinging his axe above his shoulders and bringing it down to cleave the ropes in one cut. Three more axes fell in unison and the cage lurched to the starboard side. Dropping their axes, Aeschere, Saeric and Nazar grabbed hold of the cage low down on the inboard side and, as it reached the rails, heaved upwards with all their might. As the ship wallowed over to that side, the lift was enough to overbalance the cage and it rolled into the inky depths.

From below there was a sudden scream of "Master!" A crash resounded and then running feet, the three Foresters turning just in time to see Amalric leave his shirt behind in the hands of the sailors who had tried to grab him as he lunged for the side. Without breaking his stride, he leapt up with one foot onto the rail and then on and out into the water in a long dive.

"Lost Souls!" Aeschere cried in horror, hanging on for grim death to the side as he searched the waves for any sign of de Loges. Even the twins, normally unshakeable, had gone pale at the sight of Amalric's suicidal leap, and for a moment everyone froze. Then reality returned as the ship righted itself and the light winked again on the horizon.

"Everyone except those on the wheel, get below right now!" the captain commanded. "No-one else is going overboard!"

The wheel was protected by a curved wooden shelter which could be rotated within a deep groove in the deck to match the direction of the wind. The captain now retreated there with the wheel men, who all wore safety ropes. Everyone else was barely below decks when the storm-front hit. From below it felt as though the whole ship was picked up and thrown forwards. A ferocious crack made them fear the steering was gone, and if anyone was left above there was no sign in the wild movements of the ship. The speed they were travelling at was now beyond any the ship could normally achieve, and there was a crackling sensation in the air all around them.

"Trees! What is that?" Saeric yelled over the din. In the blackness that surrounded them an eerie glow had begun.

"It's like Arthur described coming from the Scabbard," his twin yelled back, and indeed it seemed most intense in the region of the strong room where the Scabbard had lain. At that point, though, there was a dreadful crunching noise from beneath them that had nothing to do with magic and everything to do with the bottom being ripped out of the *Grendel*.

"Brace for impact!" a voice in the dark called out. But in that instant the whole of the front of the ship seemed to explode inwards and darkness enveloped them.

Chapter 10

Learning to Lead

Prydein: Aer-Yule – Yule

In the days after the flight from the battle and the survivors' encounter with the farliath, Ivain had never been so cold, wet and exhausted in all of his protected life. He, along with the rest of the men who were retreating on foot, seemed to walk in a daze. His whole day was occupied in focusing on putting one foot in front of the other, and not sliding into frozen-over patches of marsh and streams. By night they camped near water in the coombes of the moors, as protection against the war-mage's sendings, and where there were trees to get firewood from against the subzero temperatures.

For the first couple of days he was ready to just lie down and die. In a life of feeling like a spare part to be shunted around where required, he felt he had plumbed new depths. Yet he did not die. The Knights and enlisted men were experts at survival, and once they began to recover their equilibrium after the shock of the betrayal and defeat, things began to improve. Many were superb shots, bringing down many of the wild geese on the wing which regularly flew over the moors from the marshland to the west. The rich, greasy meat had never been a favourite of Ivain's when prepared by the royal cooks and slathered in rich sauces. But cooked over the open fires it was something else. The grease was collected as it ran off, and was used on the men's boots against the wet, while the remaining thin veins of dark yellow fat provided much needed reserves of energy to keep them all going. Other men would disappear off to one side as they walked and return with pockets full of nuts and berries, so that if food was not plentiful, it was certainly enough to stop them starving and to enable them to keep on the move.

After eight days the company came to the River Fret, and to their astonishment saw riders in the Order's uniform heading towards them with speed. The leader of their company, whom Ivain now knew to be Commander Eremon, signalled a halt and went to meet the riders on the road. His total bemusement at the riders' news was written across his face as he turned back to the others. Beckoning everyone forward he raised his voice so that all could hear.

"We wait here," he announced to their amazement, but continued even as questions formed on the lips of the company. "Master Hugh has heard of the battle from scouts who followed Brion's men out from Trevelga. He's sent a bird to Freton with orders for an immediate evacuation!" There was a collective intake of breath. "He fears that Duke Brion may be so emboldened as to feel he could attack Freton after his success against us, and the Master knows Freton is not meant for defence. Those riders are chasing after the men whom we were *supposed* to join with to attack Mullion! Ealdorman Hereman is following with the whole of the Freton garrison who are a day behind, since they have the wagons with all the supplies on. His orders to Commander Breca up ahead are to wait wherever it's safe until they can join up, and then this time we are going to take Mullion!"

A ragged cheer went up at this. The loss of their friends would not be wholly in vain if something in the way of a victory could be salvaged from the mess. As Eremon continued to explain that the idea was to then make a stand at the eminently fortifiable Mullion, Ivain was confused, but the men seemed to understand what was going on and the lifting of spirits was almost tangible. As they found a sheltered spot by the roadside to wait for the main column, Ivain made sure he was seated next to Pauli and asked the question that was vexing him.

"I'm sure it's me just being stupid again, but how can we take Mullion if it's so defendable? Surely we'll be cut to pieces even trying."

Pauli smiled. "No, it's not a stupid question. Did de Loges tell you nothing of the reasons why we were sent to take Mullion?"

"No. ...Or to be more precise, Hugh told me we were going to take Mullion because, he believed, Brion was so sure that we lacked the ability to resist him that he wouldn't dream we would attack his own stronghold. Hugh thought that Mullion would be poorly defended, with Brion taking most of his men with him to seize my palace and the capital. But once we were on the road Amalric said that that was stupid. That he'd had a dream that showed Mullion still fully defended. That it was Trevelga that Amalric thought would fall easily, and so we could recapture it before Brion had chance to fully defend it."

Pauli's brow creased in perplexed concern. "De Loges told you that?"

Ivain nodded.

"Sacred Trees!" Pauli breathed softly. "I wonder…"

"What? What is it Pauli? You look as if you'd seen a ghost!"

The older Knight ran a hand across the several days' stubble on his chin, gave Ivain an appraising glance and then took him by the arm and led him over to where Eremon sat. "You'd better hear this," he said to his leader, and then repeated what Ivain had told him. Eremon and the five captains with him all reacted as Pauli had.

"What is it? Tell me please!" Ivain pleaded. "Why does everyone keep doing this to me? Everyone keeps giving me bits of information, or telling me to go here or there, but nobody ever tells me *why*!"

The desperation in his voice registered with the professional soldiers, and Pauli suddenly felt very sorry for the young king. It had never really occurred to him to think what it was like for Ivain. Somewhere along the way he had acquired a stylised idea of what it must be like to be king, but he was beginning to see a very different reality.

No doubt Ivain's grandfather (the previous king of Prydein) had ruled his court with a rod of iron, getting his own way over most things and playing the Maker with the lives of the small folk. But poor Ivain had inherited when only a boy of eight. Throughout his childhood there had been no question of him assuming the mantle of power, but now he was a young man of twenty-five. Yet it was becoming clearer with every statement from Ivain, that it had proven impossible for him to wrest the power out of the hands of those who had governed in his name during his youth, in the seven years since he had come of age. Pauli could now see that the young king had been just one man alone, fighting webs of intrigue and power-brokering, with no allies prepared to back him without taking something else from him in return.

"I'm so sorry," Pauli apologised, and meant it. "We've been talking over your head like you aren't here. That's not acceptable, and we wouldn't have done it to another Knight." The apology was for himself, but his words were also a strong hint to the others, and it with was with relief that he saw embarrassed awareness dawn on them too. "I'm sure things would've been very different had de Loges been taking over after the death of his predecessor," he told Ivain. "We would've had to find a solution quickly or put up with him how he was. But Master Hugh was still there, and more of the senior men had served with him in real conflicts than with de Loges, so for the most part we could, and did, by-pass de Loges so that he's become just a figurehead."

Eremon smiled wanly at Ivain. "I suppose things would also have been different if de Loges had been seen as a battle-hardened leader. From what Hereman has told me, I think Master Hugh saw de Loges as someone who would be able to negotiate the mire of the court intrigues and keep the Order's influence strong, and so he wasn't bothered at first that de Loges wasn't a fighter. But then we've come to this crisis, and we need a leader. A *real* leader! And that's made it clear to de Loges that it's Master Hugh who still holds the reins of command in the Order, no matter who holds the title. You should know that de Loges was hardly ever present at the planning meetings, and showed no interest in Mullion's real strengths and weaknesses."

"You've probably noticed that those of us who've been in the Order for years only use one name," Pauli continued explaining. "It shows that we've forgone any of our family associations and are wholly part of the Order. Admittedly Oliver still keeps his family name, but that was primarily because there were so many Olivers in the year he joined they had to find some way of distinguishing them! But he's still simply Oliver unless there's a need to specify who he is. Yet we still refer to Amalric mostly by his family name, rather than as Master Amalric, which is partly because no-one thinks of him as totally absorbed into the Order anymore. But it's also partly come from him. Once he was at court, increasingly often he reverted to using his family name so that he was seen as being the same as the other nobles – or at least that was the excuse that he gave to the ealdormen."

"I don't think anyone was totally convinced that he was fraternising with the nobles in the Order's interests," agreed Eremon. "I think the truth is more likely that he realised that he regretted losing his former noble status. He used to always be on about how he had the king's ear." With a visible jolt Eremon seemed to suddenly realise that now he was talking to that very king in the unassuming young man before him. "Your ear," he corrected himself.

"And yet he told me nothing," Ivain said, every word carrying years of frustration in them. "Hugh was better, and yet he said I should learn how to rule first and that he would fill me in on the details later on. But 'later on' never happened. Once upon a time I thought Amalric was fond of me in a strange sort of way. I was never sure whether it was fatherly, like Hugh, or something else …well …until a few weeks ago, but that's even more confusing!"

"Did you know that Oliver and the rest of us hauled de Loges' arse out of the palace dungeons?" Pauli asked. "Or that he was as much use as the turnips in the cart we shovelled him into?" Ivain's open-eyed astonishment told Pauli that this was not quite how Hugh had told him of the events. "He was utterly spineless, lying whining in that cart. We'd never have got him moving when we saw Brion's men coming for us. Your young queen was marvellous! She put a sting in him that had him up on a horse, and riding over land we'd never have got the cart over."

The mention of Alaiz was another knife twist in Ivain's soul. Another bitter regret that he might never get the chance to put right, but he had no time to linger on that, for Pauli threw another surprise at him.

"What we're all worried about now is what happened to de Loges in those dungeons." Ivain was even more surprised when Pauli added, "We know Calatin broke de Loges. But now you've told us of this dream de Loges had, and so we're all thinking that maybe Calatin kept some strand of control in de Loges' mind. We thought Calatin might have watched us, but this dream business might mean he was even closer!" Ivain felt his heart sink somewhere into the sodden soles of his boots as Pauli spelt out the implications.

"You see, that would mean that Calatin *knew* we were coming. Mullion certainly is almost empty, and could well have fallen to us, but would Brion and Calatin want us to get a firm foothold somewhere? No, of course not. So Calatin had de Loges think it was his own idea to march on the 'undefended' capital. How easy would it have been then for Brion to march out to meet us? He would've known exactly how many men we had with us. And it wouldn't matter if he emptied Trevelga of all but the wounded, because he was assured of an overwhelming victory that would render us incapable of making any further attacks on it."

"So that's why Hugh is sending us to take Mullion!" Light dawned for Ivain. "There'll be very few to hold the defence of the walls against us, but when we march in with the whole of the Freton garrison it can become impregnable again?"

"Exactly!" Eremon confirmed. "And without his spy in our midst – as we can now tell Ealdorman Hereman – we have a greater chance of success."

A day and a half later the company of weary survivors had joined the huge column of men heading north, and their lives improved greatly. Now they had extra clothing and food, and the security of being able to set proper guards at night in short shifts that did not leave men too exhausted to walk the next day. Eremon spent much time in conference with

Hereman and the captains, and even Pauli seemed to have friends among the rest of the company, leaving Ivain to his own devices for hours at a time.

It took two whole weeks to reach Mullion, not least because the day after the two forces had joined up, they spotted a dark swirling cloud on the horizon. Luckily they were already surrounded by the dense woods of the Fret valley, and the men hauled wagons off the road under the cover of the snow-laden boughs. For a tense afternoon everyone remained silent, the men with the horses constantly soothing them to stillness, as flock upon flock of black birds flew across the landscape.

Once night had truly fallen and the birds disappeared, everyone breathed again, speculating that Hugh's prediction had come true and Brion's men had ridden on to Freton. Finding it empty, the war-mage was now scouring the countryside to find the missing men. That night the leaders decided that their tracks were too noticeable to not be seen and a new ploy was decided upon. The men who had escaped the battle once again donned their tattered uniforms and lay on top of the wagons, while other men carried some of the supplies formerly contained in the wagons.

When daylight came the birds returned with it, but what they saw was a tattered column of wounded men hardly making any progress in the winter snow. The main company lay camouflaged beneath the trees, unmoving and undetected. For a whole day the birds kept returning, causing the main body of men to have to march all night in order to catch up with those creating the blind.

Yet another day of cat and mouse ensued, sapping everyone's spirit, for they feared this would continue all the way to Mullion. When the birds appeared for a third day, the leaders decided that something more drastic was called for. Overnight, the tattered uniforms were filled with clumps of dead foliage and left in attitudes of many men frozen to death. One cart was overturned as if it had fallen into a ditch while others were left as if abandoned by the frozen corpses. Ivain's suggestion of letting the horses go free was also adopted, for the Knights knew they would not stray far when the wagons contained their feed.

Calatin's spies therefore saw nothing worth further scrutiny by the dawn light, and by late morning were a mere speck on the horizon heading east. Yet over these days the column had barely covered ten miles and everyone was worn out with the tension and cold. As a precaution the column camped under the cover of some hollies and holm oaks, ready to loose the horses and resume the pose of playing dead, while all but the sentries got much needed rest. However, the watchers in the skies did not return and on the next day the march was resumed in earnest.

A week before Yule therefore found them camped on the rocky ridge above the coast, looking down on the vast bulk of Mullion Castle. The main castle was an enormous grey-stoned square keep, guarded by an overhanging firing platform which ran around its circuit at the highest level, well out of the reach of ladders, but containing wicked murder holes through which defenders could shoot, or pour boiling water or oil. It sat on an arm of the ridge they were on, which protruded towards the sea. Two circuits of walls ran around the rocky finger beneath it, one at the base and one halfway up. Beyond the castle the town of Mullion huddled in a depression in the rocky coast, with none of the houses raising their heads above the protection of the headlands, to be seared by the icy wind blasting up the sound between Prydein and Kittermere. There was little movement in either place, and Breca reported that it had been that way ever since he had reached it.

Hereman sent scouts down under the cover of the afternoon twilight, who came back reporting that things were indeed as quiet as they seemed. A full three-quarters of the houses seemed deserted, and the Knights could only assume that they normally served as additional quarters for Brion's men for much of the year. It also seemed that many of the women had chosen to march on in Brion's wake to Trevelga, following their men or hoping for rich pickings, who was to know? Whatever had happened, the scouts reported open movement between the few townsfolk and the castle until well after darkness had fallen, with no sign of anticipated attack.

Hardly able to believe their luck, Breca and his men slid down to the walls and around to the gate before dawn, falling upon the hapless gate-keeps as they opened them in the morning. By midday the rest of the force was flowing in through the gates, finding themselves quarters or ensuring that nobody from the town snuck out to warn Brion of the disaster. Many of those left, it transpired, were the old, the very young and the lame, all none too pleased at having been abandoned to take their chances in the depths of winter. Several were only too willing to point out those who, despite this, still had strong sympathies with the departed Duke, enabling these to be segregated and brought into the castle for guarding.

That night the walls of Mullion stood fully guarded once more, and a message sent off to reach Hugh telling of their success – the messenger birds having been a particularly precious cargo brought with them. As the men celebrated by getting a good night's sleep in the warm for a change, those above the rank of captain, and some chosen men, met with Hereman in what had previously been the duke's private solar. A blazing fire stood in the huge grate, warming the whole room and burning so hot that anyone stood too close was in danger of singeing. All told, alongside Hereman, Breca, and Eremon, there were twenty-three captains and commanders, half a dozen trusted men like Pauli, and Ivain. As most congregated around a table to get a hot drink, Ivain approached the three main leaders who were studying a map on a desk at the back of the room. At his appearance they looked up.

"I have a request," Ivain said, hoping his voice sounded more assured than he felt. "Please don't tell anyone who doesn't already know who I am."

"Why ever not?" Hereman asked in amazement.

Ivain looked to Pauli for support and the older Knight drifted across to join them.

"I don't want anyone else to die on my account," Ivain said.

"Sire, it's our duty to protect you, come what may," Breca said carefully. "That may mean fighting and there can be no assurances that some will not fall."

"That's precisely what I'm talking about," Ivain tried to explain, feeling all the old frustration settling back upon his shoulders. "And in trying to protect me you'll end up splitting your forces, and men who would've fought without restraint to guard the backs of their friends and companions instead will hesitate, maybe fatally. That can't happen! If we're going to win Prydein back, you have to be able to fight without constraints, and I'm the worst constraint you could've had wished upon you. If I was my father or my grandfather you'd have had no hesitation about letting them lead men into battle. In fact with grandfather you'd have had no choice! He'd have told you that was what he was doing and hang the consequences!"

A sad smile appeared on Hereman's face. "Indeed he would! But he was a seasoned warrior, sire. You're not your grandfather, though sire, nor even your father."

"No, I'm not!" Ivain replied through gritted teeth. "But I'm not going to be either if everyone keeps wrapping me up in swaddling clothes! When my father was my age he'd been bloodied on a dozen battlefields – against the Attacotti, against the DeÁine, and against pirates and raiders from farther away. Me? I can't even go for a ride in the country without a bodyguard! How in the Underworld am I ever supposed to gain the respect of my nobles, and leaders, to win my Island back, if I'm seen as some kind of congenital idiot who can hardly go to the privy by himself?"

"He's right," Pauli's quiet voice carried into the stunned silence, causing them to blink in further surprise. "Think about it, gentlemen. Prydein suffered a near disaster when we lost the old king and his heir, and his heir in turn – this young man's older brother – all in a couple of years. Understandably everyone wanted to keep the younger prince safe. He was our security from descending into chaos. But we went too far – or at least those who had any say in the matter did. In these last couple of weeks I've come to understand what a dreadful prison they created for Ivain. And it has to be said that many, if not all, of those charged with his care as a child have wanted to keep him that way as much for their benefit as his. When they should've been helping him take over the reins of governing, they've instead kept him as far away from doing anything as possible. And what can one man do when the whole court is working against him?

"His father and grandfather were openly encouraged to develop the skills they would need, but they were in the lucky position of having siblings alive and equally being brought along to serve. They were never the one and only candidate. But now, through no fault of Ivain's, the chaos has come and we're all paying the price of keeping him isolated. He has no cadre of young warriors he's spent his youth training with like the old king, and yet he has to face up to a cousin who's been allowed to develop what amounts to his own little kingdom within the Island. Brion has his sworn friends and allies. Men who know him *personally*.

"Did you ever wonder why it was so easy for Brion to substitute a ringer for Ivain on the scaffold in Trevelga, on that fateful day when we thought he'd killed the king? I know it didn't occur to me to think hard about it – any of it. If anything, I suppose I assumed that Ivain must've been so hopeless that none of his own court had cared to lift a finger to help save him." He gave Ivain an apologetic smile. "But the truth is, that couldn't have happened to his father or grandfather, because too many men of influence knew them personally. They'd have spotted that something was wrong, and raised too many questions amongst too many people for the ruse to work. But with different factions all working to keep Ivain from their opponents, he ended up with no-one he *could* turn to."

"Sire, I'm so sorry. I had no idea!" Breca was genuinely appalled at how easily his young king had been isolated. "But how can we put that right at this late stage?"

"You can let me die," Ivain said and received an instant chorus of refusals. He held up his hands and with effort the older Knights restrained themselves to listen. "I don't mean I'm about to go off and commit suicide!" Ivain said in exasperation. "Pauli has given you a clue! Listen… The ordinary people think I'm already dead. As far as they're concerned, the brother of your Knight, Hamelin, whom Brion executed in my place, truly was me. Now we could waste a lot of time and energy trying to convince people that I'm really me, and alive, by the grace of the Spirits. But how long do you think that would take? All Brion has to do is keep putting about rumours that I'm an impostor. Even with the Order openly backing me, he can twist it to his advantage by saying you're using the situation to put your own puppet in control of Prydein. I know I'm not the tactician my grandfather was, or Hugh is, but to me that seems like a game we can't win. Please tell me if and how I'm wrong, but I don't see that there's any circumstance where you can use me as a figurehead to rally support around."

For a minute the three senior Knights were lost for words, and belatedly Ivain realised that there was silence in the room behind him. Turning around he saw that every eye in the room was on him. So much for silence and secrecy!

Hereman exhaled heavily. "Don't be so quick to dismiss yourself, sire, that's as an astute piece of reasoning as any your father or grandfather ever made. I wish it wasn't so, but I can't think of any way around what you've said."

"Then let's keep me dead," Ivain ploughed on resolutely. "If we can't do anything positive with resurrecting me, the least we can do is not give Brion a weapon to beat us over the head with. If we can't win the hearts-and-minds battle, then why engage in it at all? Surely we'd be better exploiting the indignation that Alaiz reported from the ordinary people that I should've been killed? Let's win back Prydein first, then we can worry about how we explain my remarkable reappearance."

"Make's sense," an unidentified voice from the group behind said, and there was a general murmur of agreement.

"But for that to work we can't have any report getting back to Brion that the Knights have someone they're guarding like he was made of glass." Ivain's reasoning was inexorable. "The one person who truly knows I lived beyond the execution is Brion! And if your assumptions of Calatin being in control of Amalric are true, then Brion also knows I rode to the battle next to Amalric. We therefore have to make *him* think I died there for real, and so I have to become invisible to him."

"What are you proposing then, sire," Hereman asked, with the expression of one who knows he might have to swallow a very bitter pill.

But Ivain smiled, and with that smile he won Hereman and the others over. It was the kind of smile which would have hard men smiling with him and strong-minded women melting, Hereman thought. He had known Ivain's father – a man who was always smiling, yet somehow the smile had never reached his eyes. There had been something Hereman had never quite trusted about Crown Prince Geraint. An air of duplicity about the man that had had Hereman wondering how often he had smiled in someone's face only to stab them in the back moments later.

And as for old King Mordred, he had been a sour old man, never once smiling to Hereman's knowledge. Of course, Hereman had only known both when he was still low in the ranks of the Order. They might have been very different with those they perceived of being of more equal status to themselves. Yet that would not have saved them had they ever been in Ivain's current position, Hereman realised. Men instinctively knew when they were being looked down upon, and it rankled even while the correct observances were being made. Ivain, on the other hand, would win ordinary men willingly to his side with that smile, which came from inside and made no distinction on whom it was bestowed.

"Well for a start off you can let me become an ordinary Knight!" Ivain was saying. "I desperately need more training. I never, ever again want to be in the situation I was in in that battle! Nothing is more terrifying than being swept along in that maelstrom with no idea of what to do, or what anyone else is doing. Train me, I beg you! I know you can't put into a few days what it normally takes years to learn, but I've been taught how to handle weapons well enough – what I need is the battle tactics. And for Spirit's sake stop calling me 'sire'! My mother told me that the year following my birth every dairymaid and merchant's wife called their sons after me. She hated it, because she'd chosen the name because it *wasn't* common in Prydein, but now it might just save my life more than all the subterfuge. There are more 'Ivain's' of my age than even Brion can keep track of!"

Hereman and the others breathed a sigh of relief. This at least was all easily possible, and all within the room agreed to remain silent as to Ivain's true identity. However, before they could get down to further tactical discussions a man hammered on the door and entered, breathless from running up the long flight of stairs.

"A message from the Master! Relayed from Bittern!" he puffed, thrusting a slim coiled paper into Hereman's hand and retreating immediately. All eyes were on the ealdorman as he uncoiled it and read it.

"Well this is news!" he muttered, then looked up at Ivain. "I know what we just promised …but Master Hugh writes that he's sure you perished on the battlefield."

Ivain closed his eyes in distress for a second. "Poor Hugh! I had no wish to cause him such pain."

"Do you want me to tell him you live?" Hereman asked.

Ivain sighed but shook his head. "No. Hugh's already been through the pain. I can't save him from that now. And what if your message was interrupted? Anyway, the same goes for Hugh as the rest of the Order. He'll do much better if all that amazing tactical experience is focused on winning back Prydein, not working with one hand tied behind his back all the time trying to protect me. At least this way, if I die trying, he won't have had his hopes renewed only to be snuffed out again, as well – not that I intend to die! But who knows what might happen? What is Hugh doing, anyway, does he say?"

"Wizard baiting!" Hereman said cryptically. "Or trapping, more like! Doesn't give details – but like us he wouldn't say much in something that might fall into the wrong hands. He says that if we've taken Mullion, we should try to secure the western coast and link with Bittern as soon as the weather allows. Whichever, he wants Brion's remaining men bottled-up and unable to spring any surprise attacks."

And from then on the evening was filled with making plans for securing western Prydein. In the days that followed, Ivain was worked as hard as he could ever have wished for by the Knights around him. The ordinary men seemed to accept without question that there was a new addition who was being put through a rigorous training scheme. For the first week he was never allowed out of the walls of the castle, and although he appreciated the intense workouts he was given by masters-at-arms he did wonder if Hereman was, in effect, keeping him safe despite their conversation. But in the second week he was allowed out on patrols in one of the larger companies. For the most part they scoured the countryside, visiting the small fortified manors and farms of Brion's lesser landholders, ensuring the men were really away, and confiscating any hoards of weapons found there. Pauli was Ivain's permanent escort throughout this time, and for the first time in his life Ivain found himself making a friend who wanted nothing from him because of his position.

Yet strangely, in the midst of all this activity, for the first time he also had chance to put his life so far into some kind of perspective, and what he saw appalled him. Until this point he had never realised how much he had been conditioned to accept his position. As he sat quietly in the hall at night, listening to the conversations ebbing and flowing around him, he was forced into the realisation of how rarely he had had any choice in anything.

Of course he had had no choice about becoming the heir to the throne and then inheriting – that was just his bad luck. But it was the little things which began to niggle at his memory. Time and again he met men who had had no choice but to enter the Order, forced by the necessity of having an uncontested succession to this estate or that title. Yet once in the Order they had had choices. One had decided that he had little interest in the warrior skills, but loved horses and had trained as a farrier. Despite his noble birth, having renounced all claims and associations, there was subsequently no bar to him pursuing a more manual skill. Similarly, another former noble had quit the training to enter the kitchens, and now produced breads and cakes which would have been the envy of the court cooks. Others who had been of quite lowly birth, or who had even entered simply as enlisted men, had found no bar to them rising through the ranks as their ability allowed.

Each had had some say in how his life would continue despite the initial act beyond their control. For Ivain, though, there had not even been this much. From early childhood he had been trained and channelled down one path so rigorously, and immutably, that he had never even thought to question simple things.

Why, for instance, did all the court have to have the same thing as him for breakfast? He had absolute freedom to choose whatever he wanted on the one hand, yet if he chose unwisely there would be complaints about his selfishness and inconsideration for others. Yet here among the Knights the cooks produced a reasonable selection from which everyone picked what they liked. So why had it never occurred to him to change the court convention? It was so simple. So obvious. And yet he had never even realised that such an option was open to him. He was the king. If he wanted to change the custom then it was perfectly within his prerogative to do so, but no-one had even as much as hinted to Ivain that he could, instead immersing him in these rigid conventions from infancy.

It was frighteningly insidious, he realised. In a blinding flash of insight he also saw that his mother had been too frightened to step outside the conventions set down by her father-in-law and his ancestors. She had been the unwelcome Attacotti bride, always under suspicion no matter how often she proved her loyalty. In fear of being removed from the side of her only remaining child, she had chosen to subsume herself into this artificial culture, never questioning or changing anything, and never daring to speak out. Her passive acceptance had been handed on to him by example, and with his advisers and guardians all wanting a compliant king over whom they could hold sway, every time he had dared show curiosity as to how things could change he had been brought back to heel. Trained and trained, so that in time he had been mentally incapable of imagining options away from those imposed upon him.

Alaiz had been right he now knew, albeit for different reasons. She had been right to challenge his view of their life together. He was now appalled at how easily he had been willing to accept that he must continue with his childhood playmate as a wife – married when they were both too young to know what marriage might require them to do with one another. *Spirits!* Ivain thought, *no wonder she was so distraught! Alaiz at least kept her wits about her enough to feel there was something wrong between us. Not like me. What a fool I've been! Sacred Trees, I should've put my foot down years ago. The alliance with Kittermere was never that meaningful once Rathlin was in the hands of the rebels – Kittermere's no longer our stepping stone to our other island. I could've insisted on an annulment for both our sakes. Arranged for her to have lands of her own wherever she wanted, let her live her own life, not keeping her chained to me, caged up like a wild bird pining for her freedom. I wish that I could see her once more to let her know I never did it deliberately.*

And why had he never thought to simply nominate an heir? The question plagued him, for he could see that if there had been a clear succession marked out, there would have been less of a gap for Brion to exploit. Choose an heir, and one more to succeed in case of an early death, instead of this farce of forcing all the responsibility of producing one onto himself and Alaiz. And why had he never seen that his grandfather's way need not be the only way of ruling? On the night before the start of Yule, Ivain got happily and massively drunk for the first time too, and as an amused Pauli helped his wobbly king up the stairs to the bedchamber, Ivain confessed another of his burdensome secrets to his friend.

"You're my bestest friend, Pauli, d' y' know that?" he hiccupped merrily. "Firshht time I've done this for real. Always faked it before!"

"Why in the Islands would you want to *pretend* you were drunk?" Pauli asked, even as he laughed with his young friend.

"Women!" Ivain said with drunken solemnity, even as his knees developed an independent life of their own and threatened to pitch him back down the stairs. " 'S all to do with women." They tottered unceremoniously through his bedroom door and over to the bed, Pauli yanking back the covers just in time before Ivain keeled over onto it like a felled tree. As Pauli hauled his boots off, Ivain carried on.

"...'S the problem with being the king, y' see." He wagged a wobbly finger in Pauli's direction. "They all want to be the one who's bedded the king. Spirits! You should see some of the s'posed ladies I've seen with their kit off! Scary, Pauli! Very scary! One minute y'r walking in a long-gallery with the daughter of the house on a wet afternoon, and the next she's tripped you flat on a chaise, got her skirts up 'n' declaring undying love 'n' ...'n' ripping off y'r breeches! Never could perform like that! Always had to pretend I'd been at the wine cellar.

"Only way out, y' see? Can't tell 'em they scare you witless! Can't tell 'em they're as ugly as a cow's arse! 'N' the pretty ones're the worst 'cos they know 'xactly what they're doing, 'cos they've had men at their beck and call all their lives. 'M the king! Have to be a gentleman 'bout it. Bloody gran'father's fault! Went around tupping half the women in the Island claiming the right of seni … seniori…ori…ority! Half the fucking Island thinks 'm a total souse, drunk all the time, for not fucking their women witless and fathering bastards on 'em. …Can't bloody win!"

At which he suddenly fell asleep, leaving a bemused Pauli to strip him of his outer clothes and throw the covers over him. *Well he's certainly going to experience his first hangover tomorrow*, Pauli thought with amusement. *He definitely won't have to fake that!*

Then he thought some more about what Ivain had told him. Trees! What a mess! On the one hand barely being trusted to get on a horse without breaking his neck, and on the other not even having a choice about the women he bedded. Some young men Pauli had known would have set to working their way through the women with a vengeance, regardless of the consequences or the lives they might wreck, or create, in the process. That was one side of old King Mordred he had not heard much about before, but it did not surprise him. The old man was just the sort who would have abused his position like that, and he had certainly not been the kind of man women would have taken to for any other reason. Mordred had always had a cruel streak he did little to conceal.

And Prince Geraint had been too much the ladies' man from what gossip reached the Knights. No doubt Princess Gillies had lived to regret her love match with that one. *Sacred Trees, what did she plant in her son's mind after an experience like that*, wondered Pauli? It said much for Ivain's personality that he was still a likeable man after all the messing with his head that had been done.

Come the morning Ivain honestly thought he was dying. He staggered downstairs at the ringing of the breakfast bell only in the hope that the sooner he got down, the sooner it would stop its skull-splitting racket. Then the sight of fried eggs and bread had him running for the latrines, and a long conversation with his Maker down the privy chute, which was where Pauli found him.

"Oh Spirits! I'm dying!" groaned the prostrate Ivain.

"No you're not," Pauli said firmly.

"Stop shouting!"

"I'm not," Pauli laughed. "Here. Get this down you. …No, don't look at it! Close your eyes and knock it back in one go."

"No," Ivain moaned, retching dryly. "It's no good. Just leave me for the Abend. There's nothing else they could do to me that's as bad as this!"

"Nonsense! Come on, down the hatch!" Pauli tilted Ivain's head back and poured the mixture he had carefully carried out in the leather tankard straight down Ivain's throat. Ivain could have sworn that his eyes jumped out of their sockets and made a complete circuit of his head before returning, as the fierce concoction hit his raw stomach with all the gentle finesse of a thunderbolt. For the next few seconds he tried to cough, vomit, sneeze and scream, all at the same time without managing to do any of them. Then for the first time that day, the world seemed to settle back into something like its regular orbit.

Had his eyes not been so full of tears that he could see nothing, he would have seen Pauli doubled up with mirth, stuffing his fist into his mouth to stifle the hoots of laughter. Of all the men he had successfully given his secret hangover cure to, Ivain's reaction was quite the most spectacular. However, despite being a deep shade of puce from his exertions, Ivain was now definitely back in the land of the living.

"Is there some heathen god of strong drink I offended last night?" he croaked, cuffing the tears from his eyes. "I swear I'll never touch another drop!"

"Ah but you will, lad, you will!" Pauli spluttered joyously, even as he helped Ivain to his feet.

With Ivain still leaning on Pauli's arm, they walked up to the battlements of the keep. The wind was keen and they stood in the lee of the roof looking out to the Straits of Kittermere as Ivain gulped in the fresh air. In the distance the land lay in a soft haze of greens and greys.

"That's it!" Ivain suddenly said with such finality that Pauli wondered what in the Islands he could be referring to, and tightened his hold on Ivain's belt in case he was about to jump off the roof. "That's where I ought to go," Ivain explained instead, pointing a finger to Kittermere.

"Sacred Root and Branch, why?" an astonished Pauli asked.

"Because I have to do something myself. If I stay here, I'm still doing what I've always done. I'll be waiting for men like Hereman to win my throne back for me. I can't do that anymore, Pauli, I just can't. Once upon a time, and not so long ago I'd have thought it enough to pick up a sword and go where someone else pointed me, and have thought I'd done enough to prove myself. But not now. If I'm ever going to go back as king, it has to be on my terms, do you see? I have to have the confidence in myself so that I can change things for the better – not just for me. For the people of Prydein, for Alaiz and for my mother. I have to be able to go in and say 'I've done this...,' and for it to be enough to at least gain their respect for long enough that they listen to me."

"Alright," Pauli agreed cautiously. "What are you thinking of, then?"

"I know I can't be anything more than a small cog in the big wheel that needs to turn in order to win back Prydein. I'm not such a bighead that I think I can do better than Hugh and Hereman at reclaiming the main island. But what about the other islands? If Brion left Mullion unguarded, what of Alaiz's old home? Her oldest brother, Turstin, we know is in Trevelga with Brion. But what of the younger of the two, Gorm? No-one has seen him on Prydein. What if Gorm still holds Osraig? We can't leave him there. He'll always be a threat to our security, and what use is it clearing the coast on this side, if our enemies can sail across the Strait and fall on us that way?"

Nor could Ealdorman Hereman fault the logic of this when Pauli had led Ivain into him, and they had told him of Ivain's request to be allowed to retake Kittermere.

"What makes you think you can pull this off?" Hereman asked guardedly, and got the winning smile again.

"Because I went to Osraig a few years ago on an official visit. Alaiz was ill and didn't come, but her brothers were so full of themselves they gave me the full tour of the place. I've been all through Osraig Castle! While Turstin was pulling the wool over Amalric's eyes, Gorm took me around the lower reaches of the castle. He's not overly bright, so he was quite happily boasting of how the only weakness of the castle's was the shit chute!"

The Knights looked from one another in surprise.

"You actually know the full layout of the castle?" Hereman asked, becoming a little more convinced of the possibility.

"Why the shit chute?" Breca could not refrain from asking, even though he was expecting some trite reply about the place where even the king must go alone. Instead Ivain's reply gave him pause for thought.

"Osraig Castle was originally built right on the coast," Ivain explained, positioning a beaker of caff to represent it on the desk. "But over the centuries the sea has deposited soil eroded from our side of the Strait. So," he moved a piece of string along the desk, "instead of being here …the coast is now out here with this big spit of land sticking out to the north side. Well originally, the castle privies emptied straight into the sea, but that no longer happens. Instead it all falls to the bottom of the castle walls, and stays there."

"Sacred Trees, I bet that stinks in summer when the wind's in the wrong quarter!" Pauli thought aloud.

"It does!" Ivain confirmed. "And that's why they have the lowest of the low come and rake it away. It gets shovelled up and carted away, but there's a ramp of sorts made up of the …em …leftovers of previous years. Now Gorm boasted that it's so treacherous only a fool would attempt to climb up that way in fighting gear. Apparently every so often they lose some poor soul from among the rakers when it gets unstable and they sink in."

"What a way to go!" Breca was appalled.

"But look at the weather now!" Ivain said triumphantly, and suddenly they could see what he was telling them. The slope would be frozen solid. Even men in armour would be unlikely to sink in this iron hard frost.

"By the Trees! You've got something!" Hereman told Ivain, whose pleasure at the compliment was written large in his grin. "I don't suppose you know how many men they normally have over there, do you?"

Ivain thought for a moment. "There were two full companies there when we visited, but Turstin must have taken at least half of them with him when he joined Brion. He could hardly have come empty-handed and still hoped to share in the profits, could he? I know it's only a guess, but I doubt there can be more than fifty men still in Osraig, and they won't be prepared for an attack."

Hereman and Breca withdrew to the window for an inaudible conference before returning.

"Very well," Hereman agreed. "You get to go, but Breca will go with you." Some of the excitement faded from Ivain's eyes and Hereman felt compelled to explain. "There has to be someone of recognised rank leading this, si... Ivain. Someone the men know and will follow unquestioningly into battle. They don't know you well enough yet. You're a quick learner, but Breca has firsthand experience of skirmishes, set battles, and taking the odd fortified settlement of the Attacotti." Hereman smiled sympathetically. "Let him teach you a thing or two, eh?"

Despite Ivain's eagerness to be off and doing the job, he now found himself effectively apprenticed to Breca, and being introduced to the realities of moving large numbers of troops around. And Breca was a thorough man. He first had Ivain draw him plans of Osraig Castle, explaining at each stage why he needed to know – for things like how much rope they would need to carry, and whether he would need to set men to guard against men coming out of any small picket gates as well as the main one. Then there was the matter of supplies. They swiftly decided that there would be only limited amounts they could seize locally until they actually got into the castle, and hungry men were weak men, so they would have to carry goodly amounts of food with them.

Brought up on bards' tales of heroic epic undertakings, this was all a revelation to Ivain. He had somehow had the idea of romantic and dramatic sudden departures to counter threats. Of knights leaping onto horses and charging out of the castle gates in barely the time it took to strap on a suit of armour. Now he knew the bards had left out the boring bits! The hours of counting arrows, and then getting the fletchers to make more, so that they would not run out. Working out how many loaves of bread they would need per man, and getting them double-baked so that they would not go mouldy in the men's packs. At least Breca was sympathetic, knowing that Ivain's ignorance was genuine and not stupidity or idleness.

"We're all a bunch of romantics too, you know," he told Ivain when the young king confessed his unrealistic expectations and where they had come from. "Who else would be willing to risk life and limb for a bunch of ideals? And if ever we get a minstrel passing through, you'll hear the men calling and stamping for more after all those epic song-poems. The last thing they want to hear about is all the mundane stuff they know only too well. They want to remember the high points. The moments when you feel like it's wine running through your veins instead of blood, and you feel like you and your friends could fight your way into the Underworld and back. But they also want someone to tell them that it's all worth it. That the friends they lost weren't sacrificed for nothing.

"I was a young page at Moytirra, you know. Scariest bloody battle I've *ever* been in. And the biggest! I lost most of the friends I'd trained with that day. The price we paid for that victory was huge. But at least there's some consolation in knowing that we were part of the force that saved not just our Prydein, but all of the Islands. It's more recognition than we get for most of the lesser skirmishes and running fights we have, even though men die just as hard in them.

"When the bards sing about the heroes of Moytirra, I don't think about people like Brego of Ergardia and Jarl Harald of Rheged – the big names ordinary folk know about. I remember squint-eyed Howie, and little red-haired Billy, who fought like a man possessed. And big daft Sid, who went into battle with his boots on the wrong feet because he'd taken them off against orders, and didn't have time to put them on right again. There're some men who you'll think are the hardest bastards walking this earth, who'll suddenly start weeping like little lads at some song, because it brings back the memories of their mates who aren't here anymore. But they wouldn't thank you for getting the singer to stop! So there's nothing wrong with those ballads and epics, it's just that there's a whole heap of practicalities that have to happen in real life if you're to even have a chance of winning!"

Finally, though, Hereman agreed that they could depart on the first day of the New Year. Enough fishing vessels had eventually been commandeered to ship two hundred men of the Order across to Kittermere, and even the choice of those men had been complicated. So many of those from Freton had been still in training and had never seen a real conflict, whilst those who had fled the battle were often the remnants of lances who had been together for years, and found it hard trying to develop that understanding within a new lance at short notice. Half the force was therefore from those Breca had led out from Freton, while the other half was made up of newly created lances which mixed the recruits with the veterans from Bittern. Three days' training together was not much, but it was a start.

It was going to be a sober New Year for them all, for Hereman had decided that he would leave Eremon in charge of a force of defenders, while he led the remaining major portion of the men out on a vigorous sweep of the countryside to the south. By making such a show of force in that direction, rooting out dissidents, it would not be obvious that the small flotilla was sailing directly for Osraig. So a lock was put on the wine cellar, and only weak beer served to the men that night, but these men hardly needed strong drink to raise their spirits. There was a real feeling that at last they were doing something positive towards reclaiming their homeland, and even the men who were only going on the patrol were filled with a determination to make it look good, in order to give their companions the best possible chance of success.

The biggest worry was the great storm which began to build as the evening wore on. It came screaming out of the west, and men feared that it preceded a heavy fall of snow. Yet right up until midnight it still remained only high winds tearing out of the west, although for their purposes that was little comfort, for the wind was so strong it would have dashed any boat back against the coast of Prydein. Hereman, Breca, Ivain and Pauli went up onto the castle roof to take a look as the midnight bell rang and the rest of the men were offering one another their best wishes for the coming year and for luck in battle. High up, they could see the ragged remains of clouds being chased across the sky at an incredible rate.

"I don't like the look of this at all," Hereman said with a worried frown.

Ivain's heart sank. Surely this would not mean that they were further delayed? Although he had to admit to himself that he did not fancy being tossed about on a boat in this weather, but Breca's qualifying comment brought him up with a jolt.

"No, there's no way this is natural. It's too fast for even the worst gale and it's coming in a straight line, not swirling about like it should."

"Look where it's coming from too," said Eremon, coming to join them. "We never get westerlies at this time of year normally. I don't like that this is coming straight from the direction of New Lochlainn."

"You think the DeÁine are causing this?" Ivain asked in dismay. "But how would this serve Calatin? Look! We're not even quite under the southern edge of that big cloud that's coming. It's going to miss most of Prydein altogether."

"Maybe it's not Calatin that's summoned this?" Pauli wondered. "There are others of the Abend abroad, and that storm has already passed over Brychan and is heading for Ergardia and Rheged. There could be trouble ahead for those Islands too."

At the mention of Rheged, Ivain thought of Alaiz and offered up a silent prayer that she was tucked up safely somewhere beyond there. But Breca was staring hard at the cloud.

"What in the Underworld is that cloud?" The worry in his voice made the others look hard again.

"It's like it's alive!" exclaimed Pauli.

"Everyone below, *now*!" Hereman ordered. He leaned over the parapet and bellowed down to the sentries on the wall beneath. "Get everyone inside now! Pass the word to those on the lower wall too. Every man is to be inside *immediately*! The coming storm is enchanted!"

As he was hustled down off the roof, Ivain heard the pounding of feet as men hurried to obey. Breca and Eremon disappeared off at the first landing, and he could hear them shouting to men to lock the window shutters and bolt the doors. By the time he reached the main hall everyone was standing in expectation, celebrations forgotten. Men ran forward to Hereman reporting that other men were secure within the curtain-wall, signals having been passed between the groups already, and not a moment too soon.

Suddenly the wind hit the castle, funnelling down the great chimneys and fanning the flames of the fires into spitting menaces. Men hurried to stamp out flying sparks which settled on the wooden floors, even as they noticed that the wind seemed to carry voices. Eldritch howling and wailing echoed around the stones, chilling the listeners to the marrow. By pure chance it was traditional to burn a log of each of the sacred trees at the change of year, so good blazes burned in each of the castle's fireplaces, and later men came to believe that saved them.

It seemed to go on for an eternity, and yet it could only have been half an hour or so before the noise abated and the wind backed off a degree. Shortly afterwards there was a hammering at the door and a man calling for

Hereman. They opened the door with great trepidation to find only a worried looking soldier from the lower wall.

"Sire!" he gasped. "All's well amongst our men, but something terrible's happened in the town! When the wind eased off we could hear fearful screams and shouts – but these were human, not like the voices on the wind. A couple of men volunteered to go up on the wall and have a look. There are dozens of bodies lying in the streets where they died!"

Chapter 11

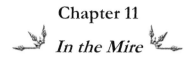 *In the Mire*

Ergardia – Kittermere: Yule – Eft-Yule.

In the midst of Caley celebrating the imminent New Year, the Order's war ship again slipped out of harbour and began the rough crossing from Ergardia to Kittermere. She was not best equipped for winter travel, having little in the way of shelter on deck except for some protection around the wheel. The forecastle had been designed more as a fighting platform than for any accommodation role, and those who were not on duty did not linger up there, nor in its twin structure on the aft main deck. With the ferocious winds, it was even impossible to rig tarpaulins as protection against the spray and sleet, for they caught the wind as sure as any sail. Soldiers and sailors huddled together below deck in mournful misery, while the cook struggled to keep the galley fire alight enough to at least provide warm food to fight the bone-numbing cold.

Once more Alaiz was utterly prostrate with seasickness, but at least it meant that she was so incapacitated that she failed to notice the rising fear amongst the men on the fourth day out. They had set out with the wind in their favour, and although the tides were strong it had promised to be a straightforward, if rough, journey. It was on New Year's Eve, as they caught their first sight of the coast of Kittermere, that things went badly wrong. Suddenly the wind backed as night fell. Then from out of nowhere a new wind came howling up from out of the west, piling up waves broadside on to the ship. It was only because the ship was already battened down for a rough crossing that they survived, for had the hatches and ports not been closed they would surely have shipped water and sank. As it was, the sailors frantically fought the sails down to the minimum for steerage, and then worked the pumps like men possessed as huge waves hit the ship's sides and swamped the decks.

The soldiers willingly lent their strength to helping pump out the brine, which endlessly seemed to wash in through even the smallest of gaps, and ran in salty rivers down the ladders and into every corner. In the midst of fighting to keep the ship afloat they heard chaos on deck, followed by a sailor running down below yelling something about the Wild Hunt coming. Men looked wildly from one to another, and Talorcan could see the panic begin to spread. Sailors were notoriously superstitious, and this was the time when old wives tales said the Hunt rode, but he imagined it to be only some form of the storm that had played on their fears. Shouting for calm, he left the others with orders to carry on pumping, and went on deck to find Captain McCormack to help restore order.

What he saw when he emerged into the black night he would never have believed had he not seen it with his own eyes. Above them the last high tatters of the storm clouds scudded past, showing glimpses of the moon and stars with clear skies behind in the west. But beneath those clear stars a great bank of cloud was being driven towards them at a frantic rate. At its leading edge it took the form of a vast army of horses and riders, with hounds at their heels, their leader clutching a great scythe.

The captain stood paralysed in horror until Talorcan grabbed his arm, yelling,

"Everyone below! Now!"

"What about my ship?" McCormack cried.

"It'll have to take its chances, and us with it," Talorcan bellowed in his ear to make himself heard over the rising howling of the gale.

The last man slid below and Talorcan slammed the hatch shut just as the storm hit them. The passage of the front only lasted a few minutes, but nobody who was there ever forgot the sounds, or the eerie light which seeped down through the planking. Maybe it was their terrified imaginations, but it sounded as though a herd of horses had landed on the open deck and were galloping across it, their riders shrieking for blood. No-one doubted that had anyone been up there, their soul would have been harvested by Jolnir, the Lord of the Wild Hunt, condemned to eternally ride with him, and never find the true afterlife. Drauger, the Islanders named these living dead – a fate feared even beyond consignment to the Underworld, and it had men clutching the dragon-headed crosses they wore around their necks, or making the sign of that cross over their hearts.

Even after the howling ceased and the night was filled with more natural cries of the wind, it took sometime before anyone dared venture up onto deck. When they did it was to more frantic activity. The sudden manic thrust of wind had pushed them far off course, even against the tide, and dangerously close to the coast of Kittermere, which now loomed blackly off the larboard bow. In an exemplary display of seamanship, Captain

McCormack wrestled with the elements to bring his ship under control, even as he still shook from the terror of what he had witnessed.

Within two turns of the hourglass they found themselves drifting into the lee of Kittermere. The distant bulk of its rolling western moorlands deflected the worst of the remaining gale, whilst ahead of them lay a maze of water courses as the vast marshes drained into the sea.

"I knew the Wild Hunt were supposed to ride during Yule," McCormack confided to Talorcan, as he took a restorative swig of fiery rum. "But I always thought it a tale to frighten children with. That…," he shuddered. "…That was something else! Rowan protect us all, I never want to see the like of that again!"

"And on the stroke of the New Year too!" his sailing master agreed. "By the Trees, that's an evil omen, if ever I saw one! Thank the Great Oak that protects it's offspring that we ride on, we didn't sink, or we'd all be drauger riding behind the Dark One instead!"

As Barcwith joined them, Talorcan pondered aloud.

"Well, whether that was really Jolnir, I don't know, but real or a glamour – some arcane sleight of hand on a grand scale – my money would be on the Abend conjuring it up!"

"Why?" the captain asked aghast.

"To frighten Islanders!" Barcwith concluded with certainty in his voice, catching his commander's train of thought. "Whatever that was, it travelled with great speed. It must've already passed over Brychan. With the width of that storm front it must also have passed over most of southern Ergardia, where the majority of that island's towns are, and it was heading straight for Rheged. Do you think it's coincidence that it happened on the one night of the year when you can guarantee that, across *all* of the Islands, folks will be up and about at midnight? The DeÁine have been fighting us for long enough to know our customs. You can bet that they know the stories of the Wild Hunt. I don't see the witches worrying whether Jolnir is, or was, real, do you? Or worrying whether they can contain him if they really did summon him?

"My gut instinct is that they would know that this is one of the few times when pulling a stunt like making everyone's nightmare image of the Wild Hunt come to life, would sap Islanders' morale. Sap it more than any threat of an army. We're a stubborn lot. They know that from hundreds of years ago when they first came. Take our lowlands and we'll retreat into the hills and the heather, and fight to the last man. Do as the king and his

Donns did and fight us head on, and we'll fight back even against impossible odds, and cost them dear for every acre gained. But those four evil bitches are more subtle than that, and I'd bet Lorne Castle on them being behind turning our own childhood fears back on us."

As Barcwith had been talking, more of the sailors had stopped what they were doing to listen, and a murmur of anger rippled through the assembled men as he finished. For an awful moment Barcwith wondered whether it was against him, but then realised that it was at the thought that they had been played for fools.

"Fucking bastard Abend!" a grizzled and battle-scarred sailor swore, and different variations on the curse echoed around the deck.

"Right! Let's get this ship into the marshes, then!" the captain commanded, once more in full control of himself and his ship.

For the next few days, life on board took on an unreal quality. The ship glided under minimal sail through the shallow waters of the vast sea marsh. The masts rose high above the rushes which masked the edges of the channels, but for those on deck the rush heads grew above the height of the sides of the ship, cutting them off from the rest of the world. Sometimes the channels were the size of great rivers but slower moving. Other times the rushes came so close that they almost brushed the sides of the ship.

At times like that, the sailors reached over the side and harvested the bulrushes to make torches from, until they had great bundles stored on the deck, with the heads carefully being soaked in oil. A canvas tilt was spread over them to stop them getting soaked in the frequent squally showers which drenched the travellers, but the captain would not risk taking the rushes below deck for fear of fire. The preparations were not simply done on the off-chance, though. During the days after the fey storm, daylight was covered on many occasions by clouds so dense it was barely lighter than night, and several times they needed the torches just to navigate safely with.

On the second day they came to a huge open space, although whether it was a true lake or somewhere where the rushes had yet to take hold of, the men could not guess. The soldiers hoped that a few more sails could be set to speed across the open water, yet the captain ordered torches lit and men to the bows. Standing looking over the sides it was sharp-eyed Tamàs who first pointed out the rotting tree stumps protruding just above the water's surface. Then later they spotted strange shapes in the distant gloom.

"Rowan protect us," breathed Ad, "what evil are they?"

"Aye, this is an evil place," Decke solemnly replied. "Some work of the Evil One no doubt,"

"Nay," Tamàs calmly disagreed, screwing his eyes up to peer at them. "Look! That 'n' has wings!"

"Ah, messengers from the Underworld," was Decke's sage interpretation. "See! It disappears beneath the water! Back to its master!"

A passing sailor laughed. "No, mate! Just cormorants. Wait …there he is! See? He's got a fish in his beak. They can dive deep, those birds, and they thrive here where the fish are plentiful. I've seen them at sea where they'll dive and then fly off. Here they don't need to fly far, so they sit on the tree stumps to dry their feathers. See those over there?" He pointed to a group off the other side, who resembled black crosses above the water as they stretched their wings out from off their individual perches, with beaks held up high.

"Sacred Trees, Decke! Cut it out!" Galey grumbled. "It's bad enough crawling through this gloom without you seeing the Lord of the Underworld at every turn! You'll have us all jumping at shadows before the day's out at this rate!"

"Ah, the righteous have nothing to fear from him," Decke mournfully intoned, not to be quashed.

The others left him to his gloomy pondering and went in search of what the cook had managed to concoct. However, Alaiz woke up in time to hear Decke's pronouncements and asked,

"Is he always like that?"

"Only when he's got too much time on his hands, miss," Tamàs told her. "Different folks copes with grief in different ways. Some lose their faith when they lose everyone they care about. Others, like Decke, find it and hang onto it to keep them going. He's alright when he feels he's helping to rid the Islands of evildoers. Then he's too busy to start thinking too hard about what it all means."

"He doesn't seem to find much consolation in his faith," Alaiz mused. "Not like Andra."

"Aye well, they're different sorts," Tamàs reasoned. "We reckon Decke was never the cheerful type, even before his loss, so he carries his faith heavy. But you'll not shift him from his path, and it'd be cruel to take away the thing that keeps him sane in the dark hours."

"And what about you, Tamàs?" Alaiz was curious about her carer. "What keeps you going? You always seem so calm."

"Me?" He stopped and thought for a moment before answering carefully. "I believes that what goes around, comes around. Them as does evil to others sooner or later has evil done to them."

"I've never heard that preached," Alaiz mused.

"Aye, maybe not. I'm not book-learned like Decke, and where I grew up was thin on churches. Too close to the DeÁine, happen. But up in the hills you found out that sooner or later, them as took out their temper on their animals came to a bad end. Maybe as simple as getting into a temper when they was out trying to find a lost sheep, and not taking care about where they stepped, and ending up at the bottom of a bank or cliff." He stopped and thought again before continuing. "Decke believes in the Spirits crying out for vengeance. Me, I think that vengeance is a people thing. I'm not much good at putting these things into words, but I suppose I believe in a natural order. A balance, if you like. I does my best to do the right thing, as near as I'm able to tell, and I reckon that's the best anyone can do. In return, sometimes them as does evil – and is knowed to be evil – gets directed into our path, and we even things out a bit again. Just one cog in a big wheel, but restoring the natural balance, see?"

"I like that," Alaiz said with a wistful sigh. "It's more reassuring than hoping that something bigger than you happens to think exactly the way you do. And for what it's worth, your best is plenty good enough for me, Tamàs. You're a good man."

It took twelve days in all to negotiate the channels of the Kittermere marshes, not least because each time they crossed one of the open lakes, it took several goes to find the channel back out. The captain had maps aplenty, and when the weather permitted he took sightings to check their course. The trouble was that channels seemed to shift. Some which had obviously once been quite broad were silted up and filled with a treacle-thick gloop which stuck like glue to the ship. On one occasion, having mistakenly gone in a bit faster than intended, the only way they got the *Craken* out was by putting the ship's boat over the side with a towing rope. The sailors in the boat had rowed for all they were worth, while everyone who could find a pole tried to find something solid enough to push against. A whole day was lost in this way, and by the time the ship was back in clear water, all anyone was fit for was crawling into their hammocks.

Finally, though, they came out into a broad water at dusk, to see the lights of a small town twinkling in the distance. It had to be Ceos, for there was nothing else remotely of that size in the whole of eastern Kittermere.

All lights on board were immediately doused, and the ship slipped across to a headland on the far bank which they could remain hidden behind. By the strength of her hull and her sleek lines, the *Craken* would never be mistaken for anything other than a warship, and, as Kittermere had none of her own, would be assumed to be hostile. All sails were taken down, so that the only thing likely to be visible above the land was the main mast, and in the current filthy weather that would be reasonably indistinct from a distance.

A major decision now had to be made. Did Talorcan's party disembark and go on horseback through the countryside, or should they assume that Taise and Alaiz' joint guess at where the Bow was was sufficiently certain? If that was so, then they could try to take the ship at speed past Ceos and down river, then hug the Kittermere coast to stay clear of Mullion until they reached the next great out-fall from the marshes. This would be faster than riding. Much faster. But, once committed to it, it had two disadvantages. The first was that the ship would have to make a very quick landing to put the riders ashore before Osraig, and then sail down the narrow sea channel with all speed, as they would be closer to Duke Turstin's men. It was then committed to taking the long way all the way around southern Kittermere, where the currents were worst, before they could hope to safely make another landfall and collect the riders once more to take them on to Rathlin. The second problem was that having made themselves so obvious, there would be little time for the riders to explore before soldiers from Osraig came to find out who they were. This was fine if they only had one place to search, but not if they came up empty-handed there.

With the moderating salt air, the danger of ice on any track-ways was negated, and although there were still marshes around Ceos for the first couple of days' ride, after that they should find themselves on lightly wooded moorland. The deciding factor was therefore whether Alaiz was fit enough to ride again. Once they had been off the rolling sea her health had improved visibly, especially as she had slept solidly for days, yet in the mornings she still found herself dreadfully nauseous. But as each day went on she now improved, and by midday was almost her old self. Her companions went off into a huddle and then Tamàs led as they came back to her. He looked uncomfortable as he asked her.

"Will you be all right to ride, miss?"

"Yes, I think so," Alaiz said thoughtfully. "I'm hardly going to be seasick on dry land! I might be a bit slow getting going, but it's not the sort of country you can ride fast over anyway."

Tamàs fidgeted. "Aye, but would you be better if we waited a day or so?"

"No," Alaiz answered, puzzled. "I can't think of anything that's going to change much in the next few days that would make a difference."

"Can't you, miss?"

Tamàs, Galey and Barcwith looked as puzzled as she did. It was only as they turned to go, shrugging their shoulders, that she remembered a conversation with Taise.

"Oh!" she gasped. Then started doing some mental counting. "Ohhhh…. Oh no!"

"Something wrong, miss?" Galey asked innocently.

"Today …it is the fourteenth, isn't it? I haven't miscounted while I was so out of things?"

The men did a quick check and confirmed that they were pretty sure that it was indeed the fourteenth of Eft-Yule. Alaiz gulped and looked distinctly shaken. At first the men thought she was going to start throwing up again, but then Tamàs caught on to what was racing through her head.

"Missing something are we, miss?" he asked with a smile beginning to appear.

"Oh dear!" Alaiz muttered, feeling the dreaded blush starting to rise once more. "…Oh dear! …Errrr …yes …a few actually."

Barcwith and Galey caught on too at this point, and also began to grin.

"What're you lot grinning at?" Decke asked perplexed.

"Alaiz is missing something that ladies have every month," Galey explained, rolling his eyes to Ad at Decke's confusion.

"So?" was Decke's response.

"Spirits! Even I know what that means!" Ad said in amazement at Decke's naivety. "She's going to have a baby. How can you not know *that?*"

"Ah well," Barcwith said to Alaiz, trying hard not to sound amused. "Better hope that your husband's no better on these things than Decke here, eh? That way you might convince him that these things take twelve months instead of nine!"

The implications hit the others too.

"Better hope he can't count, more like it!" Galey added.

"Oh, I don't think there's much wrong with Ivain's counting," Alaiz worried. "Or his knowledge of how long it takes. …And even if there was, I think even *he* knows that he's supposed to play *some* part in the process …and what it entails!"

"Ooops!" Barcwith's humour faded slightly.

"Mmmm … 'ooops' is about right," Alaiz sighed miserably. "My so-called husband never was my 'husband' in the proper sense…"

"He wasn't?" Barcwith and Galey gasped in unison.

Alaiz shook her head sadly. "No. …And not from any rejection on my part either. He just said he didn't think that way about me. He did his …'growing up', for want of a better way of putting it, with some of the other ladies at court. But never with me. Not ever."

"Silly bugger!" was all Barcwith could think of to say to that. What kind of man would go messing around with other women when he had a nice lady like Alaiz given him as a wife? He had not even had to earn her affection! Talk back at Lorne had been that she had taken up with the young Knight because her husband had rejected her, but none of her current companions had ever dreamed that it had been quite so complete or for so long. The king of Prydein was obviously a total idiot!

It was Tamàs who broke the spell by wondering,

"Maybe that's been why you've been so sick when you never used to be before?"

"Ohhh!" Alaiz groaned as the realisation hit her. Then felt such a fool for not having thought of it before.

"So, should we take the ship, now?" Galey asked her.

"I don't think it makes much difference," Alaiz said glumly. "I know riding's supposed to not be advisable when I'm …well, like this! But, to be honest, I don't think I could take another fast journey on board like the one we did before. If I retch any harder, I think I'll turn myself inside out, and that can't be doing me any good either. In truth, I think I'd rather ride. At least then, if I don't feel well I can at least get off the horse and walk for a bit. I should stop being so sleepy soon, too, I hope! Surely we aren't likely to be pursued until we get right close to Osraig, as long as we're careful getting round Ceos unseen?"

Her companions agreed and went to tell Talorcan of their decision, who had known what was going on, but had firmly declined to have any part in the conversation.

The upshot was that the horses were swung back onto dry land that night, to give them chance to un-stiffen from their confinement and to graze. In the wan light of the dawn, the companions bade Captain McCormack and his crew farewell, and left them to find their way back through the marshes. The ship would navigate the north Kittermere coast, and then beat its way southwards down the western coast to their arranged meeting point. McCormack was confident that on this route they would be able to pass unnoticed, and that the bay he had chosen for the rendezvous was safe and viable for them to linger in. Talorcan could give him no estimate of the time it would take for the riders to reach him, and so the facility of a fresh water source near to the shore was vital. Food they had aplenty, but water was both heavy and cumbersome to store in great quantities, and so they relied on being able to replenish the ship's barrels regularly.

As the *Craken* slipped surreptitiously away from the shore, the riders waved farewell to their companions of the last weeks and then turned inland. Talorcan led with Decke by his side, bow at the ready. Ad and Galey flanked Alaiz, while Barcwith with an equally prepared Tamàs brought up the rear. A low bank of ground rose on their left, providing them with some cover from prying eyes from Ceos. More fortunate was that the fields through which they were riding were waterlogged from the endless rain and snow, and in no fit state to be worked. Not a soul stirred in the countryside, and Galey told Alaiz that most folk would probably be doing jobs close to home, like repairing ploughs, or nets for fishing on the lake.

What the lance did not tell her was that they were as much on the lookout for crows and the like, and it was to their relief that they saw no sign of abnormal activity in the air. As they made camp on the first night in a copse of alders, Barcwith and Talorcan privately spoke of their hope that this might mean that they had stolen a march on the Abend. Travelling through territory regularly scoured by Turstin and Mad Magnus was quite enough to contend with, without the Abend throwing their weight around too.

It was fortunate that there were plenty of small stands of timber and woody shrubs on this side of the island, for everyone was in desperate need of a good fire at night. Immediately on leaving the loch-side near Ceos, the going was wet for two complete days, with the only advantage being that the land was so sparsely inhabited there was no danger of being spotted in getting a good blaze going. The few cottages they saw were pathetic places, made from the same peat that they rested upon. What little stone there was was reserved for the great stone chimneys which sat solidly at one end, and where the men told Alaiz the families would be huddled. Cattle herded into what were mere substantial lean-tos at the opposite ends of the cottages, provided another source of warmth for the families.

The only thing still in their favour, as far as Alaiz could see, was that lowland Kittermere rarely suffered from hard frosts or long standing snow. The all encompassing salt water on this side of the island kept the temperature moderate in comparison to what they had been experiencing on Ergardia. Unfortunately Alaiz knew that once they were closer to Osraig, and the highlands which passed as Kittermere's hills, the snow would return.

For a couple of days they then found themselves on rolling moorland that was firmer underfoot, and where the air felt fresher and less sodden. Then they were back down amongst river channels and picking their way carefully. Time began to lose meaning for them, for it took an inordinately long time to cover what were only a few miles when seen on a map. So often they would take what they thought was the firmest route, only to find their way barred by an open stretch of water, which forced them to retrace their footsteps and try again. This tried Talorcan's patience beyond words, and after a week on the road, he was fit to throttle the first stranger who crossed him.

Also, to his chagrin, Alaiz was turning out to be far from the liability that he had expected, and his men now looked to her as often as him for confirmation of their route. The closer they got to her old home ground, the more confident she became that they were heading in the right directions. With no stars or moon for night after night, and the sun hidden under a constant bank of solid cloud, the soldiers had nothing to give them a sense of direction to match to the maps they had. It was Alaiz who increasingly confirmed that some feature they saw was something named on the map.

Her morning sickness was still lingering, but she was always quick to let them know as soon as she felt able to mount up for the next day. On several days she could not face riding on a swaying horse until nearly midday, but with someone leading her horse, and another walking with her for her to hold onto for support, she gamely walked so that they could at least begin moving. She might have then dozed in the saddle, for the horses could not go at any speed over this terrain, but she always rode on. Even Talorcan had to admit he was impressed by her will power. Nonetheless, he was greatly relieved when they fought their way out of the second maze of marsh land, and Alaiz confirmed that that was the last of them.

It then only took another couple of days before they crested a long ridge, and found themselves looking down on a long valley.

"Well this is it," Alaiz told them. "This is Llin Rossing, or Glen Rossen if you want to call it by its old name."

"Where do we start?" Barcwith asked, as much to her as his commander, and to Talorcan's irritation he himself had no idea, but Alaiz did. Pointing to the northern end of the valley she told them,

"We'll have to go that way first. If it's still there – and I can't imagine the locals letting it fall into disrepair – there's a good solid wooden bridge over the river. If we cross over and come back down the other bank, there're the remains of a road running right down to the water's edge. Before the land slipped and submerged the valley, there was a town down there. This is very different rock to where we've come from. It's all porous. Higher up the rivers disappear into the rock and come out lower down. There are caves all over the place. This valley must've been riddled with them, because one day the whole valley floor just gave in. The river had undermined a great stretch of its route over the years."

"Gosh, aren't you clever knowing all that," Ad gasped in awe.

Yet before Talorcan could say she must have read it somewhere, Alaiz herself replied with good humour. "No Ad, actually I was the despair of most of our tutors. I only remember this because we had one who was really keen on rocks, and he was nice to me. Most of them found it a pain to have to tutor the little sister along with my brothers, but this one was quiet and the boys made his life hell. I think he was quite relieved when they disappeared off to weapons practice, and he could study what he wanted – the only condition being that he took me with him and kept me out of mischief.

"He told me that the whole place sank. Straight down! That's why some of the buildings are still pretty much upright under the water. Apparently it's written down in some of the local holy books. That's how he came to tell me what the old name for the place was. Considering he was educated by the monks, he was quite sniffy about the fact that the Church uses it as an example of what the Spirits will do to unholy and disreputable places. The simple homes have long since been washed away, of course. Wood and wattle and daub don't last once they've been totally submerged. But the big stone places like the market hall and the church are sometimes quite visible."

And indeed when they arrived at the road which led down into the water, they could all see what she meant. Even in the turgid water of winter, it was easy to see that the water was having to flow around certain obstacles. Part of the town of Rossen must have been solidly built, for the top of a church tower was even now just visible. Unfortunately how they would get to it, let alone search the rest of the building, was beyond any of their imaginations. In summer it would be an easy swim, and a good swimmer would be able to dive into the depths without too much difficulty, but not now.

They were all standing on the bank contemplating this problem when Tamàs cleared his throat apologetically.

"I hates to say this," he said mournfully, "but how long's this been like this?"

"What do you mean?" Barcwith asked cautiously, sensing impending doom.

Tamàs tapped his own bow. "Well, we're supposed to be finding a bow that Master Brego thinks we can use, aren't we? Does anyone know what this special bow's made of? 'Cause even yew's going to be bugger-all use – beg pardon, miss – after it's been in the water for decades, maybe even hundreds of years."

"Oh for fuck's sake!" Talorcan exploded, without any concession to Alaiz' presence. In frustration he picked up the largest rock he could grab and hurled it with all his force at the distant church. "What a bloody fool's errand we've been sent on!"

Even Barcwith could think of nothing positive to say, and instead shied another rock into the waves. More by luck than skill, it dropped neatly within the crenellated tower top, and from the watery depths there was the muffled sound of a bell being hit. As if it had suddenly been dislodged from something by the jolt of the falling rock, the bell now began to move in the current and to knock against something. It was hardly ringing, but the bell must have been well made, for even muffled by the water it gave an audible metallic, rhythmic clunk – and it did not stop!

"Shit!" Barcwith swore, embarrassed. "Come on! Let's get out of here before we make ourselves any more noticeable!"

In a foul temper, the two senior men led a rapid retreat from the valley and up into the rolling sheep pasture. But before they went far Galey's voice was calling to them to stop. Looking back in irritation, Talorcan and Barcwith saw him sitting back at a small cross-road with Alaiz, and the others strung out between them.

"This way," Galey called, gesturing them to the left-hand track.

"And why, in the name of the Hunt, is that?" Talorcan demanded, as he rode back to Galey.

"Because Alaiz has given me an idea," the redheaded man-at-arms answered, unfazed by his captain's glare.

Talorcan's, 'Oh?' carried a weight of sarcasm, but Galey was undeterred.

"Look, Tamàs is right! No bow left in those conditions would survive. Now from what Alaiz' tutor told her, this natural disaster happened many centuries ago. That means it would've been long enough ago for the people who lived here to still be aware of the importance of the Bow, don't you think? So are they really likely to have left it there to rot? No, of course not. Her tutor said the surrounding churches had the disaster written down. Now the Church might be doing the whole doom and gloom bit over the valley these days, but what if it was written down in the first place to ensure that the Bow *wasn't* lost forever?"

Alaiz was nodding encouragingly to all this, and now chipped in.

"While we're here, there's a big old monastery only two valleys away. It's nothing much now, and there are only a few brothers keeping the place going, but you can tell from the size of the place and the stonework, that once upon a time it was really important. I bet they have a copy of a holy book with the disaster in it."

"Does your brother ever go there?" Barcwith asked, his mind working furiously.

Alaiz shook her head. "No! Absolutely not! Turstin hates monks. The only thing he keeps one eye on the Church for, in all its forms, is for the land and money they have. This place lost most of its rich land long ago, and they certainly don't have precious things – gold and silver crosses and stuff – and he wouldn't think of books as having any value at all."

All eyes were now on Talorcan.

"Come on, sire," Barcwith urged him, rallying at the prospect of something positive to do. "We've got this far. We've got nothing to lose following Galey's idea." He was careful to make it Galey's, knowing that his leader would be less resistant than if he credited Alaiz. Barcwith could not fathom why Talorcan was so antipathetic to Alaiz, except that she seemed to personify this wild-goose-chase of a mission. For his own part, he was starting to wonder if he dared push his luck and tell Talorcan to get a grip on himself, for this was certainly untypical behaviour. The severe Knight was normally courteous and considerate to women, even if he was not interested in them.

"Very well," Talorcan conceded grudgingly, "the monastery it is. Will we reach it before nightfall?"

Alaiz nodded, "I would've thought so, and that would give us a good reason to stop there, wouldn't it? Even a monastery running on few brothers will still be offering hospitality to travellers. It might be a bit basic, but they're still unlikely to turn us away."

"And if they do, we'll know who's been there before us, won't we!" Talorcan added, remembering Calatin's presence in Prydein, and wondering if the fiendish priest in disguise had ventured this side of the Strait of Kittermere.

It was already dark by the time they rode up to the gates of the great monastery, which were firmly barred. In such a troubled land no-one was taking any chances of inviting the lawless in. Talorcan escorted Alaiz to the small inspection hatch in the left gate, as Barcwith hammered on the right-hand one. A frightened face appeared at the hatch and it took some time, and the appearance of his senior monk, before the lance gained admittance. Even then the men were sure that had they not had Alaiz with them, they would have been refused entry.

Within the compound, they could see that Alaiz had been telling the truth as to the state of the monastery. The stonework was beautifully wrought, with the door to the church being wreathed in arches of intricately carved foliage and the heads of fabled animals. And the windows had rare coloured glass in them, speaking of great expenditure when the buildings were raised. Yet decay was all around. Well-worn paths ran between a few buildings, but aside from the direct crossings, the main courtyard flagstones were disappearing beneath weeds which were creeping up around the edges. Many windows looked to have been shuttered for years, judging by the rust on the nails and the fading of the wood, even going by what the men could see in the flickering of the torch-light.

Assessing the nervousness of the brothers, Talorcan decided not to mention wanting to see any books that night. Indeed, had there been any locks on the doors of the rooms they were shown to, he felt certain that they would have been locked in overnight, the brothers were so afeared. The lance spent a night barely more comfortable than in the open. The mattresses were damp, and it was only their own bundles of fire wood that got anything like a decent blaze going in the meagre grate of Alaiz' room, into which they all huddled until they were forced by weariness to their own assigned beds.

Luckily the morning light put everyone in a better frame of mind, and the brothers were more receptive to hear their guests' request. Consequently, while the rest of the men tended to the horses, Galey accompanied Talorcan and Alaiz into the monastery library. Here the prior, a painfully thin young man, attempted to lift a vast tomb off one of the shelves only to have to stand back and allow Talorcan to bring it down. Galey and Alaiz straight away pounced on it and began investigating the end papers, which were covered in annotations. But Talorcan could not refrain from asking,

"When was the last time you had a decent meal, brother?"

The frail figure shrugged as he admitted that supplies were desperately short. The monks ploughed the fields immediately next to the monastery, he said, but had given up on trying to work the fields farther out. Every time they had something worth harvesting, others came and stole it before the brothers had a chance to savour the fruits of their labours. The young prior said he thought it was Turstin's men collecting the taxes the brothers could no longer afford to pay.

"Fool!" Talorcan spat out. Then seeing the young brother blanch, quickly added, "Not you, brother! Turstin! All he's doing is driving you out, and who'll pay him anything then?"

"Oh, he has one of his henchmen set to take over," the prior admitted wearily. "The place may be going to wrack and ruin now, but it was well enough built that it wouldn't take much to set it straight. And if you saw it on a better day, you'd see that we're in quite a pretty spot. It's nicely sheltered here, and we have a natural spring over on the far side of the enclosure."

"Do you, now?" Talorcan pondered. "Well, well, quite the defensive site isn't it!"

Turning on his heels he strode out to the others.

"Barcwith," he barked, "take Decke and Tamàs and see what you can hunt in those woods!"

His sergeant looked up in amazement from the horse's hoof he was de-stoning.

"Sire?"

Talorcan by now was close enough for Barcwith to see the anger smouldering in the dark eyes, and he wondered at the cause until Talorcan snarled,

"That bastard Turstin is trying to starve these brothers out! Our queen's big brother is empire building on his own account, it seems!"

"Is he, by the Trees!"

"Well that's what *he* thinks, anyway," Talorcan was looking his most wolf-like – and positively cheerful at the thought of wrecking Turstin's plans. Something far more worthwhile than the task at hand! "It occurs to me that Kittermere has long been lacking the presence of the Order, don't you think? And this would make a first-rate preceptory – they even have their own water source away from any possible contamination or cutting off! These brothers could stay and serve as priests to our men and still be better off."

"So we're going to provision them so that they're still here when we come back?" guessed Decke.

Talorcan briskly clapped him on the shoulder. "Exactly! I'll send a message to Master Brego with McCormack when he's dropped us off on Rathlin. Ideally, I know this is Master Hugh's territory, but he seems to have more than enough on his plate at the moment, and the Prydein Knights have never attempted to expand into Kittermere even in the good times."

"Mmmm …but don't you think he'd object nonetheless?" Barcwith wondered.

"How could he?" an enthused Talorcan argued. "It's all part of the remit, isn't it? To help and to serve? Well these people haven't been helped or served in more years than anyone can remember, so Hugh would be pushing it if he objected to us taking on the responsibility. … So off you go, then! A nice big stag that they can hang and cure would be good, or the odd wild boar if you can bring it down!"

Shaking his head at his leader's mood swing, Barcwith waved Decke and Tamàs to follow him and led his horse down to the gate.

"You're helping them?" Alaiz' amazed voice sounded from Talorcan's side, making him spin round to face her. The dramatic change in his demeanour made her start, he appeared so different. Gone was the permanent sardonic sneer, and the cold eyes, and in their place was a genuine smile that was not just on the surface. Suddenly Alaiz saw what Kayna found so attractive about this Knight, having until now found it a total mystery why any woman would want to associate herself with him.

"Yes, we're helping them," Talorcan said positively. Then, seeing Alaiz' surprise, felt rather chastened that his behaviour had evidently led her to have such a poor opinion of him, and felt compelled to explain.

"I did take my vows, you know! And I take keeping them very seriously. These monks desperately need help – and here and now, not some vague promise for the future. If we don't help them, they won't survive the next few months and Turstin will walk all over them. They, of all people, don't deserve that. Although we're on a mission, the little time it will take us to help these brothers will be well spent. And even if it wasn't, there'd have to be a really compelling reason for me to turn my back on them in their current state."

"Oh? …Oh, quite!" a startled Alaiz agreed, then remembered what she had been coming to tell him in the first place. "Ermmm… We seem to have hit a problem." Talorcan raised an eyebrow in question and she winced as she reluctantly admitted. "Well it's like this. We found the records easily enough. The bad news is that we've hit another one of those riddles – the anagram things. The good news is that Galey was right. The folk who lived here centuries ago still knew the value of what was in their keeping. They couldn't leave the Bow to rot under the water, so they moved it, and tried to leave something as a clue for whoever might need to find it in the Islands' hour of need."

Before Talorcan could say anything in reply, Galey joined them at the trot.

"I've spoken to a couple of the brothers," he informed them. "None of them can think of what the anagram is really meant to be. I've left one of them hunting out some old maps that they have buried away, so that we can see if there's some old settlement that nobody now knows of, but it's not looking hopeful."

Talorcan shook his head wearily. "This bloody Bow is a pain in the neck!" He walked away a few paces, shrugging his shoulders in circles to try to rid himself of the tension which was returning to tie him in knots across the back of his neck. Then stood with his hands laced behind his head, starring at the grey sky, as he thought. Galey gave a watery smile at Alaiz and tried unsuccessfully to look optimistic, but could think of nothing worth saying to either of them. Suddenly, Talorcan dropped his arms and spun back to them.

"So you're saying this is going to take time to figure out?" he demanded. Both nodded. "Right, in that case I think the best thing we can do is give it our best shot for the next day or so while we get the brothers set up. If nothing makes any sense by then – and that's more than likely – we'll ride to meet McCormack. I want you two to make a copy – no, make that two, just in case – of this anagram and any maps you think might help. If I'm sending McCormack back to Master Brego with all speed, then he can take this information to Taise and the others back at Lorne. We can't afford to linger here, it's not safe."

"I thought you said this place was defendable?" Alaiz said in confusion.

"It is! Very defendable! But if Turstin hears you're here and decides to do something about it, we aren't equipped to fight off anything more than the smallest of patrols. We'd be forced to retreat behind these walls and sit any siege out. We could end up trapped here for months on end, and that's no good. The DeÁine could invade the Islands and we'd be no farther on to finding the Island Treasures than we are now. We must keep on the move. A couple of days to give it our best attempt is one thing – Brego would expect no less – but then we need to go after the Arrows before it's too late."

True to his word, Talorcan gave Barcwith and all except the more-learned Galey three days to forage, even joining them himself on the last two expeditions. In that time the brothers were provided with four deer and many game birds, while Ad proved adept at snaring the local abundant rabbit population. All the brothers were kept busy hanging, salting and smoking to preserve their new hoard. On the final day, the men rode further afield and spotted a distant manor house, which they guessed belonged to Turstin's man who had his eye on the monastery. The house was well situated, but nothing in comparison to the monastery either in size or quality.

However, closer to the small wood whose cover they were observing it from, was a large stone barn the loft of which turned out – upon closer inspection by Decke and Ad – to be filled with sacks of milled corn, and some boxes of late-harvested fruits and vegetables. As dusk fell, the lance led their horses down to the barn and strapped as much as the beasts could carry onto their backs, then slunk away again without even a bird chirping to draw notice to them. It was long after dark when they reached the monastery, but the brothers now had enough grain to keep them in bread for many weeks.

On the following morning, the last day of Eft-Yule, the little band once again set off. The rest had been a much needed tonic for Alaiz, and mercifully her morning sickness had now receded. It was just as well, for the weather had turned for the worse and they would need to keep moving. Overnight the temperature dropped markedly, and an icy wind was blasting in from the north bringing snow showers with it. Galey was appointed chief navigator, having had the most chance to pore over the maps at Blessed Mungo's – as the monastery turned out to be named.

In consultation with the brothers and Alaiz, he had decided that it would be foolish to attempt a crossing of the highlands in the centre of Kittermere. It was not that they were particularly high in comparison to those on Ergardia, or Celidon, which they were so used to. However, those high mountains had recognisable tracks, because they were the only ways through visible passes. Here the island was so sparsely populated there was nothing but a maze of sheep tracks, going nowhere in particular over rolling hills. The potential for getting hopelessly lost was just too great.

Instead they would continue south-west for a while, hugging the low foothills until they were level with Osraig, where they could take a long broad valley across to the west coast. This had the undoubted danger of taking them close to Turstin, but the monks were pretty sure that he and most of his men were still with the revolting Duke Brion. The biggest unknown quantity was Alaiz' nearer sibling in age, Gorm. No-one had heard hide nor hair of the younger brother for months – although that in itself was encouraging, since he was a passionate hunter, and, had he been at Osraig the whole time, it was unlikely that he would not have been seen out in hot pursuit of some poor creature. Without even his presence, it was unlikely that the men left to guard Osraig would stir themselves to go on patrol in such foul weather. Yet Talorcan still felt it behoved them to ride past the brothers' home territory with all possible speed, and they spent several long, cold days in the saddle, riding hard.

At night, though, they no longer needed to camp out, for the prior had gratefully written them letters of introduction to several of the monasteries and granges they would pass along the way, ensuring them a warm welcome and beds for the night. Their first stop was a generously proportioned farmhouse from the days when the Brothers of the Sacred Cross had had great flocks of sheep in the hills. Once more it housed far fewer men than it was capable of containing, although being built in the local timber with wattle-and-daub style, it was commonplace enough to have escaped the acquisitive advances of the thugs in Turstin's pay.

The brothers here were poor but not starving, which was much the way they found things at the tiny churches they stopped at on the next few nights. None warranted the title of monastery, being little more than a church with living quarters attached, and a priest plus a couple of brothers, and two or three lay brethren to help with the farming. Isolated from the main Church, they had more dealings with the widespread farms they ministered to than any central authority, but it meant that they were generally well-informed as to the appearance of strangers in the area.

At first Talorcan worried about this, concerned that as soon as they left someone would be setting off hotfoot for the nearest manor. But it became increasingly clear how deeply Turstin was loathed by the majority of Kittermere's population. Few places had escaped having crops or livestock seized to feed an army that did nothing to protect the locals from Attacotti raiders – indeed, were often more of a menace, since they were not restricted by wind or tide to get there.

To his profound embarrassment, Talorcan often found that as soon as it was revealed that he was a Knight of the Cross, he was treated like visiting royalty, and had pleas for the Order to send men to aid the islanders pressed upon him – both verbally and in writing to pass on to his Grand Master. Alaiz was even beginning to be convinced that maybe Brego had spoken the truth when he had said Talorcan's bark was worse than his bite, for no matter how often he told his men not to mention the word 'Knight', sooner or later the locals would somehow find out. Yet she never heard any of the lance being chastised or being given punishment duties.

Finally she plucked up courage to ask him why, as he escorted her into a farmhouse while the men attended to the horses. For a second the black brows lowered in a scowl, and Alaiz thought she had misjudged his mood, then he gave a sardonic half smile.

"Hmmm …so you've noticed," he growled, but without much vehemence. Steering her to the fireplace, he gestured her to sit and then stood before her, one elbow propped on the mantle. "I suppose you've been used to the soldiers around the court or Master Hugh's Knights?" he said thoughtfully. "Well that's one way of soldiering. Big armies engaging in big battles. When that happens, discipline is everything. Men drilled until every set piece is second nature are less likely to fold under attack, and it means that whoever's directing the battle overall can keep the orders simple, so there's less likelihood of misunderstanding.

"The thing is, though, that sort of fighting only happens once in a while. It's fine for a sudden invasion or the like, but it doesn't help when you have a constant threat from an enemy who refuses to be brought to a set piece battle. That's how the DeÁine have been since Gavra, and how the Attacotti have always been. We've been far more in the front-line of

DeÁine skirmish attacks than ever Prydein has been, and they're far too damaging and dangerous for us to just dismiss.

"That's why we fight lance by lance. But when you fight in small units, every man depends on the others for his life. We have to have men who can think for themselves. If a captain, knight or sergeant is cut down, there isn't another officer just down the line who'll take over. They're on their own, and they have to get themselves out of whatever the situation is, not just sit there like sheep waiting for the wolf to devour them because the dog's gone. But when you have men like that, you can't expect them to think and act for themselves only when it suits you. If I trust Barcwith or Galey or Tamàs to take over if I died or was wounded, then I have to trust them now too. They grew up in communities like this on Rathlin and Brychan, Alaiz – I didn't. They know how these people will react without hardly having to think about it – I don't.

"Now, I don't like the idea that I'm giving these poor folk, whose lives are hard enough as it is, some kind of false hope that the Knights of legend will be only a few days behind me, bringing them peace and freedom from their dire lords. But the men evidently think that it brings the people more to our side, and less likely to tell anyone we've been here. And who knows, maybe they're right? I can't prove they're wrong, so I have to remember that they've not been wrong in situations like this in the past, and trust them. Does that answer your question?"

Alaiz nodded, then thought of something. "You know, you've made me see something in a new light. Back at court, I never understood why Ivain and Amalric constantly clashed over the way Ivain treated the archers and their families when he went out and about. Amalric was always telling Ivain he must keep more of a distance, and I used to think Ivain was just being stubborn, and ignoring a more experienced commander's advice because he was so used to getting his own way. But now I can see that maybe Ivain was just doing things a different way. He used to read accounts of old battles over and over again, and he said that once the first volley was over, the army relied on the archers skirmishing around a battle and acting on their initiative to pick off prime targets, and that they should be treated accordingly. He said just what you've said, that they wouldn't have some officer telling them what to do but had to think for themselves, and so he needed to know how they thought in case he was ever in charge of an army, like his father and grandfather were."

"Well, well," a surprised Talorcan murmured. "If he figured that out for himself in the face of such opposition then maybe he's not a total fool after all!" Then a thought occurred to him too. "Wait a moment. Did he actually go and speak to the archers in person?"

"Oh yes!" Alaiz confirmed. "That was the worst of it as far as Amalric was concerned. Although, having seen now what a useless sort Amalric is in real danger, I'm wondering whether that wasn't more than a slight touch of jealousy on Amalric's part."

"Oh, I'm sure you're right about Amalric," Talorcan dismissed the acting Master of Prydein, "but what I was thinking was that the archers might be the only people who Ivain can really rely on, apart from the Knights who still look to Hugh instead of Amalric. If they know him … *really* know him, and recognise the real man – not just a figurehead king – then that willingness to trust them might end up by saving his life. The news from Prydein before we left Lorne was confused and grim, but Ivain might yet survive the whole thing. Such men as the archers don't switch allegiances. They'll stay true to Ivain, not just whoever wears the crown. For once in his life Ivain looks like he's done the right thing."

"I hope so," Alaiz wished sincerely. "Whatever our differences and problems, I don't wish him dead. I wanted to be free to live my own life the way I wished, but there are far worse men who could be king, and one of them is close to getting there."

With only one more day to reach the bay where Captain McCormack and the *Craken* hopefully would be waiting, the movements of Brion and the false priest who was known to be the Abend Calatin, preyed on everyone's thoughts. While nobody wanted to see civil war on Prydein, they all hoped that the focus of the Duke and the warlock was on the east, and that the Knights were giving them a run for their money. The last thing they needed was for Prydein to have collapsed, giving Brion chance to think about the west. No-one knew whether he would attack the Attacotti or try to make an alliance with Mad Magnus, and that unpredictability made him doubly dangerous.

It was therefore with considerable relief that they found the trusty captain and his crew waiting as planned, and with news that they had seen no sign of activity from Brion. As soon as they embarked, Talorcan persuaded McCormack to part with one of his few messenger birds to send a minutely copied version of the words containing the location of the Bow to Lorne. Then the two men pondered what was the best route to take.

The *Craken* had had several near misses with Magnus' ships on the way round, and only by island hopping and diving into estuaries had they remained unseen. At present the *Craken* lurked at the inland end of a long sea loch, which had scattered small islands at its mouth. The islets made for wicked currents in the winter seas, and it took a captain of McCormack's calibre to even venture near them, let alone steer a course through them. This had more or less guaranteed that the ship would remain undiscovered, but once they left the treacherous tidal races behind, they were vulnerable once more. On the open sea there was nowhere to hide.

The quickest landing was straight west across the short stretch of open sea, but that led directly into Magnus' home ports of Droman, Reiff and Kylesk. A southern passage would be fast with the wind whipping down from the north, but left the lance with a long and arduous trek across Rathlin's bare craggy highlands. Even at the mention of such a journey, Galey and Barcwith were vehemently in opposition to it, as being too dangerous in winter to even consider. That left little choice but to beat north and sail virtually into Temair harbour itself.

What worried everyone about this was that they would be sailing along sea-ways regularly travelled by Attacotti vessels. McCormack was confident of sailing far enough from the coast to avoid being spotted from land, but there was no guarantee that they would not come across other shipping. The debate raged back and forth until Tamàs suddenly spoke up.

"Why don't we sail straight up to Brychan?" he asked. "If we head that way we can sail to Farsan. It's a friendly port. All we have to say is that we're on business for the Grand Master. The *Craken*'s an Order ship, after all, so why would they question one ship? It's hardly likely that we'd be seen as a threat on Brychan. That way, we'll be so far out in open seas that if we do encounter any Attacotti ships it won't be obvious where we're going. Then all we have to do is drop down to Temair."

"By the Spirits! Yes! That's the solution!" McCormack enthused, while Talorcan gave Alaiz a 'see what I mean?' look, while clapping the older archer on the arm in approval at his solution. And as the sails were trimmed and the navigational sightings made, Talorcan permitted himself a small moment of optimism that this mission might turn out well after all.

Passage of the Storm

Chapter 12

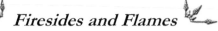

Firesides and Flames

Brychan: Yule

Berengar's announcement at the Yule festivities gave everyone cause to think hard. For Roger it was now some consolation that the man who was leading the party was as committed to bringing Edward down as Cwen, and was unlikely to leave her carrying the blame if things turned nasty. For Jane it was worrying that her daughter had once again fallen in with someone with a complicated life. The difference, for her, being that his secret was really that – a secret. Neither Edward or any of his cronies had any idea of Berengar's association to the royal family, and Berengar himself seemed keen for it not to be revealed. There was at least the possibility, then, that Berengar could complete this mission and then return to his former life, without anyone else being any the wiser as to who his half-brother was.

For Cwen herself it brought a feeling of a deeper and stronger bond with Berengar. The knowledge that he was personally driven, and not simply going through the motions because he thought his duty demanded it, made a big difference to how she now thought of him. Now she knew beyond a shadow of a doubt that he would be alongside her in the fight, irrespective of what anyone in his Order said.

For Swein it was a different kind of revelation. With every turn Edward was turning out to be a dreadful aberration. No wonder he had exhibited superhuman strength in dismembering his poor half-brother if he was a DeÁine. Yet what terrified Swein maybe even more was the knowledge that Edward might not be a one-off, but part of a whole army, all predisposed to predate upon the unsuspecting people of Brychan. His own experience of Edward's sexual appetites had not been soothed by Berengar's talk of what seemed like an endless succession of raping and molesting. More than anything else it brought home to him the desperate need to remove Edward from a position of power before he could entrap the whole Island into becoming a new part of the DeÁine Empire. Edward on his own was terrifying enough, but what he would be like if he had the backing of mighty warlocks and witches just did not bear thinking about.

During the next few days everyone thought about things in their own way, but the *Brace of Brachets* was way too busy for anyone to do anything but fall into bed by the end of the day. A week after the end of the old year, festivities at the inn were once again building up to the major celebrations for the New Year. This time the inn would be open through to the early hours of the following morning, and in light of that remained closed to all but resident guests on the Eve day until the sun went down.

That in turn meant that everyone had the first chance in days to get up at a leisurely pace, instead of rushing around to be ready for the normal late morning opening. Even when they did open, Jane was not providing cooked meals. In the interests of ensuring that their customers remained something like upright at least until midnight, she was preparing trays of savouries which could be eaten in fingers. There was therefore much baking of breads, and other gloriously aromatic things which Cwen was busily involved with, but almost nothing for Swein to do.

Having realised that the best tactic was to stay from underfoot, he wandered out into the yard with Eli to where Berengar and Jes were attempting to get the stables cleaned. With the gates to the yard shut, there was only a limited amount of room to move the horses around, and with every stall occupied it was turning into a complicated dance. Eli naturally partnered up with his older brother, and Swein quickly caught on to what he was doing and began to do the same for Berengar.

While Berengar raked out one stall, Swein took the water bucket and washed it out and refilled it, leaving it by the horse in the yard. He would then get the next horse out while Berengar put new bedding in, and once that was done he would put the first horse back in its stall and fill its manger, while Berengar began clearing the empty stall. At first he wondered whether Berengar would expect him to take over the smelly job of removing the old bedding, but the practised easy with which Berengar was getting the job done was something Swein could not hope to match. He did tentatively offer, but Berengar just laughed and shook his head, raising Swein's slender arm and with a twinkle in his eye pretended to try to find the biceps.

"You need a bit more of Jane's home cooking to build you up before you start hefting soggy straw about!" he said kindly. "Quicker all round if I carry on, I reckon. Then we can both go and get fed!"

With the four of them working at it, the stable was cleared by midday, and going into the inn they found that Cwen had plated them up food in the back room out of the way. The brothers wolfed their food down, then rapidly disappeared to go and find their friends for a few hours before they would be needed again. Esclados had put in a brief appearance with Roger, but the two of them were now in the middle of the important job of checking the barrels for the coming night. Nothing would be worse than draining one barrel and then finding that the next one had not settled and was undrinkable. For once, the whole of the back of the main bar was one long line of barrels, which were being tilted on chocks as their levels required, and carefully broached and tested. Esclados was in his element, and with his strength was an asset as he could move the full barrels with greater ease than any of the normal staff.

It left Swein sitting alone with Berengar as the two without a job. For a while the silence lingered uncomfortably until Swein plucked up courage and spoke.

"Berengar? Can I ask you something?"

The ealdorman had just about been dozing off, but something in Swein's tone made him sit up.

"Yes, of course."

Swein wriggled uncomfortably, wondering whether he should have spoken, but it was too late now with Berengar awake and watching.

"It's just that," he began tentatively, "I was talking to Jacinto …about his past and what it was like for him as a child. …And I don't understand – why were the Knights so hard on him?"

"Hard on him?" Berengar asked in amazement. "What in the Islands has he been saying to you?"

Swein squirmed on his cushion, mentally kicking himself for starting this conversation. "Well …why did his foster family keep him separate from the other children? …Why wasn't he treated like a member of the family? Why did he have to sleep in the kennel? …You and the others have been kindness itself to me, and I'm *nothing*. Jacinto seems to be everything I'd expect you to want in a squire, but he says he gets nothing but punishment duties. I just don't understand why that should be. …Or shouldn't I be asking?" he said nervously as Berengar sighed heavily.

"No, there's no reason why you shouldn't ask," Berengar replied sadly. "In fact I'm glad you've spoken up. I had no idea that that was the picture Jacinto had painted of his life." He stopped and wondered how he was going to explain this, then realised that Swein was probably interpreting what Jacinto had said in the light of his own experience. The young man sitting next to him was still verging on frail despite the decent food and lodging he had had since travelling with the Knights, and he remained tormented by dreadful nightmares on an almost nightly basis, as was testified by the screams they all heard.

His voice softened by sympathy for the appalling life Swein must have led, Berengar started again.

"You mustn't take what Jacinto said at face value, you know – and by the way, you're not 'nothing'! You're as important as anyone else! Now, I don't know how he painted the picture, but this is pretty much his story in brief. After the Battle of Moytirra the border was drawn up between us and the DeÁine. In the next year the villagers all along that southern stretch of Brychan started to rebuild their lives. Many families had suffered terrible losses while the war had raged backwards and forwards, and there were a lot of orphans. Some of them were just small children whose parents had been killed, and where it was impossible to find a relative to take them in.

"In other cases women found themselves pregnant, sometimes by a husband who wasn't around any longer to provide for them, or by some soldier who'd raped them – more often that meant the DeÁine. And by DeÁine I don't just mean the ones like the Abend. Wherever they came back from, Swein, on the way they'd acquired a huge army of slaves, and many of them were drafted into the army to be thrown at ours as expendable to try to wear us down by sheer weight of numbers.

"Many of them were sallow-skinned, olive-skinned, or dark-skinned like Jacinto, and many also made a run for it as soon as they saw a land beyond where the DeÁine had no control. Some of them settled and made a life with the local villagers. Others stayed until they could find a ship heading away from the Islands. I'm guessing Jacinto's father was one of the latter, because Jacinto appeared on the doorstep of one of our granges as a boisterous toddler of, they guessed, about three.

"Like all the other orphans we took in, he was found a place with a family in the married quarters. Unlike them, by the time he was five he was already a handful. I read the report of the garrison commander. The wife who was fostering him came in to see the captain in tears when he was eight. They had two other little boys and a girl, and had raised two children of their own, with their son already a promising page in the Order. She said she couldn't cope with Jacinto anymore. The final straw had been when the other boys had been playing a board game, and Jacinto had turned up and wanted to join in. When they told him he could have a go the next time, he flew into a rage and attacked them. One child ended up with a broken arm and ribs, and the other with two black eyes and a nasty swelling on his knee, as well as other bruises between them."

Swein was looking pale. He remembered only too clearly his older brothers, who had bullied him mercilessly, flying into rages over similar things as children. All of a sudden Jacinto was looking a lot less like himself. Berengar noticed his pallor, but decided that having started there was nothing to be gained by stopping. Better to get it over and done with.

"He went to another grange and another family – this time of a retired soldier who'd had a good reputation for being able to straighten out problem recruits. Jacinto was way younger than anyone he'd normally fostered, but the commanders at the time thought it would be worth it if it nipped the behaviour in the bud. Because Jacinto was already showing promise of being not just big, but well co-ordinated and a quick learner."

Berengar sighed. "They tried everything. The thing with the dogs was simply that they wondered whether he'd respond to having some responsibility. Most of the other kids loved to have a dog or a horse or a bird, and – as long as it's properly supervised so that the animal isn't neglected – it's a great way to get them used to taking a bit of responsibility for something else.

"Not Jacinto, though. He took it that they were trying to foist the dogs off onto him so that they didn't have to deal with them. He apparently said that they were treating him like a kennel-man! They weren't, of course. All they'd done was offer him *one* dog! *He* was the one who decided he'd show them up. Show the rest of the garrison what they were doing behind everyone's back. Or at least that's how he rationalised it when it all came to be put on record. By then he was full of ire that 'others' stood by and did nothing. Yet he was the one who *chose* the little room by the kennels because he saw himself as the outcast – the odd one out.

"Honestly, Swein, I don't know where all that anger against the world came from. If there was a bad way to look at anything, Jacinto would find it. Even worse, he appears incapable of seeing anyone else's viewpoint. He can't seem to bond with anyone. He never seems to feel any sympathy with anyone unless he can twist it to fit in with how he sees himself."

"Could it be something that happened when he was very small?" wondered Swein, frantically trying to find some distinction between Jacinto and his own thug-like brothers.

"Who knows," Berengar sighed heavily. "Maybe. Maybe not. Only he can tell us if it is – but he has to trust us enough to start talking, even if the full story takes some piecing together, and that hasn't happened so far."

Berengar eased the knots in his shoulders and leaned forward over the bench table to Swein to keep eye contact, continuing in a weary voice.

"As for when he joined up …well …all I can say is thank the Trees we've never had another recruit like him! It's not all about muscle, Swein. We make vows when we become Knights that we take very seriously. We're here to protect and serve *anyone* in need – unless, that is, they turn out to be a criminal or someone who's a danger to others. But to do that you have to be able to see people for what they are. You have to be able to put yourself in other people's shoes, so that you can work out whether that aggressive person in front of you is really a threat, or someone frightened half out of their wits who's snarling at you in the desperate hope that if they look fierce enough *you* won't attack *them*.

"Now no-one expects that to come straight away. Obviously it takes practice and experience. If you want to see an expert at it, watch Esclados when he's helping Roger tonight. He's a canny old bear, and he can sniff out a bad 'un quicker than you can say 'knife'. But to get there you have to *want* to help others. Some recruits are born to it. Others find it comes when they get their first taste of the chaos and damage that wars bring, and see people with nothing left but the clothes they're standing in. With Jacinto, though, it was as though he thought it a sign of weakness to be …aach, well …so downtrodden, so reduced in circumstances. That if those refugees hadn't been so pathetic, and shown a bit of spirit and fought back, then all would have been well!

"The trouble is, you see, Jacinto has never met anyone bigger and stronger than himself who really means him harm. At weapons training, if he got beaten then he'd go away and practice and practice until he could go back and beat the person who'd bested him. In a way it's unfortunate that he's got nature on his side, having grown into a very big man. If he'd been your build, then he'd have had to revise his view of life long ago."

"Bloody right!" Swein said with feeling. "I've been pasted around more rooms than I can remember, by men who thought it would be funny to have some sport with the girlie one!"

"Well we can help you avoid that happening again," Berengar said sympathetically. "A bit of training is all you need." Then seeing Swein's sceptical expression, "No, really! Not every Knight is built like a castle gate, as you've now seen, but it would be a fool who thought the smaller, lighter-built ones were anything but deadly fighters. But coming back to Jacinto, you do see what I mean, don't you? That arrogance of his is more of a barrier to him getting on in the Order than the clumsiest fighter. Them we can train eventually, but, if you don't care about anyone but yourself, no-one can gift you with the ability to feel compassion. The punishment details we handed out in desperation were treated as physical obstacles to be overcome. Trials of strength and hardness! No matter how often I explained to him *why* he was being punished, I could never get through the brick wall in his mind – and neither could Esclados! When we left Vellyn he was on trial. I'd told him if I didn't see an immediate improvement he was going to be expelled from the Order forever."

"What?" Swein exclaimed in astonishment.

Berengar had the grace to look embarrassed as he said, "I told him I was putting him personally in charge of your well-being. He'd been arrogant enough to turn you away when you and Cwen desperately needed help, and I hoped that if he could start to see you as a real person then it might ...just might ...open the door into his mind a crack."

"Oh it opened a crack all right!" Swein muttered darkly, "but it wasn't in his mind!"

Berengar nearly spat his mouthful of beer across the table as he choked in his astonishment. His realisation of the real relationship between the two young men suddenly shifted dramatically. Then a dark thought crossed his mind.

"He didn't force you to do anything you were unwilling to do, did he?" Berengar asked, dreading the answer. Swein gulped, but managed to keep his voice almost even as he weakly replied.

"Not forced." This suddenly felt most bizarre. He had never had this kind of conversation with a man who did not share his tastes. It had never felt safe to speak out in mixed company of the kind he had encountered beyond Edward's inner circle, for fear of retribution at being considered a pervert. Yet Berengar's concern did not seem to be about what they had done, but whether or not he had been hurt in the process, and he was still sitting and watching Swein with an expectant expression.

"The first time it just ...sort of happened," he tried to explain. "At first he seemed more surprised than I was. It's only been later on that I started to wonder what was going on in his mind. I don't think I got any closer to the person inside than I did on that first night." He laughed bitterly.

"Would you believe it? Edward let me see more of himself than Jacinto did. The main difference *there* was that I didn't really realise what it was that I *was* seeing until it was too late."

"Well, if you'll take a bit of advice meant in your best interests, keep the distance you've now got from Jacinto, Swein. Because once he's got used to you being there, he'll start to regard you as his property. Even worse, he'll keep putting you in situations where he forces you to decide between him and something else. It's like he has to keep on testing people, and he's just waiting for you to put a foot wrong so he can pass the blame for any failures onto you. And you'll never be able to anticipate what it is that he really wants – not unless you're a lot smart than me, anyway – because, like you've said, he never lets you get close enough to find out."

Berengar levered himself off the bench and walked around the table, pausing beside Swein. Placing a hand on the thin shoulder, he could have been a father imparting advice by his kindly tone as he said,

"You've had more than your fair share of people mistreating you already, Swein. You don't need to be setting yourself up for another basket full of trouble. Hard as it seems to believe now, there are people out there who'll accept you as you are and care about you, without trying to turn you into their pet lapdog, or expecting you to stand being beaten black and blue."

Swein was beyond astonished. He sat open-mouthed as Berengar ambled out to find Esclados. Had anyone previously ever told him that one of the most senior men amongst those Knightly epitomes of masculinity would give him such unprejudiced advice, he would have laughed in their face. But maybe – just maybe – it meant that there was a slim chance that things might eventually get better for him. If Berengar could be genuinely concerned for him as a real person, who else might be?

He was therefore feeling unexpectedly festive as the evening came around. As soon as the doors opened there was a steady stream of customers arriving, and he was soon kept busy washing out an endless stream of tankards. Not so long ago he would have spent the time fretting on how low he had sunk to be doing menial work, but in the cheerful atmosphere of the kitchen it was impossible to slip back into his old ways. Jane and Cwen often rolled their sleeves up and helped him out when the backlog looked like overwhelming him, laughing and joking as they dunked mugs in the hot soapsuds.

At first Swein wondered how they were ever going to keep this pace up all night, but slowly it eased off. Cwen and Jane explained that many locals would arrange to meet for a drink with friends at different times, moving from inn to inn during the early part of the evening as people tried to meet as many as possible. As the New Year drew closer, though, people began to stay put. And an hour before midnight, Swein found himself with no more mugs to wash. Cwen tucked her arm through his and escorted him out of the kitchen.

"They've got enough spares to be going on with for quite a while now," she told him. "We'll do some clearing up at the end of the night, but a lot of it can wait until the morning."

In the main bar they found Roger and Esclados controlling the proceedings from behind the bar, while the rest of the family took the money, mopped up spillages and generally kept the place looking something like respectable. Just moving around was difficult. Not only the main bar but the side parlours too were packed with people. Roger's expertise as a brewer was obviously making this the inn of choice for many people to see in what they all hoped would be an auspicious beginning. Squeezing between burly farmers and tradesmen and their wives and families, Cwen and Swein found Berengar standing guard over the family's drinks at the far corner of the bar. Jane appeared behind them and Berengar handed her a mug of a light clear beer, and then proceeded to thrust a similar one into Swein's hand.

"Don't drink the winter ale if you don't want a thick head!" the ealdorman warned him with a twinkle in his eye. "Roger's Old Yule Ale is strong enough to fell an ox if drunk in pints! Deceptive taste to it, too! All smooth and malty, and before you know it you end up like him over there."

Following Berengar's nod of the head, Swein saw two men, obviously journeymen spending a bonus from their master, but now slumped on the far bench, propping one another up. One had his head on his friend's shoulder, fast asleep, while the other was trying to desperately uncross his eyes and focus on which of the several mugs he was seeing in front of him was the real one containing the beer.

"What's this, then?" Swein asked warily, peering into his tankard.

"Oh, don't worry," Jane reassured him. "This is the honey beer. It's strong enough to keep well but you'd need several pints to get in that state."

Eli shouldered his way to the bar with a bucket full of cold, wet towels, which Esclados hauled over the bar and began exchanging them for the rapidly drying ones currently cooling the barrels. That made Swein realise just how hot it was in the room. Looking over to the grate he saw in surprise that the fire was well down. He had expected to see it roaring away, but the newest log was only just beginning to smoulder. It was obviously the body heat of so many people packed so close which was generating the warmth.

In the castle, Edward would never allow the room he was in to become so crowded. And suddenly Swein realised it must have been because in such a press it was impossible to see more than a few feet in front of yourself, let alone the other side of the room – and Edward always liked an audience. In fact Swein had always thought that the New Year would be accompanied by much country dancing outside of the court. Yet now he could not imagine anyone even being able to take more than a few steps without colliding with a neighbour.

"What actually happens at the, ehmm, New Year …the midnight hour …whatever?" he rather embarrassedly asked Cwen, not wanting to show his ignorance and put his foot in things.

"Well it's getting pretty close now. Now he's got the cold towels for Pa, Eli is going up to the attic room that looks out to the church tower. When he sees the candlelight in the tower he'll run down and tell Pa …"

Before she got any further Eli's head popped in through the small gap by the door and gave his father a thumbs-up sign. Roger immediately went to a great brass bell hung in the middle of the bar and rang it vigorously. The room swiftly fell quite, with only one or two soft murmurs circulating. Everyone stood listening intently, then through the frosty night the church bell rang out, and everyone let out a great cheer and began shaking hands, or hugging and kissing each other as their relationships determined. Swein found himself on the end of a head-spinning round of embraces which left him feeling quite giddy. Suddenly he realised that the doors had opened, and people were spilling out onto the street to find more room to move.

In desperate need of air, he slipped out and looked up at the crystal clear sky. The full moon hung like a festive lantern high above, lighting the street almost as clear as day. Standing in the doorway, Cwen and Berengar came to join him, and he was just about to wish them a happy New Year when something made him look back up. A dark shape flapped across in front of the moon, and then they heard a strange noise.

"What's that?" he asked instead. But before anyone could reply, more dark shapes appeared, and then the noise distinguished itself as cawing.

Suddenly a whole flock of crows, rooks and ravens appeared over the roofs heading east.

At Cwen's exclamation of, "Sacred Trees!" drew the attention of others, who saw them looking up and turned to see for themselves.

"Lost Souls! Ravens at night!" Berengar whispered in horror.

"What is …?" Esclados came to the door and stopped in his tracks as he saw the birds. "Hounds of the Wild Hunt! That's an evil omen! Nothing natural made those birds take flight at this hour."

The birds were moving at great speed, and despite the vast numbers in the flock were soon gone from sight. But that was not the end of it. The wind continued to build and suddenly a huge bank of cloud appeared over the roof tops. The temperature plummeted as it rolled across the sky, blanking out the moon and stars, but it was not dark, for a sickly, greenish light began to build at the leading edge. Then someone screamed and pointed before collapsing. From beneath they could see what seemed like thousands of hooves, paws and feet, and was it imagination or did the wind sound like hounds baying and horns blowing?

"The Wild Hunt!" someone screamed and people began running in all directions, even as the bank of cloud passed and tore on its way eastwards.

Suddenly there was a shriek from within, and they rushed back to find that the previously quiet fire had erupted into a roaring blaze, sending sparks flying out into the room. Jane and Yvette were frantically stamping out glowing embers which kept landing on the wooden floor, and were throwing cushions across the room from those benches nearest the blaze. From the sudden shouts of alarm coming from outside the same must have been happening in many other houses too. In a blink of an eye the revellers had dispersed, then moments later the church bells set off again, but this time with a more frantic and continuous ringing.

"Fire! Fire!" they heard voices calling from outside. "Help! Fire! Sound the alarm!"

Esclados had had the presence of mind to grab the bucket of soapy suds from the kitchen, as being the nearest thing to hand, and thrown that on the main fire, quenching the sparks but leaving unpleasant smelling smoke behind. Eli and Jes ran in with more buckets, and soon there was nothing left but some smouldering logs and a lot of mess. But it was clear that others were not so fortunate. Leaving the women behind to bolt the door after them and continue with the cleaning, the men quickly exited the inn to offer aid to other townsfolk.

The houses on the little square were all solid stone constructions, and it seemed as though most of their owners had either been at home or in the *Brace of Brachets*, where they could get home in a hurry. There were therefore no fires out of control in the immediate vicinity or in the main square, although there was a strong smell of smoke and burning cloth. The same could not be said of the outskirts of the town. The houses of the poorest were often ramshackle timber affairs, and one particular enclave to the west seemed to be well alight already – perhaps because it had been the first area the strange flight of birds and the unearthly cloud had passed over. Jes flung the inn's gates open wide, and Roger yelled to Esclados and Berengar from within the stable yard.

"Quick! Come and give us a hand!"

Roger and his sons were harnessing the family dray horses to the wagon and standing empty barrels on it. When the wagon bed was full, they pushed up the sides and dropped the holding-pins into place. Roger got onto the driver's seat and waved Esclados up beside him, before cracking the whip over the horses' heads. With no further encouragement, the horses leaned into their harnesses and the dray made a rapid exit from the yard and was turned towards the river. Berengar jogged after it with the lads.

After a mighty sprint they reached the wharves along the river bank, and found folks already there filling whatever vessels they could find that would hold water. With great expertise, Roger wheeled the dray then reversed the horses to a wider jetty. Gus and Jes immediately began taking down a barrel between two of them, scooping the freezing river water into it and then heaving it back onto the dray, while Eli walked the full ones into the centre of the wagon. This was work where Esclados and Berengar's strength paid off, for they were able to handle a barrel each, even though they were sweating heavily by the time the dray was filled again.

Without further ado Roger set the horses moving again, and soon had the dray moving at a formidable speed. The two Knights now understood why there was a brass bell mounted on a wooden frame beside the driver, for Eli leapt up beside his father and rang it with great vigour to warn others of their coming. With the dray moving at that speed, there was no way that Roger was going to be able to stop it in a hurry if someone was foolish enough to step in front of it. However most of the locals seemed familiar with what was happening, and flattened themselves against the sides of buildings as the dray thundered past. Berengar and Esclados contemplated following on foot, but realised that they would never keep up, and left the younger men to do the running. Instead, they began to help others fill their containers at the river. Before they knew it the sound of the bell warned of Roger's return.

"How's it going?" Berengar called to him, even as he was hauling the first barrel back down to the river.

"It's bad!" Roger called mournfully. "There's no way that everyone could've escaped. In those old shacks the flames spread like wild fire. It just leapt from roof to roof. The whole district must've been ablaze within minutes. We can't even get close the source of the fires. All we can do is drench the houses one street in from the inferno, and stand by with pitchforks to keep pushing away any falling burning beams."

"Sweet Rowan!" Esclados prayed. "How many souls lived in there?"

"Hard to say," Roger said regretfully. "The town guild has been trying to get those hovels moved for years, but no sooner do we find work and shelter for one lot, than other people seem to creep in at night and take over where the others left off." He sighed. "You can't blame them. Most of these people are from right up on the DeÁine border, or over it. Some of them have been edging slowly east for years, carrying what little is theirs on their backs. And there's rarely any trouble from them – maybe that's the problem, it's too easy to overlook them."

"What a terrible thing to happen," Berengar lamented. "To spend so long fleeing persecution, and then just when you think you've reached safety to die in a fire."

"Indeed," Roger replied as a parting comment. "I fear we may have lost over two hundred souls this night."

"Two hundred!" Esclados gasped, as Roger and Eli disappeared into the night once more. "That's a desperate loss, Berengar!"

"That it is, old friend. Even more so because I fear that this was no natural accident. I can't help thinking about those birds. By the Trees, Esclados, they were travelling fast, don't you think? Too fast to be moving under their own power. That wind seemed to be driving them east. And what was *that*? That wind was what fanned the flames of all the fires. There was some mischief attached to it, and if it wasn't started by a DeÁine then I'm no Knight."

"I wish I could say you're wrong, but I can't," Esclados sighed mournfully. "Any more than I can dismiss this as just a bad twist of fate. Behind the bar I've kept hearing people wishing for good luck, and that the Lord Jolnir and his Wild Hunt would stay away tonight. It seems to be a countrywide legend that he harvests the souls of the unwary at this time, and makes them living-dead."

"Then if that really was Jolnir, how come we're still here?" wondered Berengar. "Somehow I don't think that was Jolnir, but if certain evil-minded schemers knew of the legend, then I'm thinking they've made the best of their timing in sending that apparition on this of all nights. That was a sign saying 'the DeÁine are coming' as bright as day, to me. What worries me is what was it meant for? Are they really coming, or is it meant to put us all in a panic for some other reason?"

"Mmmm…" Esclados pondered. "The birds – that was a sign. But that cloud? Just a sign? I'm not so sure."

"Why?"

"Well do you imagine the Abend would worry about whether they could control the Lord of the Underworld if they opened the way for him to come through into this world?"

"You think that was real?"

"Over two hundred souls just passed over in one quarter of this town, Berengar. Two hundred dead in one go. Not to mention the ones whose hearts stopped from fright in the rest of the town, or any drunken brawls in the rougher quarters. Multiply that out across the rest of the towns that thing passed over, and then tell me you're convinced that wasn't Jolnir harvesting reinforcements for his army."

Come the morning after the fire, the full state of the damage was revealed. The shanty town was gone, and the people who had hidden there were among the ashes. Elsewhere, whole families were left destitute in the freezing midwinter weather from isolated house fires, or where a small cottage row had gone up in flames all together.

In a strange way, though, it made the decision for the travellers easier. There was nothing to be gained by staying, for the job of rebuilding would take months – months they could not afford to delay by. The little help they could offer over a few days would make little imprint on a disaster of such a scale, but by vacating their rooms they could leave them free for those in more need. Packing their things as quickly as they could, they then helped to move the remaining paying guests up to the small family rooms, leaving the large rooms below available. The *Brace of Brachets* was built to sufficiently generous standards that in the better rooms there was space to sleep a small family at a push, and it was not long before that became reality. It grieved Berengar and Esclados to leave Cwen's family to cope with the stunned survivors, but at least Roger and Jane seemed familiar with what would be needed, and it was encouraging to see the way the little town had instantly closed ranks and begun pulling together.

Even as Esclados began apologising for leaving them to it, Roger was swift to silence him.

"No, no, you must go!" he said emphatically. "This isn't the first fire the town's had. Everyone knows what must be done." Clasping Esclados' hand he went on, "But you, my friend, you have a much more important job to do. I feel it in my bones! I may only be a country innkeeper, but I know there was nothing natural about those fires last night. What Berengar told us that night ..." he sighed and shook his head, "that scares me much more! I see now, you must stop King Edward before it's too late. We can't afford – Brychan can't afford – for him to be in charge of this Island if the DeÁine are coming! You have to discredit him. Make the other nobles and the Churchmen see him for what he is, before it's too late! Go with my blessing, and look after my Cwen!"

Esclados could only nod his thanks, then mounted up beside Berengar. Sybil reluctantly came to her seat on the pommel of his saddle, having spent a joyful holiday ridding the stable of mice. After a quick ruffle of her feathers, she coughed and spat out the ball of bones from her last meal, before settling more comfortably for the ride.

"Yuck! Does she always do that?" Swein asked queasily.

Berengar laughed. "Oh that's birds of prey for you! Never ones to stand on your dignity!"

Leaving her family was desperately hard for Cwen. Until this moment she had not realised how much she had relaxed in the comfort and security of her old home. It was only Richert's memory and her ever growing faith in her companions that tore her away this time. This was no exciting move to a new home. All she could see ahead was darkness and danger. Then the thought of those horrors overwhelming this happy corner of the Island made her shudder. But the hope of protecting everything that she held so dear was enough to get her up on Twigglet's back. Swein edged Bracken close to her and reached across to squeeze her hand.

"If I were you, I don't think I could face leaving here." he said sympathetically. "I wish my home was like this. I think you're being very brave."

That almost opened the floodgates on the tears she had been struggling to hold back. Luckily Berengar led them out before she could change her mind, and the three men kept quiet for the first part of the day to let her regain her composure in peace. Away from Radport they soon realised how bad the weather had become. Even on the main roads the passable path was only a single track in the middle, where riders had kept it trodden down. By the sides of the road, the banks of snow rose in powdery slopes, which threatened to slither down and engulf the unwary traveller.

The fastest they could safely move the horses at was a walk, and by the time the winter sun was lowering, everyone was weary and glad to take refuge in a village inn. Berengar and Esclados had decided, in view of the reports which had come in from travellers, not to take the loop of road north around the great Pen River estuary. Instead they were following the river eastwards to Pencrick, where the River Rad joined the neighbouring Pen at the sea. From there they would catch a boat across to Penbrook, leaving a shorter ride up to Arlei.

In the drifting snow it took three days just to reach Pencrick, but the good news there was that the sea was unusually calm for the time of year. A merchant sailor, short on trade due to the closed off roads, was happy to take four passengers and their horses on the simple day's trip across the estuary. Any money was better than sitting in the harbour waiting for goods that did not come. Once more the two ponies distinguished themselves by placidly allowing themselves to be led aboard the swaying boat, while Berengar and Esclados' more spirited mounts had to be calmed and cajoled to get them aboard.

The wind had been steadily blowing from the west for days, their captain informed them as they got under way, which was wonderful for a quick passage but left the four feeling twitchy. Standing in a huddle at the stern they pondered the meaning of it, out of earshot of the crew. It was unnatural, Cwen assured them, for at this time of the year the wind was normally more often than not coming from a northerly direction.

"Bloody wizards!" Esclados muttered feelingly.

"Maybe," Berengar mused, "but perhaps it's not all bad news." The others all looked at him expectantly. "Well if the Abend wanted news *back* they'd have to have let that wind drop, wouldn't they?" he reasoned. "This wind only helps the birds get to wherever they're going. Even ravens would be hard pressed to fight their way all the way back to New Lochlainn against this sort of headwind. It must mean that whatever action they're thinking of taking hasn't started yet."

"Dear Spirits, I hope so," Cwen prayed, as the others nodded their assent to that hope.

By that evening the boat had tied up at Penbrook, and the horses were disembarked with greater speed than they had gone on. Standing on the quay the four were conferring as to where to spend the night when a man appeared out of the gloom.

"Ealdorman Berengar!" he exclaimed with undisguised relief. "Thank the Rowan we've finally found you!"

Berengar spun to face him and searched his memory for the name to go with a vaguely familiar face.

"Ah yes, its Scully, isn't it?" he said as the information clicked into place.

"Yes sire. Sire, you must return to Garway at once!"

They all stiffened at this and Esclados' hand instinctively slipped to his sword's pommel. Berengar groaned inwardly. This was most difficult. How could he disobey a direct order from the Grand Master.

"I'm afraid that won't be possible," he said, trying to make it sound as reasonable as possible and dreading that it might come to blows. Yet Scully's next words took the wind right out of his sails, and of the others too.

"No sire, you don't understand. Something terrible happened after you left. Master Rainer called men to him. We think it must've been whatever you said to him caused him to send birds out to all the castles along the border and east. But sire, someone put poison in his personal supply of mead. The Grand Master's dead! And so are the castellans of Seigor and Craws!"

"Sacred Trees protect us!" Esclados gasped in horror.

The others could only stand in stunned silence. Scully continued, voicing their thoughts.

"I know, it's beyond belief! Poor Captain Turville is driven to distraction trying to hold everything together. Before Yule we sent as many birds out as we could. Luckily those going west went before this evil wind started, and had it to their backs on the return. The word has come back from the border as far as Wolfscar, would you believe. The far north has sent back nothing yet, but that's hardly surprising given the snows. They may know nothing of the crisis. But Tarah, Redrock, and Laon all agree with the others. You're to be acting Grand Master until a vote can properly be held."

"What?" Berengar breathed in shock.

"You're to be acting Grand Master of the Order, sire. The other commanders thought that as you were the only one in full possession of the facts of the crisis, whatever it is, that you were best equipped to make any decisions."

Suddenly Esclados began to chuckle. "Sacred Root and Branch, my friend, this is a turn we could never have anticipated!"

Berengar turned to look at him as though he had lost his mind, until Esclados pulled him away from Scully and said softly in his ear. "Wake up, man! This is the best thing that could happen! Can't you see? Now you can move the whole Order against Edward! It will have to be done carefully, I grant you, but as acting Grand Master your word now carries weight. You don't have to say it's just our fears any more. You were one of the last alive to speak to Rainer. No-one will be any the wiser that any actions you order weren't what Rainer was planning anyway!"

"By the Trees!" Berengar whispered back, "you're right!"

"Sire," Scully interrupted them, his voice still urgent. "We've been looking for you for ages! More of the men are at the inn down the road. We were heading for Dinas Castle tomorrow morning to tell the captain there we hadn't found you – he's been co-ordinating the search around here. We need to let him know you're here."

The unspoken reproof was also there that Berengar needed to tell everyone what the next move was too.

"You're right, Scully. Forgive me." Berengar shook his head in wonderment. "This is all so unexpected. Lead on. We've nowhere planned to stay tonight, so your inn is as good a place as any, and we shall all no doubt think clearer in the warm with a meal inside of us."

Once inside it took until after the meal was past for Berengar to be able to plead for some time to think, and to escape to a room upstairs. Esclados kept Cwen and Swein downstairs for a tactful hour before pleading weariness, and leading them to their rooms. Of course, no sooner were they out of sight of the troop of soldiers than they hurried to Berengar's room. He opened the door to Esclados' soft tap and motioned them in.

For a moment there was an awkward silence as they all found a seat. Cwen found she could not trust herself to speak. After all they had been through, this seemed to be so unfair. It was the one summons she knew Berengar could not ignore. And although she could see that having him as Grand Master seriously aided their cause, at the same time she dreaded losing him as the leader of their own quest. Esclados went and clasped Berengar by the shoulders.

"Oh my dear friend, this is a weight for you to bear and no mistake. And only you can decide what you're going to do. I wish I could help you, but I've a feeling anything I say will only make things harder for you."

Berengar gave a wan smile, briefly gripping Esclados' hand before turning to the others. Seeing Cwen's pale face, he went to her and took both her hands in his as he sat on the bed beside her.

"Actually," he said addressing them all, "I've already made up my mind."

"You have?" Swein wondered in surprise.

"Oh yes! It wasn't so hard. Obviously I have to go back to Garway, and as fast as possible. For a start, with Craws and Seigor leaderless, I need to get men installed there as fast as possible, but at least I can make sure they will be men I can count on to act as I see fit. Esclados, you'll come with me to Kiln and then go with some of the men to Dinas."

He saw the other two's puzzled expressions and explained. "Dinas is only small, but it is the nearest castle the Order has to the capital. Esclados, I want you to put the captain fully in the picture. Edward is to be watched from now on. Then I want you to go on to Laon to explain to Ealdorman Warwick there. Redrock is sufficiently clued up as to what's happening to make do with a message. Cwen, you and Swein will go down to Tarah Castle for the same reason. That means Edward will be encircled by Knights who now no longer trust him and will watch him like a hawk. I don't want that bastard escaping justice!"

Cwen gave a ragged gasp and threw her arms around Berengar's neck. "Oh thank you!" she sobbed. "I feared duty would drag you away and tie you down."

Enjoying the embrace, Berengar held her tight as he replied.

"Duty, yes! But not away from you or what needs to be done." He stroked her hair comfortingly – an action that did not escape Esclados' gaze. Holy Spirits, he thought, he loves her!

However, Berengar then eased Cwen away from him so that he could look not only into her eyes, but also those of the others. "This changes nothing, do you hear me? Nothing! I have to make sure our border with New Lochlainn is secure for when the snow melts in the spring, but that won't take more than a couple of weeks once I'm at Garway. Then I'm getting at least a battalion and we're riding on Arlei. I want at least half a battalion from each of the places you're going to to join me at Dinas by the last week of Imbolc. That gives us seven weeks to congregate our forces. I'd plan for sooner if this weather wasn't so awful, but I don't want to march on Edward with fewer men than he already has at his call in the countryside around Arlei. We have to encircle him, and then get all the major nobles and Churchmen to a court gathering. Move too soon and it'll look like we've imprisoned Edward for weeks, and that might get him some sympathy. In front of the assembled court I intend to expose him as a DeÁine infiltrator."

"You think they'll believe you?" a stunned Swein asked.

"Yes. In fact it was you, Swein, who gave me the idea."

"Me?"

"You said he boasted about his hairlessness. If necessary I'll have him stripped naked and paraded through the Great Hall at Arlei for all to see. Stripped of his finery they'll have to look at the man. And what they'll see is someone unusually pale and hairless with colourless eyes, which is a combination no natural Islander ever has. There'll be no way that Edward can claim pure descent from the Mar family. What none of you know is that at a secret location, known only to the Ealdormen, we have three DeÁine defectors. I intend to bring these with me when I ride on Arlei. Stood next to those DeÁine, who all senior Knights can swear to as being the real thing, Edward's bloodline will be blindingly obvious.

"Even the most self-serving noble surely won't be dumb enough to openly support Edward under those circumstances. I don't care whether they then vote to string him up from the nearest battlement, or bury him in a dungeon for the foreseeable future. We then have time to gather more evidence, but more importantly, if the DeÁine attack we can organise a defence by men who will stand, not fold and let them in."

Comforted, Cwen shortly allowed Esclados to escort her to her room, with Swein leaving in their wake. Yet afterwards Esclados returned to his commander.

Berengar wearily opened the door but admitted, "I thought you left too easily. I should have known you'd have more to say."

Esclados closed the door and leaned on it, folding his arms across his ample front and giving Berengar a very knowing look.

"Did you think I wouldn't catch on?"

"About what?"

"Oh come on, Berengar, after all these years did you think that I, of all people, wouldn't notice when you fell head over heels in love?"

This time it was Berengar who was lost for words. Esclados gave a conspiratorial grin.

"Oh, don't worry, I won't tell, and for what it's worth I doubt she realises the depths of your feelings for her. It's why I'm sure she has no idea that you're sending her to Tarah to keep her safe. That *is* what you're doing, isn't it?"

"Curse you, you crafty old man," Berengar grumbled, but without any malice. "Alright, yes, I am sending her away to keep her safe. If I had my way, I'd ship her way off to Ergardia on the next boat – except that she'd come straight back!" He groaned and sat heavily on the bed. "Does life always have to be this complicated? I want nothing more than to wrap her in goose down and put her somewhere so safe that she'll never be hurt again. But that amazing spirit of hers, which draws me to her, is the very thing that would have her running a mile from me if I did that. I have to let her be the person she is, don't I?"

"Unfortunately, yes you do," Esclados said, coming to sit by him. "For what it's worth, I think you're doing the right thing. You have to give Cwen something to do or she'll take herself off, and who knows what she'd get mixed up in. But I too want her as far away from the court as possible when we tackle Edward. I've been thinking all along that she and Swein need to be invisible when we actually bring that bastard down. It has to be a legitimate move. There can't be a hint of revenge, or it might all backfire on us. It still might do, and those two have sacrificed enough to bring us this far. I'd never forgive myself if either of them came to any harm. I think Tarah is an inspired choice. In fact, if you keep on like this I wouldn't be at all surprised if they don't make you Grand Master permanently!"

The next morning was stressful beyond belief for them all. Berengar had split the searchers into two, with one group as escort for himself and Esclados, which would then divide again when he and Esclados went their separate ways. However, over half of them were going under Scully's command as escort to Cwen and Swein. For the first time in his life, Swein found himself wrapping his arms around a sobbing woman as he held Cwen and comforted her. It had come far too quickly after having left the loving warmth of her family's home for her to cope with another separation with any composure.

Luckily Scully was a decent and kindly man who caught on quickly to Swein's brief explanation, and allowed Cwen an extra hour to have a mug of caff and calm down before they too set off. As they rode off southwards towards Tarah, Swein made sure Bracken was side by side with Twigglet so that he could reach out every now and then and give Cwen's hand a squeeze. The men-at-arms surrounded them and it was an otherwise quiet day's ride. Indeed the whole journey took on an unreal quality. Halfway there the snow suddenly disappeared. One minute they were walking the horses between banks of snowdrifts, and then the next they were out into fields that had barely seen a frost. All of them stopped and looked back in amazement at the snow-covered landscape behind. It was as though a straight line had been drawn across the countryside.

"That can't be natural," someone said, voicing all their thoughts.

"No, and it probably isn't," Scully spoke earnestly, "so the sooner we get to Tarah and warn them the better."

And on the clearer roads they were now able to move at double the speed. A mere eight days after leaving Berengar, the troop rode in under the great gate of Tarah Castle to a warm welcome by the captain in charge. This far from the dangers of the DeÁine, Cwen expected to find some old Knight on the verge of retirement in command, sent to one of the easier spots to guard for his last few years service. It therefore came as something of a shock to learn that the commander was a real firebrand who regularly ran off Attacotti raiders, and who had set off days ago for Arlei, after a message arrived saying that Edward was purportedly leading an army out against a DeÁine threat. Word had come of Edward's departure hard on the heels of the strange storm at New Year, and the commander had set off determined to find out what was going on.

So much for guarding against Edward, Cwen's thoughts howled in frustration. The young captain left in charge was awaiting replacement, as he was only newly risen from his sickbed having lost a leg in a running skirmish with a heavily armed band of Attacotti before Yule. Even as she smiled sympathetically at his frustration at not being able to be more help, Cwen wanted to run outside and scream at this setback. Luckily Swein made some excuse she did not even register, and managed to get her away from the men, and up to the guest rooms which looked out over the sea.

Once there and alone, Cwen spent several minutes punching out her frustration on the mattress until she could trust herself to speak. Swein was startled at her actions, but could not help thinking that his life would have been so much better if the people in his past life had pummelled a bolster of feathers, instead of him, when things got too much. Finally she sat up, flushed, and with strands of hair escaping from her plait.

"Sorry about that," she said with a ruffled smile, "…just got too much!"

"Quite," was Swein's disconcerted agreement.

"Oh Swein, what are we going to do?"

He shrugged and went to look out of the window for a moment before he spoke. "I guess the one good thing is that the commander of this place could be at Dinas when Esclados gets there. Or maybe they'll even meet on the way there, so he'll hear the whole thing from someone with more authority than we have. That way he can't dismiss us or drag his feet about doing what Berengar wants, can he?"

Cwen heaved a sigh of relief and gave Swein's arm a hug as she joined him by the window. "Oh my, that's a comforting thought, isn't it? So maybe it isn't all going quite so bad after all."

Berengar himself would have been heartened by the faith his beloved had in him, for life was getting more complicated by the day. Esclados and he had ridden with their escort with the best speed they could muster in the appalling weather, and had congratulated themselves on reaching the grange at Kiln by the end of the third day. However, the captain in charge of the grange was effusive in his welcome, and not simply because of the news that the new Grand Master had been found alive and well, and was on his way back to Garway to take command. Barely giving the weary travellers time to ease off cold wet clothes and sit down to a much needed meal, he sprang his own news.

"Sire …I don't know what this means, but an army passed through here five days ago, just after Scully left us."

"An army?" Esclados exclaimed, almost choking on his dinner. "Where in the Islands did an *army* come from?"

"It was the king. The king's mobilised as many troops as he can find and he's heading for Caersus. He must've done it with speed, because the men stripped the town bare, and none too gently."

Esclados and Berengar looked at one another with total shock. However had Edward found out they'd been to Caersus? All this time they had been worrying about getting men on their side, had they got it all wrong? Should they have tried to depose Edward, and then worry about justifying it afterwards?

In a ragged voice Berengar asked, "Did they say why the king marches on Caersus?"

The captain shrugged in puzzlement. "The men we spoke to said they'd heard there was a *DeÁine* army on the way, and that they were going to stop it, if you can believe that."

Berengar and Esclados exchanged glances again. So Edward was not making it clear to those around him why they were going to Caersus of all places. Was that because he knew he was on shaky ground? Was he also hoping to get the evidence that they had sent to Tarah with Cwen and Swein, and then justify his movements afterwards?

"How many men were in this army?" Berengar asked out of curiosity.

"That's the odd thing, sire," the bemused captain told him. "By my men's nearest approximation there were around four thousand all told, most of them foot soldiers, hardly any cavalry. What sort of army are they planning on fighting? If the DeÁine are invading they'll be coming in their tens of thousands, won't they? Anyway their army will surely have to be mounted for the most part, because a march from New Lochlainn in this snow and ice would take so long half the troops would die on the road."

"Indeed," Esclados solemnly agreed. "It seems unlikely that there is really a DeÁine threat, because no experienced general would lead men into battle so outnumbered."

"Oh, and that's something else," the captain remembered, "there were no generals with them!"

"No generals?" Now Berengar was really alert. What was Edward up to? This sounded as though they had him on the run, for why else would Edward go into battle without experienced leaders? And four thousand men? The captain was right, it was no force to pit against an invading army of DeÁine, but it was a neat superiority of numbers to send against the men he had led to Seigor. It would enable Edward to take control of the situation with little loss of life on his side, and keep anyone who might let slip the truth cooped up until he could deal with them.

Suddenly he realised the captain was speaking to him again, "…so what are we going to do, sire?"

He covered his inattention with a cough as Esclados came to his rescue.

"Well, you were quite right to think it's unlikely that the DeÁine were on the attack. Ealdorman Berengar was consulting with Grand Master Rainer because we'd heard that King Edward might be hatching some plot to make history repeat itself, and dissolve the power of the Order."

"Sacred Trees!" the captain and his men swore.

Berengar caught on to where Esclados was going with this. "Precisely. Caersus is almost certainly a blind in order to make a strike at Seigor and then Garway. It's rather convenient, don't you think, that both stand leaderless just at this moment? Captain, I want to you to send word with all haste tomorrow to all our places east of here. Tell them to pull back from the granges and any preceptories lacking heavy defences. Get word out that any between here and Arlei are to make for Laon, Redrock or Tarah. I'll not have our men losing their lives because of random attacks by a maniac! We mustn't give that mad man any opportunity to strike at us and take the initiative. Get everyone to safety and then let's see what he's up to. We mustn't be seen to be taking the bait.

"We have to force his hand and make him come out in the open. I'm sure the reason there are no senior officers with him is because he knows he's on dangerous ground, and that they'd want proof of whatever he intends to accuse us of before they'd sanction military action. We, however, will leave before first light and ride with all speed for Garway. The Order must be prepared for the worst." He sighed, "I never dreamed I would become Grand Master, let alone in circumstances such as this."

"What puzzles me," Esclados pondered, "is how he got the army assembled and on the march without the top officers? Surely at least one or two of them would have been in Arlei or nearby? Wouldn't they think it strange if part of the army just upped and marched off without them? Unless…"

The word hung in the air, pregnant with meaning, but all were thinking of the sudden demise of their own Grand Master. If Edward could engineer that in the heart of the Order's own most secure castle, how easy would it be to murder the army generals in the relaxed security of the capital?

Chapter 13

 Subterfuges and Seductions

Brychan: Aer Yule to Yule

Jacinto stared moodily into the cup of rather tepid nettle tea. For days now he had been cooling his heels in the refectory at Garway. Chaos had broken loose in the castle, and with the Grand Master now dead, everyone seemed to have forgotten about his existence. A week had gone by since Swein and Cwen had left, with Berengar and Esclados hard on their heels. At first Jacinto had been delighted to see the back of them. The two Knights were the only ones who might let on how closely he had come to being dismissed as a squire from the Order. In fact it was bliss not to have to watch his every move in case one or the other of them was watching him. At least at first.

Then day by day the realisation had dawned that nobody was watching him at all. For someone who had been used to being at the centre of some sort of attention for most of his life, total anonymity was an unnerving experience. An experience which gradually turned to anger. How dare they ignore him! Did they not realise that he was the only one left who might be able to tell them what had been behind Berengar's sudden and acrimonious departure? Not that he really understood what was going through the ealdorman's mind, but at least he had been there on every step of the journey so far, and that made him important from his own perspective. Yet despite his every effort to reach whoever was now in control, he constantly found himself back here in the refectory in isolation.

Had he known it, the harassed captain left in charge of sorting out the wreckage was being shielded by some very competent sergeants. All of them realised the severity of the situation facing the Order and the weight which had for now been thrown onto one junior officer, who, despite being a very promising and able leader, was nonetheless utterly unprepared for the situation he now found himself in. So, while he tried valiantly to deal with the larger issues at hand, they fielded all matters concerning the everyday running of the castle. That included making sure that a pompous squire, with inflated ideas of his own importance, was not given the chance to take up precious time with his whining complaints. Some of the men who had come with Ealdorman Berengar had let it slip that Jacinto was regarded as a grade-one pain in the neck by everyone from their leader down. And given that many of these were men with impressive records and considerable experience, they were listened to.

The consequence was that Jacinto was ignored by all and sundry, in the hope that one day he would just disappear, and save them all the trouble of deciding what to do with him. Ten days after the others left, Jacinto did just that. In the depth of night he collected his things, raided the kitchens for a generous supply of food and, as soon as the gates opened for the new day, took a horse and left. His luck held in that his departure coincided with a milder spell in the weather. The worst of the snow held off for the best part of a week, and he was able to make good time as he set his horse on the road to Arlei. Deep within him there was a burning desire to get to the capital and the king. If no-one else would listen to him, then surely the king would want to hear about those who were plotting his downfall, and how they aimed to do it?

By the time of the Yule festivities he was on the last stretch of his journey. The last day of the old year was spent riding his now exhausted horse through freezing rain, taking shelter that night in an isolated shed normally only ever used for lambing. It was a bitter and miserable end to a year he wanted to be able to forget as soon as possible.

However, come the morning the horse bared its teeth at him and snapped whenever he tried to mount up. The mare had had enough of her heavy-handed rider, and had picked up the scent of other horses and decent fodder on the wind. In the final attempt to mount up the beast won, and made it past him to bolt out of the door and out into the winter morning, where she set off in pursuit of better things. Swearing bitterly as his saddlebags disappeared with her, and the supplies they contained too, Jacinto set off on foot. That night he had to break into the back of a country inn and hide in a dark corner of the wash-house to get out of the cold, stealing breakfast as he slunk out before anyone noticed in their hung-over state from the ongoing festivities. By the end of that day, though, he had managed to get a lift from a wealthy if still inebriated merchant into the capital, and found himself within the massive walls of Arlei.

To his amazement here the festive season seemed to be taking a back-seat to other activities. It did not take long to find out that the rumour was that the DeÁine were going to attack. It also did not take him long to realise that when he told the people he met that the Knights were not coming, but that he was a Knight who had come alone to help fight, that he was treated as a hero and had food and drink bought for him. As he tried to find his way into the palace, he stopped at a different inn at each midday and each evening, oblivious to the increase in panic that he left behind him at each stop. Soon the rumour was spreading like wildfire that the Knights had retreated into their mountain castles and had left the people to fend for themselves. Everyone knew someone who'd talked to a lone Knight who had confirmed the story, it seemed.

In the hidden recesses of his subconscious, Eliavres was directing Jacinto on his mission to reduce the Arleians to panic with relish. He had originally planned to send the ambitious squire straight to the palace, but that was hardly necessary when the king seemed to be doing all his work for him without any prompting or aid. Now he was far more valuable inciting the populace to panic.

Up in his eyrie King Edward paced the floor by day, and ravished his way through his companions by night. Part of him was consumed by a burning excitement at the thought of approaching DeÁine, for the rumour had soon reached the palace, and Eliavres had subconsciously primed him to be receptive. Finally he would come into his own! This was the opportunity he had been waiting for the chance to get rid of the pestilent churchmen who held onto the exchequer and curbed his spending. They would be the first the DeÁine had hung! The ranks of their precious martyrs were about to get added to in some numbers! But most of all – best of all – the overbearing, sanctimonious Knights would be hounded to the Underworld.

Yet he still had to be cautious. To overplay his hand now was to lose all. He must be seen to be doing all in his power to protect his people. Edward had every intention of coming out of this with a glowing reputation that would go down in the written histories, and of being spoken of for generations as the saviour of his people. So this was going to be handled with great finesse, and Edward flattered himself that when it came to such things there was nobody better. However much it galled him so be inactive, he was going to sit tight and let the people of the capital see in great detail how he was calling troops to him, how he was having the captains drill them and bring them to a state of full readiness.

How he had refrained from laughing in the faces of the pompous Churchmen who had come to see him, he would never know. Puffed up with their own importance, they had presumed to tell him – him, Edward the Great – that he should send to the Knights for advice, and hand on all the intelligence he had concerning this new threat. He wished he could tell them that there was no intelligence, or at least not of the kind that they thought. It was his own brilliance which had deduced the threat! His incredible intelligence! The dreams that came every night now were so stunning in their clarity. So detailed! Beautiful in the simplicity of their plans!

He had always felt a kinship with the DeÁine, and as he had grown older he had observed his body developing differently to other young men – and by the Wild Hunt he had taken advantage of the bodies of enough of them to know! He remembered early feelings of inadequacy as the teenage boys around him had boasted as their genitals had developed, and grown hair around them, while his had remained baby smooth and small. But by the time others were also gaining facial hair, he had realised he was not abnormal but special. No, more than special – unique! He had remained in a pure state by his way of thinking, even though his sex drive was, if anything, even more aggressive than the most randy of his contemporaries. And then he had found the fun that could be had with dildos and other toys, and had never felt he was missing out on anything ever again!

In the midst of his adolescent sexual explorations he had encountered a young soldier, fresh from the frontier, who had put things in a whole new light. The soldier had become even more excited as Edward had undressed, proclaiming he had always wanted to fuck a DeÁine. Of course, having pumped him for details as he allowed the soldier show him new variations on pleasures which had been learned as a prisoner, he could not let him live. The man had disappeared into an unmarked grave, but leaving Edward with a tantalising new possibility before him.

Over the years Edward had then traced people who had worked at the manor where he had been born, and others who had cared for him in infancy. It had taken years, because Edward knew that if everyone started dying too close together people would get suspicious. Now, though, he was confident that there was nobody left who knew that the babe born to the Earl of Mar's mistress was a DeÁine. But he knew! And he was convinced the DeÁine would know as soon as they saw him. He was sure he was a pure blood – after all, his mother had been raped by one or more of a pack of DeÁine Hunters, and they were an elite. No common slave could ever have reached such a peak of destructive artistry. That had to be where his sophisticated talent for pleasure and pain came from. Just the thought of it all was making him excited, and he called for a servant.

"Bring me a woman!" he commanded.

"A woman?" the servant, who was new, asked in astonishment. He had been told the king only ever took men to his bed.

"Yes, a woman, you dolt! …I feel like a change! Make sure she's young."

"A virgin?" the servant asked nervously.

"Jolnir's balls! No! I don't want some whimpering, snivelling thing that won't join in the fun! Get me a high-class whore. The best dissembler the local madams can provide!"

"Dissembler ….whore …yes sire," the servant cringed, wondering how in the Islands he was even going to go find out which were the best whore houses, let alone find a young, attractive whore in the time his master was likely to give him.

Luckily for him, the other servants were better prepared for their master's whims. An old hand, by virtue of his survival for over a decade in the precarious position of the king's household, sent a messenger to a place that gloried in the name of Dirty Nelly's.

"Are you sure?" the new servant asked as he gnawed at his fingernails in terror. "With a name like that aren't they likely to all be poxed to the eyeballs?"

"Doesn't matter if they are," the old timer replied with confidence, "you don't think he's going to use his own tool, do you?" Then took in the new man's flabbergasted expression. "Look, you'd better get used to this and quick! That girl, whoever she turns out to be, is never going to live out the night. His lordship occasionally likes to have a whore or two because he says they're better at pretending he's the best fuck they've ever had (not in those words, of course!). But he's not going to take the risk of her going back to the whorehouse, and telling every poxy soldier who ploughs her after that, that the king's got the smallest one she's ever seen. So small she couldn't even tell he was there! And I know that 'cos one gasped it to me with her dying breath – wanted me to let the girls know that he couldn't pleasure any woman she'd ever met, in order to get her revenge on him for her suffering. …So don't stare if he's disrobed when you take his bath water in! It's the only way to keep your head on your shoulders round here!"

"Sacred Trees!"

"Not round here, sonny! They left this shit hole to its own destruction years ago! If you feel like praying, go to one of the chapels in the town. They might hear you then! And speaking of the town …that's why we use the whorehouses where no-one knows or cares who goes missing. The good houses won't send anyone these days! A good girl with a bit of talent, who keeps herself clean (and has the wit to spot a poxed customer before he gets to her), can earn a fortune for the pimp or madam. There used to be the Underworld to pay when Him up there started sending back bodies in bits! Some of the whorehouse owners got pretty nasty – threatened to go elsewhere, like Dinas. Close enough for them to catch the capital trade, but not close enough for Himself to grab their best earners. And to add insult to injury, the bodies which came back whole enough to be inspected showed …well …no signs of a normal man's pleasure…"

"…Then how does he …?"

"…Some very nasty toys if he wants to penetrate them, and I mean nasty! Some wood, some metal, even some with barbed bits on 'em! I've even heard he uses some so big they split folk open! Though that usually goes on down in the dungeon! But I've seen some strong men come up from guarding that place as white as sheets and needing several stiff drinks before their hands stop shaking. The only person he could find to do the clearing up down there without passing out, or puking all over it, is an old slaughterhouse-man whose sight's going. He carts the worst out in sacks, and then others go in and sluice the walls and floor down after Himself's had one of his real bad sessions."

"Sacred Trees! Oh Spirits! …Oh Spirits… Oh crap!" The man gulped convulsively just at the thought.

"Yes, so be prepared for the worst if you're still on duty when he's done with her. If you think you might puke, don't have dinner tonight. And remember – that won't be the worst he's done."

The young servant nodded mutely, and went to beg a mug of ale from the kitchens to fortify himself with for the events to come.

Oblivious to the discussion below, Edward had had the fires in his rooms stoked against the winter night and was now wandering through them in impatience, stark naked beneath a fur-lined velvet wrap. Until, that was, he came to a framed old map on the one wall. It showed the full land mass of Brychan – even though the part the DeÁine had held for so long had little detail on it – and it showed just how big the whole Island really was. Taking a sip of strong sweet wine from the glass he had been dangling from one hand, he placed it on a window ledge, and took a drag from his ornate small pipe filled with smoking poppy seed in his other, before he began masturbating before the image.

"Mine all mine!" he panted, his excitement rising as he imagined himself being proclaimed as a lost prince of the DeÁine, and being processed in splendour into a city where an array of slaves of every imaginable kind were paraded naked before him for his personal selection and delight. Luckily for the whore, he had been sucking on the pipe the whole time, so that as he orgasmed he also passed out, and was insensible by the time she arrived.

In a nearby dwelling Eliavres' body lay equally inert, but in his case this was because his spirit had left his body and had risen to watch the spectacle in the royal chambers. Unfortunately for the whore, Eliavres needed to feed his disembodied self, and so, when the servants sent her in through the door of the main chamber without looking, they were not to know that what happened was not their master's doing. The poor girl found herself enmeshed in a writhing white mist which then, oblivious to her screams, sucked her life force without conscience, leaving her a battered, empty shell.

Satiated, Eliavres drifted to the prostrated king. What exactly he had been thinking as he had climaxed, Eliavres did not know. Entering a resistant, conscious body could not normally be done without loss of its life, for the shock was too great. He therefore had to wait until sleep or something else rendered his target insensible. However, Eliavres was getting to know the twists and turns of Edward's mind quite well after so many nights, and the map was a good clue.

Sliding into the king's mind, Eliavres began sifting through the new information which had appeared since his last visit. What a puny race to think that so few men amounted to an army! Even with the new company which had just arrived, the force at Edward's command was not even a third of the DeÁine army that approached the border. Walking the streets the previous night to listen to the effects of his rumour-mongering, Eliavres had had a brilliant idea, and now he prepared to put it into play. The four female members of the Abend were approaching with speed, having driven the snow clouds before the DeÁine army to prevent any falls slowing their passage, but also to isolate the dreaded Order of the Knights of the Cross in their high castles. Their destination was Caersus, for Eliavres was sure the Gorget still lay hidden there. But now he insinuated a thought into Edward's mind.

Tell your army to march immediately, he told Edward. *March with all speed on Caersus and you shall have a great victory over a DeÁine army! Don't worry, it's only conscripted slaves – they won't put up much of a fight – but your generals and the Knights aren't to know that. Give the people of Brychan a decisive victory over the DeÁine and you'll be fêted in the streets! And who'll be able to say you don't know how to win a war then? The DeÁine won't mind. The slaves mean nothing to them, and it'll show them you're a man to be treated with respect! Act decisively and the Divine Power will be with you! Neither snow nor ice will stand in your way, and that will show your favour with the higher beings for even the most foolish to see.*

Like a dreaming dog, Edward already began moaning and twitching on the floor in his excitement, and Eliavres withdrew, smugly considering how easy it was to get things done when you had such compliant tools. Of course there would not be any easy victory at all. With any luck the Brychan army would be wiped out, but Eliavres looked forward to the chaos which would ensue when it was discovered that the king of Brychan was languishing in a DeÁine dungeon. It might even produce a premature and ill prepared strike at New Lochlainn to try to get him out – which would suit the Donns and the DeÁine army nicely, thank you very much. And he, Eliavres, would take the credit!

He was even happier when the next day dawned to frantic activity in the capital. No sooner was there light to see by, than companies of soldiers were seen heading out of the gates. Taking a walk down to a pie shop on the main street to find breakfast, he overheard two men, whom he took to be very senior captains or even commanders, talking as they sat on their horses watching the men file out.

"Spirits! I wish Earl Richert were still alive!" the one said with heartfelt sorrow.

"I know what you mean," his companion replied. "He'd soon have put a stop to this nonsense. What in the Islands are we marching on *Caersus* for anyway? Does anyone except the king know?"

"Doubt it!" his friend grumbled. "Bloody fool's errand if you ask me. And look at the weather! We're going to freeze our nuts off in this snow! Where, in the name of all that's sacred, does he think we're going to billet the men each night? If they have to camp out, half of them will be crippled with frostbite before we get there."

"I know, I know! But nobody knows where General Wensome is. He hasn't been seen since the summer. And General Murgatroyd is walking around like a ghost. You can't get two sane words out of the man. Someone said the rumour in the barracks is that his three young sons were fetched to the palace – and you know what Himself is like for the kiddies!"

"Dirty bastard! It's about time one of his fancy boys did us all a favour and cut his dick off while they're playing in that dungeon! …Oh sod it! Here we go." The last foot soldier had passed them, and a line of cavalry came up which the two men urged their horses out in front of. "Oh well, better make the best of another shitty wild goose chase, I suppose."

Eliavres took a bite of the apple and dried apricot pie, and savoured it with delight. The world was good today! Not only was Edward's army going to be outnumbered by more than three to one, but they were probably not even going to be fit to fight when they got there. The DeÁine army might hardly lose a slave let alone a soldier, and that would make the Donns very happy with Eliavres! Not much chance of the king's body guard keeping him safe either! *And who will take the credit for that little coup?* Eliavres thought smugly, *and, oh look, here he comes…*

King Edward himself appeared, dressed in sumptuous furs over a totally impractical, jewel-bedecked breastplate and gold-plated armour, on a pretty prancing white horse. Except that Eliavres could see that the ostlers had obviously given Edward a sprightly mare, which would create the right impression of a dashing rider, without actually entrusting a fully trained war-stallion to such an inexperienced handler. The DeÁine warlock chuckled to himself as he watch Edward go dancing off to his doom. Then remembered he had to get the fool to Caersus on time, so hurried back to his rooms with a second pie to do something about the weather, and to inform the others to expect the company of the king. For good measure he also sent his minion into the ranks of the army.

Jacinto was welcomed with open arms as an experienced fighter, and soon found himself as second-in-command to a young captain in charge of a company of foot soldiers. This was more like it! Straight from squire to officer rank was proof to himself that he had made the right decision to come here. Of course he was not looking forward to the march – that promised to be cold and miserable – but there was the chance of a battle at the end of it. A real battle against another army, and Jacinto knew that in real battles men got promoted fast when others fell. He did not think he had much to worry about when it came to his own safety. After all, he was bigger and stronger than almost anyone around him, so all he had to do was watch his back and fight at his best, which he was sure would be better than any of the opposition.

As he strode along with a smile on his face he heard hooves behind him. Turning to look up at the rider he saw the most resplendently clad man he had ever laid eyes on. For his part Edward could not believe his luck. Reining in his horse to walk beside the strikingly dark and wonderfully muscled young man, he demanded his name.

"Oooh, Jacinto is it," he purred when the reply came. "Well when we make camp you just report to my tent, Jacinto! I'm sure we have lots to talk about and I'm sure you won't be disappointed." Then more softly as he spurred the horse onwards, "I know I won't be!"

Jacinto also felt deliriously happy, and could not understand why the captain asked him if he was actually going to go. The man was mad, why would he *not* go? Why camp on the hard ground when, for doing nothing more than he had with Swein, he could sleep in comfort. He was not that naïve that he did not realise what the king wanted him for. After everything that Swein had said about Edward's tastes he had almost been counting on being spotted, but he would not be such a wimp as Swein had been. Edward would find out what it was like to have his equal between the sheets! Although he was betting that out here the king had furs on his bed, not sheets. Jacinto had always wondered what it would be like having sex on real fur – all soft and silky and rippling! Oh yes, this was going to be a time he never forgot!

As the New Year celebrations got underway two days later, Eliavres knew that his message had got through to the four witches. They had always had much greater success at handling the weather than he had. He was watching the cavorting in the street below his window when he saw people stop what they were doing, and point up to the sky and start screaming. In the far distance he could see a huge flight of rooks wheeling and diving, presumably sent to find where Edward's men were. But then he realised why the rooks had all headed off to land when he saw the storm cloud behind them. He could not help but laugh! Those four could be so inspired! Tonight of all nights to summon the spectre of the Wild Hunt was just too delicious for words!

The first of the howling gale and its riders screamed overhead as Eliavres capered at his window. But then something did not feel right and stopped him in his tracks. What *was* that up there? The leading edge of the storm had been sculpted with the Power, and that had temporarily blinded his sense to the glamour attached to it. Something he had most definitely *not* asked for, and he hurriedly reached out to Edward's army to shield it. The blast of the wind then reached up to the city and rattled the house, and he knew that it would have cleared the path for the army, even if he was beginning to have some worrying thoughts about what else it was doing.

For behind the animated cloud he could also already see the sky low on the horizon tinged with red, and then he began to smell smoke. Was that the outskirts of Arlei burning or the towns beyond turning into infernos? Then he looked upwards again. What had the witches done? Suddenly Eliavres shivered and began to wonder whether they might be working to their own agenda. None of the four were exactly trustworthy or subservient. Were they making their own bid for power and about to undermine him if he was not careful? Could they really have summoned some ancient demon of these lands? Struck some deal with a malevolent spirit? To carve up the Islands between them?

An even nastier thought occurred to him. Rumour had it that the very earth of Ergardia was toxic to those DeÁine with the Power, so had those witches offered the least useful Island to another force in exchange for help in gaining control not only over the Islanders, but to steal a march on the other Abend too? Curses! That could ruin all his plans! But now the attached glamour descended from the clouds and touched the ground just in front of the city walls in a sheet of septic light, and he could feel a gut-wrenching compulsion rolling off it. *Kill!* it said within his mind as it brushed over his lodgings, and beneath his window he could begin to see mayhem breaking loose on the streets. *Sacred Temples*, he thought, *what have you witches done? You'll wreck everything if you're not careful!*

Then the smell of smoke pressed itself more urgently on his senses, and he realised that a more immediate problem was how to get out of the city before it all went up in flames and him with it. Near immortal he might be, but even his body could not withstand cremation. Grinding his teeth with frustration, he pulled in more Power of his own, and prepared to batter his way out of the maelstrom of writhing humanity which tore at one another oblivious to the approaching firestorm.

Chapter 14

Seeking Redemption

Brychan: Eft-Yule

A week later Jacinto wondered what he could possibly have been thinking of to ever have wanted to be with Edward. His body screamed in agony in places where he had not known it was possible to feel pain. And it was not just the shock of walking for a dozen miles a day, sometimes knee deep in snow, when he was used to riding. The gnawing cold, frostbite, and the aching muscles of marching in the freezing conditions, were nothing to the sufferings of the nights. *Where does Edward get his strength from*, his mind silently screamed?

When they had undressed together for the first time, Jacinto had believed that being twice as broad as Edward would ensure that he remained in control. Nothing could have been farther from the truth. The first time Jacinto had used his strength to try to pin Edward down, after Edward had slapped him, he found himself being flung across the tent like a toy. And then a punishment, one of many, had followed. To his horror, Jacinto had found himself screaming like a child in Edward's hands. The man knew all the pain centres of the body. He could have Jacinto jack-knifing in agony time and time again, until he thought his muscles would rip and his bones break apart, without ever leaving him so incapacitated that he could not march the next day. Nor did Jacinto's screams bring anyone to his aid. All those in the immediate travelling household were too used to Edward's ways, and too downright terrified of him, to dream of interfering.

After only one night Jacinto's feelings about Swein had already changed beyond his wildest imaginings beforehand. The frail little man he had so despised, and been so willing to use, had stood years of this treatment, when each coming hour repeatedly felt more agonising than Jacinto believed he could survive. Now he wished for this to stop more than he had ever wanted anything in his life. Indeed, it brought home the realisation that he had never really wanted before. All his previous demands now seemed petty, and far too easily gained, to have ever prepared him for his current torture. And alongside that, he had come to realise how stupid he had been, which tortured his soul as much as Edward wracked his body.

It was all too clear, now, that Berengar and Esclados had had a much clearer understanding of what Swein had been through, and he saw their sympathy for the other man in a very different light. And as for punishment! In an awful moment of revelation in the darkness before dawn of the first night, as Edward slept and he cowered in a corner of the tent, it came to Jacinto just how kind the ealdorman had really been. The shock of which made him retch. All his previous railings against authority had sorely tested those around him, yet they had never even begun to make him suffer as they might've done.

Even at the end, after the way he had behaved towards Swein – as such an absolute bastard, he now realised – had Berengar treated him even faintly like this? No! All Berengar had done was put him in close contact with Swein in a desperate attempt to reason with him. His eyes tearfully swung to where he knew the monster lay again at the thought of Swein. Too late, he now knew that Berengar had been trying to make him see how bad things could really get for someone through no fault of their own.

And that hurt as well. Because as he lay there, too traumatised to sleep, he remembered Swein telling him how he had run away from home and been picked up by the king and his men before he had even got inside the city walls. Poor beaten and lonely Swein had had his torment thrust upon him, without any chance of avoiding it. He, on the other hand, had arrogantly walked to it with some stupid, stupid notion that he could do what others had not – that he would tame Edward!

All his life Jacinto had shovelled off the blame for the mishaps and upsets in his life onto someone else. Anyone else but himself. Therefore being confronted with his own rampant folly was bad enough on that first night, and he had marched mechanically through the next day, with his mind still reeling as much from that as his body attempting to cope with its own experiences of the night. Yet in the following nights, when Edward finally slept and Jacinto hovered on the edge of terror and exhaustion, the whole sorry mess of his life unravelled before his mind's eye in gruesome detail. Every excess of Edward's dredged up some counterpart of his own from the past, as if each ill deed had been stored up to later be revisited upon him tenfold and all at once.

In a couple of nights Edward had achieved what years of the Knights' kindness had failed to do – he showed Jacinto himself, and Jacinto did not like what he saw. And if he had ever thought the men in the preceptories had ignored him, he now found out how wrong he had been. For, to the rest of this army he marched with, that one night in Edward's tent had rendered him invisible.

He left Edward's tent too late in the morning to eat at the camp fires, and nobody kept him anything, because they all resented the fact that they thought he was gorging himself on dainties at the king's table. At night it was no better, for he was summoned as soon as the tents went up, and Edward may have had foods of the finest quality prepared for himself, but he ate sparingly. The scraps Jacinto was picking up would have left him ravenous on a quiet day. On a forced march in arctic conditions, Jacinto was quite literally starving to death as his body rapidly burned what little food he got by marching and trying to keep warm, and then resorted to using all his reserves. In the depravations of this week alone his pants already hung off him, and the sleek and polished appearance he had prided himself on was gone in the haggard and exhausted man he caught sight of in Edward's mirrors.

However, the mirror Edward had held up to the man within was much more shattering. Jacinto's life was crumbling and being revealed in a cold hard light that hid nothing anymore. In sleep-deprived delirium, the people who had been around him all those years appeared in sad procession, each one sighing and shaking their heads at him. *We tried to warn you*, they seemed to be saying. *We feared it would come to this, but would you listen? Would you learn?* And in silent agony Jacinto mouthed the words "I'm sorry, I'm so, so sorry," over and over again to the shades of those who were not there.

But most of all, if he lived long enough, he wanted to tell Swein how sorry he was. That was, of course, if Swein could even bare to be in the same room as him anymore. For it was a measure of how swiftly and far Jacinto had fallen that he now saw their roles reversed. Swein was the one with the moral high ground. Swein had gone through all this and so much more, yet could be so brave as to go with Cwen to try to stop Edward. In his ravaged soul Jacinto suspected that, had he been in his place, he would have taken off in the opposite direction at the mere thought of taking on Edward at any level, and not stopped running until he reached the sea. He felt utterly worthless, even in comparison to those he had once despised the most.

Having attached himself to the string of camp followers, Eliavres also found Jacinto's state of mind vexing. The man never achieved a state of sleep deep enough for him to link minds with, and he had not done it often enough beforehand for it to be sufficiently familiar to Jacinto for him to allow it when only semiconscious. By now, with Edward, the king had barely to close his eyes before Eliavres could slither inside, but that was because Edward welcomed the visitor who came after his nightly exercises with the new toy. Yet Eliavres found it hard to gain a true sense of what was happening in the camp from Edward. The king had a warped perspective on everything, for his ego was central to all he saw. He saw his army as a shining example of rugged determination to fight for their king, first and foremost, and then their country.

No use at all to Eliavres, who wanted to know exactly how exhausted and demoralised the troops really were. He had counted on being able to use Jacinto for that, but whatever Edward was doing to the would-be Knight it was quite successfully destroying him before Eliavres had had his use out of him. Nor could Eliavres find a new minion. In such a cacophony of minds, all under stress, it was impossible to single out a new one, let alone find out if it belonged to someone who could be of any used. The nearest he had come to making a connection had turned out to be a drunken cook who was being beaten by the men for gobbing in the stew. That night Eliavres had had to throttle a lone, aged whore just to ease his frustration, and replenish his wasted psychic energy from the encounter.

On the second of Eft-Yule, the great mass of men had passed like a storm through the already traumatised town of Kiln, earning them the curses of the citizens, as freezing soldiers raided those unburned houses for every blanket and piece of food they could carry. Even Eliavres had been able to see that all was not well with the troops from such behaviour. Yet it hardly helped him. Such behaviour was absolutely normal for a DeÁine slave army on the move, but he had no idea whether that was the same in the Islands. The reactions of the local civilians hinted that it might not be, for instead of the passive acceptance at losing their hard-earned stores – as happened with the weary population of New Lochlainn – these folk attempted to fight back and barred their doors, sometimes successfully.

It made Eliavres wonder whether this army would stand and fight. The DeÁine armies were more frightened of the commissars at their backs, waiting to report anyone wavering to the Abend and their acolytes, than anything any enemy could throw at them. The pure-bred DeÁine had so successfully fostered a climate of fear and suspicion among their conquered people, that as long as there was a pure-bred DeÁine nearby, there would never be any question, even with a great army, of not going where they were pointed and then fighting. Edward's army, however, seemed to work on a very different basis. The officers were trying to maintain some semblance of discipline, but morale even amongst them seemed very low. When the troops ravaged Kiln, many officers were to be seen going round afterwards handing out purses in compensation, and telling locals to go to Arlei and draw replacement food from the army depots there. Yet they were also worried enough about the welfare of the men to be heard complaining that they had to have more food if they were to travel in such weather. Would such officers be willing to throw their men at overwhelming odds without a care?

Not that it was essential that the DeÁine army actively engaged Edward's, but for Eliavres personally it would be much better if he could be seen to give them a resounding victory. The DeÁine Donns could be distinctly dense at times, Eliavres knew, and he wanted to din it into their minds that he was the one who played by their rules. If the DeÁine army walked into Brychan unopposed, then the Donns were quite likely to miss the point that it was Eliavres who had told them about the Gauntlet in the first place. He had to be able to point to information provided by him which enabled them to be victorious, in contrast to Anarawd and Quintillean's defeats. Which all meant that Edward's army had at least to put up the appearance of wanting to fight, and in turn that meant that if they needed stirring up a bit he needed to know in advance.

When they reached Foel on the night of the sixth, Eliavres had dreadful palpitations that it might all fall apart, for he saw the army melting away into the town. The dread thought that the entire army might be deserting en masse drove him near to distraction for an hour, until he reached the walls of the town himself. Then he saw the state of the place, and almost thought about kissing Helga the next time he saw her in person, he was so happy.

The town was a scene of complete devastation. In the darkness of the winter night nobody had spotted that the town was burnt out within its stone defences. The wind which had roared through on New Year's night combined with Helga's glamour had hit Foel full on. Bodies entwined in the throes of death lay where they had fallen, many then rendered down to charred bone by the intensity of the heat from the fire which had indiscriminately devoured the living and dead alike. Many of those murdered by their neighbours were only distinguished from those who were solely victims of the fire by the arrowheads or sword remnants still embedded in them, or the bony fingers which still grasped one another's throats. And the ravenous army found nothing.

From there the force swung south-west for the three day march to Radport. Where the remnants of Foel's population had got to was immaterial. That was until the army began to encounter the stragglers of refugees on the road, where upon the officers had their work cut out for them. The men by now were desperate, and their hope at seeing the civilians in front turned to anger as they realised that they carried nothing but a few tattered clothes, and were as hungry as they were. Officers rode horses, who themselves were stumbling with lack of food, up and down the line trying to prevent angry scuffles and worse, with only minimal success. Many of the women were saved from violation simply because the soldiers were so driven by hunger as to lack the energy for lust. Then Radport came into view and the swollen, starving army of soldiers and refugees surged forward.

For Jacinto the march had become something out of a drunkard's nightmare of the Underworld. On the night that the army had camped within Foel's battered walls, it had struck him that Edward might have gone well and truly mad, even by his warped standards of sanity. No sooner had the royal procession found a place to pause, in what must once have been the main market square, than Edward ordered his tent erected. In the midst of the chaos, the royal servants scurried frantically to prepare the royal bed and bring in food. Yet as soon as Jacinto had been dragged into the royal presence, and the servants thankfully made a hurried exit from the tent, Edward had fallen face forward onto the bed in a stupor. Casting about him nervously, Jacinto spied the great basin of steaming water and, having checked that Edward was truly comatose, took advantage of the situation to bathe his cuts and bruises with the blissfully warm water. Had there been a razor to hand he might just have cut his own throat to end his torture, but Edward had no need of a barber himself, and had had one come to shave his pet on alternate days rather than leave a blade within anyone's reach.

A nervous hand whipped back the tent flap and shoved in a folding table with hot soup in a large goblet, and a whole duck which had been cut up and char-grilled over a camp fire. With eyes downcast the servants never even noticed Edward was asleep, or that Jacinto was standing unwatched for a change. From the bed there came a whiffling noise, and Jacinto saw Edward now twitching and writhing on his back in his dreams. Whatever the dream was, it was pleasant going by the state of Edward's rising state of arousal, and Jacinto only took a second to think before pouncing on the food and soup. He devoured everything of the duck, even cracking the bones to suck the marrow out of the larger ones. The hot soup warmed his belly for the first time since they had left Arlei, and afterwards he gulped down the sugary honey treats from the side plate, grimacing at their cloying sweetness but welcoming the much needed energy.

He slid the table back out without lifting the tent flap to reveal his face, and was washing the duck grease off his face when he was seized from behind as Edward wrenched his pants down and entered him. Expecting wrath for his theft of the food, Jacinto was shaken to the core to hear Edward laughing wildly with every thrust. After the first climax, Edward threw back the rear tent flap and looked out on the desolation of Foel, which only seemed to arouse him once more. To Jacinto's amazement, Edward capered in naked jubilation, before dragging him forward and ravaging him again, with the nauseatingly overpowering smell of wood-smoke and burnt flesh filling the tent. In the second he had looking Edward full in the face before he was once more on his hands and knees, Jacinto gasped at what he saw, for the king's eyes were swirling with a smokiness behind the lens as if the burning had crept within him.

Even stranger was that the king disdained to use any of his sex toys. Normally Edward's physical arousal withered long before his twisted mind had had its fill, and Jacinto had come to dread the king's collection of toys which he used to supplement his inadequate member with. Yet on that night the king had not paused even to don one of his ornate condoms, which in one way was easier on Jacinto by far, yet the other man's hands also explored every inch of Jacinto's well-endowed genitals on and on into the night in a way that Edward had never done before. And all the time the king only ever paused to look on the desolation that had been Foel, and laugh with maniacal delight, convincing Jacinto that he had indeed lost what little sanity he had ever had.

What Jacinto could not know was that on that night Eliavres temporarily took control of Edward. The sight of the carnage had driven Eliavres' need to know what Edward knew with such urgency as to prompt Edward's early descent into sleep, as the DeÁine war-mage hammered into his consciousness. What Eliavres found there only confirmed what he had suspected, and he now had great hopes for what might have happened at the Knights' great castles further down the road. So deeply had he plumbed Edward's depths that he found himself still entwined as the king awoke, and suddenly he realised that as long as he was careful he could share the king's body for once.

Eliavres' experiments with the Power had rendered him sterile, as was usual for one of the Abend, and feeling Edward's lust flowing through his body brought on a sudden longing for what he had lost. His own hunger fuelled Edward's and together they buggered the hapless Jacinto with none of the king's normal preambles. And, as Eliavres had not previously lingered for Edward's usual nightly exertions, he failed to realise how out of character it was for Edward to behave as he did. Of course Eliavres would have preferred it if Edward had been entertaining a woman on that night, but years with such sensory deprivation meant that even Jacinto was welcome when he could be relished firsthand. It was Eliavres' delight that Jacinto witnessed, for he could see how little opposition the oncoming DeÁine army could expect now, and the submerged Edward drank in the exaltation and was intoxicated by it too.

Come the morning, a shattered Jacinto crawled out of the tent exhausted, but at least with a fur-lined jacket hidden under the old cloak that he had also managed to filch while Edward finally slumbered again. Clutching the old cloak tight around him, he managed the next day's march largely due to the hidden jacket giving him some desperately needed warmth for the first time since his ordeal began. When the camp was made the next night he worried what to do with his ill-gotten gains. He had no baggage of his own any more, and anyway he feared that the other servants might steal it while he was in the royal presence. Finally he decided to undo the jacket so that he could shrug it off with the cloak as he entered, and then drop it by the entrance where Edward would ignore it, but far enough in to stop petty theft by the servants.

This time he got little in the way of food, but Edward too must have been exhausted after the strange night before. No sooner had he eaten, than the king strolled to his bed and toppled onto it fast asleep. A stunned Jacinto could hardly believe his luck, then pulled the covers over the slumbering king and began to explore the contents of the tent. No weapon presented itself again, but he wrapped himself in several of the rugs and curled up by the heaped up brazier to get his first proper night's sleep in something that passed for warmth.

The morning bugles gave him plenty of warning, and he escaped before Edward fully woke and could question him. The next night saw resumption of Edward's more normal habits, but with no mention of the two previous nights to Jacinto's relief but puzzlement. Yet it did give Jacinto some cause for hope. Every day brought him a bit closer to Caersus and once they reached there he knew from what Berengar and Esclados had said that there was a grange there. If he could just hold on for a bit longer, and if Edward's decline continued, then there might come a point when he could affect an escape from this living nightmare.

With the next day came the prospect of Radport, and that night the army streamed into the riverside market town like the plague. For hours total chaos reigned. The famished troops looted and plundered, taking over houses as they came to them, and with the latecomers willing to fight those who had seized houses first for the chance to spend a night in the warm and dry. Wild animals would have behaved better, and the local people alternately wept and fought to preserve what little they had. Here too the hand of the Abend witches had struck heavily in the poorer quarters, but the main body of the town – built with better materials, and whose citizens had not been so drunken as to be easily manipulated – had survived unscathed until the army arrived.

The officers soon gave up any attempt to instil order, and instead hurried to find fodder and stabling for their cruelly deprived horses. Edward took over the largest inn in the main square for himself, and was soon joined by his leading men who, having finally arrived at the chance to pause for breath, now presented Edward with their vociferous complaints at the way the whole campaign was being conducted. For this night Edward had his hands too full to be able to worry about Jacinto, who was taken under instruction to the next inn by the residue of the royal household and several bitter soldiers deprived of the chance to plunder, to await his master's pleasure. The inn seemed to have been acting as a refuge for those who had lost everything in the fire, but these poor souls were now ejected to face the winter night to make way for the incomers.

Leaving the others to gorge themselves on the ample cellars and food store, Jacinto scrabbled for long enough to get himself a share of the food and a flagon of beer, and then retreated to the top of the building, as far from the press of billeted soldiers as possible. In a tiny attic room he found what was obviously a store of the owners' family treasures, moved there for safety while the refugees were quartered below. And for the first time in his life he suddenly felt revulsion at what was being done to someone else's home, and compassion for the dispossessed.

Wedging a heavy chest against the door to prevent anyone surprising him, he sat down on the sagging old bed and reverently picked up a needlework sampler which had been stretched onto a frame to be hung on a wall. It commemorated the birth of a son called Eli, and Jacinto hoped that whoever Eli was he was far away from here tonight. This had obviously been a loving family who had given their children the kind of home Jacinto now realised he could have had, if only he had allowed the people who had taken him in to help him, instead of biting their hands at every turn.

Yet the wave of self pity which began to rise up fell apart with a chilling shock as he looked at the third sampler. The birth of a daughter named Cwen was recorded in a wreath of rambling roses and daisies. As if he had been doused with icy water, Jacinto suddenly recalled walking in under a sign which proclaimed the inn to be the *Brace of Brachets* – the self same name that he had heard Swein's Cwen refer to. In horror he now remembered that she had said she was from Radport. He was sitting in Cwen's home! Not some random stranger's but Cwen's! Cwen who had actually tried to be nice to him. The same Cwen who, with Swein, was trying to bring that lunatic, Edward, down. Cwen whose courage put his own posturings to shame, he now knew, and he regretted every unkind thought he had ever had about her. Then an even worse thought occurred to him. Where were her family? Where were they in this town filled with marauding soldiers?

Frantically stuffing the precious samplers under the bed where they might not get damaged, Jacinto downed the beer and wrapped his remaining food in a blanket which he slung over his shoulder. As silently as he could, Jacinto crept out of the attic. From below came the sounds of drunken carousal and arguing. By the sound of it many more men had found the delights of Cwen's father's cellar, and as one lot passed out in drunken stupors, more came to drain the store of good beer. Yet at least it guaranteed he would be unlikely to be missed.

On the next floor he got to the end of the corridor, to where the far window looked down onto a roof which led to the stables. With care he eased the shutter fully open and opened the leaded casement. At his proper weight he would never have made it through the confined space, but having grown so thin he was able to wriggle out and lower himself onto the slates. With care he crept along the ridge, and then lowered himself down onto the next section of roof, which was a wing of the stable connected to the inn. However, this looked down onto someone else's yard on the side away from the inn's yard, and while the inn's was full of horses gorging themselves on bags of hay and oats, the other was full of soldiers getting drunk.

Luckily nobody was looking up, and Jacinto managed a slow crawl to the junction of the roofs with the main stable block. Beyond, there looked like there was an orchard, but he needed to get onto the other roof in order to be able to get down. As he slithered across onto the slate tiles, three came loose under him, and he made a frantic grab for them before they shot off the roof and hit the floor to draw attention to him. He caught the tiles, but as his face pressed to the hole in the stable roof, he suddenly realised he was looking into several pairs of very frightened eyes hidden in the hayloft below.

"*Shhhh*! Don't scream!" Jacinto hissed. "Please don't scream!"

With care he managed to ease a few more tiles up so that he could drop down into the loft. There he found himself face to face, or at least as near as he could tell in the gloom, with several members of what he assumed was Cwen's family.

"I won't harm you," he whispered, but they looked doubtful. "Are you Cwen's family?" he tried again and saw a flicker of interest. "I knew Cwen while I was still with the Knights," he tried for a third time, and this time heard a sigh of relief.

"Who are you?" an older woman's voice asked.

"My name's Jacinto."

"Phaa! The one Swein and Berengar and Esclados talked about!" a young boy's voice softly exclaimed in disgust. "On your way, troublemaker! We're not so desperate as to need the help of the likes of you!"

"Hush, Eli!" the older woman reproved, then to Jacinto, "but I would like to know what you're doing here?"

"I've been held captive by Edward," was the best thing Jacinto could think of to say that would not alienate them instantly. "I was here under guard, but they're all getting drunk on your beer, so I climbed out of the window. I was in the attic and saw your samplers. That's when I remembered what Cwen had said and realised this must be her home."

"What's left of it!" a younger woman's voice said, the bitterness not softened by the lack of volume.

"We can rebuild, Yvette," the older woman consoled.

"Yes you can," Jacinto softly agreed, "which is better than those from Foel can. There's nothing there now!"

"Sacred Trees!" another female voice whimpered.

"How many of you are there here?" Jacinto asked, as a drunken roar of many male voices suddenly spilled out into the inn's yard.

"Myself, I'm Jane, Cwen's mother," the older voice replied. "My daughter-in-law, Yvette; my youngest son Eli; Bethan and her sister Gail, who help me in the kitchen; and Eli's friend Zeek who was stopping with us." Then the voice quavered. "My husband and two middle sons, with Zeek's father and his wagon too, were taking refugees to our oldest son's farm. They have a big barn they emptied so that some folks could go there, and leave us room to take in more from Foel. The first fleeing from there arrived days ago."

Jacinto thought frantically. "Where is the farm?" he asked, praying it would not be on the road to Caersus.

"Down the coast on the other side to the road to Pencrick," came the reply.

"Then we have to get you there," Jacinto said with more firmness than he felt. "There's no way you can stay here. Not even for the rest of tonight. The army will be scavenging through every nook and cranny. You won't be safe."

"But our Ma and Pa are in town!" a tearful girl's voice protested.

"Then best hope they've had the sense to get out," Jacinto told her gently, in a way he would only too recently never have thought to use. "The best thing you can do is get to safety first. The army won't be here for long, and then you can come back and look for them. But these soldiers have marched for days with no proper food supplies. They're cold and they're angry, because they don't know what this is all about, or why this whole thing is such a shambles. Or what attacked Foel – because that could be the biggest threat of all, and that scares them because it's so unknown."

"It was the DeÁine," Jane whispered back. "Berengar and Esclados said the wind at Yule came from New Lochlainn and was sent by something they called the Abend. Some kind of coven of DeÁine witches and wizards."

Jacinto was stunned. So the threat of the DeÁine was real! Quite why he had never really thought it real before he could not say. Maybe he had just been too arrogant to see it? Or was there something in the back of his mind which he had deliberately shut out, and even now refused to come forward enough to be anything other than a ghostly whisper? Why had he given all those warnings over something he had never believed was real? What in the Islands had he been thinking? But he had not really had a serious reason to think hard about it at all before. Now, though, it chilled him to the marrow, and he understood Swein on another level yet again.

Edward was bad enough on his own, but coupled with the DeÁine there was a whole new series of permutations, none of which were good news.

For a second he was too frozen to move, and then he heard in his mind Berengar's weary voice desperately trying to explain, for the umpteenth time, the principal of doing service to aid others that went beyond any consideration of self. And horribly late in the day, Jacinto suddenly realised what he had meant. If his life was to count for something more than an endless succession of self-indulgences, he had to do what he could to save Cwen's family – no matter what the cost to himself.

He pulled a bale of hay to the hole in the roof, and climbed on it to look out into the yard. It was full of men, but men reeling in drunken stupor around the milling horses, and none of them looking upwards.

"We have to go over the roof," he whispered to the cluster of people behind him. "Eli, can you and Zeek get up onto the ridge if I give you a leg up onto the roof?"

"Suppose so," Eli agreed cautiously, "why?"

"I'm going to hand the girls up to you, so that you can help them over the top of the roof so that they can slide down into the orchard. It was quiet back there when I just crept along the roof. Then I'll hand Mrs…?"

"…Jane…"

"…your Ma, up to you. I'll come up last. If we get spotted, I'll try to hold them off for as long as possible. Get out of the town on the fastest route. Don't try to go in the direction of the farm if it means taking a street through the town. You can loop round once you're clear. Come on, Zeek! Grab the edge of the roof!"

And with that Jacinto hoisted Zeek up to the hole in the slates, and supported the lad until he had wriggled through and crawled up to the ridge. On Jacinto's instruction he lay flat, with his legs dangling down the other side of the roof to present the least target until Eli had joined him. The girls had more trouble because of their skirts, and Gail turned out to be a very girlie girl who had never climbed anything in her life. For a horrible moment, Jacinto thought she was going to get stuck and start screaming, but the two lads caught her hands and hauled her bodily up the roof.

Without waiting they swung her over the ridge, and slid her down the other side to drop with a squeak on the ground beyond with Yvette. Luckily there was too much general noise for her crying to be heard once she was in the orchard, and she calmed down more once Bethan had joined her. Hardest of all was Jane, for her buxom figure required the removal of another pair of slates, yet at least she did more to help herself than the younger girls had done, and bore the discomfort in stoic silence.

Jacinto had to join them on the ridge to lend his strength in lowering Jane down to the guttering, and in the end he had to slide past her and drop down himself in order to be able to help catch her. Eli and Zeek bravely took time to slide slates back into place to make it less obvious that someone had been on the roof, before they too dropped down into the orchard. The boys then led the way under the cider apples, and out into a deserted alleyway.

With them providing directions and Jacinto adding tactical help, the little party slipped through the shadows of ravaged Radport. On many occasions they had to wait for groups of scavenging soldiers to pass, but Eli and Zeek had chosen a good route, and they were soon passing the last of the buildings on the side of a fast flowing mill leet, which breached the defences on the southern side that were guarded more by the river than the walls. However, they then came to the end of the leet as it flowed into the River Rad, and encountered the next problem. Somehow they had to cross the river. A small stone packhorse bridge lay off to their left, just wide enough to carry the hay wagons from the outlying farms coming into market, but even in the dim light they could see that it was guarded.

"Provost's men," Jacinto whispered, "there to make sure none of the men desert that way."

"There's a wooden footbridge a bit further down on our right," volunteered Zeek.

"I guess that will have to do," Jacinto conceded reluctantly, although he was already worried about how exposed they would be once they got there.

Sure enough the wooden bridge was soon reached, and they had plenty of cover near it from some huge coppiced elder bushes between the bank and the wall. Less helpful was the fact that the river hardly wandered at all here, and the men patrolling the stone bridge would have an uninterrupted view of the far end of the wood bridge straight along the water.

"Which way would you go to the farm once we're across the bridge?" Jacinto asked.

Again it was Eli who took the lead in answering. "There's a path running alongside the river bank, but if we make a dash straight into the trees there's another path back within them which runs parallel to the river one. It's there for when the river's in flood because it's a bit higher. We've got to go left on it, because going right only takes us up onto the main road close by the west town gate, and that will be watched, won't it?" Jacinto nodded agreement. "Alright, so we have to go left, but there's an open stretch where the paved road from the stone bridge does a right-angled turn to the left, and it joins it on the right. To get to the farm we then only have a short stretch on the road with hedges on both sides, then we turn off down a long lane that looks like it's only going to be a gap in the hedge at the road end."

"Good!" Jacinto said with some relief, glad that at least once the imminent danger was passed the family had a good chance of making it to the farm.

There was little of the moon showing tonight, which was a help, too. As a good heavy cloud drifted across its face, Jacinto sent the boys across one at a time, each holding the hand of one of the younger girls. Jacinto had learnt his lesson from trying to get the girls over the roof, and had no intention of sending them across alone, where they might freeze in full view of the soldiers and endanger them all. The boys had strict instructions not to linger in the scant bushes by the banks, but to make a dash straight for the woods. Zeek turned out to be able to do a passable imitation of an owl's hoot, and so Jane, Yvette and Jacinto stayed back until they heard him make the call to let them know all four had reached the safety of the woods. That way, Jacinto had told them, at least some of them stood a chance of escape if they were spotted. With the next cloud he sent Yvette up onto the bridge, only waiting until she reached solid ground and could risk breaking into a sprint before he ushered Jane across.

He was already becoming quite fond of this comfortable motherly lady. She had been all common sense throughout the ordeal, even though Jacinto knew it must be horrifying for her to have her home invaded and her family split up. Jane had backed his insistence that the youngest go across first, despite knowing that she could not hope to keep up if it came to a chase.

"They won't bother with an old woman like me," she had declared firmly at the youngsters' protestations. "But you young girls, they'll rape you if you get caught! All they're likely to do is rough me up a bit. Bruises soon heal."

But from the glance she gave Jacinto he could see in her eyes that she knew that was not true. No woman of whatever age would be safe tonight in this town. She knew it and it terrified her, yet she could put a brave face on as long as her children were safe. For his part, her courage tore at Jacinto in a way he would not have believed possible until his own victimisation, and his heartfelt silent vow was that he would not allow Jane to be taken while he drew breath.

Yet by some miracle they all made it across the river without a single cry going up to reveal they had been spotted. The walk along the woodland path allowed them to get their breath back, as they had to take it slowly for fear of breaking fallen twigs and branches underfoot, and signalling their presence. As near as Jacinto could judge, it took them about half a turn of an hourglass to reach the junction with the paved road coming from the main bridge. Now, though, they had another problem, for there were more provost's men than they had anticipated lingering between the town and the stone bridge.

"Can you get off the road any earlier than the lane? Through the hedge into the fields?" Jacinto asked, looking at the tall hawthorn hedge on the right-hand side of the road.

"Not along here," Eli said regretfully. "That hedge is in front of a bank. It's not a big bank, only about your height, but at the top you'd be in full sight from the town walls, and there's no room to crawl along behind the hedge until you get to the lane. Actually you'd be hard pressed to get through it at all, because no-one ever gets to the back of it to cut it back like they do on the road side."

"Then we do the same as before," Jacinto declared. "You four make a dash for it when I say so. Don't stop on the road whatever happens! Get to the cover of the lane where you can get out of sight before you wait for us. The provost's men are more worried about deserters than civilians. They'll only chase you so far because they can't leave the bridge unguarded. Remember that once you're on the lane you have an advantage. You know this place, they don't! Eli, Zeek, use your knowledge! If there's a wood you can hide in, or a bank you can get down behind, do it and wait for them to give up. You folk aren't important enough for a full scale manhunt. These men are scavengers like the rest. They'll take what they can if it's easy prey, so don't make it easy for them!"

With that Jacinto led the foursome to the road edge. Zeek and Bethan hared across the open stretch first, then when the nearest provost's men turned for their second patrolled walk back along the bridge he sent Eli and Gail out. Gail had not stopped crying since they had set out, which was perhaps why she did not see the pothole. One minute they were running and the next she had sprawled headlong, crying out as her ankle was twisted in the ground. Jacinto heard the women by him stifle gasps and prepared to sprint out himself, but Eli, used to the heavy work at the inn, turned and yanked her to her feet. As if she was a bag of oats for the horses, he flipped her up onto his shoulders and ran with her the last stretch into the darkness. Cupping a hand to his ear, Jacinto could just about make out the receding sound of Eli's feet.

But the damage was done. Even as they heard the soft hoot of Zeek's call, telling them Eli and Gail had made the lane, it was almost drowned in the rapid march of booted feet on stone.

""I tell you I heard someone!" a voice said insistently.

"Man or woman?" another asked, already closer.

"Woman I'd guess," said the first.

"I could do with a good woman!" a third commented.

Jacinto ducked down and risked a glance out of their shelter and saw three men.

"Don't see nothing," the second voice said.

"Well she ain't goin' to be stood there in the moonlight just lifting her skirt for you, is she?" his friend sarcastically replied. "She'll be in the woods. ...Aren't you, sweetie? ...Here pussy, pussy," he called with a nasty laugh, and they all took a step closer.

"Shit! They're going to search!" Jacinto swore. "If I distract them can you two run for it?"

"To keep away from them I could run all the way to Arlei!" Jane declared stoutly, "but what about you?"

"I can handle three men," Jacinto told her, although already his mind was reminding him that he was not quite the fighter he might have been. "Are you ready? ...Go!"

As Yvette and Jane lifted their skirts and hand in hand made a dash for it, Jacinto launched himself out of the brush straight at the men. Taken totally by surprise, the three soldiers were completely stunned by the appearance of the tall dark warrior hurtling straight at them snarling. His momentum carried him straight into two of them, hurling them to the ground with him on top, driving the breath out of them. All the practice paid off as Jacinto rolled without even thinking about it and came to his feet, driving his fist into the face of the third man, who had expected to catch their assailant off balance and was instead caught out himself. The man fell across one of those on the floor in a tangle of limbs, and Jacinto stamped hard on the other, hearing ribs crack and a strangled scream. But the flurry of activity across the bridge hadn't gone unnoticed and the pounding of running feet on stone alerted him just in time to spin round and see six more men already on the bridge, and closing in.

On the winter air the sound of another owl call echoed briefly, and Jacinto guessed that Jane and Yvette were safe with the others. But now he could not lead these men to them! So he turned on his heels and ran back the way they had come. Back into the trees and back towards the wooden bridge. There were shouts from behind him now, and he could hear his pursuers blundering through the wood making no attempt at silence. Could he lose them here? He looked at the alders and willows and made a dash off to the left, only to find the bank Eli had spoken of looming above him again. He could have scaled it with little effort, but that would take him into the fields, and he did not know if that would give his followers a sighting of the fleeing family. Not that way then!

He pounded back onto the path, aware that his detour had cost him some of his lead. He was also having more trouble running than he used to. Edward's deprivations had left him with little in the way of reserves of strength, and he knew he was already panting harder than he should have been. His legs were starting to feel wobbly too – something the Jacinto with the perfect physique had never known before. Stumbling over an outstretched root, he went flying and had to scramble to his feet again, losing even more ground to his hunters. Then the trees thinned out and he was on a short, steep uphill run catapulting himself up onto the road to Caersus. In the instant he stumbled into the open, a thrown rope net enveloped him and he fell to the ground, hopelessly enmeshed.

Rolling onto his back he looked up to see four riders sneering down at him, one of them carrying a second net identical to the one he was entangled in.

"Well, well, what have we here?" their leader grimaced. "The king's current pet making a run for it! His lordship won't like that! You're supposed to be honoured to have his prick up your arse, boy, not be running away! Come on lads, we'll get a fat reward for catching this one, I bet, and I for one could do with a drop of decent food and good wine. Tie him up and let's get out of here, it's too bloody cold to be pissing about with perverts like him!"

And with that Jacinto was bundled up in his net and thrown onto the back of a horse, to be led back into Radport and to Edward.

261

Chapter 15

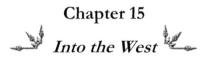

Into the West

Brychan: Eft-Yule

Berengar and Esclados left the grange at Kiln with all speed the next day, with an increased escort. The two lances which had travelled with them from Penbrook had now been substantially augmented with four more from the grange. The captain insisted that he had sufficient men left to pack up all the stores they could carry, and still provide escort to the south to Tarah for Cwen and Swein, without those four Knights and their men – but that he did not want to go down in history as the man who had lost the Grand Master as soon as they had found him! And within minutes, as they reached the gates of the town, they were glad of the extra lances. An armed militia of local men stood belligerently at the gates denying them access. Luckily Berengar and Esclados had no need to go through the town, but Berengar still rode close enough to converse with the men.

"If you want to guard your town from worse than has already happened get *behind* the gates," he called. "Post watches on the walls, not down here on the road. Barricade the gates and only allow in those whom you know or who are obviously refugees."

"What do you care, soldier?" spat the leader.

"I'm not a soldier, I'm a Knight!" Berengar riposted. "And I do care! I care that you've been brutalised by an army led by the man who dares to call himself your king. But worse is going to come! I'm going west to do what I can to stop him, but the main body of the Knights are snowed in. We will come to your aid, but until then prepare for the worst."

"Worst!" another man exclaimed. "What could be worse than the last week? That wind on New Year drove men mad and burned whole blocks of the town! Then we get an army stripping us bare! We've no food, hardly any blankets, too many widows and orphans, and too few men to man the walls!"

Berengar looked at Esclados in despair. If it was like this on the eastern side of the Pen estuary whatever was it going to be like further west?

"They'll never survive if Edward brings a starving army back through here," whispered Esclados, desperately trying to think of a solution.

Then Berengar had an idea. "If you can't hope to hold Kiln," he called, "then don't try." An angry growl rose from the civilians but he waved them down. "Get everyone together and head south for Penbrook." He turned in his saddle and called to one of the Knights. "Go back to the grange! Tell the captain to send an order in my name to Dinas. They're to evacuate the preceptory and aim to meet your own captain at Penbrook. Together you'll then escort these people to Tarah." He turned back to the militiamen. "We're evacuating our grange down the road. My captain has more supplies than our men can carry. Summon your people! You can collect what you can carry and have an armed escort to safety. But be warned! We'll tolerate no hoarding! Those supplies will be shared evenly amongst all. Anyone who has a problem with that can stay behind and take their chances, as can any man not prepared to fight under my men's directions."

The relief was tangible amongst the men, one calling out, "Bless you, sire!"

While another called, "Thank you! But who are you? Will your order be really be obeyed, or will we find the grange closed to us?"

"It flaming well better be obeyed!" Esclados growled loudly. "This is the new Grand Master of the whole Order! And what Master Berengar says goes!"

And with that they wheeled their horses onto the Foel road while the lone Knight galloped back to the grange, determined to deliver the message and still catch up with his new Grand Master. By this first showing, things were going to get interesting around this man, and the Knight had no intention on missing out on the action, having a shrewd suspicion that the coming events might be the stuff legends were made of.

Meanwhile Berengar was quietly chastising Esclados.

"Was that really necessary? You didn't need to proclaim it to the world that I'm the new Master! The 'senior' officer around here would have sufficed."

"Would it?" Esclados asked with a sympathetic grin. "Get used to it, my friend! From now on your words carry a lot of weight, but you also need to believe you're the Master. The title will get you so much respect, but in the current climate of chaos you have to grab it with both hands and be prepared to use it to the full. You made the right decision back there, just as the remaining ealdormen and captains made the right decision in choosing you to lead. Other Masters may've had the luxury of not having to act until the word of their promotion had spread, and their names had become known, but you're going to have to do it for yourself on many occasions, I fear."

None of which made Berengar feel any happier, even though he knew Esclados only spoke the truth. In short order the messenger Knight returned at the gallop, confirming that the captain was redirecting the men at the grange to pack the entire store into manageable sacks for the displaced citizens of Kiln. Thereafter they increased the pace, and found themselves approaching Foel in the evening three days later. In horror they reined in their horses at the sight of the open gates and the desolation within. With swords drawn they rode in, every nerve taut and expecting ambushes, but not a thing stirred except the tatters of cloth blown onto ragged beams by the winter wind.

"Abend?" Esclados breathed to Berengar, who nodded.

"Looks like the same storm we saw had a field day in here," he sighed sadly, then spotted detritus piled up at the side of a square. "But I'm guessing Edward's army has been through here since, going by that mess! That's not been burned at all, and we're on the tenth of the month, aren't we? Well that's not ten days old. Look, it's hardly started rotting!"

One of the men-at-arms jumped off his horse and poked around in the garbage with a stump of burnt wood. "I'd say three or four days old, sire, no more," he reported.

"I'd guess they're in Radport by now then, Oak preserve it!" one of the Knights estimated.

"Radport?" Berengar and Esclados exclaimed in unison, both swinging to look at the Knight.

"Aye," he said, somewhat worried by their reaction. "You did say the king was heading for Caersus didn't you? Well the main road to there goes south-west through Radport – the straight-on road is the one you want to Seigor, remember? They'd have to get off the straight road if they were going to drop down to Caersus. Even the king isn't so mad as to take an army off-road across the moors, is he?"

"No lad, not so mad as that," Esclados confirm in a choked voice, while Berengar was rendered speechless at the thought of the kind folk they knew there at Edward's mercy. "It's just that the Master and I were helped only days ago by some good people there," he explained to the men, but was not able to continue any further.

"Then may the Sacred Trees protect them in their hour of need," another of the Knights prayed. "And if not, then we shall avenge them tenfold once our men from the mountains rejoin us."

"Make it so!" several voices intoned with feeling.

They found a place of shelter for the night that had not been too badly polluted by Edward's army, but Berengar found his thoughts plagued by worries for Cwen's family.

"Are you sure you're all right for me to leave you tomorrow?" fretted Esclados.

"Yes. …Yes, I am," Berengar reassured him. "I hate to let you go, old friend, but I need you to do this for me even more." He leaned in close to Esclados and spoke softly so that only he could hear. "You must get to Laon! You know Laon is the headquarters of the Foresters in Brychan, but did you know it has hidden secret reserves?" Esclados' surprised raising of his bushy eyebrows said not. "Ah …well it does! You must get to Ealdorman Warwick and tell him of all we know – and get him to put that bloody book you're carrying somewhere safe! Warwick is a different man to Rainer, and not only because he's a Forester. The last time we all met, the two of them nearly came to blows over Rainer's willingness to get the Order so tied into court politics. Warwick will understand without you having to labour the point why we have to bring Edward down.

"But equally important – may be even more, Esclados – is that the Foresters know the secret ways through the mountain caves. If we need to cut Edward off, I may need to send men through the mountains to Laon from Garway, once we have the men from the snowed-in castles on the frontier. It would allow me to catch Edward in a pincer movement. In a sad way it's done us a favour that Foel is already destroyed, because it's the prime spot to trap his army, but now without us having to worry about the citizens. Once he starts to move back east, as long as we have the extra men, we can drive him from behind straight into the other half of our force, that's gone by the underground route to Laon and then come down from the hills in front of him. But to do that, Warwick has to open the hidden passages from his side. They were always meant to stay hidden from the west because of the DeÁine threat, and nobody at Garway knows the routes east, anyway.

"You're the only one I trust to tell this to, Esclados. The passages are only known about by the ealdormen, but I don't have the time to go to Warwick myself. I can't explain why, but I feel a pressing need to get to Garway and sort things out there. So if I can't go myself, then at least I feel better sending the man I trust most in this world!" And Berengar clasped his old friend's hands tightly in fond respect.

Esclados could think of nothing to say to that, and when they parted ways in the pale morning light, he prayed with all his might that this would not be the last they ever saw of one another. In the back of each of their minds still loomed the possibility of a DeÁine threat, but without further information they were forced to focus on other more pressing matters.

And so it was that Berengar and his escort ploughed their way west along the snowbound road over the moors, in a straight line towards Seigor. Here there were few inns, and because of their slow progress they found themselves spending alternate nights huddled into shepherds' refuges. Eight long days they struggled along the frozen highway, with the high mountains encrusted in their icy, winter tomb up on their right all the way. Seeing the weight of snow on the slopes clearly for the first time as the clouds lifted, Berengar fretted even more about what he would find at Garway, and how long it would be before he could even hope to see men from the Order's fortresses further along the Castles Road. If he was to go up against Edward he needed more men than he could assemble from just Garway, Seigor and Craws if he was not to leave them undefended.

With great relief they finally saw the great towers of Seigor Castle rising before them on the horizon. The central keep was a massive affair, capable of holding virtually all the garrison if dire need required it, while surrounding it was probably the most substantial curtain wall in Brychan. Great stone revetments supported it throughout its circuit, while the five towers and the gatehouse protruded far enough to provide archers with a first class angle from which to fire upon besiegers attacking the main wall, and vice versa. Even as they rode across the winter landscape towards it, the party heard a trumpet sound on the clear air alerting those within of their approach. At the drawbridge they saw that the portcullis was down barring the way, and they were challenged by sentries unseen behind the arrow slits. However, the mention of Berengar's name brought a rapid change of attitude, and even as the great iron grill was being winched up to allow them in they could hear the excited shouts of the men being relayed back through the fortress.

No sooner had they ridden into the bailey than a grey-haired commander came hurrying down the keep's steps to greet them.

"Berengar! By all that's sacred, it's good to see you! Or rather Grand Master, now, isn't it."

Berengar laughed, "Ranulf! It's good to see you too! And unless we're in formal company, it's still Berengar to you. We've known each other too long to stand on ceremony now."

His old friend clasped him warmly by the hand. "As you wish. Congratulations! I can think of no better man to hold the post in such troubled times. But I fear celebrations will have to wait. Have you heard the latest news? Aagh! No, of course you won't! You would've already been on the road when I sent the birds out. We've had word from Cedric at Craws. Foresters based there were worried by that storm at New Year and went out scouting westwards. They came back all of a lather – it was lucky they went out on skis and made a fast return – for there's a DeÁine army on the way!"

Berengar stood in stunned horror. "You're serious? A *DeÁine* army?"

Ranulf nodded and did some quick calculations. "By now they can't be more than a couple of days away from Roch. Luckily the Foresters were senior men and so they had the authority to tell the garrison at Roch to get out of there fast! Cedric's message to me said that the civilians were on their way out too, and heading north to Fold. The Roch garrison is going to escort them and supplement the garrison at Fold."

"Sacred Trees and Blessed Martyrs!" Berengar swore. "That gives us barely eight days before they reach here!" Then he remembered why he had come here in the first place and groaned even deeper, causing Ranulf some concern.

"Berengar? Are you all right? You're not sickening after your dire winter's ride are you?"

"No, no, old friend – or at least not sick in body! Oh Ranulf, even worse news arrives with me! Edward has brought what he can of the Brychan army west and must now be somewhere around Caersus."

"*Edward*? At Caersus? Why?"

Berengar took his friend by the arm and headed for the keep steps. "Come! We have to talk and I need your experience to add to mine if we're to avert total disaster. But how quickly can you send scouts out? I must know what's happened to Edward's army."

Ranulf was becoming more anxious with every passing minute at the unfolding events and immediately responded with, "Right now! I can send two lances out on each of the roads – two towards Marloes, two south on the road that eventually goes to the coast and Pembrey, and two on the Caersus road." At Berengar's curt nod Ranulf stopped and turned to call to his men. "Achiad company, first six lances! Prepare to depart! Captain Mitchel to my office immediately!"

Ushering Berengar into the warmth of the office, he called for refreshments and quarters to be made available straight away, while giving succinct orders to a keen young captain who had come bounding up the stairs on their heels. Captain Mitchel received his orders, gave a crisp salute and disappeared with even more speed than he had arrived with, so that Berengar was much relieved to hear the sound of departing hooves shortly afterwards. As he gratefully sipped a mug of scalding hot caff, Berengar told Ranulf of what he had discovered along with Esclados, Cwen and Swein. The veteran captain's jaw dropped further with each revelation until by the end he was staring at Berengar in open-mouthed horror. For a moment silence hung between them, then Ranulf asked,

"But how *could* Edward have known about the DeÁine? We didn't and we're right on the border! If we'd had even so much of a whiff of them you *know* we'd have been sending out warnings long before this!"

"Yes, I know you would," Berengar reassured him, "and I think there's no blame to be attached to any of our lookouts. This reeks of long standing plotting to completely marginalise us and subvert any plans we might've made for such an eventuality. What worries me, Ranulf – what really, *really* worries me – is how complicit Edward is in all of this? I can't for the life of me figure out whether he's just a pawn – someone whose flaws are so well known that it's been easy to manipulate him in some way to the DeÁine's advantage. Or whether he's in it far deeper.

"You see it makes much more sense if you think of him as a DeÁine himself. Swein told us that Edward regularly bragged about his DeÁine attributes, and how he thought them much the finer race. What if this idiot has invited them in to Brychan thinking that he's removing 'unhelpful' advisors like the generals, the churchmen, and us, and replacing them with a people much more like-minded to him? As far as I can gather, he's just about daft enough to think that he would still remain at the top of the heap, so to speak, with the DeÁine here and in control. It then makes much more sense of him dragging an army through the land in appalling conditions if he doesn't actually want them to fight to win!"

"Shit!" Ranulf swore. "Shit, shit, *shit!* Edward's actually handing Brychan to the DeÁine on a plate!"

Berengar nodded regretfully. "I fear he is. Otherwise, why not send us a warning? Tell us to hold the Gap and then make an organised advance, with the army properly equipped and with us ready to hand out supplies along the way? Our men at Kiln had enough in the stores to help, but they dared not open their doors because Edward's host was so hostile. Now he has an army that can barely march, much less fight. What can he possibly hope to achieve with that except defeat?"

"Then you're not going to feel any better when I tell you how many of the DeÁine are about to appear over the horizon," Ranulf said mournfully. "Rowan only knows, it scared me stiff when I heard!"

"That bad?"

"That bad!" Ranulf took a swig of his own caff and shuddered. "Fourteen thousand! That's what the Foresters estimated!"

"Fourteen thousand!" Berengar yelped, utterly stunned. This was no token sword rattling but a real attempt at invasion!

Ranulf nodded sagely. "About ten thousand of that's the usual slave army, but there has to be the best part of four thousand veterans at the core. Ten thousand useless buggers, but that's still ten thousand who are more terrified of the drivers behind them than of us in front of them. Ten thousand the DeÁine can afford to be slaughtered like cattle, because they'll still take a fair few of ours with them."

"And even then that still leaves four *thousand* veterans for us to deal with," Berengar fretted. "How many men do you have here, Ranulf? I'm not up on garrison numbers in the south anymore."

"Oh, we're up to our normal full strength of a complete regiment of two thousand in two battalions. We didn't lose any of our fighting men when we lost my predecessor – you remember Commander Clarke, don't you? – in the coup that took out Master Rainer. The only men we're technically short of are the company of ten lances he took with him to Garway as an escort, who are still up there – he thought it wise given the implications of danger in the message that summoned him. Didn't help him though, did it?" he said sadly.

"No," Berengar sympathised, "but at least you've been second-in-command here for long enough to have been able to pick up command without any real problems. Is that the same at Craws?"

Ranulf wearily ran his hands through the stubble of his cropped, receding hair. "Yes …yes it is, and you'll be glad to know that Cedric had no problem picking up the reins there except for the unexpected suddenness of his promotion. His experience made him the blindingly obvious candidate even though he hadn't already been second-in-command there – the post was vacant."

"Thank the Trees! I admit I've been having nightmares that I might find you two had moved on, and some young hawks temporarily in charge at both places. Our stop here before Yule was too short for me to have time to ask after you, and of course Clarke was still very much in command then – and then events have just kept moving faster and faster. You've no idea how much better I feel already knowing you two are here!"

"Thanks for the vote of confidence," Ranulf said wryly, "but how does that actually help anything?"

"Because you're both old enough to have been in real battles with the DeÁine. I don't have to worry about misguided heroics from either of you! …Especially as I fear I'm going to have to give you an unpalatable order."

"Oh? … That doesn't sound good."

Berengar got up and walked to the window and looked out across the snowy landscape, a mixture of fear and adrenaline pulsing through his veins. "We can't fight the DeÁine with the men we've got here, Ranulf. Even if Craws is also up to strength, and Garway, that gives me a maximum of six thousand men to put into the field. Against ten thousand I think we'd be lucky to get through the slave army with anything less than a thousand casualties, and more like two, even accounting for our better training."

"So? Grim losses though those would be, that then makes it even odds against their veterans."

"But that's assuming we can get the men from Craws and Garway here before the DeÁine arrive. And what if there's a second wave of DeÁine behind that which our Foresters didn't see? I could even take the risk of that if I knew that Edward would fight with us. But what if he comes up behind us and attacks our rear while we're engaged with the DeÁine? All the information I have points to him having the best part of four thousand men with him. Captain Scully thought that each battalion of a thousand had been pulled from Delving, Beluss and Shipfold, with a rough estimate of a mixed thousand foot soldiers and some cavalry from Arlei, and all I've heard since then backs that up. Even if half of those are so incapacitated by frostbite and cold that they can't fight, they could still swing the balance horribly against us."

"Would his men fight against us?" Ranulf asked in horrified disbelief.

"I should think it depends on what he's told them, wouldn't you? If they think *we're* the ones allied with the DeÁine they might very well, don't you think? At least the DeÁine and most of their slaves *look* foreign. If it comes to an occupation they'll all be pretty visible, but what if you thought some of your own were selling you down the river into slavery to the DeÁine? You'd rather they were dead beforehand, wouldn't you? At least you wouldn't be jumping at shadows and watching your back at every turn!"

"Sacred Trees! Put like that I see what you mean! What a mess! Yes, they may well feel that they have no choice but to fight us." Then a nasty thought occurred to him and he rose to stand by Berengar, staring at the white, flat killing ground to the west. "But they don't even have to fight us, do they? All they have to do is stand by and do nothing!"

"You've got it," Berengar said bleakly. "Even if the DeÁine send the slave army in separately – which would be an unlikely first – and we deal decisively with them, by the time we've fought our way through them to the veterans, that will still leave the remains of the slaves to be regrouped and thrown at our backs. They're not just going to sit down in the snow and wait for the battle to finish, are they? Not with their slave drivers riding their beasts-of-battle amongst them! And we both know that it's far more likely that each great wave of slaves will have a hard-core of veterans mingled in with them to keep them going. Even *if* I can get the men from Craws and Garway here, we'd still be outnumbered more than two to one, and three to one if Edward's men weigh in on the DeÁine side.

"But what if the DeÁine arrive while our reinforcements are on the road to here? We could be trapped in here to watch our friends be massacred separately on the road. Because the men from Craws would be more likely to meet them first seeing as they're coming from further west. Or even worse, what if Edward besieges us here? We'd be immured here in this castle as our tomb, totally unable to even lead a sally out of the gates to die beside them! Then there'd be nothing to stop the DeÁine until spring comes and the mountain castles could get out of this fell fall of snow. We wouldn't even be able to lead skirmishers out to harass and weaken the DeÁine in preparation for a counter attack."

"What are you going to do?" asked an appalled Ranulf. "Is there anything you can do?"

"I'm going to give you the order to evacuate Seigor," Berengar told him sadly.

"And that's going to *help*!" Ranulf exclaimed in confusion.

"Yes …or at least it's the best of the piss-poor options I have!" Berengar growled. "Look at it, Ranulf! That bloody great flat plain heading west! Seigor was built right here to launch attacks *out* of. But it's a sitting duck for a siege. You've got the thickest walls in Brychan for a reason! And that reason is in case of a siege – but I don't have enough men to hand to risk having two thousand of my best incarcerated and out of action. Now Garway is impossible to besiege! Even the DeÁine can't bring enough in the way of siege engines close enough to its walls to be effective, and if they used the Power to blast holes in the curtain wall, we can just retreat into the mountain itself and pick off the poor bastards they send in to try to root us out. Garway even has its own springs! Fresh water that won't run out and can't be contaminated like a well.

"If I pull your entire garrison back to Garway along with the men of Craws, *then* I have a force I can do something with. I can guarantee – and yes, I do mean *guarantee*, Ranulf, for reasons I haven't told you yet – that I'll have six thousand men I can get out from behind my walls to actually fight with! Moreover, I don't have to worry about whether any defectors, or spies, from Edward's army have crept amongst our ranks who are likely to open the bloody gates one cold night, when we're all too frozen to be alert!"

Ranulf looked utterly miserable, but nodded his head in reluctant acknowledgement of the truth of what Berengar had said. "What do you propose for the castle itself, then? Are you going to leave a few volunteers to try to hold it to make a showing of resistance?"

"No." Then Berengar saw the look of shock on Ranulf's face. "I know, it goes against all my better instincts too, Ranulf, but look at the length of your walls! I'd have to leave no less than five hundred men for it to even begin to look convincing – any less and they wouldn't stand a chance of holding anyone off for more than a day, because there'd be huge gaps in the wall left unmanned. And I'm not prepared to sacrifice that many men for a futile gesture which would only hold off the inevitable by one day."

"What, then? Will you lock and bar the gates, or do you plan to leave them open too?"

"That depends on what news your men bring back."

"Sacred Trees, Berengar! You aren't really planning on leaving the gates open are you?"

Berengar rubbed his tired eyes. "Maybe. If Edward's troops are closer than the DeÁine to here." He took in Ranulf's aghast expression and tried to explain. "I'm counting on there being some men among them who've fought against the DeÁine before. Without us there as a distraction, the

DeÁine will be the focus of their attention. So I'm also counting on them having the sense to look at the overwhelming odds coming straight at them, and realising that their king and leader has lost what little of his mind he ever had. Those men don't deserve to die, Ranulf, but I can't save them! *We* can't save them. But what I *can* do is give them a fighting chance of some of them surviving.

"So if Edward is closer than the DeÁine, we're going to march out of here and leave the gates open, so that those lads with some sense can make a mad dash for the safety of these walls. If five hundred or a thousand soldiers make it in here and shut the gates, they're in with a better chance than anywhere else on the plain. And for that reason, we're going to leave half the stores behind. I'm mightily afeared the DeÁine may have at least one war-mage with them and/or the witches, which may mean the Power gets used on any resistance, but those who retreat inside here will make them pay the cost for taking Seigor and do the holding up for us. It's a cold and harsh decision, but it's the best odds I can give them."

"Flaming Trees! May I never be in your position to have to make a choice like that!" Ranulf invoked. "So let me get this straight. We're going to abandon Seigor and retreat to Garway, where we'll fight a guerrilla war – at the very least – until the lads from the Castles Road in the west can join us. If the DeÁine will get here first, you'll lock the gates and strip it bare. But as that's less likely than Edward's army arriving here first, you plan to walk out leaving the gates open, and allow the poor bastards who have some sense to get out of the field to die behind these walls when the DeÁine wizards do their stuff and blast them with Power. Is that it?"

"Pretty much," Berengar sighed.

"In which case, may the Trees protect us and you, my friend, if this all goes wrong!"

And with that Ranulf left to give the orders to begin packing and to face the resistance he knew he would meet. Meanwhile Berengar leaned his weary head against the chill of the window to ease the ache inside. *Do you hear that, Trees?* he thought. *I surely hope you are on our side, because if not I may go down in history as the briefest Grand Master in the Order's records! Berengar the Barmy who opened the gates of Seigor and let the DeÁine walk into Brychan. What a bloody epitaph that would be! The acting Grand Master whose every act was wrong.*

However, they got their first answer quicker than expected. As night fell, the sentries called the approach of a large group of men coming closer along the Caersus road, but this was no army. At their head flew the standard of the Order. Berengar realised this must be the captain from the grange outside of Caersus acting on his old order from Yule to evacuate if the king's army approached, and sent men out with fresh horses to help them. By midnight the two companies totalling one hundred men were safely within the castle walls, and Berengar and Ranulf got their first news of Edward's army in days.

They had crossed with the two lances who had just left from Seigor, the captain reported, who had carried on to a refuge along the road where they would be able to look down towards the city and see what was happening. He had passed them only hours out of Seigor and had been able to tell them little of what had happened in the last day or so. He could, however, report that there was general unrest amongst Edward's army, especially amongst the veteran soldiers who could see disaster looming. The last they had heard, Edward was scouring the town for something, but no-one knew quite what, although Berengar had a shrewd suspicion which he kept to himself.

Then in the midmorning of the next day, the first of the patrols came back. The men whom Ranulf had sent towards Marloes reported all was quiet on that road, as did their colleagues who had gone towards the coast. There was therefore little doubt that the DeÁine army was coming straight for Seigor from Roch, and making no attempt to avoid a direct confrontation by taking the southern route to avoid the fortress. Then the men sent on the Caersus road came hammering back in through the gates, calling out that they had seen in the distance the first of Edward's army already beyond Caersus and heading this way.

"Looks like you were right," Ranulf said to Berengar.

"I almost wish I hadn't been," was his reply. "Call all the men to the bailey, will you? I feel I should at least tell them why we're doing this."

"I already did that," Ranulf reminded him.

"I know, but if this all goes wrong I want every man who survives to know that this was my order alone, and not your responsibility."

"You don't have to do that, Berengar. I've not questioned your order – formally or in my heart. You've made the only choice possible, and with better reasoning than Rainer would have. It's no fault of yours that you have no good choices left."

But Berengar insisted, and so an hour later the entire force stood in the open court before the steps of the keep as he briefly told them why they must depart. As he told of his hope that some of Edward's men would find refuge in the spot that they now stood on, he could see some of the men nodding their heads in understanding.

"I want everything we're taking packed and ready to go by tonight," he told them. "We leave for Garway tomorrow with the first light, and I want the last man out of here by midmorning at the latest. That gives us a clear start of a full day before the earliest any of Edward's men can be here. I want us up into the first of the foothills before his scouts can even see us, because I don't want that fool of a king thinking he can have a quick victory over us, just to whet his appetite before he starts on the DeÁine. And I don't want any man in either of our armies having to face the decision to fight his own countrymen, when the real enemy is only a few days away. We leave at daybreak!"

In a bitterly cold, clear dawn the entire garrison of Seigor rode out, heavy-hearted and silent. Berengar sat on a borrowed destrier by the gate to make sure every last man left. He had not wished to offend his friend by saying anything, but there was a small part of him that had feared Ranulf would not leave his beloved Seigor if he was left to check the rearguard. And Ranulf was well liked amongst the men, so that if he stayed, Berengar knew that he would not be alone. So worried was he, that he actually went back in to the bailey and stood listening for a few moments in case there were any stragglers. However nothing could be heard except the crunching of retreating horses' hooves on the frozen snow, and the faint chinking of metal from the harnesses. Wheeling the horse back to the gates, he made sure they were well propped open, then cantered back down the line to join Ranulf at the head.

As the sun came up on their right, it bathed the snow in golds and reds without a cloud in the sky, although Berengar could find no joy in the glorious day.

"Nothing proclaims to me the closeness of the DeÁine than this weather," he sighed regretfully to Ranulf. "We've had foul weather upon foul weather, and then with no warning we get a day like this. I fear that the Abend have controlled the clouds to their every advantage – snow to hamper our every move, and now it's clear to allow them easy passage and to allow their scouts to easily spot our movements. We must make haste to be off the plain by tonight!"

Luckily the men and horses were rested and fresh, so that with the improved weather they were able to ride on into the night. However, when they did stop, clustered around a small, wayside Order-hostelry, they were well within the rolling foothills of the mountains. The heavy snowfalls had made the going very heavy, doubling the time it had taken Berengar and Esclados to make this journey when they had come with Swein and Cwen; and Berengar and Ranulf had regularly rotated the riders who were breaking trail at the front to give those horses some respite, but even so their passage had been slow.

"Do you think we'll make Garway by tomorrow night?" Ranulf asked Berengar quietly, as they studied a map in a corner of the back room.

"I think we have to!" Berengar replied, worry written all over his face. "In any other circumstances I wouldn't dream of pushing the horses so hard in this deep snow, because we're going to have to ride on beyond midnight to do it. And if I thought we'd have to fight, I couldn't take the risk of the men being so tired either. But – if I've guessed right, and Blessed Trees let that be so – I don't think the DeÁine will bother about us if they see us retreating, and I think it's better to get these men behind Garway's walls as soon as possible."

The following day proved a trial for everyone in many ways. As they climbed higher into the mountains the snow got even worse, forcing their pace to what felt like a snail's crawl. On top of that, though, in the bright sunlight the higher they climbed the greater the visibility became, not only for them looking back down to the plain, but for anyone down there looking upwards. Berengar was horribly aware that so great a body of men as he was leading, would stand out as a long black snake strung out along the white mountainside. At times hillocks provided cover, but even then some part of the long column was always still exposed.

Leaving Ranulf to carry on in the lead, he paused at midday on a small promontory with three lances of Foresters as his escort. While the men filed past, he and the Foresters scoured the plain below to make what observations they could. From their vantage point they could pick out the dark bulk of Seigor left in lonely white isolation, but not for long. Already another black line was heading its way, tiny as ants on the move from this distance, but unmistakably the army Edward led.

Berengar's heart went out to the ordinary men down there, for it was blindingly obvious that all was far from well with them. Instead of a neat, tidy column marching in good order, he could see small groups straggling off to each side, and even the main line was not a coherent body.

"Flaming Trees, the DeÁine will chew them up and spit them out without even pausing for breath," one of the Foresters breathed in dismay.

"I know," Berengar replied sadly, "and all we can do is hope that Seigor's walls give some of them a place of safety to weather the storm."

"And the storm's coming!" another declared pointing with outstretched arm to the sky in the west.

Following his gesture the others now saw small wheeling clouds approaching with more speed than the wind.

"Birds!" several men proclaimed in unison.

"That has to be the Abend spying out the land," one of the Foresters added.

"Which means they're not far away now," Berengar agreed, just as another of the men drew their attention to more flocks away to the east and south.

"Let's just hope they don't come up here," the Knight said, which sounded more of a prayer than any expression of hope that they would be so lucky as to escape scrutiny.

They turned and hurried to join the column, but barely an hour later flickering shadows and cawing heralded the flight overhead of a flock of rooks, and for the rest of the daylight they were afflicted with several more visitations. Only with the coming of darkness were they able to march on in peace, although it did little to relieve anyone's anxiety, for all knew that the DeÁine must now realise they were heading for Garway. The only consolation was that, knowing that the DeÁine army had not yet been visible on the last inspection, they were too far away to physically hinder the Knights' progress. Also, a strange benefit was that, with the Abend keeping the skies cloud free, the light of the partial moon was reflected off the snow and gave them something more than just the torch-light to ride by.

However, everyone was more than thankful to turn up into the ravine which housed Garway, in the dark early hours well before dawn the next morning, and to see the bulk of the castle rising above them. Almost more delighted were the remaining senior officers in charge of the headquarters, grateful to have someone once more at the helm of the Order. Moreover, the hawks which Ranulf had sent with the warning that nearly two thousand men would be descending on the castle, had arrived in time for hurried preparations to have already been put into place. Exhausted men and horses were therefore soon heading for food and rest, leaving Berengar to make his way up to the Grand Master's office.

As he opened the door and walked in it felt very strange, and the circumstances of his last visit crowded in on his memory. Walking to the window he looked down on the scenes of activity below, thinking that if anyone had told him the last time he had looked out that he would return within weeks, and as the Grand Master, he would have thought them mad. Yet this was now all his to command, and he needed to think how best to use it. However, he had barely sat down at the desk before a young soldier knocked and entered without being called in to hand Berengar a message.

"This came by hawk, sire," the man gasped. He was too young to have seen action before, Berengar realised, and by the uniform he was one of the men seconded to the aviary, so this was possibly the first time he had had to take a scroll from the leg of one of the killer battle-hawks. No wonder his hand shook! The lad was probably wondering who to be more scared of, Berengar or the hawk! Yet Berengar's own blood ran cold and his heart sank even further when he read the hurriedly scribbled shorthand:

Craws Castle, 22nd E-Y. DeAine army passed Roch yesterday, est. now 20,000. All routes cut off, order sent by hawk to Fold to evacuate to Hirieth. Craws under siege. No way out, do not attempt rescue, Abend using Power-fire – we die with valour! May we meet again beyond the veil in the Summerland. † Cedric.

PART 2

RHEGED

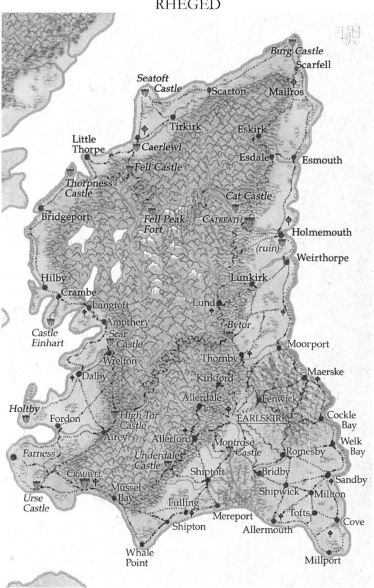

Burg Castle
Scarfell
Seatoft
Castle
Scarton
Mailros
Tirkirk
Eskirk
Little
Thorpe
Caerlewl
Esdale
Esmouth
Fell Castle
Thorpness
Castle
Cat Castle
Bridgeport
Fell Peak
Fort
CATREATH
Holmemouth
(ruin)
Weirthorpe
Hilby
Lunkirk
Crambe
Langtoft
Lund
Amothery
Bytor
Castle
Scar
Einhart
Castle
Moorport
Wrelton
Thornby
Dalby
Maerske
Kirkford
Allerdale
Holtby
Fenwick
Cockle
Fordon
High Tor
EARLSKIRK
Bay
Castle
Airey
Allerford
Welk
Farness
Montrose
Romesby
Bay
Underdale
Castle
Castle
Shiptoft
Bridby
Sandby
CRAUWEL
Shipwick
Millton
Mussel
Urse
Bay
Fulling
Tofts
Castle
Mereport
Cove
Shipton
Allermouth
Whale
Point
Millport

Chapter 16

 Husbands and Wives

Rheged: Aer-Yule – Yule

For Matti and Kayna the ride to the coast of Ergardia was something of a relief, and it was hard not to feel exhilarated at the prospect of the mission ahead. Neither of them had realised quite how depressing it had been to see their friends and loved ones leaving. Indeed, by the time they reached the castle of Ferryfort they felt quite guilty at how little they had thought of Alaiz. Despite their sympathy for the young queen's plight, it was difficult to find something encouraging to say every day when it was obvious that there was no prospect of her getting what she most desired. So it had been a welcome change to spend the ride discussing possible courses of action with Iago and Elidyr. Brego had been in agreement with them that they should avoid the normal crossing between the Islands from Ferrybank to Bridgeport. That way was too open to being discovered by Oswine's and the DeÁine war-mage Tancostyl's spies.

A small fleet of fishing vessels was waiting in the loch beyond Ferryfort Castle to transport the men of the Order, whom the redoubtable Ron and Edmund were bringing across Rheged to find refuge in Ergardia. It therefore made sense for the four to make the journey to Rheged with the flotilla, and creep into the small fishing port of Little Thorpe which lay across the loch from Gerard of Urse's castle of Thorpness. At Ferryfort they were received with all hospitality by the ealdorman in charge of the area, and made comfortable. It was probable that they would cross in a few days' time, for he had already had a message from Gerard saying that the troops were not far off, but even so the foursome had trouble containing their eagerness.

Happily the message to summon the boats came the next day, and on the third morning they slipped out of the loch for the overnight sail to Rheged. With a fair wind in the summer it would be possible to do the trip quicker, but in the high winds and awkward tides of winter it tended to take more than a full day, and now the crossing was rough. As the only passengers the four had plenty of space, but they pitied the returning soldiers who would be packed tightly in the holds reeking of the fish they normally contained, and taking the worst of the pitching and rolling. Under the cover of the early darkness the small flotilla slipped into the waters of Rheged, and tied up along the quaysides at Thorpe, the local fishermen having moved the smaller boats down into the quiet waters of the loch to temporarily make room for so many visitors. No sooner had the boats been made fast, than a stream of men appeared out of the darkness and began to slip on board, silent, grim-faced and battle-scarred.

However, the four arrivals had no time to gaze at them. A bear-like figure prowled out of the darkness and enveloped Matti in a huge hug which she returned.

"By the Spirits, it's good to see you again, Matti!" Gerard's bass voice growled in her ear as he swung her off her feet. "Rosin's been worried sick about you!"

"It's good to see you too!" Matti replied, feeling happier than she had expected at seeing her old friend again, and gave him another tight hug. "This is Sergeant Iago. He's the one who got me out of here safely the last time."

"Iago!" Gerard spoke with real warmth. "You're very welcome for keeping Matti safe." Then he peered closer in the gloom. "Aren't you one of Ruari's men from way back?"

"That's right," Iago answered with a grin. "We've met before. Years ago. Chasing Attacotti raiders down on the south coast, I think?"

"By the Trees! So it was!" Gerard remembered, then realised that there was another woman standing there whom he had not spotted muffled up by a thick cloak.

"This is Kayna," Matti introduced her friend. "She's been around the Knights all her life, and one called Maelbrigt trained her to fight as good as a Knight."

"Really?" Gerard was surprised but impressed. He was even more impressed when the fourth member of the party, a slim Forester whom he vaguely recognised, said,

"That's *the* Maelbrigt she's talking about. The one MacBeth's spoken about."

Gerard's eyebrows went up, but then, ever irrepressible, he could not resist adding, "Well the local lads won't be pinching your bottom, then!"

For a second Kayna almost bit at what she took to be a facetious remark, until she saw the twinkle in his eye and realised he was pulling her leg in much the same way Maelbrigt used to. And so with a grin answered back, "Not unless they want to lose their fingers, anyway!"

Already she was feeling relaxed in this amiable company, and by the time they reached the inn where Edmund was waiting, she felt that she had known Gerard for far longer. Although Matti had told her of the contrast between the two friends, she was still surprised to see it once they were in the well-lit, snug room. If Gerard was a friendly, great shaggy bear of a man, Edmund was slim, neat and tidy, despite weeks on the road. He too gave Matti the most affectionate of welcomes, and Kayna felt a twinge of jealousy at Matti's having a cousin who so obviously cared deeply about her. Kayna was not even on speaking terms with her two sisters, and had been dismissed as a hopeless cause by the rest of the family when she was so small as to not have any real memories of them. The young tomboy had not even been summoned back from her playmates down at the grange when rare visitors had come to Luing, so completely had she been written out of her sisters' families.

Then Edmund was facing her and she was looking straight into mesmerising cat-green eyes. With Kayna being on the tall side for a woman and Edmund being only average height, they were very much of a size, making the eye contact very close and Kayna felt a twinge of lust. Something she had rarely felt for the men surrounding her in Celidon, with the honourable exception of Talorcan. Most of them had been far too easily intimidated by her fiery independence, and Kayna had never wanted someone she could walk all over.

Edmund, though, was someone she already knew would be more than a match for her in spirit from Matti's descriptions – she had just not expected him to be so attractive with it. Matti herself was silently amused to see her normally suave cousin as bowled over at the meeting as her friend was. They would be good for one another, she thought, and resolved to get Rosin helping her to throw the two together.

Arriving at Thorpness on Yule Eve, they were received with delight by Rosin and Gerard's boisterous family. To Matti's delight, Osbern's estranged wife, Ismay, was there, and looking healthier and happier than at any time during the years when Osbern had been nearby. However, it struck both her and Rosin that Edmund was terribly torn. On the one hand they had always suspected that Edmund harboured a soft spot for the fragile wife of his friend, and the way Ismay cheered up whenever he visited led them to believe that she felt the same. Yet now Edmund was confronted with the temptation of the feisty Kayna, aided by the fact that there were no obstacles to prevent any relationship going where it would. Edmund seemed to spend the whole evening being solicitous to Ismay, and at the same time drawing Kayna into conversation. Luckily, Matti could quite legitimately ask how things were going with Ismay and her marriage, not having seen her in months, so sending the message to Kayna that this was not Edmund's wife, and with no immediate prospect of being so either.

"How is our favourite religious fanatic?" Matti asked wryly.

Ismay rolled her eyes. "Oh, as full of fervour as ever," she said wearily. "I swear he wears out the knees of more breeches than any man I've ever heard of with all that praying. And before you ask, yes, he still confesses everything to that viperous old priest of his – may he rot in the Underworld when his time comes! That one has a lot to answer for for ruining what little we had of a marriage."

The four arrivals looked from one to another. So nothing had changed, Osbern must still be treated as compromised. The brief silence came close to attracting comment until Elidyr saved the moment by saying, "Stupid man, there's much better things I can be thinking of to be doing on my knees, especially with a pretty wife!"

It instantly made Ismay blush.

"Blessed Spirits!" Rosin whispered to Matti, "He's not making a play for Ismay alongside Edmund is he?"

Matti quirked an eyebrow, "Well that would make things interesting, wouldn't it? Ruari did hint that Elidyr is quite one for the ladies, and he's definitely easy on the eye, isn't he."

Rosin gave Elidyr an appraising up and down glance. "Mmmm… Very pretty …but I prefer my men with a bit more meat on their bones. How slim are those hips? He's fit, though, I'll give you that. I bet he could keep going all night! But then I've heard the same said of your cousin Edmund."

Even the normally unshakeable Matti felt herself start to flush at that. "Sacred Trees, Rosin, who did you hear that from? …Not Ismay, surely? It hasn't gone that far, has it?"

"Oh no, not Ismay," Rosin replied with an airy dismissal of her hand. "No, it was when the Huberts stopped here on their way back from Earlskirk after last Yule. The oldest daughter's married to some dope from the south-east who spends most of his time hunting. Edmund travelled back with them under the pretext of coming to see us, but the two nights they were here he was definitely in her bed, and she told me she hadn't had a decent night's sleep since her husband had gone off to visit his family. Dead happy about it she was too! Came down both mornings like the cat that'd had the cream!"

"Lucky cow!" Matti said with feeling. Then realised what that sounded like and hurriedly corrected herself. "Getting some attention, I mean. Not that I want to do it with my own cousin! Spirits forefend!"

"How is dear Will, by the way?" Rosin asked.

"*Aaagh*," Matti began with frustration. "Honestly, Rosin, the man's impossible! I'd just got to the point where I was dismissing him as being beyond all hope, and he goes and gets all soft on me. Over in Lorne he was actually *talking* to me, can you believe that? He was genuinely concerned! Worried about the way he'd treated me for all these years."

"You're joking!" Rosin exclaimed. "Mr thick-as-a-brick-wall has finally woken up to the fact that he's been as much use to you as a wet straw in a gale? Wonders will never cease!" Then she saw the look on Matti's face. "Great Maker! You don't actually fancy him now do you?"

"Well just a bit," Matti admitted. "If I thought he could be like that all the time, I could almost start thinking we could have a proper marriage."

"You don't have to stay married to him, you know," Rosin protested.

"Oh really? And how exactly do you think I can get out of it, short of him getting himself killed?" Matti asked sarcastically.

"You could get your marriage annulled on the basis of his infidelity," Rosin suggested.

Matti looked at her as if she had lost her mind. "*Phfaah*! You must be joking! Honestly Rosin, you've spent far too much time up here in the wilds if you think that! Every other man of breeding is shagging someone else at court – usually someone else's wife. The entire court would be getting marriages annulled on a yearly basis if that law really held! …Oh, I know, the Church says marriage is forever and faithful, but they don't even begin to comprehend the problems of political marriages, where you can end up stuck with someone you've hardly met and like less. For most people, affairs are the only way to stay sane. I'd be laughed out of the law courts – even the Church ones – for trying to leave Will for that.

"We're only unusual in that I don't play the court wife game. It's *me* who's seen as the aberration. The freak of a wife who *reads* and whose husband is actually scared of her. He'd be the one who got all the sympathy if our married life became public knowledge! I'd be ostracised by even those few who speak to me now, and I'd never get another proposal of marriage from anyone of standing. I'd be as good as penniless. So you tell me, how bad would it be to make things work for Will and me in that case?"

"Mmmm …well don't start counting your chickens before they've hatched," her friend cautioned her. "This is Will we're talking about, don't forget! Hardly the reliable type except in battle! And if you'll take my advice, don't turn down the chance to have a bit of a fling yourself in the meantime. If, against all odds, it does work out between you and Will, you'll go back much more happily if you can honestly tell yourself it's not because he's the only one on offer."

"Why in the Islands do you say that?" an astonished Matti asked.

"Because Ismay's not the only one that rand young Forester's eyeing up!" Rosin told her with a grin, savouring her frequently all-too-controlled friend's rare disconcertion as she caught Elidyr casting glances her way.

However, as the evening's festivities got underway on the lead up to midnight and the commencement of the Yule celebrations, Rosin began plying her guests with her home-brewed, heady mead. With the youngest children already in bed, the proceedings got distinctly inebriated as the adults and older children got into the spirit of the night. So much so that towards midnight Gerard managed to pull his wife to one side.

"What in the Islands are you doing?" he hissed urgently in her ear. "Are you trying to get them all pissed as rats?"

"Yes!" Rosin hissed back, then saw Gerard's total incomprehension. "Look," she explained, "you remember what Edmund was like last Yule?" Light began to dawn for Gerard. "Do you really want him to end up in bed with Ismay tonight? Or even worse, what if he goes with Kayna tonight and Ismay sees him coming out of her room tomorrow morning? Can you imagine how she'll react?" Gerard groaned. "Exactly!" Rosin declared. "So I want him so drunk all he'll do is crawl into his own bed, and Ismay sufficiently hazy that she won't remember he was making suggestive glances at Kayna. As for Matti, it's about time she let go of some of that self-control for once. And anyway, it's not all of them – look at Iago, he's still stone cold sober, and that Elidyr is hardly even tipsy."

"You're a crafty, conniving woman, did I ever tell you that?" Gerard laughed affectionately, planting a kiss on her lips before taking the jug of mead from her hand and drawing her out of the room.

They returned to their guests by the time the midnight celebration happened, although Rosin looked distinctly ruffled and Gerard was exceedingly cheerful.

"How do they do it?" Edmund asked Matti as he hugged her and wished her well. "How in the Islands do you keep a marriage going like that for all those years?"

But Matti could not find an answer for him, and when she crept into her chilly bed alone an hour later, she felt awfully lonely. Despite her brief reconciliation with Will, here she was again on another Yule night lying in bed by herself. *Nothing's changed*, she thought bitterly, *how stupid was I to think that it ever would? Where's Will? Off on some mission again! And Ruari? Where's he? He's never going to be around any more than Will, unless they chain him to a desk at the Order's headquarters. And how grumpy would he be at that?*

A tear trickled down her cheek. *Oh shit, I'm maudlin drunk!* she realised, but the tears were well in flow now. *I'm never going to be first on the list for either of them. I'm going to go into old age just the way I've lived life so far, all alone. I might as well die in battle, because there's not much to look forward to beyond this.* And she rolled over and let the pillow soak up her tears. Which was why she did not hear the door open softly and someone enter, until the mattress dipped beside her. Before she could say anything a pair of soft lips was kissing hers, and went on doing so for some time. When she could finally draw breath, the voice beside her said softly,

"A brave lady like you shouldn't be so sad on a night like this."

Soft, long hair fell across her face. Elidyr! So Rosin had been right! Part of her thought what a contrived comment it was, and wondered how many times he had used it before, but the other part did not care.

"That's a dreadful seduction line!" she reproved him, then kissed him hard back.

"I know," he laughed as they broke for breath, even as his hands were pulling her night-gown off.

Just for once she wanted to lose herself and forget what and who she was, and so she closed her eyes and let him take over. When she woke midmorning he had tactfully disappeared, for which she was rather glad. However nice it would have been to repeat the night's activities – and they had been good ... very, very good – she wanted to sort out her own feelings. The night had been a blissful relief. A chance for her to at least get a glimpse of what she had missed out on. However, she had no illusions that Elidyr harboured any deep seated love for her. This was not even a romance, and it would be idiotic to think of it as anything more than a very enjoyable night. Yet as she snuggled a little deeper beneath the warm quilt, she resolved that she would not feel guilty for enjoying it either. Neither

Will nor Ruari might come back from their missions, and both of them had had their chances to take comfort where they would. One night was little enough to take in kind – and Elidyr was very experienced and very considerate, and a lot of fun!

Although when she went down to the hall and saw him standing at the window, she found it much harder to be composed than she had hoped. The long black hair was hanging loose rather than in its usual braided queue, making him look much younger. And dressed in just a thick shirt and breeches, she had a first rate view of the slim hips which had reduced her to quivering delight only hours before. He must have seen her come in by the reflection in the glass, for he turned and gave her a warm smile, reducing her knees to jelly. *For Spirit's sake, woman*, she told herself sternly, *he has to be ten years younger than you! Get a grip on yourself!*

Then she did some mental calculations as she heaped bacon into fresh crusty rolls at the table to hide her confusion. No, he must only look that young, because if he was a full Knight in the Foresters that would have put him into his twenties before he achieved rank, the same as any Knight. Moreover, Ruari had referred to the missions Elidyr had been on with him, so he was no newcomer to the Foresters. Taking a crunchy mouthful she wandered over to stand near him, and under cover of eating took sly glances at him. Close to, there were tiny lines around his eyes and the odd grey hair. To her further consternation she realised he must be around thirty, only a handful of years her junior if that – less gap than there was between herself and either Will or Ruari. Even worse, she knew that if he offered to take her back upstairs right now, she would accept in a shot.

Mercifully she was saved by the appearance of Iago and Gerard seeking replenishments of caff from the pot warming on the great fire, and both of them were summoned to the library. It did not stop Elidyr's hand caressing her buttocks as she preceded him through the hall door, though, causing her to splutter on her own caff. Within the library, which also served as the family's map room and music room, however, it was all business. Kayna and Edmund were already pouring over a detailed map of Rheged.

"Good, now we're all here, I'd better give you the bad news," Edmund said, looking up briefly. "There's no way we're going to be able to move about openly. I fear that Tancostyl has been able to use the Helm, or at least is using it to draw Power. Rheged is split in two. Those who have been exposed to him seem to believe his ludicrous stories – even those whom I know would normally question things. He has to have bewitched them in some way, although it's anyone's guess how. He now has a small army at his disposal. Pretty much all the men of the lords who were hanging around Oswine's court, actually.

"The good news is that in the far north and north-west there is strong resistance. When I met Ruari's soldiers over on the north-east coast, even the ordinary folk were not taken in by the tales they were hearing and gave us every help. But we have to be careful. It was one thing to make that one-way journey, but we need to be able to look around, and I don't think Master Brego ever intended us to endanger the ordinary people by them getting caught hiding us."

Iago looked at Kayna and Matti, "Edmund was saying that he doesn't think we'll be able to go straight down to the spot where the Spear was probably last hidden. It's as I feared, we're going to have to do a lot more paper chasing before we can hope to go and start searching on the ground."

"Although he's being watched closely, I think we have to go to Jaenberht," Edmund sighed. "If anyone would know where there are old maps and things it's him. There's just no way we can go and look openly down in the south."

Gerard shook his head regretfully. "I know, but it's going to take us a good two weeks to get up to Scarfell." He tapped the map just below Scarfell and said to Kayna, "Mailros is here. You can see there's no way through the mountains that would shorten the journey. And that means that I don't think we can wait here until the New Year. Much as I want to be here with my family, I think we have to leave tomorrow."

"I'm sorry too, but I agree," Edmund said.

"There's just one thing," Iago interrupted. "Should we really take the west coast route?"

"I was thinking the same thing," Elidyr spoke up. "If Jaenberht is being watched, won't they expect someone to take the route farthest from Oswine's men? I can't help thinking that we'd be a lot safer taking the route up over Fell Peak."

"But that takes us right past Fell Castle, Fell Peak Fort and Catraeth!" Matti protested.

"Yes it does," he replied, "which is why they won't think we'd try to get through there. But that way we'll only have ordinary men to deal with. Ordinary men who hopefully will be getting drunk and laid over the festive season! It always takes weeks to shift the whores out of the barracks at Catraeth after Yule, what with it being too dark to get the men out on exercises much too. Which would you rather face? A man who has a hangover and is daydreaming of the night before, or one of Tancostyl's creatures that never sleeps or loses sight of its prey?"

With memories of Will and Ruari's experience of being followed by rooks and crows also in mind, it was reluctantly decided that Elidyr and Iago were right. Fell Peak Pass was the right route to take. To Kayna and Matti's disgust, it was also decided that they would travel as four soldiers with their two whores.

"If you think I'm walking in the depths of winter with my bosom exposed, you've got another thing coming! I'm not getting frostbite on my sensitive parts no matter how desperate the mission!" Kayna told them in no uncertain terms.

"Oh I don't know," Edmund teased. "I think you'd look quite good in a bit of skimpy lace." Then quickly backed off at the look in Kayna's eyes. "Only joking! …But you do need to be in skirts. Those black leather breeches are very sexy," he added with an appreciative stare, "but you'll stand out a mile dressed like that! And you, too, Matti. You'll have to look more the part."

However, they finally reached a compromise, with the two women agreeing to wear more revealing tops as long as they had warm scarves, wraps and coats. But they would keep their breeches, and wear those instead of underskirts beneath long skirts. The men were convinced of the sense of that once it was pointed out that if they had to make a run for it, layers of petticoats would make it impossible for the two women to keep up. If push came to shove, both of them would cut the skirt ties, leave them, and run in proper boots and breeches which would let them make a decent stride. The rest of the day was therefore spent in making preparations and finding outfits for Matti and Kayna. Ismay, being more attracted to the frilly sort of clothes, found her travelling chest being plundered by the pair and Rosin, and, once she had got over the surprise, joined in with enthusiasm. She proved to have quite an eye for picking which things went together, and being smaller than either Matti or Kayna, her clothes were appropriately tight on them where it mattered.

That night Matti half hoped that Elidyr would appear again. However, when he stayed away, despite her disappointment she was in some way relieved. They were going to have to travel and maybe fight together, and she was not too sure of how she would do that, and keep her mind on the job in hand, if things flared up into a passionate affair.

The next morning's early departure from Rosin and Ismay was uncomfortable as well. Matti had never been the one to take her friend's husband away into danger before, and she was acutely aware that Gerard and Edmund were with them as much out of loyalty to her as any to Brego's commands. After all, they were not Knights, and had said no oath of loyalty to the Order as Iago and Elidyr had.

"I'll do everything possible to keep him safe and sound," Matti promised Rosin, meaning every word.

"I know you will!" Rosin replied with a hug. "I don't like him going, but I know what's at stake. I keep telling myself I don't want my children growing up in a world ruled by the Abend, and this is what my Gerard has to do for his part to make sure that never happens. And you take care too. I want to hear about your night-time visitor when you come back!"

"Is there nothing that happens in this castle that you don't know about?" Matti asked in amused wonder.

"Listen, with Gerard's sons around I've learned to sleep lightly!" Rosin told her. "Tuck them up in bed and five breaths later they're out and off trying to scale the towers again. I know every night-time shift and bump of this old place – *and* when the floor boards creak because someone's up and about! And I assume he was both *up* and *about?*"

"Rosin!" Matti protested, trying to hide her blushes, and feeling very relieved when Edmund turned his mount and led them out of the gate.

They rode out of the castle on local shaggy ponies, except for Gerard who, because of his size, was on a hairy fetlocked farm-horse. There was no way they could take the better horses without giving the game away that they were far wealthier than any ordinary soldiers. At least the roads were relatively clear of snow, having been well trafficked in the run up to Yule. However, the price of inns was a nasty shock, even though they had been prepared for it. For the first two nights they got preferential treatment because Gerard was a well enough known and respected figure to be recognised. The sixth night, though, had them gasping at the price the landlord of the tatty wayside inn near Fell Peak Fort was asking. He obviously thought that anyone stupid enough to be travelling on New Year's Eve was worth fleecing for all he could get. Luckily both Gerard and Iago knew of a mountain hut not far from the Fort, and they declined to pay the price.

It was dark, but with a cloudless sky as they approached the Fort, allowing them to see it clearly. From within there were the sounds of merrymaking, and, keeping to the shadows made by the stone wall which ran along the road, they were fairly sure nobody would be keeping a close enough watch to spot them. Skirting the fort off the road, they slipped up into the side valley which would eventually lead to a pass which crossed to a great loch to the south. Infrequently travelled, it did not justify a proper paved road, but there were enough folk passing that way to warrant the hut, since travellers could hardly ask for hospitality at the army base. It was well into the night when they reached the stout wooden cabin, and there was evidence that someone else had used it not long ago, for the wood was relatively freshly replenished. Iago soon had a fire going in the wide stone grate, and they were able to heat up water for a hot drink.

It was Elidyr, who had been back out to the horses, who spotted that they could see down to the fort from the yard. Once upon a time the view would have been blocked by the mountain, but there were signs of several rock-falls over the years, and now the view was unobstructed. He reported that the whole fort was lit up and much activity going on, but nothing more sinister than the expected festivities, and so they relaxed. Since they were all hungry for a warm meal, they decided that they too would sit up to see the New Year in, which would give the sausages time to cook in the fire. At first they sat chatting companionably, but then noticed that the wind was getting up.

"It must have backed," Edmund observed, as the fire spluttered with a gust rushing down the chimney. "It has to be coming from the west or south-west because it's funnelling straight up this gap."

"Yes, and it's funnelling straight down this bloody top too!" Kayna swore, but allowed Edmund to pull her to him and wrap an arm around her.

To Matti's surprise, the prickly would-be Knight was succumbing to Edmund's charms, although whether anything lasting would come of it, it was too soon to tell. For the moment they had more to worry about with keeping the fire under control. As a precaution they moved anything likely to catch fire well away from it, and moved to the sides of the fireplace rather than sitting in front of it.

"I hate to say this," Gerard said a little later as they were munching piping hot sausages, whose juices were making the hard bread much more palatable, "but I think we're going to have to set a watch tonight. This wind has made the fire too unstable to leave it unwatched, and we banked it up with too many heavy logs before it got rough for it to burn out soon.

Anyway, in this weather we need the warmth, but we don't want to be burnt to death in our sleep either."

Having eaten their fill, they settled down for the night with Iago taking the first watch. He was just waking Elidyr to take over when the most awful noise began to rise outside. The two of them wasted no time in rousing the others, for they feared they might have to make a hurried escape, thinking an armed patrol was inexplicably heading their way. However, as they opened the shelter's door, the gust of wind nearly knocked Gerard in the lead over – no mean feat in itself given his weight. The door flew out of his hands and crashed back against the walls sending them all reeling.

From within the shelter they saw a terrifying sight. The wild bank of cloud covering all overhead seemed to be alive. It writhed and tumbled in all directions, with the wind making such a fearful racket that they did not hear the screams at first, putting them down to the shrieking of the wind through every nook, cranny and crevice outside. Then as their eyes adjusted to the night they began to make out hooves, paws and boots, as if they were watching an army on the move from beneath. The sound of tortured souls screaming in agony was woven into the wind, rising and falling with the gust, as though the tormented rode within the clouds.

For the first time since meeting her, Matti heard real panic in Kayna's voice as she asked, "What *is* that?"

A strangled voice she took a moment to register as Edmund's replied, "The Wild Hunt! Scared Trees protect us! It really is the Wild Hunt."

Staggering to his knees, Gerard crawled to the door and slammed it shut, leaning his weight against it even as Iago launched himself at it too and dropped the bar across it. All of them retreated to the back of the cabin, although they were soon stamping out sparks as the remains of the fire went berserk in the furious gusts howling down the chimney.

"The Wild Hunt?" Kayna asked breathlessly as she scoured the floor for stray burning shards of wood. "I always thought that was just a tale to scare naughty children with. It scared me stiff when I was little."

"Well what else can it be?" a worried Elidyr countered. "It's supposed to ride at the end of Yule, isn't it? And did you see the size of those clouds? They were across the horizon for as far as you could see! And the speed it was moving at? That was never natural!"

Then for an awful moment they were stunned into silence as a crash sounded on the roof. The men seized their weapons, and Matti and Kayna fumbled frantically in the packs where their swords were hidden. It sounded for all the world as if a horse had landed on the slate roof and was prancing on the spot. The dust of ages showered them from the rafters, blinding them with bits in their eyes as they were looking up, and they retreated to the walls, fearful that the roof would come in. An eldritch cackle echoed down the chimney, freezing their blood, and then it was gone.

Wiping streaming eyes, they remained glued to the wall until they were sure it had gone. The wind seemed to be slowly dropping too. With great caution Elidyr risked a glimpse outside, as Gerard and Iago stood poised to slam the door shut if necessary, but nothing sinister appeared. Opening the door fully, they could see the tail end of the cloud moving away. But it had not finished with its nasty surprises. Rising up from the ground a little way off was an eerie column which looked to be made of very much the same stuff as the cloud, and joining the end of it. As they watched, the last remnants of the trailing end rose from the mountains, and were absorbed into the clouds a moment later.

Before anyone else could ask what it was, a white-faced Elidyr turned to them. "The Fort!" he croaked. "I've heard it said that when the Hunt's Lord Jolnir gets as many souls in his army as there are of us alive, he'll return to do battle and take over the world, so that he can escape the Underworld where he was sent by the Maker as punishment."

"I've never heard that," Gerard said shakily, disbelieving what he was hearing and fearing what Elidyr was implying.

"I have," Matti heard herself saying, feeling as though someone else was operating her quivering lips for her. She cleared her throat and tried again. "It's in some of the older books I had at the castle. No-one tells it anymore, a bit like the tales of the Island Treasures."

"So like the Treasures, there might be something in the old tales," an anxious Kayna wondered.

"Yes," Elidyr agreed, "and like the Treasures, the tales of Lord Jolnir have been thought worth passing on because of the fear that they contained some germ of the truth in them. Well if Jolnir wants souls, how many do you think were down in the Fort? And wasn't that tale end of cloud rising from the Fort valley?"

"Could he do that?" an appalled Edmund asked. "Can he actually kill people?"

"I thought it was only those who were unfortunate enough to die on the nights he rides whom he could harvest," Matti argued, forcing back tears of fear. "If he could actually kill people, then how come he hasn't gone on a killing spree and got all the souls he could ever want in one go?"

"No, you're right, he can't kill," Elidyr gasped, forcing his breathing to calm down and taking Matti's trembling hands in his. "Well remembered, Matti! He can't. He can't kill!" although even he would have admitted it sounded more like a mantra he was repeating to calm himself, than something he believed with any conviction. "I must've imagined that cloud rising," he muttered as he pulled her close and held her tight, stroking her hair comfortingly.

They all breathed a little easier, but nobody felt like remaining isolated on the mountain now, and they would have the perfect excuse to seek refuge at the Fort. Iago was the first to grab his bags and head for the ponies. At his exclamation of 'oh Spirits!' the others all rushed round the corner of the cabin. The ponies must have kicked down the door and escaped into the mountains in their terror, but that was not what Iago was looking at. Instead, the veteran had walked over to the wall where there was the best view of the Fort. As the others joined him they understood what had rooted him to the spot. Fires burned in parts of the Fort unchecked, but not a soul moved in the compound. More than that, the whole place was silent. Even from where they stood they could see what looked like heaps of bodies sprawled everywhere.

"Sacred Trees and Blessed Martyrs!" Gerard prayed. "Are they all dead?"

"There must've been a full battalion of a thousand soldiers there, not counting all the cooks, farriers and ostlers and the like," Edmund gasped in horror. "They can't all be dead! Not all of them?"

"I fear they are." Iago's voice carried a dread finality to it. "I haven't seen a single creature move down there. I don't know how, but they're all gone. If that was Jolnir, he just got himself a half a regiment in one go!"

Chapter 17

Tales of the Departed

Rheged: Eft-Yule

In a daze, the six of them staggered down the snowy hillside towards Fell Peak Fort. None of them wanted to believe that not a soul survived below, and all felt compelled to go and make sure nobody needed help. It was a totally surreal experience slithering down the slopes, for the howling gale had erased all signs of human passage and left the snow pristine and untrammelled again. Matti felt like they were the only people left in the world, then found that so terrifying that she automatically reached for Elidyr and Iago for the comforting reassurance of touching someone alive. Kayna too, she noticed, was hanging on to Edmund and Gerard as though they might suddenly be sucked away from her. The crunching of their boots across the surface sounded unbelievably loud. So loud that they could not believe that anyone around would not hear their approach.

Stumbling onto the main road, they saw the gates to the fort hanging drunkenly from their hinges. The iron bands holding them had burst apart as if some monster had torn his way in by hand. In shock, they walked in unchallenged. It looked like a scene from some deranged painter's idea of the Underworld, and even the battle-hardened Iago stood aghast at the sight. Everywhere there were bodies. Some heaped up, others lying singly. Some with arrows or spears sticking out of them, stabbed by their own comrades. Men seemed to have fallen on their neighbours and friends and torn one another to pieces. Others still lay where they had fallen, each still clutching the dagger they had stabbed their partner in death with. And so many. A thousand men seemed a huge number when they were on the move, but there was something even more overwhelming about seeing that number of dead.

Yet only parts of that number were actually out where they could be seen. Many must have died in the buildings which were now blazing infernos, and the ghastly red, flickering light kept bringing new scenes to a weird but static life. Suddenly they would see a man's arm thrown up as if reaching for help, only to realise it was the light moving and not the arm. It flickered in sightless eyes, too, unnerving everyone. A loud crash nearly made them jump out of their skins with fright, until they realised that the fire was beginning to really take hold across the fort, and that a large beam had fallen in on one of the barracks.

"We haven't got long!" Iago warned them. "Luckily the main walls and the keep are big, old, seasoned oaks, and they'll take forever to catch alight, but the rest will go up in earnest soon. Let's split up. Gerard, you take Elidyr and Kayna and go left. The rest of us will go right. Stay in your threes, go round the parade square, and keep to the outside unless you definitely hear someone – and I mean *hear*, as in proper words! Don't risk your lives because you think you hear a vague moan or groan. The buildings collapsing will make plenty of those, I can tell you from experience! Just keep calling and listening. We haven't time to search all the buildings before it gets too dangerous to stay."

Gerard immediately caught on that Iago was separating the two attachments which had formed, and chivvied his partners off. Away from the distractions of Edmund and Matti, Kayna and Elidyr were more focused and they worked with a will, calling into those buildings which were not already blazing furiously. Harsh though it seemed there was little point in even looking into those firmly ablaze. Nobody was likely to be there, and, if they were, there was no way that the three of them could affect a rescue. Yet if anything it was even more depressing that, by the time they had worked their way around the left-hand buildings which surrounded the open parade ground in the middle of the fortress, it was obvious that no-one living was left. Every so often they saw Iago, Edmund and Matti on the opposite side, and each time their hearts lifted in the hope that it might be someone else before seeing the shaking of heads signalling failure there too.

When they met at the east gate, Iago's group looked even more shaken.

"Even the horses are dead," Iago said, appalled. "It looks like the men went mad and cut the poor animals throats where they stood in their stalls."

Suddenly Kayna's head came up and a fierce glint came into her eyes.

"That's it!" she announced firmly. The others looked at her in astonishment, both at her words and her sudden turn from sorrow to anger. "That's how it happened!" she declared. "You were right, Matti! Jolnir can't kill the living. He can only harvest those who happen to be at the point of death when he passes. But something made these men kill themselves at precisely the right moment, and that something was the Abend!"

"How can you know that?" Matti asked in astonishment.

"When we were travelling to Ergardia and we got to the abbey where Maelbrigt and Labhran fought the grollican, the monks told us of brothers going mad. Maelbrigt and Labhran said on one night back then that the Abend strike at people through their fears. That thing we've just seen may possibly have really been Jolnir, but what's the betting he was summoned by the Abend?"

"Bastards!" Elidyr exclaimed, mentally kicking himself for allowing himself to be so overwhelmed that he had failed to think clearly. "Why didn't I see it? Which direction was the wind coming from? The west!" he carried on, working out his thoughts aloud for the others to follow. "Of course the Abend wouldn't do this just to do Jolnir a favour. We've had proof that some of them are on the hunt here in the Islands. Aach, this reeks of their plotting! Turn us on ourselves on the night when men are too drunk to resist the spectres whispering in their ears. Let the armies take the lands close to New Lochlainn, and let the rest of us destroy ourselves so they can just walk in."

No-one could argue with that, and in a strange way it made them all feel just that bit better. Knowing it was still the same enemy they had set out to fight brought them back to earth. However, it was now imperative that they leave the fortress with all speed. The heat was becoming unbearable, and only the remaining winds driving the smoke on in gusts stopped them being enveloped in it. They hurried through the east gate and on down the road. When they finally paused to look back they could see that Iago had been right. The main walls still stood, but from within them a column of flame rose that filled the orbit of their dark frame. It stood out like a vast beacon in the night which would be visible for miles.

"We'd better get out of here," Gerard warned. "That blaze is going to be easily seen from Fell Castle, and they're bound to send a troop out. And I wouldn't be surprised if the watch at Catraeth didn't spot something with this pass being so high. We don't want to meet anyone coming up the valley. How would we explain how we escaped?"

But they saw nobody. By a stroke of good luck they found the ponies nervously cropping the exposed grass under a rocky overhang two miles down the road, and managed to catch them. However, the saddles were still up at the refuge, and nobody felt like going back for them. Luckily the bridles had been left on as halters, with only the bits removed to allow the ponies to feed, and so they soon had them in a state where they could be ridden. Riding bareback was not ideal in the conditions, but then they were going slowly anyway.

That night they found another mountain refuge, and the same the night after. By this time they were becoming increasingly bothered by the lack of traffic on the road. Surely by now someone from Catraeth should be coming to investigate? On the fifth night they approached the small watchtower of Cat Castle in great trepidation. They had still seen nobody on the road, and the approach to the isolated castle was uncharacteristically silent. Only when they got right to the cluster of small huts at the foot of the castle did they see signs of life. Terrified villagers crept out of their homes to greet them in stunned delight.

"We thought we were the only ones left in the world alive!" one shaken old man told them.

"What happened to the garrison?" Edmund asked.

A stocky farmer struggled to find the words. "It was Yule. ...We celebrated as usual. ...Most of us have stock to tend to, so once the midnight bell had struck and we'd wished one another well we went to our beds. The soldiers went on carousing."

"Drunk as usual!" a buxom grey-haired wife denounced them, folding her arms disapprovingly under her ample bosom, but with less venom in her voice than the newcomers felt she might usually have used.

"Yes, drunk," the farmer conceded, "but nothing outrageous. Nothing to cause alarm! They were always well controlled, and the watch were *never* drunk on duty. ...But that night ...oh Spirits, that night!"

"The storm came!" a rabbity-faced girl squeaked.

"We saw it too," Gerard confirmed solemnly, at which there was a collective breath of relief from the villagers. They had not been alone! And these strangers would need no convincing that they were not losing their minds. The farmer continued.

"We've talked it over. It was the noise of the storm that began to wake us, but up here we get some vicious winds at this time of year and we build to withstand them. It was the screams that really woke us up! Sacred Trees, they were dreadful!"

"We could see them!" the buxom wife joined in, her voice now quavering with remembered fear. "There were men on the battlements fighting ...strangling one another! We could see them in the torch light!"

"And the watch kept calling to them to stop..."

"...but they turned on the watch..."

"…killed them…"

"…tossed some of them off the top of the walls! Their own…"

"…their mates! Killed them…"

"…stone dead! Ran mad inside the walls!"

A babble of voices overran one another in their haste to tell the tale.

"A big column of smoke…"

"…or cloud…"

"…went straight up from the castle…"

"…up to that cloud thing!"

"The last of the watch died bravely," the farmer concluded. "They chopped the ropes holding the portcullis, trapping themselves and everyone else inside the castle. They saved our lives! They stopped the mad ones getting out. …We heard them being torn to pieces …" He stopped and swallowed convulsively at the memory. "It was horrible! Like something out of a nightmare, only it was real."

"The same happened up at Fell Peak Fort," Edmund told them gravely, and received a collective gasp of horror in response.

They found themselves being hustled into the barn-like building which passed for the market hall of the village, and had food and mulled wine pressed upon them as they were made to recount their own tale. As Gerard and Edmund told it for the second time, Kayna and Matti sat to one side looking around. It was obvious that many of the villagers were sleeping here now, going by the number of bedrolls, seeking safety in numbers. They could see old folk and children clustered near the large hearth, and many of middle years, and young women, but no youths. As Gerard drew their tale to a close, Matti ventured to ask a question.

"Tell me, please, did you lose any of your own?"

There rose a muffled sobbing from parts of the hall.

"Most of the young men, we think …the unmarried ones. They liked to celebrate with the men in the castle," the farmer replied, grief written across his face. "About half a dozen of our sons were inside as guests." He paused, struggling with his sorrows and fears. "We don't earn much out of farming up here," he explained. "The children always work on the farms, so it's not like they ever have to go out of their way to learn the business when they get older."

Then shook his head and tears stood in his eyes. "Most of the lads go down to Catraeth to work as servants at the barracks for a few years while they're still single. Happen it helps us out, see? One less mouth to feed when it's a big hungry lad makes a difference. And they get to see a bit of the outside world. Calms them down a bit, makes them grow up, having to stand up for themselves in a big place full of strangers. Them as is a bit free with their fist up here, soon learn as there's bigger and tougher men than them down there. A few like it and go for soldiering, but most come back. ...But not this time ..." He broke down and a friend came to clasp his shoulder and carry on.

"Thomas' son is ...was ...down at Catraeth," he explained. "Every day we've hoped to see someone from down there come up to see what's happened. Now we fear the same's happened down there as here."

"Spirits! You've not heard from Catraeth?" Edmund asked in horror, and received shaking heads as his answer. "What? ...*Nobody?*"

The friends looked at one another in growing disbelief. If the same had happened at Catraeth, then one of the biggest garrisons in the whole of Rheged, possibly in the whole of the Islands, had been wiped out in one night. No, not even one whole night! In a mere hour or so! As they stood struggling with the vastness of the tragedy, a thin, red-eyed woman plucked at Edmund's sleeve.

"Please sir, can you get into the castle? Can you go and find out? Can you tell me if my boy is really dead? So I can bring him back and bury him? Please?"

Her plea touched all their hearts. However bad Fell Peak Fort had been, none of them had had someone they cared for in there, and knowing what that had been like, they could not refuse.

Iago looked to Elidyr. "Can you scale the walls?"

Elidyr went to peer out of the door at the great mass of stone beyond, then nodded. "I should think so. It's not like it needs to be done at speed. Those walls aren't defended anymore, and there are plenty of handholds with the stone being so old and worn."

"If you can lead the way, I can probably follow," Edmund volunteered. "I'll need a rope to help, but if you get up and then give me something to grab hold of in a crisis, I should make it."

"And me," Kayna chipped in, to the locals' surprise. "Don't look at me like that," she chastised Gerard and Iago. "Gerard's kids aren't the only ones to cut their teeth climbing the walls of their own home, you know. I spent all my childhood evading nurses by swarming up the walls where they couldn't follow! I bet I've had more practice than all of you at climbing castle walls!"

That nobody could argue with, and so the next morning the three of them were sent to form a reconnaissance party into the castle. Matti, Gerard and Iago waited anxiously at the bottom as Elidyr carefully ascended the wall. Before the end of the rope had even reached Edmund's grasp, Kayna had reached up and grasped a hand hold in the stone. To their amazement she was as quick as Elidyr climbing up, never once having to resort to the rope next to her. Edmund followed more slowly, several times having to grasp the rope for a moment to steady himself, but finally reaching the top without mishap. At that point the three scouts disappeared from view and those below hurried to the gate to wait.

It seemed like ages, but in reality it was only a short while before they heard the others behind the great oak barricades.

"Elidyr's climbing up to the winch," Kayna called to them. "It looks like they cut the rope close to the portcullis, so there should be plenty of slack left for us to let it down and reattach it to the eye-holes at the side of the iron grill. Edmund's hacking the old knot off now," and much clanging and banging bespoke the truth of this.

As everyone stood in nervous anticipation, they took reassurance from the fact that they could hear the voices of the three within conversing, even if they could not quite hear what was being said. Then there began an asthmatic creaking and some tortured, metallic groans. These were followed by the sounds of heaving and struggling at the gates themselves, which then swung in to reveal the three climbers looking distinctly sooty.

"Some fool lit a fire right under the portcullis," Edmund explained. "All the lubricating grease has run off from the winch and the pulleys, and the slot in the arch the iron grill goes into is choked with soot."

Edging in through the gate, it was now apparent that the portcullis was up just enough for men to duck under without having to crawl.

"Don't worry, it's secure," Edmund reassured them. "There's nothing wrong with the brake, we just couldn't raise it any further with only the three of us. Get half a dozen strong men on it and some grease on the winch, and it'll go back up properly."

However, the villagers were streaming past them into the bailey of the castle, and then crying out in horror at what they saw there. Following them in, the six travellers could only sympathise with their reaction. Had they not already seen the same at Fell Peak they too would have been stunned by the ferocity of what had happened within. Here too, man had fallen upon man, friend killing friend in a senseless and manic frenzy.

"There's no-one left here either," Elidyr softly said to the three who had waited outside.

"Then there's nothing we can do to help," Iago sighed. "We'd best make for Catraeth tomorrow."

"But what will we find there?" Matti worried.

That night they willingly accepted the shelter of the grateful villagers, and replenished their dwindling supplies from the castle. The big difference from Fell was that here nobody had managed to burn down the wooden buildings within the castle walls, and the stores remained un-destroyed. At the same time, Gerard and Edmund pressed upon the villagers the need to take the garrison's bodies out to the tilting yard beyond the walls, and simply cremate them all together.

"You have to move them now before they become a focus for disease as they rot," Gerard insisted. "With the ground frozen like iron you can't hope to bury even a handful of them, let alone the two hundred plus in there."

And reluctantly the villagers agreed.

It was with heavy hearts that the six rode on the next day, leaving their distraught hosts with such a grisly task. It was only a day's ride to Catraeth, yet the snow for most of the way still remained undisturbed and pristine. Only as they ventured towards the outskirts of the large town which serviced the barracks did they see signs of life. At least here, though, there were signs of real activity. A nasty smell clung on the breeze coming from several controlled fires dotted around the landscape, unseen themselves but identified by their plumes of black, oily smoke.

"Thank the Trees someone's begun the clearing up here," Iago said, even as he coughed on the smoke.

Closer to the barracks they found a hive of activity, and at least here in the throng, their appearance attracted no attention. Dismounting, they led the ponies through the mass of dazed people until they were close to the great fortified barracks. The gates here stood thrown open, and within was a sight to quench the most ebullient character. The whole of the great conglomeration of sleeping quarters, stores, practice halls and administration buildings lay in smouldering ruins. Nothing stood unless it was stone or the charred bulks of vast oak timbers. The exterior walls stood as they always had in lonely remembrance of its former function, for it would be many months if not years before Catraeth was fully operational again.

A constant flow of haggard town and country folk moved about. Those coming out of the gates carried makeshift stretchers, with human forms covered with any piece of cloth or blanket which could be pressed into service. Those going in had empty stretchers awaiting their next grim load.

Without a word the six turned and walked on past the garrison perimeter walls. There was no need to inquire what had happened here – the tale was too familiar by now. Nor did they see a single man in uniform until they got to a large inn almost on the southern edge of the town. There a harassed captain was pouring over a map propped on the stone horse trough, his sergeants about him. Edmund brushed his hands over his travel stained coat and smoothed his hair down, then approached them.

"Good day," he said calmly.

"I can't help you, stranger," the captain said without looking up, his voice reflecting the stress he was suffering. "I have no men and too much to do."

"I know, I'm not looking for help," Edmund reassured him. "All I wanted to do was save you a journey in vain."

This got the captain's attention, and as he looked up they could see how young he was. Edmund's calm assurance seemed to register and he straightened up, brows furrowed in curiosity.

"A journey?"

"I know this isn't what you want to hear," Edmund carried on, "but we've been travelling through the mountains. We got to Fell Peak Fort the day after New Year and all that's left is the walls and charcoal – just like here." The soldiers let out a collective moan of horror. "Last night we were at Cat Castle, and the villagers there have just got into the castle and are starting cremating the dead. I wish I had better news, but I regret to tell you that no-one seems to have survived at either place. We'd hoped things would be better here. That it was just local. I'm guessing you were hoping the same?"

"*All* gone?" the young captain cried in disbelief.

"Sacred Trees, we're cursed," one of the sergeants choked wearily.

"Was it just the north-west, do you know?" Edmund asked. "Have you heard from south of here? I have a brother down at Crauwel," he improvised. "I'm worried sick for him. We thought it was just some freak accident at Fell, but then we got to Cat and now this? How far has this gone?"

"We've no idea," another sergeant replied, grey-faced with strain. "We were on the road ourselves – down at Lund. The storm passed us by, but then we were all asleep – the monks don't go in for revelries much. We heard of unrest in Winton and beyond, and so came up here with all haste. We had a message for the captain here to call out all the men to hunt for some traitors. A message from the king no less."

"Traitors?" Matti gasped, having no problem looking frightened. It had to be them the message referred to.

"Aye miss, traitors," his friend said. "Although whether it was really from the king, or that strange fellow who's always at his side these days, I couldn't say. We were just told to ride with all speed so as they were caught as soon as possible. Well that's gone by the board now! We'd best hope the raiders over in the east have gone too, because if they're still there and hear of this, we'll have more than one or two bad lads of our own to contend with. At the moment we couldn't fight off a flock of sheep, much less armed raiders!"

"Spirits!" Gerard exclaimed, both at their near brush with disaster and the state of affairs in general.

Wishing them good luck, the six left the soldiers and rode on until they were well out of sight.

"Phew, that was a narrow escape!" Gerard said, reining in his plodding horse. "Why did you risk speaking to them, Edmund?"

Edmund shrugged. "What did we have to lose? Those villagers at Cat aren't going to forget us in a hurry, are they? It seemed better to tell that captain he didn't need to go there at all. Keep him thinking about the big picture, not worrying about why six strangers were making such a journey in the depths of winter. And it paid off, didn't it! Now we know we were compromised from the start."

"I know! But how did Tancostyl know we were in Rheged?" fretted Iago.

"Maybe Ruari's men attracted his attention," Matti wondered. "He may not have been worried about them since they were so clearly leaving the Island, but just left his creatures watching to make sure. We must've been spotted arriving."

"But how?" worried Elidyr. "Think about it, we arrived at night. None of the birds were about, and my old companions are too thorough to have left a strange person hanging around. Yet that message must have left *Earlskirk* the very same day we reached Thorpness. It couldn't get here by road any quicker!"

"Then it's Thorpness that's being watched!" Gerard interrupted in horror, thinking of his family.

"Yes, but I doubt your loved ones are in danger," Matti reassured him. "After all, in themselves they represent no threat. And we weren't there long enough to have put them in peril. Once we left, Rosin and the boys will have gone on doing the normal domestic things they always do. They won't be behaving suspiciously, will they?"

"And that wasn't only what I meant anyway," Elidyr emphasised. "Don't you see what this means? Either that cursed war-mage has a hold on the mind of someone in the castle, so that what they see he sees, without any delay in time. Or someone knew we were coming, and sent the message by more normal means even before we set foot in Rheged. Because in this weather, how long would it take a rider to get from Thorpness, across the mountains and into Earlskirk? More than the three days it took us to ride from Little Thorpe to Thorpness, that's for certain! More like three weeks in these conditions, surely? Which means the Abend either have a spy in Lorne to have known that early on – which isn't possible – or there's magic at work here."

Gerard conceded to this, but still looked worried sick for his family and rode in silent misery beside Matti. Edmund, Elidyr and Iago, however, were still worried on a different score. As they rode onwards, the three chewed away at the problem of how they had been betrayed like dogs worrying a bone.

If someone within Gerard's household was under Abend influence, why had Ruari been able to hide there, and why had the arriving men of the Order not been waylaid before they could reinforce Ergardia? Edmund was quite certain that nobody new had joined the servants in over a year, let alone more recently. Rosin and the children were above suspicion, beyond a doubt, but it was Kayna who finally pointed the finger of blame at Ismay, as they were settling the horses down in the shelter of an isolated barn as darkness fell.

"No!" Edmund exclaimed, appalled at the idea.

"Who else is left?" Kayna demanded. "You've been blinded by her sweet innocence, but the innocent can sometimes do the most awful things simply by not comprehending the evil some men can do. What if she wrote to Osbern telling him that his friends were due back? Rubbing his nose in it that *he* wasn't there but you, Edmund, *were*. You've told us how insanely jealous Osbern is nowadays. Maybe she wanted to pay him back for all the hurt he caused her by letting him twist that knife in his own gut?"

"Oh Sacred Trees," Edmund sighed, "but I suppose it is possible."

Matti looked over the back of her horse as she lifted the saddle off. "Of course it's possible!" she chaffed at them. "Honestly! You men! She's not some fey little creature. Some Sacred Martyr. Ismay's flesh and blood, and even someone as even-tempered as her can be pushed beyond their limit of tolerance. Kayna's right. Ismay may have no idea of how or why Osbern is compromised, or that he couldn't be trusted not to betray his friends. She would never think that letting him stew in his own juice might rebound on us. Yes, she knows that priest is trouble of the worst sort, but she could hardly have known that he answers to one of the Abend until we told her – and by then the message must've gone. In fact, if she wrote at the same time as the message was being sent to Ergardia to summon the fleet of boats, the letter could have been sent as early as the middle of Aer-Yule."

"Hounds of the Wild H… Spirits! I won't ever use that curse lightly again," Gerard gulped. He coughed then continued, "But Ismay did write! …After I sent the first message to Ferryfort to say that the men were expected. I didn't question what she was writing, because the letter went back to *her* house at Hilby." He shook his head in irritation at himself. "I should have thought! …Curses! We all know how controlling Osbern is with her. I should have guessed he'd have his spies close to her still."

"And if one of those spies was the priest, it makes even more sense," Kayna added.

"In fairness to Ismay, he may not have been at Hilby when she left home," Matti said thoughtfully. "The priest may have turned up unannounced after she'd left, and the servants would hardly have had the authority to turf him out. From what we're guessing, he won't be the sort who would have scruples about reading a letter not addressed to him. The letter could have reached there in under a week. A message by bird from there would have had time to get through…"

"…or if the priest is one such as Ruari and I saw at Montrose, then Tancostyl could have read it through his familiar's eyes for himself," Edmund concluded. "No time need have elapsed at all before that bastard wizard knew enough to put two and two together and make more than four!"

Elidyr gazed in unfocused concentration at the roof timbers. "That would work," he agreed. "That would still have left him the best part of a fortnight before Yule when that captain arrived at Lund, when we know Tancostyl had men out on the roads looking for us. Yes, that definitely fits! It gives Tancostyl a couple of days to get his plans in place and to get Oswine to give the order, then the riders time to start making their way north."

"But what about my Rosin?" a frantic Gerard asked. "What'll happen to her if the priest decides to go to Thorpness? Tancostyl's ire could fall on my family!"

Yet Tancostyl had other things on his mind at that point. For since the turn of the year, he had been driven as near to despair as he had ever known in his long life. In one misbegotten night his plans had been reduced to total wreckage. As the cloud had appeared over the mountains to the west of Earlskirk, he had anticipated trouble. But even his darkest premonitions could not have prepared him for the chaos that ensued.

At his insistence, his puppet king, Oswine, had assembled all the troops at his disposal at the two great garrison towns of Crauwel in the south and Catraeth in the north, and in the capital, Earlskirk. Between them they were to launch attacks which would throw Rheged into civil war, under the cover of which Tancostyl had intended to move the Helm across the Island to Crauwel, there to await a ship to Brychan. With an army on the move, nobody would spot the lowlifes and dregs of society who would flock in his wake, drawn by the tainted energy which would wash over the countryside from the emergent Treasure. He and the Helm would move unhindered to their destination.

Moreover, the army was to have been Tancostyl's personal bodyguard on a grand scale, and not just from the petty thieves and vagabonds who might be drawn to try to steal the Helm. To his rising frustration, he had been unable to find out exactly who the person was he kept hearing of, but someone of high repute as a leader had appeared out of the wilderness, and seemed to have found out more than Tancostyl liked about his own plans. It had to be a native Islander to have gone to ground so expertly and without a trace, and Tancostyl disliked mysteries. The last thing he needed at this delicate stage in the proceedings was some cursed, charismatic rebel leader stirring up those who had not yet fallen under his spell into an effective resistance.

He had been forced to concede that he was working with very inferior raw materials with which to craft his masterpiece from. The idiot Oswine had a positive talent for alienating those who had supported his father, and far too many of the leading nobility had quit the court before Tancostyl had been in a position to blackmail, or bemuse, them into subjection. As individuals they posed little threat, but, were they to combine, the number of men they could rally to their cause would tip the balance decidedly in their favour in any open conflict. Nor had he anticipated that the monastic order would prove to be quite such a thorn in his side. That bumbling fool of an archbishop, Fulchere, had assured him that the spiritual guidance of the Islanders was his sole purlieu – and the idiot had truly believed that, since no-one could have hidden a deliberate misdirection given the depths of Tancostyl's mental probing.

In reality Abbot Jaenberht was proving to have a far more wide-ranging and effective influence than Fulchere. Moreover, the abbot had proved impossible to silence. Oswine's bungled attempt to have him and his leading churchmen ambushed and killed, had only served to alert the wily old man to the depth of the danger he was in. And even worse, far from being intimidated, Jaenberht had gone on the offensive using his considerable influence to persuade nobles of the danger of going to court, thereby depriving Tancostyl of the chance to enchant any more of them into subservience.

Yet at that point all had still been to play for. Jaenberht and this mysterious stranger – or maybe more than one of them – assumed that Tancostyl was aiming to take control of Rheged, and were acting on that premise. Tancostyl, however, had no intention of lingering any longer than possible in this benighted corner of the world. He could therefore afford to be reckless with the men at his disposal, and if pushed intended to be. There was no need to retain enough men to hold onto his gains – in fact it hardly mattered if they were decimated, or even slaughtered wholesale, in the process of getting him to the boat. And once aboard, he could hardly have cared any less about what happened to those he left behind.

But then New Year had come. By the twitching of his senses at the ripplings in the Power, Tancostyl had known the cloud boded ill. He could sense the glamour even if he had not yet made out what its purpose was. Like Eliavres, his first thought on seeing the Wild Hunt manifest itself in the skies of Rheged was one of humorous delight at the idea of rendering the Islanders panic-stricken with their own legend. That was, though, until it reached his vantage point in one of the castle towers, and he saw its effects on the men below. What in the Underworld had possessed the witches to add such a compulsion to the illusion? These were the men he needed! Needed alive! Alive and capable of defending him. Yet now they were falling on one another like rabid curs.

Frantically drawing the Power to him, he had cast a shield in front of the edge of the glamour, forcing its energy up and away from those on the ground. Sweat pouring off him from the effort, he spread his shield as far across the land as he could while still maintaining its integrity, using the near bank of the great river which flowed past the capital as his anchor point for its edge. The shield drained him of everything he had, and even as the storm passed on into the east and dissipated, he slid to the ground unconscious.

When he woke it was to initial relief. The early reports revealed that almost two thirds of the force he had had in the capital had survived, and for the first day he felt thankful he had caught the glamour in time. But then the reports had started coming in. First was a bird from a spy of Oswine's in Mussel Bay, near to Crauwel, speaking of seeing the flames of Crauwel burning even from that distance. Hard on its heels came news of the complete and total loss of all the force gathered there. At this point Oswine had had hysterics, and Tancostyl for the first time had begun to comprehend the depths of the disaster which had happened.

By the time the news from a man outside of Catraeth arrived, he was apoplectic with anger. Which one of those stupid bitches had come up with this? On the Sacred Temples of Lochlainn, he swore, he would rend each of them limb from limb when he reached New Lochlainn! What raging incompetents! In one rash move, they had deprived him of the means to bring one of the DeÁine's most important weapons out of the hands of the forsaken Islanders.

Tancostyl had ground his teeth and torn his mattress to shreds with his bare hands in his fury. Had he not been so desperate to hang onto those men he had left, he would have sucked the life force out of as many as he could take, and hurled a sending of his own back at the witches that would have rattled their teeth. Instead, those beggars and poor folk of Earlskirk who had survived the night met their end in their dozens, as Tancostyl projected his alter ego out of his body, and went on a feeding frenzy to replenish its lost reserves of energy. Gone was any hope of a covert departure, and his temper was at its limit, so that when Oswine made some fatuous remark, Tancostyl pounced upon him. All his frustrations bubbled over and he physically bounced Oswine off the throne room walls, punching and shaking the hefty young man as if he were no more than a feather pillow.

By the time he stopped, Oswine was bloody, near insensible and terrified out of what little of his wits were left. Crouched in a corner of the room, he rocked and whimpered, deserted with speed by those he once thought his friends and supporters. Most fled the castle that night, let go by Tancostyl as being of no use anyway. He had their men, and that had been their sole attribute in his mind, being too ignorant of the lands they held to even be useful to him for information. The men were ordered to prepare to march, and in the morning exactly a week after the New Year, Tancostyl rode out of Earlskirk in a litter lined with warm furs, cradling the Helm in his lap, and surrounded by the small force which would now have to serve as his army to get him to the coast. His sending to Helga in the night had been savage, his rage pouring down the flow of the Power and leaving her writhing in agony, his message clear. *The boat! Send the boat! Now! Fail and you die!*

As Tancostyl's litter exited the city gates, in the deserted throne-room an elderly man, muffled in a heavy cloak and leaning on a sturdy staff, walked rheumatically to the collapsed would-be-king of Rheged, who recoiled away from him along the floor.

"Come, come, my son," a gentle voice spoke. "You have nothing to fear from me." He reached down, and with a sturdy hand grasped Oswine's arm. "Up you get! That floor's too cold to stay sitting on, and besides, I can't bend down enough to tend your cuts if you stay there."

Oswine allowed himself to be pulled to his feet, and tottered to a bench which the old man had righted and set against the wall. Retrieving the cleanest cloth left, which had adorned a table set with food, the old man also found a flagon of strong wine, and began to use the wine to clean Oswine's cuts and bruises. The wine stung horribly, but the old man insisted it was the best thing they had to hand. It shocked him to realise that the pale stuff he was washing away was, in fact, Oswine's blood, which instead of being bright red was almost colourless in the weak candlelight of the hall. He had heard of someone being bled white as a saying, but the reality was worrying. Was that the result of close contact with the Helm, he wondered? Then he pressed bread into Oswine's hands with a cup of wine and made him eat, taking the same for himself.

"What am I going to do?" Oswine suddenly wailed piteously. "What's happened? Why did he do that? I did everything he told me to! Why didn't he tell me if he wanted different?"

"You've fallen in with evil men, my son," the calm voice replied, pushing his hood back to reveal the head of an elderly monk. "You forgot the teachings of your father and grandfather. You allowed yourself to be seduced with promises of grandeur and riches, without ever thinking of how they would be paid for."

Oswine looked aghast and yet uncomprehending.

"I don't mean just in money," was the monk's gentle reproof. "That sort of power comes with obligations, as your father well knew. You took the life of leisure and let the control slip away out of your hands. And now it's all gone. You let it go because it was too much bother to keep it, and now the man who beat you has control of all you once had, and has cast you aside as having outlived your purpose."

"Will he come back and kill me?" wailed Oswine in terror.

"I have no way of knowing," the monk said calmly, passing him another hunk of bread.

"But what am I to *do*?"

"You can repent, and help those who've been working all along to prevent this disaster," the monk suggested. "But this will be no easy ride, I warn you. This time you cannot lie on your couch while others do the work. However, *these* men do not want you in order to take what you have. They won't treat you the way Tancostyl has."

"Who's Tancostyl?" was Oswine's confused question.

"The man who's been acting as your counsellor, your chief adviser. …The priest… The one who just near beat you to death"

But Oswine's expression remained an addled blank. *Sacred Martyrs and Spirits*, Father Walter thought, *his wits have truly gone!* And as if on cue Oswine asked,

"Where's my father? Why isn't he here? Why do I have to do this? He should be the one taking charge. I don't know what to do!"

"Your father is dead, son," Father Walter said as gently as he could.

"Don't be silly! He was here only last week."

"Last week? My dear boy, your father died fighting raiders in the east two years ago."

"No! No, he couldn't have! He was here only last week!"

"What year do you think this is?" Walter asked cautiously.

"What a silly question! It's the year 539 of the Current Era, of course."

Walter sighed sadly. "No, my son, I'm afraid it isn't. We've just passed the New Year into the year 542. You've lost over two years of your life in which a wicked war-mage took over your life and clouded your mind."

Oswine whimpered in terror again and began mechanically shaking his head, as if doing that would make the truth change.

"I'm sorry, it's the truth. In that time, you became King Oswine and, under the influence of that war-mage, you alienated all your father's trusted advisers. Those you didn't have killed! You may have no memory of those things, but I assure you that your subjects will take a very long time before they can forget much of what was done in your name. Few would throw you a line if you were drowning, and many would stamp on your hands as you tried to climb out of the water and kick you back in."

"What's to become of me?" Oswine cried, truly frightened and disorientated now. Ghosts of memories were beginning to float across his mind now, but it was as though he was watching someone else walking around in his body. Then another thought came to him. "If I was so bad, why are you helping me? Are you helping me, or are you just waiting to get your own back like those others? Who are you?"

"I'm Father Walter, and I used to be prior of Maerske Abbey under Abbot Jaenberht. You knew him, although I doubt you remember that now. As for why I'm helping you …I've known many folk who've died and not deserved to, but I can't bring them back to life, and if the Divine Maker and his Spirits choose not to either, then I have to believe that it's all part of some greater design. That our small lives are part of a wondrous web that we can barely see the most insignificant strand of. By that creed I therefore have to believe that they have chosen *not* to let you die now, and if the Sacred ones want you to live then I must help you do so."

Although, Spirits help me, I could willingly put a few more dents in your miserable pate for the ill you've done! Walter thought. *Well might you howl for your father! He was more of a man at twelve than you'll be if you live to be ninety. Tancostyl wouldn't have found Michael half so easy to lull into a daze, and as for your Uncle Ruari…! I hope whatever misbegotten gods the DeÁine pray to are ready to receive Tancostyl's shrivelled soul in short order if Ruari ever catches up with him, because if I was a betting man my money would be on Ruari winning hands down.*

He looked at Oswine, still rocking in childlike misery, a string of snot running unchecked from each nostril, and tried not to think how long this journey was going to feel whilst caring for one such as this. *Spirits, have I led such a life as to require a penance such as this?* he wondered. Then, remembering the state of Oswine's blood, looked twice to make sure that it was not blood running from Oswine's nose. It did not seem to be, but the state of Oswine's health might complicate things even further. Sighing deeply he pulled on his woollen mittens and saw a thick cape that would do for Oswine.

"As for what will happen to you …come, we'll go to the stables. We have a long journey ahead of us into the north, and neither of us is fit to walk that far. All the horses have gone, but when I rode in earlier, there was another mule to keep my old girl company. I'm too old to fight and I lack Jaenberht's energy, but I'm not in my dotage yet, and I promised my friend Ron I would come here and see what I could learn of you. However addled your wits are, you're still the legitimate heir to the Rheged Jarldom (let's forget that 'king' nonsense, shall we?) and in the light of that we need to take you to safety. Come! You, my son, are going to Abbot Jaenberht, where you can be kept from doing yourself any further mischief!"

And putting a firm hand under Oswine's arm, Walter pulled him to his feet, and led him out of the wreckage of his short-lived kingdom.

Chapter 18

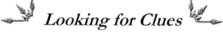 *Looking for Clues*

Rheged: Eft-Yule

For the band of travellers their luck took a turn for the better the following morning. None of them had had a particularly good night's sleep after the disturbing conversations they had had that evening, and Gerard looked positively haggard with worry come the morning light. However, as they were leading their horses out of the barn, on the road below them in the valley they saw a substantial column of men with an equally large number of monks riding in their midst. Moreover, at their head flew a beautifully wrought banner, which the others assured Kayna was the emblem of Jaenberht's monastic order.

With haste they mounted up and headed down to intercept the column, only to find that the escort was taking no chances with the safety of the monks, as they became surrounded by grim-faced soldiers. Keeping their hands well away from their swords, Gerard and Edmund explained that they were seeking Abbot Jaenberht on a mission of some importance from Master Brego, hoping that the combination of that name along with their own reputations would be sufficient to guarantee their safety if nothing else.

However, the person whose name worked the greatest transformation on the attitude of the soldiers was Matti's. As soon as she was introduced, the young acting captain became profuse in his apologies for the threatening behaviour, although Matti was possibly the more startled of the two. Indeed she felt somewhat mortified, given that she had previously berated Will for the behaviour of men she had assumed to be under his command. That increased when she realised that, even when he had been most deeply affected by the presence of the DeÁine Helm, his first order to those men still supporting him was to look out for her and take her to safety. Yet she had hardly had chance to absorb the startling truth before the soldiers parted, and they found themselves in the presence of Jaenberht himself.

"My lord abbot!" Edmund exclaimed. "This is an unexpected pleasure! We feared we would have to search for you."

"MacBeth told us of Oswine's aggression towards you," Gerard added. "We thought you'd be directing things from within the security of some stout walls somewhere. What brings you out here in such dangerous times?"

Jaenberht parted the front of his robes to reveal a substantial chain-mail vest beneath, and smiled.

"I think anyone attacking us might find me a might harder to dispatch to the Spirits' care than they thought," he said with a twinkle in his eye. Then more sternly, "And I couldn't remain at Mailros once I'd had the message about what happened at Catraeth. Rheged might be on the brink of civil war, but I still have a spiritual responsibility to the people, and I have to bring what comfort I can to the poor souls at the camp."

The others exchanged glances before Iago asked,

"My lord abbot, how much did your message say?"

Jaenberht gave him a quizzical stare. "Why do you ask?"

Matti took a deep breath. "Because there's nothing left of the garrison at Catraeth for you to minister to – only the folk from the town and surrounding countryside who are trying to clear the chaos."

"What?" Jaenberht exclaimed, echoed by gasps of amazement from his surrounding escort.

"I'm afraid so," Iago continued, "and it gets worse. We were by Fell Peak Fort when that thing struck on New Year's night. The trailing edge brushed by us and we were lucky to escape, but when we went down to the fort there wasn't a single soul left alive. Not even the animals. Back then we thought it a local disaster, but since then we've passed Cat Castle and the whole garrison there is gone too, as well as the main barracks at Catraeth."

"There was some sort of glamour attached to it which preyed on the minds of anyone susceptible," Elidyr continued. "Not just the feeble-minded but anyone a bit taken with celebratory drink. The lucky ones were those who'd already gone to bed and only woke as it was passing, or those like us who'd remained sober."

"Great Maker!" Jaenberht gasped. "All? ...Everyone? ...But that must mean..."

"...thousands of souls," Iago finished sadly for him.

For a moment even the normally unflappable Jaenberht was lost for words. When he could speak, though, the others could see he was rapidly thinking through the consequences.

"Then there's little point in continuing to Catraeth," he contemplated. "But what of Earlskirk? And further south? Has anyone heard of

Tancostyl's movements in all of this? It makes no sense for him to be behind this." Then he typically returned to concern for the ordinary folk. "Did you say that there were people trying to clear up the mess at these places?"

"Not at Fell Peak," Matti told him. "Up there the garrison is too isolated, and the whole place was a blazing inferno the last we saw of it. There can't be anything left except ashes within the Fort, if even the walls remain. But at Cat Castle the villagers were for the main part still alive, if mourning the sons they'd lost who'd got trapped in the mayhem inside the castle. I'm sure the village priest would appreciate a hand. He must've known almost everyone he's having to say the rites over, and probably needs as much consoling as those he's trying to comfort."

"And there's a poor young captain trying to make some sense of the chaos at Catraeth," Kayna chipped in. "When we came through, all anyone was able to do was carry the charred remains out and cremate what was left. Everyone looked totally stunned, as if it was all too much to take in. I bet the few priests they had around the town must be overwhelmed with the task in front of them."

Jaenberht wasted no more time debating, and with characteristic decisiveness immediately detailed those priests he had with him, with most of the monks as support, to take the fastest route to Catraeth to give what aid they could. A third of the soldiers went with them under the command of a senior captain and two very able sergeants, both as an escort and in case the Catreath captain needed aid in keeping law and order. Jaenberht was realistic enough to know that it was likely that even in the face of such a disaster, there would be a small minority likely to see the opportunity for a spot of looting.

Then he turned back to the new arrivals.

"This changes everything, and I'm eager to know why Brego sent you here. Will you ride with me to Lund? My abbot there is very capably holding the fort, as you might say! Or at least successfully fending off Oswine's thugs. I can't make any plans until I know more, and he may have had word from Earlskirk by the time we get there."

It was the best thing the six companions could think of doing too, and so on the four following days they briefed Jaenberht and puzzled over the turn of events as they rode. Frustratingly, none of them could imagine why Tancostyl would have acted in such a way until Kayna, with her usual perceptiveness, commented that surely it was more likely that the Abend's left hand had not known what the right was doing.

"From what Maelbrigt used to tell me, that bunch have more twists in their minds than a willow basket," she declared. "He always said that the worst thing that could happen was for them to actually agree on something, because most of the time they didn't trust one another further than they could spit."

"My word! I do believe you've hit on it!" Jaenberht agreed. "Yes, that would make so much more sense of it, wouldn't it?"

"And would explain why the storm came from the west rather than from the south where Tancostyl was last known to be," added Elidyr. "If he played no part in summoning whatever it was, then we don't have to wrack our brains wondering why he would leave the capital, or destroy an army he already had control over."

Rather more worrying was the fact that Jaenberht had no idea that an Island Treasure had even existed in Rheged, and was sure that he had never come across a reference to anything being hidden in the mountains of the south. For good measure he consulted several of the brothers travelling with them who had worked in the scriptorium, but none of them recalled seeing strange markings on any of the maps there. But the biggest puzzle of them all was how Oswine had been alerted to their presence on the island. Having confided their suspicions over Ismay and Osbern's actions, the friends were dumbfounded by Jaenberht's declaration that the current priest to the Braose household was actually one of his own men.

"I can see why you would've thought the way you did," Jaenberht said, "but Brother Lionel is a most pious man who's spent most of his life at Mailros. He never went near the capital."

"But why did you appoint him to Osbern's household?" queried Kayna. "Surely it would be more normal for the bishop or archbishop to deal with allocating such a post?"

"Indeed it would," Jaenberht confirmed. "But Osbern came to me himself. He said that he'd heard some very unsavoury rumours about Archbishop Fulchere – rumours which unfortunately have a fair founding in the truth, I'm sorry to say. He told me he'd been very unhappy with the last two men Fulchere had sent, and had a suspicion that Fulchere was trying to find soft places for some of his cronies in the major households, after the last man was found drunk in Osbern's wine cellar several times.

"Given that, I thought it quite reasonable – knowing Osbern's piety –

that he would want someone with their mind a bit more on the job. So I was only too happy to send Lionel. And that was three years ago. I've also seen Lionel myself since then, when I was in the west eighteen months ago, and again barely nine months ago, and nothing in his manner gave me any cause to wonder at any change in him. I'm sorry, but I don't think Lionel is the source of your betrayal."

Which left everyone stumped. Gerard and Edmund agreed that Osbern himself had shown no uncharacteristic behaviour, and had been the usual gloomy, sanctimonious man of the last several years. And in the months leading up to Ruari's return, they had been around him long enough for it to have been hard for him to dissemble for that length of time. Yet that did little to ease Gerard's worry for the safety of his family, for the consequence of that reasoning meant that somewhere close to his home had to harbour Tancostyl's spy.

Arriving at Lund, however, there were surprises which altered everything. The abbot informed them that the messages he had received from the south confirmed that the carnage had been widespread. Messages relayed through Iago's former temporary retreat of Allerford, reported that Crauwel had fared worst of all. There the townsfolk had also perished – either alongside the garrison in a suicidal frenzy, or soon after in the firestorm which had rendered town, port and barracks down to ashes. The blaze had been fierce enough for the folk of Mussel Bay and Airey to see the glow on the horizon when they recovered from their own nightmares. How many had perished they were unable to say, for there was nothing left to count when they went to investigate. Despite the excellent natural harbour, it seemed unlikely that anyone would want to rebuild on the site of so much death from unnatural causes, and for now Crauwel had been left to the ghosts.

Yet against the odds, Earlskirk had got off lightly. After a brief burst of mayhem on the outskirts of the city in the shacks of the poorest, the storm seemed to have passed the capital by. And although the casualties amongst the very poor had been exceptional high for a night of revelry, among the greater populace and the troops there had been limited deaths.

"So Tancostyl had to protect his own," mused Jaenberht as they conferred the next morning, "interesting, very interesting!"

And there could be little doubt of that, since afterwards the mage had collected what army remained about him and marched them out of the city heading south, and had not been seen or heard of in the capital since.

"What in the Underworld is the fiend up to!" growled Gerard. "By the Spirits, I have increasing sympathy for Ruari! Trying to outguess these bastards is like trying to track a ghost through an invisible maze!"

"Well at least he isn't heading anywhere near Rosin and your children," Matti consoled him. "The only ways he could take an army north are past here, or over the passes Iago and I took across the mountains, and he couldn't go that way without the brothers at Allerford seeing them."

"And they've not seen a soul either," Iago backed her up. "But moreover, Gerard, just think. … If he's got a whole army to handle, he's not going to have time to worry about any reports from a minor spy, regarding a handful of people in a place he's already washed his hands of."

That relieved Gerard greatly the more he thought about it, and Matti too, for she had been feeling increasingly guilty at the thought that she might have brought disaster down on those who had only wanted to help her.

"I wonder if he's actually leaving Rheged?" Elidyr proposed to the assembled friends and Jaenberht's leading men.

"You mean he's taking the Helm away?" Edmund wondered. "That's a bit of a worrying prospect isn't it? I mean, who can we warn? And where's he going to go with it?"

"Well Tancostyl was always one of the more daring of the Abend," Jaenberht mused, "so I wouldn't be surprised if he took a ship. He'll be as sick as a dog all the way, which is probably why he's got his own bodyguard with him. No doubt he'll use the Helm to subdue them into total subservience before he leaves dry land, so that they'll protect him without question when he's incapacitated. From what Hugh and Brego have told me, Quintillean would be too suspicious and cautious to make such a move, and if it was him we were dealing with we'd have to be looking for plots within plots. But Tancostyl will take more chances. And I don't think we need to worry about him going to Prydein, because Calatin is there, and apparently Tancostyl and Calatin can't stand one another."

"What's odd about that?" Kayna snorted. "I didn't think any of them got on!"

"No they don't," Matti explained, "but Ruari, Brego and Maelbrigt reckoned that Tancostyl and Eliavres at least look at things the same way when it comes to getting control over physical things. And Tancostyl and Anarawd are both lecherous old goats who try to outdo one another over whom they've seduced. It's hardly getting on, but they do have some sort of common ground. Whereas Calatin is downright weird – even by their standards! As near as the Covert Brethren could ever make out, even the other Abend haven't figured out what Calatin really wants, and it gets them mad, because he'll suddenly refuse to join in on one of their scheme for some bizarre reason that only he understands. So I think Abbot Jaenberht is right – Tancostyl won't go to Prydein if he knows Calatin's there."

"Shall I send a bird to relay a message on to Ergardia?" the abbot of Lund inquired.

"I think that's a reasonable precaution," Jaenberht assented, "even though we have no hard information as to where he's gone. At least Brego can send out alerts to his southern ports in case Tancostyl gets diverted by winter storms."

"In the meantime I think we should go to Earlskirk," declared Elidyr. "Who knows what information we might glean from whatever he's left behind?"

Jaenberht agreed that much might be achieved by a visit if the capital was now relatively safe, for an archive of his own order was there along with one of the Church's.

"If there's anything at all about this Spear," he told them, "it's most likely buried amongst the old papers down in the vaults." Moreover, he informed them that he would come with them. "I want to have a stern word with that fool Fulchere!" he said with such resolve, that none were in any doubt that Fulchere would rapidly regret supporting Tancostyl.

Yet that night as they congregated in the refectory for the evening meal, the final surprise arrived. They had barely sat down when the main door was thrown open and Father Walter limped in, saddle-sore and weary, leaning on his staff and a lay brother for support. Behind him two more of the lay brothers from the stables half supported, half carried the bemused form of Oswine. For a moment Gerard and Edmund failed to recognise the young man they had disdained to call king until Walter said to Jaenberht,

"I thought I'd better bring young Oswine to you for safe keeping."

For a moment nobody could make themselves heard in the babble of excitement, then Jaenberht's voice rose above the others and instilled order once more. A chair was hurriedly found for Walter and piled with soft cushions for his aching bones, into which he sank with a moan of relief. Meanwhile, Gerard strode round the table to come face to face with Oswine to confront him. Yet, by the time Walter had been revived with a mug of caff and felt able to tell his tale, Gerard was already walking back shaking his head sadly.

"I thought I would throttle the miserable little shit if I ever got my hands on him," he confessed to Edmund, "but even I wouldn't have wished this on him. His wits have totally gone, and the bits he does remember make me wonder if he's really known what he's been doing for years."

"I confess my sympathy has worn thinner on the journey," Father Walter admitted ruefully to Jaenberht, but in the hearing of the others. "Sacred Martyrs, Abbot! It's been a wearisome task to get him here! And there are many of the old Jarl's family whom Tancostyl would've had a harder time subverting to his cause. This one was a spoilt brat who never wanted to work at anything even before the mage got his hands on him, and all he's done all the way here is whine for his father, and complain that it's not fair that he should've had to shoulder the responsibility for the Island. I've near worn my prayer beads away – if only to give my gnarly old hands something to do other than grab him round the throat to shut him up! I fear I have much penance to do, Father!"

"Nonsense!" Jaenberht declared. "You did your penance along the way! But my dear old friend, whatever possessed you to go to the capital in the first place? Even the journey there must've been agony for you!"

"I couldn't rest," Walter told them. "I can't explain it, but after MacBeth went – you do know he's alive don't you?" he suddenly thought to ask. Jaenberht nodded and confirmed he had seen Ruari in this very monastery on the night Will had reappeared. "Oh good! … Well, then Ron from *The Mermaid* came, and said that he and some of the others were bringing the men of the Knights back from the east. It was after that that I kept having this niggling feeling. Several times I could've sworn I half caught sight of something out of the corner of my eye – once it was definitely a person – and something half whispered about records. The only thing I could think of was that Ruari would need something that was in the Grand Master's office, or at least the main preceptory. So I went back up to the abbey and got Millie the mule out of her stall. I think the brothers thought I'd gone mad, but I couldn't rest, I really couldn't.

"Funnily enough the itching in my mind eased as soon as I got on the road for Earlskirk. I couldn't rush – neither Millie nor I are up to that any more – and I had to make sure I stopped in plenty of time to lodge at a proper inn each night. I'm not daft enough to think I can rough it anymore.

Anyway, I got to Earlskirk just in time for Yule. The brothers were very kind to me at Blessed Martyrs' hostel and found me a comfortable bed, but try as I might I couldn't get near the Knights' old places because the whole city was in chaos.

"I was near to despair and then the New Year came. Great Maker! I never want to live through the like of that again! And from what I've heard on the way here that was nothing to what happened to some poor souls – may they be received into the Spirits' care! The very air seemed to crackle and spark. And the skies! Dear Spirits, the skies seemed to boil! Then as suddenly as it started it stopped.

"When morning came the brothers went out and began doing what they could for the distraught and injured. I still couldn't get anywhere because the army was out on every street getting ready to march. Only when they'd gone did I realise that the whole palace complex was unguarded. I only thought to get to the Knight's headquarters, but all around the front of that is wrecked. Then I saw the Great Hall was left open, and went in and found Oswine. After that I could hardly leave him, and so I decided to bring him to you. I feared I would have to drag him every miserable mile all the way to Scarfell and Mailros! I don't think I've ever been so relieved to find someone as when I heard yesterday that you were here!"

Given that their conversation had been punctuated by undefined wails and moans from Oswine, everyone's sympathies were with Walter. He had obviously not exaggerated the strain of caring for the befuddled former king, who sat staring vacantly into space when he was not swatting away invisible beings, all the while drool running unnoticed down his chin. Jaenberht lost no time in ordering Oswine away to the care of the infirmarers along with permission to keep him in a separate chamber where he would not disturb the other inhabitants. There was obviously little to be gained from questioning him when his sense of time had become so disjointed. Even if he remembered something there was no way of knowing whether it had happened two weeks ago or two years.

However, Elidyr was much intrigued by Walter's compulsion, and once his five companions had congregated in the room set aside for the two women he brought the subject up again.

"I think Walter was on the right track, you know," he said thoughtfully. "I can't explain it, but I have a good feeling about it. We keep hearing about the power of the DeÁine Treasures, but maybe our own have more than we credit them for."

"Are you saying that they …well …*want* to be found?" Kayna asked, her curiosity piqued.

"I don't know," Elidyr admitted. "Put like that it makes it sound as though they have a consciousness, and I'm not sure that that's right." He paused and tried to form a coherent reasoning. "But don't you think that a handful of anagrams are pretty lousy protection for something as important as they're supposed to be? Don't you think there should be more than that?" He ruffled his long hair with his fingers as if trying to shake some thoughts loose in the process, but creating a moment of more earthy lust in Matti, who was finding that one night harder to dismiss than she had expected.

"I mean …I'm a pretty good fletcher," he went on, "yet I wouldn't know where to start to make something imbued with the kind of power the Arrows are supposed to have. So the person …people …who made the Treasures had to have skills way beyond anything we have. In which case, do you think they could've created some kind of watching device? Something infinitely more complicated than a simple puzzle? The puzzle …that was made *by* men *for* men, just to remind folks *where* the Treasures were. I'm betting that getting *at* them will be much more complicated. And in that case, do you think that Walter was being directed to where there's some kind of clue as to how to do all this?"

"Cross of Swords!" Edmund gasped. "That's a thought isn't it! By the Trees, though, Elidyr, I fear you may have the right of it! Certainly the bit about the anagrams hardly being much protection, anyway. But what are you suggesting? Something like a glamour that actually recognises friend from foe?"

"I can tell you now that Jaenberht will say that it's the Good Spirits on our side that Walter saw," Matti said emphatically. "You'll never get him to believe in some mystical voice from the ancient ones."

"No, I'm sure he wouldn't," Elidyr agreed, more confident now that his companions had not simply dismissed his idea as mad. "But then he's been conditioned to see things that way, hasn't he? Yet it was the Grand Masters who held the keys to where the Treasures were hidden – not the Church or the monastic orders, they're all too recent arrivals in the Islands to have been involved in that very early process. Back then the Church was barely getting a foothold in this territory where most folk would've believed in the power of the Sacred Trees. On the other hand, every chapel of the Knights that I've ever been in – and that's quite a few – have *only* had carvings of the Sacred Trees in them."

Kayna shook her head in surprise. "I can't believe I never noticed that," she gasped. "All these years I've been around the Order and yet that had never occurred to me! But you're right, there are no Martyrs or dedications to the Spirits anywhere in the Knights' chapels. That has to be significant." Then paused to think before asking, "So are you thinking of something like a spirit, that was once living? Or something made – like the Treasures from inanimate things – and then infused with some sort of power?"

Elidyr shrugged. "Who knows? Hopefully we'll find out before it's too late. But for now I think we have to get down to Earlskirk and find a way into that preceptory, because I don't think we can afford to ignore the hidden message in what Father Walter thinks he saw and felt."

The result of which was that their small band, accompanied by Jaenberht, some monks and an armed escort, rode virtually unchallenged into Earlskirk on the morning of the twenty-first. Father Walter had declined to remain in the same abbey as Oswine for the sake of his sanity, and had accompanied them muffled in furs and blankets in a litter with the valiant Millie tethered behind. Some of Gerard's own household were amongst those attempting to provide a kind of security at the city gate, and once he was recognised they were waved through with much relief. Edmund and Gerard then felt beholden to hang back and try to restore some sort of order, even if it was only getting men to clear the undergrowth so that the gates could be closed once more. So Matti and Kayna rode on with Iago and Elidyr and the monks up to the great complex on the hill at the heart of the capital.

With characteristic energy Jaenberht refused to rest, but instead went straight to the cathedral to survey the destruction there. Having ascertained that there was no structural damage, he set his monks to begin setting all in order and sent the soldiers to find any local monks who had stayed, but who had remained in hiding after the New Year's terrors. As night fell, the doors of the cathedral were flung wide open to reveal an interior brightly lit with candles, and the bells once more rang out across the city calling the citizens to prayer. And they came in their hundreds. From out of the alleyways and streets, people of all sorts thankfully hurried towards something which finally spoke of some sort of return to normality.

"He's a shrewd man, this abbot, isn't he," Kayna remarked to Matti as they stood on one of the palace balconies looking down on the sight.

"Oh yes!" Matti agreed. "You'd have to get up pretty early in the morning to catch Jaenberht out!"

"He's certainly got the ordinary people sized up alright," Kayna added with unconcealed admiration. "Some sympathy for what they've been through, and something to pin their hopes onto, is going to get them up and functioning faster than any amount of bawling and shouting by soldiers."

"And we're going to need that good will," said Edmund's voice from behind them, as he and Gerard came into the room defrosting their hands around hot mugs of caff. "Spirits, but it's a mess down there! The gates are closed tonight for the first time in years, but it's going to take months to set the whole place to rights. Have you found any hints as to where the old nobles who served under Jarl Michael might be now? Great Maker, but we could do with Will here now instead of him being off in Brychan!"

"I'm afraid the people are going to have to do much for themselves," Matti said sadly. "We found some orders for executions. Apart from Earl Havar and Earl Brusi whom we knew about, it looks like Earl Erhman and Earl Norvik died at Tancostyl's behest, and poor old Einar's heart finally gave out only a month ago. I hate to tell you this Gerard, but you're one of the most senior men left!"

Poor Gerard looked as though the roof had just fallen in on him. "Me? *I'm* one of the most senior? Flaming Trees!"

"I'm afraid so," Matti confirmed, "and we'd better find Osbern Braose pretty quickly too, because he's another one!"

"Do we trust Osbern to be in control?" Elidyr asked, voicing their concerns.

"I don't see how we have much choice," Edmund answered. "After all, given what Jaenberht said about the priest being blameless, we have nothing at all to connect Osbern to our betrayal. It's not a crime to be nasty to your wife or a religious fanatic – even though maybe it ought to be! We'd have to have a lot more hard evidence before we could tell anyone outside of this group what we suspect, and to be honest, Osbern's not corrupt whatever else he is."

For his part Elidyr had to report that he had had little more success in getting into the Knights' headquarters.

"Our old Grand Master must've seen trouble coming three years ago – or at least his closest men did – because that place is sealed up like a tomb!" he complained. "Oswine's, or more likely Tancostyl's men, got as far as breaking down the front door onto the cathedral square. The anteroom is absolutely wrecked, as are the couple of offices which led off it, and the room that I'm guessing the Grand Master used to meet people in. The problem is that the walls are all stone, and there were trick doorways to get beyond there. Ruari told me some of the ways in before he left in case I needed them, but there's all sorts of rubbish to get out of the way first, and the trigger to one of the ways has been hacked off the wall along with other decorative bits of stone by some moron with an axe! When I've cleared all the bits of masonry away from the surface and the floor, I'll be more able to tell whether it'll still work, and if the panel will move. To be honest, though, it's going to be a long job."

"Then I think that helping you has to be a priority," Iago announced. "I'm sure Jaenberht is more than capable of organising the citizenry, and frankly, at the moment they'll probably take direction from someone known as a good and holy man more than they would from nobles like you, Gerard. Let's win the battle for control of the Island first before we start worrying about how we're going to rebuild it."

And when they caught up with Jaenberht later that night he agreed with them. Steepling his long fingers before him, he regarded them from under his brow creased in a frown of concentration.

"Iago is right," he declared, "you have to continue on the course Brego set you on, but may I make a further suggestion? I can let Elidyr have half a dozen of my brothers along with Father Walter to help with the cleaning up and searching, which will leave the rest of you free for a day or so. What worries me is where has Tancostyl got to? Nobody here has heard any more of him since he rode out just after New Year. Why don't the five of you ride down to Montrose Castle? I'm sure, Matti, that you wish to pay your respects to the bereaved families on your estate, and you'll be able to find out from Osbern if he's heard anything of Tancostyl. That monster must've passed Montrose to go west – unless he was heading east, and I can't imagine why he would do that – since he's not been seen crossing the river at Allerford."

Everyone agreed that made a lot of sense, and so come the morning the five of them set out on the road once more. As they came into sight of Montrose Castle three days later, Matti broke down in tears at the sight of the blackened battlements. Nothing she had been through had quite prepared her for how it would feel to see the wreckage of her own home. Even Edmund, who had seen its sad state before, found it no easier to return to, but was even more perturbed at the uncanny silence.

"Where is everyone?" he wondered. "Sacred Trees and Blessed Martyrs, they can't all have been wiped out by the storm, can they? When I left they were coming on a treat with the repairs ...and where's Osbern?"

When they got to the ford the evidence of the repairs was clear. Edmund made them pause at the edge, and when they stopped to look closer they could see that the stone pavers had been returned to their original wandering course. However, all the horses baulked at setting a hoof in the water, and when Iago dismounted and disturbed the surface they found out why. Oily ripples surged and writhed at the passing of something unseen, making him hastily step back. But Elidyr neatly vaulted off his horse with an enigmatic 'Ah-ha,' and rummaged briefly in his saddle bag before walking down to the water's edge. Throwing some grains of salt in, he watched for the effect they had and then turned round and pronounced to the others,

"They've got a baneasge here!"

"A what?" Gerard said.

"One of the Abend's pet monsters," Elidyr explained, recalling to the others that he was an experienced Forester despite his seeming youthfulness. "Nasty little buggers! Nothing really outrageous mind, like a bansith or a bleizgarve which can go just about anywhere, because these things can only survive in water. In fact, that's why they're weaker than the other monsters. The Abend really can't cope with water, but they needed something to guard their waterways against their enemies, so they came up with the baneasge. It doesn't have a defined shape because they can't control it well enough for that, but it can be dangerous, nonetheless, because it just consumes anything living that comes its way. The good news is that this one would've expired fairly soon anyway, because it's obviously feeling the effects of being separated from its master's control – which I think we can take as a good sign that Tancostyl is far away from here and not likely to return. And if you give me a moment I can get rid of it completely."

With that he turned back to the water and began to chant softly, during which he three times sprinkled something from a small flask he had produced from his baggage into the water. The process was accompanied by initial churning of the water, and then steam issuing from one part of the ford, which was followed by an unpleasant, smelly scum rising to float inert upon the surface.

"All clear!" Elidyr declared, and without waiting, remounted and heeled his now willing mount down to the stone pavers.

Approaching the castle itself they were heartened to see the newly repaired gates were still standing, but then less so to see them standing ajar with no apparent guard. And still silence encompassed the whole promontory. Passing between the gates, Gerard then dismounted and swung them shut, dropping the bar to prevent anyone coming in behind them and taking them by surprise. With swords drawn they entered the castle itself and found absolute desecration. In the great hall a great host of men had obviously worked their way through the remaining castle stores, judging by the discarded barrels, pots and sacks left strewn across the floor.

"Well at least this looks like human activity," Kayna said in a half-hearted attempt at optimism for her friend's benefit.

Surprisingly, a relieved sounding Matti agreed with her. "Yes it does, doesn't it!"

She waded through the detritus, intensely concentrating on the floor until she reached the far side. "Do you know, there's no blood here!" she declared. "Whatever else happened, there was no killing in here."

Iago did not have the heart to caution her that the Abend did not need to shed blood to kill, but Matti was already on the move. Hurrying out through the far door, she led the others rapidly through the ground floor and out to the walled gardens at the rear of the castle. Bounding up the steps of one of the far gazeboes she leaned out and looked down to the base of the wall.

"That's it!" she cried gladly. "The bushes here are far more flattened than when Wistan and I made our escape. I'd guess that some of the men lowered the older folk and children down and then jumped down, because that little path is totally trampled by the passage of people."

"Then where did they go?" wondered Iago. "The messages from Allerford said nothing about refugees from Montrose."

"Probably to Bridby," Matti speculated. "Most of our tenants had some sort of family there, and that was our nearest market. And if they saw that storm coming out of the west they probably would've headed away from it. Bridby has good, stout walls but no garrison. No soldiers to worry about! Yes, I'm sure that's the way they would've gone."

"But where's Osbern?" Edmund fretted.

"Well if the ordinary folk legged it for Bridby, I'd bet Osbern headed for the chapel," declared Gerard.

"Of course!" Matti exclaimed, and led them on another hurried tour through the castle and up the stairs to the little chapel where Ruari and Edmund had found Andra. This time, though, there was no-one hiding beneath the altar or anywhere else. The beautifully embroidered altar cloth was gone, and the tiny stained glass window lay in shards on the floor, so that only the simplicity of the room had prevented further desecration.

"Where in the Islands is he?" Gerard exclaimed in frustration, concern for his friend overriding any previous suspicions.

Then Edmund realised what Kayna had picked up off the floor and was about to put on the altar.

"That's Osbern's prayer book!" he cried in horror.

"Are you sure?" Kayna asked. "It looks just the same as any priest would have."

"Yes, but we've never had a resident priest here!" Matti declared. "Andra was the last person to take a service in here as far as I know, and he did it from memory not a book."

"And it's unmistakable," Edmund said, holding up the slim volume and pointing to a cut in the leather cover. "That's where it saved his life by stopping the second arrow that would've killed him. Those conniving priests used it as a symbol of a divine desire to save him! Without it taking the arrow for him, they would've had a harder time twisting his mind so much."

"And ever after that he'd never be parted from it," Matti confirmed, with tears of worry returning once more. "Oh Osbern, where are you?"

Chapter 19

 The Man Inside

Rheged: Eft-Yule

Osbern watched the approaching armed force with mounting distress. What could he possibly do to save the people in the castle from as many soldiers as these? There was no good reason that he could think of which would have an army on the move the week after New Year, and in freezing weather. At the moment they were congregating at the edge of the ford, which worried Osbern even more, since it implied that they knew of the existence of the monster and were waiting for someone to come and deal with it. And that someone had to be a DeÁine, if not an actual member of the Abend, against whom he could not possibly hope to stand his ground alone.

Then he remembered the way over the garden wall which some of the men had been using to go and fetch supplies. Turning to the two former stable-hands standing beside him, he sent them hurrying off to gather everyone, along with anything they could grab on the way, and to lead the escape over the wall.

"Go! And don't come back until someone you know comes to fetch you!" Osbern ordered them. "Preferably a Forester who'll know how to deal with whatever this DeÁine might leave behind!"

With sword drawn, Osbern kept watch in the lower ward until the last man had gone into the garden and shut the gate behind him. Hurrying back through the gate into the main ward, Osbern dropped the bar across it, so that it would look as though it had been barred from the inside to prevent invaders coming in that way, rather than others fleeing. Running, he now went back to the kitchen doors to the garden and barred those, along with the little picket door on the other side of the castle. Then shutting the main door, but not barring it, he went to the chapel and began to pray like he had never done before.

Please let the ruse work, he prayed. *Let the people get to safety. Make whoever this is think that I'm just some stupid old fart who's had some misguided idea about defending the home of a friend single-handed. Great Maker, let them pass us by untouched! Good Spirits please hear me now, if you've never heard me before. I know I've been a fool these past years. I've pushed away my friends and family by sitting in judgement on them when I had no right to. Instead of continuing to fight for good, I've hidden away and let evil walk in. I've expected you to show me preference I don't deserve, and pretended that I don't have any responsibility for my own life by making you the excuse.*

He clasped the old prayer book in his hands and kissed the cut on it reverently. *You saved me then because I was helping others – not because I was better than them – and I see that now so clearly. Please forgive me! Guide my steps back towards the right path.*

Yet at that moment the door to the chapel crashed open and he was seized and dragged outside. His struggles only got him a pounding from their fists, so that blood running from his split brow part-blinded him as he became aware of a presence in front of him.

"This is the only one, your Greatness," he heard a man beside him say, and vaguely registered the strange monotone of the voice. Enchanted, he wondered? Then a spine-chilling voice answered, sibilant as a serpent,

"One? Is that all?"

"Yes sire."

"Hmmmm…"

Tancostyl looked down on Osbern with undisguised disgust. He was sure that the last time he had bothered to turn his attention back to this benighted rock there had been more people here, and certainly one man could not have made the repairs alone. That was why he had left the baneasge on guard, for he had thought it possible that the troublesome general or the mysterious stranger might turn up here. But instead there was only this fool on his knees praying to some inferior god instead of defending the gate.

He contemplated scouring the man's mind for information, then looked at the blood flowing down the forehead and could not be bothered to clamp his hand onto it to force the connection. The trouble with blood was that it took so much washing to get off afterwards. All very well in his own torture chambers where he was dressed for such things, and with a steam pool on hand to cleanse himself with afterwards, but not in this draughty hole with cold water.

"Take him away." He dismissed Osbern with a haughty wave of his hand. "Throw him in with the other prisoners. We'll have to take him with us so he doesn't go squealing to the rebels and that cursed abbot the minute we've left, but I'm not wasting my energy on him." *He's obviously nobody,*

331

Tancostyl thought, *or he would've been fawning round that fool of a king, not stuck in some backwater.*

For his part, Osbern could not believe his luck. His heart had sunk into his boots when he had realised it was Tancostyl himself standing before him. *I've got no chance of hiding anything from him if he forces his way into my mind,* he had thought in despair. *Then he'll know all about Ruari and the escape plans and everything. And if he uses that Helm thing I might not even remember what I've done! Dear Spirits! Save me from that at all costs! I mustn't betray the others!*

Yet nothing of the sort had happened, and he found himself being led away not even to the dungeons which Will's ancestors had had built, but to the kitchen store room. There he was thrust in with nearly two dozen others and forgotten about until the morning. During the night one of the young women gave up the fight for life against the cold and lack of food, and two others who turned out to be her sisters set up a heart-rending keening. Whether that alerted Tancostyl or not, Osbern never knew, but the mage was at the door when they were chivvied out by somnambulant guards whom he berated soundly for not having fed the prisoners.

"They're to be kept *alive,* you dolts! What use are they as hostages if they're dead?" he screamed in their un-registering faces. "Go and fetch them *food!* I want them fed every day! Do you understand? *Every* day!"

Whereupon he turned on his heels and stormed out, black robes flying around him. However, his words must have registered because as the prisoners were marched out they had bread thrust into their hands, despite the rumbles of discontent from nearby soldiers who had obviously had their own hoards raided by the guards. Osbern divided his bread between three women who looked the worst off, saying that he at least had eaten in the last day and needed it less than them.

By that night, though, he was glad of the watery soup when it arrived along with some rock-hard bread, although the next day they fared somewhat better at the expense of the poor folk of Shiptoft. A grim forced march over four more days brought them to the barred gates of Mussel Bay. Being on the coast, the town walls were substantial as a deterrent to Attacotti raiders, and the residents had no intention of letting a bunch of poorly disciplined soldiers inside their defences.

"No matter," Tancostyl declared dismissively, "we won't waste our energy on them. We'll dine well at Crauwel, for there must be something left with no soldiers there to eat it all."

His rage three days later on finding nothing but ashes was near apoplectic, and his entire escort trembled in fear. They could not know that he had planned to meet the ship which would take him from Rheged here, and had assumed he would be able to wait behind the security of the walls until its arrival. In his fury he drained the life force out of ten of his soldiers and sent a searing message on the Power to Helga. "*Where, by the Sacred Temples of Lochlainn, is that boat? I need it now!*"

"*Well you'll just have to wait!*" was her scathing riposte. "*Even with a conjured wind in its sails, there's only so much speed it can take without falling apart. Do you want to ride home on driftwood planks, soaking wet? Because that's all you'll have if I push it any faster! If you've got yourself in a mess then that's your problem – I've fulfilled my part of our bargain.*"

"*Bargain?*" Tancostyl's mental scream tore back at her. "*Was it part of our bargain that you raise a glamour that had my entire army destroyed by its own hands? Fool! Idiot! If you want some of the Power that the Helm can give, it has to be safe in our hands. Not bobbing on the waves when the great battle comes! And don't think you can reach out and use it while I'm incapacitated on the sea, because you won't be able to reach out and use it either! Even down here on the beach it's become unstable. You get the Helm with me or not at all! And as none of the others appear to have lived up to their boasts and found the other pieces, I seem to be holding the winning hand! So get me that boat!*"

But just at that moment Helga had quite sufficient on her plate without worrying about Tancostyl's temper tantrums. Nine days earlier the four women had joined the army which they had summoned from New Lochlainn, and had begun the wearisome trek east. Even Geitla had had too much to do to enjoy the plentiful young male flesh around her, for they had all been kept busy facilitating the army's swift passage. Now more than ever they felt the loss of the great numbers of acolytes at the debacle at Gavra Pass, for those left were too few and too inexperienced to be able to cope without at least one of the witches being present at all times.

Helga and Masanae had often wondered about that slaughter in their private meetings, for both of them thought it too much of a coincidence that the best of their acolytes had been the first targeted by the cursed Knights. However stupid the acting DeÁine king had been, his betrayal was unlikely to have included the names of the Abend's finest students. That spoke of someone observing their movements over a longer period of time, and with greater concentration than he had been capable of. Yet no amount of probing had brought any name to light and the two witches could only assume that, whoever the spies had been, they too had perished. That was little consolation for the massive setback in their ability to channel vast quantities of Power, though.

Therefore the four witches had their hands full without thinking about where their male counterparts had got to. And that left Tancostyl cooling his heels on the coast of Rheged with a small army which was rapidly starving to death. Even as he fumed he realised that he had to do something. There was no way that he could remain in the ashes of Crauwel. Sooner rather than later he feared, that the cursed abbot would rally men and come hounding him, and with no leaders amongst his men he would have to fulfil that role himself.

Yet Tancostyl was no military man when it came to directing armies. War-mages acted alone or with others of their kind in solitary acts of mass destruction. None of his training had given him a clue about using huge numbers of others – that was what the Donns were for – and even he had to admit that such battle tactics were his weak point.

So there was no way that he could afford for his followers to become entangled in an open fight – especially with no cover or place to launch surprise attacks from. On the other hand he could keep marching westwards. That way he would at least find new places to plunder, and hopefully some of his hostages would have family around those parts which would dissuade the more bloodthirsty local nobility from attacking. Going west also brought him closer to the ship coming from New Lochlainn, so that if it could go no faster at least he could cut one, or maybe two, days off its voyage. And so they marched onwards.

For his part Osbern had been stunned by the desolation of what had once been a thriving barracks, town and virtually impregnable castle at Crauwel. Yet as they were hustled onwards, he suddenly woke up to the reality of their location. From the road Tancostyl was taking, they could only be on the way towards Urse Castle, which was somewhere he knew very well from frequent visits to Gerard and his family going right back to when they had both been boys. Next to his own family's homes, he knew Gerard and Edmund's almost as well.

Wake up Braose! he scolded himself. *You're a bloody soldier, not a milkmaid all afraid! Start thinking about escape routes, because you'll likely never get a chance as good as this again. Where will they put us? Maybe the dungeons – but only if that cursed war-mage is going to sit there and wait for whatever he thinks is coming. Why would he wait at Urse, though? No idea … but can I take the chance of being incarcerated in the dungeon for days or weeks? No! So I have to make a break for it before then. Once I'm free then I can think about freeing the others, so it doesn't have to be something that gets us all out at once. ...The quarry! It has to be the quarry!*

For three more miserable days the forlorn army trudged onwards, only goaded on by fear of the demented wizard in their midst, who seemed to have eyes in the back of his head. Had any of them had any idea of the toll it was taking on Tancostyl, maybe more of them would have rebelled, but he cleverly covered the way it was draining him. As the light faded on the third day they saw the towers of Urse Castle appear on the horizon and Tancostyl increased the pace. Osbern's heart went out to the Urse family's tenants in the small village on the roadside, for they were swiftly plundered of everything. But Tancostyl had also learned that there was nobody at the castle except the elderly steward and the servants, which was just the sort of place that he wanted – a well-stocked estate with no defenders.

Turning down the road to the castle, the strung out line of troops had to pass through a twisting defile in the rocky coastline. When Urse Castle had been built centuries ago the stone had been locally quarried, leaving a deep cleft in the earth where ragged, natural walls of stone rose either side of a roadway. The Urse family had found it a useful defence, since once in the defile there were only two options for an attacker – to go on in the face of archers raining arrows upon them from the security of the cliff top, or retreat. Even now the younger men at the castle had obviously had advanced warning of Tancostyl's army's approach, for they bided their time until the troops were well and truly sandwiched within the rocky walls and began to shoot arrows down into them.

In the dusk, chaos ensued. With more experienced leaders amongst the men it would not have been so bad, but Tancostyl was near the front and by the time he had realised what was happening many of the rear ranks had simply turned tail and run. Half befuddled by Tancostyl to keep them passive, the men lacked the common sense to count the number of arrows falling, and to see that there were far fewer defenders than their fear and the half-light led them to believe. So, while Tancostyl raged and attempted to restrain his panic-stricken men, Osbern made a break for it. Elbowing the nearest guard in the face, he shouldered a second into a third and dived for the undergrowth, clutching the last guard's knife in his bound hands.

Limited light, and the drainage water from the higher ground above, had resulted in the defile becoming home to all manner of ferns. Little ones clung in pockets in the rock walls, whilst the floor had larger varieties which rose several feet tall to make a cascading jungle. Into these Osbern made his escape. From their childhood days he remembered that there were overhangs which virtually constituted caves along this route, from where the boys had mischievously waylaid passing guests. No-one but a local would have known that the rock walls were not straight up and down, and Osbern counted on this now. Within seconds he was tucked away in a dark corner of one of the bends, well out of sight and quiet as a mouse.

His first job was to saw through the ropes at his wrists and those hobbling his ankles. His guards had been thinking of someone trying to run for it in the open, not hiding in dense cover, and were nowhere near him. He took a handful of the well-composted leaf mould and smeared his face with it to prevent the paleness of his skin showing up, just in case someone came searching. However, Tancostyl's tactics to keep the men compliant meant that nobody bothered to report to the war-mage that one of his hostages had escaped, since they assumed he was all-knowing.

Once he was sure that the last of the men had passed him by – or at least all of those who still followed Tancostyl – Osbern crept out of his hideaway. He had resolved to go to the edge of the quarry nearest the castle just to see whether Tancostyl looked as though he would set up a more permanent camp there. That way he would be able to give anyone pursuing the army something to act upon. Yet to his horror, no sooner had he begun to slink along the wall then a hand clamped over his mouth and three other strong arms held him still.

"Keep quiet!" a voice hissed in his ear. "Not a sound or I'll break your neck! Now back up following our lead, and don't struggle."

All kinds of thoughts galloped through Osbern's mind. Were these some of Tancostyl's men who had seen an opportunity to do a little hostage taking of their own? Or some kind of rear guard he had known nothing of? But then why were they not taking him on towards the Abend mage? Then reason kicked in. These men seemed far from befuddled. In fact they sounded very alert and competent, and his purloined knife was already gone. So maybe they were nothing to do with Tancostyl's force at all, in which case they might well be men he could ally himself to, with the result that he temporarily complied with little resistance.

Back at the entrance to the quarry, he was dragged off the path and into the surrounding bushes. Then a small lantern was unshuttered just enough to shed a little light upon his face, and the grip on him was relaxed a little.

"Who are you?" the same voice asked him.

Clearing his throat he answered, "My name is Osbern of Braose. I was taken prisoner at Montrose Castle." Then he decided to take a chance. "I hoped that if I could get free, then I would be able to get into Urse Castle later on and free the other prisoners. Or if not, then at least to be able to fetch help, although Spirits know from where. Maybe Abbot Jaenberht has rallied support."

His statement was greeted with silence, then a strained voice from the undergrowth said, "I believe him."

"Strangely enough, so do I," a third voice said from right beside him, so like the second that for a moment Osbern wondered if he had been captured by the fae-folk, before reasoning that there must be at least three very mortal men with him.

"Well, Osbern of Braose, what do you know of the …person …who leads those who took you captive?" the first voice asked.

Osbern sensed the testing nature of the question.

"It's Tancostyl, one of the DeÁine Abend," he replied. "He came to Montrose Castle six days after that fearful storm at New Year. I think he's quit Earlskirk for good. I'm not sure, but I think he might be moving the DeÁine Helm. A friend of mine, who's a Knight, said that that was what the crown was which appeared for the first time at the coronation. Most of the men around Tancostyl here seem to be enchanted, and I've been wondering whether the Helm was used to make them so submissive."

"The *Helm*? Cross of Swords!" the weaker voice swore, while the first voice asked,

"What's the name of your Knight friend?"

Osbern took a deep breath and mentally grasped the cross at his neck even if his arms were still being held too firmly for him to do it physically. *Please let this be the right choice! Spirits help me if I betray Ruari by this revelation.*

"His name is Ruari MacBeth." *At least I haven't given his rank, so if they don't know him he could be any one of the rank and file.*

But this time Osbern had made the right choice.

"MacBeth?" Aeschere said in surprise. "I know of MacBeth! In fact I even met him once, describe him to me!"

"Tall, rangy …blond hair that never stays straight, however well his uniform looks …blue eyes that can stare into your soul…"

"That's him," Aeschere confirmed to Saeric and Nazar. "All right Saeric, you can let him go," and Osbern found himself released.

"Who are you?" he asked his captors.

The lantern was fully uncovered, and he found himself looking at three men who all looked as though they would be useful in a tight spot. Two were obviously twins going by the remarkable similarity. But one of them was sitting down, and by his stillness and pallor appeared to have been wounded.

"We're Knights, Foresters, from Prydein," Aeschere said by way of introduction. "We were on board a ship when the storm at New Year hit us. The ship was wrecked on the rocks and we were flung overboard. Saeric," he indicated the young man standing next to Osbern, "and I found ourselves washed up in a small cove below a castle to the west of here. Nazar wasn't so lucky. We spent a whole day trying to find him before we found him hanging onto a rock with several of his ribs broken. When we finally got him up to the castle, the Underworld seemed to have broken loose inside.

"At first we thought it the result of some political struggle, but then some of the men woke up and spoke of hearing voices in their heads. They were distraught at what had happened to their friends, all the more for fearing that they'd been the culprits for many of the murders. For several days we stayed there, with them helping us search for members of the crew from our ship. We found about half a dozen in the first day, but after that only bodies, including that of our brave captain. The cold had killed as many as drowned.

"Then some of the men came back talking of a madman they'd found wandering on the nearby headland. His description fitted that of a man we'd been guarding, who'd been completely under the spell of another of the DeÁine – the war-mage called Calatin. What became of Calatin's body we don't know. Salt water is toxic to the Abend in any form, and it defies belief that he could've survived total immersion for hours even if he didn't drown. What worried us was that Amalric – the man we were guarding – was said to have what might best be described as 'abilities' that he certainly didn't have before."

"We've been tracking him ever since," Saeric picked up the tale. "Unfortunately, Nazar's pounding on the rocks has meant that on many days we've had to leave him in the care of some cottager while we hunted, but then had to return at night. We've lost our man Amalric several times because of that, but we've not dared leave Nazar for long because we haven't known who to trust. Amalric had wandered back and forth with no purpose, it appeared, until three days ago when he suddenly seemed to straighten his course and headed this way."

"I don't like it that you've now told us that another member of the Abend is right here," Aeschere added. "It sounds too much like Amalric sensed something that he recognised and headed straight towards it."

"Then you'll like it even less when I tell you that three days ago we found the wreckage of what's left of the huge fortress of Crauwel," Osbern said. "Even tied up out of the way, we could hear Tancostyl's screams, and at one point he seemed to be having a one-sided conversation with someone. At the time I wondered whether he was in such a rage that he was letting slip into words things that he was thinking …or maybe thinking *at* someone!"

"Cross of Swords!" Aeschere swore. "That would make sense."

"But do you think your man is keeping a prearranged meeting or acting upon instinct?" Osbern asked the three men.

They paused to think and then almost as one shook their heads before Saeric answered for all of them.

"I don't see how it could be prearranged. Calatin was definitely after the DeÁine Scabbard until we trapped him at Yule. If he'd intended to meet Tancostyl here at this time, he would've had to make a move away from Prydein before then. It was only our ship losing control that drove us here so fast, and he couldn't have counted on that happening. No, he must've just sensed Tancostyl's presence and been drawn to him."

Osbern looked at his new allies.

"In that case, are you sure that the Scabbard remains hidden in Prydein?" The three nodded emphatically. "Then can you think of any way we can stop Tancostyl taking the Helm out of Rheged? Because try as I might, I've been unable to think of a way that alone I could prevent that. He just has too much power – of all kinds! In fact, I can't see a way that I'd be able to get close to him, he has too many men under his spell. Do you even know a way we can loosen his grip on them? One that he can't immediately counter and have them turn back upon us?"

Aeschere and the twins had to admit that there was nothing they could do in the face of direct opposition from Tancostyl.

"However, as soon as he gets aboard his ship, I reckon we could break the bonds then," Aeschere said with confidence.

"Well that's something," Osbern said hopefully, "because I'm betting that he'll leave them with some compulsion to create mayhem to cover his retreat."

"Undoubtedly," Saeric agreed, "but where is he going to get this ship to take him back to New Lochlainn from?"

"I'd guess Farness, the castle you've come from. There are no big natural harbours this side of Rheged until you get a bit further north to Fordon, and that's well protected by Holtby Castle on the headland. They have some big trebuchets along the walls that can lob rocks far out into the sound. I would've thought in the time that Tancostyl has had here, he would've realised that an alien ship would have little chance of getting into that harbour unnoticed. There's a bit of a fishing quay here at Urse, but it's horribly shallow for any seagoing vessel, and Crauwel's jetties got incinerated with the rest of the buildings."

"Good." Aeschere was feeling more positive at this news. "Then we need to herd the men down onto the beach and if possible into the surf. They only have to get damp – we don't need to risk drowning them."

"How do you propose doing that, though?" asked Osbern.

"It'd be easier on horseback," Nazar spoke up. "If we can get horses then I could ride more easily than I can walk, and crowding them with horses would be one way of forcing them down to the beach."

"Then one of you come with me," said Osbern with a grin. "I know exactly which field the Urse steward will have hidden the horses in!"

Leaving Saeric to care for his twin, Osbern led Aeschere around the side of the quarried rocky outcrop to a large field nestling in a shallow valley which led down to the sea. There they found a dozen sleek thoroughbreds with their halters still on. Osbern even remembered that some spare tack had usually been left hidden away down there in a small cleft in the rock, which they found wrapped in protective oil-cloth, and fashioned bridles and lead-reins from.

"If we each ride one and lead two we can make a good line to force the men back with, as well as moving fast," Aeschere told Osbern as they quickly buckled straps together.

As they were liberating the horses, Tancostyl was once again in a towering rage within the castle after communicating with Helga. He would have to get to Farness, she had told him, if he wanted to get on board any quicker, for that was the first possible landfall. He was also none too pleased to realise that the four witches were virtually attempting a conquest of Brychan without a single male member of the Abend being present. With any luck Eliavres would meet them somewhere near the border, but Tancostyl did not like that much, either, given that Eliavres was always far too susceptible to following Magda's lead. His role of pupil to her tutor had never fully been dispensed with.

Where, by the Sacred Temples of Lochlainn, Anarawd had got to was beyond Tancostyl to work out. The fifth male member of the Abend was no war-mage, but he was capable of standing his ground against the witches, which was why he had been left behind and in control in the first place. Venting his frustration by flinging several servants high against the stone walls and sucking the life force out of them, Tancostyl soundly cursed Anarawd. How typical of him to go wandering off on some obscure mission of his own instead of concentrating on the main task at hand! The trouble with Anarawd was that he could never get past his own thirst for domination to see that if he helped the others first, he might actually achieve something, instead of his endlessly ill-fated convoluted schemes.

He was so angry he nearly wiped out the soldier who came cringing into the hall, with two others behind him dragging a third man.

"Your Greatness, we found this man wandering outside who asked to be brought to you," the soldier said in a terrified voice.

For a second the full implications of what had been said eluded Tancostyl, but then he suddenly whipped back round to stare at the newcomers.

"He asked to see *me*?" he demanded. "The leader, or me by name?"

"You by name, oh Great One," the soldier dithered, waiting for his head to be struck off or be turned into something unnatural.

Then the third figure spoke in a voice which wavered, but whose words were sharp and irritated.

"It's me! Don't you recognise me, Tancostyl?"

"Recognise you? Fool! I've never seen you before! How could I recognise you?"

The figure gave an impatient gesture. The gesture of one not used to ever having to be tactful or conciliatory, which suddenly rang bells in the back of Tancostyl's mind. He had seen *that* gesture before, somewhere, but the voice prompted him further.

"No, you imbecile! Of course you've never *seen* me in this form! I've only taken it in desperation! I said *recognise* me! I felt you on the Power from miles away, can you not do the same for me standing next to me? We've chewed the lotus leaf and smoked the agaric often enough together within the temples!"

Suddenly Tancostyl reached out with his senses and received a mighty shock.

"*Calatin?* Is that you Calatin?"

"Of course it's me!"

"What are you doing in *that?* Where's your own body?"

"At the bottom of the ocean."

But beyond that Calatin would say no more of the circumstances of how he had come to be forced to change bodies, although Tancostyl could guess that once again Calatin had underestimated the cunning of the lesser folk he rode roughshod over. It would not be the first time, and Tancostyl harboured a secret glee that the normally supercilious war-mage had finally been forced from his haughty assumption of superiority over the other Abend. Maybe Calatin had studied the Power with an abstract purity lacking in the rest of them, but he would have fallen long ago without their protection from even the other highborn DeÁine, let alone the common herd. Tancostyl also guessed that the body Calatin currently inhabited had been in the water with his old body, going by the blisters and burns on the exposed skin. What Calatin did say was,

"This creature was one of mine who followed me into the waves. The water almost broke the bond," omitting the truth that for a few desperate moments Amalric had actually broken free completely, and begun to swim frantically for the shore which had risen up to meet him. It had been the realisation that this body was coping with the water which had led Calatin to reach out to it. In his sickening state he had had terrible trouble focusing, but had been able to channel enough weak threads of Power to hook the cage onto the trailing anchor of the ship.

Rushed along in the wake of the storm-tossed ship, he had nonetheless almost expired until he had felt its first juddering on the rocks, and the spark of hope from the man that the shore was in sight. Calatin knew that he would die if he remained in the cage and in this body, and so he gathered every last ounce of Power and launched himself in his entirety into the man. The expending of all his Power probably saved Calatin, for it gave Amalric time to get ashore before the toxic effects of newly drawn Power began to radically alter his body chemistry, leading to the reactions with the salt water.

Such explanations were not for Tancostyl's ears, though, and instead Calatin reached out to probe him and also felt the presence of the Helm.

"You have it!"

"Yes I do," Tancostyl replied with considerable smugness.

"Let me have it! I need it!"

"No!"

"No? What do you mean, no? Let me have the Helm and I can regenerate. Healed I can help you get it to safety!"

"*Phfaa*!" Tancostyl snorted in derision. "Do you think I'm that stupid? Once you put the Helm on that'd be the last I'd see of it! You'd be off on some lunatic scheme of your own, leaving me to fight my way out of here. I know you, Calatin! I know you too well! Always off with your head in some cloud, and looking down your nose at the rest of us for getting our hands dirty down on the ground. Well getting my hands dirty has paid off! And if you think you can just crawl in here and take the reward from me, you're even more deluded than I thought! I'll let you draw Power through it because you can be useful to me in helping to get out of here, but the Helm is mine and mine alone, do you hear? Mine!"

The two war-mages continued bickering and hurling insults at one another through much of the night, only stopping when Amalric's body shut down of its own accord and went to sleep, leaving a fuming but trapped Calatin inside, who was forced to wait until morning to start again. By that time, though, Tancostyl had got his men up and ready to march. The castle's stores had been stripped, and the men set out on the road once more with Tancostyl's anger a flail at their backs.

With Calatin's new body slung in a litter, Tancostyl set him to work the moment he awoke, drawing Power through the Helm. With the way Tancostyl had set things up, only a trickle found its way into Calatin's body while feeding the inner mage, which was barely enough to enable Calatin to make essential repairs to the damaged body. He begrudged having to expend the effort on one so inferior to a DeÁine in physique, but knew that to try to transfer again so soon would only result in his essence becoming disembodied, and left to ride along the tides of the Power.

As the armed force hurried north-west, Osbern and his new allies kept pace with them, although they had taken a chance on this being the right road and so were ahead of their quarry. Osbern's local knowledge and the acquisition of the horses paid dividends now, for he knew where the few road junctions were. And so once the leading men had passed each of these, the four riders were able to hurry to the next – often cutting across fields instead of sticking to the winding lanes – and then allowing Nazar to rest while they waited for the foot soldiers to slog through the snow. By the evening of the second day, Osbern assured them that there was now nowhere else but Farness that the troops could go, except backwards. Consequently the four rode on into the night, but were able to alert the folk of Farness of the danger approaching before dawn.

With the watery light of day creeping over the horizon, Aeschere set the bemused locals hurrying to the shore to fill every vessel they could lay their hands on with sea water. By early afternoon the battlements of the old castle were lined with probably the strangest weapons it had ever known. Barrel after barrel of brine was poised to be emptied down on those attacking from below, but most were clustered around the small trebuchets located on the towers.

"Hammer the lids down," Aeschere instructed the men anxiously experimenting with the siege engines, the experts having died at New Year. "Launch the whole barrel out into the middle of the men. From this height the barrel will explode on impact and shower everyone around with brine. It should be enough to break that warlock's hold on a couple of dozen men at a go. You don't have to be accurate! This isn't subtle stuff like firing a bow. Just wait until a big group heads your way and let fly. You'll soon get a rough idea of what the range is like, and if nobody comes your way just wait. Don't bother trying to adjust the firing position."

Saeric had personally set each of the four towers' trebuchets up to give the optimum angle of fire and range knowing the inexperience of the operators, so it was down to luck now.

As the sun made its final brief appearance of the day, the ragged army appeared around the bend in the road just as the sails of a ship were seen coming closer towards the shore. From their observation point on the south-east tower, the four soldiers suddenly felt as much as saw a change in the troops heading their way. Nearly dropping with fatigue and hunger, the front men nonetheless broke into a trot and headed straight for the little harbour where fishing boats bobbed at anchor.

The watchers assumed that Tancostyl must have told them to clear a space for the approaching ship at the quay, but these men had evidently never handled any sort of vessel before, for they simply cast off the lines and pushed the small boats out into the water. Soon the harbour had scattered boats all over the place and Tancostyl could be heard screaming in frustration that things had only been made worse. Then the watchers felt a rippling, tingling effect upon the air.

"Sacred Trees! He's going to use the Power to clear the way," breathed Nazar, and seconds later a ball of Power-fire flew out from the midst of the men and exploded into one of the larger ships. The shock-wave sent waves ricocheting out and swamped some of the smaller boats in passing, while a second, then a third fireball took out more of the larger ones. Many of the locals wept at the sight of their means to earn a living disappearing to the harbour floor, but Osbern consoled them that at least the swamped boats could be re-floated, and that while Tancostyl was flinging fire in amongst the ships, he was not aiming it at the folk. The remaining soldiers accompanying the warlocks had been spread out to form a guard along the roadside, and the watchers could see two figures hurrying along the cleared path as the strange vessel came within the harbour walls.

"Well there's not much doubt about it," Saeric sighed. "Either Amalric has become enchanted by another member of the Abend, or Calatin has somehow managed to insert himself into Amalric's body. Is that possible?"

Aeschere shrugged. "I've never heard of such a thing, but then we know so little of what the Abend do outside of their wartime activities. As far as I've ever known, the Power extends the life of their own bodies, rather than simply their souls being transferred from body to body as each one wears out. But that doesn't mean they don't know how to do it. Does it matter?"

"Well it might if our unloved leader is still in there, mightn't it?" Nazar said thoughtfully, having picked up on his twin's train of thought as so often happened with them.

Aeschere turned to look at them in undisguised horror.

"Lost Souls! That's a fearful thought I hadn't had!"

"You mean the original man might be trapped inside and unable to get loose, while one of the Abend makes free with his body?" an appalled Osbern asked. "Poor bastard! Is there any way we can tell? And is there any way we can set him free?"

"Cut him off from Tancostyl and then use more salt water!" Aeschere exclaimed. "Nazar? Can you take charge of this trebuchet and change the angles to keep freeing men from Tancostyl's hold at the rear? Now rather than once he's boarded?"

The wounded man nodded and painfully rose to his feet to walk to the firing position, while the other three raced down the steps. Without being told, Saeric tore off towards the next tower to do the same with the next siege engines, while Aeschere called to Osbern, "Follow me!" as he raced for the gates.

"As soon as the wizard has passed, start dousing the men," he called to the locals, then to Osbern, "can you fight?"

And for the first time in years Osbern felt his old resolve return and rise up.

"You just lead on," he told the Knight. "You're the Forester! Go for the mage. I'll watch your back for you, never fear!"

Swords drawn and a small pin-barrel each under their arms, they ran out of the postern gate and hugged the wall as the first of the big barrels began to land amongst the soldiers. For an awful moment Osbern thought that they had got it wrong and that the brine would not work, as men shook themselves in surprise and then laughed at being soaked in nothing worse than water. But seconds later the same men began to double up in pain and then suddenly straighten up with looks of total bemusement on their faces, as though they had no idea how they came to be where they were. Most just stood in astonishment at the sight of two armed men running past them lugging pin barrels which would normally have held beer, and neither of the two had time to shout orders.

Ahead of them they saw the ship, now inside the harbour, lower a boat rather than wasting time trying to dock. Tancostyl, with his DeÁine stamina, was almost at the quayside, but Amalric was trailing far behind as his battered body ran out of energy.

"De Loges!" Aeschere roared, and saw the body twitch and almost turn. "Cross of Swords! He's in there!" the Forester cried, and sprinted forward.

Behind him Osbern had one eye for the men surrounding them, but was rapidly coming to the conclusion that they presented no threat. The able field commander that he had once been surfaced once more, and he raised his voice to command them, "Lay down your weapons!" The authority and assurance in his voice meant that virtually all the men around him complied without even stopping to think, allowing Osbern to hurry forward to Aeschere's side.

The combined Calatin/Amalric had his sword up and waving around, but the eyes were all over the place instead of focusing on aiming the weapon. Aeschere was keeping up a continuous dialogue aimed at the suppressed Amalric, while attempting to engage the sword blade and disarm him. It enabled Osbern to move to Amalric's right as Aeschere distracted him to the left, upon which Osbern let his sword hang by its lanyard, yanked the lid off the pin and doused Amalric in brine. As salt water descended over his head once more, a gut-wrenching, tortured scream went up and the sword clattered to the floor forgotten.

Amalric staggered away from them, fingers clawing at his face as the skin came up in huge bubbling blisters. His foot caught on the coping stone of the roadway and he fell backwards as Aeschere came at him with the second barrel. The water caught him squarely in the chest, sinking straight through his already sodden clothing and for an awful moment the two pursuers thought they had killed him as the agonised howling abruptly ceased. Then there was a ripping sensation which was felt more than heard, and an electric tingling on the air as if lightning were about to strike. A smoky shade of vaguely human shape seemed to be torn out of Amalric's chest, and then with a fading, eldritch cry, shot off high into the air to disappear in a massive static discharge.

Afterwards, the twins told Aeschere and Osbern that they saw Tancostyl stagger and almost fall, as Calatin was torn from his physical existence, but then practically dived into the boat which rowed with frantic speed back to the ship. For their part, Osbern and Aeschere rushed to the side of the prostrate figure.

"Oh Spirits, he's not breathing!" Aeschere cried, and began pumping Amalric's chest in between forcing breaths into his mouth. Osbern hurriedly loosened Amalric's belt and the neckerchief he wore tightly around his throat. Nothing happened and Aeschere redoubled his efforts, but then Amalric gave a weak gasp and then coughed. Seconds later he was crying out in pain and Osbern wondered whether they had done the right thing in reviving him given the extent of the burns from the water. However, the blisters soon began to lose their inflamed appearance, so that within minutes, although the former Grand Master was still covered in great bubbles of fluid, there was no inflammation beneath them.

Osbern swiftly ordered some of the bemused soldiers to make a stretcher, and they loaded Amalric onto it and took him into the castle. Leaving the Foresters to deal with him, Osbern set himself the task of sorting out the ragged remains of Tancostyl's army. Rapid questioning revealed that most men remembered up to the disastrous New Year, but then little beyond. Moreover, most were appalled that they had been bewitched into fighting for the man they at least knew of as the sinister priest who had corrupted their Jarl. So as night fell, Osbern found himself with over half a battalion of soldiers only too anxious to return to Earlskirk and take part in its defence if necessary.

"What do you intend to do?" he asked the three Foresters, as they shared in the hastily concocted hot stew which was being passed around. "Will you return to Prydein now?"

"I don't see how we can at the moment," sighed Aeschere wearily. "It's hardly as though there's a ship around here capable of making the journey across the open sea in winter. And I'm afraid it will take a while before either Amalric or Nazar are fit to travel anyway."

"Then may I make a suggestion?" Osbern ventured. "Why don't you leave Saeric and Nazar here with Amalric? The soldiers who don't have family in the capital can stay here under the twins' command, with the other hostages too weak to travel, and put this place into good order. They can keep an eye on your former prisoner at the same time – just in case there are any vestiges of Calatin lurking in some dark forgotten recess of his mind. Then you can come with me and help get these lads back and doing something useful."

"Where are you going with them, then?" Saeric asked, before Aeschere could swallow the mouthful of crusty bread he had just dunked, and be able to comment.

"I'm going to take them up the coast and see what's left of Fordon and Airey," Osbern told them. "I doubt it will be good, but at least I can take an accurate account back with me. Then I'm going up to High Tor Castle and over the mountain tracks to come down to Allerford. I'm hoping the abbot there will know where Abbot Jaenberht is, and I'm hoping even more that he's come to the capital, because he's the only hope I can think of for getting Rheged back on its feet. He's not a military man, but he's a superb organiser, and if Tancostyl has the Helm to use as he wills, I don't think Rheged dare remain undefended."

Chapter 20

Order Restored

Brychan: Eft-Yule – Imbolc

After the fell storm of the New Year, Hugh watched the seas anxiously with Tiny Arthur for the return of the *Grendel*. Then finally a fishing boat limped back into Boddigo bringing news of the annihilation of Crauwel across on Rheged, and everyone suddenly had even more to worry about. Hugh had taken Arthur with him when he had left before the New Year to inspect Bittern, and they had felt the storm's passage while at a roadside refuge. They had therefore been relieved upon their arrival at Bittern, on the first of the new year, to find that apart from a desperate lack of men, Dabhi had the place in good order. So much so that Hugh had set out the very next morning to return to Boddigo to collect Haply, Grimston and the Scabbard, with the intention of hiding the Scabbard at Bittern for the foreseeable future.

He had fully expected to see the *Grendel* tied up in the harbour as they'd ridden back along the coastal stretch of the road, and had worried when the full extent of the storm at sea had been revealed. Many of the fishing boats had been smashed against the stone jetties, and the few out at sea had not been heard of since. The almost certain loss of Aeschere and the other men was a sore blow to them all, but the news from Rheged made them realise that although their own problem had been substantially reduced, there were still others to be dealt with. Calatin might be gone, but Duke Brion remained a thorn in Prydein's side which Hugh now resolved to extract. Moreover, with him gone they would be free to help the other Islands.

Word had already appeared from Mullion announcing the successful capturing of Brion's home castle by Ealdorman Hereman and the men from Freton. Another light in the gloom was that the men had left the huge training camp just in time, and had met up with the contingent led by Captain Breca with few casualties. Despite Amalric de Loges leading the men of Bittern to their untimely death, the Knights of Prydein had therefore retained much of their original strength. Something which Hugh felt Duke Brion would not be expecting.

"I'm sure he's been blinded by his reliance on Calatin," he told Haply and Grimston as they warmed themselves by the fire of the inn which was temporarily their quarters in Boddigo. "And if Calatin simply dragged his information out of Amalric's mind, then we're really in with a chance of defeating him. The one thing we cannot afford to do is give Brion time to get his second wind. A winter campaign is hardly ideal for us, but it's no better for him now that his tame sorcerer is gone."

"Where are we going to start?" Haply asked. "You surely can't ask Hereman to bring his men on another long winter march so soon."

"No," agreed Hugh. "But then Hereman is just where he can do most damage to Brion's ego. His message said that he's already started scouring the countryside for Brion's henchmen – so even by normal methods, messages from Brion's spies should've dried up, and that should worry him. Furthermore, although Hereman understandably didn't want to put much in a message, he hinted that he's had information that's led him to believe that part of his force, under the command of Breca, stand a good chance of taking Osraig."

"Yes!" Grimston punched the air above his head. "Give that little shit Turstin something of his own medicine too! This is more like it!"

"Indeed," responded Hugh, unable to suppress a responding grin. "The whole reason why I asked for Breca for the original attack on Mullion is because such operations are his strong point. So I'm going to let them get on with the jobs those two do best. Meanwhile we, gentlemen, are going to take this cursed Scabbard to Bittern for Dabhi to lock in his deepest dungeon, and then ride for Treliever. It's a bigger and more sheltered port than Boddigo and I'm hoping that there was less damage there from the storm. We should be able to commandeer a ship to take us with all speed around the coast to Rosco."

"We're joining Piran?" guessed Haply.

"Yes we are," Hugh confirmed. "I shall ask Dabhi to send a bird to Thorold at Vellan to get him to bring up as many men as he can during that time. Today is the eighth. I want us to be at Treliever by nightfall on the thirteenth and sailing by the following day. With the right ship it should only take five days – seven at the absolute maximum – to get to Rosco. We shall ride straight away from there for Tancross and I'll ask Thorold to be there by the twenty-fourth. We may be delayed by a day but no more than that barring magical interference.

"I want him to bring the standards, and before we sail, I shall attempt to get word to Rosco and Bera so that every man rides in full uniform with our standards at our head. I want Brion to know exactly what he's unleashed, and the price he's going to pay for the lives he's cost. The people of Prydein will see who it is who cares what happens to them, and that it isn't that twisted duke."

True to his word, Hugh had them on the road bright and early the next day with the escort which had travelled with them from Quies. Arthur was something of a problem, for Hugh had no desire to take the young lad into battle with him. Yet leaving him behind was just asking for trouble, and so Arthur once again rode in front of Hugh. Dabhi took charge of the Scabbard at Bittern and placed it in one of the ancient torture holes at the bottom of the lowest level of dungeons. Once used to throw the worst prisoners in and forget about them, it seemed an appropriate resting place for the DeÁine Treasure. Everyone breathed a sigh of relief as the heavy iron grill slammed down on it, and they shut door after door behind them as they trekked back up through the levels of Bittern until they appeared into fresh air. As Haply said with relief, it was rather like visiting the Underworld and then finding you were not dead after all!

An uneventful ride later they reached Treliever, and once Hugh's name was cast abroad a ship was swiftly found. The *Madeline* was a sleek vessel used to making fast passages with perishable cargoes, with a dashing young captain who relished the challenge of getting the Grand Master of the Knights to his destination in record time.

"Safe and in one piece will be just fine," Hugh assured him, beginning to regret his emphasis on speed at the time of asking.

However, the young captain knew his ship and the coastal waters of Prydein. The *Madeline* fairly flew across the waves, her sails catching every breath of wind, leading Arthur to declare that when he was old enough he was going to have a ship just like this one. As her keel sliced through the wave crests, Arthur was delighted to be shown how to navigate and steer, while the older men gratefully remained below decks where it was drier than being soaked by the icy spray. Arthur's only complaint was that the experience was over far too quickly, for they raced into the harbour below Rosco around midday on the fifth day, a good half day ahead of even Hugh's most optimistic estimate. Hugh even offered Arthur the chance to stay on board, hoping that the irrepressible youngster would accept, but Arthur was not having that.

"I wanta see the Knights go inta battle!" the young gang leader declared with determination.

"I fear you'll end up riding out with him in front of you!" an amused Haply said softly to Hugh, who rolled his eyes in desperation.

"So do I," he sighed. "I think we'd better see how small the armoury can fit some chain-mail, don't you?"

To Arthur's wild delight the armourer at Rosco found an ancient surcoat made for some nobleman daft enough to want to take his small son into battle. There was even a small chain-mail helm, a touch on the large size for Arthur, but then that was better than it being small. The armourer put a couple of links in the top of the helm to hold the edge up so that it would not keep falling down over his eyes, and it was all they could do to get Arthur to take it off to go to bed. As it was, he insisted on having it ready at the foot of his bed in case the call to arms came during in the night.

"Sacred Trees, the lad's enthusiastic, isn't he?" Grimston sighed wearily, as the three of them shared a mulled blackberry wine before retiring.

"I want to say he'll feel different once he's seen a real fight," Haply agreed, "but I fear that Arthur's already seen so much brutality and bloodshed in his little life, that it's not going to come as much of a shock. Spirits! What a childhood! To have to fight for every scrap of food and avoid men who want to hunt you like you were vermin. How do such things happen? We're supposed to be a civilised society! There are churches everywhere you look in Trevelga, and yet turn the corner on all that piety and it's a running sewer."

"Well when we've stopped this mad grab for power, I'm going to personally hold this Island's reins for a while," Hugh declared. "I've never wanted this to happen, but someone has to put Prydein back on the right course. I know many of the leading churchmen, and thank the Spirits here in Prydein they aren't as self-serving as on some of the other Islands. If anything they've been trying to swim against the tide of corruption for years, but haven't had the power to influence anything outside their own walls. Together we surely must be able to make a difference until some sort of leadership can be sorted out."

Haply yawned largely as the warm wine relaxed him, then apologised, "Sorry! That wasn't meant as a comment! For what it's worth I think we're long overdue for a return to a chancellor ruling with a group of his equals sitting as his council of advisers. It's worked well on Ergardia and Celidon, and even on Rheged until that cursed Abend stuck his fingers in the pie. Is it coincidence that the two Islands which have had recent civil wars are the two where the chancellor's been made into a king, and the council dispensed with?"

"I'm sure not," Grimston agreed as he led the way to their sleeping quarters, also yawning. "Trees, I'm glad I've never had kids! I'm shattered and we've only had Arthur around for a few weeks!"

Hugh laughed. "I think that has more to do with Arthur than with children in general. From what I've seen he's exceptional by anyone's standards. I just hope he doesn't have us up before dawn wanting to be off!"

On the five day ride to Tancross, Arthur's enthusiasm never wavered, leading Haply to declare that the sooner they added him to the ranks of the recruits the better. The little lad's high spirits seemed to infect all who came into contact with him, and the sight of the tiny figure in his mail coat riding in front of the Grand Master brought a smile to many weary faces.

At Tancross, Hugh found Thorold waiting for him with the first solid intelligence of Brion's movements. The renegade duke had returned to the capital after wiping out Amalric's force near Haile in Samhainn. Yule had then been accompanied by wild celebrations in the capital. However, many of the citizens' festivities had been blighted by drunken rampages by Brion's troops, who seemed to feel that, having 'freed' the Island from its king, they were entitled to take whatever they wished. Many of the richest merchants had apparently left the city if they had premises elsewhere. For the less wealthy, and those for whom Trevelga was the only home they had, the start of a new year had been nothing to rejoice over. The enchanted storm had passed them by but they had suffered nonetheless.

However, something had changed within the royal palace during the festive season. The departure of the strange priest had been noted just before Yule began, but after the start of Eft-Yule Brion had begun sending men out searching for him. The search had been concentrated in the north but had also gone east and west, yet the stranger seemed to have disappeared. For a couple of weeks it seemed as though Brion might just give up – although Thorold had to admit this was not information from within the palace.

Then, however, he must have had news of the Knights massing at the River Tan. Trevelga was no place to get trapped in, for the city was too large to defend easily against a siege, and too many of the citizens sympathised with the Knights and would have found ways to let them in.

The reports said that Brion appeared to be stripping the palace of everything of value preparatory to leaving, and they speculated that he must by now have heard of the taking of Mullion. However, the holding of the Knights' army at the Tan seemed to have made him think that they were still wary of advancing to engage him in a head on battle.

"Well he's going to learn just how wrong he is!" Hugh announced. "Are the men in good shape?"

"Fine!" declared Thorold cheerfully. "All the better for the weather easing off since the turn of the year. We've been rotating them in and out of the towns too, so that they haven't been camping out for the whole time. The people of Tancross, Crossways and Lanfarn have been wonderful. Young King Ivain did us proud, Great Ash save his soul. They were his to a man, and they hate Brion with a passion for what he did to Ivain."

"Bless his soul indeed," Hugh agreed, feeling again the burning anger deep inside for the loss of his young protégé. "So Brion plans to make a run for it, does he? Has he sent any men westwards yet?"

"No, none at all. We think he'll go in force and all at once to retake Mullion," Thorold said, "but he's not moved yet."

"Then let's force his hand," Hugh decided. "We can march through Pendrim to Coombe and cut him off as he flees west, or try to bring him to battle at Moorcross."

"Why not do both?" Thorold suggested. "Send half the men to Coombe, and then the other half can advance on Moorcross, but fast! We'll have to make sure he doesn't retreat behind the walls of Mithian Castle or it'll take months to starve him out!"

"Then I want you and Piran to take the men you have up here in the north, westwards tomorrow," Hugh declared as a cunning plan formed in his mind. "It'll take me six days to get down to Lanfarn if I'm collecting men as I go. You should be past Pendrim by then. Just make sure no scouts of his live to tell him of your passing! We'll pick up our pace after then too. I'll hope to make Moorcross in three more days which would put us another three days away from Trevelga.

"I can send men to cut off the approach to Mithian. I want him to come out to us full of confidence that he's only facing a small force of what he believes are the remaining Knights in Prydein. If we give him a bloody nose then, I think he'll retreat and try to make sure any full battle comes at his time and place of choosing. But that won't happen because he'll get out of

Trevelga only to find you waiting, and then he'll find that Knights don't die so easily when the odds are more even!"

To Hugh's relief, by the time they'd got down to Lanfarn the lying snow was much lighter. The heavy falls which had made travelling a nightmare on the west and north moors had barely touched the southern uplands, which had only normal light dustings of snow. Morale was high within the ranks of the Knights, infecting even the horses, so that the ride to Moorcross was made in the three days Hugh had planned.

Pausing for a day to rest most of the horses, Hugh sent those who had only joined them at Lanfarn under Wulfric's command off on the road to Mithian by night. He had men milling around on the start of the road to disguise the signs of the passage of the several companies of men, for he had no intention of underestimating how many spies Brion might have this close to the capital. The following morning the remaining massed men rode out of Moorcross to the cheers of the locals – all heartily sick already of being raided by Brion's thugs – and many a soldier was thrown mistletoe for good luck.

The great standards rippled in the light wind, each displaying the wheeled cross, with the fierce dragon upon it worked in grey and silver, and the silent motto beneath. What Hugh had never revealed fully to Amalric was just how many men in the Order were in the eastern castles – and now, he belatedly realised, Amalric had been too disinterested in the ordinary men to ever ask. Bittern and Quies were small fortifications which had held only one battalion each (each battalion consisting of two hundred lances, with every lance being lead by a Knight). Amalric had assumed that Freton was the odd one out having two battalions because it was the Knights' training base. Therefore when Calatin had scoured Amalric's mind he confidently reported to Brion that Vellan, Rosco and Bera only had a thousand men in each, giving Brion's men the advantage of outnumbering them a minimum of two to one in any engagement.

However, Amalric was wrong in his assumption. The three great eastern preceptories held a full two fighting battalions each, plus many ancillary soldiers. In the current situation, Hugh had pulled all six battalions – plus the remaining half one from Quies, which had just evacuated to Rosco – out into the field, safe in the knowledge that the three eastern castles were still occupied by sufficient men to hold them until help could come, in the unlikely event of a siege. Even when two and a half had gone with Thorold and Piran to cut off the escape route, and one with Wulfric, three battalion standards flew displaying bygone battle honours behind Hugh's unadorned one as the Grand Master. In the winter morning, the sun shone on woven blues, greens and reds, and reflected off gold and silver, while the tassels at the base of the white standards fluttered like hawks' wings. Every Knight wore his red surcoat with the white dragon-headed sword emblazoned upon it, while the regular soldiers wore plain white over their mail.

In the winter landscape there was something almost unearthly about the great host, for at times the white surcoats blurred with the white of the countryside making them seem to partially disappear, and then suddenly return in flashes of blood-red. Cresting a small rise at the end of the first day, the men saw in the slanting low sun a rider galloping frantically towards Trevelga.

"Go on," Hugh laughed. "Tell your master just what he wants to hear – that the three thousand men of the east have come to fight!"

And sure enough Brion seemed to take Hugh's bait. The temptation to repeat his total victory at Haile was too much for him to resist. Unlike when Amalric had led the men of Bittern to their doom, this time Brion had had little warning. And as his army rode out to meet Hugh's across the undulating farmlands, it was clear that he had not had chance to mobilise the full seven thousand men the Knights now knew he had at his disposal. However, a good five thousand approached – no doubt in Brion's mind a sufficient superiority of numbers to guarantee victory. Their progress was slower than the Knights', owing to nearly half of Brion's force being on foot, but Hugh knew that most of these were the hardened fighters who had spent years battling the Attacotti on Kittermere. These men would more than likely attack the horses' legs to bring the riders down to their level. There would therefore be no superiority just from being mounted, and Hugh swiftly decided that he would not imperil valuable horses by ill-considered massed cavalry charges, but keep most of his men on foot.

He therefore halted his own force well before dusk at a small tributary of the River Drima and made camp. Ahead was a large water meadow which would be ideal cavalry ground. Again, Hugh was deflecting Brion away from his real intention, and once night fell he had the horses of his infantry led away to safety. The Knights' trained war-horses were brought into the centre of the camp, and pickets were posted all along the river bank. Sure enough, just past midnight there came the sound of men wading the shallow river, and heading for where they might expect the horses to be tethered. Hugh's men shadowed the creeping marauders until they heard them whispering their confusion at finding no animals, then killed them before reporting back to Hugh that Brion had once more taken the bait and was expecting cavalry.

Before the late winter dawn, the men-at-arms and the archers were, in their turn, wading across at the shallow fording points they had spied out the day before. Those few Knights who would be fighting mounted let the foot soldiers have a good hour's start before they carefully took the horses across. Hugh had spotted the rises of several lynchets at the far side of the meadow, and his foot soldiers lay in wait in the shadow of those small banks as the sun came up on what would be another fine day.

As the rising light revealed the Knights without their supporting men, riding slowly across the meadow, there came a savage roar from only a few hundred yards ahead of the hidden men. Brion's men had also crept forward during the night, and now his archers stood up and prepared to take aim at the horsemen. Instead, they suddenly found themselves the targets of a killing volley from the Order's archers, who in response rose from the grass on either flank. Screams of pain echoed on the morning air as the barbed arrows found their mark, but the Kittermere men were not routed so easily. They turned to attack the Order's archers, swords and spears brandished in their fists as they broke into a run, but now a clear trumpet call rang out and the Order's hidden men-at-arms rose from the cover of the lower land, broke over the bank like a wave and ploughed into the distracted enemy.

Faced with this new attack, Brion's men suddenly found themselves fighting for their lives. Hugh's surprise attack had confused Brion's men's who had not anticipated fighting an equal force on foot, and the easy victory they had been promised vanished like the dawn mist. Totally organised, the men of the Order were a very different opponent to the men who had been taken so off guard three months earlier, and Brion was swift to realise it.

As Hugh rode forward with Arthur in front of him he saw a figure in the distance, who he assumed must be Brion, wave his riders around the mêlée now taking place between them. As predicted, they came around to Hugh's right where the lynchet was lowest, and he turned his own cavalry to face them. The Order's horsemen must have looked a tempting target, for Brion still had near enough two and a half thousand men mounted up, whilst Hugh only had around six hundred now that his regular soldiers were fighting on foot.

Brion's riders started heeling their horses to a canter before they had all even managed the wheel around the mêlée of foot soldiers, and although they came down the slope at the gallop, their ranks were still unformed as they had to turn again onto the meadow. The Knights on the other hand had turned with the precision born of endless practice, and now formed a perfect line three riders deep. As one the Knights brought their horses up to a canter, the long lances came down in a single sweep and the horses accelerated a gallop. The ground shook with the pounding of hooves and before Brion's riders had time to form up properly Hugh's men were upon them. The Knights' trained destriers ploughed into the lesser horses like scythes through corn, knocking the lighter horses over and trampling, them as the Knights first impaled the riders on the lances and then drew swords to continue the attack.

In a blaze of carnage the Knights went straight through Brion's riders, wreaking havoc as they went. Discipline told as the Knights refused to become distracted by riders beyond their left or right, and their swords swung in an economical rhythm where every blow counted. Whereas the foot soldiers were evenly matched, Hugh and the mounted Knights were outnumbered four to one, yet Hugh did not lose a single rider.

When they were well clear, Hugh wheeled them back to face the enemy, and as they swung round saw on the horizon the glint of armour from Wulfric and his men. Brion obviously saw them too, and suddenly the retreat was being called to his men. As Brion turned his riders to plough up the lynchet and into the Order's foot soldiers to free his own men, Hugh's infantry broke off the engagement as planned and allowed them through. With many of the foot riding pillion behind the cavalry, Brion's men beat a hasty retreat straight back towards Trevelga.

Many bodies lay upon the ground from the melee and the Knights rode back to lend assistance to the wounded. To everyone's relief few of the dead and wounded amongst the foot were from the Order, and once the head count had taken place it transpired that only around two hundred of the Order were wounded and less than fifty dead. On the other hand over five hundred of Brion's foot soldiers lay dead on the field, and another hundred were wounded prisoners. From amongst over two thousand cavalry, Brion had lost close on another five hundred men and almost half that number in horses. By the time Wulfric caught up with them to report that Mithian remained untouched by Brion, another dozen of Brion's horses had had to be put out of their misery from irreparable wounds. Most of the other stray beasts, however, were rounded up and added to the Knights animals.

The sun had not yet reached midday, and so those Order's horses which had been held back were brought forward, and the whole force rode forward at an easy pace. Hugh had no desire to overnight his men amongst the carnage of the battle, and it was important to keep the pressure on Brion. By the time they made camp they were within sight of Trevelga's city walls, which Hugh judged should be sufficient a hint to Brion that they had not finished with him yet. The Order had never kept very many men inside the city, but nobody had forgotten those from amongst their ranks who had lost their lives when Calatin had attempted to seal them into the city after Amalric's defeat. Most had made it out alive, but there had still been fatalities and every one of those was one too many.

Before daybreak, people from the city came out to the Knights to tell them that Brion was leaving by the west gate. With the coming day the Knights therefore made a triumphal entrance into Prydein's capital. However, if the residents were overjoyed to see the Knights back, the soldiers were appalled at the signs of destruction everywhere. A small troop went to investigate the first of their own buildings and came back ashen-faced, declaring that there was nothing left but ruins. Only when the Knights had reached the central square, and Hugh had dismounted to talk to the bishop of the great cathedral, did he hear more of what they found. Arthur was enjoying being left sitting on the great war-horse alone, and so the five Knights managed to get Hugh out of Arthur's hearing.

"They hung some of his gang from the spikes on the stable walls," one told him. The seasoned soldier was near to tears at what he had found. "May the Underworld take Brion and torment him for eternity," he swore. "To do that to those little children!"

"We think another six of them might have been alive when the buildings were put to the torch. Burnt little corpses behind a locked door!" another equally distressed Knight added in a choked voice. "That wasn't just Brion! That was those savages who follow him. I'll show them no quarter, no mercy!"

"No quarter! No mercy! And that's an order you can pass along to the others out of Arthur's hearing," Hugh told them with restrained savage fury in his voice, "but make sure he doesn't get wind of it or he'll be asking why."

But the Knights were already adamant that the little fighter would be spared as much as possible, and so for once Arthur remained oblivious to the word that spread through the ranks like wild fire. If the Knights had previously been prepared to treat Brion's followers as simply misguided, they were certainly not from now on. The men fanned out through the streets of Trevelga hunting for any laggards, but despite the willingness of the ordinary people to help hunt those who had made the last months a misery, nobody was found. Bidding the bishop farewell and temporarily commending the care of the citizens to him, Hugh led his men out of the west gate in pursuit.

Until the discovery of the small bodies, Hugh had planned to let his men rest within Trevelga for a day, but he knew his men and sensed the outrage amongst them. With only half a day's head start, Brion's men were soon in sight upon the horizon, and they could see the panic begin to set in on the hindmost troops. Confident that they would catch them and knowing that Thorold and Piran were up ahead, the men of the Order were prepared to rest for the night, but Brion's men obviously marched well past darkness falling and started before the dawn.

Yet over the second day Hugh's men once again made up the difference. The state of mind of the men they were pursuing was evident from the dropped spoils by the side of the road. Sumptuous woollen rugs, pillaged from the houses of merchants, lay abandoned beside ladies' finest dresses, and boxes of now broken tableware.

"What did the stupid bastards think they were going to do with those in a marsh and rock pigsty like Kittermere?" Hugh heard someone comment behind them.

"They wants 'em 'cos if they has 'em the rich folks don't," Arthur called back, trying to turn around and getting lost in his helmet. "It ain't what it's worth to them," he said earnestly to Hugh, as being the only person he could see, "it's what they know it means to them as has it. They know them folks'll be aggrieved, and that's what makes it worth carting all this junk across the Island."

"I'm sure the head of the weavers' guild wouldn't appreciate you calling his grandmother's carpet a piece of junk," Hugh remonstrated – although in his mind's eye he was tickled by the thought of the reaction of the pompous and mean merchant if he ever encountered Arthur and his forthright comments. Hugh had never enjoyed the company of the man on the rare occasions when duty had forced him to visit the guildsman's house. To start with the man had had everything money could buy, and yet getting money out of him to fund charitable acts had been like trying to get blood out of a stone.

Maybe he'll start to understand what it's like to go without, Hugh thought hopefully, then thought again. *No, that tight-fisted bastard will have something squirreled away – he has the luck of the Demon Lord. Oh, but it would give me great satisfaction to find that he collaborated with Brion thinking it would give him some advantage. It would give me an excuse to throw him into the darkest dungeon in the palace for a month and see him come out half the size he went in. I know that's not a thought befitting my station, but after what's happened to Arthur's little friends it's the way I feel. Trees, but I'll root out every turncoat and make them wish they'd never been born! First Ivain and then this! Someone is going to pay!*

As the sun sank low in the west they began the descent to the river valley, and saw Coombe nestled by the crossing. To everyone's delight they could see Brion's men halted in confusion, for spread out ahead of them was a long line of the Order. Thorold and Piran had sprung the trap! The river was too wide to ford except by the town, the road to the north was only accessible through the town, and Piran's men were blocking the way to the road south. The tables had been turned and now Brion's men were the ones left with no alternative but to fight. Even without the men Hugh had left behind in Trevelga to guard the prisoners and the wounded, there were still six thousand men of the Order in the field, and they could see their trapped enemy looking back and forth trying to work out where all these men had come from.

"You didn't expect this did you, Brion?" Hugh chuckled softly. "Not to your liking at all is it, fighting with only even odds!"

And given the losses sustained earlier, Brion's men were now the lesser number by several companies' strength.

"Do we wait until tomorrow to fight them?" Wulfric asked Hugh. "There can't be more than an hour's light left."

"No," Hugh replied. "I've had enough of this. If we wait until morning, half of them will have escaped across the fields in the dark, and you can bet that they'll be the ones who did the worst deeds. It'll be the sheep who are left to be cut down by us, and they're not the ones I want. Sound the advance!"

Across the valley the trumpet call rang out, and from down below they heard calls ring out a heartbeat later like an echo, signalling that Thorold had been prepared and was bringing his own men forward. The mass of Brion's mob seethed and lurched first one way and then the other. Some tried to make a run for it and the archers with Hugh hurried forward and shot them down as they ran. No message was necessary to Thorold, and the archers with him took their cue and similarly dispatched those who ran their way. By the time the archers had all escape routes covered, the enemy's men had realised the futility of trying to run and stayed within the force. Then Brion's archers came to the front ranks and prepared to fire. Hugh raised his arm and waved his own forward in formed ranks this time. Many of them had the range in the light winter breeze down to a nicety already and, before Brion's archers could get a shot off, volleys from the Order were falling in a lethal rain on them. Casualties were heavy, and before long only the occasional arrow flew from out of the enemy ranks.

Now the ranks of the Order fanned out and formed the line of battle which was mirrored by Thorold's men. In the evening hush all that was heard was the jingle of harnesses and the rhythm of hooves, which rose to a trot and then a canter. As Hugh's men came down off the steeper part of the slope onto the valley floor, the great horses leapt forward into a thundering gallop and the battle cry went up,

"For the Order, the Rowan, and Prydein!"

And on Hugh's cue the massed voices added, "No quarter! No mercy!"

Across the valley, Thorold was in the centre of the men already rising from the canter to the gallop as he heard the second cry. *Sacred Trees!* he thought. *No quarter? No mercy? Whatever has Hugh discovered? I've not heard that since we fought the DeÁine!* Then raised his own voice and bellowed the order,

"No quarter! No mercy!" and heard it echo out along his own ranks.

Many of Duke Brion's men huddled together to wait for death to take them as they heard this, but the wild men of Kittermere came out fighting. If they were going to die anyway, they were determined to take as many with them as they could. In their savage war-bands they pounded out, foot soldiers running at the stirrups of those mounted. Yet they were not used to fighting disciplined troops who held the line and did not waver in their attack. The Knights tore into them giving them no chance to attack the horses, and then returned to attack again, leaving those who had ridden between the larger war-bands to close ranks and attack the main body.

Hugh found himself facing a band led by a thug who looked more pirate than soldier. Arthur had been strapped onto the back of Hugh's saddle to stop the little lad being easily knocked off and to give Hugh room to use his sword. He had tried to leave Arthur at the top of the hill, until he realised the fierce lad would only run down into the fray and get trampled.

Now Arthur had one of the Knights' long knives as a sword and was lashing out at anyone who came his way. As Hugh's blade engaged with a snarling brute by their horse's head, Arthur sunk his blade into the biceps of another who had turned back to try to attack the horse's flank. Slashing the brute's throat open, Hugh turned in the saddle and sliced half the face off the one Arthur had stabbed, even as Arthur turned his attention to the other side and poked at another just raising his sword. Hugh swung the sword in an arc over Scythian's head and near severed the raised sword-arm, before swinging it back to the next man ahead of them.

Hugh could not remember the last time he had gone into battle with this much pent up fury. Like many of the older troops he had regarded the Knights' regular task of dealing with raiders as an unpleasant job which had to be done. He bore them no personal grudge. They were only trying to survive – except that they were going about it the wrong way. He had had no regrets about leaving the physical side of things to the younger men once his expertise was needed elsewhere, and in spending more time in the planning than the execution. But these were feelings from the distant past. Back to the days of Moytirra, and his anger and loathing for an enemy which took the lives of innocent people for no reason. As he bludgeoned one in the face with the sword's pommel with a backward swipe, which then put him in line to lunge straight down the throat of another, he could hear himself snarling under the surrounding din.

"That's for Ivain!" he growled, wrenching his blade out of an eye socket. "And that for Squiers," a severed hand went flying through the air, "…and that for the men you bastard's butchered at Haile!" He opened the arteries on a neck and kicked the corpse clear of his horse. "Gutless cowards! …Butchers! …No quarter! No mercy!"

And then he was facing other Knights who were also looking for the next enemy to kill. Coming to his senses Hugh called out,

"Find the leaders! Find the Duke! Find that bastard Turstin!"

As the frantic activity slowed down, men began searching around the remaining pockets of fighting. In the gathering gloom, Hugh had a horrid fear that Brion might make his escape, but then he was called from somewhere to his left, and he saw Brion being dragged forward writhing and kicking by four Knights. The renegade duke faced Hugh defiantly.

"So you wanted to make the killing stroke yourself, old man? I didn't think you had it left in you! All that nursemaiding my useless cousin! Go on then! Do your worst! And make it a clean stroke!"

Hugh looked down on him with undisguised contempt.

"That cousin you so despised was worth ten of you," he said with bitterness. "And because of that you're not getting off so lightly. I'll administer the final blow if you really want – but not here. You're not dying so quick! You'll swing from a noose from the palace balcony and your pet rat with you."

More men had dragged a white-faced Turstin to stand alongside Brion as the duke screamed at Hugh,

"You can't do that to me! I'm a duke! Hanging is for common criminals!"

"Really?" Hugh answered with silky sarcasm. "Well let me tell you something Brion. You're no duke! You aren't fit to lick your father's boots, and he was hardly a shining example of noble behaviour. You're a self-made bastard, if not by birth. You've no castle, no lands and no power anymore. So what makes you think you're a duke? And as for hanging – the punishment fits the crime."

"What crime? …What *crime?*" an increasingly worried Brion demanded.

"Think on the row of bodies you left swinging from the Baker Street preceptory to burn to death in the fires your men set," Hugh spat with venom, his face a mask of fury close to Brion's as he leant down from his saddle and inclined his head back to where Arthur sat behind him.

"That wasn't me!" cried Brion.

"No! That wasn't us!" agreed an even more panicked Turstin.

"Oh? Then who was it?" Hugh queried nastily. "Ghosts?"

"It was Calatin! He did it! He's mad he is! You find him and make him talk …you'll see!" babbled Turstin.

Hugh leant his left forearm on his thigh to support himself as he leaned out in the saddle towards the two prisoners again.

"Not you? …Calatin? …You fools! You've just admitted in front of all here that you've been colluding with the DeÁine! That's treason, and you hang for treason!"

"The DeÁine? No! No!" Turstin screamed. "No, not the DeÁine! Calatin! I told you, Calatin! He's a priest, a dark priest who knows magic!"

364

"You pathetic fool," Thorold sneered from beside Hugh. "Did you really believe that? Calatin is DeÁine! He's more than DeÁine, he's one of the Abend! You willing brought one of the Island's greatest enemies into our midst, supported him while he wreaked havoc on us, and you never once asked yourselves where he got that strength from? How somebody like that could appear from nowhere? Sacred Trees but you're stupid! A priest? Even this lad riding behind the Master had the wit to see him for what he was!"

"You closed your eyes because it suited you to," Hugh continued remorselessly. "He offered you what you wanted to hear and your own twisted greed drove you to accept. It wasn't ignorance that kept your eyes shut, it was the selfish expectation of getting what you wanted with very little effort on your behalf, and to the Underworld with the suffering of others. Well you should know that at this moment, that war-mage you hitched yourselves to is floating at the bottom of the sea. We've already dealt with him, and now we're going to deal with you! Clap them in irons! They'll hang before the people, and unlike the farce they acted out over Ivain, this really will be justice!"

Kittermere & Prydein

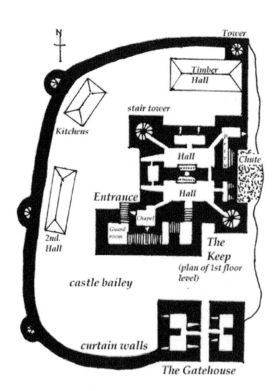

Osraig Castle

Chapter 21

A Tale of Two Castles

Brychan: Eft-Yule

At Mullion nobody was quite sure what had happened to cause the mayhem in the town, but the storm was the chief suspect. However, with its passing, Ivain and Breca had other things on their minds. Largely due to Hereman's mistrust, the sailors had been brought within the castle for the night, but that at least meant that none of the crews had been lost for the boats they were using to get to Kittermere. The raid therefore went ahead as planned, and in the morning the two hundred men embarked, lugging large quantities of kit with them.

The howling westerly wind was hardly helpful to their mission, and for the first couple of days they painfully tacked their way down the Sound of Kittermere. It would have been quicker to ride down the coast had there been anywhere where they could embark from further south. However the tide had eroded this stretch of the Prydein coast to crumbling cliffs for most of the upper channel, and then south of the cliffs had turned it into a quagmire, too thick to ride on and too shallow to sail over, once the granite changed to softer rock.

At the end of the third day they saw Hereman's force wave them farewell from the last of the cliffs, turning inland on their own mission. Then three more days of beating down the Sound finally brought them close to their target. Just as Ivain had told them, a long spit of muddy sand formed a tongue from the rocky headland out into the bay, and was slowly being populated by tussocks of hardy plants. Even on the seaward side, the water was too shallow in most of the spit's lagoon for the boats to land the Knights far enough away from the castle to find cover, and it had been clear from the outset that they would have to disembark at the solitary landing place beneath the castle.

For once the limited winter daylight was in their favour, and they did not have long to wait for darkness to fall. As the last of the light faded, the little flotilla crept into the bay and edged across to the western side where the shadows were deepest. By the middle of the evening the men were slipping off the ships and making their way noiselessly up seaweed-draped rocks onto the sheep-cropped turf.

Osraig was a dismal place. The castle was built of solid grey granite and nobody had bothered trying to make much of a home of it. It still had mainly arrow slits for windows, even on the seaward side which was theoretically its strongest side. A rocky promontory stood to its right as viewed from the sea, and a small watchtower built into this rock marked the start of a solid curtain wall which formed a land-ward horseshoe shape around the bleak keep, and ended back at the shore in a gatehouse tower as tall as the keep if less massive. The keep itself was a four-storey solid square, with each corner reinforced so that it had mini towers projecting from the wall line. On the southern side a fore-building housed an enclosed flight of stone stairs which led to the entrance on the first floor, limiting and guarding the only access. When the sea had pounded the cliffs at the castle's feet it must have been truly impregnable. Even now the keep and watchtower stood at the top of a substantial rise the height of several men above the beach.

The night was black and moonless as Ivain led the men off the turf and down onto the shingle beach. Breca had worried that their footsteps would be heard, but now he appreciated why Ivain had said that would not happen, for the choppy winter sea kept up a constant percussion on the shingle from which their steps were indistinguishable. Half the men remained hidden in the shadow of the gate tower under the command of a senior Knight, in case anyone there saw the assault on the castle and decided to join in the defence. These Knights would take care of the additional defenders and then take the gatehouse, or, if all was quiet within, they would wait until the keep was taken and then make an assault in support of the first group against any guards on the curtain wall.

Again Ivain's intelligence proved correct, for even in the icy cold their access point could be smelt from some way off.

"Hounds of the Wild Hunt! That's disgusting!" Pauli whispered in Ivain's ear. "Would it've killed someone to have got that cleared and a proper system put in?"

"It would probably have killed several!" Ivain whispered back with dry humour. "Just remember, in summer some poor souls have died just moving a year's worth!"

With picks and spiked staffs, a snake of men climbed the ice-packed, stinking slope until they reached the stone of the castle wall. Frozen as it was, they still felt their boots slipping and sliding, and decided that maybe it was as well that they were doing this in the pitch black and could not see what they were stepping in. Risking some light from a shielded lantern, they saw a wide chute sloping up into the castle on the eastern wall. Two smaller chutes dropped down at the southern end of the wall to the left of where they stood, but this one was easily double their width. Without a word, Breca pulled a bundle of straws from his pocket and held them out, but even as the men each began taking one to determine who would draw the short one and have to make the grim first ascent, Ivain tapped Pauli on the arm.

"Give me a pick and give me a leg up," he mouthed silently.

"No!" Pauli mouthed back. "You're the …!"

"…one who thought of this! I can't ask someone else to do this."

Ivain was resolute, and before Breca had realised what was happening, Ivain's pick had dug into the highest masonry joint he could reach, and the young king was pulling himself upwards and swinging Pauli's seized pick in his other hand to get a hold. Breca glared at Pauli who raised both hands in exasperation, then motioned for two others to give him picks and went to follow Ivain. Another two men-at-arms who had been reluctant to begin the grisly climb now also stepped forward, and followed Pauli and Ivain without a word.

Sacred Trees, Breca thought, *this one may not have the experience necessary yet, but he certainly knows how to make men follow him. When word gets around that the king did the first scramble up the privy rather than make someone else do it, he's going to get an awful lot of goodwill.* And the first one up did have a grim job, for they had to clear the fresh deposits out of the way. Almost worse, at the top Ivain remembered a wide board with five holes cut in it for men to sit on. The only way to get it off was for two men to wedge themselves against the back wall with their backs, and the front wall with their feet, in order to free their hands to push the board with. A singularly unpleasant spot to be in when the unaccustomed rich foods of a week's festivities had taken their natural course!

Ivain was almost heaving at the stench by the time he reached the board, despite the nose-numbing cold. With care he managed to wriggle into a position to be able to look up through one of the holes, and saw that chamber was deserted. A filthy Pauli appeared by his side and together they shoved at the board.

It was not a particularly heavy board, but trying to shift it from underneath with very little to grip made it feel three times heavier. The two men-at-arms came right up behind Pauli and Ivain, and managed to brace their legs a bit more for them by dint of leaning against them while hanging on with their picks. On the fourth shove the thing finally shot upwards and clattered off onto the flagstone floor. As Ivain and Pauli struggled to stop themselves falling, the two behind hauled themselves up over the edge of the stone seat and dashed for the door.

For a moment everyone held their breath for fear that the falling seat had raised the alarm, but nobody came. Some way off they could hear the sound of men carousing, and it seemed as though the few left to defend the castle were taking advantage of the beer cellar. As soon as Ivain and Pauli were also in the room, Ivain went to watch the door while the other three found things to attach ropes to. No sooner had the ropes gone down to the men below than they started climbing up, and within minutes the small room was full.

Easing the door open, Breca led the men out, this time insisting that Ivain stay back from the front.

"They'll smell you coming before they see you!" he told Ivain, who realised that he could not argue with that. As he held the door ajar for more men to slip through, he undid his wrecked coat and let it fall on the floor with his woollen hat. No amount of washing was ever likely to remove the stench he had ground into the fibres while moving the seat, and although the castle was bitterly cold, it was still pleasanter for him and the rest of the company without them. As the last of the men joined them in the chamber, he took the opportunity to take his turn in the file of men creeping along the corridor.

The chamber they had come up into was built into the thickness of the twenty-feet-wide walls. At ground floor level there were only a few of the tiniest of arrow slits and no other external openings, since that was the storage area. They had climbed up and entered at first-floor level on the eastern seaward side, and now made their way to the right into the north-east bastion, where another small chamber was also let into the reinforced bulk of the corner wall. This served as an antechamber to one of two oblong halls created out of the centre of the massive keep. Each of these was a good fifty feet long and twenty wide, and the central wall was as much to provide much needed fireplaces and chimneys than for any reinforcement, given that the floor rested on the huge stone vaults of the stores below.

The hall before them was deserted and they crept in. In the middle of the same long northern wall, another door led to an isolated inter-wall chamber, while at the far end of that wall a third doorway (mirroring the one they had come through) led to a spiral stair in the north-west bastion. At the far end from where they had entered, a door in the western wall led into another chamber in the thickness of the chimney-wall, which could be passed through to come out in the second large hall. A door in the east end of that central chimney-wall (directly across the shorter width of the hall from the one they had just come out of, and the wall which bisected the keep) was the only other way into the southern section of the castle, making it possible for defenders to in effect seal off half the castle if the need arose.

Therefore with care, the Knights entered the second hall but found that deserted too. From this hall, a door in the eastern wall led off to two smaller privy chutes, which were obviously for the more important residents since they afforded more privacy in two separate cubicles. Next to them a doorway in the south-east corner led to the other spiral stair. Breca left men on guard at both the stairs whilst they investigated the side rooms on this side. Where the central chamber stood in the thickness of the north wall, in the south wall steps led down a short way to an anteroom. This stood at the top of the flight of the main entrance stairs. Although very imposing and grand, because of it the whole of this floor was freezing cold in winter, and the Knights could see why the defenders had retired elsewhere. In the south-west corner, where the fore-building projected out over the entrance stairs to first floor height, were two more rooms, one of which was the castle chapel.

Not a soul disturbed their passage, and Breca sent men down the main stairs. Sounds of scuffling were briefly heard, and then a man bounded back up to report that the two half-asleep sentries had been dealt with, and the entrance of the castle was now theirs. Men now slipped silently down to the basement and found nobody except two sleeping scullions and the cook in the kitchen, who were easily bound and gagged. The other occupants were therefore all upstairs where Ivain had explained the lord's principal hall lay, with the sleeping quarters located above on the third floor. On the second floor the grand hall was only divided by the great chimney breast and two stone pillars on either side, and so the Knights ascended the stairs in both towers. Men remaining below were signalled when both leaders had reached the top, and the Knights tore out of each stairwell simultaneously.

Gorm sat sprawled in the lord's chair with a flagon dangling from one hand. The men around him were half asleep, half drunk, and never knew what had hit them. Those possessed of enough wits to fight died quickly, and the rest were subdued in no time. The drunken Gorm was hauled to his feet and dragged before Breca, but he was so far in his cups that Breca saw no point in wasting his time speaking to him. The Knights had come prepared with lengths of rope, and now the castle men were bound hand and foot, and gagged with their own scarves. A man went to the only proper window in this hall, which fortunately looked out over the sea as being the least vulnerable side. Opening a lantern, the man-at-arms signalled to a watcher below, who repeated the signal back, and went to tell the other half of the Knights that they could now take the southern gatehouse.

This was the main and only gateway into the castle ward and a formidable defence in its own right, but it had been built with attacks from outside by land in mind, not from the well-watched rear. Clearly nobody had ever anticipated men coming up from the beach and across the castle's bailey! The portcullis was down and only a handful of disgruntled men huddled around a small brazier trying to keep warm. They were swiftly overpowered and the Knights ascended the single stair to the first floor. Here there were more men, but most were wrapped up in what blankets they had, trying to get some sleep, since they were assuming they would be taking the watch from midnight onwards.

To Breca's delight they had made a full sweep of the castle and had it secured within an hour of making the climb up the chute. Not a man had even been wounded, whilst the captives were divided between the subterranean room beneath the main castle stair, and a similar one at the gatehouse. As he walked around the bailey with Ivain, who had liberated one of Gorm's coats to replace his own, it became clear why little had been done to the main castle to make it habitable. From the sea they had seen a lower stone wall running on the seaward side from the north-east bastion up to the watchtower, by the start of the curtain wall, and from the inside they now realised that a half-timbered hall had been built against it. This was the place that Alaiz had called home as a child, and if hardly luxurious it was certainly more homely. It had clearly lacked a woman's touch for many years, but even so, faded wall-paintings brightened the place up where thick wool hangings did not provide warmer cover. Above it, an open chamber with three smaller ones leading off it, contained beds hung about with thick drapes against the winter cold.

Just opposite the hall was a more spacious kitchen and store, also built against the curtain wall, which was obviously the one regularly used when the castle was fully occupied. The Knights swiftly got a good fire going in there, and a handful of men set about making a hot meal from the ample provisions. On the western side there was another half-timbered hall where the Knights found terrified servants. Once convinced that they were going to be substantially better off than under Turstin and Gorm's vicious lordship, these folk set to with a will to make beds up and light fires to warm the place up. Gorm and Turstin had meanly refused to let their workers have proper fires in this hall, saving all the wood for the grand hall which took vast amounts of logs to keep warm.

"Forget the castle," Breca told everyone. "We'll only use that in dire need. Let's get these two halls warm and usable – they're far more practical for long term use. I want men out patrolling the walls, but that means having somewhere comfortable to come back to. Men who are too cold to get a decent night's sleep are men who'll make mistakes and miss something, and I'm not having that."

By the next morning an almost festive air permeated the place. What passed for a meagre little town associated with the castle could hardly believe its luck when it woke up and found the dreadful brothers were no longer lords over them, and the Knights were treated as liberating heroes. Ivain had surprised even himself with the accuracy of his estimation of the number of men left, for aside from Gorm, there had been around thirty men carousing in the hall and twenty in the gatehouse. These men were now bundled, still tied up, along with an escort of fifty of the Order onto the boats which had brought the Knights, to be taken back to Mullion. Breca had no desire to keep them in a castle where they knew every nook and cranny, and where some of them had no doubt been blackmailing and threatening the locals for years. Fear could be a powerful incentive, Breca knew, and he wanted to avoid any of the servants being intimidated by old enemies into freeing them.

For several days, the Knights used the horses they found stabled outside the walls to make forays into the surrounding countryside. Had they known it, on a couple of days they came close to Alaiz and Talorcan's lance making their way across the Kittermere uplands. However, there were too few horses for the Knights to ride far, and there seemed no sign of the brothers' henchmen lurking on outlying estates.

"They've obviously all gone across with Turstin to make their fortunes, or so they think," Pauli speculated to Ivain, after a couple of days.

"Well let's hope Hugh gives them a nasty surprise," Ivain replied raising his mug of caff in a silent toast to his old mentor.

However, by the end of a fortnight most of the Knights were bored stiff. There was little to do, and even Breca admitted that the patrols were being done more as something to keep the men occupied than against any real threat. A message had returned from Hereman saying that they had enjoyed similar success in securing the countryside around Mullion. So much so, that in the light of Osraig being in the Order's hands, he had now sent another two companies in the boats under Eremon's command to bring the good news of Kittermere's liberation to Ceos.

"I know I shouldn't complain," Breca said to Pauli and Ivain in the seclusion of Turstin's private chamber on a wet afternoon, as they dug through what records the family had bothered to keep. "But really! The first proper engagement in years – the stuff we train and train for – and we win hands down without so much as a scratch. And now it looks like we'll be sat on our behinds for the next few months while the eastern preceptories have all the excitement of fighting Duke Brion and Turstin. I can't blame the men for feeling left out of it because I do too."

"Well ...," Ivain let the word hang in the air making the other two look up to see him grinning at them.

"Well what?" asked Pauli suspiciously.

"You haven't had another bright idea have you?" Breca said, unable to keep the anticipation out of his voice.

"What about Draynes?" Ivain said.

"I think we've had quite enough of shit chutes without adding smelly drains to our achievements," Pauli objected with feeling.

"No, no," Ivain waved Pauli's objection aside. "Not drains as in gullies for the rain. No. ...The place. ...Draynes. ...It's the other proper castle on Kittermere! In decent weather it would be about three days' good ride from here. There's a reasonable road from here to there. In fact it's the only reasonable road in the whole island! I haven't said anything until now, because with so few horses it would mean more like six days' march. But it's a valid tactical target because it's the best port the island has. Being just to the south of where the coasts of Kittermere and Prydein narrow to make

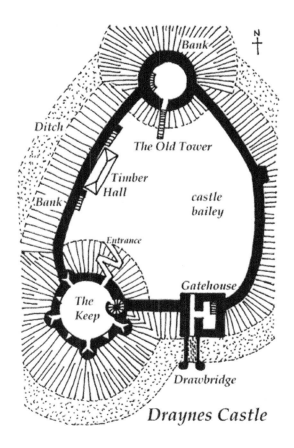

Draynes Castle

the Sound, it isn't subject to the same wicked tides that you get in this close stretch of sea up here.

"I've been thinking, though, about what Hugh said way back when we were in Quies. Rheged has one of these Abend loose and causing chaos. So what about the other Islands? Hugh always said Ergardia was secure because there was something special about it, and anyway they have the mountains to fall back into. No stranger could launch a raid into those high passes without getting into all sorts of trouble. And the same goes for Celidon. But what about Brychan? They were always the most vulnerable, being only over the mountains from New Lochlainn. What happens if the

375

DeÁine go on the offensive? Has there been any word, do you know? Rheged might not be able to go to their aid, and anyway, if Rheged's ports are compromised then we might find it difficult to use the northern ports of Prydein. Wouldn't it be useful then to be able to send men out of Draynes and up between Kittermere and Rathlin?"

"Only if you neutralise the Attacotti first," Breca said sadly. "I'm afraid they could easily not know anything was amiss and attack us just for the sport of it."

"So they might," agreed Ivain. "And the main reason why we've never gone in to sort Magnus out, Hugh said, was because Kittermere was barely compliant at the best of times. Back then he thought *we'd* be the ones starting a civil war if we tried to use Draynes as a base to strike at Magnus, and Hugh would never have intentionally started *any* war except in the direst need. But everything's changed now, hasn't it? The war's come, like it or not. And Turstin is no longer the ruler of Kittermere, whom I have to appease at every turn for fear he'll ally with my enemies. Indeed, the last time I had chance to talk of such things with Hugh, he said he feared Turstin was secretly in alliance with Magnus. So the last thing we want *now* is for Magnus to sail unopposed into Draynes, and come to the aid of those he sees as his allies against us."

"*Mmmm…*" Breca pondered, although Ivain could see that he was sorely tempted. "Put like that I suppose I could justify it to Hereman."

"There's no shortage of supplies we could take," Ivain added. "The men would hardly be going without, especially if we used the few horses as pack animals instead of to ride. And because the route between Draynes and here was so important, there's no shortage of places to stop overnight. Again it's the only place on Kittermere where you *will* find inns!"

Breca held out until the evening when he consulted the senior Knights who had come with them, but everyone was just itching for something to do and no-one protested. There were even a few men who had travelled the road before, who confirmed all that Ivain had said. In the third week of Eft-Yule, therefore, a company of one hundred men marched out of Osraig led by Breca. Those who remained behind had been rejoined by those who had gone to escort the prisoners, and so a full company still guarded Osraig under the command of a senior captain called Scrope – a man steady and experienced enough that Hereman was unlikely to protest when he found out. With less inside information as to the layout of Draynes Castle, the

Knights went prepared for as many eventualities as possible, for they had no idea by what means they might need to force an entrance.

The weather had turned slightly milder and wetter as they progressed down the southern finger of Kittermere, and for the first time their reception by the locals was less friendly. Many of those living down here had the look of Attacotti with their dark hair and eyes, and pale skin, and the Knights began to wonder whether Turstin had been purposely inviting Attacotti settlers onto the island. On the sixth evening they stopped short of the town, although they had no doubt that any defenders in the castle would have already heard of their approach. However, Breca wanted to take his time surveying the castle in the daylight. A rushed attack was most likely to fail.

With the coming day, he and those men he had fought with previously when dispersing Attacotti raider camps went on a reconnaissance, while Pauli led the rest openly down the road to the town. Pauli's group met with sullen, inhospitable stares and a few muttered threats, but nothing physical, and had soon taken over adjoining main inns by the waterfront to serve as a temporary base.

Meanwhile Breca, with Ivain at his side, was scrutinising the castle. Unlike Osraig, Draynes had never been built at the sea's edge. The waterfront here was too useful a commodity. Instead the castle perched on the headland overlooking the bay and was of a very different construction.

"My word, this is old," Breca said in surprise, as they looked down on it from a little higher up the headland. "This must've been one of the first castles ever built on the islands when our people brought the know-how over from the east." He pointed to where a tower sat perched on a great mound at the north-east end of the curtain wall. "I'd guess that was the original defensive work, then when it became too small for the purpose they built the curtain wall. See how the wall sweeps out from that one, rather than that bigger keep down at the south-west end?"

Ivain shielded his eyes and followed Breca's pointing finger. The old mound was to their left as they stood looking out towards the sea, and an egg-shaped massive wall spread out from it, broken at the right-hand far end by another mound, which was not so high but broader, and was sat upon by a round keep with four bastions. An additional steep bank rose around the curtain wall to join with those of the two keeps, and was fronted in its circuit by a deep ditch except at the old keep end. On the far side, the visible top of a square building looked like it might be a solid gatehouse, but all in all, the place looked impregnable.

"Well there's nothing for it," Breca declared. "It's going to have to be a night attack and that's going to be a swine!"

They hurried back down the slope and met the men Pauli had sent to escort them to where he had found billets for them, but on the way Ivain had an idea.

"Now we're here, why don't we make a show of going to do a proper inspection?" he asked. "That way they'll think we've come and been chased off. If we retreat back down the road tomorrow after going through the whole performance, they'll be more complacent," which was a plan that got everyone's approval.

Consequently, late that afternoon Breca marched a sizeable contingent up to the castle gate and demanded entrance. The piratical men on guard openly laughed in his face, and he made a good show of making a shamefaced retreat. The next morning the Knights made a dawn charge up the hill, the archers firing over the curtain wall and through the lowered portcullis. Their arrows clearly found several targets going by the howls of pain, but the attackers beat a hasty retreat when the defenders began throwing hot oil off the battlements at them. Muttering discontentedly, the Knights marched straight back out of the town and down the road to the jeers of the townsfolk.

Out of sight they halted.

"That went better than I'd hoped," Breca confided to the senior men. "They're obviously not used to professional attackers or they'd have seen straight through our little act," he added, "and those townspeople definitely think we've turned tail and run."

As night fell they made the trek back, but this time over the dead bracken and drab scrubland away from the road. Scouts had already gone out in the daylight to find the safest path, and were on hand to keep everyone moving in the right direction. These few men remained where they were in case a hurried retreat was needed – nobody wanted to end up running straight off the cliff.

Swinging round, the Knights approached the northern side of the old tower and carefully climbed the steep bank. It was the one place where the ditch was shallowest, no doubt because with the steepness of the slope leading straight to sheer walls, it was thought impregnable. But the Knights were not planning on assaulting the tower. Having got some height, the lead men swung grappling hooks out to catch on the curtain wall battlements. With great expertise they had four ropes in line right by the tower within minutes, and men began climbing up.

The greatest danger was that in order to make the climb the men had had to leave off their chain-mail, and rely on the stopping power of their leather and felted wool under-jackets. From well back in the line, Ivain found himself holding his breath in anticipation as the first men were briefly silhouetted against the night sky as they swarmed over the top. All remained quiet, though, and no alarm was sounded.

"Either we've taken them off guard, or they're waiting until we're really compromised with half our men in and half out," fretted Pauli to him quietly.

That only made Ivain even tenser, so that by the time the line of men in front of him began to noticeable edge forward, he was having to make a conscious effort to breathe. After what felt like an eternity it came to his and Pauli's turn to climb the ropes, and Ivain found out just how hard that was to do. He was sweating and shaking by the time someone grabbed him by the scruff and helped him up onto the parapet. Already many of the men had disappeared somewhere, and then he got tapped on the arm and pointed towards the picket door into the tower. Inside, he saw several figures lying motionless by the flickering flame of the torches in the wall sconces, then breathed a sigh of relief when he realised that they were not any of the Order's. Breca stood in the middle of the round room listening to slight scuffling sounds from above, then all went quiet until two men came down to report the top two floors were also taken.

Within minutes the remainder of the men were within the tower, the grappling hooks removed and brought inside, and no sign of forced entry remained outside to betray them. Three men came staggering in with piles of rather tatty jerkins raided from sleeping quarters above, and the Knights pulled them on wherever possible over their own clothes. The Attacotti were generally not a large people and it was noticeable that the bigger men amongst the Knights could not find disguises to fit them. To their disgust they were therefore the ones who had to remain behind to guard the tower, while the other prepared to assault the keep.

"We'll go by the southern curtain wall opposite to where we came up," Breca told them. "The first men up have been watching that side and tell me that a patrol goes out from here at each turn of the hour glass. Luckily they saw the patrol go out and came in to find the glass freshly turned, and we can therefore assume that it's every hour. They went right to the end by the gatehouse and then came back again, but all the time they were looking out to sea. We'll secure the gatehouse first and then go for the keep."

"Won't they rumble something's wrong if two or three times the men go out along the walls, sire?" someone asked.

"Probably," Breca agreed, "but we're only going to send half as many again out and have a third come back. Those first men will spy out the land and make a count of how many are inside as near as possible. With the next patrol we'll send the extra men out, but with that we should have enough to make a start on the gate. If we can keep it quiet like we did here, then we have more chance of taking the keep swiftly. I want everyone prepared to make a charge along both walls if necessary, but that's a last resort."

The men spent the interval making sure the tower was as secure as possible, and then Breca sent ten men out on patrol walking openly along the wall. Luck was with them, for it began to rain and there was no light shining out from the keep their way, and so twenty more crept along in their shadow below the level of the ramparts. As one said later, they all arrived feeling like dwarves after such a long walk all hunched up, but it worked. Four men strolled back shortly afterwards, and reported that they could hear several men talking down in what must be the guardroom by the gate. However, the concept of keeping reinforcements close at hand was clearly alien to these men, who probably did not understand siege warfare. The upper rooms, which any commander of the Order would have used as sleeping quarters for those rotating through the guard, were filled with all sorts of plunder which had probably been acquired by less than honest means.

"The biggest danger is that someone will trip and go flying over some of this junk in the dark!" one man confided to Pauli in disgust at such amateur defences.

With the rain turning to icy sleet and reducing visibility even further, Breca decided that there was nothing to be gained by further creeping about. Once they were having trouble seeing across the open space to the keep, he reckoned that all those with some of the camouflaging jerkins could openly make their way across, for in the awful weather nobody was likely to be counting. In short order, therefore, some seventy of the men had assembled in the gatehouse. Ivain was furious that as one of the bigger men there was no jerkin to fit him, and Pauli, as his minder, was forced to stay behind too, although he had had little chance of finding a garment to fit either.

Nothing seemed to happen for ages, and then they spotted movement on the short stretch of wall between the gatehouse and the keep. Then down at ground level a man appeared out of the gatehouse and stepped around the corner out of sight of the keep, then waved a pale rag above his head.

"They've taken the gatehouse!" gasped Pauli with relief, and Ivain realised he was not the only one who had been holding his breath again.

However, the keep did not fall so quietly and suddenly the muted sound of fighting wafted across on the wet night air. Then a man dashed out and managed to ring a bell they had not spotted before, it rang only once but that was enough. Even as an arrow flew out of the gatehouse and struck him down, a door was flung open, and the Knights realised that some wooden lean-to buildings had been constructed against the wall opposite the gatehouse. Men appeared and then hurried back inside for weapons.

"Come on!" Pauli called to the remaining men with them in the tower. "No need for quiet now! We mustn't let those extra men come on the lads from behind!"

And with that he led the charge out of the tower. Some of the Order used the ground floor door, while Ivain and those who had already been on the first floor dashed out of the door to the parapet and along it. A third of the way along, a flight of stone steps ran down into the bailey, and Ivain bounded down them, sword drawn and at the ready. At the bottom he encountered some of the defenders and found himself fighting a ferocious opponent.

It was the first time he had really gone in on the attack, and the first where, thanks to the Knights' tuition, he actually felt like he knew what to do. He was still scared stiff, but now the fear was mixed with a strange exhilaration, and instead of wanting to curl up in a ball and hide, he was filled with a determination to defend the backs of the Knights ahead of him inside the keep. Thinking of further consequences was not an option he had time for, and he focused on making every stroke of the blade count. Nor was there time to stop and see if he had actually killed anyone. Instead he relied on the men behind him to ensure no-one got back up and stabbed him from behind, as he used his weight to force his way forward. If nothing else, Ivain's height gave him an advantage and he made the most of it.

Before he knew it he was through the newcomers to the fight, and at the slope leading up to keep. Looking back he saw that the men behind him had the situation in hand, and so he headed upwards. The keep was reached by a zigzag path going up the mound, and Ivain raced up it and through the door. A Knight standing among several bodies whirled towards him and then acknowledged him.

"There were men coming out of another building," Ivain said succinctly.

The man nodded and gestured upwards to where there were still sounds of fighting.

"Better go and help them, then, if the others have got the entrance," he said, and led the way up a spiral stair at the rear of the circular room.

The next floor was chaotic, with a mass of fighting men filling the floor and little room to enter, but there was the sound of yet more fighting above. Ivain left the other Knight to attack the back of an Attacotti who was trying to strangle a fellow Knight, and pounded upwards. He reached the next floor just as a shaggy, bearded ruffian came snarling towards the way out. Ivain raised his sword and exchanged several brutal cuts with the man before running him through. As the man fell forwards, Ivain saw Breca slice another across the middle, and then all was calm on this floor. A moment later the sound of fighting ceased below too.

Stepping over the corpse, Ivain walked to Breca.

"Is that it? Have we done it?"

Breca looked over Ivain's shoulder to where someone had appeared signalling to him and then his face broke into a grin.

"Yes! We've done it!" He turned to the rest of the men in the room. "Anyone hurt?"

A couple had nasty sword cuts which would require attention, and several men would sport some spectacular bruises in a few days' time, but there were no fatalities. From the room below two men of the Order had been killed, but other than that the whole castle had been taken without loss of life on their side. The scouts out on the hillside were signalled to come in, and the Knights set about the grisly task of dragging out the bodies of the defenders. Unlike Osraig, these men had fought to the last one, and none had been taken alive.

As soon as the corpses had been taken away, Breca did not wait for the place to be cleaned up to start searching.

"I want to know if Magnus held this place," he told Ivain and Pauli who had joined them. "If Turstin was just employing Attacotti mercenaries then that's one thing, but if these men answered directly to Magnus then that's something else."

Together they rummaged through every nook and cranny in the keep, starting from the top and working down. Having found nothing by the time they reached the ground floor, they checked the basement and found a hoard of the Attacotti's curved bows but nothing more.

"That tells us nothing," Breca complained in frustration. "They could've bought the bloody things off Magnus for all we know!"

A thorough sweep of the gatehouse was equally unhelpful, for although the contents of the upper rooms had come from many different sources, nothing stood out until Ivain joined in the search. As a Knight held up a beautifully worked lady's dress towards Breca and complained, "This could have come from anywhere," Ivain let out a cry.

"That's my mother's!"

"Are you sure?" Breca demanded.

"Absolutely sure," Ivain said, seizing it off the man. "You see this rose picked out in freshwater pearls? She had that done on many of her dresses and she loved this shade of green because it showed off her hair so well. But worse than that. I know she packed this dress when she and Alaiz thought they were coming to Kittermere on the diplomatic mission they got kidnapped on. Which chest did this come from?"

The man pointed to a corner of the room and Ivain clambered over to haul at the chest. The other man joined him, and together they managed to lift it up and put it on top of another chest, closer to the light.

"Look!" Ivain pointed at the faded side of the chest. "That's our coat of arms!" He dug into the chest and brought out a dress which he shook loose. "This is Alaiz'! I'd know it anywhere because she hated it. She always complained when she had to wear it because it was so ostentatious, and the gold thread scratched her something shocking. There's only one place this could have come from and that's the men who seized my mother and Alaiz. No wonder they were able to appear out of nowhere! When I saw Alaiz after she'd escaped, while we were both at Quies, she said that it was uncanny how they appeared out of the blue. Well it wasn't uncanny was it? The men here must have had word from Gorm that his sister was on her way and been watching. I bet from the top of that other tower you can see right over the headland and out to sea. All they had to do was send a signal to the galley – that's if it wasn't tied up here in the bay. But we know where they went, and that was straight back to Magnus!"

"That settles it then, doesn't it," Pauli said thoughtfully. "Turstin's been playing all sides against the middle."

"Or hedging his bets," Breca grunted in disgust. "If he didn't get what he wanted off Duke Brion, he could come back here and with his other best friend, Magnus, he could've made Brion's life hell until he *did* give him what he wanted. He's a real charmer, isn't he?"

"And in the unlikely event of me winning the first round and Brion being sent home with his tail between his legs, he'd have done the same to me, I'm sure," Ivain added bitterly. "By the Trees, I hope I'm there to see him get what he deserves! I never thought I'd say this of anyone, but I want to see that bastard dancing from the end of a rope alongside my cousin!"

The morning brought an angry mob of townsfolk at the drawbridge, who tried to pelt the Knights with rotten fruit and eggs through the portcullis grill until Breca lost his temper. Then the bodies of the defenders were unceremoniously thrown over the gatehouse ramparts into the mob. Whether the mob had expected the Knights to just take prisoners whom they could then set free, the Knights could not work out, but when the bloody corpses began falling, the mob's ardour disappeared and them along with it. However, it made Breca unwilling to venture out of the castle for a day or so, and so sentries were posted to observe the goings on in the town below.

Meanwhile, those not on guard duties spent their day cleaning the place out. The undisciplined marauders had made messy tenants, and soon there were two good bonfires going within the walls which were regularly being added to.

"Spirits, this lot are worse than magpies for hoarding!" Pauli complained to Ivain, as they dragged another half broken sea-chest from some forgotten raid out to the fires.

Yet at the bottom of the old tower they found something strange. An iron grill was let into the floor of the basement, and at first the Knights assumed that it was another of the grisly remnants of an age when prisoners were incarcerated never to be brought out again. Everyone who went in the room reported having the shivers and all their hairs stand on end, and out of curiosity Ivain and Pauli went down to take a look. The room was certainly a chilling sight, for in the basement walls were still the hooks to hang prisoners on while they were tortured. For Ivain, though, something pulled at him to go to the iron floor-grill. Peering down into it he thought he could see something.

"Can we get a lantern down here?" he asked, and began working at the grill.

"You surely don't want to go down there, do you?" asked a horrified Pauli.

"No, I don't *want* to," admitted Ivain, "but there's definitely something down there – and we said we'd investigate the castle thoroughly, didn't we. Well what if Magnus' men dropped something down here to hide it?"

The other Knights could not argue with that, and so a lantern was brought. With much scrapping and chipping away at layers of dirt, the grill was finally freed and the lantern lowered into the hole. A couple of ancient skeletons lay curled up at the bottom, and the Knights were about to say 'I told you so' to Ivain when he pointed to something below the bones.

"Look it's something wrapped up," he insisted. "Get a rope! I'm going to climb down."

And before anyone could stop him he had sat on the edge and then lowered himself down to the extent of his arms and dropped. Someone hurried out to get a rope and a basket which they used to bring up the two skeletons, but then Ivain called for the basket again.

"There's something like a fragile old piece of vellum down here," he called up. "I'll put it in the basket because I suspect it's going to fall apart if I try to hand it up to you."

Lying on the floor looking down, Pauli and Breca saw him carefully lift a scroll shaped object cradled in both hands and put it in the basket, and then retrieve a second one. As the basket was pulled up out of the way they saw him reach down and pull at the other object.

"Flaming Trees, it's much bigger than I thought," he said, as they saw him start to dig around the lowest point with his hands. "It's buried in all this dusty stuff!"

He managed to move a fair amount from around the object, which they could now see seemed to be cylindrical, then gave it a strong tug. The object moved but the watchers also experienced a giddy sensation. Yet before they could call a warning to Ivain, he had tugged again and this time held up something that looked like a thick staff as tall as he was.

"Come on up *now!*" Breca ordered, and Ivain grasped the rope with one hand, and let them haul him up while he hung onto his find with the other.

Once he had arrived panting back on the basement floor, they ushered him up to the ground floor and out into the daylight.

"What is it?" someone asked over Pauli's shoulder.

"It's a bow case," Ivain replied.

"Come off it, who'd make such an elaborate case for a bow," another said.

But Ivain looked up and smiled. "You'd be surprised! Many of the archers I used to talk to over in eastern Prydein made bows, and to become a master craftsman they have to produce a test piece. Some of those bows are works of art! And the men who make them take great pride in them. They make cases like this for those pieces so that they can be kept as family heirlooms."

With great care he felt along the length until he found a join. Gently he began twisting the two halves of the case and there was a faint sucking noise. Once again the surrounding men experienced the strange sensation, but Ivain was oblivious to it. With great reverence he pulled off first one half and then the other, and then held the contents up for all to see.

"Would you look at that!" he gasped in awe. "What a magnificent bow! It's yew!" Carefully taking the bowstring he pulled it up and strung the bow. "Sacred Trees! How long has this been buried? Yet would you look at that? The string is as supple as when it was made!" Lifting it up, then pulled the string back and aimed an imaginary arrow down it. The weight and power of the bow was evident in the flexing of his arm muscles.

"Ivain, there's something weird about that bow," warned Pauli. "Can't you feel it? It's like the air's gone all tingly."

"No, I don't feel that, and I don't think it's weird in a bad way. It's like this was made for me, though. It's not weird, it's special, and I can't explain why, but I think it was waiting to be found. ...What happened to those scrolls? Do they say anything?"

Breca stepped back into the tower to speak to someone and then came back out again. "The one is in very old script, they say, and just talks about moving something to safety, and the other one is in some kind of code."

"Well if this was important enough to be moved to somewhere safe, then I think we'd better take good care of it, hadn't we?" Ivain said, carefully unstringing it again and putting it back in its case. "Anyway, you never know when a bow like that might come in useful!"

Chapter 22

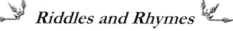 *Riddles and Rhymes*

Ergardia: Eft-Yule – Imbolc

Within the vast space of the hidden library of Lorne Castle, Taise, Sithfrey and Andra sat huddled around one of the huge work tables. The work was proceeding at a painfully slow pace, for Taise and Sithfrey had completed as near a translation of the copied manuscript as they could. The task at hand now was to try to make some sense of the whole. Some words and even whole passages of the original remained obscure, and the only hope of shedding light on them was to be able to put them into some kind of context. Context, however, was eluding them except in the most general sense.

It did nothing to help that they all felt rather left out of things. At first they had avoided saying anything outright, preferring to speculate on what was happening to their friends. A casual, "I wonder how Matti's doing?" or "How far do you think Ruari's got?" would be the opening for a lengthy discussion during the first week. But as time dragged on it was finally Andra who first expressed his deep frustration out loud.

"Oh, this is hopeless!" he snapped. "I'm no use here at all! What are we doing? Going round and round in circles that's what! And in the meantime our friends and loved ones are risking life and limb while we just sit here!"

Taise put a comforting hand on his arm. "I know, Andra, I know. We feel just the same. If it's any comfort, we need you because you're the only Islander left for us to work with, and both Sithfrey and I know we're likely to miss something that's blindingly obvious simply because we come from a different culture."

Andra sighed heavily and patted her hand back. "I'm sorry, Taise. It's not your fault, or yours, Sithfrey. I'm just so frustrated by being cut off from everything. I know I was more of a burden than a help to Ruari on the way here, but if nothing else I felt I was *doing* something."

The three of them got up and left their work table and headed for the refectory, where at least they could see something of the outer world through the window onto an inner ward of the castle. Getting mugs of caff each, they found a bench by a window and sat looking out. Thick snow covered everything in a silent blanket outside, and inside the refectory was quiet, for it was far too early for the evening meal and all the men were busy at their duties.

"It feels like time's ground to a halt," Sithfrey said morosely. "The snow makes it seem like the world's stopped turning! How long have they been gone? Two weeks? It feels like forever."

"You're not telling me you miss Maelbrigt?" teased Taise in a weak attempt at humour.

Sithfrey looked startled and then shrugged. "I guess in a funny way, yes. He scares me. ...Well all the Knights scare me! ...But him and that MacBeth are really scary! But at least when they're around, I suppose I feel like nothing truly terrible would happen without them giving it a fight."

That was so true for all of them that they sat in silence for a while, until Andra spotted a little robin sitting on a holly bush only a few feet from the window happily eating the berries. It triggered a memory of something he had heard the others talking about.

"Taise..." he said pensively, making her look up. "When you were telling us about what happened when Maelbrigt and Labhran battled the grollican, didn't you say that the berries of the rowan had a drastic effect on it?"

"Yes. ...Yes I did. ...It was something I would never have expected. The whole branch of the rowan was pretty toxic, but when that monster crushed the berries on itself they really did some damage. It was like ...well it was like they made what passes for blood in that thing boil. ...Why?"

"The poem," Andra said thoughtfully.

When they had deciphered the manuscript which Kayna and Labhran had so carefully copied, they had found one part was a poem. However, why something which appeared to be an elegy for fallen warriors should be part of the manuscript was totally puzzling, and was one of the conundrums they had been battling for weeks.

"What about the poem?" Sithfrey asked.

"Doesn't it say something about rowan berries and blood?" Andra wondered. "You see, I've been watching that robin and I thought what an intense red the berries are, and how they look almost like drops of blood on the white snow. ...Yes, I know that's gory, but I was half thinking – as we've all been doing – about Ruari fighting battles and things at that point. ...So do you think it might be about fighting the kind of battle that Maelbrigt and Labhran fought? Not just a normal one?"

By now the three of them had stared at the transcript so much they could see it in their minds' eyes without having it in front of them. They could all visualise the pieces of parchment which the librarian had given them to copy it all out onto to. For he was determined that, as Taise might be one of the last people capable of reading it, her translation should also have a permanent copy made of it. Ever modest and methodical, Taise had insisted that once more the curls and swirls of the original monastic hand be copied meticulously with her own version alongside it.

"I'm not infallible," she had insisted to the librarian. "In the future someone may come along who can do much better at it than me. You must have the original as well as my translation. Working from the original will always give greater meaning and subtleties than anything in translation, no matter how good that is."

And so the treated but as yet uncut skins now lay, still in their sheep-shapes, on one of the great desks, for once they had completed the work the glosses and annotations would be added. Then the whole thing would be bound and placed in the library for posterity. For now, though, the poem sheet of parchment had just two columns of writing, and the three were using slate work boards to write things on and then scribble them out again. Sithfrey had got so used to this that he had his permanently under his arm and a piece of chalk in his pocket, and now he wrote the translation of the stanza out from memory for them.

From Celidon the clansmen came,
Men went to the battlefield at dawn,
The wolf in his fury, the iron shone,
Eagle circled the sun, the crows await the feast,
That day when Naejling's work was done.
Blood red rowan stands in the Island,
The strength of past fallen, fire in the blood.
Aneirin sang his praise, the mead-cup's lament.

"That's it!" Andra cried pointing to it. "Look, that bit about blood. It appears twice in two lines. There are lots of ways you could describe bright reds – sunsets, fires, even the colour by name like the ones dyers use – so why choose to call it blood-red? And don't say because it's a battle poem, because why then would you have 'fire in the blood'?"

"Warrior's frenzy?" speculated Sithfrey.

"Maybe," agreed Taise, "but I think Andra may have something, although where that takes us I don't know. I mean who are Naejling and Aneirin? Aneirin sounds like he might be a bard of some kind, but we've looked through all the records here and none of the names in the poem relate to anyone we can find. No kings, no nobles, nobody."

They all sat staring at it in silence again as Angus came into the refectory with a mug and plates for washing. Seeing their downcast faces, he took his things to the scullery and then came to sit down by them.

"No change then?" he asked, hoping that at least voicing their frustrations to him would give them some relief if not help.

"None," Sithfrey told him. "For a minute just then we thought we might have had something, but it still doesn't lead us on anywhere else."

They showed him the work slate and the burly highlander read it carefully without saying a word.

"I've not seen this before, although I've heard you talk about it with Master Brego," he said afterwards. "It sounds like one of those old epics about knights with their famous swords – you know the ones with names, like old King Hrothgar had."

The three of them looked at him blankly.

"What do you mean?" Taise asked.

Angus suddenly realised that they had no idea what he was talking about.

"Have you no' heard people like yon Sioncaet singing the old songs? Aach, but I loved them as a wee laddie! Old King Hrothgar, he was the last king of all the Islands. He lived sometime during the first time the DeÁine got chased away, hundreds of years ago. The songs tell of a big battle, and how he led the army with his magic sword. Nail, I think it was called or something like that."

"Nail?" Taise leaped to her feet nearly knocking the table flying. "You mean things like swords had names?"

Angus looked puzzled. "Aye, did you not know that?"

"*I* didn't know that," Andra said, "and I've always lived in the Islands! But then I grew up in a monastery. They hardly encouraged us to learn songs about going around chopping people's heads off and things."

But then Sithfrey suddenly grabbed Angus' arm hard in shock. Before Angus could object, Sithfrey asked in a strangled voice,

"You said 'Nail' or something like that. Could it have been Naejling?"

"Aye, that's it!" Angus said cheerfully. "That's the name of old Hrothgar's sword!" Then saw the stunned look on the three faces and realised he had said something of significance. "What about it?"

"I think you'd better come downstairs with us, Angus," Taise said faintly. "In fact, if you can do what I think you're going to do, we're going to be kicking ourselves."

"Why?" a rather worried Angus asked as he was hustled towards the library.

"Because Sioncaet and Maelbrigt kept saying to us that we should just do the translation and then throw it open to everyone else, but we only thought of those who'd come here. And so once they'd all disappeared off in a hurry, we've just plodded on on our own. It never occurred to us that others in the castle would be able to help to. Oh dear, oh dear! How arrogant of us! That was so DeÁine, wasn't it? Sithfrey and I are sometimes still so conditioned by our upbringing. We still think of scholars as being a world apart and the only ones who can read and shed light on things."

"Not just you, Taise," Andra said sadly. "It happens in the monasteries as well. The monks who taught me thought the only learning worth having was the stuff in the sacred books, and that it was their privileged ground and theirs alone. Ever since I got away from them I've been learning so much about things I never even realised were important before." Then a thought occurred to him. "You see, I was right! We're no use at all sitting down in that library. I was just wrong in thinking we had to go far away, instead of just upstairs!"

The librarian and his staff were rather startled by the sight of the door being flung open and Angus being ushered in, but even more by Taise's demand of,

"Why did nobody tell us that swords and things have names?"

The librarian looked round at his colleagues in bemusement then said,

"Because that only happens in the old romances! You're dealing in histories. You're not looking at old folk tales, and stories for winter nights by the fireside."

"Maybe we should have been," Sithfrey said darkly, as Taise took Angus to her translation.

Angus leaned his gnarled knuckles on the polished wood table, and bent his shaggy head to read the parchment.

The Elegy

War came unheralded, came to plunder.
No threat before, no challenge issued.
Greed in hearts, for unlawful render,
From across the seagulls' road the bloodless ones
A warpath carved. Too few the elder ones,
No more their seasoned men, wise in battle,
No more the youthful men to bear arms,
To fight the ancient enemy.

The men of Brychan came this day
Set out at dawn, around a battle-strong lord.
Brychan where the oak is strong in the earth,
Bears its men upon the waves, ocean tested.
Hilderand was tempered by the enemies' flood,
Strong to the last, Owain bore him back.

Rheged's lords came when challenged,
Renowned men, steeds beneath them.
Rheged where the ash is tall, valued by men,
Stands firm, united though many attack.
Waelaesc fought hard in line, savage the thrust,
Urien bore him back at the last.

Prydein's men, they came in war-bands,
Braver men you never saw come before.
Yew burnished bright for the noble ones,
And for every man a joy and honour, firm in battle.
From Prydein, Fearban joined with his brother.
Herestrael came mustering summoned men,
Birch bearing seed, reaching skywards.
Peredur returned the one home.
Cynddylan, the brother to his casket.

Men of Ergardia in war-gear came,
To hunt the enemy, the hawk upon the fist.
In mountains high the thorn grows strong,

Sharp and hard to those who would it seize.
Seaxwulf came in Calic's stead, the symbol of their faith,
Bloodstained the blade that Elphin carried back.
Vanadis' tears the chalice filled.

From Celidon the clansmen came,
Men went to the battlefield at dawn,
The wolf in his fury, the iron shone,
Eagle circled the sun, the crows await the feast,
That day when Naejling's work was done.
Blood red rowan stands in the Island,
The strength of past fallen, fire in the blood.
Aneirin sang his praise, the mead-cup's lament.

Wine and mead were drunk in the hall,
Enemy scattered, weapons shattered,
Great the havoc, swift the spears,
Planted shafts, swords clashed,
The shield-wall held, valour won.
The court of the Islands was not disgraced.
Every warrior pure in heart, thought not of self,
As one they fought, united in the heart,
With a single mind they wielded weapons,
Each man a thousand, and a thousand as one,
None withstanding.

No return home for the valiant ones,
Their resting place the earth is now.
Far from their kinship they lie,
Gone but not forgotten.
Only guardians remain to watch,
Until they rise once more, united,
Called by name, the key a symbol
To wake them once more
To battle from beyond.

They came from the north and south,
Bearing arms for the land,

With rowan branch in hand,
The mighty heroes of the Islands.

"Mmm," Angus said thoughtfully. "I can see that if you didn't know even one of these names you'd be well and truly stuck."

"Oh we've been stuck alright," Sithfrey said with feeling.

"In fact the only thing we're fairly sure of is that the last verse is something someone added later on," Taise told him. "In their very careful copy, Kayna and Labhran made it clear that this was in a different hand – presumably by someone who inserted it later who wanted to add his bit for posterity. It was also the one bit that didn't need translating even though it was in a very old fashioned script."

"Aye, that would make sense," Angus agreed, "because that bit's shorter, simpler, and sort of rhymes."

"Well the rest probably did originally," confessed Taise, "but I'm not good enough to translate it and make it rhyme as well, and it was more important to get the sense of it. But the thing is, can you tell us anything at all about it? Remember that even if it's obvious to you it might not be to us."

"Right then," Angus said exhaling deeply, and Sithfrey and Andra picked up their chalks ready to make notes. "At the risk of stating the obvious, you have each of the major Islands mentioned by name. And as that wee lassie Alaiz said, you seem to have a longer entry for Prydein, so maybe this relates to a time when Rathlin and Kittermere were part of it. So maybe this is confirmation that you were right to think of that original group of three islands having two of the Treasures?"

"We sort of thought that," admitted Taise, "but we couldn't get beyond there."

At that point Brego strode in, word having evidently reached him that his personal servant had been hijacked by the researchers in the library. Coming to stand beside them, he looked enquiringly but gestured them to carry on.

"Well now," Angus continued, "you see Naejling is under Celidon, but I have a feeling that Hrothgar's seat was in Brychan if anywhere."

"Ah yes," Brego murmured as understanding came, "of course, Naejling was Hrothgar's sword. I'd forgotten that."

"So it changes the meaning doesn't it!" Andra suddenly added excitedly. "We've been thinking Naejling was a person who died and whose body was brought home by this Aneirin – whoever he was. But if Naejling is a *sword* then it connects The Sword with Celidon, which is where we thought it was, so it confirms what we found elsewhere in the document."

"Aye, but they put both in that manuscript you found," Angus pointed out, "so maybe it's telling you something more. Before, you didna' find its name mentioned, did you? So looking at the other names, do you no' think that maybe Hilderand is the name of the Shield, and Waelaesc is the name of the Spear?"

Brego nodded and added, "And if I remember something from long ago correctly, Calic is more or less the old word for chalice. So that would equate well with the Bowl, wouldn't it."

"But why would you need to know the name of these pieces?" wondered Sithfrey.

Brego and Angus looked at one another and then Brego answered,

"Well if the old legends are to be believed, the name was part of the weapon's power. All previous victories were embodied in the blade or whatever it was, so that the weapon itself brought something extra to the battle regardless of who wielded it."

"Like the ability to channel the Power!" exclaimed Taise.

"So maybe you need to know its name to wield it to the full?" speculated Andra. "That would explain why they felt it necessary to put the names in as well as the locations."

"Sacred Trees, that would make sense," Taise agreed.

"And speaking of Trees," Angus added cautiously.

"Yes?" everyone chorused expectantly.

"Well maybe you wouldn't know this because of not being soldiers, but the finest quality bows are made of yew."

"Oh!" gasped Sithfrey, "and the Bow is in Prydein, which is where you get yew turning up in the poem!"

And suddenly everyone could begin to see a pattern emerging.

"So would you have a Spear made of ash?" queried Andra.

"Absolutely," Brego confirmed. "Like Angus said about bows, the best spears are made of ash, and – although they'd be incredibly heavy to the point of being impractical – if you want a shield that would stop just about *anything*, you'd make it from oak. And you can make arrows out of birch."

"Aye, but do you not see, sire?" Angus asked Brego, careful to remain respectful in company. "The woods are in the wrong places for their affinities."

"Oh dear," sighed Taise. "Are you telling me that there's something else we missed."

"To be fair," Brego said swiftly, "if it's any consolation, it's only now Angus has said it that I'm seeing it. You do know that the Sacred Trees have their own symbolism attached to them?"

"What? Like the yew being the tree of the north and old age?" Andra asked. "Because if so, I spotted that these don't bear any relationship to the old tales."

"They're not old tales!" Angus said firmly. "You ask any Forester!"

Taise sighed heavily and wondered if this was going to be a permanent habit. "Oh I would have asked a Forester, but the one I know had already left by the time I'd got this to the point where I was satisfied that I had the right words in translation. So go on, tell me. What are these relationships?"

Angus stood with a watchful expression as Brego told the others,

"The Birch is the tree of the east. It symbolises spring, youth, promise and new beginnings, and the healing that can come from starting afresh. It also has an affinity with air. The Ash is the tree of the south and summer. It symbolises the awakening of understanding that comes with adulthood, but also – because in the Islands the place beyond death is the Summerlands, and ash is linked with summer – it's believed that ash is the wood that the bridge to the next world is built of. Long ago Islanders built funeral pyres and ash is thought to have an affinity with fire, so that emphasised the connection.

"The Oak is the tree of the west, autumn and full maturity. It's supposed to have an affinity with water, and certainly we build ships out of it – hence the reference there to waves and ocean-tested. And then there's the Yew. The tree of winter and old age. Because they live so long they're supposed to be immortal, but they also represent the rebirth that comes after death in the same way that spring follows winter. They're the tree of the earth that comes back to life after the resting time of winter. Now, the Rowan is supposed to be magical, both as a defence and for attacking. Old folk still hang rowan over the lintels of their doors as protection against evil, and a witch is supposed to be held at bay by it."

Taise and Sithfrey stood dumbfounded by all of this until Taise managed to say,

"All those years we studied and we never heard any of this! We were just taught that the people of the islands worshipped all manner of strange things. That you worshipped trees because it was a relic of your not-so-distant uncivilised past. Along with people who'd been murdered in nasty ways to remind you that it could happen again, and to keep you in check."

"Uncivilised! The cheek of it!" Andra was incensed. "And the Blessed Martyrs are much more than that! They didn't just get bumped off because they crossed some powerful thug, they were standing up for something they believed in against evil!"

"Aye, and the Trees are much more too," Angus said dryly giving Andra a sideways glance. "But more to the point, can you no' see, after what the Master has just said, that there's something wrong with where these Trees are here?"

"Oh!" Sithfrey gasped in realisation. "If you were looking for the Spear by association with the wood it's made of you'd expect to find it in the south, wouldn't you. So you'd start looking in Prydein, perhaps. And if the Bow is made of yew then you might expect that to be in, say, Celidon in the north?"

"Exactly," Angus said approvingly, "so maybe that explains the line, 'far from their kinship they lie.' Because if you needed to find them, you'd be looking in the wrong place if you went by what they're made of."

They all stood contemplating the poem in the light of this and then Taise broke the silence, saying thoughtfully,

"I can see that in that case, the first verse might well refer to the DeÁine. Not only did we come out of nowhere from across the ocean in their eyes, but we could be described as 'bloodless' because of our pallor in comparison to Islanders. In which case the 'elder ones' could be the same as those who wrote the books in this library, although I find it intriguing that it therefore implies that they and the DeÁine were enemies from a time long before."

"Yes, that is interesting, isn't it," agreed Brego. "There's still the lingering legend that the Islanders had help repelling the DeÁine the first time. And that whole bit about there not being enough of the elder ones any more to fight the DeÁine alone, makes more sense in the light of that."

"But who are the guardians?" asked Taise. "We've now guessed that you have to call the pieces by their names, but who or what is watching over them? And what 'key' is the symbol? And do we need it in order to be able to 'wake them once more'?"

She looked hopefully at Angus, but he could only shrug in ignorance.

"And I'm afraid I have another question," admitted Brego. "If the first verse is about the DeÁine, the second is about the Shield, the third the

Spear and that longer fourth about the Bow and Arrows, I have to tell you that the fifth confuses me. I know, as my predecessors did, that we have the Bowl here in Ergardia. But that's a stone-like depression. It's part of the land itself, filled with water and it can't move. I'm assuming that Calic is the name of the Bowl, and therefore that's why it couldn't be carried into battle. But what is Seaxwulf that went in its stead? A blade of some description I would guess going by the last line, but what is the thorn? For a moment I thought it could be referring to the Rowan, but that comes in the Celidon verse. And why is it a symbol of faith? Whose faith? The Bowl's or the men of Ergardia?"

The three researchers groaned. Just as they had thought they were getting somewhere another set of problems had appeared. However, Taise insisted that a large pair of slate boards with the whole poem written on them be taken up and placed in full view in the refectory. She was not going to get caught out again, by having the one person who knew something, being oblivious to what they were trying to untangle. If anyone in the castle could add anything, she wanted them to come forward. Personally she was curious to know who Owain, Urien, Cynddylan, Peredur, Elphin, Vanadis and Aneirin were, since Angus had to admit that on that score he, too, had no idea at all.

In the meantime they turned their attention to the other part of the manuscript. If the two pieces that they had partly deciphered already seemed to tell the reader how to find the Island Treasures, it seemed likely that the third section would be of significance as well. After making the day's discoveries, Brego had insisted that they take a break, and it was over the evening meal in his office that he made another suggestion.

"Please don't be offended by this," he said carefully, "but I've been thinking about this in the light of what happened today. Why don't you stop trying to unravel every minute piece of this puzzle as you go? I know it's all important, but with the best will in the world you can't gift yourselves with an exhaustive knowledge of Island culture. So, why don't we prioritise? As you've rightly reminded us so often, Andra, the two youngsters are in peril right now, so let's focus on what we can do to help them.

"In which case, why don't you read what you have purely in the light of being DeÁine? You two are DeÁine, and you know how the Abend are likely to think. So forget about what an Islander would read into this and put yourselves solely into the Abend's shoes, and see if you can come up with a reason for why they're acting the way they are. I have a feeling in my bones that you may make progress in this direction even if the rest eludes you, and that would be something we could put to practical use straight away."

Although this had been hinted at before, having actually seen that they might be better letting Islanders decipher what Islanders had written, the two DeÁine researchers and Andra agreed. For the next couple of days they discussed the writing over and over, getting nowhere again, until Sithfrey made a key observation.

"Do you think that they – the Abend – might have seen them as separate pieces?" he wondered, turning Kayna and Labhran's work over in his hands, and suddenly Taise saw what he meant.

The piece of parchment which the two had been copied onto was much bigger than the original, and had allowed them to draw the damaged outline of the original around the words. The long poem lay on one side of the original, with the seven lines they had deciphered first. The rest of it had lain on the obverse side of the enchanted manuscript, even though Kayna and Labhran had copied both onto one side on theirs.

"Would it make a difference?" Andra asked.

"Oh yes!" Taise answered emphatically. "You see Quintillean is the only one of the Abend to see the original. Anarawd only saw a copy of this and... Oh! ...Oh my life! Why didn't I think of this? He almost certainly saw only a partial copy, because otherwise there would've been no need for Quintillean to risk life and limb coming to find the original, would there?"

Sithfrey sank onto a chair and banged his head on the table twice. "Idiot! Fool! Of course! How could I not have spotted that!" He looked up at Taise. "It's so obvious, isn't it? And it can't have been the poem side, because Anarawd is the one and only member of the Abend who seems to have taken no interest at all in the Islands as far as we can tell. So it must be this other bit."

They carefully scrutinised the second translation that Taise had made.

Seers foretell what is to come, from the north to the south will be in their hands, the east to the west will be their own, their sway will know no bounds. Arise the Islands and keep the faith! Seek no sorcerer nor mystic mercenary, fortune lies in your own hands; stand fast, seek what is foretold, opposition will cease.

In the past lies the key, seen yet not seen, here yet not here, of this world and not, speech without words, linking deed to doer. Guarded by wardens in the houses of the holy, those who know the rites will succeed. Who is the keeper? From which court do they come? With whom do you desire to be united? An answerer for each question will set loose the power.

The forebear of power brings it forth to the rightful heir who bears his name. Each piece a person, each person a piece, connected by the words, connected by the purpose. Pure in blood, pure in heart, without desire for the world, they hold the fate of the Islands within them. United in mind, blood flowing as one, they are channelled and consumed by one purpose. From the four corners they will unite, each a piece of the whole. By the breath of the nine were they infused, in love were they conceived, in the world above and the world below taking form in the centre. Seven will come forth out of the three, out of the four. The past, present and future will mingle in the now, with air, fire, water and earth.

As one they will take back what was theirs. All will be well. This we pledge in heart and mind and blood.

"Knowing this is Anarawd we're talking about," Sithfrey said carefully, "I think we can assume that words like 'desire', 'heir', 'love' and 'conceived' will have been understood in their very physical form, don't you?"

"Oh yes," agreed Taise. "No doubt about that. He was always the lusty one of the male Abend, like Geitla was of the witches."

Then another thought hit her so hard it was almost physical, and she gasped.

"Taise? Are you all right?" a worried Andra asked, looking at how much paler she had gone.

"Yes," she replied weakly, "it's just that I think I've realised something rather important. I think we'd better get Master Brego down here."

When Brego arrived with Angus at his heels, Taise was feeling less faint and was able to explain more.

"We've been so blind!" she told him. "We've been trying to find meanings for everything in this and so it's no wonder we've failed. But Anarawd only saw a copy of the one side of this, so he doesn't realise that this all relates to the Island Treasures – *he* thinks it's about the DeÁine! He's trying to perform a ritual based on this to gain control of the *DeÁine* pieces. But Quintillean and Masanae now probably know that this relates to the Island Treasures. The Abend are potentially going after two different things!"

"Sacred Trees," breathed Brego, "that alters things, doesn't it. I suppose in one way it's a good thing that they're divided, but can you predict how each will react? Because if not, that will make life more complicated."

Taise thought for a moment before speaking, carefully choosing her words as she reasoned her way along.

"I think that in their arrogance, Quintillean and Masanae will assume that one of the Abend should be more than capable of retrieving a single Treasure from under the noses of mere Islanders. Let's not forget that Quintillean must have seen the original (which nearly killed me) before he went to Ergardia, and found that working in the Islands wasn't as easy as he thought. He would almost certainly have sent what he learnt from it on the Power to Masanae. So I feel that they will be acting on the assumption that Tancostyl will get the Helm, Calatin will get the Scabbard, and Eliavres will get the Gorget."

"I'd agree with that assessment," Sithfrey quickly added before Taise went on.

"Now without being foolishly modest, I really don't see Anarawd sending Hunters after me – that never felt right. But what if the Hunters came with Quintillean instead? He may well have realised that the Gauntlet is on the least populated of the Islands, and assumed that it would hardly take his great power to retrieve it."

"Or at least, if he hadn't brought them, he may have summoned them as soon as he read the manuscript," Sithfrey qualified her argument. "If there was time for him to get from Celidon right into Ergardia before we set out, then, if the Hunters were on a ship nearby in case they were needed, they could've arrived quite quickly. That sort of level of preparation is very much Quintillean's trademark."

Brego and Angus considered this and then conceded that it was a strong possibility.

"So," Taise continued with her careful analysis, "although we'll need more time to work out what Masanae and Quintillean will do, I think I can make a start on reading this through Anarawd's eyes. I'm sure all the Abend will read the preamble as being an affirmation of their right to rule the Islands. Their arrogance won't let them see it as an incitement to resistance. The second paragraph I think Anarawd will have read in the light of the third. Whatever it *really* means, he will think that 'forebear' means 'father' specifically, rather than general 'ancestor'. And he'll think that 'power' is

Power in the DeÁine and Abend sense, so that it's speaking of a male who has *the* Power who will conceive an heir.

"Now in New Lochlainn there are what we call Houses of the Holy – quite different from what you would understand by those words. Separated from the Sacred Temples of Lochlainn, the DeÁine in exile created the Houses as a temporary place of worship. The nearest description for you would be a kind of monastery, in that there is a church part and a part which is a dwelling for the priests and priestesses, and also a medicinal part. I think he'll try to have a child born within the precincts."

"Excuse me for interrupting," Brego said, "but I thought that excessive use of the Power rendered the Abend sterile?"

"It does," Sithfrey agreed, "which is why Anarawd has been trawling every ancient text for a spell that would reverse the effects. I doubt any such thing would work, but he clearly *thinks* he's found something that will."

"And that certainty in *his* mind is the key," Taise continued. "Therefore I suspect that if you had the means to find out, you would discover that Anarawd is at Tokai Palace, because that's where the Houses of the Holy are. Now as for the rest, I'd guess that he would take it that a new-born is as pure in heart as it's possible to get. And if he's fathered them all they would be united in blood. I suspect we're talking about three children, because he will be thinking of the four mentioned in that penultimate sentence as being the DeÁine Treasures.

"The nine he'll have read as the Abend – no doubt about that – and their love of ruling, and that once the spell or ritual is complete he'll have domination over the elemental forces of air, water, fire and earth in the past, present and future, and that those equate to the seven it mentions. And finally, I can see that he would think that this is a ritual that was originally intended for all of the Abend to participate in, but that if he can pull it all off himself, instead of the nine ruling he will rule alone."

Taise stopped and looked around expectantly. Sithfrey was nodding emphatically in support of her argument while Andra, Brego and Angus were deep in thought. Then Brego spoke,

"Terrifying though his arrogance is, doesn't this mean that he doesn't stand a snowflake in a desert's chance of succeeding? I mean, this was never, ever meant to apply to what he thinks it does?"

"Absolutely!" Sithfrey was quick to agree. "So what Taise has shown is that unless Anarawd has some information we know nothing about, he can't unite the DeÁine Treasures in the way he thinks he can. They'll still have to be wielded by one person each, even if that is a member of the Abend. He can't use them all at once."

"And so we still have the advantage that the Abend hardly ever agree on anything," Andra piped up optimistically.

Reassuring though this was, there was still the question of what Quintillean and his permanent partner-in-crime, Masanae, would do. However, it helped the researchers immensely now that they could discount the DeÁine Treasures, for Taise and Sithfrey had been trying to bring all they knew of those and apply it to the writing. Once it was simplified to the personalities of the two leading members of the Abend and what they, as DeÁine, would assume about the Island Treasures, the permutations were fewer.

For a week the three discussed the text in depth, trying to dredge every last nuance out of it in the light of Quintillean and Masanae's twisted minds, which was a grim revelation for Andra. However, at the end of the third week of the month they sat by the fire in Brego's office, confident that they had the best possible rendering of it. As Taise had said before, they believed the opening paragraph would be read as a statement of the DeÁine's inalienable right to rule. The idea of speech without words, Taise and Sithfrey reckoned, would be the Abend's ability to communicate mind to mind across great distances on the waves of the Power. And that this was the key which was being spoken of. The rites must therefore be referring to someone who could create glamours.

Given that Wistan and Kenelm had been Quintillean's victims of choice, they felt sure that he at least had read 'houses of the holy' to mean the Islands' monasteries in a duel link with the DeÁine complex at Tokai. With a reference to courts, along with heirs, he must have been looking for someone of royal blood and been amazed to find two fall into his lap. The 'pure in blood' would mean their physical heritage, and purity in heart without desire would emphasise the monastic setting, plus an overriding emphasis on virginity.

'Each person a piece', the three of them thought, would be seen as the potential for a person to contain the Power of a piece. Rather more worrying was that they suspected that 'blood flowing' might mean that the two Abend intended to bleed the two boys to death – something which drove Andra near to distraction with worry. Especially as 'channelled' stood a high probability of resulting in the two Abend channelling Power into them to do it, and all felt queasy at what ghoulish interpretation could be put on 'consumed'.

More optimistically, they thought that Quintillean and Masanae would be after four victims, believing that the Islanders only had four Treasures the same as the DeÁine, since they did not know of the Bowl, and believed the Bow and Arrows only counted as one. Taise and Sithfrey were also of the mind that the two leading Abend would think along the lines of control of the DeÁine Treasures resulting in the domination of the Island ones if the right ritual was used, thereby killing two birds with one stone – a metaphor which then made everyone feel faintly sick as they thought of the boys once more.

"Sad to say, if we don't rescue the boys in time, their loss of life will be for nothing – not even for evil – because the ritual won't work anyway," Taise said shaking her head sorrowfully. "The more I look at this riddle, the more I seriously doubt that any of the Abend have read it correctly. You've been right all along Master Brego. This is something meant for Islanders which relates to them, and how they are to access and use their own Treasures. Complex and obscure though it is, I think we can safely say that the Abend cannot use this formula to achieve any mastery over them.

"Of course that's not to say that, whatever the actual form of the ritual they perform is, it won't have a power of its own. None of the three whose actions we've been attempting to predict are lacking in knowledge of the arcane arts. They will undoubtedly also have consulted the extensive records of rituals and rites kept at Tokai and Kuzmin, and if the life force of people with a potent bloodline is added to that mix, who knows what will happen? All I can say is that they won't instantly gain control of the Treasures of either side."

"The bad news is also that we still have to work out what this really means as an instruction for you," Sithfrey added. "But we've all decided that to do that, the best thing we can do is spend as much time as we can talking to your men. And with those being from as many different parts of the Islands as we can find. So from now on we'll be in the refectory during breakfast and dinner, and in the halls afterwards. During the day we've got the librarian and his helpers retrieving all the old legends and tales he can find written down. We're now convinced that the truth is hidden somewhere in the fables, because they're going back far beyond where the histories start."

With at least partial success firing their enthusiasm for the task once more, the three set to with renewed energy in the following days. It helped that Brego had personally stood up in the halls before the men and explained what was needed, and so the three found themselves welcomed into groups in the evenings beside the great fires in the halls. The men of the Order sympathised with the difficulty of disentangling the puzzle, and if the three found themselves slightly overwhelmed with information, at least it was less dispiriting than working in isolation down in the silence of the crypt-like library.

As Eft-Yule turned to Imbolc, they had made some progress, if less than they would have liked. They had a shrewd suspicion from the hints in legends, coupled with Taise's astute observations, that the nine were the same as the mystery names in the elegy. What baffled them all was the correlation between these names on the odd occasions they appeared in the legends with certain animals. Having been tripped up by dismissing references to trees, they were not about to pass by ones to creatures. What worried them greatly was the growing belief that there was some saying or ritual which had been intended to be handed down which had been lost, and Andra in particular spent much time going over the religious records back to the earliest ones he could read looking for clues. Yet events seemed destined to overtake them, for a message arrived from Talorcan bearing the bad news that there was yet another anagram to be solved – and in a hurry!

Celidon

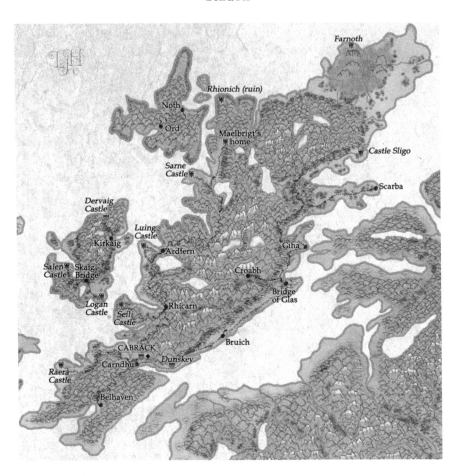

Chapter 23

Dark Ascents

Ergardia – Celidon: Aer-Yule – Eft-Yule

For days after they had left Lorne Castle, everyone was in a subdued mood. For Maelbrigt it was largely the thought that he might not see Taise again, but also worry over Kayna. While he knew Kayna was as prepared as anyone could be for the task ahead, he nonetheless fretted over where her impulsiveness might lead her. The casual conversations between himself, Will and Ruari did little to ease his mind either, since they also were concerned that Matti might be all too eager to prove herself, and throw caution to the wind. Ruari confessed that he had begged Master Brego to send someone other than Elidyr with the two women. And when pressed upon to elaborate, admitted that while Elidyr excelled at covert solo operations, he was not quite so good at taking into account the fact that others did not share his survival expertise.

"He's the man you want guarding your back in a tight spot, never doubt it." Ruari told them. "And he'd never be false! But I'm glad Brego's sending Iago with them. There's a good, solid, reliable man if ever there was one! He'll keep their feet firmly on the ground. My only worry is if for some reason they split up. Whoever goes with Iago will be safe – and I know him well enough to know that he'd never agree to the girls going off separately – but then that leaves one of them with Elidyr without any brake for their enthusiasm."

"You just have to trust them," Sioncaet gently reminded him. "Both of them are intelligent women, and there's nothing you can do to change things. We have our own missions, and it's only us who can do them. We can't go back."

"You're right." Maelbrigt managed a wan smile. "It's just in all our instincts to want to protect them, that's all."

His old friend smiled back. "I know! But you and Ruari and Will need to remember that *their* homes, *their* friends, and *their* lives are equally threatened by the DeÁine, and they have every right to want to fight for them as well! If we fail, they could die just as easily by sitting at home and doing nothing, and they're both bright enough to know that. They need to know that if the worst comes to the worst, *they* did everything possible too. You can't deny them that consolation."

"You're quite right, my wise friend," Maelbrigt sighed regretfully. "It just takes some getting used to!"

This first part of their journey was punctuated by stops at granges, and farms used to visits from the Order, and so the conversations at night remained general and avoided their missions. Then came an exhausting climb over the mountains, even though they avoided the peaks and used the shelter of the timber-lined lochs as much as possible. On the first night's loch-side camp, once they had several good fires going and the tents pitched, Ruari and Maelbrigt stood together by the central fire, as Sioncaet drew Will away in conversation.

"You're worried about him – Labhran – aren't you?" Ruari noticed.

"Yes I am," admitted Maelbrigt. "The things he saw, and the way he had to split himself in two in order to survive in New Lochlainn did some real damage. I know he feels he lost something of himself during those years that's never come back. In his mind he thinks he was only a small step away from turning into a hard and callous bastard like the DeÁine who surrounded him. Sioncaet says that wasn't remotely the case – and he should know since he knew all the DeÁine elite for decades even before Labhran arrived – and that Labhran always had far more compassion, even when he had to be at his most ruthless. Some of those things he had to do to survive, and to get the information we so desperately needed, still haunt him, though. Going back to New Lochlainn isn't just crossing a physical border for him. He's crossing one in his mind. He may have to revisit that persona he adopted, and that's going to take him straight into his own personal torture cell."

"Do you think he'll crack up, then?"

"No. …Not crack. …But what I fear, and Sioncaet does too, is that he may get Oliver and the men through to rescue the boys and safely on their way home, and then leave them."

"Leave? Why?"

"Because if he has to go back to that place in his mind he'll lose the will to live, and Sioncaet and I know the place where he'll go, and then he'll kill himself!"

"Oh no! Hounds of the Wild Hunt, no!"

Maelbrigt's sad eyes met Ruari's look of shock. "He's had as much pain as he can take, Ruari. He'll go to end the pain."

"Why in the Maker's name didn't you say this earlier?" demanded an appalled Ruari. "Brego would never have let him go if he'd known it would cost him his sanity. Never! No matter how much we needed his expertise. Why ever did you let him volunteer?"

"Because it might just *save* his sanity," Maelbrigt sighed. "He can't go on forever the way he's been for the last few years, Ruari – and it's not fair on Sioncaet, because he feels he can't leave him to wither away alone, and so he's accepted his own exile to stay with his friend. We both hope that going back may lay some of the ghosts to rest for Labhran. He's going back under very different circumstances, you know. This time he can do what his heart and instinct tells him is right. Only in the worst possible scenario would he have to adopt the guise of a leading DeÁine again. This time he'll be able to *prevent* someone's torture and pain. This time he'll be able to fight back with a bunch of highly trained and committed Knights right behind him, and at his command. We're hoping some of those ghosts die then too. Sioncaet wants to be near New Lochlainn just in case the worst comes to the worst."

"And what about Sioncaet himself?" Ruari wondered. "Will he stand up to this? From what you've just said he didn't have such an easy time of it back then either. Will he hold up?"

"Oh Trees, yes! No question! Don't forget, Sioncaet grew up amongst the DeÁine – he is one, and living proof they don't have to be evil! He was fighting for the promise of something better that he'd never even seen, only dreamed of, until he came back to the Islands with us. He had to practice far less deception too. He was long held in respect as a highly talented minstrel, with an unquestionable DeÁine birthright. Nobody would ever have asked who he was. And as a minstrel he could spy into the innermost sanctums, because his position allowed him access without question anyway – he didn't have to earn his right to be there. And no-one ever expected him to order an execution, or to order someone flayed alive, and him have to do it with his own hands in order to keep his cover intact."

"*Flay* someone *alive?* Holy Martyrs and Sacred Trees! Is *that* what he had to do? I had no idea! Poor bastard, no wonder he's haunted!" Ruari was horrified, and felt guilty for not having asked more questions back at Lorne, as Maelbrigt continued his explanation.

"Labhran was posing as a high ranking army officer, only one step below the senior Donns – we infiltrated him in place of someone he looked like, who'd been serving on the frontier and whom the Foresters took out.

That monster turned out to have a record and a half as an evil, twisted sadist, but Labhran was the only one we had who could even remotely double as him, and so that's how it went down."

Ruari gave Maelbrigt a shrewd, appraising glance. "Took out? Do you mean *you* took him out? Was it you who was responsible for getting Labhran in there?" The expression on Maelbrigt's face was confirmation enough without words. "Aaah, now it makes sense. That's why you always act as if you're responsible for him." Ruari clasped Maelbrigt's shoulder warmly. "You're a good friend to keep watching out for him, but it wasn't just your decision, you know. You aren't solely responsible for the way he is now."

"Is that Labhran you're talking about?" Sioncaet asked, coming to join them by their fire. "Because if so, the answer is that Labhran makes him feel like that. ...Don't look at me like that, Maelbrigt, it's the truth! You were the unfortunate one who took him up to the frontier and killed the real officer, but you didn't train him for the task, and you weren't the Grand Master he vowed to do the deed in front of – which nobody forced him into, by the way. You just keep getting the shit end of the stick because you're the only one left from those days who he knows anymore.

"So every time he sees you, he vents all his hurt on you. And that," the bright-eyed minstrel told Ruari with a wagged finger for emphasis, "is why I wouldn't let Maelbrigt be the one to go into New Lochlainn with Will, and be the one to dig Labhran out if necessary. If Maelbrigt failed, he'd never forgive himself. Oh I could've gone after the Sword, I know Celidon well enough by now, and it's the most straightforward of the tasks – probably!" he said with airy humour and a knowing wink. "But I know this one by now," the finger now pointed at Maelbrigt, "and I'm not having *both* my closest friends self-destructing on me!"

Ruari shook his head in admiration. He had always stuck by his own friends, but these men were prepared to do things on one another's behalf that took friendship to a whole new level. Come what may, he resolved that Sioncaet and at least one lance should go with Will into New Lochlainn now. And if it came to it, he would get the cursed Treasures back to Lorne and then come back himself, rather than let the sacrifices Labhran and Sioncaet were making be in vain.

However, the more pressing problem was getting to the ferry to Celidon. For days they slipped and scrambled their way up and down slopes heavy with snow. The horses had to be led as often as ridden and everyone, man and beast, was exhausted by the time they stumbled in through Dunathe's gates. With the approach of Yule, the amount of daylight they had to travel in had slowed them enormously in the mountains, but at least from here on they had decent roads, even if they had high drifts on either side.

Nobody could remember a winter when the snows had come so early and so heavy, and Sioncaet wondered aloud whether this was another sign of the Abend's approach. He was sure that he remembered the four witches having some talent with the weather, even if the male members of the nine had little power in such things, and no-one felt like contradicting him. To everyone's relief, though, they had seen no sign of Abend spies in the form of carrion birds and beasts – the thing Brego had worried over most, and which had ultimately determined their use of this route.

At Dunathe they were relieved to find that Brego's messages had got through, although evidently the birds had been badly delayed, and the ealdorman in charge had already begun to sort out what he thought they might need. Ruari therefore called a briefing in the refectory after everyone had eaten their fill.

"Right," he began, "listen up! This is where you find out more details about this mission. I make no apology for keeping you so much in the dark until now, for it's imperative that no-one finds out about certain aspects of what we're about." Then he looked around at the eager faces and had trouble refraining from grinning back. Instead he managed a restrained smiled at Maelbrigt. "Maelbrigt here is going to the north of Celidon in search of the Sword. That may sound like an easy journey, but it's not."

Maelbrigt himself took over the briefing. "Guthlaf and Hrethel, you and your men are with me. We move with all possible haste, given the weather, for the north of Celidon. It would take us far too long to take the roads, and so we're making a crossing of the mountains to bring us over near to Sarne. Your lances are all experienced mountaineers. That's why you were chosen for this, and we'll need all of your skills to do this with speed and in one piece. I foresee us leaving the horses at the grange beyond Giha, because there's no way we're going to get them over the passes.

"That means we'll have to look to remount at Sarne, and with luck Master Brego will have sent a message by birds to them so that they'll be expecting us – although not specifically why. What we are hoping is that if the message has got through we shall have some reinforcements. There were several other Knights like me who stayed in Celidon, and with luck the messages will get out to the granges, and they in turn will summon the men. We then ride for Rhionich. What we'll find there is anyone's guess. The original castle is long in ruins, and its replacement may not be much better. What happens there will determine our route home. Personally I favour a ship to bring us back, but that may not be possible. Our first priority is to get the Sword, however."

On cue Ruari took over. "You've all had chance to get to know General Montrose here, and the cover story for our leaving has been that we're accompanying him to find the two nearest heirs to the Rheged Jarl – I refuse to call that idiot a king!"

"Aren't you? Coming with me, that is?" Will asked, feeling rather confused, and wondering if he was going to end up going alone after all.

"Part of the way," Ruari replied, giving him a reassuring grin before turning back to the general assembly. "After we leave Maelbrigt and his team, the rest of us will cross Celidon by the main road from Giha to Cabrack where we'll board another boat for Brychan. I'm hoping to cross straight to Breslyn and get fresh horses at the Order there, and then ride north. Much will depend on what we find there, but the initial plan is that Montrose will take the northern route around the top of the mountains towards New Lochlainn in search of the boys. Unferth and Waeles, you're going with him, as is Sioncaet who will be your guide."

"I thought he was going with Maelbrigt?" an even more puzzled Will asked, and some of the men also seemed grateful he had asked.

"In the planning sessions that was what we originally decided," Sioncaet admitted. "We knew it would stop Taise worrying so much and so be able to concentrate on her work with the manuscript. She's going to kill me when she finds out I've let him go off alone!" The men chuckled at this. "But the more we thought about it, the more it was obvious that if Will had to go into New Lochlainn he was going to need someone who not only knew the way, but could give him and the men some background knowledge.

"That had to be me if Labhran was going south. And to be honest, I wanted to. Because I know how Labhran thinks. They're more likely to catch up with Quintillean, but I can slip into the towns and villages for news, and if they get caught the word of that will spread like wildfire. We're not just following a trail, we're the rescue party in case we're needed!"

"That's more like it!" Will felt far more enthusiastic at the thought of some real soldiering to be done, and his enthusiasm was catching.

"So are we with you then, MacBeth?" the remaining unmentioned Knight, Haethcyn, queried.

Ruari nodded. "Indeed you are. And this brings us to the truly covert part of this operation. Taise and Sithfrey think that the Shield is hidden in northern Brychan – most likely in the triangle of land between Nefyn, Wynlas and Roselan. Roselan is the nearest fit to what's written in the manuscript, but there's a problem. The current Knight's castle was only built a few years ago, after Moytirra, to protect the mining community up there. It's close to the coast to protect the crossing to Ynys, too. We need to see the old maps of the area, because the original castle was somewhere up on a protruding arm of the foothills, with its back to the mountains. But there are dozens of sites that fit that description, and that castle's probably no more than a pile of rubble by now."

"Is it possible the Shield was moved, like the Sword possibly was, to somewhere nearby?" Will asked.

"Anything's possible," Ruari told him, "but what bothers Brego and me is that I heard nothing about that at all when I was in the area years ago, when we were moving the DeÁine Gorget out of harm's way. You'd have thought that if the Grand Master of Brychan had had any idea of the fact that he also had an Island Treasure on his patch, he'd have wanted that moved to safety too. So we're guessing that somewhere over the centuries that knowledge has been lost – the chain was broken – and the Order in Brychan knows nothing of this. We're therefore operating more in the dark than Maelbrigt and his team, and closer to enemy territory."

For Maelbrigt's team the main necessity was to pack as much food as they would be able to carry without the pack horses once they reached Celidon. The mountaineers took the opportunity of acquiring more rope and spikes now that they knew more of the route they were taking.

"Are you going to be able to keep up with them?" Sioncaet teased Maelbrigt, as they stood watching the men testing the calibre of the ropes, and picking through the spikes to make sure none were faulty.

Maelbrigt rolled his eyes only partly in mock desperation. "Spirits, I hope so! I thought I was still fit, but there have been times over this last week when I've been gasping for breath and they hardly seem winded at all. How embarrassing would it be if they have to haul me up a rock-face like a sack of turnips!"

For all of them the luxury of a proper bed was not wasted, everyone being acutely aware that it might be some time before they slept warm and safe again. However, they could only afford to spend one night in the castle, and come the morning they were off again. On the day before the start of the Yule festivities, they arrived at Culva and made inquiries about the ferry.

At first the ferrymen were unwilling to set sail. It was only mid morning, but it would take the rest of the day to get to Giha, and would mean they spent the first part of Yule away from their families until they could return the next day. That was until they found themselves faced with quite so many stern-faced members of the Order, helmed, mailed, and very insistent. The heavy purse in compensation also did much to mollify their irate wives, who were prepared to put up with some domestic upheaval when it paid the landlords for the next two months and more from just one trip.

A biting wind seared its way up the narrow sound between the Islands as the first ferry pulled away from the shore. Normally one would wait until the other was at least halfway across before setting out, but today the first had barely cleared the harbour before the second began to cast off its lines. By nightfall all the Knights were disembarked at Giha and enjoying a hot, spicy stew in the grange, although nobody felt relaxed. The next day they would separate to go their different ways, and they knew that from now on they would need to be on their guard.

Friends sat quietly in close company, struggling to find words which were adequate when they knew it could be the last time they would see each other, creating an unnatural hush in the packed room. They all knew they should get an early night but most catnapped on the benches, determined to see Yule in with friends if nothing else. As the nearby church bell rang out at midnight, men embraced and wished one another good fortune for the weeks to come.

"If I don't come back, promise me you'll take care of Matti," Will said, his voice choked with emotion as he looked Ruari in the eyes, hands on his friend's shoulders. Before Ruari could protest Will cut across him. "No, listen, I mean it! And I don't mean just stopping by whenever you're in the area. Marry her! She loves you, you know – more than she ever has me. I didn't realise what a shit I've been to her all these years until we met up at Lorne. I haven't deserved her loyalty, and you've been a true friend. I'd hate to think I came between you after I've gone like I have in life."

Finally Ruari managed to get a word in. "Stop that! Stop it right now! Don't you dare *not* come back, you bloody fool! Curses, Will, how is it that you can hump your way through so many women and still not be able to

414

read your own wife? Yes, you've seen her at last for the woman she is, but she's seen you too! You dumb ox, hasn't it dawned on you that for the first time she's attracted to you? Honestly Will, you have the chance to finally make your marriage work. Don't screw it up and throw it away – because *I* might not forgive *you* if you hurt her like that again. And if we're talking about promises, I want you to promise that even if I don't make it, that you'll go back and give it your best shot."

As they drank each other's health, Ruari wondered why life had to get so complicated. Yes he loved Matti, but how long would it last if they were tied together as man and wife? How long would she be happy with him always off dashing here and there for the Order? That had always been one of her complaints about Will – that he was never around when she needed him most. Now, if they came through these next few months, Ruari would be almost certain to become the new Grand Master of Rheged, and his life would get even more entwined with the Order. And too many people were depending on him for him to be able to give it up and walk away. The days when he could have done that had gone forever. Once upon a time he would have given up the Order in a heartbeat for a chance with Matti, and his feelings had not changed that much, but his circumstances had. Maybe he should have done something about it back then, and if he could have his time over it might be different, but the problem with being older was that you had to live with the decisions you had already made, like them or not.

Further down the bench Sioncaet and Maelbrigt were also deep in conversation. As they saw in the festive season both were thinking of Labhran, and much of their talk had been of what he might do under various circumstances. Both wished there was some magical device by which they could see how he was coping, but then the conversation had turned to Taise and Kayna and the hope that they would both be safe and sound when they got back to Lorne.

Even Ruari did not have the heart to insist they leave before dawn the next day, so it was in the watery early light that the company assembled together for the last time in the yard. Those going with Ruari filed out and headed south on the road, while Maelbrigt's little band wheeled westwards until only the two leaders were left.

"Good speed!" Ruari wished Maelbrigt as they shook hands in farewell. "May you find the journey easier than you've feared."

"You too," Maelbrigt wished him. "Take care over there and keep an eye on Sioncaet for me will you, for as long as you can."

And with that they turned their horses and went their separate ways.

Maelbrigt and the two lances made good time for their first day's journey, and reached the grange in plenty of time to have a meal and then a good night's sleep. Come the morning, though, they found that the old sergeant who ran this small outpost was horrified at the thought of them walking further than they had to. He insisted that he and two of the young recruits accompany them for the next couple of days. That way they could all ride, and pack-horses could carry the fire wood they were going to need for the first leg of the journey. Consequently they made much better time than Maelbrigt could have hoped for, and by the end of the third day from Giha, they were making camp at the foot of the broad highland loch where any track passable for horses ended. At least for this night they were warm in tents with a good blaze going outside. Guthlaf and Hrethel pronounced themselves well pleased with the arrangement, for it meant that all were starting the first stage rested and in good condition instead of already weary and chilled.

When they left the kindly sergeant and his men, they were relieved to find that the path around the shore of the loch was relatively passable despite the snow, and in two days' marches they reached the loch head. Now, though, the climbing began in earnest. A steep ravine had been cut into the rock by the waterfall which fell from a higher loch to the one they had just walked along. The waterfall was now nearly frozen and the rocks at its edge a lethal tumble of ice. Guthlaf's sergeant must have had mountain goats for parents, Maelbrigt thought, because the man swarmed up the rock-face with deceptive ease, to be followed by the rest of the lance. Hrethel's men then sent the packs up on the ropes, one by one.

Then it came to the point where Maelbrigt had to make his ascent. Screwing up his courage, he gripped the rope in his gloved hands and pulled himself up. The first few hand and footholds were easy enough to find, but after that he was glad of Guthlaf calling instructions down to him, guiding him to where it was best to put his weight. Where in the Islands was the lad he had once been, who scaled walls to scramble over rooftops for fun, Maelbrigt wondered, as he hung on for dear life with his nose pressed against the cold stone? Halfway up he thought his breathing was already loud enough to be heard a mile away. By the time he crawled over the edge he was gasping like a fish out of water.

"Not bad, not bad at all for a novice," Guthlaf praised him. But the praise was somewhat undermined by the speed with which the next man appeared, despite the fact that Maelbrigt was fairly sure he had not been on the ropes at the same time as him.

"Novice?" he wheezed when he had got enough breath back. "I'm not a novice, I'm bloody baggage compared to you lot!"

The men laughed with him and pulled his leg for the rest of the day, but Guthlaf's mountain goat of a sergeant did admit that it had been a particularly nasty climb, and that the others had only done it so fast because they had scaled it before when they had been here on a training exercise a year ago. That at least made Maelbrigt feel a little better, although by the time they stopped for the night he felt like his strained knees might never stop wobbling.

Mercifully the next day was hard going, but on more of a continual steep slope, although that brought its own problems. On the long steep slope it was easy to miss your footing, and once sliding it was hard to stop on the fine powdery snow. Here the wisdom of being roped together was brought home to Maelbrigt, for even the experienced climbers were occasionally wrong-footed, but nobody slid far when the others could dig their staffs in and haul them back up. The one time he looked back he wished he had not. The slope seemed to slide off the edge of the mountain in a pristine white sheet, only marred by the snaking trail of their footprints. Even with a fair head for heights it was a giddying sensation, and a mistake he did not make twice.

Nightfall found them again at the foot of a loch, but this one curved along its length towards the south-west. The next day they got as far as they could go along its shore, and prepared for the long climb they would have the next day as they scaled the valley wall. At this height the temperature was dropping lower still at night, and even during the day the surface of the loch was frozen. It belatedly occurred to them as they huddled around the fire, that the next day was also the eve of the new year.

What a way to spend the festivities, Maelbrigt thought. *Freezing your balls off by a frozen loch and nothing better to look forward to for the start of the coming year! Sacred Trees, I hope this isn't the way the rest of the year is going to go on!*

Then he pulled the down-filled quilt closer around him, and tried to get some rest in the makeshift shelter they had knocked together. The quilts were a life-saver, for with a bit of squashing they packed up quite small and light to carry, but, when shaken, soon filled out and were warmer than a standard bedroll blanket. Combined with the fire they made the nights tolerable if not comfortable, and so far they still had trees around about which they could cut plenty of wood from, but this would be the last night for that.

The next morning dawned dry but rough, with a wind building from the west. Neither Guthlaf nor Hrethel were happy about making the ascent in the rising wind, but their supplies would not stretch to days just sitting around when they had no idea when it might clear again. Today they would be making a long climb up rocks which, while not a sheer vertical face, were so steep as to require spikes and ropes. The benefit of making this climb was that it cut four days off the more gentle route, and once they had made this difficult ascent they would be on high plateau for four more days, with only minor climbs before the descent to the coast began.

This time Hrethel's men led the climb, although today, because of the continuous nature of the climb, they would have to at least start it with packs on. During the morning they made good progress and the weather held off, with even some watery sunshine appearing now and then to cheer them up. They made the first break on a long wide shelf where there was plenty of room for all of them, and some shelter from the wind. The second climb was less vertical, and although longer, less taxing. However, as the sun began to lower they still had the final stage to climb, and Maelbrigt felt his heart sink as he looked up at it. This was mountaineering in earnest, for a sheer cliff loomed menacingly over them, broken only by ragged chimneys and wicked overhangs.

Even for the experienced climbers there was no way to do it safely with all their equipment on, and the group divided up into teams. The first three went up until they found a ledge where they could safely pause. Then the next team joined them while in a relay the first three made another climb. At that stage they ended up with a team at the top, two teams part way on ledges separated by the worst stretch of overhangs of the climb, and a pair of men at the bottom. The packs were then hauled up in stages and piled up at the top awaiting the climbers. But all this took time, and Maelbrigt could feel the tension mounting as the light faded with men still strung out along the cliff. Only the urgency of their mission had sent them this way for nobody would climb by night by choice.

He was lucky in that the mountaineers had felt it unwise to expect him to make the climb in one go. In the process of getting the baggage up, he had therefore accompanied the first batch of packs to the first ledge. Then part way through he had made it to the second break point, struggling over the outcrops of rock with at least some daylight to help him see where he was going. However, things were getting worse, for as well as the closing darkness the weather was now turning bad. In fact beyond bad. The wind was rising to a full scale gale, with the only consolation being that it was coming from the west, and so blowing them straight onto the cliff and not off it. He insisted on staying to help at first as the men below now needed the baggage ropes to help them up, and one time he felt weight suddenly drop on the rope he was holding as the man below lost his footing in the wind.

With everyone at least to the first stage and the last of the light gone, Guthlaf now insisted that Maelbrigt make the final climb to the top.

"This weather is getting worse and you're the least experienced of all of us. You can't help us if we need to rescue someone and you're better off up there, out of our way," he told Maelbrigt bluntly.

Fastening the rope around his waist, Maelbrigt reached up to the first handhold and began to pull himself up. He was determined that the men at the top should not have to expend their strength hauling him up in case they needed to do that for someone who got injured. Yet within minutes, he was glad of the nearby ropes for handholds as he struggled to reach the crevices in the slippery rocks, while being battered by the wind.

In the blackness of the winter early night he groped for handholds and desperately tried to remember where the footholds had been when his face had passed them. Sometimes there was a brief flicker of moonlight, but most of the time he could barely see his hands moving, let alone details of the cliff above. Each handhold came with experimental fumblings, and without the ropes on either side he would surely have fallen straight to the bottom on several occasions, for he often ran out of places to grip and had to haul himself up on the ropes. How the mountaineers had found their way up was a mystery to him, even given that the first party had gone up in full light.

Icy needles stung what bit of his face was exposed, and he was glad that he had wrapped his scarf up over his nose and mouth and pulled his hat well down over his eyebrows and ears. Even so, he got to the point where he had to pause to brush the icy deposits off his face in order to be able to see the little that was visible. More dangerous was that his fingers were so cold there was a danger he would lose all feeling in them despite the warm, felted gloves. The wind cut through everything and chilled him to the bone despite the exertion of climbing.

Once a gust nearly had him off his precarious hold, and all he could do was flatten himself against the rock-face until it slackened off a touch. It was a moment of unbridled terror as he felt the wind tearing at his clothes, and grinding his face along the jagged surface. Nothing would save him if he lost his grip for one second. This was worse than any battle. There he could react and at least try to defend himself when overwhelmed, but here he felt as in control as a dropped leaf in a storm.

Even when the gust passed, he could barely bring himself to move until he heard Hrethel calling to him to find out if he was alright. He was so focused on putting one hand and foot after another, that it came as a shock when he reached up and grasped someone's hand instead of rock. He could not see who gave him the flask for a drink, but he gratefully took a swig and felt the fiery liquid burn its way down. Immediately he was left alone, for everyone's attention was understandably on the men below, and as soon as he felt able he went to help. In the time it had taken him to struggle up the last stretch, three more men had made it to the stop below them, leaving only one making the last bit of the lonely climb from the first stage. After a brief pause to recover, these men began the climb up to the top, and Maelbrigt went willingly to the ropes to help.

By now it was pitch black and the wind like a knife, requiring the men beneath to hold the ropes steady from down below to stop them drifting. Two men struggled over the edge and staggered off to find out if there was some shelter for the rest of them afterwards. Then some time later two more appeared, leaving three below. With two men holding ropes below and four above they managed to get another one up who turned out to be Guthlaf, looking more anxious than Maelbrigt would have believed possible.

"It's no good," he told them, the strain showing in every word, "the other two are going to have to have two ropes around them and one each side for safety. That rock is turning to a sheet of ice! I've only just made it and it's getting worse by the minute! We'll just have to pull them up."

Maelbrigt would not have believed how heavy one man could feel as a dead weight, and he was only one of three on his rope. With the wind jerking the man left and right it was muscle wrenching work, but nothing prepared him for the sudden lurch as the other rope sheered on the cliff and his team took the whole weight in one yank. As the rope slithered through his gloves, he frantically grappled to regain his grip, grateful that the man behind him had the rope tied around him to prevent the end being lost and the man with it. The others pounced on the rope too and within seconds the man's perilous decent had been halted and he was on his way back up.

No sooner was he over the top then a new rope was being swung down to the last man, for nobody wanted to leave it any longer to get him up. Afterwards Maelbrigt could only think that exhaustion had worn down even the indefatigable mountaineers for the accident to happen. The ropes had taken a fearful punishment, and now they were being dragged over rocks which had been turned razor sharp by the wind honing the ice. As everyone hauled away with desperation, there came a point when this time it was Maelbrigt's rope which snapped. As his team stumbled backwards as the tension broke, he saw things unfold as if in slow motion. Just as had happened to his team, the other team found themselves with the whole weight, and the rope began to race out of their hands. But this time their reaction was too slow. As men in dazed exhaustion scrabbled to grab the rope, it kept on going until it ran out. Their anchorman was jerked off his feet, careered into another – who teetered on the brink but was grabbed by the next man – before the anchorman disappearing off into the void, the screams of the two linked men following them down. Then silence.

That was, except for the wind. Maelbrigt was not a fanciful man, but ever afterwards he vowed he saw something detach from the bank of cloud which was ripping across the night sky, and come their way. And the wind seemed to be filled with distant voices, then for a bone-chilling instant it was closer and, he could have sworn, laughing maliciously. Everyone stood frozen, too stunned to move for a moment. Then grief-stricken and shocked, the men staggered away from the treacherous edge and over to the lee of some stunted bushes. No-one even mentioned going to see if the men could be rescued. There was no way they could have survived that fall. Hrethel did a swift roll-call and Maelbrigt felt his stomach churn in horror as he learnt that the last man on the ropes had been Guthlaf's nimble sergeant. A man who had been a constant help and encouragement to him, always ready to offer him tips on how to do things easier, and patient with Maelbrigt's inexperienced clambering. How typical of the man, Maelbrigt thought, that he would see everyone else safe first and leave himself to make the most dangerous ascent. And he promised himself in his grief that now there was yet another lost life to make the Abend pay for.

Guthlaf also felt it keenly for it had been his other man-at-arms who had died with his sergeant, and he was struggling to contain his grief. It was Hrethel who took the lead and chivvied everyone to their feet and moved them a short way to where they could camp. In the shrieking wind it was impossible to get a fire going, and they had to settle for getting into the lee of some huge boulders and the bushes that clung to them. Then they huddled together with their packs stacked around them as additional wind breaks. Nobody really slept, only dozed fitfully.

None of them had appreciated that it was already past midnight when they had halted, until dawn came quicker than expected. Then they were all eager to move on away from the site of the accident, but everyone was staggering in a daze after a mile or two from lack of sleep and a decent meal. When they spotted a tiny side valley, with a stand of hawthorns and dwarf birches, everyone agreed to stop and take a proper rest. Although the wind still tore on in its heady race above the surrounding rock walls, within their sheltered spot it was thankfully calm. The thin branches easily caught alight, and made a much needed blaze in the clearing they made in the centre of the tattered copse, and soon they had tea brewing.

It was surprising how much better you could feel with a cup of spicy tea, Maelbrigt reflected as he gratefully sipped the scalding mug-full, dunking the rock hard biscuits in it to soften them enough to be edible. The dried beef was pretty chewy, too, but with the nuts and dried fruit provided much needed energy for the drained men. It did nothing to ease their minds at the loss of their companions, but it did help restore their bodies, and these men were professional enough to bury their grief until there was time and space out of danger to let it flow.

Maelbrigt insisted they post a watch, but equally insisted that he take the first shift himself while everyone else curled up to sleep. At first he busied himself with collecting more wood and banking up the fire, then went to the little stream to refill the water and set some to start warming, so that they could have another hot drink against the chill of the coming night. Once he sat down, though, he could not keep the nagging thought of that cloud out of his mind. There had been something desperately wrong with that, but he just could not put his finger on it. It was why here, in the middle of nowhere, he felt the need to set a watch. Something was ringing alarm bells in the back of his mind, yet it refused to come, and the only thing he could hope was that it would come back to him once he had had some sleep.

A week later, as they slithered their way down treacherous paths and frozen stream beds, it still hadn't surfaced, but he was pretty sure that it was something to do with the Abend. His conviction was bolstered by the length of time the wind had continued to roar eastwards. No natural storm would have sustained itself for so many days in one direction, or with such steady ferocity. In his mind Maelbrigt reviewed the map of all of the Islands, and reckoned that they probably had not had the worst of it, either.

The high mountains in the north of Brychan would have borne the brunt of this northern edge of the storm, but the aerial front they had seen stretching back southwards had gone on for miles. And that made Maelbrigt wonder if it had been long enough to pass over southern Brychan and the way through from New Lochlainn round the south end of the range. If so, he feared for what Labhran might find himself encountering. *Sacred Trees, keep him safe, keep him sane,* he prayed as he tramped along, mechanically putting one foot in front of the other.

However, the one good thing was that they'd come into land which was used as high pasture for sheep in the summer, and the mountain side was scattered with shepherds' refuges and substantial stone sheep pens which they could use at night. Even better were the mountain huts where emergency supplies were stored away for desperate travellers caught in bad weather. Maelbrigt couldn't imagine how they would've survived without these additional supplies, for they were eating their way through their own at a greater rate than anticipated due to the extreme weather. So it was with some relief that, when they stopped for a midday break on the seventh day after the disastrous climb, they found they could see the north-east coast of Celidon dimly on the horizon from their high vantage point.

They had originally intended to continue marching just below the ridge and come down to Sarne as the land fell away to the sea. But by now they all desperately wanted to get off the mountains, and there was a road far below to their left which would take them to Sarne and take only marginally longer. They were therefore already concentrating on looking for a way down, when someone cried out and pointed further south. There, snaking up the line of the road was a column of men. A large column of men! And Maelbrigt felt the tears come into his eyes as he recognised the flag at their head. His old company had come! In fact most of Luing, except for the very old, must have dusted off their boots and got their swords out of store for there to be so many.

"By all that's sacred!" Hrethel breathed in awe, "I never expected such strength still lived in Celidon! So many! I wonder that they've come after all this time."

"They'd always come!" a choked Maelbrigt answered. "All they've ever wanted is hope, a sign from Ergardia. Celidon may have been deserted by the Order, but we've never deserted them! All you had to do was ask. They've been waiting for you for a long time."

And with that he led the rapid decent down the hillside to meet the column, leaving the mountaineers to follow. As Hrethel and Guthlaf brought up the rear, Guthlaf tapped his friend on the arm and pointed to the flags, saying softly in wonder,

"Sacred Trees, would you look at that! They're not just any old companies. They're companies of *Foresters*! Nearly two whole *companies* of them!"

Hrethel gasped in realisation. "They haven't come for us, my friend, they've come for him!"

"Maelbrigt's a Forester!" Guthlaf groaned. "Of course! How could I have forgotten?"

Even the world weary Hrethel was in awe. "They must be from his last posting. In which case, I think we've done our bit in just getting him here. Whatever they were anticipating us meeting on the rest of this journey, back in Ergardia, I reckon Brego was hoping these men would deal with it. We were only ever the back-up in case the message failed to reach them."

"Then knowing what they train to fight, I'm mightily glad they made it!" was Guthlaf's heartfelt response.

The mountaineers crashing descent had alerted the men at the front of the column, and a dozen riders broke rank and came ahead to investigate. As soon as Maelbrigt was recognised he was greeted joyfully. A rider raced back to the column calling out the news, at which a great rippling cheer went up from the men and the whole column sped up to meet the newcomers. Baggage was immediately redistributed on the packhorses so that mounts were freed up for the exhausted climbers, and food handed out to them to eat as they rode.

Maelbrigt was soon at the head of the column and surrounded by men whom Guthlaf and Hrethel had never seen visit Ergardia, but who were obviously of some consequence. Neither was bothered by their exclusion from the conference that was going on, suspecting that much was Maelbrigt bringing the locals up to date on the plan. And with less and less need for secrecy, and now knowing Maelbrigt, they felt sure that he would be telling them more soon enough.

Maelbrigt himself was quite overwhelmed by the sight of the men around him. Some he had not seen in many a long year – not since shortly after Gavra Pass, in fact – others more recently but only briefly. Particularly poignant was his reunion with his former sergeant, Eadgar. When the Celidon sept had been mothballed, Eadgar had stayed at Luing on one of the outlying farms with his wife and family, and as Maelbrigt had thought it long overdue that they had some of Eadgar's time, he had left him alone.

In the subsequent years, though, Eadgar's wife had died and his children grown and flown the nest, leaving the now salt-and-pepper-haired veteran to return to his old captain. Few words needed to be spoken between them. The old bonds had been strong enough to need little renewing, proven by Eadgar's handing Maelbrigt an oiled cloth package. It was the length of a man's forearm, but tapered at one end more than the other, and was obviously weighty.

"I got them out of the vaults," he said solemnly. "A message like that could only mean trouble, in which case I knew you wouldn't want to be without them."

A flicker of pain crossed Maelbrigt's eyes before dissolving into a smile. "You know me so well! Still!"

"We all came prepared," a voice at his elbow said, and Maelbrigt turned to see another old, familiar face. Yaroman had fought side by side with Maelbrigt in the killing grounds at Gavra, and what had happened there always returned to both their minds whenever they met. Consequently, although close, their meetings had been few over the latter years. Perhaps it would have been different, Maelbrigt had often thought, had the Celidon sept continued and they had had new missions together to overlay the memories. If Eadgar was another solidly built man like Maelbrigt, Yaroman was quite the opposite, being tall and angular. How he had come to be at Luing when the message had come in, Maelbrigt could not imagine, since he normally stayed at the former headquarters in Cabrack, but he was glad – very glad.

Then another figure appeared from the past. Bosel had been a Knight when Maelbrigt was only a squire, never rising to high rank, but being the kind of extremely competent man who formed the backbone of the corps of Foresters. A bulky older man, he was still fit, and seemed none the worse for the mad dash he must have made to ride from his far flung home, south of Luing, to join the column. Beside him rode his old friend Aldred, a small, wiry, dark man who had an encyclopaedic knowledge of the specialist writings the Foresters relied upon. Between the two of them they had kept an eye on the old preceptory (reduced to the status of a grange) at Luing, and Maelbrigt had seen them as often as he could when he had made trips south.

Behind them Maelbrigt saw the mischievous grin of the much younger Raethun. Merely a newly created squire at Gavra, the younger man had fought with skill and daring, and he had been elevated to Knight a few years afterwards, only to have the sept close before he could advance any further. At first Maelbrigt had wondered why he had repeatedly refused to go to Ergardia where he could have kept his career going. Then at a chance encounter at an inn, Maelbrigt had learned that had Raethun gone, he would have had to join the ordinary ranks instead of the Foresters – the Ergardian sept being overly blessed with Foresters and too few ordinary men at the time. The young man already knew where his calling lay, though, and chose to stay with Aldred, to continue to learn while making frequent trips down the road to Bosel to have his fighting skills honed. What sort of Knight he had turned into was yet to be proven, but Maelbrigt was betting that with those two tutors it would be formidable.

The bulk of the column of men was made up of the enlisted men of the Order and almost equally divided between men-at-arms and archers, with a fair scattering of veteran sergeants like Eadgar. Maelbrigt signalled them to ride on, sitting on his horse by the side of the road with the other six Knights in order to see who had come. There was a time when he had known every man in the place, and even so he found himself grinning at familiar faces riding past, but with them were many he did not know. These were the younger men who had decided to follow the calling, despite what must have seemed a very distant prospect of ever having the chance to fight. Maelbrigt was heartened to see that the sergeants had paired each new man with a seasoned veteran, and was humbled to realise that the grange's men-at-arms had secretly continued to recruit even without formal authorisation from the Order.

On the two camps they had to make before reaching Sarne, he took the time to walk amongst the men and acquaint himself with as many of the newcomers as possible. It brought a lump to his throat whenever he found himself talking to a young man who turned out to be the son, or in one case even three sons, of someone he had fought alongside and who had died at

Gavra Pass. Most of those he had thought were new to the Order he instead found had been brought up within it, and were as steeped in its traditions as any of the veterans. They were here because they had always expected to be called to arms, and had never given up hope that one day the Celidon sept would be revived. There was therefore no sense of 'them and us' between the veterans and the recruits, which was something Maelbrigt had feared finding, for it could be a lethal weakness in combat.

In the great hall at Sarne on their first morning there, the whole company assembled to hear the briefing, Maelbrigt on the dais with the six Knights who had ridden in with him, and the Captain of Sarne and his second-in-command. Captain Heaney was another old friend, and had insisted on making up the column's numbers with his own soldiers to bring it up to a full two companies of one hundred men, even if they lacked the traditional proportion of Knights amongst them. The winter wind whistled eerily through the old castle as Maelbrigt addressed the sea of expectant faces.

"I'm sure you're all eager to hear what we're about to do," he began, and heard the enthusiastic ripple run through the assembled men. Briefly he explained the overall situation and then came onto the Island Treasure. "We're going after the Sword," he told them. "It should be somewhere at Rhionich Castle, but where is anyone's guess. Do any of you have any memory of a story of this thing? Something your grandmother may have told you when you were a child? Anything at all? Because our records perished long ago, and any little thing might help us."

He paused and let the murmur of voices from the floor rise for a moment as men conferred with their neighbours. For the most part all he saw was shaking heads, but one or two earnest conversations seemed to be going on. From one of these a man tentatively raised his hand and Maelbrigt gestured him to speak up.

"I don't know if this is any help at all, sire, but me and Berry and Hector, here, all come from up north of here. My old granddad used to tell me to look out for wild mountain thyme growing around a place – that there was something special there. Something, he'd never say what or maybe he didn't know, but it was special"

"Aye," someone nearby said, "my grandma said the same. Said it was something that made us us, if that makes sense. Something that was at the very heart of the Island. And her old friend from over the hill used to tell us lads of a story of a king who'd come back from out of a tomb when the

Islands needed him most, and save us. Back then we thought it just a good tale, but maybe there was something in it after all? Wouldn't a king have a sword?"

One or two younger men tittered at what sounded like such an old wives' tales, but the men on the dais rapidly conferred.

"I've not read about any tomb," admitted Aldred to the others, "but then, as our records are singularly lacking in any references to the Island Treasures at all, that's hardly surprising. It sounds quite plausible though. You'd think nothing of it if you found a knight or nobleman buried with his sword, would you? A case, maybe, of hiding it in plain sight? A desecrated tomb would be much easier to spot, too, than trying to watch one sword amongst many in a castle."

"What about the wild thyme?" wondered Yaroman. "That sounds like simple superstition."

"I don't think we should discount it," Aldred said thoughtfully. "Just because we don't know what it means yet, doesn't mean that it won't become clearer once we get there."

Maelbrigt turned back to the assembly. "Thank you! Has anyone else heard a similar story?" There were not many hands that went up, but enough for them to see that it was a far from isolated story in Celidon, at least. "Right, in that case keep your eyes open for tombs in strange places – I mean that quite seriously – or wild thyme, not that we'll see that much under a blanket of snow.

"Now, more pressingly, most of you now know that I encountered DeÁine Hunters here in Celidon only a few short months ago, who were seeking Taise for what she knows of the Treasures – both lots! If it was important enough to send two triads after Taise, then I think we can assume there will be more we haven't encountered yet. We have to assume that, even though the DeÁine don't know we're going after the Sword, we're likely to meet them nonetheless. The more experienced among you will know that they're not to be taken lightly. Even a dying Hunter is more than capable of killing anyone of you, so no heroics! There's no shame in going three or four to one where they're concerned – in fact it's the best thing to do.

"Even if we don't meet them at Rhionich, it's highly likely we'll meet them at some point later on. And that's because we're then going onwards to get the DeÁine Treasure from the far north." A ripple of excitement ran through the crowd. "Now it may sound dramatic, but I'm not going to tell you where that is. Not yet anyway. We have too far to go, and there's too great a danger that one of you may end up in enemy hands.

"They can't use the Island Sword against us, as far as we know, but there's no telling what might happen if Hunters get to the DeÁine Gauntlet first and one of them decides to put it on. Taise said the high probability was that it would quickly kill him, but that for a brief moment he might be able to wield it. All of you who've encountered Hunters before know that in their drug-ridden, hypnotic state they know no boundaries. Their minds have already been touched by the Abend, or one of the acolytes strong in the Power, and that may make them more attuned to the piece. Allowing every last drop of their strength to be drained by the piece in a suicide attack would be typical of their mentality, and they have the strength to do it.

"But more importantly, that Gauntlet *must* not get taken west. All the Abend are accounted for as far as we can tell, and there aren't any in Celidon the last we knew, but the piece *must not go to them*! And the Gauntlet will draw all DeÁine like flies round a midden the minute we bring it out of where it's been hidden. If they get the Treasures back to the Abend then the Islands *will* fall!"

The high spirits of earlier were now overlaid with an air of determination as Heaney announced the preparations for departure the following morning, which persisted up to the actual event. The hundred men rode out divided up into five troops. Conventional lances were not possible, for they had far too few Knights for the traditional one to four soldiers ratio. Instead, Maelbrigt had had great pleasure in announcing to Guthlaf and Hrethel that they had been promoted to captain, with immediate effect, and now commanded twenty men each; with the other three troops of twenty commanded by Yaroman, Bosel and Aldred. Raethun rode as Maelbrigt's aide alongside Eadgar, who insisted on serving as Maelbrigt's body guard. Fully kitted out and with pack-horses laden with supplies they were able to make good progress, for although the roads were often little more than tracks, everyone was familiar with the territory to some extent. Knowing that there were few hidden pitfalls, they rode on after dark by the light of the moon, or with torches when the clouds masked it.

Five days later, they turned into a long valley at the far end of which lay Maelbrigt's home. He was surprised at how strange it felt returning with a full company and without Taise, bringing it sharply home to him how irrevocably she had become entwined in his life here. The men rapidly distributed themselves among the barns and the old castle, and Maelbrigt was soon too busy to miss Taise until he lay down in his old room that night. Then the memories flooded back and he vowed once again to do everything he could to keep her from harm. He remembered their last night here and the feel of her lying beside him in the same bed, but that also brought back the memory of the two orphans they had cared for in those last days.

There at least his conscience was clear, for the men had brought word that Rob and Jakie had settled in happily at Luing once the sorrow at being parted from their friends had lessened. Both lads were quick learners and had taken on the lessons with the other children at the grange with great relish. Quite what the villagers in the hamlet down on the loch-side would say to that, Maelbrigt did not know, but the next day would provide the answers.

Securing his old home once more the next morning, Maelbrigt led the men down the right-hand kink in the valley and towards the little hamlet below it. The villagers were clustered fearfully at the roadside as the fearsome looking company rode closer, and a blatantly petrified Adam the sail-maker was shoved to the front of the group, although he could not seem to find his tongue. Before the man could summon up the courage to challenge these formidable strangers, however, a sharp-eyed Peg suddenly recognised Maelbrigt and let out a cry of delight. Maelbrigt heeled his horse forward and bent down in the saddle to greet her warmly, noticing how much more careworn she looked than he remembered.

For several moments there was stunned surprise as the villagers realised who he was, and took in the uniform of a commander of the Knights of the Order of the Cross. None of them knew that the stars above the dragon-headed cross on all the men's uniforms meant that they were of the elite corps of Foresters, but then few outside of the Order had ever known what a Forester was. For the simple country folk it was enough to see a full company from the Order, armed and ready for the fray in their village. That alone would be talked about for months.

However, none seemed to question what they were doing there. Doing a rapid head count, Maelbrigt also realised that there were even fewer villagers now than when he had left, and a few pointed questions soon had the relieved locals telling them of the strangers who had descended upon them only days after Maelbrigt had left. They had gone through the village like a storm, and had returned after finding Maelbrigt's home locked and deserted.

Despite the torturing of several of the villagers in front of their friends, the hapless folk had been unable to tell the monsters amongst them where Maelbrigt and Taise had gone since they had not been told. Several had died before the Hunters had been convinced of the truth of this, and they had ridden out as suddenly as they had arrived. Part of Maelbrigt was sickened by the suffering of innocents on his account, but another part was relieved that he had kept his own council as to their destination, for the Hunters might have caught up with them before Talorcan and his lance had crossed their path, and alone he could not have protected Taise.

Yet now was not the time to delay in commiserating with the desolate villagers, and they rode on having at least had the satisfaction of telling them that Talorcan's lance had sent the two triads to the Underworld and were no longer a threat. However, the men did not relax their guard, although the countryside remained noticeably clear of any other signs of Hunters, and in the changing landscape there was little chance of missing them if they were there.

Here in the far north-west, the forest-covered slopes leading to high jagged crags dwindled out. Instead they rode into an arctic world of low, stunted bushes on open, frozen, marshy moors and valleys. What mountains there were rose straight from the flat valley floors in to cones of bare rock, eroded by millennia of rain, frost and wind. The final two nights before they reached Rhionich were miserable beyond belief, with a howling wind screaming down from the north which tore at the tents and defied their best attempts to light fires, even though the wood they carried with them was dry enough. It sapped the spirits of everyone, and it was only the reassurances of those who had lived this far north that things would be better by the coast that kept them resolute.

On a bleak afternoon in late Eft-Yule, the column wound its way down off the inhospitable moors, and saw the sea in the far distance. As promised this was a gentler landscape, although noticeably lacking in tall timber. Isolated crofters scratched a living from the thin belt of fertile soil on the coast and every inch of usable land was under the plough. For now though, the only sounds of life they heard were the piteous bleating of sheep from dry-stone, storm-proof folds. The locals remained behind doors giving no clue as to what they thought of the extraordinary sight of armed men this far north.

What they saw when they turned a small shoulder of land would have stopped them in their tracks if they had been walking. Rhionich Castle stood black and ruined by fire, with the crumbled remains of its predecessor tumbled on a pillar of rock out in the crashing waves beyond.

"Oh no," breathed Yaroman, pressing his mail-backed glove to his lips, "we're too late!"

"No!" a horrified Raethun cried. "We can't be! How could they have known?"

"They're sorcerers, why wouldn't they know?" a despairing Yaroman replied.

Chapter 24

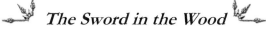 *The Sword in the Wood*

Celidon: Eft-Yule

Maelbrigt looked in horror at the burnt out shell. Then Aldred tapped his arm.

"Does that look like the Power to you?" he asked, which made Maelbrigt stop and look again.

As his heartbeat returned to something like normal, after the shock of seeing their destination in ruins, Maelbrigt began to realise that Aldred was right. This was just a fire. A normal, ordinary fire which had taken roof timbers, and scorched stone. Where the stone had collapsed it was simply where the rain and frost had done their worst on the unprotected mortar. There were no signs of holes blasted through the stone by the Power. No sign of whole sections of wall or tower reduced to pulverised ash.

Catching Maelbrigt's eye, Sergeant Edgar bellowed for quiet over the babble of worried voices as Maelbrigt stood in his stirrups to see over the heads of the men nearest him.

"Be calm!" he commanded. "Look again! Whatever might have happened here, what you can see now isn't the work of the DeÁine! Yes, we should proceed with caution, but this is old. …See? …The rain has all but washed the soot off the seaward side! Had this happened within the last months that would still be fresh, for we've had snow not rain."

Then he thought again, and caution asserted itself. "Bosel, take your men and go down that road coming up on our left, and loop round to the castle that way. Hrethel, you take your men and go with him. The rest of you – we go to just short of firing range, then Yaroman and his men will come with me. The rest will wait until we give you the all clear. …Cut a sprig off that rowan tree, Eadgar." He turned to Guthlaf and Aldred. "Your messenger will return with that. I can't think that Hunters would make the association, or would see it important enough to worry whether a messenger carried a sprig of plant. If the messenger comes back without it, you'll know he was forced."

Nonetheless it was with some trepidation that Maelbrigt and Yaroman's troop rode up to the castle. However, all was deserted.

"How come we never heard of this?" wondered Raethun as he gazed about him.

Yaroman shrugged. "This was always an isolated outpost. With our Order down to such small numbers, I suspect most preceptories and castles have been too busy ensuring their own survival to think much about anywhere else. We wouldn't have thought it strange not to have heard much from somewhere so far off the beaten track, and there were probably never more than a few dozen men here anyway."

As they rode in through the charred gates, it became evident that the major source of casualties had been the collapse of the roof. Looking at the damage it seemed likely that a fire had begun on the first or second floor, and probably at night when the smoke would have taken men before they realised anything was amiss. The skeletons had already been picked clean by scavengers and been bleached by the summer sun and salt spray. Even the most suspicious amongst them could find no reason why they should not send for the rest of the company, and Guthlaf and Aldred's men were soon with them. As soon as they were joined by Hrethel and Bosel's contingent, men set to retrieving the skeletal remains of the garrison and placing them in a makeshift mortuary, until they could find the burial ground. Others cleared the fallen timbers, and in the shelter of the bailey wall, they made a camp where the stone vaulting of the lower floors still provided roofs.

Once the needs of the living had been attended to, however, they returned to the reason for the long trek. Hrethel and Guthlaf found their skills once again in demand to access the upper levels of the towers, while others scoured the ground floor and those parts where some form of stair survived. Maelbrigt and Aldred were directed by a couple of men who had been here before to the castle chapel, and they, with Eadgar and Raethun's help, rummaged through the wreckage there. However, it was soon blindingly clear that no-one had ever been buried or entombed in the confines of the chapel. Nor, it transpired, anywhere else within the castle.

"What did they do with their dead, then?" a puzzled Raethun asked, as they all sat around the fire that night, waiting for the water to get hot enough to re-hydrate the dried beef into something like stew. "They weren't buried in the chapel, and there isn't a graveyard outside the walls like we have at Luing. You can't tell me nobody ever died up here! This endless rain and cold must have seen a few off to an early grave, if nothing else did."

The night had turned damp again, and was alternately snowing or else freezing the men with icy sleet.

"We'll just have to search the countryside round about," Yaroman morosely told him, forlornly swirling the last dregs of his tea in his mug. "Spirits, that's going to be a cold task, because we're going to have to go slowly if we're not to miss something in this weather. It might be nothing more than a series of grave mounds after all this time, and can you imagine how hard it's going to be digging each one of them up with the ground frozen hard like this?"

"Well it's a good job you're not in charge of keeping morale up!" Bosel chivvied him. "Sacred Trees, you're still a little ray of summer sunshine, aren't you? Anyway, this isn't some bunch of primitive settlers we're looking for. Oak and Ash, man, do you seriously think any of our Order would just dig a hole and drop their comrades in – except in the most dire of circumstances? Of course not! There'll be a chapel somewhere. We just have to find it."

With the fires banked up, the men settled down for the night inside the castle, feeling their most secure for many days with the gateway barricaded against intruders. Maelbrigt curled up in his bedroll and tried to sleep, but despite his weariness it was as though he had ants in his bed. Something kept scurrying past the edges of his mind just as he got to the point of nodding off. Finally he sat up with a sigh and looked about him. To his surprise he saw Yaroman sitting up too.

"So you feel it too," his old comrade asked, "it's not just my imagination?"

As Maelbrigt shook his head they saw Bosel roll over and sit up, as did Aldred on the other side of the fire, and the four exchanged glances. If all four of them had their sixth sense twitching then something was afoot. A bleary-eyed Guthlaf was disturbed by the movement as they got up, and was amazed to see them each pull similar packages out of their packs. The mysterious item handed to Maelbrigt by Eadgar turned out to be four wicked-looking knives of a kind Guthlaf had never seen before. In place of a standard straight blade, these were wavy-edged so that in the light of the fire they looked like solid flames. The blades were the best part of a foot long, with wooden handles bound with three slim bands of steel instead of the usual wound steel wire grip, and a guard which split into two spikes at the end of each crosspiece. The blade side of this guard looked as razor-sharp as the blade itself, and even in the dim light, Guthlaf could see that they had been pattern-welded. And that meant a master smith of the kind they had not had in Celidon in a generation. Someone who not only knew how to make good steel, but knew the right words to say over the blade as he fashioned it too.

He watched in awe, as the four veterans each tucked two knives into their belts, and began to move away from the fire with a knife in each hand. Raethun went to light a torch that lay nearby, but Yaroman caught his eye and shook his head. Silently as cats on the hunt, the foursome prowled out of the lean-to and into the open courtyard. One or two other veterans were already on their feet looking out of their respective shelters and noted the Knights' passage, silently acknowledging them and reaching for weapons themselves.

On the next bedroll Hrethel nearly choked when he saw that the ordinary men were pulling out wooden wands. The wands were sharpened at the end to enable them to be used as stakes and were made from the five sacred trees – oak, ash, birch, yew and rowan – which he had occasionally seen being made. All the time he had spent training and fighting had never fully prepared him for the sight, for what this moment would feel like – for the use of wands could only mean magical forces were at work.

Then from beyond the walls they heard it. An eerie half sighing, half yowling noise, which made the hairs on the back of everyone's necks stand. The men cast about them but there was nothing to see within the walls. Yet beyond, it sounded as though whatever they were had begun to multiply in great numbers and were starting to circle the walls. The horses now began to get restless and the new men were sent to calm the animals, and to stop them breaking their tethers and running amok.

Meanwhile the veterans had spread themselves around the circuit of the outer walls. Nobody was asleep now. Everyone held themselves poised for the attack, but nothing happened. The wraiths, or whatever they were, kept up their infernal yowling for the best part of an hour, yet never came within the walls and finally seemed to dissipate into thin air as swiftly as they had come.

"What in the name of all that's sacred was that, do you think?" Bosel wondered.

"I have no idea," Aldred said with feeling. "That doesn't match the behaviour of anything I've ever read about the DeÁine conjuring up."

"How could it be the DeÁine?" a bemused Raethun asked. "I thought you said that sorcerer Quintillean never made it up here?"

Several of the men looked at him with eyes that might just as well have shouted aloud 'stupid boy' for asking, but Maelbrigt whipped round to look sharply at him.

"By the Trees, Raethun, you may have something there! You're right, we have no reason to think Quintillean delayed his quest by coming this far north. If that was DeÁine magic then he must have brought at least one of his acolytes with him, but there's been no hint of any others wielding the Power. The Hunters most certainly couldn't conjure up that sort of apparition." Then he paused and looked at Aldred questioningly. "Unless that wasn't DeÁine at all? Could that have been something much older? Something left to guard the Sword? Is that why it didn't attack? Our approach triggered its appearance, but it sensed we were no threat?"

Aldred shrugged and raised his hands in a gesture of defeat. "Don't look at me! Nothing in my research has ever told me about who made the Island Treasures, or why, or what power they must have had to be able to do that. All I can say is that common sense would tell us that if something, or someone, had the skill in the magical powers to create such pieces, then it would be foolish not to think they'd have the power to protect them too."

"Then it doesn't bode well for when we go outside of these walls that it can't tell we're friendly," Yaroman responded gloomily.

The Knights speculated on the possibilities for a while, but as it became evident that whatever it was was not coming back that night, they retired to their beds once more, and this time found themselves able to sleep.

In the morning, in the chill of a thick sea fog, they ventured out of the walls and looked for signs. It was an eerie experience, with voices and footsteps muffled in the wet blanket which had descended on the headland. Search as they might, however, nobody could see any sign of a host having surrounded the castle during the night, and by midmorning the leaders decided there were better things to be doing.

Hrethel and Guthlaf were instructed to search the seaward side, closer to the cliffs than they had gone the previous day. If possible, Maelbrigt wanted them to see if they could find the old track-way which once upon a time must have led to the original cliff-top castle. Any original burial grounds would surely not have been far away from that main route, but Maelbrigt's growing concern was that it looked as though the cliff had crumbled, and if that was where the tomb might be, their quest might end in the sea. Yaroman was sent with them to provide additional Forester experience, should they need it.

Meanwhile, the rest of them were going to explore inland.

"We'll leave going along the coast in each direction until tomorrow," Maelbrigt told them. "We can divide up again then, and something tells me that either direction will be a wild goose chase, anyway. If we have to resort to that, we're only confirming that we can't find it. I'm sure it has to be around here somewhere, if only we have the wit to work it out."

The horses were mostly left within the castle. It was far too foggy to ride with any safety when gulches worn by the sea might be anywhere, and also this was going to be careful work better done on the ground. The men with Maelbrigt cast about to find the tracks leading inland from the castle, and by midday it was confirmed that there were three cart tracks and a gap in a wall. After a short break for food, Maelbrigt sent Bosel and two thirds of the men, now mounted, off down the left-hand pair of tracks climbing back up the hill, which looked as though they might have divided to serve isolated farms and would then come back together. More people might mean a chapel, they reasoned. Aldred took ten horsemen with him and began to investigate the right-hand path, which led off the track they had ridden in by, and which seemed to disappear into a gully. Maelbrigt, Eadgar and Raethun, with four men and on foot, took the gap in the wall which led off this path, expecting for it to peter out within a few yards allowing them to rejoin Aldred's route.

However, the first surprise was that it appeared that the tiny path had been used recently. Maelbrigt and Eadgar poured over the tracks in the wet grass in bemusement. There were signs of paw marks – quite large paw marks – and yet with little weight in them. The grass stalks were bent, but not crushed flat, despite the pug marks being almost the size of Eadgar's palm. It was a long paw too, more like the pad mark of a running dog like a greyhound than a big cat, with the claw marks clustered at the front at the end of long toes on the one imprint they found in bare earth. If they hadn't seen the bent grass as they stood in the gap, they would most likely have missed the tracks altogether, so faint were they.

Yet the paw marks went on a straight course. There were no diversions for an animal marking, and at one point they totally bypassed a rabbit warren in a small bank nearby. This was no wandering dog! Eadgar and Maelbrigt conferred but could not work out how fast the beast had been going, either, until Raethun, who was standing up and looking down on the marks instead of being crouched down beside them, pointed something out.

"That looks like a person ran down here, not an animal," he thought aloud.

Maelbrigt and Eadgar looked up and then rose to stand beside him, looked at the tracks and then one another and nodded.

"That's what's foxed us," Eadgar gasped. "It's going upright, on two feet, not on all fours!"

A shiver ran through the small company. Animals with paw pads walking like men did not sound like good news, and the four soldiers loosened swords in their belts, Maelbrigt mentally kicking himself for not having brought any archers with him. Proceeding with great care they followed the prints in their hasty passage.

Shortly they veered to the right, leaving the main course of the wider valley running inland towards where the others were searching, and disappeared into a tangled landscape of massive quartz boulders, peaty bogs, and ridges and dips coated with heather and bracken. The tracks finally disappeared into a ragged cluster of stunted hawthorns, whose tortured tops had been sheared to a sharp angle by the blast of the regular sea-gales which scoured this coast. It would have been stretching the imagination to call it a copse. The trees were neither high enough nor dense enough, and the now dead bracken still lay in brown swathes beneath them, allowing the trackers to spot their quarry's route through the parted fronds.

What the hawthorns did disguise, was the fact that the ground dropped away sharply on the other side to a totally hidden vast depression. Suddenly, protected by the high slopes around them, there were real trees. In this deep, secluded bowl in the terrain, even oaks grew tall and straight, and the little group stood in awe at the edge of a small wood. Down here the wind was inaudible, and a silence descended on the place making them want to whisper.

"This place is old!" one of the men said, staring at the girth of the stag-headed oak before him. "Would you look at the size of that thing! It's enormous!"

"Hundreds of years old," the man beside him agreed.

And it was warmer down here too, and not just because they were out of the wind off the sea. Frost had hardly touched these trees despite the harsh winter beyond. The leaf litter of autumn lay where it had fallen like a thick carpet, not driven into heaps by the wind. However, it also meant that the tracks had disappeared, for there was no way of telling where their light-footed quarry had gone. Cautiously they continued their descent, although the slope was very shallow now. A tiny stream crossed their path and Maelbrigt stooped to scoop a handful of water.

"Clean," he said softly. "Cold but not icy. Must come from a spring down here somewhere."

As Raethun watched him, something flicked at the corner of his eye.

"Don't move suddenly," he murmured, "but we're being watched! Right of the big oak two trees back on our left. I think we've found our furry friend!"

Maelbrigt stood slowly, making much of brushing the leaf mould off his boots to allow him to surreptitiously scan the area. Sure enough there was a faint scurry of movement, but it seemed more timid than threatening. Then he saw it briefly for a second and gasped. His first thought was 'squirrel'. A very big squirrel! About the size of an older child or very small adult. For one second it had stopped on its haunches just like a squirrel, but there was something very strange even so. The back legs were large and powerful, with the front paws smaller and more dexterous, in a squirrely sort of way, but as soon as it moved it stood up and ran instead of scampering on all fours. The tail was totally wrong too, being thin and whippy, and it stuck straight out behind when the beast ran. Yet that was nothing to the head. Instead of pricked ears, they stuck out from the side with fringes of fur half hanging down mournfully. But strangest of all, rather than a short muzzle, the face ended in a long horny protuberance that looked more like a beak than a nose.

For a moment Maelbrigt was too stunned to move, and going by the gasps behind him the others had seen it too.

"What in the Islands was that?" a stunned voice asked.

"Something out of legend, if my guess is right," a wonder-struck Eadgar replied. "Although how it came to be here is beyond me! I thought them something of the distant past like, dragons and elves. I never, ever dreamt I should really see a squint."

The others all turned to look at him in astonishment.

"You're not serious, are you?" a grey-haired veteran demanded, trying not to laugh. "That's something out of children's fairy tales!"

Maelbrigt had been frowning in concentration. "Well, maybe that's the only memory of them that we have any more. But Eadgar's right, it does fit the description. And what else would you think that strange combination of beast and bird could be? It's nothing indigenous to these Islands, that's for sure."

"I've never even heard of a squint!" Raethun declared. "What are you talking about?"

Eadgar looked vaguely embarrassed as he tried to explain. "Alright …so, when you were a little lad, did anyone ever tell you bedtime stories?"

"Aye, my mom and sometimes my grandma," a still sceptical Raethun reluctantly admitted.

"Well among them, did they ever talk about the fairy folk?"

"Sometimes," Raethun grudgingly conceded, although Maelbrigt noticed that the three others apart from the veteran were listening carefully too.

"Right, then. Well, if you talk to Aldred, you'll find that some of the scholars who wrote the books he reads thought that there was something in those old tales. That the fairy folk weren't cute little things lingering to dance in forgotten woods. They thought that the tales recalled another race, long gone, who we should more properly call the fae folk, because they had skills we can't even imagine anymore. If I remember right, there was even one writer who thought that they might have been the original inhabitants of the Island – a people so technically advanced that it would look like magic to us.

"Another believed that some great disaster befell them. That they overstepped some kind of natural boundary and that they were shunted into some kind of other reality. So when we think we see them it's when the veil between the worlds is thin, and we can see them and they us. They try to talk to us to warn us against going down that path in the future. Now those same writers think that the squint was a creature they bred to pass beyond the veil before the disaster. That somehow they were able to start from scratch and build a living being to do their bidding."

"Sacred Trees!" one man breathed, "that's playing at being the Maker!"

Maelbrigt took over. "Yes and no. The Church would have you think so, which is why the sanctimonious ones preach that the fae folk were – are – evil. But there's a fragment of an old tale that says that the squint, along with other strange creations, was never quite right. That even with all their skills, the ancient fae couldn't make a true living being. Instead, the squint is permanently trapped between worlds. Sometimes it's more here than there, and sometimes the reverse. That would explain why the creature we tracked here made so little impression on the ground. A beast of that size, even a bird, would have trodden more heavily on the earth. That's why I think Eadgar's guess is right."

"An old …no make that an Elder race…" Raethun wondered. "Could they have been the makers of the Island Treasures? And is that why, of all the places in Celidon, we should see another of their creations just where we think the Sword is?"

Maelbrigt and Eadgar grinned in response, and understanding dawned on the others.

"Bugger me, we found it!" the veteran breathed.

"Well, not quite," Eadgar cautioned, "but we're surely on the right track. Look around you; has anyone else noticed what this wood is made up of?"

They all turned to gaze about them. They stood on the edge of the great oaks on the western edge of the bowl, and were aghast as realisation set in. In the pantheon of the Sacred Trees the oak was the tree of the west and represented autumn and maturity. While to their right they could see a copse of ash trees, just where they should be in the south, the tree of summer. Tall as the warriors' spears they made, there they stood, symbolic of vigour. To the left, in the north, stood the brooding darkness of the ancient yews of winter and old age, massive in girth and still carrying their berries. Old legends told of the yew being associated with the fairy folk, who were known to be able to disappear in the darkness beneath old specimens, and it was missed by none of them that this was the way the Squint had last been seen heading.

There must a space of some sort ahead, they agreed, for the light was clearest there, but beyond that they could just make out the silver bark of birches. Not only the Sacred Tree of the east and spring, but also associated with the fae they recalled. And scattered in spaces between the larger trees and around the edge there were rowans everywhere.

"Aren't rowans also supposed to mark dragons' dens?" a worried Raethun asked, clearly thinking that if one creature from mythology could suddenly be found alive and well, the potential was there for more to appear.

"I don't know about that," Maelbrigt said, "but I do know that they grow around all the stone circles I've ever seen in the north, and we don't know what most of those were used for. Some people are reputed to have disappeared walking through the centre of a circle at the wrong time of year. Or should we think of them as having been fae folk who made it here almost fully for a time?"

Someone coughed nervously.

442

"Well we'll never find out standing here," Maelbrigt decided. "Come on, let's make our way into that clearing."

The seven of them walked cautiously out into the open air and were astonished at what they found there. The chapel was nothing like they had expected. In the midst of the clearing stood a small, round building with a domed roof. The outer walls were unadorned except for a tracery of beautifully wrought ivy, which scrambled up the walls and then wove its way around the base of the domed roof to create a decorative guttering. It stood isolated in a perfect green circle devoid of grave mounds or markers.

At first they thought that someone must have cut the grass around it, or brought in sheep to graze on the close cut turf. Only as they stepped out onto it did they realise that it was, in fact, a dense carpet of low growing thyme which circled the place. As they stepped forward, the thyme they crushed beneath their feet filled the air with its pungent scent. Someone might approach this place silently, but short of flying there was no way to avoid stepping on the thyme and releasing the fragrance.

"Wild mountain thyme!" Raethun was amazed. "That old tale was right!"

"And what a simple, clever defence!" Maelbrigt marvelled. "Even one man – and even in the dead of winter – would create a discernible fragrance by the time he'd got from the edge to the chapel. Plenty of warning and so subtle you might not notice what you'd done until it was too late!"

They advanced with care while circling the building in an attempt to find the door. Finally, having passed around to the north and then the east, they came on the door on the southern circuit of wall. A beautiful arch was wound around with what they suspected were vine leaves. Grape vines grew poorly in the cool climate of the Islands, and none present had ever seen them in real life, but the bunched fruit made it likely that that was what they were. Intertwined amongst the branches were tiny faces looking out. Some were exotic looking birds eagerly devouring the fruit, while other were animals but with almost human expressions. Suddenly Raethun dug Maelbrigt in the ribs with his elbow, forgetting his junior position in his excitement.

"Look! A squint!"

Sure enough, right by the door handle was a beaked face which was almost identical to the beast they had seen earlier. Right on cue, behind them they heard the frantic pattering of feet. Into their midst scurried the little creature, chattering unintelligibly. Maelbrigt had had his hand outstretched to the handle and now withdrew it, instead reaching out to the little beast which seemed to be doing its best to chase them off, flapping its front paws and snapping its beak – although whether that was just part of the way it spoke or not, they could not tell. For a second the men's hands went to hilts, then they looked at the beast and to their utter amazement saw tears in its eyes and stopped in their tracks.

"It's alright," Eadgar said in a reassuring voice, just as if he was talking to a distressed horse or hound. "Steady now, we're not going to hurt you."

Something in his tone of voice may have conveyed itself to the distraught creature, or maybe it was the men moving their hands away from their weapons, but the squint seemed to calm a fraction. That was until Maelbrigt's hand made contact with it, just having time to register the shock of touching soft, warm fur. It let out an ear-piercing squeak and leaped back, while Maelbrigt was thrown backwards into Raethun, who just about managed to prop up his commander without falling over himself. The men seized their swords once more as a dazed Maelbrigt shook his head.

"No! Stop!" he commanded as the men began to draw. "Put your weapons away! Now!"

He stood up, swayed, rubbed his forehead, then bent down more to a level with the squint.

"It's all right little chap, come on, we won't hurt you," he said gently, this time keeping his hands clasped in front of him. Without breaking his gaze on the dazed squint, who had retreated several paces after their encounter, he spoke to his men. "That was my fault. I didn't think. He's between existences, and my touching him pulled him to me, and me to him. Neither of us meant to hurt the other, but we did. He's terrified! I felt that. It was like we were linked for a second. I tell you, he's worried that if we go in there that we'll destroy something."

"We wouldn't be sacrilegious!" an appalled Raethun protested.

Maelbrigt shook his head. "No we wouldn't, but I don't think he even understands that concept. It's simply the act of entering. That's all it will take, or at least in his mind that is, for us to harm something inside. The trouble is, I don't know how to tell him we have no choice."

However, if the brief touch had shown Maelbrigt something of the squint's mind it seemed to have done the reverse too. For a moment longer the squint stood shivering, and shimmering in and out of focus, then crept forwards towards Maelbrigt like a dog that had been beaten too often being shown the hand of kindness. The men stepped back and let the wary squint edge closer to Maelbrigt until it stood before him. Its head went on one side as it regarded him, ears twitching, and sad eyes tearing. Then it moved between him and the door, but only so that its paw touched the door before him. As the squint attempted to press the lever, Maelbrigt's hand reached over and enclosed it as he too depressed the handle.

There was a *clink*, and a hiss as if air had been let out, a second before the door swung inwards. Yet there was simultaneously a dizzying shift in the air which seemed to crackle with energy, and for a second it was almost as if the whole chapel had rotated half a degree and then returned to its original position. Men cried out in alarm and the squint gave a howl of pain and collapsed in Maelbrigt's arms. For the first time he felt the full weight of the creature.

"Oh Rowan!" he cried, "We've forced it fully into our world! Quick! Help me get him inside, and someone run back to that stream and get some water for him."

Eadgar and the old veteran grabbed a hefty back paw each and helped Maelbrigt carry the squint inside. They were so taken with caring for the beast that for a moment they failed to look about them, but once Maelbrigt had held a burnished blade to the squint's beak and it misted with breath, they looked up.

"Someone run and fetch Aldred!" he commanded, and one of the men turned to do his bidding.

Inside, the chapel was breathtaking. They had expected to see the long-familiar carved images of the sacred varieties of trees, but nothing had prepared them for this. For a start off, it was much bigger than it had appeared from outside, for a good third of the chapel was below the outside ground level. But what was astonishing was the amount of real foliage within the space. The stone of the roof had a translucent quality which allowed light to filter through it, but it was also now apparent as to why the guttering was necessary. For around the walls there were minute pinholes of light from outside. In some cunning fashion tiny passages had been incorporated into the carvings, so that behind a bunch of rowan berries, or from beneath an oak leaf, instead of shadows a glimmer of light shone.

At the moment the chapel was filled with the scent of the thyme from their approach, but complementing the sights and smell were soft whisperings. The same tiny channels were allowing the woodland breeze to drift in and over other carvings which were acting like wind chimes. Tuned to perfection, the sound never seemed to be still or irritating, but gave the chapel a feeling of being alive, as though it was almost breathing. In this living stone space, real plants thrived. At the base of the walls, where a shelf ran which could have been meant to be used as seating, there were all manner of ferns. Some had strap-like leaves, others delicate fronds in browns or greens, with the smallest creating individual seating divisions in the circular seat, and the largest at the foot of the basin in the centre. This was surrounded by a lip only one stone high and within it a little forest spring bubbled clean and fresh.

Nothing hung from the roof, but up the walls the carvings of the tree trunks and branches had been craftily curved to make small pockets, which allowed plants which would naturally have grown high in the tree canopy to make their homes. In the shelter of the chapel, plants from far-off countries survived the Islands' winter, and draped the carvings in exotic foliage of their own.

The squint lay on part of the bench, his breathing shallow and ragged, but alive. Just possibly more alive than he had ever been before, Maelbrigt thought. As the man ran in with his water bottle filled from the stream, Maelbrigt gently dripped water into the squint's mouth and stroked its fur reassuringly.

However, Eadgar and Raethun had chance to look around more, and what they saw in the central pool brought Maelbrigt to their sides the moment they called. There at the bottom of the pool lay a sword, and what a sword! In the northern Islands there remained the memory of some Attacotti coming screaming out of the cover of the heather-clad hills wielding great two-handed swords, and this was of the same breed. It was a monster! The hand-grip was meticulously laid roped wire with a curved cross-guard, braced where it would not get in the way of the holder. The blade tapered in the normal fashion for the first third of the blade, but then there was another crosspiece like a pair of daggers, wicked and still looking razor sharp despite its immersion. From then the rest of the blade was barbed down to a vicious point, and the whole thing would have stood as tall as any of them.

"Spirits! Would you look at the size of that thing!" Raethun said in awe.

Eadgar tentatively reached out with his hand, but the second his hand touched the water it seemed to go solid. For a moment all was as still as if the sword had become encased in solid glass, but then, beneath the surface, something began to shimmer. A face came into focus and turned its gaze onto those looking down on it. An old face with a thin white beard, it spoke with an old man's querulous voice.

"Who comes to disturb my rest?" it demanded. "How did you get past the watchers? Where is the key? Why has no-one come to take my place? Who are you?"

The three looked at one another in surprise, then Eadgar answered for them, just in case whoever was perceived as being the leader came under attack.

"We are Knights of the Order of the Cross. We've come here seeking the Sword."

"Why?" the old face demanded.

Eadgar blinked but rallied to reply, "The Islands are under threat from the DeÁine. We fear they may use their weapons against us and destroy all of us."

"DeÁine?" the white whiskers spluttered. "Don't be ridiculous we drove them out, far from the Islands! They can't have come back so soon. You lie!"

The three looked at one another in confusion.

"No, no word of a lie, I promise," Maelbrigt insisted. "They've come from New Lochlainn. They're going to launch an attack through the Gap of Brychan."

"Rubbish!" the talking head argued back. "New Lochlainn? No such place! Never heard of it! You lie!"

That threw the Knights. How long had this figure been here? His eyes were searching the interior of the chapel as the querulous voice called out, "Key? Where are you? Summon the watchers! Get them out of here!"

"You do *know* of the Battle of Moytirra?" Raethun asked carefully.

"No! You lie! You will die!"

"Shit!" Maelbrigt swore. "Everyone out, now! And that includes you Raethun!" He knew better than to try to get Eadgar to go, but all the others retreated to outside of the door. Nothing happened though, which made Maelbrigt wonder whether it was waiting for either himself or Eadgar to move.

In the tense silence they suddenly heard the crashing of hooves coming down the hillside, and they vaguely registered that the man who had gone for help had begun calling the moment he was out of the wood. Aldred must have been returning and been right nearby for him to be so quickly on his way down. Meanwhile Maelbrigt and Eadgar said nothing, worried in case they broke the stalemate, while the disembodied head continued to call for the key as though it were alive.

After what felt like an age, but must only have been minutes, they heard the men outside calling to others and telling of what they had found, then Aldred's familiar silhouette appeared at the door. Cautiously he walked in to stand beside Maelbrigt and raised an eyebrow in query. Maelbrigt leaned in to him and softly whispered into his ear what had transpired, at which even the normally unflappable Aldred looked nonplussed for a moment. Then he carefully leaned over the pool.

"Would it violate your instructions to ask who ruled Celidon the last time you heard?" Aldred asked.

"Ha! A trick question!" the face chortled. "The same king who rules the rest of the islands, of course!"

The three men took a step backwards.

"King?" hissed Eadgar. "There hasn't been a king in hundreds of years!"

"Sacred Trees, how long has it been since anyone came here?" wondered Maelbrigt. "Can you remember the names of all the old kings, Aldred? Because I'm sure I can't!"

"No," Aldred replied slowly, deep in thought, "but maybe we don't need *all* of them. Think about it. You said he thinks the DeÁine have only just been defeated, and when would it be most likely that the Sword would have been hidden? Straight afterwards, surely?"

"Which would make it King Hrothgar?" Eadgar said, wracking his memory for what he had been taught as a child.

Aldred nodded. "And didn't Hrothgar have a great sword, supposedly made by the immortal smith Weland?"

Maelbrigt stepped to the pool edge again and stared down at the face.

"Was Hrothgar the king when you were …left …here?" he asked. "Because if so, I hate to tell you this but over five and a half centuries have passed since then. There are no more kings! The line died out and now each Island rules itself. Thirty years ago the DeÁine began to launch aggressive attacks into western Brychan, having overrun the east of the Island with their slave armies. Then twenty-six years ago we fought a great battle at Moytirra, and used the old castles in the mountains to seal the Gap of Brychan, but since then the DeÁine have been a constant threat.

"Now we know they've been searching old manuscripts for anything that might give them a clue as to where their pieces of Power might be hidden. Their war-mages have come undercover into the Islands and are searching even as we speak, and if they find them we have no power to resist them."

For the first time a shadow of doubt flickered across the face, and Eadgar pressed home the advantage. "That's why no-one has come to relieve you. Nobody knew you were here. Over the years the existence of a guardian was forgotten. I don't know when or how you should have been replaced, but even by then the knowledge of that had long gone."

The face creased into a frown, and for a moment they thought it was about to accuse them of lying again, but then the eyes shot open in surprise. The three men were still staring into the pool so hard they had not heard the squint come up behind them, and the reflection of its sad pointed face made them start as much as it did the disembodied face.

"Ah, Key! There you are! What have you done?" the head demanded of the poor distressed beast.

The little squint chirruped and chattered frantically at the face, his beak getting lower and lower until its tip grazed the hard surface. Instantly the glass seemed to dissolve back into water.

"*Aaaaagh*," the old face moaned, "so long! It's true then! All those years have passed?"

"I'm sorry, yes they have," Aldred said sympathetically.

"It's come, and in the time of my caring," the old face said and shook its head in sorrow. Then Aldred noticed that the face seemed to be ageing faster now the squint had broken the spell.

"Quickly!" he spoke insistently. "You must help us! What do we do now to get the Sword?"

"Only the one who will wield it can take it from the pool," said the voice, already beginning to sound like dusty leaves. "He, and he only, has the power to use it to the full. Others may take it once it's in the world, but for them it will only be a sword as any other."

"How do we get it out of the pool?" Eadgar demanded urgently, for the face was now in danger of disintegrating.

"Speak its name!" the voice crackled. "Speak the sword's name ..." And the face disappeared as if blown to dust and settled in the water at the bottom.

"Shit! Shit! Shit!" Eadgar exploded, turning and pounding his fist into his palm. "The bloody thing has a *name*? And how are we supposed to know that?"

Maelbrigt and Aldred had both gone pale at the disappearance of the talking head, looking in dread at one another. Then Aldred gasped.

"Hrothgar! What was the name of Hrothgar's sword? That has to be it!" And ran to the door and called the question out to the assembled men waiting outside.

Raethun appeared at the door,

"Naejling! I think Hrothgar's sword was Naejling!"

Maelbrigt leaned over the pool and declaimed 'Naejling' as he thrust his hand down into the water. The pool was deeper than it seemed and he was up to his armpit in the water without touching the sword, but at least it had not frozen over again. As his friends rushed forward, he took a deep breath and immersed himself in the water.

For one awful moment, as his hand grasped the hilt, they thought it might not come free. Then they saw it move, but now the problem was the weight of the thing. Maelbrigt was unbalanced and could not pull himself up and the sword as well. Eadgar grabbed his free hand, while Aldred and Raethun seized his belt and pulled, but the surprise was the squint. He went nose first into the pool, sinking his claws into Maelbrigt's collar and pulling his head up so that he could breathe, but seemed to bring something more than simple strength to the act.

All of a rush, the Sword and Maelbrigt came over the edge and clattered onto the floor, and everyone fell over themselves. The squint shook himself and showered the chapel with droplets of water.

"Don't do that to me!" a shaken Eadgar remonstrated with his former captain. "I'm too old for you to scare me witless like that again!"

Maelbrigt shook the water from his hair then gave a huge grin.

"Yes, but we've got it haven't we! We've got the first of the Island Treasures!"

The word spread outside and a cheer went up, but Aldred was looking thoughtful, causing Maelbrigt to give him a quizzical glance.

"You do realise what this means, though, don't you?" Aldred asked. At Maelbrigt's blank look he went on, "You're the one who has to wield it in any battle we have with the DeÁine. It was only ever going to come free for the right man. That doesn't mean that there was ever only one person who could pull it free. But once free it belongs to one man only, and now that's you!"

In stunned surprise, Maelbrigt got up and tottered outside lugging the huge sword, followed closely by the squint.

"And that's not the only thing that's attached itself to you!" Aldred murmured in amusement as he followed the unlikely pair outside.

Chapter 25

Sent on the Wind

Celidon: Yule – Eft-Yule

For days after leaving Maelbrigt, the rest of the party which had departed from Ergardia rode down a road which felt never ending. The illusion was largely created by the lack of change in the scenery, for the road followed the west coast of Celidon right down into the southern waist of the Island. In the distance on their left they would catch glimpses of the slate-grey sea across the frosted landscape. To their right rose the mountains, foothills piling up to jagged peaks, all covered in a thick layer of snow making one heap of rocks look much the same as another. At the end of the fourth day's ride they reached the small port of Bridge of Glas, where they were hospitably entertained by the men of the grange. Ruari was able to pass on the good news that Master Brego intended to send men to revitalise the Order in Celidon, which was immediate cause for celebration. Had it not been for the urgency of the mission, Ruari felt they would have been detained there for the whole of the festive season, they were so welcome.

It made him feel terribly guilty that few in the Order on the other Islands seemed to have thought what the effect of closing the Celidon sept would have been on the ordinary soldiers left behind. Committed as any Knight, they had been left in a dislocated limbo, not knowing when, or even whether, the preceptories would ever be fully functional again. It brought a lump to Ruari's throat to see how loyally these men had held on to the way of life and had tried to keep the standards going, even to the extent of carrying on recruiting and training younger men, when there was so little hope. Even Will was affected by the knowledge.

"By the Trees, Ruari," he softly commented when they got a moment alone. "How I wish I'd had troops this loyal! Oswine would never have got a foothold in Rheged with men like this."

"Don't sell our own men so short," Ruari gently chastised him. "Here they live a very isolated life. There are more people in Earlskirk alone than are left in every town on Celidon put together. They've worked miracles here, but from what I've heard from Ron, our men did wonders keeping the granges functioning in the face of such aggressive action by Fulchere and Tancostyl."

"Granted," Will conceded, "but what impresses me here is the sheer length of time they've kept going. Who knows what your men would have done if there'd been no prospect of a Master ever being elected?"

"Oh indeed!" Ruari agreed. "Here they had three years on minimal strength, and then they've had five more struggling on alone. At home ours have only had a year and a half with people making acquisitive moves against them, and at least our sept had the backing of powerful men like Jaenberht, who stopped anyone getting too carried away. And, more to the point, it's been in the interests of those who wanted us powerless to keep the infrastructure intact because of the money it generates. We've been lucky to live on the most fertile of all the Islands, and to have been given extensive grants of land over the generations. Here, nobody is that wealthy, and every grange has to be self-sufficient. That must make it so much harder to keep going when the level of man power drops through the floor, as it did here after Gavra Pass."

However, despite their deep desire to stop and help rejuvenate the grange and others like it in Celidon, there was no choice but to ride on. Luckily they were following the main road which everyone took if travelling from Ergardia to Celidon's capital, Cabrack, and so there were plenty of wayside inns in contrast to the rest of the Island. On the eve of the New Year they rode into the yard of a long, low, stone-built hostelry. Massive block-stone walls rose in a single storey covered by a steeply sloping slate roof, regularly punctuated by chimneys and the windows of the accommodation upstairs. The soldiers filled the place, but the landlord was glad of the trade. Miles from anywhere, he only had the local sheep farmers and their families coming down to celebrate, and they would not be stopping overnight.

Will, Sioncaet and Ruari shared one room, and Unferth, Waeles and Haethcyn another, with the twelve soldiers squeezed into the three remaining rooms and a couple of truckle beds down in the smaller public room. If they had been unprepared for the reception they got from the grange, they were even more stunned by the jubilant reception they got from the local people. They were given a heroes' welcome, with everyone eager to know when they could expect to see more men arriving.

The night therefore took on an air of even more excited anticipation, and Ruari resigned himself to the fact that all of his men were going to have mammoth hangovers the next morning by the way they were having drinks pressed upon them. At this rate he would be lucky if anyone was fit to ride before midday, and, with daylight in such short supply, he was dreading the thought that it might be easier to spend another night here than risk getting caught between inns in the freezing weather, since even on this road those were spaced a full day's ride apart.

In a valiant effort to ensure they rode on, he insisted that his men retire to bed as soon as the initial celebrations at midnight were past. The two unfortunate men who had been destined to have the truckle beds were faced with either being left to get hopelessly drunk and then struggle to keep up with the others if they stayed downstairs, or sleep on the floor upstairs and get some rest. Tempting though the landlord's excellent spiced beer was, they feared Ruari's wrath more and resigned themselves to a hard night on the floor. Everyone had therefore settled down and drifted off to sleep, despite the ongoing celebrations, when a commotion downstairs woke them.

Ruari, Will and Sioncaet all sat up, jolted into awareness.

"What in the Islands was that?" Will exclaimed.

"Sounded like someone screaming in pain," a dazed Sioncaet said, struggling off the truckle bed to light the lone candle in the flame of the dying fire.

Then another series of shrieks and howls rent the night. Without a word the three of them hauled on boots and jackets, grabbed their swords and dashed out of the door. In the corridor they encountered the rest of the men, all as perplexed as them, although those nearest the stairs were already dashing down them towards the sounds of a violent affray. A horrified, 'Lost Souls!' had them all racing to follow, and they found themselves in a bewildering tangle of folk.

"Help us!" the landlord pleaded, spotting the Knights.

"What's going on?" Ruari bellowed across to him.

"Spirits only know!" he cried. "One minute the last of them were getting ready to leave, then some of those who left a few moments earlier came charging back in and started trying to kill everyone!"

"Men! Pin down all those with coats on!" roared Will across the chaos, and the trained soldiers weighed in and began subduing the riotous locals.

It was soon obvious who the troublemakers were, since those who had only been defending themselves instantly backed off when confronted with trained fighters. The ones who had returned to wreak havoc, however, fought on like men possessed, and, with the other folk retreating from the fray, there developed small pockets of flailing limbs as two or three soldiers attempted to subdue one of the others. The soldiers quickly realised that stopping them was not an option, though, and began simply laying out the opposition. In short order there were seven unconscious local men and three women, and everyone breathed a sigh of relief.

"Thank the Trees you were here!" was the openly expressed and heartfelt opinion of the rest of the people.

"But what happened?" a puzzled Sioncaet asked them.

Everyone looked blank or shrugged, and the landlord tried to explain.

"The wind really started getting up something wicked after you went to bed. The old folk left there and then, but most folk lingered a bit. Then it started to get really rough." For the first time the men of the Order noticed that the wind was howling and shrieking around the inn outside, and that the fires were guttering and sparking in the ferocious gusts.

"Well then everyone decided they'd better get home. This lot left because they were all going to walk together since they were the worse for drink. They have to cross a wooden bridge over one of the mountain streams, and they were worried in case someone got blown off – it's not a long bridge but the drop's very steep. So off they went, and everyone else was getting their things together and saying their farewells when back in they came. They didn't say a thing. Just charged in snarling like wild animals and started laying into folk!"

Another voice said tremulously, "Hamish is dead! Ewan cut his throat like a sheep before he knew what was happening! They were friends. Why would he do that?"

"And Jamie and Seth!" someone else added. "But Seth was trying to kill him too! Jamie's over there."

They turned to see a tearful woman kneeling beside the bloody form of an unconscious young man. Unferth immediately went across and inspected the inert man.

"He's hurt badly," he told the assembly. "I don't think we should try moving him at all. Let's get some blankets down here and keep him warm. His arm's definitely broken, and the cut on his head needs stitching, but I'm worried what's going on inside. I'm sure he has broken ribs, but I don't like the way he's breathing even so. I'd rather he woke up and told us where he feels pain, or if he can even tell us anything at all."

"Is he the worst casualty, among the living that is?" Ruari asked.

A quick check of those sitting on the floor or benches confirmed that although there were several broken limbs and nasty cuts, the man called Jamie was the only one with wounds likely to prove fatal. Ruari had his men attend to the locals, since all had rudimentary knowledge of how to treat battlefield wounds, then drew the three Knights and Will and Sioncaet together on one side.

"I don't like this, not coming on the night of our arrival" he said, but got no further.

The door of the inn burst open and a wild-eyed couple staggered in.

"The Wild Hunt!" the woman screamed. "The Wild Hunt is riding!"

"We saw it!" the man gibbered. "We were up in the glen and it went past. We saw Seamus, Willy, Bob and Dougie fall on one another and start tearing one another to pieces!" His voice rose hysterically as he told them, "Then there was this cloud. All wild horses and riders and hounds!"

"And we saw a piece of it come down and take each of the boys as they died!" shrieked the distraught woman. "He's got them! Jolnir's got them!"

The six senior men looked at one another, then charged for the door, drawing their swords as they went. Overhead the sky was now clear, although there was still a ferocious wind blowing. Then Sioncaet called out and pointed southwards. There in the distance was the edge of an immense cloud, totally different in character to the natural formations to the north.

"Holy Spirits," breathed Haethcyn, "what in the Islands is that?"

"I don't want to believe it, but I fear those two may have been right," a disconcerted Waeles said, sounding as though he was desperately hoping someone would tell him otherwise. Yet nobody could think of any sane explanation for what they were seeing.

"I don't feel so good," Will suddenly said.

Ruari and Sioncaet whipped round to stare at him questioningly.

"I've got that itchy feeling again in the back of my mind," he told them, "like when we were back in Rheged and that bastard Tancostyl was trying to make me jump through hoops. I haven't had that since I crossed the water until just now. Not even last night. I've only just realised it because I thought it was just being woken up and being thrown unexpectedly into the fight, but now I'm sure it's not that."

"How bad is it?" Ruari demanded anxiously.

"Not as bad as Rheged," Will reassured him. "Nowhere near as bad as that, that's why I didn't catch on immediately. And it is fading …slowly. It's fading with that bloody cloud! The further it goes the better I'm feeling."

"The Abend!" Sioncaet and Ruari exclaimed in unison.

"There's something afoot!" Sioncaet declared. "This has to be the witches! It's right up their street."

"Then you don't think it's Jolnir himself?" Haethcyn asked, trying to keep the relief out of his voice.

"All I've ever heard of the Wild Hunt and Jolnir says that he himself cannot kill," Ruari said thoughtfully. "I wouldn't put it past the Abend, but just think what we've seen here tonight. Is it any coincidence that the worst affected are the young men? The ones who've been drinking the most heavily, leaving them the most suggestible? The ones who form our fighting force! There's not one older person amongst them, but most of the maturer folk were only a bit tipsy and they sobered up fast. What's the betting that at the front of that storm is some invisible cloud of a spell that makes men fall on one another and commit murder? It's guaranteed to cause havoc, and look where it's heading – straight for the most inhabited part of Ergardia and then on to Rheged."

"Aye, and there's no end to it going south," Sioncaet observed. "It goes right on beyond the horizon. I'd add to what Ruari's said with the thought that that thing could have come through the Brychan Gap, or at least the worst of it. Some of it must've come over the empty mountains, but I fear for what this means for southern Brychan."

With that dire warning in their minds they turned back towards the inn. Ruari was at the rear and paused for a final look up at the sky. In that moment the clouds to the north parted and the moon was revealed, shining bright, and he felt a tug at his spirit. He heard no voice or sound, but deep within him he felt something reaching out to him and summoning him to go north. Was it fancy or did he see, low and barely above the mountain top, a light suddenly appear, bright and piercingly clear, which blazed for just a second or two and then fade? Almost as if a signal light had been flashed to him alone?

Not enough sleep, MacBeth, he told himself sternly, *West, my lad, that's where you've got to go, and quickly going on tonight's goings on!* Yet, even as he wrapped himself in the blankets and tried to get some sleep for what was left of the night, the thought would not go away that he ought to be going north instead.

They left early in the morning, but not before seeing to the locals. Those who had run amok the night before woke with no memory of what had happened, totally bemused as to why they were tied up. After close

457

questioning they were released and Ruari had the unenviable task of telling them how many they had injured, and explaining to their victims that there had been no knowing intention behind the deeds. The news of the Abend's bewitchment was greeted with anger and consternation, but there was too much sorrow on both sides for anyone to feel much relief that there was little chance of the same happening again soon.

The troop rode on, worried about what they would find at the next stopping places. By the time they rode into Cabrack a week later, they had stopped three lynchings of befuddled murderers, and a near riot of confused locals against the beleaguered grange at Dunskey Castle, whom they blamed for mysterious deaths in the village. There it had not been helped by the fact that a bird from Brego had obviously got through, and the men of the grange had earlier been seen arming themselves and putting everything in readiness for new troops. Without knowing why all the activity was taking place, the local folk were already fearful that the soldiers might have decided to launch a bid to become masters of the area, or just leave them to it and had given up on the Order altogether. It was with great relief that they heard from someone whom they saw as having authority that nothing could be further from the truth, and that the Knights were finally returning.

However, as soon as they passed through the southern gap into the west of the Island the tales of the Hunt dried up. Here they had only experienced a vicious, but normal, winter storm with no apparitions attached. All the way, though, the riders had been plagued by foul weather. The wind had driven the snow off the mountains into drifts across the road, and periodically new falls had added to their misery. Had the road not been so well defined, and marked out by tall poles against the eventuality of drifting, the men felt sure that on several occasions they would have lost it altogether.

Once in Cabrack they were heartened to find that the messenger birds from Brego had got this far too. The former head of the disbanded Order, who was now chancellor of the Island, was courtesy itself, and had already set things in motion for their sea journey. Down in the harbour several hefty merchantmen wallowed and rolled despite being tied up to the quays, and nobody fancied a trip in them. However, there was also a sleek man-of-war tied up, which rode with ease those choppy waves which made it into the sheltered harbour.

Ruari was delighted to learn that this was ready to sail on the following morning's tide with them on board, and so they enjoyed a relaxed night in the comfort of the great castle which dominated the town. The ship was as good as she looked and the captain a canny seaman who was not fearful of putting to sea in such adverse conditions. For two days and nights they hugged the coast of Celidon heading south-west towards the north-east spur of Brychan, taking shelter from the worst of the wind, which in any case was blowing them away from the jagged cliffs and not onto them. However, they reached a point when there was no alternative but to cross the open sea on the narrow stretch between the two Islands. For two days they pitched and rolled at anchor in the shelter of a small bay, but finally the captain declared the storm had abated enough to risk the open sea. Ruari had intended for them to anchor at Breslyn itself, but now the wind was against them.

"I'll land you on Brychan never fear," the captain told him, "but Breslyn is out of the question. With this wind, we won't just go into the harbour – we'll be flying into the harbour, up over the quay, and be spread in broken bits of wood up the hill behind if we try it! We'll make the race across, aiming between the main headland and the first island to the north, then come around once we're in the lee of the whole of the peninsula. On that stretch there are lots of tiny harbours for the fishermen which hardly warrant a pin prick on the map. One of them is barely a day's march from Breslyn."

And with that Ruari had to be content. But the captain was as good as his word, and with great skill he manoeuvred the ship for another two exhausting days in gale-force winds and ferocious seas, safely into the waters of northern Brychan. Here the worst of the continuing high seas were muted since the westerly wind was being blocked by the land, as their captain had suspected.

It was something of a damp landing on a small natural rock jetty, done in a mad scramble as some of the crew held the ship close to the rock with ropes and poles as the soldiers hurriedly jumped off, other sailors throwing the packs down to them. Then the ship was gone, pulling swiftly out to sea and away from the dangers of the rocky shore. Mercifully the cloud was high and light, and they could navigate by the moon and stars once the daylight had gone. There was nowhere to take shelter and so they pressed on, for it was warmer walking, and they were eager for the warmth within the castle at Breslyn.

It was therefore with a jolt that they pulled up at the top of the crest, which should have looked down on the castle, and saw the blackened ruin by the moonlight.

"Sacred Trees! What happened here?" Ruari gasped, shaken to the core at seeing the immense castle he had previously visited so devastated.

"Whatever it was, it wasn't recent," Sioncaet observed. "Look, the snow is all over the floors and wreckage. That hasn't been disturbed since it fell."

They hastily descended to the ruin and began exploring. Someone had obviously been back and carried out burial duties, going by the neat row of hummocks near what had once been the chapel. Equally, though, there was nobody here now. It was a severe blow to Ruari, for he had counted on getting horses here, but more importantly there was no shelter for the rest of the night. Some rummaging around unearthed enough wood to start a reasonable fire, which was laid and lit in the angle of two walls, where the remnants of a stone-vaulted roof gave partial cover. It was a squeeze to fit all eighteen of them into the cramped space, but packed together their body heat was beneficial to all of them, and if it was hardly comfortable at least they were not going to freeze to death.

By morning, though, Ruari had no further idea of what to do next. From memory there were no other preceptories in the neighbouring countryside who they could go to for horses, and local farmers were unlikely to be able to provide sufficient horses for all of them. On foot it would be a long cold walk, and they had not come prepared with enough supplies for a long trek. It was Sioncaet who came up with the best solution when he suggested that they see if they could signal to the ship. With the westerly wind still blowing hard, and with no urgency anymore, he thought their captain might well have chosen to lie off shore and wait for the wind to change to a more favourable direction. So they set off on the weary trek back over the headland, retracing their own footsteps until they were looking back down onto the cove.

Everyone breathed a sigh of relief when they saw the distant shape of the warship and set to with a will to build a signal fire. It took the rest of the day to attract the attention of the sailors, and for them to then tack the ship back to shore. As night fell the weary soldiers climbed into the ship's boat and were rowed in two parties back to the ship. The captain was appalled to hear of what they had found and could offer no explanation, confirming that when he had been this way in the summer the castle had been intact, for he had stopped there for fresh water. However, he was willing to take them further north to Roselan, since he would not risk trying to fight against the wind and tide to cross back to Celidon while the sea was being driven so hard through the separating strait.

For Ruari this was in many ways saving time, for his search lay in the countryside around Roselan. But Will's quest to track Quintillean and the two young hostages could be seriously compromised by landing so much farther north. He and Sioncaet had intended to ride straight for Nefyn where many roads joined. If there had been no sightings of their quarry passing north through this narrow bottleneck, they'd intended to ride south at least as far as the Knight's castle of Vellyn. Just north of Vellyn was a lonesome trail which headed up into the mountains, and on over the high passes and sheep trails of the Brychan Line into New Lochlainn. Although they were fairly sure that it would be impassable in the current heavy snow, once that way was ruled out, if the fugitives were still missing then they had to have gone round the north coast, or for the southern route being covered by Oliver and Labhran. Now though, Will would have to assume that they had gone north, for there was no time to ride back even as far as Nefyn, let alone Vellyn, and yet still hope to catch Quintillean before he made DeÁine territory if indeed he had come this way.

It took four days to sail to Roselan with the first three in calmer conditions. Luckily they had already tied up to the quay in the morning when the winds began piling up the seas again in the afternoon. They were warmly welcomed by a surprised captain of the castle and found beds for the coming night, whilst over a lunch of hot and filling smoked-fish soup he explained what he knew of the demise of Breslyn.

"It's Ealdorman Berengar you need to speak to – at least if he still lives, Sacred Trees protect him! He was the one alerted to what had happened. A Knight passed through here under his orders warning of the possibility of a member of the DeÁine on the loose, and a powerful one at that."

"A DeÁine?" the new arrivals cried as one and the captain looked startled.

"We also hunt one of the DeÁine who took two youngsters hostage far off in Ergardia," Ruari explained.

"Well this happened back in Winterfalling," the captain told him. "Could this be the work of your DeÁine?"

"Winterfalling?" Will exclaimed. "No. In that case it couldn't be. The one we were hunting was spotted still in Ergardia in Samhainn. There's no way even one of the Abend could be in Brychan in Winterfalling, get all the way to the west coast of Ergardia and back to where he was seen, and it still be only in Samhainn."

"One of the *Abend*?" The captain and his men looked appalled. "Not just any DeÁine? Sacred Trees, tell me that isn't so?"

"I'm afraid it is," Sioncaet said sadly. "What your Ealdorman Berengar might not have known back then is that we have every reason to believe that the Abend are up to something. The war-mages have been spotted on other Islands. Tancostyl is certainly on Rheged posing as a priest in the royal household. Abbot Jaenberht over there also had word from Master de Burh that Calatin's on the loose in Prydein. We're on the trail of Quintillean, which means it's pretty certain the one who razed Breslyn must be Eliavres. Anarawd, we've heard, remains in New Lochlainn with the witches, but for who knows how long?"

"You must send messages out to your Grand Master that a DeÁine attack may be imminent," Ruari insisted, but the captain only looked sicker.

"Then I fear we are undone!" he cried in a low voice. In answer to the newcomers' surprise he told them, "The Grand Master of Brychan is dead!"

"What?" Ruari gasped. "Are you sure?"

In answer the captain got up and went out, returning shortly with a message in his hand. It was in the tiny cramped shorthand that all the Order's message writers used to squash as much as possible into something which could be attached to a bird's leg. On the fine vellum lay a spider's web of words, and Ruari found himself wishing he had arm extensions as he held it out to try to read it, and silently cursed getting older.

"By the... No, surely not! ... Sacred...! Cross of ....! ....No!"

"Will you stop doing that!" exploded Will, looking over his shoulder. "You're driving us all nuts! For Spirit's sake tell us what the bloody thing says! You know I can't read your infernal codes!"

"Grand Master Rainer was poisoned along with the commanders of Seigor and Craws and their aides back in Aer-Yule at Garway. Actually *in* the Order's main headquarters! How could that happen?"

Ruari's party all sat in shock as the distressed captain tried to explain.

"From what we've heard since, Berengar arrived there with many men and Esclados of Rhue – a totally trustworthy, veteran Knight – and with them a young woman and man. They had some urgent message for the Grand Master and went immediately into his office with the Master and his two Seconds. Unfortunately those men are now dead too, so we don't know what was said. The girl and man left, Berengar and Esclados followed them in a hurry leaving others of their party behind, and going who knows where. They are innocent of what happened, as far as our messages tell, for it was after that that Rainer called the captains to him. They drank poisoned mead while in conference, probably put there by a squire who, it turns out, Berengar was about to expel from the Order. One Jacinto by name. However, Jacinto too has disappeared.

"The Order is in chaos and the castles of the western chain have been snowbound since before the murder. Everything's having to be done by bird, and we're using the few hawks we have trained for such work, as they're the only ones strong enough to fly in this weather and not be prey to the flocks of rooks and ravens we've been plagued with since New Year. If he can be found, it's been agreed that Berengar should become Grand Master, at least for the near future, since he seems to be the only one who has the faintest idea what this is all about. And now you tell me the Abend are on the move. Things could hardly be worse!"

"Oh yes it could!" Will said gloomily. "The Abend seem to have conjured up something that may or may not be the Lord Jolnir and his Wild Hunt! It passed over many of the Islands on New Year's Eve and into New Year's Day."

"We saw nothing of it here," one of the local Knights exclaimed in amazement.

"No you wouldn't have," Ruari told them. "You're beyond the northern extreme of where it travelled. We've only seen the edge of it ourselves, but that was bad enough. The Abend wove some sort of glamour into the leading edge which drove folk to turn on one another, killing blindly."

"Sacred Trees!" several voices invoked.

"We fear greatly for what may have happened in southern Brychan on that night. Have you had any messages from the far south since then?" Sioncaet asked.

With great relief the captain said that, yes, they had had messages at least from Redrock, and that they had relayed a message which had come from Dinas in turn with no mention of a massacre – and that had to have started out at least a couple of days after the turn of the year. It had mentioned a terrible fire at Arlei on New Year's Day, though, which had claimed many lives and destroyed many buildings.

"The same thing, no doubt about it," Ruari said pensively, "What we saw must've gained some momentum as it fed off the departed, but the end result is every bit as bad. It's bound to affect Brychan's ability to defend itself. Were many troops lost?"

"No," the captain told him, almost afraid to add, "but only because the army wasn't there."

"Not there? Where in the flaming Underworld had the bloody army gone then?" Will asked, barely able to contain his frustration at the scale of the disaster looming.

"To Caersus. The army went to Caersus. And before you ask me, I have absolutely no idea why King Edward should call out all his reserves, and march on a town whose only claims to fame are a castle and the biggest cathedral in southern Brychan. But two days before the New Year, my message said King Edward rode out with all his men and headed west. Since then we've heard that they passed Dinas, so they were definitely heading west, but from then on we have no castles on their route, and so we've had no word of them. Now, with what you've told us, we must fear that they may have perished in the storm."

"Maybe not." Sioncaet was staring at the ceiling and obviously thinking hard. "What do the Abend want? Not the DeÁine, I mean, but the Abend in particular." The others all looked at him expectantly. "Let's think about it. ...How much bad odour have they been in with the Donns and the other pure-breds at court since the fiasco at Gavra Pass?"

As someone went to answer him Ruari shushed them to silence. Maelbrigt had told him that when Sioncaet thought aloud like this the wise man shut up and listened.

"The Donns have been spitting blood at the defeat – no doubt about that! The Abend must have spent the last few years totally out of the royal circle – unknown disgrace for them. *Mmmm*... That would prompt the kind of moves we've seen already. ...A lone attempt to grab power. ...But who have we here and what would they do? ...We've been after Quintillean who would never consider power sharing, but what of the others? Tancostyl's as bad as Quintillean, but he's been in Rheged for a long time. Calatin was always the dreamer. The one who wanted the Power and as much of it as he could get, but cared nothing for earthly prestige. But what about Eliavres? *Mmmm* ...he's crafty and he likes his creature comforts..."

"You sound like you know them personally!" a startled Knight could not refrain from exclaiming before Ruari could stop him.

Sioncaet blinked and then smiled distantly. "*Mmmm* …yes I did, for over a century actually." The castle Knights gaped at him in astonishment, which he registered enough to try to explain. "I was over there you see — before Gavra that was. And what most people forget is that those nine are as much in competition with one another as anyone. Quintillean wants to remain head and to that end spends much of his time plotting with Masanae. Those two hardly ever deigned to speak to the king, let alone the Donns or the Arberth who do most of the day to day governing, and in the process they got right up the noses of all the pure bloods. You have no idea how infuriating someone can get when you've had to put up with their funny ways for the long lives of the DeÁine. The Abend might be the ones who focus the Power – which all DeÁine admittedly see as their divinely given right, or inheritance – but the Power hasn't helped any of them that much since they came back to the Islands from the barren wastes of the far south."

"The far south?" the captain mouthed silently to Ruari. "He knows where they came from?"

Sioncaet saw him. "Yes, I know, and I know because I came with them young man, and before you ask, yes I am DeÁine." That stunned everyone else into silence, and Ruari and Will to smug grins. "Now since the arrival in New Lochlainn the pure bloods have been getting a bit short on patience with the Abend. They want their Treasures back and they want to rule again, but the Abend haven't come up with a solution. Magda is, to all intents and purposes, going steadily insane, but she still remembers a time when the Abend were feted by all the DeÁine, and she hates their retreat into solitude. She's one of the ones who still talks to those of rank and isn't seen as threatening. Helga's too cold to make any alliances, and Calatin is downright eccentric even for the Abend. But Magda trained Eliavres."

The assembled company gasped, even Ruari. This was new to all. "Now Eliavres is a different kettle of fish. The others tend to underestimate him, but he's more dangerous than Anarawd by far. He's dangerous because he listens. He listens to the other DeÁine. I was always catching him sitting quietly in some alcove listening to the random conversations of those at court.

"Now I wouldn't be at all surprised if young Eliavres has been listening to the Donns and their complaining. And knowing him, I wouldn't put it past him to have come up with some plan that would tickle the palate of the Donns. (I doubt there would be anything that Anarawd could say that would induce the Donns to move for him again. He wrecked his chances for the next century or two with his double-dealing at Gavra Pass.) But Eliavres would know just how to plant bait that the Donns would bite at."

Suddenly Sioncaet was totally focused and making eye contact with the rest of those around him. "What if Eliavres has offered them an easy victory over the army of Brychan? Haven't we all been saying how unseasonable the weather has been? The witches have a real skill with the weather, and Eliavres would know how to offer titbits to them to get them to snow-in the Knights. How often have your forts been this badly snowed-in so early in the year?"

"Not in living memory," the stunned captain replied. "There wouldn't have been any point in building the castles there if they were always cut off! The odd few days yes, but not like this! That's why they're where the mountains are already descending into New Lochlainn – the castles only get cut off when there's been heavy snow in New Lochlainn first."

"Well not this year, I bet!" Sioncaet said emphatically. "In fact I wouldn't mind the odds on there not having been enough snow to wet a mouse's paws over there. They've swept it all straight to the hills! And with it they've cut off the most formidable part of the armed force of Brychan. Now the snow's here, and with the coldest couple of months ahead they're not going to get out before spring either, are they? Which gives a DeÁine army time to have a nice easy victory over King Edward and his toy soldiers, walk into Arlei, and get themselves nicely settled in before the Knights can even act.

"And the worst of it is, you can't do a thing about it now, can you? That perverted king of yours wouldn't listen to reason even if you could get a bird to him in time. Meanwhile the Donns get the victory they've been craving for decades – it won't matter that it's small and easy, any victory is good news after the catalogue of disasters they've suffered. Eliavres gets a big step up in the pure DeÁine's estimation and carries Magda up with him, and suddenly all the DeÁine start remembering why they ever supported the Abend in the first place. After that it will be near impossible for Quintillean to speak for the Abend on the council, or anywhere else. Eliavres will be the one who has the ability to get backing for any further plans the Abend might have, and you can bet that he'll wring every concession he can get from Quintillean before he'll do a thing for him."

For a moment everyone sat in awed silence. Put like that it all made so much sense. Then a Knight at the back of the room spoke up.

"So what are we to do? How can we just sit back and do nothing?"

"I said you couldn't *prevent* it. Not that you couldn't *do* anything." Sioncaet corrected him. "I think you should send those birds out again. Tell those snowed-in on the western line exactly what's going on. That way they may be able to make some kind of move down into New Lochlainn earlier than they could back into Brychan. It might be possible to cut the DeÁine army off on the New Lochlainn side, do you see? Because the spring will come early there if they've had no snow. A few miles through drifts, and then an easy march, is a very different proposal to struggling down that great long mountain road in drifts up to your armpits, and they may not even know New Lochlainn is snow free. They might not think to look, either. This way they can at least send out scouts to find out. Warn them a whole DeÁine army could be heading their way!"

Chapter 26

 *The White Hare*

Brychan: Eft-Yule

From Roselan the party from Ergardia began to search in earnest. Each day Ruari rode out with Haethcyn and his lance, Will with Unferth's lance, and Sioncaet with Waeles'. Although they all knew their individual tasks, at this stage they were looking for any clues which would help with either mission. A week of finding absolutely nothing had them all tearing their hair with frustration, and then in one day everything happened at once. Ruari had ridden almost straight west from the castle into a long low valley that did little but reach a high pool, which then drained from the other side back down towards the road. The valley had been ignored up to now because the local Knights had said it went nowhere but back onto the road, and it had no flat areas where any building of consequence could ever have been, but now they were grasping at straws. However, Haethcyn's sergeant spotted an old man out trapping rabbits and had gone to chat to him. His excited call had the others joining him at the double.

"Quintillean was here!" he told them. "This man put up a stranger and his two nephews only the day before we landed!"

"What? It's taken them two *months* to get this far?" Ruari was suspicious.

But the old man was not to be doubted. He told them that the younger of the two boys had told of how their 'uncle' had been seriously ill for two whole weeks after they had landed. All their spare money had been used up and then some, so that the older lad had gone off with the shepherd of the farm they had last found lodging at, to work for over a week helping to round up the last of the flocks in payment. The old man told them that the younger boy had told him that he had tried to run away at that point.

"The lad whispered it to me in the night when the others were asleep. Said that he'd only been gone a day when his 'uncle' made a miraculous recovery and came after him and dragged him back. Was none too pleasant when he found the other one was gone as well, but that one was assured of coming back on account of being with the shepherd – and what could he say when the lad was paying the bill for him?

"Nasty piece of work that uncle was! I tried to offer the youngest a place with me. Poor little mite showed me where his 'uncle' had given him a beating for running off. 'Uncle', my arse! But he was a big brute and there was something about him that made you think twice about taking him on, especially at my age I'm ashamed to say."

"You were wise not to," Sergeant Aytoun told him. "He's murdered for less, at least this way you've lived to tell us so that we can follow him."

"Has he?" the old farmer muttered darkly.

"And he's certainly not the boys' uncle," Haethcyn added. "The whole reason we're chasing him is because he's kidnapped them."

"Then you'd best hurry up," the farmer said. "That youngster's in a bad way. They had to stop again with me because after the beating he took sick for days. I reckon that bastard did him some real harm 'cause he's thin in a way that doesn't look like it's his normal way, if you know what I mean."

"Oh Wistan!" Ruari's voice was full of regret. "We should've protected you better than this."

"Don't worry, sire," Haethcyn said firmly. "A week's no time to make up, and all the better for there being fewer ways to miss him now that we know he's got this far."

Yet Ruari was not destined to follow his heart and rescue his young half-nephew. As they entered the refectory having hurriedly kicked the snow off their boots, they met an equally excited Will talking animatedly to Sioncaet and Waeles, with Unferth and the lances around them.

"We've found something!" Will called as he caught sight of them.

"So have we," Ruari replied, "although I don't know whether you'll feel like celebrating too much at our news."

The others were as appalled as Ruari and Haethcyn's lance had been when they heard of how the brave Wistan had been treated for trying to evade his captor. However, Will's news was more pleasant. Having reached a tiny hamlet at the limit of another dead-end valley, Will had decided to accept the hospitality offered by the few inhabitants who were glad to have visitors to relieve the tedium of their isolation. In his inimitable style Will had begun flirting with the farmer's wife – although carefully given that her husband was there – in the course of which he had hinted at their quest to find the old castle. At that point the villagers had taken him to the old grandmother sitting knitting by the fire.

The old lady might have been half blind and deaf but there was nothing wrong with her memory. Delighted to find someone who wanted to hear one of her stories for a change, she had cheerfully given the Knights the whole thing in detail. How as a little girl she had gone up to collect the wild thyme which grew up on the little plateau in the hills. Her parents had scoffed at her when she said that she talked to the watcher in the woods, and whenever she had taken them up there he had not appeared. But she really had seen him, she told Will. How else could she have known that he was guarding someone called Hilderand? Was that the sort of name anyone from round here would have? No, of course not! So she would hardly have made something like that up, would she?

It had taken the rest of the afternoon to get away from the old lady who had a whole fund of other stories to tell them, but her family had been delighted at the gold crowns Will had pressed on them for their help.

"You can go back tomorrow and her son will take you up to the plateau!" Will told Ruari triumphantly. "You'd best take Waeles and his lads because it sounds like it could be a bit of a scramble in this weather, but the locals say it isn't impossible."

"Only if you and Sioncaet promise to set out first thing as well after Wistan and Kenelm."

"Of course we shall!" Sioncaet promised. "And with all possible speed. We can ride hard knowing where the granges and castles are, and that we can get fresh mounts there."

"I'll send Jensen with you," the captain of Roselan added. "He was Berengar's messenger and he's travelled up to Wynlas already, so he'll be recognised. That way you'll be given priority for whatever you need over anyone else. And I've a first rate lance under Sergeant Neil – good men every one – they can go with you just in case you need them. They're all marksmen archers, and the Knight they trained with before he died at Gavra Pass was a Forester, so they know a trick or two."

Ruari thanked him profusely, but nonetheless had trouble getting to sleep that night worrying about the two captives. It was drifting in and out of sleep in the long hours, though, that a memory (or was it a dream?) came to him. Maybe it was Will's tale of the hill-farm family telling stories that had done it. Whatever it was, he was back in the modest house he had shared with his mother outside of Earlskirk away from his father's court – a small boy sitting by the fire as his mother told him tales. He always remembered her as the beautiful blonde-haired woman she had been in his childhood, not the frail invalid eaten away by growths who he had visited at the infirmary of Maerske Abbey in Abbot Jaenberht's care the last time he had seen her. She had loved to tell him the stories of her own people from the land in the far north. Tales of giants and trolls, dwarves and fabled animals, living in a white world very like the one Ruari was now travelling in. But in among those there was something else.

He could remember her leaning in to him, secretive but smiling, the flickering flames of the fire dancing in her eyes as she said, "And always watch out for the wild mountain thyme, Ruari! It's a special plant for special places! You never know who you might meet there, so keep your wits about you! Doors open in those places."

"Doors?" the young Ruari had asked. "How can there be doors on a mountainside?" All the time knowing the answer, but wanting to hear her tell it one more time, because it sounded so much more exciting when she said it.

"Doors into other worlds. Not wooden ones like in a house, but places where the skin between our world and the next gets thin. Places where the *other* ones can slip through for a time. Sometimes they're people that look like us but are different. Sometimes they're animals."

"Like what?" the young Ruari had prompted, quivering with excitement.

"Like the squirrel who can run up and down the great pillar of the world from the Upperworld above and through this middle earth to the Underworld below! Or the stag who grazes in the Sacred Forest to keep the lesser plants from overwhelming the Trees. Or the badger who digs through the earth to make sure the Underworld stays buried. Or the goat whose milk is the mead of the gods," and she would then tell him another of the old northern legends.

Ruari had liked the old gods too. Not as much as the animals admittedly, but the gods sounded a lot more fun with their battles and feasts than the Sacred Martyrs the priests who taught him talked about. Except that he had learned not to talk about the gods to them. The priests got desperately wound up when anyone talked about the old ways, let alone the idea that there might be a whole pantheon of gods instead of one Great Maker, and so the maturing Ruari had gradually forgotten.

That was until tonight, when it suddenly did not seem so odd to be remembering the old ways. Sitting up in bed in the dark he kindled a candle, now very much awake, and tried to dredge every last memory back up. Weapons had names, it suddenly came back to him! The great heroes always had a sword with a name that was part of its power, something that made it more than a piece of metal. So maybe Hilderand was not a someone, maybe it was a some*thing*? A shield-shaped something!

Come the morning he was hardly refreshed for the exertions of the coming day, but he was going out with a great deal more of a feeling of certainty that they were on the right track at last. Will and Sioncaet met him in the refectory for breakfast, already carrying their saddlebags.

"So this is another farewell," Will said, but with all his old vigour, in contrast to the dazed wreck of a man Ruari had retrieved from Rheged.

"So it is," Ruari replied, hugging his old friend. "You be careful, Will! One brush with the Abend like you had is enough for any lifetime. Don't forget that, of everyone in your party, you'll be the most susceptible to Quintillean's glamours and spells of misdirection. No-one will think any worse of you for retreating if you get that feeling he's doing something strange – it's not cowardice, it's common sense. Trust to Sioncaet, even if all your senses are telling you otherwise. He's the least likely of you all to succumb."

Will grinned back with his roguish smile. "Don't you worry about me! That bastard Quintillean is due some cold hard steel and he's going to get it! Now I *know* I'm not going daft when the world starts to feel strange, and I know what it feels like when one of them lot starts their magic-making. I won't get caught so easily again!"

Ruari turned to Sioncaet. "You take care too! I now have some idea of what you're walking back into, and that it holds its own set of dangers for you. Take no chances of being recognised, please. I know I'm not Maelbrigt and I don't have his experience of dealing with forays into New Lochlainn, but if you need me, send for me and I'll come, I promise."

He turned to all of the men going with them.

"I'm not going to tell you men what to do – you all have too much experience for that. But just keep something in mind. Quintillean wants those two boys alive for whatever he's going to do. Wistan may not be well, but Quintillean can't afford for it to become fatal, and the *last* thing he'll do is kill them. So don't risk yourselves needlessly against him, however much you might be tempted to do so, to relieve the boys of their sufferings as fast as possible. And I know what a temptation that will be because I feel it already! I'd rather you followed him for a week before you can get the boys out with none of you being on the receiving end of what he can throw at you. I've seen firsthand the DeÁine on the attack, and some of the things they've done have left men taking weeks to die in screaming agony. Open confrontation is not an option!"

Nonetheless, his mind was more on the party heading north and the three they followed than on his own quest, as he rode out with Waeles and his lance. Just for a change it was milder than it had been for the last month, and a soft mist floated around them at first. However, as the daylight broke fully, the sun appeared and its warmth dissipated the haze. As they rode into the valley they could tell the location of the hamlet by the wisps of smoke from the houses' fires which rose lazily into the clear air. Three of the men from the village greeted them warmly and were ready to set off straight away.

"Best get you out of here before old Nan knows you're here," the one joked, "or it'll be sunset before we can free you from more of her stories."

"She hasn't shut up since your friend left," another said in something that hovered between amusement and desperation. "She'll never let us hear the last of the fact that one of her tales has turned out to be important."

They joined the men of the Order, riding stocky mountain ponies which barely came up to the withers of the Order's horses, but who led the way with sure-footed ease on the step paths. Higher into the foothills of the mountains they rode, following the courses of small streams which climbed steadily. The local wildlife was out in abundance making the most of the break in the weather, and Ruari remembered how back in Rheged it had been unnaturally quiet when the Abend's creatures had been abroad. Nothing to fear here, then. In fact there was something quintessentially Island about this broad defile. The trees were rowan, hawthorn, hazel and birch, with thick stands of bracken beneath that even the heavy snow could not quite smother.

High on the thermals above the mountains ahead, eagles and red kites were gliding in circles, waiting for something worth eating to appear below, whilst amongst the trees, blackbirds and thrushes squabbled over the last of the glistening berries. In the distance they saw a fox pad out into an open patch of snow covered grass, stand and look back at them, and then disappear back into the bracken, while occasional rabbits would scurry across their path. Under other circumstances it would have been a lovely winter's day ride. As it was, even Ruari found his spirits being lifted despite his worries. As they followed the path around a small outcrop of rock, a white hare appeared at the top of it and sat up on its hind legs.

"Sacred Trees, would you look at that!" Waeles' sergeant, Dynevor, said in awe. "Look at the size of him!"

"Not him, *her*," one of the locals corrected him, "and your mission must be blessed! We rarely see white hares down here, and the sight of one is said to bring good luck."

"Well thank you kindly, ma'am," Ruari said politely, making a small bow from the waist towards the hare who had not moved. To everyone's total amazement the hare in turn bowed her head down, as if in a regal salute, and remained sitting to watch them pass.

"They'll never believe us at home!" the youngest of their guides sighed in awe. "That truly was a fey hare, and we saw her! I've actually seen *the* white hare!"

For Ruari there was also a sense of disquiet that he kept to himself. The men were right, there was nothing malevolent about the hare, but he had had the distinct feeling that it was him personally it had appeared to. Something in the way it had met his gaze, eye to eye for a moment, that had been knowing and directed, not wild at all. But then they entered a belt of woodland and Ruari registered that these were birches which rose much taller than those they had passed by until now. Waeles tapped his arm and pointed to the slope beyond.

"Are my eyes deceiving me, or are those oaks growing up yonder?"

Dynevor replied even before Ruari. "No, there's nothing wrong with your eyes, those are oaks growing where they normal never would. But look south! Those are ash trees. Whoever heard of ashes growing so high either?"

"But exactly in their own directions," Ruari gasped in wonder, "exactly where their sacred positions might demand they be. Ah, look ...yews! Up there in the north!"

Then suddenly they came out onto a wide open space. The ground was a flat expanse of snow except for a semicircle of burial mounds at the rim of the slope they had just climbed. The mounds were swathed in snow, but by their height Ruari guessed they were very old. The soil had settled down and in one or two cases it looked as though the supports of the chamber beneath had probably collapsed, lowering the height even more and the odd sapling sprouted from them. Through the bare branches of the birches, to their left now, they could see east, and the keen-eyed could just make out the tower of Roselan in the distance. Then suddenly Ruari caught a whiff of something herblike as the horses came fully into the open.

"Halt!" he commanded and vaulted from his saddle. With his gloved hand he quickly brushed the snow aside and saw low growing greenery, somewhat bedraggled after such a deep freeze. Pulling off his glove he rubbed some of the stems between his fingers and then sniffed them. "Thyme!" he declared. "Wild thyme! This is it! Everyone dismount!"

Leaving the guides to eat their lunchtime pasties at a boulder on the perimeter of the space, Ruari led his men forward on foot. Their boots crunched on the deep virgin snow as they walked into the centre of the space.

"Where is it then?" wondered Chandos, one of the archers, in bemusement turning round in a full circle. "I don't even see any fallen walls, or anything that would indicate that a building ever stood here."

"I'm as sure as ever I can be that this is the right place," an equally puzzled Ruari replied, "but you're right, there's no sign of a building. I'd have thought walls would still show up even with this much snow on the ground."

"What's that up there," the voice of the other archer, Heuglin, came from behind them. Turning round they saw him pointing further up the hill, and sure enough, on a rocky promontory which looked down on where they stood, they could see what looked like masonry.

"Break out the ropes lads," Waeles ordered. "The quickest way is going to be to go straight up. We could stumble around all day in those woods and not find a track leading up. Looking at the size of these trees, they may have grown right over the road which must've once led up there."

In short order the ropes and spikes had been unpacked and Malek, Waeles' other man-at-arms, had sprung nimbly up to the first handhold. No sooner had he disappeared from view amongst the oak branches, than Dynevor was following him. At the base of the rocks, Ruari suddenly felt a kinship with Maelbrigt. The other Knight had expressed his fears that he would never keep up with his mountaineer escort, and Ruari realised that, in the long years since he had been in high mountains, he had forgotten just what such men could do. Maelbrigt had had every reason to feel trepidation, Ruari thought, as he watched the third man swarm up the rocks as if he was out on an afternoon's stroll. Then Waeles was waving him forward.

"Up you go, MacBeth, the rope is secure now so use it. Heuglin will be right behind you."

"Is that wise?" Ruari asked wryly. "I think he's in more danger of me falling on him and squashing him!"

Waeles just laughed and handed him the rope, so there was no way to go but up. It was a great relief to find that the climb was not as sheer as it looked from below. It was more of a very steep slope than a vertical wall, and Malek had done a good job of finding the easiest route up, going around rather than over some of the bigger boulders on the rock-face. Scarlet in the face from the exertions in heavy winter clothes, Ruari staggered up over the edge and got helped to his feet by Chandos, who had somehow made the climb with his bow and quiver of arrows still slung across his back. Heuglin appeared in a moment, similarly equipped, and once Waeles had joined them they all turned to the fallen stones.

Heuglin had been right. This was definitely the remains of the original castle, and Ruari admired the tactical skill of its builders. Even when its walls had been standing to their full height, it must have been well camouflaged against the rock of the mountains when viewed from lower down the slope. Yet from up here they had an unrivalled view right down to the coast. Roselan was visible straight ahead, but they could see north and south a long way as well, giving them a commanding view of the main road yonder.

Chandos stretched an arm out and pointed, and following his direction they saw tiny specks of figures riding hard on the distant road. "There goes General Montrose and the others," he declared, and Ruari was heartened to see how far they had gone already.

Returning to their own quest, however, they scoured the remains without finding anything that would help them. It took them into the afternoon, and they would soon have to leave the valley before they lost the light on the ride back down. Yet the lengthening rays of sun proved to be their friends. Again it was the archers, standing together at the rim talking quietly who suddenly stiffened and began to peer harder down at the thyme circle below. Then Heuglin beckoned them over.

"Look at this," he called. With the low winter sun now shining along the plateau rather than straight down on it, the long shadows were throwing up lumps and bumps that the men had not seen before. "The centre of the thyme carpet is lower than the rest," Heuglin pointed out. "It could be that there was a building down there. See? There's an outer circle which is more of a bank than a ditch, but then at the heart of that there's a regular circle that looks lower than the rest."

"Well spotted!" Ruari congratulated them, "but how will we ever find it when we're back down there?"

The archers just grinned, then strung their bows and proceeded to lay down a neat circle of arrows between the two seen in the snow.

"Your lads are bloody marvels, Waeles!" Ruari grinned back.

"I know they are," he answered with a laugh, "and to prove it they'll even get you back down in one piece!"

Getting down was harder than going up, but shortly Ruari was back on the plateau and running for the circle of arrows. Dropping to his knees in the centre he began digging the snow away with his hands, looking for all the world like a big blonde dog about to bury a bone as the snow flew away from him.

"Ice!" he cried as his fingers hit something harder than snow. The rest of the men joined in, and the men from the village produced small portable shovels from out of their saddlebags and helped with the clearing. With the nine of them working at it they had soon uncovered the surface of a pool. At its edge there was a beautifully worked stone rim which they had not noticed simply because of the depth of the snow all around. The floor beside it was lower than the ground outside but the snow had piled right up in a thick layer which had packed down and frozen level, misleading the Knights into thinking that they were still on the green sward outside. However, their biggest problem now was where to start looking in the remains of what they guessed might once have been a chapel.

"Do you think anyone was ever buried in here? I mean, was *It* placed here alone, or was it buried with someone?" Heuglin asked. "Because it's going to be a swine digging out graves with the ground this frozen!"

"And what about those mounds over there?" Malek added. "Do you have any idea whether this thing has to actually be in a building, or just in the proximity of it?"

They were careful to just call the Shield a thing in front of the villagers, for nobody wanted to have the Island Treasure mentioned by name in case they had to leave and return with more men. The villagers would be unlikely to be in the Abend's pay, but such news would be impossible to keep contained within the hamlet, especially when the villagers had already said they were going to the big market in Roselan town the next day. Opportunist thieves, who had no idea of the significance of what they were going after, were the last thing the Knights needed to have added into the mixture of problems they had.

"Sacred Trees, I don't have a clue," Ruari growled in frustration. He drew his sword and drove the point down onto the ice, but it hardly made a chip. He leaned instead upon the grip and tried to think, the villagers standing looking expectantly at him and the other men with furrowed brows of concentration. "It's no good," Ruari sighed, "we're losing the light too much now. There's no point hanging around thinking. Let's get mounted up again. We'll have to come back tomorrow."

The villagers led the way to the horses, leaving Ruari and Waeles standing in the circle.

"You'd think that if *It* was meant to be used in an emergency then it would be easily accessible, wouldn't you?" Waeles reasoned. "I don't mean just lying around in the open, of course, but at least visible for those seekers who knew where to look in the first place."

"I know, I thought that," Ruari agreed. "But what worries me is that so much time has gone by. Do you have any idea how long a magic warding can last for? I don't. It may have been meant to last for a century, or a thousand years, or forever. Equally it might've been meant to last forever but only if certain things were done on a regular ceremonial basis – you know, perhaps every fifty years, or when a new warden got inaugurated, or when one died. That old lady Will spoke to was talking about an old man when she was a young girl. Whoever he was he must have died over fifty years ago. And was he from an unbroken line of wardens? Was he fully trained? Or was it like our Foresters, where certain of those words that Maelbrigt remembers have only been learnt by rote? Something you have to say under certain circumstances – but you don't know what they mean, or *specifically* why. The warden might have needed to recruit a replacement and never done it. Do you see what I mean? It's all so fuzzy!"

As they began to walk to their horses, a blur of movement made them turn and look back. The white hare sat at the edge of the circle to the side of the horses and she was watching them again. Ruari took another step away and she stamped her hind paw as if to drive him back. He paused, then took another step and received another stamp in return. Totally perplexed, he looked to the others for help.

"I don't think she wants you to leave, sire," Malek called.

"Well I don't want to bloody leave either, especially empty-handed!" a frustrated Ruari protested, half to the men and half to the hare, "but what are we to do? We can't see anything through all this snow, and we haven't got enough light left today to start just randomly digging. Anyway, where would we start?"

The hare stood motionless for a moment, regarding them with ears twitching, then took off in a flurry of movement out into the centre of the pool, which she landed on with a thump of her large back paws. For a second nothing happened, then the hare leapt for the edge as an enormous crack appeared in the ice with a deafening report, and a stentorian voice from the icy depths demanded,

"Who disturbs my rest?"

The villagers yelped like scaled cats and clapped their heels to their ponies' sides. They shot off down the mountainside, and Ruari would not have been surprised if he had seen them still going when they reached the sea. Even the trained soldiers looked disconcerted and more than a little worried. He cautiously turned back to the pool, where the ice was breaking into more and more fragments.

"Who are you?" Ruari asked.

"I might ask you the same!" the disembodied voice replied in an irate tone. "Come here where I can see you!"

However, even when Ruari was at the pool's edge nothing was to be seen. He saw the hare, standing on the rim at the other side, push at a piece of ice with her front paw.

"What? You want me to lift the ice out?" Ruari asked her, and got a brusque bob of the head in reply. With great trepidation he reached in and lifted one of the pieces out and dropped it onto the snow behind him. Far from looking into an inky darkness, the pool suddenly seemed filled with a bright sunlight coming from somewhere within its depths. Waeles had come up beside him and gave Ruari a startled glance, then the two of them started lifting more ice out. The four soldiers, who had cautiously waited further back in case their leaders needed rescuing, saw that there was no obvious trap and dismounted again. Dynevor and Malek trotted to the other side of the pool and began to help removing ice chunks, although Heuglin and Chandos stayed back with arrows nocked and ready just in case. There almost seemed to be some sort of current within the pool, for the ice fragments kept drifting to the side from the centre – which was just as well since the pool was far too wide for any of the men to have reached into the middle.

With all of the big pieces out of the way the men found themselves looking down into crystal clear water that seemed to be reflecting the image of a long lost chapel wall and ceiling which was filled with light and plant life. In its midst they stared down onto a be-whiskered face of an elderly man. Just the face – nothing else.

"Are you the warden?" Ruari ventured to ask.

"Yes I am!" was the irate and emphatic reply. "But what do you want?"

Ruari took a deep breath to force himself to a calmness he was far from feeling. What would they do if this querulous guardian refused to give up his ward?

"We're seeking the Islands' Shield. The DeÁine have returned and we fear – or rather, we are certain – that members of the Abend have come into the Islands seeking the Treasures that were theirs and which we hid from them. Others are already on missions to try to ensure the DeÁine Treasures stay out of their hands, but we – and others elsewhere – have come looking for the Islands' traditional protectors against such weapons. Old manuscripts led us to believe that we would find one here."

"Did they!" the grumpy voice snorted. "*Hummph*! And I suppose you think that you'll just come in here and march off with it, do you? Well it's not as simple as that! Even if I had it, what sort of warden would I be if I let any ragamuffin who wandered by take this thing?"

"No guardian at all," Ruari replied with forced patience. "But you have to understand that many long years in the lives of men have passed since the Shield was hidden. I can't come here and simply recite whatever it is you were expecting to hear, because no-one knows that any longer! I'll stand here (freezing my arse off, by the way!) to answer as many questions as you need to ask to convince yourself of the legitimacy of our quest. But you're going to have to tell me what it is you want to know."

"And what if I don't?"

Shit! The bloody warden's gone senile, Ruari thought with growing horror, *what do we do if he just refuses?*

"Well you'll just have to sit in your frozen hole for the rest of eternity, won't you – while the Islands fall to the DeÁine and our people become just one more race to be enslaved, lose their identity, their history, and have their homes become wastelands. I don't suppose you can see much lying down there, but let me tell you that we've had the worst and earliest snow storms for generations this winter, because the *Abend* are controlling our weather. You do know who the Abend are, don't you?" The warden's sour expression said that he did. "So you can help us, or resign yourself to looking at the underside of an ice-flow for the rest of your days. Because the Abend already have the power to keep this kind of thing up for several months, and, once they have the Treasures, the amount of Power they'll have access to will mean that they can make it permanent."

"You're trying to trick me," the querulous voice replied.

Ruari groaned and pounded the fist of one hand into the palm of his other in frustration, looking to Waeles for help, but the other Knight was as confounded as him. What could they say to convince the warden? Then Ruari had an inspired thought.

"Would it help you if I told you the Shield's name?" The warden remained silent, but the eyes were suddenly very focused on Ruari. "The weapons of great strength all had names, right? Well this shield was made in the days when it would've been unthinkable to have made it and not given it a name that enhanced and embodied its very being."

Even Waeles and the men were staring at him in astonishment now.

"The Islands' Shield is called Hilderand," Ruari declared, and there was a definite sensation of something shifting beneath the snow. A tremor in the ground. Then beneath the image of the old man's head they saw a shimmering and slowly there appeared a round shape which materialised into a metal-bound wooden shield. Indistinct through the water, the men could see that there were fine decorations in metal across its surface, and a great embellished boss at its centre. With great care Ruari extended a hand and broke the surface of the water. Instantly a small patch of ice appeared around his glove and he snatched his hand quickly away.

"You are not the one!" the voice bellowed. "You shall not have it!"

"Oh shit," Ruari made the aside to Waeles, "what do we do now? You try! Maybe you're the one!"

"Me?" gasped an appalled Waeles.

"Well it seems it has to be a specific someone, and it isn't me!"

But suddenly the hare took charge of the proceedings. Leaning in she slapped the water with her front paw making the warden look to her. When Ruari questioned the others afterwards they all agreed they had only seen the reflection of the hare, but he saw reflected back the figure of a beautiful woman with ashen blonde hair. Ageless and yet in an indefinable way of great age, she took Ruari's breath away. In some strange way that he could not put into words she was familiar too, even though he had never seen her before.

"My lady!" the warden said reverently, "I had no idea you were here."

The white hare said nothing but gestured towards Ruari.

481

"You wish him to have Hilderand? But he's not the one! He's of the wrong blood. He cannot wield it." But the hare was not to be gainsaid and Ruari saw the reflected eyes look directly at him most emphatically. The warden was disconcerted too. "Oh! He is your servant! My pardons, Lady," then to Ruari, "then you must take it. But understand this! You are not the one who can wield the power of Hilderand. You have the blood of the far north in your veins, and only those of the Islands can truly bond with this piece. Moreover, should the wrong person try to use it it will be the worse for them! Madness lies that way! Hilderand will know its rightful user. Do not let others try to force the matter. The right one will feel the bond, and Hilderand will make it clear to those who witness the bonding. You may bear this with immunity because of your bloodline, but do not tempt fate by trying to use it – even you would suffer dire consequences in that event – so you must avoid the DeÁine while you carry it."

At that the face faded and the Shield floated to the surface of the pool, which began to freeze again beneath it. With great care Ruari lifted the Shield out, grunting with the effort as he took the full weight of it as its last edge came away from the water. Ruari was a big man, standing over six feet tall, but even on his arm the Shield looked large. It showed no sign of the effects of being immerse for centuries, and the steel band around its edge gleamed in the red light of the sunset, while the wood looked newly waxed.

"We'd best get out of here," Malek said, noticing how low the sun was. "As it is, we'll be lucky to get down the track and onto the proper path before darkness comes."

They hurried to their horses and mounted up. Waeles contemplated leading the horses, but decided that the animals were probably more sure-footed in the dark than the men. Letting the horses set their own pace, they set off into the gloom of the trees. It was fortunate that the route back down the stream beds was hardly overhung, and so what little light there was was not blocked out. Therefore they reached the path to the village as the last of the light disappeared and the stars came out.

Waeles led the riders, with Chandos immediately behind him guiding his horse with just his legs, whilst he swept before them with his bow nocked and ready to let fly. Ruari rode behind them with Dynevor and Malek at his back, and Heuglin riding like Chandos brought up the rear. Everyone was silent, too deep in thought at what they had seen, and yet alert for danger now that they had their precious cargo, to talk.

Ruari had used the leather from part of his horse's harness to fashion a strap, which allowed him to wear the Shield on his back while he rode, for it was so heavy as to put a strain on the horse had he held it on one side for any time – not to mention the strain on his own arm. He was aware of a vague tingling feeling between his shoulder blades which was noticeable, but not distressing. However, it took very little imagination to think what it could become under other circumstances, and he took the warden's warning seriously. And what had he meant by the Lady's servant? Even as he had lifted the Shield from the water, Ruari could have sworn he saw her blow him a kiss in the disturbed ripples and smile.

And even more worrying, what of Sioncaet and Will? He had promised his aid if needed. *What do I do should they need me if I can't go near the Abend?* he fretted silently. *Am I fated to let all my friends down? All those I care most about? Why do I have to be the one who puts the greater good over the path my heart tells me I should take? I'm trapped by cursed duty again!*

All those years ago I went into the Order for my father's sake, and although I admit I've had a good life, because of that I was also deprived of Matti. I was too bound by orders and conventions to save Michael, and then I was too far away to save his son. Oh Wistan, I'm so sorry! And you Kenelm! I should've made more effort to see you more often. Prepared you better. Made you more wary of those who would do you harm. All those years of doing my duty to Rheged and the Order, and yet I've let you two down so badly. The two of you for whom I was the one and only person in the family who could take an interest in you without exciting comment, or interest, which might have endangered you further.

And now I'm likely to do it again to Will and Sioncaet! What happens if they come to grief with Quintillean? I promised Sioncaet I would come. I promised! Who else is there to go if I don't? Maelbrigt is too far away – and anyway he has his own mission. But I promised him I'd look out for his friend. Oh Sacred Trees! Another promise as like to be broken! "Is my name destined to become a byword for faithlessness?" he said aloud without intending to.

His spirits were sunk as low as he could remember. Not even in that year on the run, in the wetlands of the east after Michael's death, could he recall feeling quite so swept along by the tide of fate with so little choice. There was little joy in apparently being the chosen one of some greater being, he felt – although he did wonder, in the light of what had been said about his bloodline, whether that had been why he had been the one who had remained unharmed all those years ago when moving the DeÁine

Gorget? Yet there was little comfort in remaining sane after such an encounter, only to be tormented by subsequent events.

At the hamlet they dismounted, but Ruari let Waeles go and do the explaining to the awe-struck locals. Instead he walked to the dark edge of the surrounding wood, lost in his gloomy thoughts. So lost that he completely failed to register that there was suddenly someone with him in the dark. It was only the soft, husky voice that jolted him into awareness.

"Never fear, Ruari, I wouldn't ask that sacrifice of you," came from beside him, and looking up he saw the woman from the pool. Her silver hair reflected the starlight, and her gown was made of no material Ruari recognised, yet she seemed very much of the world. Her face was full of sympathy as she told him, "I know you fear for your friends. It is a cruel choice you seem to have to make, but I tell you this, Hilderand must never come near Quintillean! He is sure to feel my presence, and that I cannot avoid. But in doing so he may mistake the ripples that Hilderand has made in coming back into the world as being nothing more than my interference. He must not know the truth!

"Take Hilderand to Ergardia! The one who must wield it will become apparent sooner or later, but you do not have to take the place of the Guardian permanently until then. All you must do is get it to a place of safety on Ergardia. The Island itself will protect it after that, and you may leave it in good conscience. After that you are free to come back and seek your friends!"

Ruari felt some relief at this, but could not refrain from asking, "But will I be in time to save them?"

The woman stepped in close to him and lifted her head as if to kiss him lingeringly full on the lips. Involuntarily Ruari went to clasp her to him but his hands passed right through her shimmering image making him stumble as he unbalanced. Moving back beyond arms' length her laugh was rich and warm at his look of surprise.

"No, I'm not really here, but I will make you a promise! I shall follow your friends since you cannot. There will be little I can do openly against Quintillean, but I will do what I can to keep them safe, and when you return to Brychan I will direct you to them. Look for me in my familiar's guise! I will take you by the fastest route to them if they need your help."

With his breathing returning to something like normal, Ruari's mind began working furiously again, and fretting.

"But Lady! It's taken me the best part of two months to get here from Lorne. If I do as you say, then admittedly it won't be so long if I only go to the west coast of Ergardia. But we still have to find a ship, cross to Celidon, and then cross to Ergardia. Even if we're lucky, it's likely to be a week before we leave Brychan's shores! We could then cross straight to Raera castle, but that way we'd have a grim ride through mountains to reach the road. Alternatively, I suppose, we could sail round the Celidon coast to Belhaven, but we couldn't do that in these winds. And whichever way, it's at the very least another week on top of that before we could make landfall on Ergardia. Realistically it's going to take me three weeks to get there, and that means another three to get back here before I even start following my friends. We're talking two months in all probability, and with Quintillean in the picture a lot can go horribly wrong in that time. I fear for them, I truly do!"

She brushed a lock of her long hair back from her face and smiled sadly.

"I understand your fears, and it does you much credit that you don't think of yourself. But consider this, my brave one. What can you do to help them if they do get into trouble? These men with you are valiant and true, but only five in number. Can you empty the castle below? No. For you would have done it already rather than send the others off as you had to. You must trust to your friends to do what they can, and that they have the sense to refrain where they must."

Ruari snorted. "This is Will you're talking about! Restraint isn't one of his virtues! ...But he *is* my friend. A very dear friend, and I've sacrificed so many of them over the years, Lady, that the ones left become more precious."

Her ethereal hand drifted to stroke his cheek, feeling like a faint cobweb had brushed past him. "My poor Ruari, I seem to ask a lot of you, don't I? But I have a very special task for you, and only you can do this."

"Why me?" Ruari demanded. "We've never met. You know nothing about me!"

"Oh but I do! You may not have seen me, but I've been watching you all your life! And your dear mother before that. You are probably the last who will have the blood of the north running true enough in your veins to be able to do what needs to be done. And as for why? Several of us made a great sacrifice a long time ago to help the lesser folk of the Islands when the DeÁine first came, then found ourselves trapped. If it comes to a great battle between the Islands and the full might of the DeÁine, then it is doubtful that you will win – even with the pieces such as you carry here. We can even the balance – no more than that – but we can give you a good chance of success, as long as all pull together and remain true to one another. The outcome still hangs on a knife edge. You cannot afford for any to falter, or at least not for long.

"Now I must go! It costs me dear to appear before you even for this short time." She seemed to gaze off into the distance at something beyond Ruari's sight. "However, I see that one of the boats from the north folk comes! Since it pains you so to fail your friends, I offer you an alternative. Travel to the isle of Ynys and the castle of Camais on the eastern tip. There you will find this ship. With these westerly winds you will fly east. Ask the captain to land you on Celidon's coast on the land between the isles of Laggan and Eyrs. The men of Celidon remain true. Strap Hilderand to the saddle of one of their island ponies and let others take it on from there. You should reach there in a week, and then get ships to bring you back to Laggan and Ynys with little trouble and more speed than going overland. I offer you three weeks delay. Then, if your friends remain safe, you must follow me. Does that soothe your soul?"

Ruari's face broke into a smile. "Thank you, Lady!"

Yet even as she laughed she melted into thin air, leaving him with her distant voice calling, "Remember, I have work for you!"

In the mountains far beyond, Quintillean stopped abruptly and stood stock still. What was that he just felt? He quested on the air with his Power, frustrated that he was still weak from the effects of Ergardia. Who would have thought the Island could be so poisonous?

When Eliavres' predecessor, Alvares, had nearly died all those centuries ago when he had tried to take control of that Island, the other Abend had put it down to his age. He was, after all, ancient even by their standards, and he had already been replaced as head of the Abend by Ushant. Alvares was weakening, they had reasoned, and he had certainly never been quite the same afterwards.

But Quintillean was still in his prime. Nothing he had ever encountered had sapped his strength the way Ergardia had. The more he tried to pull the Power into himself, the worse it had got. He could not understand it. His capacity for the Power had been substantial, yet he had been as Powerless as the newest novice by the time they had staggered off Ergardia. To have to make a sea crossing straight afterwards seemed to have been the finishing touch, and he had languished as weak as a new born kitten for two whole weeks after they landed on Brychan.

Even now he was far from up to his usual feats and he used the Power sparingly, for to pull too hard at it was still likely to floor him, even if not as badly as on Ergardia. The effects were taking a worryingly long time to wear off, and although he would never have dreamt of voicing his fears, they lingered on the prospect of repeating Alvares' fate. And now to feel that certain something made him even more jittery, for his memory told him that it too came from the past.

Then he remembered. It was Her! Or was it? Could it really be Her after all this time? Surely she and those with her had paid the price for setting their precious Islanders free? The last he had heard from his spies before the current return, nobody had seen neither hide nor hair of that coven for so long that the Islanders had forgotten who they were. At least no-one had forgotten who the DeÁine were, and that had to mean something. If those strange northerners had truly won the day, as the DeÁine Emperor in the old homeland thought, then surely they would have ruled the Islands thereafter? What point would there be in throwing out the DeÁine as overlords if there had been no intention of taking their place? Yet in all those centuries, nobody had filled the DeÁine's gap.

And yet it felt so like Her taint upon the Power. Her own particular signature in the ripples. Faint to be sure, but no matter how he strained his senses, he could not distinguish whether she was faint because of her distance from him; her weakness in the Power after all this time; or his own shaky control after his experiences sending him false indicators. He cursed her soundly, and also the other members of the Abend, for there was nobody here he could ask to check for him.

And he doubly cursed Anarawd for losing so many acolytes at Gavra Pass. Not so very long ago he would have had his own coterie travelling with him, for whom he could have set a training exercise in tracking the source of the ripples to confirm his finding without revealing his own weakness. Now here he was on his own, with two useless boys whom he had to drag with him if they were to be his sacrifices. He was in no position to meet one of his old adversaries, and he worried even as he turned and chivvied them onwards. Could it really be the White Lady come again?

Chapter 27

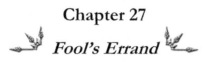

Fool's Errand

Brychan: Eft-Yule

"*You?* …Leave me? How *dare* you!" Edward screamed. "I say what happens and when, *not* you! I *own* you! I own you body and soul! I say when you live and I say when you *die*! You are mine, do you hear me? *Mine!*"

The lash made of fine, whippy canes came down on Jacinto's back again, raising another spray of blood and flesh. His back was already a bloody pulp and he was drifting in and out of consciousness. He was strung up, with his hands above his head, by ropes thrown over an exposed beam in an upper room of the inn Edward had commandeered for his own use. In his agony, which had his mind close to switching off in order to end the torture, Jacinto's legs had long since given up being able to support him. But that brought an additional torment, for his arms now took his whole weight. Earlier his hands had grasped the ropes, but now he dangled by his wrists, cutting off his circulation, while his shoulder joints felt like they might rip apart at any second. His head lolled backwards, and the hair from his long, black dreadlocks had been shredded into the savage cuts on his back.

All in all Jacinto would quite happily have given up the fight that night and died. Seeing a future for himself which went beyond the pain was now impossible. Meanwhile, the salve to his conscience was that Cwen's family had escaped, and in aiding them he had at least once upheld the honour of the Order, meaning he had fewer regrets to live to correct. Their escape he was sure of, for at some point when he was still capable of taking notice, a provost's man had entered to report that, whoever the woman was whom the men had heard with Jacinto, she was nowhere to be found. Nobody had even guessed that it had been four women and two lads who had escaped.

Yet he did not die …quite. Somewhere in a pain-filled semi-consciousness he was aware that later on he was cut down and thrown across a horse's back. In a hazy detachment, he heard men arguing with Edward about whether he should be brought along. They were sure he would die before the day was out, and could see no point in dragging him along. Why not leave him here to die, they argued. Overriding them, though, he heard Edward's hysterical scream,

"He *won't* die because I won't *allow* him to! Do you hear me! *I'll* say when he dies! He won't dare die until *I* say so!"

So he was strapped onto the horse like a sack of fodder, while the men muttered darkly in quiet voices about the king's madness. Yet the blurred events of the five day ride to Caersus marked a turning point of sorts for Jacinto. For now it was no fun for Edward to rape a man so ravaged as to be insensible, and he turned his nocturnal attentions elsewhere. His only continued interest in Jacinto was to demonstrate his superiority by his hold over Jacinto's very existence, and that meant that he was now merely peripheral to Edward's attentions. However, for the men newly charged with watching over him, the state of Jacinto's abused body finally elicited some sympathy.

"I don't care what he's done," Jacinto heard a voice beside him say as he was hauled off to a tent on the second night. "Even a shirt-lifter don't deserve that! Not even if he's shagged his way round the camp. If the poor bastard's lived this long, I'm not standing by and letting him suffer even more. ...Sacred Trees! ...Would you look at the state of him! There's not an inch of skin left unbroken on his back!"

And so, by the weak light of a flickering lone candle held by a man whose hand shook at what he saw, an old sergeant began the slow and painful process of removing the hair, splinters and cloth from Jacinto's ravaged flesh. Some rough wine which was closer to vinegar, and unpalatable to even the desperate soldiers, was used to clean the wounds, drawing more screams from Jacinto. Yet even that helped him, for Edward believed his men were now having fun with his former toy, and was content to believe that Jacinto's torment continued. Instead, the experienced campaigners among the ordinary men retrieved maggots from rotting meat when they found them, and bound them to the wounds, where the small larvae munched their way through the decaying flesh and kept the wounds clean. Without the men and their field knowledge Jacinto undoubtedly would have died, and even so he spent the last three days of the ride to Caersus wracked with fever.

Consequently he missed Edward's travesty of a majestic entrance into the cathedral town, and the furious arguments which ensued with the keeper of the royal castle and the dean of the cathedral. When he finally awoke to a freezing cold, clear dawn it was to find himself lying face down on a bed which was tucked into the corner of the monk's infirmary. In a while a young monk appeared accompanied by a bandy-legged old soldier.

"Ah! You see, brother! He lives!" chortled the older man. "Never underestimate the usefulness of maggots. They've saved many a soldier's life in my experience!"

"How long have I been here?" Jacinto croaked faintly.

"We – that is the army – got here three days ago," the old soldier told him, "and whatever it was the king thought he was going to find here, it hasn't appeared! Bloody fool! Half the army is still recovering from lack of food and frostbite, but if we don't move soon, even a town the size of Caersus is going to start running short of food."

"I can't imagine how they're all fed at Arlei," the young monk despairingly wondered.

"That's because normally they aren't *all* at Arlei," the soldier answered, as he helped Jacinto wriggle onto his side and then into a sitting position. "Normally the army is spread out in barracks in towns throughout southern Brychan. Me, I'm normally out at Beluss. There's others at Deepscar and Delving and Shipfold too. But something funny's been going on. First, all the top commanders disappeared. We didn't think it odd, any more than the lads from the other barracks did, because we just assumed our general had gone to court for some reason. But now we've been thrown together, we've worked out that they were all summoned in succession and haven't been seen since!

"Then the call came to march to Arlei on the pretext of quelling some riot planned for the Yule celebrations. So we took no supplies because we thought we'd be back in a few days. Then we get to Arlei and there's no riot, and we all get marched straight out on this fool's errand."

"Fool's errand?" Jacinto queried. Despite feeling awfully weak his curiosity was piqued. "Why a fool's errand?"

The monk handed him a mug of hot soup as the soldier went on. "Because nobody here's heard hide nor hair of a DeÁine army!"

Jacinto looked up at him and felt a twinge in his back as the newly knitted skin pulled under the mass of scabs, but still said in surprise, "But that was all we kept hearing about in Arlei!"

"Well wherever the king was getting his information from he was wrong," the soldier told him. "The only excitement they've had here was some high ranking Knight coming in and disrupting the place a few weeks ago."

Jacinto had his wits about him enough to keep quiet about the fact that he knew only too well what that was about. Then the memory returned of his swollen pride at declaring that the Knights would not march against the DeÁine whilst in all those in the taverns in Arlei, and he felt a huge surge of guilt. No wonder the Knights were not marching to war! There was no threat! But he in his own way had helped create the panic that Edward had seized upon, which he now regretted for all the suffering he had contributed towards by putting these soldiers through on the dire march west. Then the monk spoke up.

"The only excitement, that is, until the army arrived. Then something terrible came with them! Someone, or something, forced its way in here. Into the cathedral and the cloisters! Some of the brothers heard a commotion in the library late at night and went to investigate. The Spirits only know what they discovered, because all we found was their bodies in the morning, thrown amongst the scattered ancient corpses in the crypt. But down in the vaults something has torn every crypt apart!"

"Soldiers?" asked Jacinto in surprise, but both men shook their heads.

"There are only three ways into the cathedral close," the brother told him. "One is directly in front of the west front, which is the double gateway that worshippers come in through for the main services, but those gates are always barred and bolted from within apart from those times. Other than that there's a portered gate on the north side and one on the east, but because the army was in town those gates had been locked too, and each porter has a small, barred peephole to see who might be ringing the bell. Even if someone shot him, it wouldn't do them any good, because the peepholes look out from the rooms built into the thickness of the enclosure wall, not part of the gates. They were deliberately made that way so that nobody could put a hook through them and draw back the bolts from the outside."

"And the gates were still bolted in the morning," the soldier continued. "The enclosure wall is huge! And it's topped with iron spikes to prevent anyone ungodly getting in that way."

"Not very trusting, are you brothers?" Jacinto grimaced. "So much for caring for the poor and needy! Poor buggers would be hard pressed to get close enough to even ask, let alone receive!"

The monk had the grace to look embarrassed, but the soldier chuckled. "That's pretty much what I said when I brought you in here on the first evening. Luckily the great and mighty of the Church were too busy with his highness, and so we dealt with the infirmarer himself, who's a kind man. But I have to confess there are some among the surviving brethren who think you might be to blame."

"Me?" a stunned Jacinto gasped. "How could I be responsible?"

"Well they've led a bit of a sheltered life in here," the soldier said with a wry snort. "They think you should've died of your wounds, and that because you've survived it's the work of some evil spirit. While you lay unconscious, your 'wicked accomplice' apparently left your body and went on a killing spree!"

Jacinto was too stunned to argue.

"We have to get you out of here for your own safety," the brother told him.

"What? …Why?" was all Jacinto could get out.

The soldier handed him a soft, loose shirt and then a monk's robe to go over it. "Just loop the waist cord loosely around your hips, so it's visible but not holding the shirt and robe against your back. …More of the monks were killed in their beds in a small dormitory adjoining the main one. They died without making a sound to alert their brothers next door what was happening. That makes the survivors very scared indeed, but that nutter of a king of ours has made everything ten times worse.

"At first he was in a towering rage with the prior, because some Knight got his hands on the royal family records they had kept here. Spirits only know what the significance of that was, but he nearly strangled the man – it's still touch and go whether the prior will live! Well you can imagine the outrage over that! Then the unseen monster wreaked havoc amongst the brothers that night – so everyone's nerves were threadbare. But to cap it all, King Edward seems to have lost what was left of his mind, and came barging in here yesterday demanding to know where the treasure is!

"At first the brothers thought he was after money, or gold and silver he could melt down – not that the ordinary brothers have any idea where the money is kept, and the king had already throttled the only one who might know! Anyway, it turns out it's something specific he's after. The only problem is that no-one here has the faintest idea where something called 'the gorget' might be. And it seems to be a particular gorget he's after, because after he was here he forced his way into the castle's armoury, took one look at the heap of ordinary gorgets piled up there and said it wasn't amongst them. How in the Islands he could tell with one glance is beyond us all, but since then he's been positively frothing at the mouth!"

"If anyone's possessed it's him," the monk declared, "but nobody dares say that to his face. But as you can imagine, anyone even remotely connected with him is now unwelcome in here to the majority of the brothers. So you must leave before someone gets pushed too far, and decides to do something rash in their fear."

"But where shall I go?" Jacinto worried.

"Back with us, I'm afraid," the soldier told him. "The good news, though, is that his highness hasn't asked after you in days! If you keep your head down and stay away from the main tents, we reckon you can just disappear into the main mass of the army before he even notices."

"Who's we?"

"Me and my mates who brought you in here. My name's Harry, by the way."

For Eliavres things had not been going well either. Until the army had reached Caersus he had been full of optimism, confident that everything was going to plan. He had linked with the witches and been delighted to learn that the DeÁine army had made good time due to the lack of snow in New Lochlainn. Their first contact with him had come even as he had been joined with King Edward, and taking his pleasure from Jacinto in Foel. The main DeÁine army had marched from the capital and had met the four women at the junction of the ancient road to the east that very night. In the ten days it had taken Edward's army to reach Caersus, the DeÁine army had continued to march with speed far outstripping anything Edward's could manage. But then Edward did not have the witches flaying every ounce of Power out of their acolytes to clear the occasional snow drift which had had the temerity to fall short of the Brychan mountains and block the way.

By the Donns estimate, the witches informed Eliavres on the night he had entered Caersus, the DeÁine army was now only five days from the border town of Roch. They had already passed the junction with the road leading into the mountains to Wolfscar Castle, and could confirm that away from their route they could not even see the high road for heavy snow. The Knights were going nowhere! What had rocked Eliavres on his heels had been a blast of needle-fine Power directed at him afterwards from Masanae – a blast that deliberately excluded the other women and was from her alone.

In the town there is a convent, her voice seared into his mind. *Within it are two women I want very much! My spies tell me they are there beyond a shadow of doubt.*

However my minions do not have the skill to extract them. You will therefore do it for them! The one is a novice there – albeit a recent and very reluctant one. She goes by the name of Sister Alma, but her real name is Breizh. The other is her older sister, known as Heledd, who's been sent there after disgracing herself with the man who was to be her husband. Bring Breizh and Heledd to me, Eliavres, and don't mess this up or it will be the worse for you when Quintillean finds out! And with that she snapped the connection.

Quite what that was all about Eliavres could not imagine, but during her sending Masanae could not hide from him that, whatever it was, she was genuinely in league with Quintillean. Moreover, it was something that she had a personal passion for rather than simply backing another one of Quintillean's schemes. That meant that Eliavres had little choice in the matter. If he could have relied on Magda to unite with him he might have been in with a fighting chance of resisting them, but his recent mental contacts with her had revealed an alarming increase in her instability. Alone he, who was weakest in the Power among the Abend, could not hope to stand against two of the strongest. He therefore had no choice but to comply.

However, he was infinitely glad that his contact with the witches had come before he had had chance to go into Caersus and go hunting on his own account, for he could not have hidden the scale of the disaster from them. The Gorget was not there! Moreover, he could find no trace of anything of Power having ever been there! Getting into the cathedral precinct had been easy enough. He had simply slipped into the mind of a sleeping gatekeeper and got him to open one of the portals before sending him, still asleep, back to his bed. Within the compound he had begun to have his doubts when he could feel nothing, but by the time he had walked all the way around the outside of the cathedral and then the inside, without feeling so much as a twitch, he was truly worried.

In his panic, he had summoned a grollican up from the Underworld depths to tear first the crypt apart and its associated catacombs, then the tombs within the church itself. To exercise so much control over one of the fell beasts took a great deal of energy, especially when he himself could not stand idly by but had to search the library and other safe places above ground. He therefore mercilessly sucked the sleeping monks of their life force to feed his need.

Yet by the end of the night he had found nothing. Not a hint, not a record, nothing! In despair he manipulated the other gatekeeper to let him back out and then found a quiet room to hole up in. His former minion was beyond using now thanks to Edward's viciousness, and so Eliavres had to link minds with Edward himself again. *Where else could it be?* his thought blasted into Edward's mind, but Edward had no idea either. Instead of letting go, he rode in the back of Edward's mind the next day as he directed him to scour every other location in Caersus without success.

Sick to his stomach, Eliavres now realised that he had summoned the DeÁine army to retrieve absolutely *nothing*! And they were only five days away from entering Brychan! A mere five days to go before he had to explain why he had dragged them all this way on a fool's errand almost on the scale of Anarawd's disaster! What was he going to do?

Then it came to him. Whatever else happened, the DeÁine army would have to have its resounding victory. For the Donns the recovery of the Gorget had probably always been secondary, and it sounded as though Masanae and Quintillean had something of their own planned which had nothing to do with the Gorget either. Yet from rummaging around in Edward's head, he now knew that many of the officers had had the effrontery to question whether there even was a DeÁine threat. Well Edward would have to prove his leadership, for both their sakes.

So, come the morning he had Edward call his officers to him to tell them that he had received word that the DeÁine army was a matter of days away. Many men questioned how Edward knew, but were brushed off with imperious disdain. Easier to counter were those who asked, why they did not wait for the Knights to join them if the threat was so grave? How would the Knights even know there was a threat, Edward demanded? Snowed-in in their eyries they could have had no word, nor could they hope to come to Brychan's aid. Many there looked troubled at this. When it came to the DeÁine, Brychan had never attempted an armed engagement without the Knights' formidable strength, yet the logic of Edward's pronouncement was unavoidable. If they waited for the Knights, the DeÁine might already be in Brychan before they could arrive.

Reluctantly the officers agreed that they could not take the chance that the DeÁine were not there. Mad as a hare they might think Edward by now, but even the crazed had to be right occasionally. And if this was the one time when he had the right of the situation, then they had no choice but to march on. Caersus was a good fallback position, but the obvious place to fight was in the centre of the Gap around Seigor. The orders were therefore given, and the weary army dragged itself out into the snow once more, and far back in the ranks a stumbling Jacinto marched with them.

Three days later the army had reached the vast stronghold of Seigor which, to their amazement stood empty to the wind. Edward refused to allow the men inside, where he might have trouble getting them out again, his provosts forming a line of guards as a precaution, while his scouts made a cursory inspection only to declare it emptied of anything of use. Berengar had had his men leave what they could, well back in the second or third storerooms against just such an eventuality, reasoning that men caught in a siege would have the time to search more thoroughly. So as Eliavres flayed Edward onwards from within the depths of his mind, the men's morale sunk even lower with the fear of the tales of the Knights refusing to fight coming true.

Jacinto could hardly believe what he saw. Surely the Knights would not be so cowardly? He was hoping like mad that nobody now remembered his proud boasts of being one of the Order for fear of retribution. As it was, his back was a constant reminder of the cost of getting Cwen's family away, and he was sure he could not take another beating. The constant movement of marching chaffed his scabs, and he kept feeling them crack and starting to weep, so that by the first night his shirt had stuck to him with dozens of separate oozings. Yet thanks to Harry and his friend Burt, who had been the one with the maggots, Jacinto had had no further return of the fever and it was healing, if messily.

At the camp fire beyond Seigor, the little knot of men who regularly congregated around Harry and Burt huddled together to brew up the thin soup, which was better for drinking than eating. Many were deeply despondent at the departure of the Knights from the castle, yet Harry and Burt seemed surprisingly optimistic.

"Now you listen up, lads!" Harry hissed, as Burt signalled them to silence and to draw closer around their own little camp fire. "If this daft bugger really does find us some DeÁine, then you remember that castle!"

"Why, serge?" a squint-eyed runt of a recruit asked.

"Because we're going to run like fuck back to it if things start really going wrong! That's why!"

"Ain't that desertin'?" another, obviously too young to have ever fought before, wondered.

Burt sucked his buckled teeth in a theatrical show of exasperation. "Vhey don't know what it's like, do vhey Harry? Listen, cloth-ears! Vhe DeÁine don't come strollin' in 'ere wiv just a few men like vhey was on a high-day picnic, ye know! Vhey bring slaves. *Fousands* of 'em!"

"And all of 'em scared shitless of the nasty buggers behind 'em! More scared of them than us," Harry carried on. "How many men we got 'ere? Three or four thousand, tops."

"Free or four fousand!" Burt agreed. "Nuffink to what the DeÁine'll bring."

"They'll have that many slaves just to soften us up before the real troops get here! We'll be lucky to survive the slaves before we ever meet the real army," Harry continued. "So once the battle's got going, you lot watch me and Burt! If it all starts going tits up in a hurry, we're heading straight back to that castle, shutting the gate and sitting it out. Fighting reasonable odds is one thing, but where are the proper officers? Have you seen anyone much above the rank of captain who looks old enough to have been in any of the big scraps? No! And why's that? …'Cause they ain't here, that's why! There isn't a single officer with enough experience to lead us to a decent victory, even with good odds. Somethin's wrong here, lads. Somethin's very wrong!"

At this point Jacinto felt he had to say something too. "That's why the Knights left," he said softly. "They'll fight anything, but they won't commit suicide! If they've left it's because there's some good tactical reason why it's better to lose one castle, or make the DeÁine think they've run away."

"Why's that?" someone asked with a hint of sarcasm.

"I don't know," admitted Jacinto, "but then I'm not a master tactician like most of the ealdormen are."

Some of the men started to laugh at him, and he was beginning to regret speaking, when Harry cut across them.

"No lads, he's right. Never mind what some of those idiots in Arlei were telling you, this lad's right, the Knights don't give up and they don't just run away. If they've left Seigor empty it's for a purpose. I don't know what that is either, but if we end up in a massacre, I'm not goin' to argue as to why there's a good stout wall to hide behind a few miles back."

And when it came to arguing neither was Eliavres, however daft he thought Masanae's demands were. His last few days had been the stuff of nightmares even for a member of the Abend. Following Masanae's imperious demand, he had investigated the outskirts of Caersus and found that there was indeed a convent. However gaining access was quite something else. The woman who kept the tiny porter's gate into the high-walled compound was only lacking the Power to be as frightening as Masanae herself, and he only knocked once to ask for entry. Having been sent away with her scathing retorts ringing in his ears, he walked the full circuit of the walls to see if he could find a way in.

Unfortunately for him, whoever had built this compound had had the lascivious thoughts of men closely in mind, and there was no way that Eliavres could see that he could get in by. Cursing fluently under his breath, the only plan he could come up with was using the Power to blast a hole straight through the walls. But he could hardly risk doing that until the army was well out of town. The last thing he needed was for them to turn around to investigate sudden explosions.

Curse Masanae! How did she expect him to get in? He was hardly surprised that her agents, whoever they were, had failed to gain access. He had entered the royal court with far greater ease than this place, and the court had been heavily guarded by experienced soldiers! Nor could he imagine what she could want with these young women that made it so important. Surely she had her pick of thousands of slave girls if it was for one of her – or more likely Helga's – nasty little experiments? Shivering in the bitter wind, he trudged in depressed frustration once more around the walls until he reached the main road which ran into Caersus from Marloes, and there his luck changed.

Ploughing their weary way towards him was a party of monks with what looked like a large group of lepers. Like all DeÁine, he had a natural immunity to the disease and therefore despised those Islanders so cruelly afflicted, even though the DeÁine had been the carriers who had brought this previously unknown disease here. Yet now the lepers seemed to be his answer, bundled up in swathes of ragged cloths as they were. With many wearing thinly woven linen scarves wound even up and over their faces they were totally anonymous, and who would think of looking amongst lepers? No Islander would willingly put on a leper's rags for fear of catching it, and a DeÁine could not be a leper – except for now, that is.

A gangly scarecrow of a figure, close enough to Eliavres' height to be useful, limped along painfully almost at the end of the winding column of refugees. Eliavres watched him for a few minutes longer to make sure he could imitate the halting walk, then reached out with his mind to the figure.

Weakened by the disease and the cold, the man was an easy target, being half way to losing consciousness already. He put up little resistance to Eliavres' battering against his mind, and soon Eliavres had him dropping further and further back. Meanwhile Eliavres was making a crouched run behind snow-heavy bushes to reach the back of the column. For the first time he was glad of the snow as it bulked up the thin, spindly brooms' branches into a more obscuring screen.

Finally the man came close enough to him and he pounced, pulling the weak figure down into a ditch and snapping his neck with a quick wrench. Hurriedly Eliavres pulled the rags off the corpse, struggling not to heave at the smell. The man's face was near skull-like and rotting, with bits of his flesh adhering to the cloth. The detached part of Eliavres' mind registered that the unfortunate leper had added frostbite to his list of miseries, while also thinking that the caught tatters of flesh would help him in his substitution.

He was just crawling out of the ditch as a monk came rushing back to find his lost sheep.

"Come, come Gilbert! We're nearly there. Summon your strength, my friend! A few more yards and we reach safety, there are no DeÁine here! Then you may rest all you want."

And with that the monk caught hold of Eliavres' arm and began to lead him forward. For a heart-stopping moment Eliavres expected the monk to feel that he was more firmly fleshed than the leper, but then realised that the monk had a thick wad of cloth wrapped around each hand as makeshift mittens. Between them and the cold he was probably hard pressed to even grip anything, let alone feel what it was. Eliavres' put on what he hoped was a convincing show of exhaustion, stumbling along in an imitation of the leper's limp and making the odd muffled groan from within his reeking mask to cover his laughter at the monk's comment. No DeÁine? Not much!

By the time they caught up with the rest they were nearly at the convent gates, and the monk left him to scurry forward with his brothers to plead for sanctuary with the sisters. Another leper said something unintelligible to Eliavres and he responded with a noncommittal grunt, but aside from that everyone seemed too wrapped up in their own misery to bother him. After what seemed like an age, but was in fact probably only a few minutes, Eliavres saw the unassailable gate swing open and the first of the lepers trudged within. He made sure he was no longer quite at the back as he passed through, knowing that the last man would be more memorable, and was gratified to find that it was in fact a woman who was last in and who solicited concern and sympathy from the nuns, nicely distracting them.

The dragoness of a porter closed the gate with a resounding thump and dropped a huge oak bar across it. She looked as though she had spent her childhood pulling the family's plough all by herself, and Eliavres yet again was struck by the oddity of these Islanders that they would allow a common peasant into their sacred orders. Entrance to the DeÁine's temples and the school of the acolytes was reserved for those of pure blood or of proven parentage. Why would any race contaminate the sacred with mongrel stock?

Other sisters were ushering the lepers towards a small hall and a building which looked as though it might be a stable. Obviously the sisters did not normally have many in the way of guests – no doubt in fear of the ungodly stealing their 'lambs'! Even now Eliavres noticed that the younger members of the sisterhood were being kept at a distance, running to fetch food and blankets, and that it was the old battle-axes who were doing the ushering of the lepers. He snorted in amusement. As if even the randiest of novices would risk copulating with a leper – she might find herself still holding bits of him long after he had come and gone!

More irritating was the fact that he realised he would have to wait until darkness fell before he could begin to move about within the compound. He found a spot near to the door, luckily a place where few others wanted to be, and tried to imitate the lepers' awkward sitting positions. The soup that came round was hardly appetising, and he left the bowl on the floor where it was soon snatched away by another. Even the short winter's day seemed unendingly long as Eliavres waited for the shadows to lengthen, and finally descend into blackness. Just as he was ready to creep out, a bell began to toll and the lepers struggled to their feet. Moments later the monks reappeared and began shepherding them out across the frozen courtyard and into the church. A cursed service! That was all he needed!

Then he realised that it actually served his purpose better than he could have anticipated. In his ignorance he had failed to register that everyone within the walls would be there – again something that the DeÁine would never dream of allowing, since the solace of the Sacred Temples was not for the great unwashed. The lepers were chivvied into places along the north aisle with a few monks to watch over them. The rest of the monks went to the south aisle, while the body of the nave was filled with the nuns and the lay sisters. Eliavres found himself right up at the altar end of the aisle, partly hidden by a massive stone pillar. To his delight he realised that opposite him were several women who must have been incarcerated with the nuns for political reasons. Many were women of obvious wealth and breeding, who were possibly of high rank and had been shuffled away here after their husbands' deaths – no doubt out of the way of sons who wanted to run their inheritance without constant chastising by a sharp tongue! Although all had their heads covered with capacious scarves, most had wisps of grey hair showing.

That made his targets blindingly clear. The one who had been rejected by her future husband stood defiantly, making no attempt at all to join in the chanted responses. She was the only young woman not in nun's garb, and her dark hair escaped in thick strands from beneath the headscarf without her making any attempt to tuck it back under. The bad news for Eliavres, as far as he could see, was that this Heledd looked as though she could prove to be a real handful. If this bunch of frosty-hearted hellions had failed to instil some sense of obedience into her, Eliavres was definitely not looking forward to trying to drag her into the DeÁine army.

Then his heart sank even further. The gate guardian and another equally large and hefty nun marched up the central space between the standing ranks of nuns, dragging a scratching and spitting figure between them. In the struggle the headgear had been lost, and Eliavres had a clear view of his other target. Her light red hair had been brutally chopped short in a ragged bob, which somehow only seemed to emphasise her urchin-like wildness. More round-faced than her sister, they shared the same dark, flashing eyes, and while neither had the regular features of conventional beauty, they both radiated a sexuality which was almost tangible. The younger Breizh was certainly having an effect on the monks, as her loose white novice's gown pulled tightly across her full, bare breasts beneath, and she knew it! With a wicked laugh of the kind that had probably never been heard within those walls before, she ran her tongue over her lips, and in a husky voice better suited to a brothel than a convent, called out to the monks,

"Remember the edict to love your neighbours, boys!" accompanying it with a wiggle of her bosom, and some lewd thrusts of her hips in their direction.

It earned her a hard slap across the face from a sour-faced older nun at the altar which made her mouth bleed, but for the next few minutes the chants were accompanied by the sounds of rustling cloth and groans from the younger brothers' benches that had little to do with religious ecstasy. Heledd was making little effort to hide her amusement at the effect her sister was having, and after the service Eliavres was to find out why. Throughout the observances, Breizh was hauled down and up from her knees by her two guards, and at the end marched off before Eliavres could see where. He then had to wait for everyone else to settle down again before he could creep out of the mass of lepers to begin his search. And he was not sure which of the two sisters he dreaded finding first!

As it happened Heledd found him rather than the other way round. He had a fair idea as to which of the buildings housed the widows, and had begun sliding along the shadows in its general direction, when the door flew open and Heledd stormed out, hurling a leather tankard back in at some unseen person.

"Well fuck you!" she shrieked back into the gloomy interior. "You may be content to wither away in this stinking piss-pot, but I'm not!" and slammed the door shut behind her.

As she stomped across the cobbles Eliavres could hear her muttering to herself. "Shrivelled up bunch of old prunes! 'You should be content'!" she snarled in a vicious parody of an older voice. "Content to live in this frozen waste! Spirits! Their families must have been glad to see the back of such a bunch of hypocritical old moaners. 'Don't do this, you shouldn't do that!' Flaming Underworlds! You could take bets on their husbands drinking themselves to death just to get away from them!"

"I take it you want to get out of here, then?" Eliavres slid like a snake from the gloom with his tempting words.

The young woman froze, head whipping round to see who had spoken. When she spotted Eliavres, she took a step back and her head came up defiantly.

"Yes …I want to get out …but not to another prison! What are you offering and why?"

Eliavres could have screamed. The infernal woman had intelligence as well as spirit! How, on the Sacred Temples, was he to know what would appeal to this firebrand and make her come willingly? Then he had an idea.

"My older brother seeks to marry me off to some bucktoothed milch cow so he can get his hands on her family lands," he lied smoothly. "I refused. I prefer the company of other men to what I can find between a woman's legs." That should assure her he was unlikely to rape them. "He had his henchmen drag me off to go to monks to 'think about my future'…" he produced a similar parody to the one he had heard her use. "But events rather overtook us. They shoved me in through the door with those disgusting lepers and have gone off to fight with their beloved king. Ha! And they call me the pervert!"

He saw a smile lurk at the corners of her mouth and mentally gave a sigh of relief. She had taken the bait!

"Oh I know that feeling!" Heledd said with vehemence. "It all sounded so good to start with. Our brother's a minstrel, and the one day the king came through with some of his men on a hunting trip. He took a real shine to our Ben. Made him an offer to come and play at the court. 'You'll be the toast of Arlei,' he told Ben and the fool believed him. Even worse, he told Ben he would find good husbands for us. 'They'll marry far above their station,' he said, 'they'll live in luxury and never know what it is to need for anything ever again.' …I told Ben to wait. …I told him to get in touch with our other brother, Berengar, and ask him what he thought, but *no*… Ben said Berengar was always too busy to worry about us and that, anyway, *he* was old enough to take charge of the family now.

"So before we knew it we'd been packed up and marched back to the capital. We'd barely got through the flaming gates before we were separated from Ben. No doubt he's warming his feet in front of a nice fire and getting drunk on fine wines, but we got shoved off to a bunch of old viperesses. Next thing we know we're being paraded before men of the king's guard. Some nobles! I thought I'd got off lightly when one of the pretty young ones took a shine to me. It was only when he was fumbling me in the dark on the first night, that he let it slip that he spends time in the king's bed too, and I was his first woman! I was his reward, would you believe? The only thing that was getting his cock up was that he thought he was taking the cherry of his king's bastard sister!"

"What did you do?" asked an enthralled Eliavres. The king's bastard sisters? Now it made far more sense as to why Masanae would want them!

"I kicked him in the nuts and made a run for it!" Heledd spat in the snow in disgust. "Apparently he was such a notorious shirt-lifter, all his mates had gathered outside the door to check if it was really going to happen. I got as far as lifting the latch and then they grabbed me. He threw such a tantrum. I think it was only because they feared what the king would do that they didn't slit my throat there and then. Apparently 'darling Eddie' had plans for us and some other poor sod, so we got marched out here to await his pleasure. I got here first, then my sister got here about two months later." Suddenly Heledd threw back her head and laughed. "She'd been thrown out of two nunneries already for being a 'corrupting' influence."

"Why?" Eliavres felt compelled to ask, but Heledd merely beckoned him and turned to walk to the cloister. He followed her up a flight of stone stairs and into what transpired was a dormitory. Heledd led him past rows of austere beds with coarse, folded blankets awaiting the sisters. Through a door at the end they entered another room laid out the same, but now they could hear faint moans. In one of a series of small cells beyond, its door open but with the key still in the lock, they came upon a scene more fitting to the DeÁine pleasure gardens. Three naked women writhed in sexual ecstasy. Eliavres' target was in the middle, her head between the legs of a very young woman, while the remaining older woman had Breizh's breast in one hand while fondling between her legs with the other.

"Sister dear, we have a visitor," Heledd said with amusement.

A moment later Breizh's tousled head appeared and regarded Eliavres with wicked merriment.

"Oh! I was just giving the girls some extra education," she said cocking her head on one side like a bird. "Sorry, but I only do girls or I'd let you join in!"

Masanae, I'm going to find a way of making you pay for giving me this job! Eliavres swore. However, Heledd seemed to have the measure of her sister, for she said pointedly,

"He's come to discuss our futures just the way we planned."

It only took a heartbeat for understanding to appear in Breizh's eyes and for her to bound off the bed, grabbing her shift on the way.

"Sorry girls! Lesson's over for tonight. Tomorrow maybe?" And she followed Heledd and Eliavres out of the door.

Heledd led them to a secluded room on the lower floor and closed the door before turning to Eliavres.

"Alright, what are you offering?"

"I know this woman," Eliavres began, hoping like mad that he had judged this correctly. "She keeps …shall we say an 'unconventional' household, since her husband fortuitously died and left her the money to do as she wishes. Her brother and I have enjoyed one another's company, you understand." He saw Breizh's wicked grin signal her understanding of what he had implied. "This lady lives right on the border down by the sea, near Marloes. Do you know the manor?"

"No, we've always lived in the far north until we were forced down here under guard," Heledd told him.

Great Lotus Smoke! A break at last! Eliavres thought. *With any luck they won't know north from south, or east from west either, but at least if they have some idea, we'll be going roughly in the right direction.*

"When do we go?" Breizh was asking him.

Tapping into Edward's mind, Eliavres found that the army was to march at dawn. "As soon as you've got clothes fit for the journey," he told them in mock solicitousness. "If you can be ready in time, we'll slip out through the gates just before dawn."

"On no you won't!" Breizh told him emphatically.

Eliavres' heart sank into his boots once more. "Why not?" he asked, dreading what other confection of lies he was going to have to produce to get these two moving.

"Because there's a night guard, and she really doesn't sleep!" was Breizh's response. "Spirits! If it had been that simple we'd have been out of here weeks ago! We've tried every route you can imagine. They've built buildings in the way in places where the walls might be passable, there are metal spikes on others – we've even looked at the cellars in case we could dig out, but all the cellars are in buildings away from the walls. These shrivelled bitches have made an art-form out of incarceration!"

"Breizh is right," Heledd confirmed. "The only way will be if you've a strong enough fist to knock the guard-woman out."

Eliavres was beginning to get the grandfather of all headaches, and he had a nasty suspicion it was not going to go away until he had handed these two over to Masanae.

"I think I can manage the guard," he said with confidence, although the girls looked sceptical.

In the depths of the night, he had the two of them wait back from the gate while he went forward alone. With a fine blast of Power he fried the guard's brain, and laid her out where the two would not see that he had not touched her. Gesturing them forward, he unlocked the gate and led them out. By the time they had made a partial circuit of Caersus they could see the tail end of Edward's army marching off, and Eliavres concocted another ruse to justify following them. But by the first night he had had quite enough of Heledd and Breizh, and when Masanae contacted him to find out whether he had them, he asked if she needed them alive.

You realise you have selected possibly the two most irritating women in the Islands, he told her. *Wouldn't their corpses be enough?*

No they wouldn't! Masanae screamed back. *They're to get to me alive, do you hear Eliavres? Alive! And it will be the worse for you if they don't. Much, much worse!*

Then how long are you prepared to wait while I drag them every step of the way? he spat back in annoyance.

That gave Masanae pause for thought. *How far away are you?*

Eliavres had trouble hiding his exasperation. *The army you're going to wipe out is about two days from Seigor, but at this rate it's going to take me twice that to get these two there if you don't want them damaged.* He ground his teeth in fury. *You can tell the Donns they should be able to have their battle in about six days' time. When do you want these two? Midsummer?*

Masanae withdrew briefly then returned to inform him, *You may use a glamour on them. Only a mild one! Just enough to make them compliant. When I get my hands on them I want no hint of damage to their minds or tainting by the Power, do you understand! Nothing that will leave a permanent marker in their bodies!*

Very well. Nothing permanent, Eliavres agreed wearily and withdrew. What were those two up to? Such insistence on an uncorrupted state spoke of something ritual, and once again he had picked up on the hint that he would have Quintillean to answer to, as well, if things went wrong. Viewing the recumbent bodies of Heledd and Breizh, he wove a small glamour and inserted it into their minds, hoping against hope that it would be sufficient.

It was, but only just. The two women were a force to be reckoned with, and a glamour that fitted Masanae's requirements was barely up to the task of making such strong-willed personalities responsive. Nor was he helped by Heledd's sex drive. He had expected more trouble with the younger one, but with no women around Breizh merely grumbled and sulked. Heledd, the other hand, was man mad, as he discovered on the second night when he caught her in the embrace of a trailing soldier. All he could hope was that Masanae was not expecting virgins, because he was quite sure that neither woman had been that in a very long time.

Then a wicked thought occurred to him. So be it. He would keep them away from sexual adventures whilst they were in his care so that he could say in all truth that he had allowed nobody to defile them. Masanae had never bothered herself much with Island customs, and so she would be unlikely to believe that the bastard sisters of the king himself would be free to copulate like bitches on heat with whomsoever they chose. No high ranking DeÁine girl would even get the chance to behave that way, so let

Masanae believe what she would. And then, when whatever nasty spell or rite she was planning failed, that would teach her to take more notice of him when he told her things about the Islanders. As for his two captives, their fate once they left him was of no interest to him at all.

Chapter 28

Outfoxing the DeÁine

Brychan: Eft-Yule

For the next two days after arriving at Garway, Berengar fretted and paced the Grand Master's office. He allowed scouts to go out, but only half a day's ride out, and was most firm regarding the punishment he would meet out to anyone foolish enough to disobey.

"Half a day's ride gives you all time to come back here at speed," he told the scouts at their briefing on both days. "Make no mistake, this is serious! The DeÁine army that's making its way across the Gap is the most serious threat we've had to face since Moytirra. This is no DeÁine scouting party to be chased back with their tails between their legs by a few bold Knights! We have to be cunning and considered in our actions, not hasty and overreach ourselves. I promise you, we will fight back! But not against these odds. When we fight it'll be to win and win decisively.

"So, galling though it is, I want you to observe them. I want to know how fast they're moving. I want to know how many slaves and slave drivers are amongst them, and how many there are of their shock troops – the real veterans who'll give us most trouble. We saw the birds on our way here, so they can't have been far off. Our valiant friends at Craws have already become besieged, and prayers will be said for them tonight in the chapel, but nothing we can do now will save them. But I need to know if that was the main DeÁine force heading our way, or if it's a splinter group who've just detoured to take out Craws while the rest march on somewhere else. Go only as far as those highlands which will give you a good view down onto the plain. If they think us cowards hiding behind our walls, all the better, for that means they're underestimating us."

Yet it tore at Berengar more than he would have believed to stay in the office and not act. He just about managed to stay put there, knowing that it would do morale no good if the men saw the Grand Master prowling around like a caged bear, but he missed Esclados terribly. To his old friend he could have confided his doubts without fear of the confidence being betrayed, but even Ranulf was looking to him too much to lead for such confidences to be possible.

On the first day the scouts he had sent westwards towards Craws reported that the castle was totally surrounded, but seemed to be intact. Several thousand were camped around its stout walls, but there was no way that they could be all of the force that the Foresters had reported on the move. Their colleagues who had gone south reported that, surprisingly, Seigor appeared to remain empty, and that they had seen the stragglers of Edward's army still moving along the north-west road. That was confirmed by the scouts who had taken the road between the other two groups. Edward's army was marching as if heading for the major crossroad on the plain, and there was a dark smudge on the horizon that might be the DeÁine, but was as yet too far away to be distinct.

By the second evening the situation had dramatically worsened. The scouts sent to Craws came back with tears in their eyes, talking of great holes rent in the castle walls. Fires burned unchecked within the curtain wall, they reported, and even in the keep there was no sign of movement. Moreover, the DeÁine were moving away, but not up the steep climb up to Garway. They were marching with speed and order on a direct course to towards the crossroad.

"They have to be veterans," the young Knight told Berengar. "A good three thousand of them. They're marching without anyone goading them, and at double time while still keeping in the ranks. Not a man is falling out or behind."

"Flaming Underworlds!" Ranulf cursed beside Berengar. "If they can have three thousand veterans peel off for a separate attack, how many have they got in the main body?"

"I know," Berengar fretted, once he had dismissed the scouts with thanks. "Trees preserve us, but it sounds as though there may be far more veteran troops to deal with than even we feared."

He did not know whether to be glad or sad when the other scouts finally got back. The whole of the rest of the DeÁine army was heading straight for the crossroad all right, and the estimation of twenty thousand looked like being horribly correct. The only good news was that until those who had attacked Craws joined them, there was a higher than normal percentage of slaves. Normally, as all the histories recorded, there were two or three slaves to every veteran and this appeared to be the same composition. Around four thousand veterans currently marched within an army of around twelve or thirteen thousand slaves. Added to this were several hundred slave drivers who would not fight unless it became desperate, plus a strange core unit that one old sergeant believed might be the royal guard, or something like it.

"They weren't the normal companies of shock troops," he told Berengar calmly, although Berengar and Ranulf noticed a slight tremor in his hands as he pointed to the map. "But they were a big step up from the slave companies. And they were one big unit – probably near to one thousand men I'd say, so that's double the size of the usual companies of veterans. And they were totally surrounding something I've not seen since Moytirra." That made the senior men present really sit up and take notice.

"Those of us old enough to remember know the slave drivers ride those big grey, leather-skinned beasts with the two horns, or those abominable beasts with skin which overlaps like armour plating, a low head, and funny snuffling snouts. But the beasts here were huge lizards – that's the only way I can describe them! They had scales and toed feet that end in wicked looking claws. They were prowling, and not very fast, but it was the kind of pace that I bet they could keep up for hours beyond any horse.

"Four at a time were tied together by great webs – leather, rope, I don't know what, but it was thick – and slung between them were things that looked like a cross between a huge litter and a smallish tent. I reckon at least some of the Abend are in them and there must be some acolytes travelling close to them, because as each 'litter' passes, the snow around it melts – like each one is travelling in a pocket of warm air. And I don't think that's just for the Abend. Those lizard things must need to keep warm or they'll hibernate in the cold like our little native ones do. But kept warm I bet they can't half move! Which is probably why the Abend have litters not carts. Those straps look like they'd hold under tremendous pressure, so as long as the lizards' riders keep them all heading in the same direction when they take off there'd be nothing like a shed wheel, or a broken axle, to slow them down."

"Well with that and the holes blasted in Craws, I don't think we need doubt any longer that the Abend are here, then, do you?" one of the Garway officers said in a choked voice. "I can't imagine the royals making this kind of journey in the middle of winter."

Berengar leaned over to stare down at the map, feeling as though the burden of his office was dragging him down towards it. "No, no doubt at all," he sighed bitterly, "and there's nothing we can do about it for the time being. That fool Edward will lead good men who don't deserve to fight such overwhelming odds to their deaths, and I can think of no way of saving them." He tapped the crossroad on the map and looked up at the scouts from both days' reconnaissance, who he had asked to join him to ensure consensus over the information.

"Would you all agree, then, that by tomorrow evening Edward's army will have reached the crossroad?" The two separate groups of scouts who had gone that way all nodded. "And that the DeÁine will reach the same point sometime within a few hours of them?" The other scouts grimly gave terse nods. "Then may the Trees preserve us all! Because there's going to be a slaughter that I won't even dignify with the name of a battle!"

The following day Berengar did not even bother sending out scouts – there seemed no point. Lookouts were posted close to Garway on the off-chance that the DeÁine would feel emboldened by their easy victory, and come looking for a second, but Berengar doubted that would happen. Why waste time on a siege that they could not win when the whole of Brychan lay ripe for the picking? Instead, he redoubled his efforts to put Garway on a war footing. The first of the chambers running back into the mountains were inspected, and Berengar was appalled to discover that his two predecessors had paid little attention to them. Without delay, all the men not on specific duties were set to sweeping them out, replenishing torches and clearing old birds' nests out of the air vents.

For an awful hour or two Berengar's memory deserted him when he was confronted with the Grand Master's personal vault, and he could not remember the sequence in which the keys in the complicated locks had to be turned. Yet he had to get in there, for inside were the plans for the labyrinth of chambers within the mountains – chambers he was sure he remembered someone telling him were on at least seven levels, yet at the moment were only known on two. He was one step short of ordering the strongest men up with crowbars, when it suddenly came back to him. Before he could forget it he dashed back to the vault and opened it, feeling an intense rush of relief when he hauled on the massive door and it swung stiffly back on its hinges.

"You had me worried there," Ranulf said with studied calm.

"You were worried? I was nearly needing a change of underwear!" spluttered Berengar, so relieved that he made no attempt at maintaining an appearance of composure with only the two of them present. "Lost Souls, Ranulf! I never expected to have to use that information! And you know how it is when you've had so many other things to think of in between, it just seems to evaporate!"

"Well you're in now," reassured his friend. "The question is, is the stuff you wanted in here?"

Propping the door firmly open, and with Ranulf now in possession of the keys' sequence as a back-up, they began to investigate the contents of what was in effect a small strong-room. Luckily there was some order to the rolls and rolls of parchment stored inside, and they quickly found those that contained drawings of the various holdings of the Knights. Berengar eliminated the smaller scrolls on the basis that he knew the hidden network was vast and would therefore require large numbers of plans, and on the sixth attempt found them. Hurrying to the outer guardroom he laid the drawings out on a table and began to pour over them.

"Great Maker!" exclaimed Ranulf, as he stared over Berengar's shoulder. "So many! I had no idea the works were this extensive! And look at all these side rooms too!"

"Now you see why I wanted these plans," said Berengar with a smile. "See here? …There are stables for all our horses and many more. We don't have to leave them vulnerable to attacks by the Abend's Power down by the lower gate, we can bring them to safety in here. And see …here …and here …they've marked where there are access points to clear the chimneys, so that they don't get clogged up with soot in the event of a long siege. Come on! We've got work to do!"

Before the end of the day, even elderly and senior Knights found themselves with their sleeves rolled up hoicking old hawks nests out of vents, and ancient soot out of chimneys. Or making torches to light the darker corridors, where even the cunningly crafted shafts let no light in that was discernible in the weak winter hours of daytime. Every broom or rake in the fortress was pressed into service, while other men helped haul all the animal feed and bedding up into the mountain. The castle's cook was fetched to set two kitchens which he had never known about before into order, and to get the store rooms fit to be used once more.

Through the next day too, the frantic activity carried on, and no-one could complain because nobody worked harder than their new Grand Master. Yet as he sank exhausted into his bed that evening, he felt reassured that Garway was now almost ready to face a long incarceration cut off from the rest of Brychan, until the snow eased, or a miracle happened and the DeÁine went home. As he propped his boots up beside the bed, just in case he was summoned during the night, Berengar offered up a heartfelt prayer to the Trees.

"Keep Cwen safe at Tarah," he beseeched them firstly. Then, "and get Esclados to get a move on! Please don't let anything have happened to Warwick at Laon that would prevent Esclados from getting the ancient ones' tunnels opened again. If we're to fight off the DeÁine and keep your people and the sacred groves safe, I need that way through the mountains!"

For his part Esclados was also offering up more than the odd prayer. After he had left Berengar back at Foel, he had done his best to hurry, but even before Berengar had reached Seigor, Esclados and his escort had been fighting the snow on the rapidly climbing road. Once they had passed the road heading back down to Tern, they had been forced to slow down dramatically to what felt like a snail's pace. They had reached a wayside inn that night, and then been stuck there for over a day as news came in that the road ahead was blocked. Although normally not a common occurrence this far south, an avalanche had poured down into the steep-sided valley from off the snow-laden slopes.

"It's the sheer quantity of it," the despairing landlord told them. "Up here it's just snowed and snowed without it having a chance to settle and compact. It's still like powder, and once it starts moving under its own weight, it flows like a river in torrent until the pressure comes off. This is the third in as many weeks!"

It did nothing for Esclados' sense of frustration, even though there was some sense of relief that it was natural rather than another infernal trick of the Abend's. Luckily the local men managed to carve a way through the next day and reluctantly let the Knights go forward, even though they deemed it too unsafe to let ordinary travellers through yet. As the little party entered the path it felt like descending into a snowy tomb. Pristine white walls hemmed them in closely on both sides far above their heads, and there were constant tiny rivulets of crystals slithering down on them. The horses were plainly frightened and only going on because of their training, which Esclados thought was probably not far off the mark for most of the men too. He personally found the experience intensely claustrophobic, and had to consciously work to keep his breathing steady.

On the other side they stopped and turned back to look at the way they had come, and suddenly appreciated the locals' warnings. Piled up behind the little manmade gulch were ragged heaps of snow, rising to several times the height of men. But worse than that, high above, great windswept peaks of snow balanced precariously on the rocks just waiting for the wrong gust to send them crashing down into the valley.

"Let's get out of here before that lot gets moving!" Esclados said with feeling, and nobody else needed any encouragement. Yet no sooner had they reached the next inn when they ran into the same problem. Where the rocky valley narrowed on the climb up to Laon, the snow had virtually filled it. The villagers of the tiny hamlet in a protected bend in the valley had done the best they could to begin clearing the way, but it also required the Knights at Laon to dig downhill to meet them. For another whole day, Esclados could do nothing more constructive than put his shoulders behind a shovel shifting snow.

"After this is all done I'm asking for a transfer to somewhere where they never get snow!" he said with feeling to a young soldier, as they dug side by side. "I've seen enough of this white stuff to last me a life time! As far as I'm concerned it's very overrated – one white mountain looks just the same as another. Even the bloody animals are white up here! Look at that!"

And he pointed to where a white fox had appeared on a rocky outcrop above them and was watching them work. To his amazement, the young soldier dropped his shovel and made a deep obeisance towards the fox.

"Gods' speed to you, Master Fox," the young man intoned respectfully.

"What in the Islands are you doing?" an astonished Esclados demanded.

"Paying my respects," the young man told him, as if it was the most obvious thing to be doing on a freezing cold winter's morning, then realised that Esclados was looking back blankly. "I come from up in the mountains," he explained, "and my grandparents always said that white animals like that one were fey."

"I thought it was just camouflage," Esclados said with noticeable cynicism. "All the better to hunt with, and all that."

"Oh, it is," his companion agreed. "And for the most part the white animals you see are just ordinary animals with their winter coats on. But that one was all white. There wasn't a fleck of anything else on it. With the natural animals you'll still see tiny bits of their normal browns or greys flecked amongst the white. And where did it come from? This whole mountainside is a death-trap. Do you see anything worth risking death to hunt for? No. …And look at the slope above us. He didn't come past us did he? But look up there. Do you see any tracks? Because I don't, and even a fox would've left some sign of his passing on a pristine slope like that."

Esclados had to admit that the lad had a point.

"Well what is it, then, if it's not a normal animal?" He had a nasty thought. "This isn't some trick of the DeÁine's you see up here is it? I've never heard of anything like that, but I wouldn't put it past them!"

"No, no! Not the DeÁine," the young soldier said emphatically, "definitely not the DeÁine! Grandma said they were the familiars of the old ones, the people who lived in the Islands before we came. Sometimes they appear, like they're checking up on us. She said that although some superstitious folk blame them for various misadventures that befell them, she'd never known them be anything but benevolent. Sort of like a guardian Spirit, but older and more rooted in the Islands."

"Well in that case I hope they're portents of good news," Esclados sighed, "because we surely need some!" Then he looked back up at the slope, and saw that the fox was still watching them with none of the normal wariness. "Do you hear that, Mr Fox?" he called out. "We could do with a spot of help here. I've got to get up to those Knights in the castle, because my friend is expecting me to come to his aid over in the west. And soon! Not in the spring when this cursed stuff melts! I don't need a long road to march an army *down* – which you'll know if you're the smart fox this lad says you are – just a little gully for me and my men to get *up* through." The young soldier gave him a nudge in the ribs, forgetting the older Knight's rank in the presence of one of the fey. "…Please. …If it's not asking too much," Esclados added after the prompt.

With unnerving knowingness the fox nodded his head and turned to trot off up the mountainside.

"Well there he goes… Bugger me!" Esclados exclaimed, as the fox disappeared behind a small mound of snow and then never reappeared again. "Where did he go?"

"Told you so …sire," the young soldier said with cheerful smugness. "Definitely fey! She knew a thing or two did my grandma!"

Esclados grunted, "*Hmmph*! Don't suppose she knew a cure for infestations of DeÁine amongst those other pearls of wisdom, did she?" he asked with dry humour.

The young soldier's enthusiasm faded. "No sire, I'm afraid not. They killed her on a raiding party through the mountains."

Esclados wished he could have swallowed his words. "I'm so sorry, son. Maybe one day we'll give those bastards their just desserts. But in the meantime, you just keep prodding me any time any of her wise words come back to you. You're grandma might not be with us in body, but her wisdom might well help us even from beyond the grave."

The young man's smile came back, and together they picked up their shovels and began digging again. However, they had barely begun again when a frantic yelling behind them alerted them to impending danger.

"Get back here! Now! The snow's on the move again!" one of the watchers was yelling repeatedly to all the diggers.

Grabbing the tools, Esclados and the soldier pelted back down the short stretch of slope and under the rocky overhang which protected the corner turn in the road. Even as they were running they could hear an ominous rumbling behind them and felt a growing chill. As they were joined by the last of the diggers and watchers, the rumbling rose to a roar and the view backwards disappeared into white. The locals ushered them further back around the corner to the safety of a shallow cave, and from there they saw the snow appear like a white tidal wave.

For a heart-stopping moment Esclados thought of the poor folk on their previous stop lower down the valley, for it occurred to him that they were right in line for another icy deluge. Yet it was as though the snow was also being guided. With the snow came a searing wind that swept it towards the western slope of the valley away from the road. The steep river bed of the mountain torrent, which raced down the steep slopes when it was not frozen, now carried a towering flood of snow, and the huddled diggers could hear the rocky bed being carved deeper by the force of it. The rocks themselves seemed to scream in protest at the weight of snow, and on several occasions, Esclados was sure he saw huge boulders being carried along in the thundering snow. Then as suddenly as it had begun it stopped, and a deathly hush descended upon the valley.

"Is that it?" Esclados asked one of the locals, realising that he was whispering as if the noise of his voice would start another downfall.

Instead of answering, the man and a handful of his neighbours crept cautiously to the sheltered bend and peered round it.

"Sacred Trees!" one of them exclaimed, and the remainder of the diggers saw the men straighten and step out into the open to stand in open-mouthed amazement.

Hurrying forward they were all greeted by something none of them were prepared for. The whole deluge of snow had been swept to one side leaving a narrow but passable path wending its way up the mountainside. Even more astonishing was the state of the snow. Although the mountains were still heavily covered, in the valley the remaining snow had been packed down hard, so that although it ran in a steep, solid sheet almost to the top of the valley walls, there was no longer any danger of fresh avalanches. Then, far above them on a shoulder of the valley, they saw the distant figure of the fox.

"The White Fox is back!" the young soldier cried, pointing, and as one the villagers went down on one knee and bowed their heads as a sign of respect.

The soldiers needed no prompting to join them, and as he knelt on the snow the thought occurred to Esclados, *I think I've been looking to the wrong spirits! All these years I've been bending my knees to the Blessed Martyrs and wondering why they had no place in our chapels. But the old men were right. There's something older in these Islands that still has great power if only we'd open our eyes and see it. It's not just the Trees – they're merely a visible symbol of it. There are animals and even the land itself. Are the tales of Ergardia true?* it occurred to him to wonder. *Is the very land toxic to the DeAine? And if so, is that because the old ways have never died out on that Island like they have elsewhere? Do we give to these spirits something in the way of energy by the strength of our belief? I have to tell Warwick about this!*

As the fox disappeared into the snowy landscape once more, Esclados clambered to his feet with all the speed he could manage and called to his men to fetch the horses.

"Aren't you going to wait for the locals to check if it's safe?" one of the Knights questioned him.

Esclados shook his head. "Look son, if that fey fox went to all the trouble of shifting that weight of snow, I think we have to trust him to have ensured we aren't going to slither off at the first bend in the road. This is as good as it's going to get, as far as I can see, so let's make the most of it."

Thanking the villagers for their hospitality, the small band of Knights and men walked their horses briskly onwards up the mountain road. As Esclados had suspected the way remained open. A shallow coating of snow still covered the road, but nothing that the horses could not cope with, and although the walls of snow sometimes came almost onto the road the worrying little cascades of loose stuff had gone. Before, even the sound of the horses' hooves had been enough to cause small slides and ripples in the surface, but now they were able to clatter along with increasing confidence. Their joy increased when they turned another bend and almost walked into another band of Knights coming down. With picks and shovels strapped to their saddles, they had evidently been attempting to clear the road from their end too.

As delighted greetings and introductions took place, the newcomers told Esclados and his men that they too had had a visit from the fox. He had stood in their way and barked at them until they had got off the road to safety in one of the large caves that lay along the upper road. They suspected that the river of snow must have started from above the castle, for when they had emerged, it was to find that the route behind them was clearer than all their efforts had left it. However, Esclados communicated the urgency of the mission, and without hesitation the leading Knight turned his men around and they all rode up to Laon with speed. As they clattered in under the portcullis, the Knight was calling for word to be sent to the ealdorman, and no sooner had they dismounted and begun to walk towards the keep, than the door was thrown open and a figure was silhouetted against the light.

Esclados had seen Ealdorman Warwick on several occasions although they had never spoken much, and he was glad to see that the man he now knew was the head Foresters in Brychan looked much as he ever had. Easily as tall as Esclados, in contrast, Warwick was an angular man who carried not an ounce of extra weight. His dark skin and tightly crinkled black hair proclaimed his DeÁine slave ancestors, even though his family had lived in Brychan for years. The ealdorman had never forgotten, though, the tales his mother had told him of the family's flight when she was young. How the few men had chosen to stand and fight when the fleeing slaves had been caught near the border, to give their families the chance to make a final run for it, even though they knew they had no chance of winning against DeÁine Hunters. And how a patrol of Knights had thundered down on them from seemingly out of nowhere to save the day. Too late for Warwick's grandfather who had taken a mortal wound, but in time to escort the exhausted group back to a castle, where they had been tended to with kindness and understanding, and helped to start a new life away from constant fear.

As Esclados relayed Berengar's message to Warwick, the man fixed him with an intense stare, and a fire seemed to smoulder in the dark brown eyes.

"So Berengar believes that pervert Edward is DeÁine," he hissed and shook his head. "There was always something about that lily-white snake that gave me the creeps – and not just the knowledge of what he does to those too weak to resist him in that dungeon of his. Trees, why didn't I see it! Those colourless eyes should've screamed it at me if nothing else did. *Aach*! It just goes to show that so often we only see what we expect to see. And you say you have proof of this?"

Esclados pulled the book from within the folds of his tunic, and carefully opened it to the witness list. Part of him was waiting to have to snatch it back after witnessing Rainer's reaction to it, but Berengar had been right, Warwick was a very different man. He took it in with one intense sweeping glance and sat back.

"Well that's going in the castle vault for safe keeping straight away," he declared. "Sacred Root and Branch, it's blindingly obvious, isn't it! He's a bastard by birth as well as nature! No wonder he's got himself into such a froth if he thinks that, against the odds, you lot have found the evidence to bring him down." A grin of satisfaction spread across Warwick's face. "I surely hope I'm present when he comes to the reckoning," then it faded as he added, "although Richert's death is a sad loss. He would've made a fine leader for Brychan. I met this girl you speak of, you know."

"Really?" Esclados was surprised. "I thought she kept well away from court?"

"As I do! Or as much as I can. No, this was actually at Amroth. As head of the Foresters I needed to speak to Richert away from the court, and in a place where nobody would wonder why the commander of a lonely hilltop castle should need to be far from his territory. So he invited me to Amroth. He said that if I was trusting him with my secret then he would trust me with his, and that was Cwen. I liked her enormously. Such a nice, sensible girl, with both her feet securely on the ground. She was just what Richert needed. It was the only time I ever saw him when he wasn't having to keep looking over his shoulder. I think it says everything about her character that, distraught though she must be at losing him, she would decide to take action instead of weeping in her widow's weeds – and she is Richert's widow no matter what the court might think! That nasty baggage he got married off to will never lament the passing of the man as much as she will."

Esclados breathed a huge sigh of relief. Without knowing it Cwen had paved the way for him, and he wished that he could turn back time and have them come here first. Then Cwen and Swein would never have had to endure the cynical finger of doubt and blame Rainer had pointed at them, for Rainer would have found it much harder to dismiss them with two ealdormen, and all the Foresters, at their side. Then he remembered Berengar, and hoped that if he could get lucky once it might happen twice.

"I think you should know," he said to Warwick, "that our friend Berengar is much taken with Cwen too."

"And why not, she's a good person."

"Errr ...not that kind of taken. Emm ...smitten might be closer."

Warwick's eyes opened wide and then the grin reappeared. "By the Trees! Is he really? Well, well, I can think of no-one better to take Richert's place. ...Does she know how he feels?"

Esclados sighed. "I'm not sure," and then suddenly realised that he would have to tell Warwick of Berengar's family connections for an explanation to make sense. Taking a deep breath he plunged on, relating why Berengar had been so distressed at the news of the actor's death, although he refrained from mentioning that Berengar's mother might have had DeÁine blood in her veins. "So you see they now have the bond of a lost loved one in common," he concluded. "At the moment I don't think Cwen sees it as anything beyond that, but it is a bond that draws her to him."

"You've brought me nothing but surprises! Are there any more?" Warwick asked in wonderment.

"I think that's about it," was Esclados' wry response. "I think I've used up my surprise quota for several years at this rate."

Warwick pondered on the news for a moment, and then went to call for a pot of caff and several mugs to be brought up, and certain of his key men to be summoned. As they waited for the men and the caff to arrive, he said thoughtfully,

"It's funny, but I always thought Berengar and Richert were alike in many ways, and yet although we now know that they're related, it's by association not blood."

"Indeed," Esclados agreed. "From our discovery it's evident that Richert's own father and mother had no blood connection to Edward, since he was sired by a DeÁine on the mistress. And therefore, although *Edward* and Berengar shared the same mother, there's no blood link between Richert and Berengar." All the while keeping his fingers crossed that any thoughts of Berengar possibly having DeÁine blood remained absent from Warwick's mind.

Mercifully he was saved from further speculation by the arrival of half a dozen commanders and captains, and a huge pot of caff. Used to seeing

Foresters in riding gear, Esclados had forgotten that unless they were on horseback the Foresters' uniform was the kilt, and the captains' entrance was accompanied by the swirling of thick, pleated, dark green tartan. One of the captains carried a rolled map which was unfurled across Warwick's desk for all to consult. The Foresters discussed the network of caves and tunnels in matter of fact tones, and now it was Esclados' turn to be surprised. The network was truly awesome, and it dawned on him that there was room for virtually the entire Brychan sept of knights to withdraw into if the need arose.

"Did we make all this?" he felt compelled to ask. All eyes turned on him. "I mean, I can see that the cave areas were probably made by natural forces – a bit like Berengar tells me they've expanded at Garway. But what of all these connecting tunnels? Some of them – well most of them, actually – seem to be following routes that are too convenient to be caused by underground rivers."

"You're right," a grey-haired, stocky man to his left answered. "The caverns are, by and large, natural. Between here and Garway they've been uncovered by a deliberate policy of exploring, and then enlarging accesses, to bring many of them into use. Since the Battle of Moytirra there's been a feeling that we would need them sooner rather than later, and so we've focused on bringing them to a state where they can be fully utilised. But it has to be said that we didn't do the initial exploration. The very reason the Foresters of long ago chose Laon to be their home was because of the existence of a passageway network. An earlier building – we still don't know if it was a place of defence like a castle or not – seems to have been on this site."

He pointed to the map. "And you see these which lead through the mountains? Well those were here long before any Forester found them. They found them because of an old mosaic at the cave entrance here mapping the routes. Whereas the route from here to Garway is fully underground, this long route which seems parallel to the Castles Road isn't. It tunnels underground to just above Merbach, then comes into the open. If you cross the river and follow what looks like a dead-end valley, there's a hidden entrance to another tunnel. That goes underground above Hirieth and High Cross, with side routes down to each of them.

"In the river valley above Blass it emerges again and you have to cross the river in the open. In theory there's then another passage to Wolfscar that's marked on the map, but despite our best efforts we've never been able to find it in the valley by Blass, and we've never wanted to dig around too much by Wolfscar without knowing where it comes out. Wolfscar's too close to the border for us to risk giving the DeÁine a way to creep behind our lines without us knowing where they might appear."

"And what about this route that seems to go from here over to Redrock and on to Bere?" asked Esclados, tracing the route with his large finger.

Several of the Knights shrugged and another answered him. "Sadly it's another lost route. We're sure it's there, but we've never been able to find it. Our best guess is that the ancient race built them to save them struggling through the mountains in winter. Wait until you see some of their handiwork – it's far superior to anything we could begin to hope to produce. It's amazing! The corridors seem to know you're coming! You start walking and it's all black up ahead, and then the lights start to come on! And they go off behind you too."

"All by themselves?" an astonished Esclados asked. "And what sort of lights?"

"Oh that we knew," Warwick said sadly. "They're somehow concealed in the walls and ceilings behind a thin layer of rock. Long ago someone chipped their way into a couple to try to find out. But all that happened was that the damaged light went out along with those on either side and never came on again, and they found nothing except some little crystals. For fear of wrecking something wondrous in our ignorance we've refrained from further delving. Unfortunately, as you may have already guessed, with the weight of snow we've experienced in the last weeks there may be no chance of us getting to the other castles. The gateways at Merbach and Blass must be under the Maker only knows how many feet of snow and ice. We'll be even luckier if there are no rock-falls to clear come the spring."

"But you can still get to Garway?" queried Esclados anxiously.

"Oh yes, Garway's no problem!" Warwick confirmed confidently. "When do think Berengar will get there?"

"I doubt if he's there yet," Esclados replied doing some quick calculations. "I left him on the eleventh and it's only the twentieth now, even despite my hold ups. He would need to have had a remarkably clear journey to reach there much before the twenty-fourth, because I'd be surprised if things have got much better on the ground since we last trekked eastwards. He should be at Seigor by now, but not much further."

"Well that gives us time to get organised," Warwick said. "I don't wish to go barging in through the walls of Garway frightening the life out of the men there when they're not expecting us. Those tunnels haven't been fully used in generations, and I suspect most of the garrison at Garway don't even know they're there, or if they have heard of them they'll think it's just the stuff of legend. Best give Berengar chance to get there, and let them know that if they see a bunch of dusty figures coming up through their cellars that they aren't ghosts, or something worse! It's about a three day march through the tunnels to Garway. We'll aim to set out from here on the twenty-fifth, it might take an extra day's march if the ice has permeated deep into the mountainside and makes the going slippery."

"Can it do that?" worried Esclados.

"There are plenty of fresh water springs which provide drinking water," Warwick told him, "so in theory if they start to freeze then, yes, we could find ice down there. I'm ashamed to admit that we've not done enough forced marches down there in the depths of winter to be able to say with certainty, so we have to allow for the possibility."

At least Esclados had the consolation of watching Warwick putting well-planned preparations into action over the next couple of days, thus reassuring him that the Ealdorman was not just putting him off with kind words. Indeed, he was heartened to see a band of men, whom Warwick told him were trained in caring for the wounded, and those suffering from frostbite and the effects of the cold, march off ahead of them to set up a way-station. The ealdorman was obviously taking no chances if they should have to bring any wounded back that way, and they had to admit they had no idea of what Edward would do once he had got to Caersus. Would he attack Seigor? Esclados had already mentioned Berengar's order to the granges to evacuate in the face of aggressive action by the demented king, and Warwick feared that Edward would show no mercy to fleeing men.

"Berengar's not a man to leave wounded men to be hacked down," he commented to Esclados. "So we have to consider the possibility that Berengar may have had to fight some sort of action, even if it's only to rescue and retreat. In which case he may well have wounded he would want evacuated to safety, leaving all his men free to strike back. We may be guessing wrongly, but we have to allow for the possibility."

However, before they could shoulder their packs on the morning of the twenty-fifth, a soldier raced up to Warwick clutching a message.

"An exhausted hawk flew in during the night, sire," he gasped, breathless from his dash up the many flights of stairs. "We found her this morning with this on her leg. It's bad news, sire! Very bad!"

Warwick seized the slim scroll and began to read, the colour slowly draining from his face as he did so.

"Sacred Root and Branch! May the Trees protect them," he intoned, then looked up and raised his voice to pass on the news to the senior men who were gathered for final orders. "Craws is besieged by a *DeÁine* army!" Uproar filled the room for a moment, and then discipline reasserted itself and all waited for Warwick to continue. "This speaks as though another message was sent out, but we've received none. It's from our brothers stationed at Craws. They say they can now confirm the number of DeÁine at twenty thousand." He stopped and gasped, and everyone else with him. "*Twenty thousand!* Hounds of the Wild Hunt! That's a bloody huge army! ...Oh Trees have mercy on them! All routes are cut off, they can't get out." The collected men bowed their heads in sorrow. "And the *Abend* are using *Power-fire!*"

The heads whipped back up, alert and seeking confirmation of what they thought they had heard. For his part Warwick ran his free hand over his face and then squared his shoulders.

"Well gentlemen, this is the time we've trained for. So the Abend are leading a DeÁine army into Brychan are they?" He turned to Esclados. "In many ways I wish you were wrong, but this just confirms your suspicions that Edward really is DeÁine, doesn't it?"

Esclados merely nodded but added, "I'm worried sick now as to what Berengar has walked into going west. When did the message leave Craws?"

"The twenty-second," Warwick told him, and Esclados could see the other men all doing the calculations of the distances between the castles. "So with a bit of luck Berengar's made it to Garway. But we can't guarantee that now. Gentlemen! We delay our departure, but only by half a day! I'm now declaring Laon and the Foresters officially on a war footing. I'm increasing the number of men we're taking to half the garrison." He turned to a massive Islander with a mane of untamed red hair. "MacSorley, as our most knowledgeable about the arcane arts, you'll be in charge of Laon while I'm gone. I want this castle to have every protection against anything you think the Abend might throw at us, up and active and in triplicate if necessary, by the time we get back.

"Fintan, you're to be his second, Lulach, you're with me as mine. Llywellyn and Dafydd, as your men are already kitted-up, I want you to get them to draw full weapons from the armoury and be ready at the gate to the tunnels by noon. Owen and Meurig, I now want your companies ready to follow us, with Lulach bringing up the rear. Gwilym, Cadel, Iorweth and Emlyn, you're here with MacSorley and Fintan. Owen, I want you to swop your second with Gwilym so that you now have Hawise and her lot as your second company, and the same with you Dafydd and Cadel, so that Elen and her girls also march with us."

"Girls!" Esclados nearly jumped out of his skin. "You have *women* fighting in the Foresters?"

"Too right!" MacSorley said with a grin. "None better for some of our work."

"I should warn you, Hawise is his daughter," Lulach added with a mischievous twinkle in his eye, "and she's nearly as big as you, so I'd keep quiet with any chivalrous thoughts about the weaker sex because she packs one almighty punch!"

Feeling rather sorry for the older Knight, Warwick added, "But seriously… after Gavra Pass, Hawise came to me and said that maybe we should consider having some women amongst the ranks. She made the convincing argument that as nearly half the Abend and their acolytes are female, it could make tactical sense to have someone who would think the same way as them. I'll admit many of the men were unhappy about it at first, but the girls have proven they're more than able to keep up even over the toughest trials. And they've proved to be some of our most able students when it comes to learning the old crafts. Hawise is in charge of a company because she's proved she's fit for the rank, and her company are the most formidably equipped to meet the Abend witches. Maybe they've just tried harder because they feel they have to prove themselves, but there's no doubting the results they've produced.

"One lass has even begun to decipher some of the old language, and is now MacSorley's leading apprentice up in the watchtower where we experiment. Mercifully Nettie's so tiny there can be no question of her going into battle and she knows it – otherwise there'd be the Underworld to pay if she thought she was being excluded from something, and I'd have to find a way not to risk my best researcher. She's known as MacSorley's terrier, but only behind her back! She's got more fire per pound of body weight than any of the men! I have this strange feeling that one day she'll end up running the Foresters, combat capability or not."

Poor Esclados felt like the world had shifted on its axis and no-one had told him. It went against all his sensibilities to have women in a fighting unit, but he felt marginally better when he met them – or rather, got run into! He had wandered down to the gate to await the companies, whilst Warwick discussed a few last minute details with MacSorley, and was quietly munching on a cheese pasty when he heard approaching feet. From one corridor came the regular tread of men marching in step, but from an adjoining one came the pounding of many feet at the run. Around the corner careered two of the biggest women Esclados had ever laid eyes on, followed by many more. They skidded to a halt almost nose to nose with him, and it was disconcerting for Esclados to find that the two leaders could look him straight in the eye – something no other woman had ever done before.

"Captain Hawise reporting for duty, sire!" the flaming redhead barked with skull-splitting, unbridled enthusiasm.

Esclados peered round her broad shoulders into the grinning faces of one hundred women, all armed to the teeth. If their turnout was less pristine than their male counterparts who appeared moments later, it was clear that they had packed their backpacks first and worried about their uniform last. As they stood in line they tucked in shirts, fastened sword-belts more securely and buttoned up jackets, while the men behind them shook their heads in weary resignation.

"You just had to be first, didn't you Hawise," Dafydd said, strolling up to the front. He rolled his eyes at Esclados in mock exasperation. "I suppose I'd better introduce you, although I've no doubt that you'll wish I hadn't before today's out." For which he got smartly elbowed in the ribs by the other girl, who also must have stood six foot in her socks and weighed as much as Esclados. "Ouch! …This thug is Anna, Hawise's second-in-command." The blue-eyed blonde gave Esclados a stunning smile which he found hard to resist returning. "And this is Captain Hawise, and if she's as much of a pain in the neck to the DeÁine as she is to us, they'll never know what hit them!"

In answer the redhead gave Esclados a broad wink as she turned and kissed Dafydd on the cheek. "Aach, …you know you love me really Uncle Dafydd," she said mischievously. Then her expression hardened. "As for them DeÁine, those witches are just too long overdue for a taste of their own medicine. The likes of them give women a bad name." She turned and called over her shoulder, "What do we do?"

"We hunt the DeÁine!" the raised voices chorused back.

"What comes next?" Hawise yelled

"We kill the bitches!"

"And what's the *best*?"

"We slaughter the *witches*!" the rest howled.

"Sacred Trees!" Esclados mumbled to Dafydd, "They mean every bloody word, don't they!"

The captain sagely nodded his head. "Oh yes, it's personal with them. I don't know the ins and outs, but it has something to do with some old record Nettie found squirreled away about some women prisoners. Up until then the girls were just fired up to do their best to prove themselves to us lot, but afterwards there was this extra something. They won't tell you even if you ask, but they all know and whatever it was it got straight up their skirts!"

"Kilts!" Anna corrected him pointedly. "You get right snitty if someone calls what you're wearing a skirt. Well skirts are for wee girls, and *these* are kilts for fighting women!"

"Kilts then," Esclados sighed, feeling exhausted by their presence already. Yet he had to admit that there was nothing feminine about their clothing given that, like the men, the kilts came down below the knee, while thick woollen, knee-high socks were overlaid with shin guards tied on with criss-cross laces. The stout, felted jackets buttoned up to the neck preventing any glimpse of cleavage, and Esclados could see standard issue chain-mail coats strapped upon their packs.

He was saved from further embarrassment by the arrival of Warwick. With the appearance of the ealdorman everyone, including the exuberant Hawise, became businesslike, and orderly ranks were reformed. Upon Warwick's command, MacSorley stepped forward and unlocked the pair of metal-banded oak doors, then flung them wide open. It hadn't occurred to Esclados until then that they had no torches, but as Warwick stepped forward into the blackness, suddenly light appeared, and Esclados' breath was taken away by the sight of what greeted him.

Chapter 29

 *Unequal Fights*

Brychan: Eft-Yule

As the already exhausted army was forced onwards on their march the next day, Jacinto desperately tried to think of an escape route. What Edward was leading them into did not bear thinking about, because by now Jacinto had little doubt that there really was a DeÁine army up ahead, no matter how unlikely that had seemed not so long ago. The purposeful way that Edward was driving them forward filled Jacinto with dread, for his own experiences of Edward's deluded preoccupations led him to the conclusion that the insane king would think it possible to win, even in the face of impossible odds. Harry and Burt seemed to think the same, and the three of them discussed the white, snow-laden landscape as they marched, each hoping that the others would see a hiding place that they had missed.

Bit by bit, Harry and Burt edged their little coterie back along the line until they were nicely in the rear. It was not much, but they reasoned that when the Underworld broke loose they would at least have some warning. As they marched westwards from Seigor, the land rose once more onto a higher plateau of open moorland.

"Look at it!" Harry said in disgust. "No bloody cover for miles! All sodding stunted bushes even a rabbit'd be hard pressed to hide behind!"

Burt scuffed the frozen ground morosely. "Too bleedin' froze to even dig an 'ole in," he sighed.

"No mate, we'll be diggin' no trenches this time," agreed Harry.

By night there were not even enough bits of dry scrub to make fires hot enough to cook on, and men were constantly rushing out of the lines to drop their pants and squat as the semi-frozen, half-cooked food took its toll on their stomachs. After the second day from Seigor, each morning there were men who simply did not get up again, while others collapsed at the roadside while marching, too weak to carry on or fight the cold. Pack horses were slaughtered in an attempt to give the men something to keep them going, but by Jacinto's estimate they had already easily lost a tenth of their force and the number was escalating with each day. On the fourth day they came across a young captain slumped on the ground in a bad way – the first officer they had seen succumb to the conditions. Burt went to check him over and stood back up saying nothing, but shaking his head.

However Jacinto went to speak to the man.

"What kind of force is the king expecting us to fight?" he gently asked the fading captain.

"Dunno," the man replied faintly. "Says he'll save us all …kill us all more like." He wheezed raggedly. "…Say's victory is ours. …Don't think he really knows. …Voices in his head. …Glad it's warmer now, though…"

Jacinto grabbed his hand and found it ice cold, just as the man gave a wisp of a sigh and gave up the fight to live. Returning to the troop Jacinto relayed what he had learned.

"Listen, there's a crossroad up ahead," he told Harry and Burt. "It runs up into the mountains to the Knight's headquarters at Garway. When we get there, let's make a run for it. If we go at night, I doubt there's anyone who'll have the energy to chase us."

"I'm wiv yer on vhat," Burt said. "Anyfink's gotta be better vhan vhis."

"When do you reckon we'll come to it?" wondered Harry.

"We can't be far away," Jacinto guessed. "Surely within the day."

Yet as dusk came, they crested the ridge leading down to the crossroad and almost fell down with shock. Before them was the biggest army any but the oldest veterans had ever seen.

"*How* many?" Jacinto heard his own cracked voice whimper in shock.

The army was alien beyond any of his imaginings. When he had dreamed of fighting the DeÁine, he had somehow thought that they would be a regular army like the one he served in – men in armour in neat ranks, the full Knights and squires with their liveried weapons, and the rank and file armed with plain swords and spears. This was a seething mass of humanity in a riot of garish colours which defied making any sense of. In places there seemed to be something that might be ordered ranks, but at the forefront, which was all they could see in detail, a jumbled mass of men of every size and skin colour, wielded weapons whose only common factor was a sharp edge somewhere.

As his heartbeat stubbornly refused to settle down, Jacinto realised that even what might be described as swords came in a mind-boggling array of designs. Some were straight, others almost sickle shaped, and either could be thick or thin, broad or narrow, long or short; and his mind scrambled erratically to recall if anywhere in his training he had been taught how to deal with the odder shapes.

"It's Moytirra all over again, only this time we're going to lose," a nearby veteran's ageing voice whispered in horror, recalling him to the present.

Then Burt was tugging at Jacinto's sleeve. "Is vhat yer road we was takin'?" he asked with outstretched finger pointing northwards.

As Jacinto turned to look at the road he felt all hope die, for there on his escape route was another band of warriors, alone equal to all of Edward's force, and all marching with brisk purpose. Here there was the order lacking in the front-line of the others. Men who appeared foreign beyond belief with their flattened, painted faces and sallow skins, who wore helms in the shape of a strange birds' heads, the beaks of which formed their face guards. Loose woven chain-mail protected the back of their necks, but as it moved as they marched, it revealed that either they were bald or shaved their heads, for no hair was to be seen. Only black brows and strangely plaited side-whiskers, dyed red and decked with beads, revealed that they had hair and were not themselves some kind of Power-wielding DeÁine.

Long, wicked scimitars hung at their belts, but what shook Jacinto more was the shoulder armour which appeared to have razor sharp spikes on the outer edges, and the gloves which each had half a dozen tiny spiked balls on short chains attached to the knuckles – these becoming visible every time a man lifted a hand to adjust his hold on his weapon by the way they swung around. Looking like miniature clusters of morning-stars, Jacinto needed little imagination to see that a backhanded swipe from one of those would rip exposed skin open like ripe fruit, or entangle a blade leaving its wielder incapable of defending against a killing cut from the scimitar.

"DeÁine shock troops," the old veteran commented in such matter of fact tones Jacinto guessed that he must have completely given up hoping he would survive the coming battle. "And you'll never outrun *them*," the old man added.

"I could give 'em a bloody good try," was Harry's heartfelt response, but then they saw the old man was pointing not at the army en-masse, but at great lumbering creatures which were coming to the fore.

Even the ebullient Burt was utterly lost for words at the sight of creatures which seemed to have sprung straight out of a drug-induced hallucination. As the despairing troops watched, the men riding the weird beasts began to wield long leather whips and chivvy groups of men into a run – not directly towards Edward's troops, but to the side. Suddenly one rider goaded his beast too hard and it leaped forward. Harry's troop watched aghast as the beast lurched into an incredibly fast charge, stumpy legs eating up the ground at an amazing pace. It was not a gallop like a horse – nothing so graceful. Instead it ran, head held low, snout almost grazing the ground, with tiny ears pricked and a flat tail held equally low. The rider managed to turn it back to the DeÁine lines, but not before the watchers saw that its very skin seemed to be some sort of horny armour plating.

"Bastard Hounds of the Wild Hunt! That thing's got its own built in armour!" someone cried in despair.

"However would you kill one of those?" Jacinto asked of no-one in particular, but the old man replied.

"A spear in the belly if you're very lucky, or up its arse, or, if you're a very good shot, an arrow through one of those tiny eyes. Those are the only weak spots, but you've got to get to them first!"

Night fell, and Edward's little army huddled together for warmth and protection, everyone believing that the next day would be their last. Nobody slept much, for throughout the night the ground shook with the beat of passing feet as the DeÁine army swept around them and surrounded them. For his own part, Jacinto added another awful realisation to his growing catalogue of past mistakes. The old Knight Esclados, whom he had dismissed so disparagingly, had fought against just such an army as this, and *lived*. No wonder he had thought Jacinto an arrogant fool! Time and again he had tried to tell Jacinto that a real battle against the DeÁine would not be the short burst of dashing glory that Jacinto envisaged, but his words had fallen on deaf ears. Now though, as he huddled shivering on the icy ground waiting for death to find him, Jacinto would have given anything to have Esclados' calm presence beside him telling him what to do.

"Time to go," Harry whispered as the moon disappeared into a large bank of cloud.

Like terrified mice, the little band crawled away. At first there were provosts everywhere trying to stem the tide of fleeing men, and it took all night, but with Harry and Burt's guidance they finally made it past the perimeter. After that the biggest worry was the sudden appearance of the DeÁine riders with bands of soldiers blocking their way. Several times they had to lie low for a while, but then they also got beyond the edge of the

DeÁine. The old veteran had attached himself to them, and now said that those had been slaves with their drivers.

"If they'd been the real troops we'd have never got through," he told them, "but the slaves just go where they're told. It's too dangerous to think for yourself in those companies, because the DeÁine want complete compliance at all times. The only way to survive is to watch the slave-driver, and do exactly what he says without question."

"How do you know all this?" Jacinto asked him in a hushed whisper as they hurried along, casting fearful glances over their shoulders all the time.

"Prisoners after Moytirra," the older man softly told him. "The DeÁine just retreated and left the poor bastards to fend for themselves. Some ran after their masters, too numbed to do anything else. Others saw the chance for something else for the first time, and were only too willing to come back to Brychan – those that didn't try to get back to their original homelands."

With the first hint of light a dreadful racket began to the east of them. The drumming was bad enough, but at least it was a sound the men could identify. More penetrating on the cold winter air were strange ululating metallic sounds, and from their site slightly uphill position, Jacinto and his companions saw that these had to come from great curling horns some of the bigger slaves carried. To their horror they also realised that although they were now almost at the road to Garway, the way ahead was still blocked by the northern flank of the DeÁine army. The only consolation was that they had not followed the majority of their own deserters, who had gone straight back the way they had come and had already been cut off.

Now, though, the drumming changed from a wild and frenzied incitement to mayhem to a steady rhythm, and the vast army began a measured and inexorable progress forwards. Towards where Edward and the nucleus of his army were still attempting to make a stand.

"Sacred Trees! He's actually going to *fight!*" sobbed Jacinto in disbelief. "Great Maker, why doesn't he surrender? Does he *want* to die?"

But then after that he had no more time to observe others. The tramping of feet alerted him to the approach of the edge of the army closer to him, and he turned and drew his sword.

"Keep together lads," Harry called, "Shoulder to shoulder, back to back. Let them go past us if you can."

Suddenly over the brow of the little hummock they were on came an endless sea of alien people. In the core were some swarthy, olive-skinned men who carried their weapons with unnerving assurance, and Jacinto found his skills being tested to the utmost. With them came hundreds of tall, muscular dark-skinned men, and for the first time in his life Jacinto did not stand out because of his size. Several of them had strange scarring on their faces, and from somewhere in the depths of his mind Jacinto realised he knew that they came from some sort of initiation ritual.

The sense of familiarity shook him to the core – all the worse for being accompanied by a sense of childhood dread he had never dreamed lay within him. Equally terrifying was the realisation that their language sounded familiar even if he did not know what was being said, bringing with it a desire to curl up in a foetal ball and hide.

Screams in many strange tongues filled the air beyond the small patch of ground where they made their stand, and Jacinto's ears ached from the constant assault of sound. Even worse was the din of metal constantly hammering on metal as swords clashed, spears locked, and shields were used to batter at others as well as for defence. And all the time Jacinto found himself only able to fully see the man in front of him. The first olive-skinned soldier engaged him for only a matter of breaths before being forced on by the tide behind him, and Jacinto found himself swimming against an oncoming tide of soldiers, with no room for fancy blade-work or tactics. All he could do was batter back at those who would have knocked him down and speared him like a wild pig.

His breath was coming in frantic gasps now, seen briefly as white mist in the icy air, so that the men looked like human dragons breathing out white smoke. And despite the freezing cold he was sweating like mad with the exertion. Then came another noise from his childhood nightmares, and he found himself facing one of the creatures and its rider. From out of nowhere an image came into his mind of having faced one once before, and involuntarily he screamed before he realised that he was seeing it from a different angle. Now he was up almost on a level with the eyes, not down by the snout, and a fear-driven rage he had never known before boiled up from deep inside.

With a wild, snarling scream, he hurled himself forward and, grabbing his dagger from its sheath, used his shield arm to drive it into the creatures eye. Giving an ear-splitting shriek, the creature began to thrash its head back and forth, knocking Jacinto to the ground. Making a blind stab upwards, he felt his sword connect with something but not penetrate, then felt a cut to his back slice his pack straps, and rolled away to see the slave-driver stabbing at him with maniacal fury, even as he tried to hang onto the reins.

Scrambling to his feet, Jacinto slashed at the slave-driver, vaguely aware that the animal's thrashings were also dispersing the DeÁine troops around him. He managed a savage cut to the rider's leg and saw the skin peel open, but was unable to follow on as he realised that someone was behind him. He pivoted just in time to block a cut from a snarling slave as big as himself, and the two hacked at one another with blind desperation until the big slave's eyes suddenly went blank. As he slid down, Jacinto saw Harry withdraw his knife from the slave's back, at the same time as he felt an almighty thump through the ground as the beast collapsed behind him.

"The road's clear!" Harry screamed. "Come on!"

Jacinto slashed at another slave and then another, as they came at him, aware that the men he now thought of as his friends were making good their escape. The little pox-marked lad stumbled and fell as he was attacked by another slave, and Jacinto leapt in to block the attack as the old veteran hauled the lad to his feet, and half dragged him onwards. Turning again, Jacinto was just about to run after them when he saw another of the creatures coming thundering straight at them. Seeing the fleeing men, the rider stood in his saddle and used his goad on the beast, which leaped forward. Jacinto saw a spear lying on the ground in the hand of a dead man and grabbed it, hefted it in his hand and launched it at the rider, impaling him through the middle.

"Run for it!" Jacinto yelled to his friends. "I'll cover your backs!"

The beast was still on its headlong charge, only slowed down by stumbling over the men of its own ranks whom it ran down, and Jacinto hunted frantically for another spear. Making do with a kind of pole-arm, he ran straight at the creature, aiming once more for the eye but missing. However his momentum, added to the animal's, shot the blade along its armoured skull up to its ear, and Jacinto had the presence of mind to twist himself so that the angle of the blade shifted and it went in. Not as deep this time as the knife, but deep enough to stop the creature in its tracks. Withdrawing the blade with difficulty, Jacinto drew it back and was making the killing blow at the eye when he was knocked off his feet. Someone had run into him, and was wildly grappling with him for control of the weapon. All he saw was a wild snarling face draw back from him, and then the attacker head butted him and he blacked out.

On the road, Harry saw Jacinto go down but still chivvied his men onwards. The strange young man had saved them all by taking out the rider, and there was no way they could go back down to save him, if he even lived. The best tribute he could give Jacinto was to get to safety, and ensure the young man's bravery was remembered by those who lived on because of his courage. The exhausted men stumbled on until they were over the brow of another ridge, and could not believe their luck when in front of them they saw a large stone sheep pen. Hurrying to its sheltering walls they all collapsed, panting, to wait for the battle to pass them by.

By the time Jacinto came to, he had already been tied up and bundled onto a cart, although that did not last for long. His involuntary groans alerted a guard, and he found himself being manhandled off other unconscious men, and prodded into line with a string of other manacled prisoners. The pace was not fast, but it was relentless, and for the rest of the day it was all he could do to avoid stumbling, which only earned him a lash of a whip. On his barely healed skin it was torture, and he willed himself onwards after the first time, something deep in his mind telling him that he could not afford to weaken now. That night they were fed slops before being chained together by the legs to prevent escape.

To his confusion Jacinto realised that hushed whispers were going on in a foreign tongue around him. These were not Islanders who had been taken captive, but runaway slaves from the DeÁine army! For a moment he could not understand what he was doing in amongst these people, and then it came to him. The DeÁine slave-drivers had seen his dark skin and hair, and tall build, and taken him to be one of the hundreds of slaves he had seen similar to himself in the front line. As nobody came near them all night there was little he could do, hog-tied as he was. But by the light of the strange lanterns the slave-drivers carried, he could see that they were going around slitting the throats of the Island wounded. If things were pretty dire being mistaken for a slave, he needed no prompting to see that they would get a whole lot worse if he let on that he was one of the opposition, and kept quiet.

In the centre Edward could not believe what was happening. His beautiful army was being wiped out with hardly any casualties to the opposition.

"Fight you gutless bastards!" he screamed at his men as they died like flies.

Then in front of him appeared one of the weird beasts with its rider pointing his spear straight in Edward's face. Edward took in the man's features and yelled at him,

"I'm one of you, you bloody fool! Imbecile! Can't you see? I'm DeÁine!"

But the rider simply grinned nastily and drew back his spear ready to throw it. That was when two enormous lizards appeared on either side of the beast. Edward's torrent of abuse died in his throat, as a forked tongue flickered out of one of the mouths towards him and was retracted just as quickly. It belatedly occurred to him that the likelihood of this being real was so remote that he might be going mad. His suspicion was confirmed when something inside him seemed to take over his voice for him. Whatever it said, though, it seemed to work, for the rider lowered the spear and a dark-haired woman appeared from the flame-red tent strung between the lizards. Of middle height for a DeÁine, her heart-shaped face creased in almost childlike delight and, bizarrely, she giggled.

"Oooh, Eliavres, you absolute poppet!" Magda cooed, in delight. "The king of Brychan as my very own present! Aren't you a good boy!"

"I'll be even better when I've found Masanae and given her her pestilent captives," Eliavres said through Edward's mouth. "Is she left or right of you?"

Magda pointed an elegant finger over to the right.

"Thank the Graces of the Temples for that!" Eliavres said with feeling.

"Why's that sweetling?" his former tutor asked innocently.

"Because now I don't have to fight my way across the length of the line to get to her," snarled Eliavres. "Let me deliver these pests to her, then you and I must talk. They're up to something!"

"Who are, poppet?"

"Quintillean and Masanae. I don't know what it is, but they want these particular hostages, and it's hardly likely to be to negotiate with, is it?"

Eliavres felt Magda's understanding even as he broke the connection with Edward. Out on the right edge of the army he now used the Power in a weaving familiar to all slaves of the DeÁine that informed them that one of the Great Ones was present, ensuring his uninterrupted passage straight towards Masanae.

Meanwhile, Edward felt something leave his body, and was truly frightened as two burly men seized him and bound his hands and then his feet. To his horror he was slung from the poles of the litter at the back, in the same way that he had often seen trophy animals carried home from the hunt. His head lolled back in a painful way, leaving him looking upside down into the maw of one of the lizards, whose tongue flickered out to investigate him. It was clearly eyeing him up for dinner, and its saliva burned his skin, but its rider tapped the tongue with a switch and the lizard retracted it. It left Edward to swing along like excess baggage, forgotten by all, and, for the first time in many long years, he began to cry as all the false courage instilled in him by the departed Eliavres' dripped away with his tears.

Eliavres, meanwhile, towed his two captives towards another of the tents, questing ahead with his mind as he did so. *Masanae, come and get your cursed baggage! I've hauled them this far and from now on they're all yours!*

Are they intact? Masanae's mind finally connected with his.

Oh yes, they're intact! Eliavres spat back bitterly. *I've been clawed and spat at by both the vicious little cats – I'm cut to ribbons by their talons!* And instantly was forced to focus on the woman in each hand by just such another assault.

"Curse you, you whelp of a slave!" he swore, as Heledd landed a kick with her solid boot right on his shin. "By the Sacred Temples! You'll get your comeuppance when Masanae gets her hands on you!"

"Lying, twisted bastard!" Breizh screamed, beating his arm with her free fist and digging her heels in every inch of the way. Where did this man get his strength from? Both she and Heledd had tried several times to kick or punch him in the genitals, which usually slowed most men down, but he did not seem to have anything there to hurt. Nor was it possible to break the hold of even one of his fingers as he grasped their arms.

Heledd was now swinging her free arm and pounding Eliavres' face with her fist, hurling every ounce of her strength and body weight behind the blows, but to no avail. A trickle of blood was running from each nostril, but his nose should have been splattered across his face by now with the pounding she was giving him. Her knuckles were already a mess. And not once did he free one of them to deal with the other. Even worse, he was still managing to drag them both forward to some unknown destination, even with both of them attempting to pull him backwards.

Both girls were by now totally panic-stricken, as the battle raged off to one side and this utterly alien army just kept on coming. Suddenly they were in a pool of calm in the midst of chaos, and to their horror they found themselves faced with two of the giant lizards. A slave rushed forwards with a set of steps to the exotic tent strung between the creatures, and then grovelled abjectly in the dirt. The front of the tent was swept back by unseen hands, and a tall imperious woman glided out and down the steps. Ignoring the squirming slave, she waited for Eliavres to drag them forward. Looking down her haughty nose at them she commanded them,

"Kneel!"

"Fuck you, bitch-face!" Breizh snarled, hoicking up a gob of phlegm and aiming it straight in her face.

Eliavres never knew how he refrained from hooting with laughter, and the memory was a source of delight for long afterwards. He could not ever remember seeing Masanae so affronted, and felt her instant drawing of the Power to fry the young woman on the spot.

"Now, now," he quickly said with glee, "remember what you told me, they have to be alive and unsullied by the Power!"

Masanae gave him a look of pure hatred, but managed to stop herself just in time. And suddenly Eliavres was not in quite such a hurry to leave the girls and go – especially as Breizh wheeled on one foot, and launched a high kick which caught Masanae on the hip and left a filthy, muddy footmark all down her immaculate dress.

Masanae's mask of calm dissolved into a rictus snarl, and her hand shot out to claw at Breizh's cheek. But even as her blood-red talons dug into the young woman's face, Breizh's head snapped round, and quick as a flash her teeth latched onto one of Masanae's fingers. The ensuing struggle did what all of the girls' efforts had failed to do, as Eliavres lost the fight to keep his composure and let go of Breizh as he roared with laughter. With both hands now free, Breizh did what Masanae never expected. Instead of trying to pull away, the young woman launched herself at the DeÁine witch, leaping up and clamping her legs around Masanae's waist. Her hands grabbed handfuls of the witch's hair, intending to use it as a leverage, but the wig came free. Flinging it far to one side, Breizh simply transferred her grip to the witch's ears, and then let go of the finger to sink her teeth into Masanae's throat.

The two of them went down in the mud in a writhing tangle of limbs, as Masanae attempted to wrest the clawing, snarling she-cat off her. Eliavres had to admire Breizh, for by getting in so close she was giving Masanae little opportunity to use her superior strength. Having had more experience of the two girls' dirty fighting, he had automatically redoubled his grip on Heledd, and had both her arms pinned behind her back even as she screamed encouragement to her sister. When he thought Masanae had had enough humiliation, Eliavres signalled two of the huge male slaves over and told them to remove Breizh. Like taking a bone off a naughty puppy, the one guard squeezed Breizh's jaws and freed their grip on Masanae's throat, at which point they were able to haul her bodily off and stand with her still writhing and spitting between them.

With as much dignity as she could summon, which was not much, Masanae picked herself up out of the dirt, batting away the hands of the slaves who belatedly remembered that maybe they ought to be helping. Many still stood in open-mouthed amazement, never having seen such a wild and open display of insubordination to one of the Great Ones before. Masanae herself had been taken totally unawares, and for the first time in his memory Eliavres saw the senior witch struggle to formulate her thoughts.

"*You* asked for them," he could not resist saying. "I can only assume that it's necessary for whatever you have planned to have two whose life force is so virulent, because you're going to have an interesting journey getting them anywhere without leaving them permanently damaged."

Masanae shot him another look of incandescent hatred and disdained to answer him, instead ordering her bodyguards,

"Tie them to the back of the howdah," before turning her back to stamp back up the steps.

Even then, the two girls had not finished with their surprises, for even as Eliavres sauntered away in search of Magda to share his amusement with, there came an almighty ruckus from the direction of Masanae's entourage. Turning to look he was enthralled to see that the sisters had obviously co-ordinated their efforts. Strapped at either side at the back of the howdah, they had been separated by enough distance from one another to prevent them aiding each other and were near the corners. Furthermore, unlike Edward, although their hands were tied to the howdah's base they had been sat on the edge, which turned out to be a mistake. Intrigued by these strange creatures, the rear lizards had once again flicked out their long thin tongues to taste them. As one Heledd and Breizh had clamped their legs around the tongues and were now twisting for all they were worth.

In shock at the unaccustomed pain, the great lizards were attempting to pull themselves free of the painful grip on their sensitive tongues, which meant pulling sideways away from the howdah. As they were incapable of lifting their heads very high it had to be a sideways motion, and they endeavoured to swing their rear ends further out to be able to back away.

Their panic-stricken keening was also having an adverse effect on the two at the front – along with the next set of lizards with the howdah to their left – so that with the contorting of the howdah pulling on them as well, the front pair also began to thrash around. With a thunderous crack, a side support of the howdah gave way under the strain, pitching the silken tent and it occupants towards the icy mud. Breizh's lizard now had room to pull free of her and attempted to make a run for it, although it was unfortunately still attached to the howdah by its harness. The howdah bumped a few steps its way, freeing its companion lizard at the rear, who now tried to pull in the opposite direction. In a thrashing mêlée of lizards the howdah was bounced here and there, scattering slaves as it went, some of whom got trampled on by the panicked lizards.

As he felt Masanae pulling in Power once more to sheer the webbing on the lizards' harnesses, Eliavres turned away chuckling happily. He did not have to think of a way to make Masanae suffer for what she had put him through, for he could not hope to top what the girls had already achieved in less than one turn of the hourglass. He surely hoped that whatever it was that Masanae needed them for it was really important, because that would ensure that she would have a journey of the stuff that even DeÁine nightmares were made of. Oh yes, he thought, please let her think that it's worth getting those two back to Mereholt, or wherever they're going, in one piece so that there's no quick end to the torment those two will put her through!

Chapter 30

In Self Defence

Brychan: Eft-Yule – Imbolc

Unfortunately Cwen and Swein found that their initial brief burst of optimism faded rapidly the longer they were at Tarah. It was infuriating that after their mad dash back and forth across the length and breadth of the Island, that they were now forced to sit and do nothing. Yet Cwen could think of nothing positive that they could do. All she could do was trust that Berengar and Esclados would now stir the Order into activity. So for the first three days she paced the castle like a caged beast with Swein at her heels, unable to sit still or settle to anything.

"I can't explain it," she apologised to Swein time and again, "but I have a feeling like we're just sitting here waiting for a storm to break over us. Like the way you can sometimes feel a summer thunderstorm coming on even when there isn't a cloud in the sky."

On the morning of their fourth day Burgin, the wounded captain, called them to him.

"I'm sorry to have to summon you to me," he immediately apologised to them as they came in through the office door, "but unfortunately I can't manage the spiral stairs well on my crutches. I do hope you weren't offended."

Both had developed increasing sympathy for the young man left in such an unenviable position on all accounts, and assured him that no offence had been taken.

"Well I have news for you," he continued as they were joined in the office by the faithful Scully. "I don't know whether this is good or bad, but my commander, Commander Jathan, arrived at Arlei on the tenth. His message is brief but says that the capital is in chaos. The king has indeed marched out with an army, supposedly in response to a DeÁine threat. What sort of DeÁine threat nobody but the king seems to know, but they left in the middle of the Yule festivities."

"In the middle of *Yule?*" Swein gasped. "Why then?"

Both he and Cwen were doing rapid calculations, and realising that the likelihood of word reaching him of their seizure of the Book by that time was unlikely, given the state of the roads, unless a message had gone by bird.

"Why indeed," Captain Burgin sighed, "but then much of what our king does remains a mystery to me. ...However, this message was sent to us from Dinas. It appears that Commander Jathan rode on to Dinas to see if he could find out more. All the message then says is, 'Kiln sacked by king's troops, going with Seisyll' – that's the commander of Dinas – 'in pursuit'. What they hope to do, or how, he doesn't say."

Scully too had been doing some calculations. "Well the good part is that if the king left Arlei during Yule, unless he got caught in that infernal storm, he must have been close by Kiln at New Year. That puts him well ahead of Ealdorman ...no, make that Grand Master Berengar. So we don't have to worry about our new Master getting overtaken by a hostile force!"

Scully had been quite emphatic with Burgin as to Berengar's suspicions about Edward, and what needed to be done about him, so that nobody in the room doubted that Edward had to be regarded as hostile. Cwen and Swein breathed sighs of relief at the realisation that their friends were probably in no immediate danger.

"It's even possible," Scully continued, "that Jathan and Seisyll may catch up with the Master and provide him with a large armed escort. I'm sure the Master must be a good four or five days ahead of them by now, but that's not an impossible gap to make up if they realise he's in front of them."

The four of them spent the morning discussing this new development, feeling quite buoyed up by it, and Cwen even felt herself starting to relax a little. Was this a sign that things were starting to run their way for once?

In the afternoon three days after the message, they were greeted by another surprising development. Along the road appeared a long line of people. Riders hurried up to the castle with the news that the entire garrison of Penbrook grange, along with all of the refugees from Kiln, were now about to descend up on them. The captain from Penbrook had appeared to tell them that all this was by Berengar's order, and, as neither he nor Burgin had seniority over the other, they undertook to share command of the troops.

For her part Cwen suddenly found her feet again. Dealing with refugees was something she knew all about from the ones who occasionally turned up at Radport, and she promptly took over the organising of resources within the castle to deal with them, the two captains being happy to let her do so. Neither of them were experienced in such matters, and were only too glad that at least someone knew what they were doing. As Burgin said, it was quite one thing to have the standard Order training sessions on what to do upon discovering refugees, and something else entirely to have had practical experience. And so it was that Cwen found herself virtually the new commander of Tarah Castle.

A piece of news that she did not discover, until she sat down for a much needed mug of caff with Swein in the middle of the next day, was that from Dinas. He had taken it upon himself to go in search of a bunch of weary men who had come from Dinas to join up with Captain Emlyn from Penbrook, and question them.

"Apparently," he told Cwen, "as soon as Berengar found out about the state of Kiln, he decided that Edward must really be on the warpath. Dinas is only a small castle, and he didn't want it to become besieged when Edward eventually turns for home, so he told Captain Iolo at the grange at Kiln to relay an order for the Dinas garrison to fall back with him. Iolo sent the bird off alright, but by the time they got the people from Kiln down to Penbrook, only a handful of men had appeared from Dinas. Their Commander Seisyll had taken all except the minimum needed to man the walls with him. What's more worrying is that Jathan and Seisyll can therefore have no idea that Berengar's been found. The men from Dinas say that they'd gone before the bird from Penbrook got to them, telling them about Scully meeting us there."

He paused and took another swig of caff to fortify himself before telling Cwen the worst. "The thing is, Jathan and Seisyll still think that Edward has gone to *fight* the DeÁine ...so they're trying to join him!" Cwen nearly dropped her mug in surprise. "And that's not the worst I'm afraid." He put his mug down and went to put his arm around Cwen's shoulder in what he hoped was a comforting gesture. "Apparently Edward is heading for Caersus ...and that means he'll be taking the road that runs through Radport."

Cwen gave a howl of pain. "No! Not that monster in my home town! No!"

Swein hugged her tight. "I'm so sorry Cwen."

"But after what he did to Kiln...?"

"...I know. It's almost too horrible to imagine. But it also means that if Jathan and Seisyll follow Edward, after Foel they'll be on a different road to

Berengar, which means that they might not know the truth before it's too late."

Cwen gave another howl. "No! No, this can't be happening! …It can't all be going wrong again!"

She buried her head in Swein's shoulder and sobbed unashamedly for several minutes, until he said, "I think we should launch a rescue mission for your folks."

For a moment she did not realise quite what he had said, but when she did she fished her handkerchief out of her sleeve and blew her nose, then fixed him with a determined look.

"A rescue mission? *Hmmm*! Swein, that's a wonderful idea, but how are we ever going to get those Knights to agree to it?"

Swein managed a small smile. "Well they've been letting you take the lead up to now. Why don't you keep on giving them orders and see how far that gets you?"

Cwen gave a little giggle. "Sacred Trees, that's going to take a bit of nerve to carry off."

"Well you were as good as the Earl's wife," Swein said, hoping he was not going too far with such a suggestion. "You could've ended up in a position to be in charge of a big castle. Try keeping that in mind while you do it. I'm sure, thinking back on it, that's the reason Edward got away with so much was because he acted as though nobody had the right to question him." He gulped, "And I've got a plan!"

"You've got a plan?"

"I've got a plan," he repeated with more confidence than he felt. If he failed to convince Cwen then he was obviously totally on the wrong tack, but his time with Berengar and Esclados had given him a rapid education in planning. "I've been looking at the maps," he said firmly, "and I've been talking to the men about how long it takes to get between the different towns." He took a deep breath. "Now we can both make a good guess as to why Edward has gone to Caersus. All the experienced troops think that he'll be there by now, so the big question is, what will he do when he finds out that what he's looking for has gone? If he turns round and comes back we haven't got time to go overland to help them without meeting him."

"Overland?" Cwen picked up on the word and began to see where Swein was going with this.

"But what about by sea? You see I've been thinking. All the local men say that Farsan is a big port and so is Eynon. If we could get our captains to go to them, do you think they could persuade the captains of some of the big merchant ships to sail round to Radport? They could fit a lot of people in those big ships, and although it wouldn't be comfortable it would only be a short trip back, wouldn't it?"

Cwen gasped. "By the Trees, Swein, you have been thinking haven't you! Well done! That's a brilliant idea!" Swein went bright red at the enthusiastic praise. "Yes, that might well work! The captains would never agree to leading a force out to Radport for the very reasons you've said, but a sea rescue would be pretty well danger free. The only thing is, it can't be the really big merchant ships because they can't get up the river to Radport. But then the really big, rich ones are more likely to be thinking only of their cargoes and might well put to sea to protect their investments than help. The coastal traders, on the other hand, would have every reason to help us, because what happens to Radport one day might well happen to them another day. They'd also be more use because they'll have accurate maps of the river estuary – we don't want to end up stuck on a sand bank!"

With much trepidation the two of them went in search of Burgin, Emlyn and Iolo. To their surprise Emlyn and Iolo were instantly on their side.

"I think it's a splendid idea," Iolo said to Swein's amazement. "If Master Berengar thinks we should pull back to a place we can defend, then we can't leave the ordinary people stuck out there in danger. Look what happened to Kiln! Bloody savages stripped it bare! If they've done that to Radport, we need to get to the people soon before the winter finishes off what the king's men started. I'm happy to ride out for Farsan straight away."

Burgin was less enthusiastic, but as Emlyn pointed out, he was the one obliged to consider the security of Tarah, not them. "We can leave you all the men from Dinas and Kiln and some of those from Penbrook," he told Burgin, "so you'll be better off than before we arrived. There's no point in us cluttering up the ships with fighting men if we're not going to fight, and they'd be taking up room we could use for the Radport folk. If King Edward is back in town, the sensible thing to do is wait offshore until he leaves and then go in. With him supposedly having four thousand at his command, I'm not stupid enough to try to take them on with a couple of hundred. This is just what Swein said it is – a rescue mission. We vowed to protect and serve …well this is the serving, and protecting by simply moving them out of harm's way."

It was therefore decided that Iolo and Emlyn would ride at first light to Farsan, where Iolo would take the ferry across the bay to Eynon. Between them and a single company of men, they would persuade the local ship owners to set sail for Radport. More contentious was Cwen and Swein's decision to accompany them. Scully was in vigorous opposition to letting the lady his Grand Master had entrusted to his protection, go off into danger once more. It took several hours to convince him that they would be proceeding with sufficient caution that there was a minimal chance of Cwen finding herself in danger again. Even so, he insisted on accompanying her himself with two more Knights who would be nothing other than her bodyguards. Cwen found the idea supremely irritating, but as it was the only way to get things moving, conceded with reluctance.

The following day they therefore left a morose Burgin at the gate, feeling like he was being left behind all over again, and rode east. With the lack of snow on this tiny southern peninsular they reached Farsan before the following afternoon. And while Iolo and Swein caught the ferry, Cwen, Emlyn and Scully spent the rest of the day going around the market halls and merchant houses drumming up support. Emlyn's descriptions of the devastation left at Kiln added substance to worrying rumours which had already reached the busy port, and the good folk of Farsan needed little prompting to see that it could well have happened to them under other circumstances – not to mention what it was going to do to their trade in the coming year.

Iolo and Swein must have found the people of Eynon equally receptive, for on the dawn tide a whole flotilla of little ships set sail from the bay, and spread their sails in the morning breeze. The ferocious gales of midwinter had changed, and a beneficial wind from the south-east blew them on their way at a fair speed. Four days' clear sailing brought them to the mouth of the estuary and the port of Pencrick, where the leading ships put in and got their first news of the fate of Radport. Pencrick was bursting at the seams with displaced Radporters, which was encouraging for it implied that many people had made good their escape from the worst of Edward's depredations.

The townsfolk were worried that civil war might once again roll over their Island, and reluctantly conceded that a temporary evacuation to the south-east might be for the best. Consequently the vessels in Pencrick harbour also prepared to take on passengers in the form of those of their own least able to make a hurried retreat on foot. The elderly and children were hurriedly packed off with what they could carry and would be most in need of, whilst one of the quays was cleared to allow the first of the flotilla to come in and start taking off the Radport exiles.

As of two days previously, Radport had remained free from troops, and those who had dispersed into the surrounding countryside had gradually slipped back into the town to begin salvaging what they could. The lead ships therefore once more set sail and headed upriver on the next incoming tide. Overnight they tacked their way up the estuary, and in the early morning light came into view of the ravaged market town. The lead ship had barely touched the quay when Cwen hurled herself across onto the stones, and set off in a mad dash for her home. Cursing furiously, Scully scrambled off too, and with the two Knights set of in hot pursuit, somewhat hampered by not knowing which direction she was taking. Luckily the *Brace of Brachets* was not so far in land, and they caught up with Cwen as she and her mother were sobbing their relief in each other's arms.

Once he had realised that Cwen was going nowhere in the next hour or so, Scully went back to aid Emlyn organise the evacuation. What surprised them most was the townsmen's reluctance to leave. The women and children, the elderly and the infirm were hastily herded up and sent towards the quays, but a solid bunch of the men refused outright, Cwen's father amongst them. In what had once been the lovely bar of the *Brace of Brachets*, Iolo, Scully and Emlyn attempted to persuade them to change their minds, vigorously supported by Cwen and Swein.

"What are you thinking, Pa?" Cwen pleaded in desperation. "This is an army that will come back your way, not a small band of outlaws to be run off by the town militia. We'll need you – we'll need you all – when it comes to rebuilding the town. We can't afford to lose you in some fruitless show of strength you can't hope to win. I don't want to lose you!"

But Roger was adamant. "We're not so daft as to take them on," he told Cwen firmly, "and we're not arguing with you taking the others away. But we're not just abandoning our homes! You say this army is coming back our way? Well if it does we'll go across the river and hide out in the farmlands like we did before. But what if it doesn't come back? What if they go to Seigor and go back that way? Or go on and ravage Marloes and Roch? We could come back and find that people on the run from there have come here, and found it deserted and taken it over. At times like this there are always lots of refugees from over the border, too. I've got nothing against them, and we'll help them all we can. But there's a difference between helping them and handing them our homes on a plate. Or lawless vagabonds! Once they've settled in here, how would we get them out again? And what do we do if we've got no homes to come back to? Throw some other poor soul out of their home?"

That seemed to be the attitude of a substantial group of the men. All told there were about fifty mature men and strong older lads determined to hang on as long as possible. By midnight even Cwen getting on her knees to Roger had failed to move them, and the Knights were forced to concede defeat. However, one of the ships coming late from Pencrick with spare spaces to fill, brought the news that the same had happened there. Of all people it was Swein who finally broke the stalemate with a solution.

"Alright," he said firmly coming to stand before Roger. "We obviously can't force you to do this. But we can insist that you keep some ships back. We'll leave you one here now, and send a couple back when they've dropped the people off at Farsan. Why don't you tie them up across the river somewhere out of sight? That way, if Edward comes back in a hurry unannounced, you can make a run for it over the bridges into the countryside. From what you've told us of what happened that last time, he'll search the town first, so if you're not actually at the town quay, you'll have time to get the sails up and slip out by night before he has chance to send troops out to hunt for you.

"Even you can't believe that anyone who's already been attacked by Edward will come seeking refuge while he's here, and it would be a pretty stupid outlaw who came in looking for trouble as well. And if there are no ships left at the quays he won't be able to chase you by sea, so he won't know where you've gone. You can go down to Pencrick. If we do the same for them, you can all wait together. Then if Edward gets really nasty and decides to attack there, you can all get away and come east to us, but you'll only be a day away if he's only here for a day or so and moves on. Will you do that?"

"That really is an excellent solution, and I don't think you can argue with it on any point," Iolo said emphatically.

"No, you can't," Scully backed them up. "And we're going to insist that you do as Swein has suggested if you won't come with us."

"Indeed, I shall stay here with you to make sure that you keep to the agreement," Iolo surprised everyone by announcing. He looked to Emlyn. "You and Burgin are capable of organising the defence of Tarah with Scully to aid you," he told him. "Leave me two lances here and two at Pencrick –

just in case I have to knock a few out and physically throw them on board! That way, we can also do the patrolling while these folk get on with whatever it is they have to do, and we can provide an advanced warning of trouble."

Which was how they left the defence of Radport in Iolo's capable hands, and the now heavily-laden small merchant ships ploughed their way back across the waters of the great bay, and rounded the headland to Farsan and Eynon. Eleven days after they had left, the ships returned to their home ports on the morning incoming tide and began the task of disembarking hundreds of displaced people. Once more Cwen found herself at the hub of organising things, since it was obvious that they could not wish everyone onto the two ports.

Farm carts and traders' wagons were temporarily commandeered to transport the folk of Radport across the headland to Tarah, since they looked like being the longest staying guests. The people of Pencrick were distributed amongst Eynon and the bay-side town of Barwick, for they needed much of the space at Farsan for folk who had merely been passing through, and had got caught in the trouble. Many merchants who had been doing nothing more than travelling back from the huge Yule fair held every year at Caersus, had had the misfortune to be at Radport at the time that Edward's army had struck. Others had been caught a day or so later on the road and had staggered, battered and bruised, into Radport in an attempt to put as much distance as possible between them and the scavenging troops.

The vast majority were only too grateful to be offered hospitality and security, but a handful of men who were high ranking merchants still stood on their dignity. By some thought process the rescuers could not comprehend, these men seemed to think that they were owed compensation for the loss of their goods, which they should be paid by the Knights or the guildsmen of Farsan. One bombastic man, muffled in a fur coat that he had somehow managed to retain against the odds, was particularly vociferous in his complaints until Cwen lost her temper with him. Standing as near nose to nose with him as she could get, she told him exactly what she thought of him.

"You are not important!" she snarled at him. "The worst you've lost is your goods. Some of these people have lost everything they ever possessed! You can go home to wherever it is you live and carry on with your miserable, self-important life. They can't! So you just be careful! Because one more word out of you and I'm going to command the two biggest men-at-arms to pick you up and throw you, and your mangy fur coat, right back into the sea! And you can bloody well walk home on the seabed! …And don't think I won't!" she warned him as she saw him about to protest.

"Warren? Mutley?" Two burly, scar-faced sergeants, who had been enjoying watching Cwen ripping the fat merchant apart, ambled over flexing their muscles pointedly. "Any more out of this fat windbag and through me you have the Grand Master's permission to beat the crap out of him, and then feed him to the fishes! …And I don't care if he's related to the archbishop, the royal families of half the Islands, and his mother's one of the Blessed Sisters of Mercy! One squeak and you launch him!"

With which she turned on her heels and stormed back to the applauding long line of more deserving folk, even as she could have sworn she heard the harassed young man whom she thought was his son whisper softly,

"Oh go on! Push your luck, you old bastard! Just for once let's see you bite off more than you can chew!"

Glancing over her shoulder she saw that the young man's hands were clasped almost as if he was praying for it to happen. And then Swein stepped past her and she heard him say to the young man,

"You don't have to stay with him, you know. We'll find you somewhere else to stay. These are good people. They helped me, and they'll help you."

But even as Cwen was thinking how far Swein had come, she heard the young man decline.

"I can't leave him. …Oh not because I'm afraid to. One day I will leave. …But I used to have two brothers. One of them died. …Died because that vicious old bastard thought he was, in his words, 'one of those nasty little perverts!' Just like me. Just like our oldest brother. The difference was, he ran away when our youngest brother's body was discovered, but I have no idea to where. So I'll keep travelling with our travesty of a father, and acting as his clerk until I'm sure I've checked every place I can for news of Falcon. I just want to know he's alright, because he must have been in terrible shock when he left – I know I was. We're back to Kittermere as soon as we can, and then there's only one more trip I can make as a trader that I haven't covered before. After that I'm leaving. I don't know to where. There was this Knight I once knew, but where he is now and what he's doing I don't know."

"Well if you can't find him, or you need a place to stop, come back here," Swein said warmly, having no doubt at all what the father considered a pervert to be, and that by that definition he was just the same. "I've discovered, to my surprise, that there are more nice people who don't judge you than I'd ever have believed once upon a time."

Turning away he found Cwen smiling at him. "That was nicely done," she told him, tucking her arm through his and giving it an affectionate squeeze. "It's good to see you have the confidence to be yourself now. Keep this up and Berengar's likely to recruit you for the Knights!"

However, the next news they had of Berengar came in the form of a message from him, which appeared by hawk only five days later when they were back at Tarah. Burgin and Cwen were composing a letter to Amroth to request the steward to send any supplies he could to help, when the falconer arrived in Burgin's office. Ashen-faced he held out the message in a shaking hand, unable to speak. Perplexed at what could be so awful, Burgin took the rolled message and began to read. Twice he read the brief lines, the colour draining from his face until he was as white as the falconer.

"What is it?" Cwen demanded. "Spirits, Burgin, put me out of my suspense."

"The DeÁine threat," he gasped. "It wasn't a ruse! Berengar thinks that the king is in league with them. That …that army King Edward led out …they're all dead! *All* dead! The DeÁine are heading east. They're coming our way! Or at least towards Arlei. Berengar wants us to retreat while we can. We're to pack and leave within the day. He says we can beat the DeÁine to Arlei if we do, and take the road up to Redrock. If we can't get there we're to go to Bere."

For a moment Cwen sat in numbed shock, as Emlyn and Scully raced in and took the message to read in stunned surprise themselves. A deathly hush filled the room as Swein came in on their heels asking what was wrong. A shaken Burgin finally managed to tell him, at which a confused Swein asked,

"But why does he want us to retreat? We're a long way south of Arlei."

"It just says, *no Order men to be left on plain. Isolation dangerous. Mountains defendable.* And it's addressed to Jathan."

"Sacred Trees, he doesn't know Jathan's not here!" Emlyn exclaimed.

"And he doesn't know we've got three towns stuffed full of refugees already," Cwen added, slowly regaining her composure. "We cannot retreat!

There's no way that we can just march out of here an leave them to take whatever comes their way."

"But what can we do against twenty thousand?" Burgin argued.

Cwen strode to the map of south-east Brychan that hung on the wall, and stabbed at the peninsula on which Tarah stood.

"We defend this! *I'm* defending this, with or without soldiers! There's that great big rocky tor in the middle of this peninsula which will stop any army coming across the whole width. So we have the two coastal routes, the west one and the one through Barwick. Just two roads to defend. Well Barwick has stout walls like here, and we have men. Let's defend those gateways against all comers, because they won't get round it over the tor. It doesn't matter how many men they have, they can still only come on a few at a time in that space.

"On that west road, I know you brought the garrison from the *grange* at Penbrook, Emlyn, but there are still people down in its town. And the town is at the bottom of the cliff, isn't it? Whereas you Knights were at the top. So let's get to them and get them to seal off the cliff-top end of the road with the biggest boulders they can move. The DeÁine don't have local knowledge and they may not know Penbrook even exists if they can't see it, so they may be safe. And the coast road is far enough inland to not give a clear view down to the harbour. We can keep in touch with them by boat, and the road becomes defendable just where the sea and the tor nearly meet two miles up the road from here. Swein had the right of it! The sea is our strength here! It doesn't matter whether it's Edward or the DeÁine."

"But the DeÁine have the *Abend* with them!" protested Burgin.

"And even the Abend can't walk on water!" Swein stated with finality.

"No they can't," agreed Scully, "But what also worries me is where have Jathan and Seisyll got to if they're not with Berengar?"

The two commanders had ridden as hard as the conditions would allow when they had left Dinas weeks earlier. As Scully had suspected, Berengar and Esclados had been gone some five days by the time the two captains rode into Kiln, and found those townsfolk not dead already packed up and gone.

"Where have they all gone?" wondered Seisyll. "The king's army must've been just outside of here when that storm struck, yet we saw no sign of the mayhem that went on in Arlei."

"These buildings haven't suffered anything like as much fire damage as the capital," agreed Jathan. "It's as though there was a protective bubble over this bit of Brychan."

That was pretty much what Eliavres had done. Holding that in place with part of his consciousness, he had affected his own exit from Arlei and then investigated further. He had therefore sensed the full danger of the trailing edge of the glamour, and hurriedly set up a deflection around Edward's army just in time. Having been more prepared for the witches' workings, he had half expected something to happen outside of their agreement, and was therefore more successful at countering it than Tancostyl had been in Rheged.

For Jathan and Seisyll, though, there was no clue as to why Kiln had fared better and no time to investigate further, and so they rode on. At Foel they barely gave the destruction a second glance before following the army on to Radport and beyond. By the time they left Caersus, the Knights thought they had narrowed Edward's lead from nearly two weeks when they had left Arlei, down to one now. Finding the grange outside of the cathedral city deserted, they were even more confused.

"They have to have been pulled back to fight," Seisyll assumed.

"If the Castles Road is snowed-in, then whoever is co-ordinating the defence of Brychan must be using every man he can get his hands on," agreed Jathan. "We must hurry!"

They could hardly believe their eyes when they came upon Seigor with its gates open to all and empty. Hurrying in to investigate, they were more thorough than Edward's men had been and found the hidden stores.

"Someone's obviously planned this as a fallback position," Jathan said to the Knight who had just brought him down to see the cache of weapons he had found. "We'd best think of getting the defence set up."

Seisyll was in full agreement with that. They both now feared that if they had to ride so hard much further, the men and horses would be in no fit state to fight. However, they could have the castle fully prepared to take in wounded, and to provide fresh weapons and supplies if it came to a running battle. If the leader, whoever it was, was prepared to fight then there must be reasonable odds of winning, they assumed. And anyway, even in this weather, the border fortresses would have sent warnings if the DeÁine had been assembling an army of any great size on the border, preparatory to launching an attack. It must therefore only be a moderate sized force, especially as the king had only marched four thousand out with him to join the Knights. A bigger threat would demand far more men than that.

So on the morning of their third day there, they received a ghastly shock. As the pale winter sun struggled to make its presence felt through low cloud, the sentries sounded the alarm.

"What is it?" Seisyll demanded hurrying up to the battlements.

"Look, sire," a man-at-arms said weakly pointing west to the road coming down from the moorland. Spread across the horizon was an army of a size that Seisyll had never seen in his life. Neither Seisyll nor Jathan were old enough to have fought at Moytirra, and stationed down in the south they had missed out on gaining experience in the fight at Gavra Pass. Their only experience was therefore of small skirmishes not an army. Whatever had happened to the king's army, it could not have withstood the great host which now came towards them. Thousands upon thousands poured down the slope, yet had they known it an equal number had remained behind to wipe out Edward's weakened force.

"Sacred Trees protect us," intoned a man nearby, and many a voice responded,

"Make it so."

As Jathan joined them, the two leaders looked around at their men. Five hundred had ridden with Jathan from Tarah and the same from Dinas with Seisyll. Yet what could a thousand men do against a force where they were outnumbered ten to one? And yet with the speed the DeÁine were coming on they stood no chance of retreating either. In stunned disbelief they saw that just behind the leading edge of driven slaves were dozens of figures in white shapeless robes, each with their own bodyguard of professional looking troops. The white clad figures walked forwards with one hand resting on the arm of someone who appeared to be guiding them, while the other was outstretched before them as though they were pushing an invisible object in front of them. And while whatever it was remained invisible, its effects were not. A hundred paces ahead of the leading slaves the snow was melting away into nothing, so that, unencumbered by the frozen knee-high drifts, the slaves were being set a ferocious pace. If the Knights evacuated Seigor they would still be fighting snow and moving at half the pace. Behind the castle walls they might just survive. Out on the exposed plain they stood no chance.

"We're going to die here, aren't we sire," a man-at-arms said as a statement not a question.

In very little time every man had assembled in full armour in the castle bailey. As one they knelt on one knee, their dragon-headed swords held upright by the blades in mailed fists as crosses of swords, as the chaplain led them in prayer.

"Sacred Trees, help us in our time of need," he prayed, his voice wavering as he struggled to contain his own terror. "We face a fearsome enemy many times our number, and hope is gone."

He raised his hand to the west. "Great Oak. Protect all who fight this day. Give us now your strength in body and spirit. Lend us your power in defence of this land. Great Oak in you we trust."

"In you we trust," the massed men responded.

His hand crossed to the east. "Great Birch, tree of air and water. Heal the wounds of those who fight this day. May the wind that passes through your branches heal us from evil spirits, and drive away the malignancy summoned against us. Great Birch in you we trust."

"In you we trust."

Having made the cross arms, his hand dropped to symbolise the south. "Great Ash, who links this world and the next. Make a bridge of your mighty arms to the Summerlands for those who fall. Protect their souls on their journey beneath the shade of your leaves. Great Ash in you we trust."

"In you we trust."

His hand rose to complete the cross in the symbolic north. "Great Yew. Symbol of eternal life and rebirth. In your embrace may we find rest after the struggles of this life. And may the earth at your feet protect our bodies from those who would summon them for evil. Great Yew in you we trust."

"In you we trust."

The chaplain threw both arms in the air. "Great Rowan, tree of earth magic, clad in the fire of the sun and the pure white of moon-glow, aid us now! With the ice of the north, with the flames of the south, with the air of the east and the water of the west, repel all enchantments and bring the power of this land to our quest. Great Rowan …"

Every man sprang to his feet, sword arm thrust into the winter air elevating the cross of swords, roaring,

"With you we *fight!*"

THE END …so far!

If you've enjoyed this book you personally (yes, *you*) can make a big difference to what happens next.

Reviews are one of the best ways to get other people to discover my books. I'm an independent author, so I don't have a publisher paying big bucks to spread the word or arrange huge promos in bookstore chains, there's just me and my computer.

But I have something that's actually better than all that corporate money – it's you, my enthusiastic readers. Honest reviews help bring these books to the attention of other readers (although if you think something needs fixing I would really like you to tell me first!). So if you've enjoyed this book, it would mean a great deal to me if you would spend a couple of minutes posting a review on the site where you purchased it.

About the Author

L. J. Hutton lives in Worcestershire and writes history, mystery and fantasy novels. If you would like to know more about any of these books you are very welcome to come and visit my online home at www.ljhutton.com

Also by L. J. Hutton in this series:

Fleeting Victories

The DeÁine have marched into Brychan unopposed, the regular army slaughtered, and the mages are planning a terrible ritual which requires sacrifices. Can Berengar find and open the secret ways beneath the mountains to reunite his men to fight back? Meanwhile Ruari and Maelbrigt venture into icy Taineire to attempt to revive the Ancients – the only ones who knew how their arcane weapons work. Others find their courage tested in different ways. Jacinto must overcome his past, while Swein discovers hidden reserves he never knew he had. Sithfrey and Andra find themselves scaling perilous mountain heights with the covert branch of the Knights, as Talorcan attempts to protect Alaiz only to meet with Cwen and find an army in his way!

When there's no chosen one to save you, courage might be all you have left!

Summoning Spectres

Ruari and Maelbrigt venture into icy Taineire to attempt to revive the Ancients – the only ones who knew how their arcane weapons work. Others find their courage tested in different ways. Swein discovers hidden reserves he never knew he had; while Sithfrey and Andra find themselves scaling perilous mountain heights with the covert branch of the knights. Matti and Kayna face ancient traps closer to home; and Berengar has a race against time to find long-lost ways beneath the mountains, which alone will get him and his much-needed men to the coming great battle in time.

For everyone the chances of survival are slim – if one fails, all fail! Yet all is not lost as long as Will can pull off the near impossible and rally a force behind the DeAines' lines. All is still to play for and a decisive battle is looming!

Unleashing the Power

Even as Ruari and Maelbrigt rally their friends to make one last ditch attempt to save their home islands from being overrun by the DeAine and their mages, everything shifts once more. The DeAine have sent for more of their kind from across the ocean and they're on their way! Worse, despite mage Calatin dying, and Geitla also near death, new members have been elevated to the elite Abend and they're back to full strength and ready for war. But what's going on in the DeAine's lands beyond the mountains? Whose army is control there? As the last great battle comes, who controls the balance of power, and what will happen when all the magical weapons at last come into play?

And if you would like to receive the first book for free in a new (slightly smaller) fantasy quartet, set in the same world as these books, but in a different location and slightly later in date, then all you need to do is to go to my web page, follow the link, and send me your email. I promise not to bombard you with random mail – this is just to be able to let you know when new books are coming out.